City of Darkness,
City of Light

City of Darkness, City of Light

A NOVEL

MARGE PIERCY

FAWCETT COLUMBINE

NEW YORK

A Fawcett Columbine Book
Published by Ballantine Books

Copyright © 1996 by Middlemarsh, Inc.

All rights reserved under International and Pan-American Copyright Conventions.
Published in the United States by Ballantine Books, a division of Random House, Inc.,
New York, and simultaneously in Canada by Random House of Canada Limited, Toronto.

http://www.randomhouse.com

LIBRARY OF CONGRESS CATALOGING-IN-PUBLICATION DATA
Piercy, Marge.
City of darkness, city of light : a novel / by Marge Piercy. —
1st ed.
p.   cm.
ISBN 0-449-91268-X
1. France—History—Revolution, 1789–1799—Fiction.   2. Paris
(France)—History—1789–1799—Fiction.   I. Title.
PS3566.I4C58   1996
813' .54—dc20   96–24748 CIP

Text design by Fritz Metsch

Manufactured in the United States of America

First Edition: October 1996

10 9 8 7 6 5 4 3 2 1

For all the friends and acquaintances, the quick and the dead,
who taught me through their lives in the twentieth century
to understand the people of the French Revolution
in the eighteenth

Author's Note

For six days after Hurricane Bob, we were without electricity and therefore, in the country, without a working pump, without water. I was reminded every moment of the unending drudgery of life for the vast majority of people before cheap and plentiful labor not produced by slaves.

I was struck too by the authority, the tyranny of night. When the sun set, a thick and puissant darkness slid over us like pitch. This night was long, for there was little to do once we had eaten what food we had on hand (no stores were open) and wiped off the dishes. We made love and we talked. We sang till we were hoarse. Reading by hurricane lamp gave me a headache. We were bored. Looking out, we saw nothing but starshine outlining the tops of the pitch pines and the white oaks.

We are accustomed to a tamed night. Instead we sat with candles barely abrading that heavy darkness. When we returned from a candlelit house where they were sitting shiva for a friend who died in the hurricane, the countryside seemed uninhabited wilderness without the accustomed splashes of streetlamps, the lights of houses, without the occasional bloom of neon. Since many of the roads were blocked with fallen trees and torn power lines, few cars moved through the hills. We saw way off on the Truro moors someone walking with a flashlight, as once we would have seen a stranger with a torch passing.

Yet the night was not exactly quiet. Without TVs, radios, traffic, speakers, VCRs, the pump coughing on, the dishwasher churning, air conditioners humming, the whine of the refrigerator, we heard the great horned owl hunting close to the house as she normally does only in midwinter. The occasional human voice carried as if every word were significant, overtones of threat and promise. Raccoons fought in the compost pile over the rotten meat and sodden cakes and breads of our dead freezer. Furious yowling in the marsh brought all our cats to attention in the bay window.

One night as I lay in bed, our cat Jim Beam growled low. I heard something quick but heavy-footed in the rhododendrons, their big leathery leaves scorched by the hurricane. I shone a flashlight into yellow eyes. Wolf, said my blood. A coyote had come onto the patio to explore. I remembered that in the harsh and murderous winter just before the Revolution when the Seine had frozen solid, wolves came into the suburbs of Paris in search of food.

At twilight the day after, I saw a fox in this development for the first time in seven years. They abandoned their last den here when too many houses were built on this road during the mid-eighties boom. Many summer people and tourists had returned to their lives early, but even we locals were so quiet in our dark houses that the other animals reclaimed the earth.

After the second day, we lined up every morning at the dump, twenty thousand neighbors each with our two buckets to be filled. We dipped sparse rainwater out of the cistern barrel, bathing in a few cupfuls apiece. We had to bury our bodily wastes instead of flushing them into oblivion. Every small act of daily life took five times as long. Into the woods we scampered with our trowels to scatter pine needles over the mess we made. Without refrigeration or the ability we do not normally ponder to make ice, to turn on the tap and wash our hands twenty times a day, to wash after we relieve ourselves, after we cook, after sex, after touching dirt or stickiness, we became aware of odors. If we had no light and thus no color for hours from twilight to dawn, we had a great many pungent smells invading our consciousness. We all stank. How differently might I feel toward my body if I could never bathe, if washing my clothes were a major event, if even washing my hands and face used up precious water I had bought and carried up six flights of steps.

I had been brooding on the French Revolution for quite different reasons when the hurricane ripped through our town splintering houses and lives, but from that week I date the moment the eighteenth century became real to me.

All six of my viewpoint characters are historical. For four of them, Robespierre, Danton, Madame Roland and Condorcet, there is a great deal of biography available—and in Manon's case, autobiography as well. Certain scenes, such as Max's loss of his pigeon, are anecdotes in a life everybody includes. Others I have had to imagine from scratch. The lives of Pauline Léon and Claire Lacombe are far less well documented, and I have been free to create their lives from those of other women in similar situations. I have deprived Pauline of the living mother I now think she had; but when I began the novel, I believed her to be an orphan. I knew her father had died. Once I had conceived of her so placed, I could not reimagine her when, during the fourth draft, I learned there were police documents that suggested a living mother.

Some of the fates of the survivors are my interpretation, for mostly they disappear from history and we can only conjecture what happened, especially to the women who lived on. I have therefore constructed my narrative from my understanding of their characters and what little we do know. I have generally been accurate to what we know of history.

Of course there is always much we cannot know. I have changed minor names. For instance, the youngest Duplay daughter was named Victoire, not Vivienne, but I feared one too many Victoires would prove confusing; similarly, Manon was friendly with both Carnet sisters, not just Sophie, but she was closer to Sophie and I simplified. My versions of speeches are not literal translations, but try to give the effect for a modern audience as well as I can, as I have done in conversation.

Conversation presents a problem to any writer dealing with another culture, another time and place. On one hand, you do not want your people to sound quaint. " 'Swounds, perchance I might roger the wench, milord." We think and write about history because it has formed us, influences the choices we imagine available to us. On the other hand, if the people sound just like your coworkers, you won't believe they are denizens of late eighteenth-century Paris. Contemplating the amazingly vigorous, obscene language of the sans-culottes of Paris, I tried using contemporary African American ghetto language. Fortunately I was persuaded to abandon this attempt to find a corollary. I have tried to give some flavor and to avoid anachronisms of metaphor, especially those coming from a later technology. As a working rule, I have tried to be true to my sense of the characters rather than to any purely linguistic verisimilitude to 1789. The reason I was drawn to these characters to begin with was because in many ways they were familiar to me.

Occasionally I have risked anachronisms in the service of creating living characters. It is simply not possible to create lively colloquial exchanges without using colloquial language, which evolves constantly. One generation's colloquial language sounds dated in a decade or two. In some cases—for instance in referring to black people in the colonies and in France—I have translated literally, Blacks for noirs. At other times, I despaired of translating at all and used the French word. *Sans-culottes* means literally without culottes: culotte-less, if you prefer. Basically it meant the working people of Paris, since aristocrats and those imitating them wore tight silk culottes and silk stockings, and the working men wore looser trousers. You wore trousers if you did manual labor. This is a distinction lost to us, and I have just gone with the untranslated sans-culottes. I have generally not translated the place names.

On points about which there is controversy, I have chosen what I considered most likely: that Danton used royal jewelry to bribe the Prussians, for instance, and that Condorcet's fate was as described.

City of Darkness,
City of Light

ONE

Claire

❧

(1780)

CLAIRE Lacombe was fifteen when she determined she must find a way out. Her brother Pierre's friend Albert pushed her down on the floor and tried to mount her. He threw her skirts up, almost choking her as his large callused hands pawed her. She broke a bottle of vinegar on his head. Then Maman punished her for breaking the bottle and wasting the vinegar. Grandmère said to her quietly, "Good thing. Always fight hard when you fight. Don't be afraid of hurting the man. He isn't afraid of hurting you. Always fight like you mean to win." Claire listened, although she was covered with bruises, first from Albert, then from the beating. Whenever she was beaten these days, which was often enough, she planned to run away. But how? Where would she go? The only reason women ever left Pamiers was if they went off to be servants in Toulouse. If they entered a convent. If they married away.

Pamiers was small and dusty, with more history than wealth. From the edge of town she could stand and stare at the Pyrénées, crowned with snow even when the streets were sweltering. But it was a false promise. What would she do in the mountains? Hire herself out as a shepherdess? The river Ariège flowed by, a spot she frequented because Maman was a laundrywoman. Anne-Marie always had water boiling in the shed attached to their one-room house, but she washed the linens down at the river, using the wet rocks for a scrubbing board and the rocks above water level for a drying rack. Their house smelled of soap and smoke, from the fires under the huge kettles Anne-Marie had inherited from her own mother, who had been a laundress until crippled with arthritis. Now Grandmère sat by the bubbling cauldrons, stirring them or bidding Claire stir them with heavy wooden paddles.

Claire was the youngest of five surviving children. Anne-Marie had been twice widowed. The father of the three oldest boys, a hired man, died after being gored by a bull. The father of Claire and her sister Yvette and two babies who had not survived had been a bricklayer. It would have been better if she had done like the others, she heard her brother say. Died, Grandmère explained. Babies died easily of neglect. "I'm glad you thrived," Grandmère said. "Who else would I talk to?" She understood that Grandmère had taken pains to keep her alive, slipping her crusts of bread dipped in broth. In bad years, when everyone was hungry and what food there was went to wage earners, children and old people died every week.

When her father was alive, the family lived comfortably. Most of the nice things in the house—the pots in the fireplace, the hangings on the wall, the warm curtains on the family bed—were from his reign. What goes up must come down, Grandmère was fond of saying, and down he came, while repairing the octagonal clocktower of the church of Saint Antoine. She had been carrying his lunch to him, bread and a bit of cheese wrapped in a kerchief and some beans heated by the fire under one of the cauldrons and seasoned with herbs. She loved to carry his lunch because he would come down to her or sometimes take her to where he was working, and she would sit with him and eat a bite of his lunch, always better than her own, and he might give her a swig of wine and talk to her about how the work was going. As the youngest daughter, she was a disappointment (another girl) but he was often nice to her.

She had been carrying his lunch and humming to herself. She was just eleven and already tall for her age. She was looking up at the octagonal clocktower, one of the most imposing things in the entire town, and she was thinking how fine it was her own papa was chosen to work on it, when she heard the cry and looked up in time to see him fall. He fell not straight down but in a little arc, and his legs moved in the air as if he were trying to run. Then he struck the paving stones with a sickening thud she could hear yet. She had run to him, pushing through the crowd that already began to gather, to cradle his bloody broken head in her lap. It was considered a bad death, a violent death without last rites, but Papa had not been a believer. He said the Church was a soft way for lazy men to grab a living.

He liked to sing. He would accompany himself beating on the table or on one of the big cauldrons. He did not have the thick Provençal accent of Maman and Grandmère, for he came from away. If he had not been a good bricklayer, nobody would have trusted him, since he did not speak like the other men of Pamiers. He came from the Loire valley, but he never said where or why he had left. Let sleeping dogs lie, Grandmère said. He was a good husband and a good father. Occasionally he got into a fistfight, for he had a temper and he would not let anyone insult him or his family. But he never hit Claire. He liked to tell her stories. He never talked about himself but about his travels and what he had seen. Claire wanted to go everyplace and see every-

thing, instead of minding the kettles and scrubbing linen and eating only por-
ridge and beans, when they had that. Rent came first and taxes and soap.
Then food. Claire had only one skirt, two chemises and a shawl against the
cold. She lumbered through the mud in wooden shoes and woolen stockings.
Outside in warm weather the women were spinning. They took in wool to
spin. Maman, Grandmère, most of the women wore greasy black clothes green
with age. Sometimes the same worn skirts had covered the scrawny flesh of
three generations of women.

Nowadays Maman hit her often. Maman felt sorry for herself and she was
always tired. Anne-Marie was forty-two, an old woman with white braids and
a deeply lined face. Her own hands were getting arthritic now and she was
talking more and more about Claire taking over the laundry. Grandmère said,
"Anne-Marie is angry because you remind her of how she used to be. She was
a beautiful woman. Use your beauty, Claire, but don't rely on it. It goes. Be
strong. Tomorrow always does come, until you're dead." Claire had been told
she resembled Grandmère when she was young more than Anne-Marie. It was
hard to imagine Grandmère young, ever. She was a raisin.

Claire stared at the huge cauldrons bubbling on the fires that must always
be fed. Wood was expensive, so the only brother left at home, that lout Pierre,
had to go and cut it in the woods that belonged to the lord, whom they had
never seen. That was forbidden and if he got caught, that would be the end of
him. Sometimes Claire had to go with him, for Yvette had a gimpy leg, shorter
than the other. Yvette was devout. Religion was a sore spot in her family.
Grandmère was Protestant, as were many around here, some secretly, some
openly. Claire's father had been born a Catholic and had gone to mass a
couple of times a year, although he made fun of the Church. Maman had
turned Catholic for her first husband, pro forma. Both her parents shared a
deep distrust of churches, priests, monks, the whole apparatus. Only Yvette
attended church. Claire thought if she was anything, she was Protestant, like
Grandmère. Grandmère was her history teacher, her book of lore and wisdom
and anecdote, like the blue books Grandmère bought. Besides their Bible,
they had an almanac, a history of Charlemagne and Roland, two song books
and a book of fairy tales.

People in Pamiers had long memories and a suspicion of Paris and the north
and the French kings handed down from father to son and mother to daughter
like a family heirloom. People still spat when they mentioned the name
Simon de Montfort, and his name was not infrequently mentioned for a lord
who had been dead five hundred years. He was the model of evil coming down
on them from above and from away, from the north. They had had their own
religion, their own culture, their own language down here. They had been a

prosperous and cultured people, with as many ties to the Moors and to Italy as to the sword-rattling rosary-telling north.

Pope Innocent had declared a crusade against them. The fierce armies of the Capetian kings of Paris set fire to the country and slaughtered the people and burned alive their leaders, their saints, their prefects. The anger of the people had been forced underground, but every couple of hundred years, it erupted, hot and molten. A little less than two hundred years before Claire was born, militant Protestants attacked the churches, smashing icons. The royal Prince de Condé sacked the town then, burning, turning loose the casual slaughter of his troops. This history blew in the dust of the streets, in the old marks of fire on buildings, but she had Grandmère to tell her the tales as they minded the boiling cauldrons. Grandmère taught Claire all she knew about who she was and why.

Anger and rebellion were in her blood. She was born to it, as she was born to the dark hair and the sturdy bones and muscles of her people. She was strong in the back and shoulders. Her bust developed early. Men began looking at her. They began to try to touch her, to pull at her when she went by. She punched them. She cursed at them. She knew what happened if they got their hands on her. Her oldest brother had to marry his girlfriend after the men held a charivari under her window to shame her. Her second brother had been a smuggler, and from one trip, he never returned. Pierre was the only boy at home, and she hated him. He was always pinching her. They had a few chickens in the yard and an orange tabby she loved called Rougie. One day he had been teasing Rougie, who had scratched him, so Pierre threw Rougie in the boiling cauldron. He died, screaming as he cooked alive although Claire had burned her arm trying to fish him out. She hated Pierre and he hated her. He called her Big Mouth. He said she would die in a ditch with her throat cut. No man wanted a woman with a loud mouth. Fine, she did not want to be wanted.

She always paid attention to travelers, organ grinders, fiddlers, conjurors, displayers of relics, storytellers, peddlers with marmots or ferrets who performed or caught rats. That summer of her fifteenth year, a troop of actors arrived. Town people spit at them and made the sign of the evil eye, as they did when the Jews came through selling horses, but almost everyone went to the performances. Jews were horse tamers and traders, sometimes peddlers; actors were outside the law too. They could not be married in the Church. All Protestants were considered illegitimate, as were all Jews. And all actors. None could be buried in regular cemeteries.

But she thought them splendid, dressed in shining clothes and reciting fine speeches. There were seven of them, all dressed as kings and queens and great lords and ladies. The women got to talk as much as the men. One woman, who was a Greek queen, was the center of the play. Claire had a little money she had saved, and she took from her precious hoard so that she could go to every performance. Then she came home and told Grandmère how the queen spoke and everyone listened. She was fascinated by the woman who played the queen. There was one younger woman too, but she did not have as loud a voice. She could not decide which of the two important men was the most imposing. One was taller, but the other strode about like a real king must. He made the air ring. He had red hair. She had never seen a man with red hair. He was handsome and exotic and when he spoke, his voice was like perfume, like incense and oil.

She thought them the luckiest people she had ever seen. They went from town to town. If they didn't like Pamiers or Pamiers didn't like them, the next day they would be in Foix or Toulouse. They spoke words that filled her mind. Words that shone and sparkled and shook out like the richest velvet. She wanted to come close to them. She wanted to become them. They made people laugh and cry. Everyone shut up and listened. That was glory. She had a big loud voice. She could do it too. Then there would be power instead of shame in being Big Mouth.

Claire did not want to live like her mother. She did not want to be a laundress. She did not want to kneel soaking wet in the cold and the raw weather scrubbing bloody sheets until her knuckles were red and swollen. She did not want to go hungry with too many children to fill up with bread. She did not want to give birth to five loud screaming hungry children and two who failed and a stillbirth. Nor did she crave the attentions of the men in the square who called to her as if she were a dog, or the monk pressing against her at the market, or the men who tried to pull her inside when she delivered the laundry. She was tired of the dusty streets of Pamiers where the icy wind blew down from the Pyrénées in the winter and the hot wind scorched them in the summer, where the Ariège rose out of its banks to drown them and mosquitoes swarmed and the young and the old sickened and died.

The troupe had her mother wash their shirts and chemises. Claire brought them to the inn. The actors were to give one more performance and then move on toward Toulouse. She spoke to the woman who had played the queen.

"How do you get to be an actress, madame, please." She spoke carefully, like her father, keeping the heavy southern accent out of her speech. She had always known both ways of speaking, like her father or like her mother.

"You have to have a natural talent, child," the woman said loftily. On stage she had looked imposing. Now Claire could see she was middle-aged and stout. "You have to be able to read your lines or get them by rote."

The red-headed man leaned forward. "A fine-looking girl. How old are you?"

She was fifteen, but she decided to be older. "Eighteen, sir."

"So you want to be an actress? Instead of a laundress?" He laughed, but he did not seem cruel. He seemed to feel anyone would want that.

"Yes, sir, but I'd do your laundry too if you took me along. And I do know how to read." Grandmère had taught her. As a Protestant, Grandmère believed in Bible reading.

"Child, we don't need a laundress. Every town has its own."

"She's a beauty, isn't she, Jean-Paul? Flashing dark eyes, the carriage of a princess. But what about the family? All we need is to get charged with abduction."

"These poor families, they'd just as soon be rid of a girl," the older lady said. "They probably haven't the money for a dowry."

"I'll ask my mother. My father's dead," Claire said. "Where do you go next?" She memorized their route. If they would have her, she would go with them. She would let them leave, and then she would run away after them. She would not say a word to her mother, for Maman would never let her go. Maman would chain her to the cauldrons. No, she was going to wear fine costumes and speak words that rippled on the air like banners and travel all the roads of the country. That was living. That was being a free woman.

She told no one but Grandmère. Grandmère had been to Toulouse three times and told her how to go. Once she was far away she would write Maman. They would consider her a fallen woman, but if she sent money, they would not really mind. She would see the world, as her father had. Goodbye to the laundry pots, to the dusty streets, to Pierre and his friends, adieu.

TWO

Max

❦

(1766–1775)

MAX liked to watch his flock peck grain. Holding a dove gave him soft-ness and warmth, comforting, reliable. He tried never to think of his mother, since the day she had screamed and screamed upstairs and then did not scream any longer. That had been the fifth child. It had survived her three days. Nothing had ever been the same again; nothing had ever been right. His mother had adored him. She had called him her prince. He was gentle with his doves. This was Doucette. He said her name softly as she cooed in his hand. He could not bear to think of them going hungry, being attacked by a dog or cat, carried off by a hawk. He would protect them. They would not leave him.

It was harder to take care of his sisters, Charlotte and Henriette. After their father had run away, the orphans (for it was given out that the father was dead) were split up. He and his little brother Augustin were taken in by his mother's family, the Carrauts, local brewers. His father had come down in the world to marry his mother, everyone said, and they called Max a bastard. They mocked him because he had been born four months after the wedding. His father's sisters took Charlotte and Henriette, and they only got to spend Sundays together. His father had been a lawyer who, Grandpère Carraut said with contempt, entertained ambitions of entering the nobility of the robe—judges, lawyers considered less grand than the nobility of the sword, but they paid no taxes and had lots of privileges. Father had begun to style himself "de Robespierre," which meant he was making some kind of claim. Max thought per-haps the Robespierres needed all the help they could muster.

He was the oldest. He was in place of the father, pater familias. He was learning Latin at school, at the huge grim building of the Abbey of Saint Vaast, where it was always cold. It was grey and attached to the Cathedral. In front were enormous daunting steps, but the boys went in the side. He would gather them together someday, his two sisters and his little brother, and they would live in a house with a yard. His doves would have a beautiful cote like the one he had seen at the Canon's when he was summoned there because of his excellent grades and his essay on virtue.

He did not understand why it was considered a reward being kept standing and standing while the Canon was occupied and then given a speech about being extra virtuous because of his dubious background: dubious? He had stood there with his eyes on the Canon unblinking, and flung his words back in his face, silently. Dubious in what way, sir? Don't you believe my father was my begetter? Are you doubtful I was born? Perhaps I was found under a cabbage leaf, as they tell children who have not heard the dreadful cries of childbirth and smelled and seen the blood. In their eyes, he was only a child. At ten years, he considered himself almost adult. Someday he would speak and they would hear him, whether they liked it or not. Ever since his mother died, he had lived under a heavy lid that weighed on him day and night, all week but Sunday when after mass they were all briefly together.

The Canon asked him if he felt he might have a vocation for the Church. "You must make your way in the world," the Canon said to him. "The military will not do. You're a small boy, and you'll be a small man. And you must have noble quartering for four generations to be an officer. There are the courts, but you're a quiet retiring sort. The Church is your way, my son."

"But I thought you had to be noble to be a bishop."

The Canon frowned. "There are other posts in the Church. A bright young man can make his way. You might be content in a monastery—after all, you're a studious lad."

Max promised that he would consider seriously what the Canon said, but he had his siblings to take care of. He did not want to be a monk. He would be a lawyer like his father but one who made a name and enough money.

When he came home, his grandfather told him at supper that he was very lucky that the Canon was taking an interest. He must strive to be worthy of the Canon, who made recommendations to the absent Bishop, who controlled scholarships. If the Canon remained interested in him (what a phrase, Max thought, as if he were a story), then his future was made. He could go to a good school.

He confided in no one; his sisters were too flighty; Augustin, whom everyone called Bonbon, too young. Until Max had shown a talent for schooling, Grandpère meant to put him in the brewery. The smell of beer made Max gag. He drank watered wine in the season when there was no milk. His stomach was delicate. Sometimes the smell of meat made him sick. It reminded him of blood. His grandmother gave him warm milk with a little coffee in it for breakfast and bread spread with jam from wild strawberries.

Soon it would be Christmas and there would be oranges. Nothing smelled as good as oranges.

Every Sunday he let his sisters hold the doves, so long as they were careful. "Max," Charlotte said, "tell us the way it's going to be, when you finish school." Charlotte and Henriette settled down, each with a dove held gently in their hands, as he had shown them. Bonbon was too young. He was playing in the sand with a toy dog that had been Max's. Bonbon was used to playing alone while Max was at school. They did not fit into the rigid levels and boxes of the town. They were better than peasants, who were far down below, better than artisans who worked making shoes or metalwork, better than shopkeepers or the keeper of the inn. But they were less than the children of successful lawyers, less than the illegitimate son of the Canon.

"We're going to live together in a big stone house—"

"Last week you said red brick," Charlotte corrected him primly.

"This week it's stone. Stone is better."

"Red brick," said Charlotte. "You promised us red."

"Stone is better," Max said firmly. "It's more . . . elegant." It was a new word he had learned, and he had to explain to his sisters. Many of the older houses in the town were brick, with stepped facades on the roofs, so a giant could climb them, he imagined. But the houses of the rich were made of stone. "We will each have our own room. We'll have fruit trees in a glass-walled orangerie, like the abbé does, so we can have fruit even in winter."

"And who will we have to live with us?" Henriette asked. This was her favorite part. She was the second-youngest.

"We'll have each our own dog. They'll be very well trained dogs and never, never hurt our doves, who'll live in a cote attached to my room so I can always see and hear them and make sure they're safe. Every day we'll go out in the fields with our dogs and run with them, as far as we want."

"I want a spaniel," Charlotte said.

"I want a cat," Henriette insisted. "I want a tabby cat."

"Max, give us one of your birds. You have so many, and we don't have any. We have nothing of our own. In our aunts' house we're not allowed to touch anything. Just one dove for us. They're so pretty, Max, please!"

Every week they begged him and he refused them. Afterward he felt guilty. He felt guilty because he could not yet keep the family together. He had to grow up first, but it was taking too long. He felt guilty because things were not as they should be. He was the real cause of his parents' marriage. His sisters were unhappy, and that too was his fault. If only he could just grow up right now and do what he had to.

"All right," he said slowly. "I'll give you Blanchette. But you must treat her well." For the next ten minutes he explained to his sisters how they must take care of Blanchette. But when they left after supper for their aunts' house, he felt sick with apprehension. Blanchette looked forlorn in her cage, taken away from her own family, the other doves. He had condemned her to exile, as his sisters were exiled from him and Augustin.

For two weeks, Charlotte and Henriette took care of Blanchette properly. But during the third week, a storm came up in the evening, high winds, fierce cold, the north wind blowing down from the Austrian Netherlands. The girls in their beds forgot Blanchette. In the morning she was dead.

Max wept. His grandfather rebuked him. It was not manly for a boy of ten to cry over a bird. Max wept to himself after that, without sound. He could not finally blame his sisters, for they were young. And they were girls. Girls and women were weak. They took ill. They were seduced and had babies too soon. They died. Things entrusted to them died too. It was his fault. He must take better care. He must keep control. Max was the only father his family had: he who would become Maximilien de Robespierre, attorney in the Bishop's court, judge, perhaps mayor of Arras. He would save his family and hold them together.

Max's sisters, Charlotte and Henriette, were shoveled off to a charity school, to be taught to sew, embroider, pray and keep their place humbly. He himself, age eleven and always counting, got on the coach to Paris, bound for the school Louis-le-Grand, across the street from the Sorbonne. The Canon had recommended him to the powerful and absent Bishop of Arras who controlled four scholarships. One had gone to Max.

Louis-le-Grand was popular among the aristocracy. The wealthy boys lived in comfortable rooms, with their servants and valets nearby. Max was put into a dormitory with a temperature little above that of the narrow cobbled street outside. The middle-class children permitted into Louis-le-Grand were given a good education but little food and no comfort. Discipline was strict and painful, but Max had no trouble managing within the rules. Not that he obeyed every law. By the time he had been at school four years, he was reading clandestine books: not the pornography the boys passed around, but the books of forbidden philosophers. They went to church twice daily. Behind his missal he read Rousseau. He existed imaginatively in Roman history, in Rousseau's life.

He was small and narrow-chested with no interest in sports. He liked to walk, but they were only permitted to leave the precincts of the college on Sunday, the dark vaulted halls, the gloomy corridors that smelled of drains, the bleak crowded dormitory, the shadowed courtyard. He began to understand who the Bishop of Arras was: a great man, a courtier. He was received at Versailles. He was handsome and ambitious. Max had no love for his benefactor the Canon, who had never treated him other than as one might have a kind thought for a spaniel seen from a coach window; but to stay on good terms with both was important. Max won annual prizes in the school and in citywide contests. At night he dreamed of a stone house with his sisters, his little brother, doves and a dog. He dreamed of refounding his broken family. He would become a great man like his hero Jean-Jacques Rousseau, always persecuted but always virtuous, disdaining nobles and kings. Someday he would meet his hero face to face. Jean-Jacques would touch him lightly on the shoulder. "You are a true disciple."

In Louis-le-Grand he was a little mouse allowed in the house of the wealthy and proud. They pushed him out of the way on the stairs. They spoke to him as if to a servant. They never called him by name. He knew all of the aristocratic boys by name and reputation; he considered most of them stupid. The bright boys were those like him, boys of little money, threadbare clothes— although few were as badly dressed as himself—and sharp fresh talent. Boys with brains like Camille Desmoulins, here too on scholarship, like Jérôme Pétion. When they sat up in the dormitory they did not talk about imaginary conquests but about ideas, about France, about equality and justice and how a man should act. They argued about Brutus and Caesar and Augustus, as if they were acquaintances. Ancient Rome felt closer to them than the towns they had left. Camille was two years younger than himself, but their intelligence and mutual interest in Roman history and the Enlightenment philosophers brought them together. Camille got on so badly with his father he told Max he envied him, having none.

Camille had quick hands; sometimes he could pilfer a piece of bread, once an apple that they cut up between them. A Father had been overly interested in Max a couple of years before. Now he transferred his interest to Camille. Camille did not freeze and flee like Max. He had long private conversations with the Father. Sometimes the Father gave him sweets which he brought back and shared with his two friends. "What do you have to do for this?" Max asked suspiciously.

Camille shrugged. "It's child's play." He giggled. "He doesn't hurt me."

Camille's readiness to insult those who thought they were his betters got him in constant trouble. If he had not stuttered, his insults would have been worse. Max tried to protect him, but several times the rich boys beat him or had their lackeys do so.

Max must make contact with his benefactor, the Bishop. He had to rise from a name on a list into a worthy recipient of further attention. That acknowledgment could turn penury into respectability for a young man trying to make his way in Arras, where he was regarded as a demi-bastard from a defunct family. Here his unrelenting work and fierce intelligence brought him to the attention of the Fathers. But what of Arras? That town was not set up like a school with prizes to win and honors to snatch by merit.

He would never get past the Bishop's outer ring of servants dressed as he was. He was seventeen and had no clothes but the toque on his head and the shabby robe he wore at school, under it small clothes long past mending. He wrote, he rewrote, he polished a note to the Bursar. "Sir, I have been told that the Bishop of Arras is in Paris, and I would like to see him. However, I have no suit of clothes or other articles without which I cannot appear in public. I would be most grateful if you would take the trouble to explain my situation to his grace and if you would help me obtain what I must have to present myself to him. I remain, sir, respectfully, your very humble and obedient servant, Maximilien Robespierre the Elder."

The polite forms came easily to him. Camille made fun of the formality of bourgeois and noble life. He wrote parodies of the prayers and lives of the saints. His favorite was Saint Sowbelly, who mortified himself by eating bad food, spoiled vegetables, rotten meat, who went about from school to school eating the dinners of students. Camille wrote scurrilous verse about their teachers. Max had better things to do with his brain. It was the fact that he was the very humble servant of all of them that he minded, not the saying of it. More humble entreaties, more obsequious begging, and finally he was given an outfit from the charity funds. He set out walking from the Latin Quarter to the Marais, where the Bishop's family, the Rohans, had a mansion.

His presentation lasted five minutes. The Bishop was reading a letter on his desk throughout. A handsome man, a vain man. No more a believer than Max himself, although Max did not discard God. He was pious in his own quiet logical relentless way. He was sure that there had to be justice, and therefore there had to be a judge. This was no deity to whom one could address requests to find lost dogs or to cure one's pleurisy. God was a high austere judge who watched, did not interfere, but saw all that mattered. Remembering how uncomfortable he had felt when one of the Fathers had taken a too-fervent interest in him made Max satisfied by the tepid interest of the Bishop. At least he had put a face on his name. He was permitted to keep the suit of green silk.

Two letters came. His aunt wrote him that Henriette had died at the charity school. With the slowness of the mail, they could not postpone the funeral till he came. She had been dead for eight days, and he had not known. He wondered he could not feel his sister being ripped from him, that he had not known in his own flesh the moment of her death. It was his fault. He could not take her from the dreadful school. Like his mother, she was suddenly dead.

The letter from Charlotte begged him to come and save her. She blamed the nuns for not paying attention to Henriette's coughing, not taking her fever seriously. She urged him to free her from the school. He could not help her. He was still a schoolboy himself, shut up in Louis-le-Grand trying to please the Fathers. There should be something he could do, something. He was failing his family. He began to work on getting his brother into Louis-le-Grand. He had now only one sister, one brother to protect. All he could do for Charlotte was to counsel patience and promise solemnly that when his studies were finished, he would return to Arras and she would live with him.

He won another prize in an essay contest, and this time he was chosen to represent the school in a great honor. The newly crowned King Louis XVI and his young Queen Marie-Antoinette of Austria were going to stop by the school on their royal progression through Paris after their coronation at Reims. He, Maximilien de Robespierre, was the choice of the school Fathers to make a speech in Latin before their majesties. He was thrilled. He had a high thin voice but it carried well and he never had trouble making himself heard. He worked and worked on his delivery; the Headmaster wrote the speech.

The King was young and said to be faithful to his wife, unlike all previous kings within memory back to Saint Louis. He was said to want to do well for France and for the people. People talked of nothing else. Louis XV had destroyed the confidence of his subjects, running up huge debts and losing a war to England. He kept mistresses who ruled France, first Mme du Pompadour and then du Barry, who spent millions. He passed his time at a house called the Deer Park, where he had young girls brought for his pleasure. The new King was said to have plain tastes. The common people hoped this meant an end to the flagrant consumption and luxury for luxury's sake. This King would bring reform, would change the unjust system of taxation that exempted the rich and crushed the poor. It would be a new era. Max practiced his speech until Camille began to make fun of him. Finally he shut himself in the privy to say it again and again.

He thought of the privy on the great day, when he knelt in the muddy street in the pouring rain to recite his speech. He had been waiting outside the gates of the college for more than an hour before the carriage finally appeared, the mud flying out and the horses almost running him down before he could scramble clear. They were late.

By now his clothes were sodden and filthy. The mud of the Paris streets was notorious. It was composed of dirt, offal, human waste, horse droppings, garbage, soot. It was scraped off regularly and composted outside the city to be used as fertilizer. But there was always half a foot of it, rendered into stinking paste in the downpour. His black robe was foul.

The King and Queen did not step down from their carriage. He could not see them. He heard the Queen laugh once. Before he had finished the fifth sentence of the sonorous and obsequious Latin praises written by the Head-master, there was a terse order from within. The coachman shot to attention, the footmen began trotting down the street. With a sharp lurch the great coach took off, splashing mud into Max's open mouth and into his eyes. The King and Queen had decamped.

THREE
Manon

❧

(1765–1766)

MANON'S parents put her into a convent to be educated right after the incident with the apprentice. Manon had grown up on Ile de la Cité, in the center of the Seine in the center of Paris. There the Philipons lodged in a handsome house, brick like its matching neighbors and the third from the busy and always crowded bridge, the oldest in Paris, the Pont Neuf. Just along the Quai de l'Horloge was a busy prison, the Conciergerie, and law courts, the Palais de Justice. It was an important place to live, Manon thought. Their flat faced the fashionable neighborhood on the right bank called the Marais. In the workshop attached to their rooms, her father and his apprentices made fine snuffboxes for gentlemen, watch and jewelry cases. Her father was a master engraver who had as much work as he could handle. But he speculated. Since Manon could remember, her mother had sighed and commented wearily upon his belief that he was a financial genius and would shortly become rich. In spite of the workroom and studio being in the house, M. Philipon had little to do with Manon. He approved of her intelligence, her precocity, but he did not involve himself. He reluctantly paid for music lessons, for a tutor, for books. Manon saw more of the apprentices, who were little older than she. Sometimes they sang together or played cards. Always they ate at the same long table, the Philipons and the apprentices.

At first when the apprentice, Jérôme, called her over to him as she was going through the workshop—empty but for him that afternoon—she was curious. What was this thing he was urging her so insistently to see?

"Pretty Manon, come here," he coaxed. "I have something for you."

She had always liked him, for he made her laugh. He was fiddling with his pants, opening them. Then she saw what he was making a fuss about, the same thing dogs had, only bigger and he kept poking at her and telling her to touch it. "I don't want to! It's disgusting!" She ran out.

A week later, he called her over again. She did not know why she went, except she had always liked him and no harm had come to her last time. This time he grabbed hold of her, thrust her down on the windowsill and stuck his hand under her skirt. That hurt and she began to cry out until he let go of her. This time she went to her mother. It was a terrible thing, apparently. Her mother turned white and then red and made her repeat again and again exactly what had happened. Manon was terrified now instead of only upset.

"Never tell anyone. Never! He must go at once."

"But what does it mean?" she asked stubbornly. "What did he want?"

"Shhhh!" Her mother slapped her cheek. "Put it out of your mind. Forget! You're intact, thank the Virgin who watches over virgins. You must always be careful never to be alone with young men. They can be dangerous."

It was a serious thing for an apprentice to be turned out of his place, and that made her feel guilty. She did not forget. It made her wary and cautious. A young man might suddenly do violent and revolting things, might try to hurt her. She had begun to be devout right after that, but it did not last long in the convent, where life was softer than she had expected.

Afterward, she went to live with her grandmother, to learn manners. Her grandmother had been governess to the children of a great lady. Grandmère lived on the next island in the Seine, the Ile de Nôtre Dame, a quiet pious neighborhood unlike her native Ile de la Cité. Sometimes Manon missed the bustle of home. Grandmère was to polish her for finding a husband.

It was certainly quiet with Grandmère, who was more affectionate than her own mother and often kissed her. Manon was sure that she was the center of her mother's universe right next to the Blessed Virgin, but her mother showed it more by watching out for Manon's interests than by fussing over her or embracing her. Manon adored her mother, although she never seemed entirely to please her. It was far easier to please her grandmother, who was delighted to have an intelligent and accomplished young lady to dress up and show off. When Grandmère's cronies came by, she was asked to recite Corneille or Racine or some pious or pastoral poetry for them. She also read to Grandmère, who embroidered. Grandmère's neighbor had a pianoforte, on which Manon would play, sometimes fine compositions by Rameau or Gluck, sometimes simple airs they could sing. Manon played the guitar and the viola, as well as the pianoforte, but did not take music seriously. Her teacher had introduced her to a renowned virtuoso, who had been the teacher of Marie-Antoinette in Vienna. He begged her mother to let him give lessons to Manon who he said had the makings of a true performer. Her mother declined indignantly; she did not think women should have professions. Manon liked the picture of herself playing for the pleasure of Grandmère's friends, the perfect granddaughter; then she wondered if she was growing vain. She wrote to

Sophie Carnet every other day, her fantasies, her doubts, her wishes, her dreams, her self-analysis. They had become best friends in the convent and remained so.

Saturday she insisted, as she did every week, in going off to the country to see her old wet nurse, Mme Petrie. She had spent the first two years of her life with Mme Petrie and still called her Maman, as well as her own mother. "You've always been stubborn," Grandmère said. "When your father or mother would spank you when you were little, you would bite their thighs and you would never, never apologize." Grandmère thought the old connection ludicrous. Children were sent off to wet nurses, but nobody went on treating them as family. Monsieur Philipon was a master craftsman; Grandmère had been a governess. Why should her granddaughter run off regularly to see an old peasant who farmed babies? Manon refused to be shamed. Mme Petrie had been her first maman; Manon loved that cottage with its rabbits and chickens and ducks. That was one place she did not have to show off her accomplishments to be loved. Mme Petrie, who had only sons, called Manon her true daughter.

Sunday after mass, where Manon went willingly with Grandmère and read Plutarch behind her missal, Grandmère announced, "This afternoon, we are making a proper call upon a great lady. You should be impressed she's willing to receive us. I taught the children of Mme du Boismorel for eighteen years, every one of them. She's been very generous with me and she has consented to our visit today, to have you presented to her. I'm thrilled for you, Manon. This could be a great entrée for you."

Grandmère made her wear the fashionable corps-de-robe, an imitation of court gowns excruciatingly tight at the waist with a stiff bodice in which it was hard to breathe and a long wide skirt with paniers sticking out. It tended to sweep the street and pick up refuse. Grandmère frizzed Manon's hair with a curling iron, every lock, and stuck on a hat dripping feathers and ribbons. Her dress was lavender silk with a pattern of lilies; the underskirt was pale green. Grandmère wore an immense gown of pink, green and white, saved for important occasions. It took them three hours to get ready to meet the great lady. Manon had been hearing about Mme du Boismorel for her entire life. A gracious aristocrat of fine breeding, exquisite manners, superb taste: the pinnacle of everything a woman could be.

They walked, trying to keep their trains out of the mud, across the bridge to the Marais where the Boismorels owned a town house. The Boismorels had recently arrived from their country estate for the fall season. It was October, lindens and horse chestnuts beginning to turn. The sun strained through a gauzy haze and the Seine looked languid. Men were fishing and women were drawing up water. A barge laden with logs drifted under the bridge. Church bells sounded on the hour from every side, hundreds of bells from the hundreds of churches.

The town house was large and elegant. They were passed from servant to servant, then kept standing in a blue and ivory anteroom papered with columns and nymphs. Manon worried about Grandmère, who did not like to stand so long. She was looking pale by the time they were finally shown into a sitting room where a fat dumpy woman whose complexion was golden with powder and spotted bright red with rouge was cooing to her lapdog. The dog yapped at them.

"Little darling, precious honeybee, Mama's right here." Then her tone changed. It was icy, bored. "Mademoiselle. After so many years."

Manon froze as Grandmère dropped on her arthritic knees into a full groveling curtsey. "Madame. It is such a great pleasure to see you again. I wanted to present my granddaughter, Manon Philipon."

"Come forward, child." Madame turned to Grandmère. "Mademoiselle, you may sit there." Madame pointed at a low stool, something a young child might sit on. Manon approached, but she was shocked and longed to say something nasty. "Mademoiselle" was used for women of low status, poor women, servants, wet nurses, no matter what their age or whether or not they had ever married. It was a slap. Manon had never heard her mother call anyone Mademoiselle, except the maid when she was furious. It was too rude. It kept the woman addressed a child, as did the low stool. Manon stood, but she was sturdy and fifteen years old. Grandmère was an old woman with arthritis, who sat with difficulty on the uncomfortable three-legged stool.

"Manon has been reading since she was four," Grandmère was gushing. "She reads Latin as well. She knows more than I do about history. The nuns thought her the brightest child they had taught in a decade. I don't know where she gets her brains—"

"Beware of letting her read books," Mme du Boismorel interrupted, looking Manon up and down like something she had decided not to purchase. "Take care she does not become any more learned. That would be a great pity. No one will marry her, and her poor parents will have her on their hands for the rest of her unhappy life." She continued to lecture upon the proper duties of a woman of what she called uncertain family. Manon fixed her gaze on the mantelpiece. In the huge mirror above it she saw Mme du Boismorel, all flounces and lace and paint, not an inch undecorated and unadorned. Her voice was shrill, like her yapping dog who was nosing at Manon as if she were a lamppost. As Madame spoke she ogled herself in the mirror on the other wall. There were seven mirrors in this room. Manon counted them. Then she counted enameled boxes. Then she counted pictures marching up the walls, mostly pastoral scenes with naked nymphs and goddesses. Twelve paintings. No handsbreadth of silk-covered wall was without its painting, no table without Sèvres shepherdesses, marble busts of the royal family and noble Romans. She did not see a book. Not one.

Manon longed to ask Mme du Boismorel if she had learned to read herself? But this woman had fixed a small income on Grandmère, and so she must keep her mouth shut. This was a great lady. This was the personification of high society and the beau monde. If Madame choked to death on the bonbons in the dish she had not offered them, what would be lost? What virtue did she embody? None that Manon could see. A waste of gilding. A waste of lace. All this rococo plaster and satin and this hive of servants buzzing about her, and at the center, not a queen; nothing but a drone. This stupid painted woman could only behave rudely and flirt with her reflection, as vacant upstairs as her little dog.

FOUR

Pauline

❦

(1777–1781)

PAULINE Léon was born in the Cordeliers section of Paris, named for the monastery of the Franciscans whose habits tied with cords. It was an old, old neighborhood near the University and fairly near the Seine, a warren of ancient streets and a mix of decaying and new houses. The Léon family ran a chocolate shop on the ground floor of a narrow house in a cul-de-sac near the Cafe Procope, where the famous Voltaire used to hold court. The Léon family lived in a room behind the shop, cozy in winter and ovenlike in summer from the stove where the chocolate was cooked. The house was old and sway-backed. The floors groaned when even little Marie-Thérèse ran across them. Pauline was the older of only two living children. Marie was five years younger than Pauline. In between them had come two boys who had not survived their time with the wet nurse. So many babies didn't. It was better to have them die with the wet nurse before you got too attached to them, Maman said wistfully, for if they died at home, your heart could be broken. Maman, who was called Marthurine Telohau, still hoped to have a boy—to carry on the family busi-ness, she said. Pauline's father said, "Pauline is smart enough and strong enough. She can carry it on."

Maman had a bad fever that summer. Afterward, she was not in the way of women. Neither Pauline nor her mother let Papa know, because Maman feared he would go to another woman. She pretended to be having her time, and Pauline never let on. Women had to stick together. She was ten, but she was almost grown, and she was loyal to her Maman. Her Maman was popular with the women of the neighborhood, for she had a big laugh and a way of making other women laugh. She was said to have been pretty, but life wore everybody down. Her face was lined and she had lost a finger and her right arm was scarred from a kitchen accident. Where other women got stout, Maman grew lean and leathery. She never ate the chocolate, for she said smelling it all day made her hate it. Pauline did not feel that way. It was the best smell in the world. She loved coming back from errands and turning the corner of their street. Then the smell of chocolate would surround her, urging her forward: unless the sewer in the middle of the street was especially stinking.

The people above them on what was called the noble floor, who actually rented the whole building and sublet to the other tenants, were a civil servant and his wife and two sons. Except for paying rent four times a year, the Léons had little to say to them, but were friendly with the Fosse family, father (a water carrier), mother (a button maker) and three sons, who lived on the fourth floor in one room. The room in which the Léon family slept in a big canopied bed surrounded by heavy curtains, opened onto a box of courtyard between them and the buildings on the next street. It got sun in the afternoon. It had a fireplace, rarely used since they had the stove in the shop. The shop took all their time.

What learning she had came from her parents. If someone was going to run a business, they must know their numbers. She could read some, enough to make out placards and journals and bills, but she could do sums in her head. Even her father asked her to add up prices and discounts. She could write numbers and sign her name, but she could not write letters—not that she had any cause to. Everyone she knew lived within a ten-block radius. She was out in the street or in the shop all day and sometimes a good part of the night, working by candlelight and the cooking fires. Besides, there were the letter writers on every block who wrote love and business notes for a small fee.

When she had time off, she ran wild with the other kids, up and down the streets and alleys, down to the river. Once they left their neighborhood, they stole anything they could. If they ran into another gang of kids, they had pitched battles with fists and rocks. Once they caught a kid dressed up in culottes (which identified him as upper-class) and velvet waistcoat, a boy older than them, probably twelve. They beat him and took his clothes to sell to a dealer in secondhand clothes. After all, they could hardly wear that finery. They hated the aristocrats, who ate whatever they wanted, who were never hungry and lay around in beds where they slept alone in their own rooms. The aristocrats were always beating the common people, and adults couldn't hit back. Just the week before, she heard her parents say, a mason had run into a young milord on the street and spilled water on him. The milord had run him through. Nothing his family could do but curse.

She knew all the street criers who came through, the sellers of used clothing, the fishwives, the fruit and vegetable women, the sellers of patent medicines, eaux de vie, little blue books of romance and saints' lives and self-improvement, the knife and scissors grinders, all of them with their cries, repeated again and again like great stalking birds, the herons they saw sometimes on the Seine. Most peddlers were women. It was a tolerated semi-legal job. Few working people could take time out to go to the big markets like Les Halles, so peddlers resold stuff in the neighborhoods. They were all on sufferance to the police, who would just as soon knock them on the head.

It had been a hard winter. Spring brought a rise in the price of bread. Everybody lived on bread. When the price rose, their wages or what they were able to earn from their little businesses did not rise accordingly. They did without wood to burn; they did without shoes; they did without anything they could spare to have bread. In the taverns and in the street, people muttered. Someone was getting rich. Someone was hoarding flour. The ministers of the new King kept him from knowing their troubles. Turgot, the King's minister, was killing them.

The morning of May third Pauline's mother said sharply, "Something's happening." They went to the door of the shop. People were running past. After the grim mood of the preceding weeks of hunger, it seemed like a holiday. People were laughing and joking. Some were singing. "Come on, friends," the greengrocer woman shouted. "We're getting bread."

"It's trouble," Maman said, crossing her bony arms.

But Papa went to put out the fires. "We won't have customers today. I'm going along to see what's up."

"Maybe it's raining baguettes," Maman said. She closed the shutters. "I'm telling you, heads will be broken."

Anatole Fosse, the water carrier who lived on the fourth floor, came running to get his wife. "We're taking bread," he shouted. "It's time."

Maman would not go. She took Marie in back, but Pauline went off with Papa. The crowd was taking over bakery shops. People mostly paid, but they paid what bread had cost before the terrifying escalation of prices. They threw the money on the counter and took the bread and went. It was an orderly looting, with a lot of horseplay. If a baker was disliked or felt to be a cheat, he might be roughed up, but mostly they knew the bakers had little more than they did—and they had to eat.

The Watch was out but did not interfere. Some of them joked with the rioters. Around noon, having eaten their fill and carrying as much bread as they could, Pauline and Papa went home. Even after it got stale, they could dip it in broth or wine. It would silence their bellies for a while.

In the tavern the next day, Pauline was sitting with her parents when she heard the end of the story. The Watch would not arrest people, but the King's Grey Musketeers and Black Musketeers, dressed up in their finery and their plumes, would. Over the next week, arrests continued. It seemed as random as bricks falling from the skies. Jacques, an apprentice gilder, had a grudge against another apprentice, Etienne, going back to a dispute over a card game, and turned him in.

A court was set up, a temporary court without appeal. Everybody who appeared before it was found guilty. Pauline listened to the talk in the streets. It was unfair, Papa said. They were condemning men for what everyone had done—which was the point, Anatole Fosse said. They were making a public example. The trials finished the morning of the eleventh, and word spread that men were to be hanged that afternoon.

Papa took her along, saying that since she had gone to the protest, she should attend the punishment. Public executions were free entertainment. There was church and there were executions, and except for puppet shows or acrobats, there wasn't much else to entertain them. They walked in a loose procession over the Pont Neuf and across to the right bank. The Place de Grève—Strike Square, because that's where actions were organized—was a traditional spot for these spectacles, but the crowd was less jolly than usual. When they got to the square, it was not the way it always was. The scaffold for the two gibbets was built very high.

Always the crowd pressed close, to see every bit of the torture that was the best part of the show. Criminals were broken on the wheel. Sometimes flesh was pulled off their bones as they screamed; sometimes boiling oil or sulfur was used on their wounds; sometimes a famous criminal was drawn and quartered—horses were harnessed to each limb and whipped until the man was torn apart. Sanson and his son were masters of all common and extreme tortures. They were the King's executioners who took their bows like musicians. But there was no torture today. Two lines of the notorious musketeers were drawn up, one row facing the gibbet and the other facing the crowd.

Papa murmured, "They're afraid of an uprising. They know what they're doing is unfair. So this is about as fast a death as you'll ever see for a common slob. Only the nobility get their heads cut cleanly off. Nothing happens to clergy except they get moved someplace else. We hang and hang, writhing and twisting in the wind, unless Sanson is feeling kindly."

They dragged the two men in, rushed them to the gallows, put the nooses on and the priest began rattling off prayers for the dying.

"Who are they, Papa? What did they do?"

"Jean-Denis Desportes. It's said that when he left work, he and his wife entered a bakeshop near the Gobelins factory. His wife took three four-pound loaves and only paid thirty-six sous. Jean-Claude Lesguiller, an apprentice gauze maker. He kicked the door of a bakeshop and demanded that they open it. Those are their crimes, little rabbit. They are dying in our places. To scare us and keep us quiet."

"Jean-Claude looks like a boy, Papa."

"He's sixteen."

The men began to cry out to the crowd to save them, saying that everyone had done what they had, so let them loose. The priest finished quickly and backed off, holding up a cross. Sanson posed with his arms folded observing—this was a dull afternoon for him, no artistry here. The two assistants kicked the man and boy off the ladders. They swayed and bucked, flopping and turning like fish thrown on the muddy bank of the river. Sanson nodded. He was going to be merciful. The assistants stepped down and stood on the bound hands of the man and the boy. Jamming them in the stomach with their knees and jerking them down, they broke their necks and finished them off.

Papa said gruffly, "Marie Croison, accused of stealing a brooch, took an hour to die, slowly, slowly choking. Her neck was too soft, they said. It's real mercy when Sanson kills them fast."

Pauline knew that normally the crowd would be furious to have the spectacle cut short, but they just stood sullen and glowering. Some crossed themselves. Some spat, making the sign against the evil eye. Papa strode off cursing, forgetting about her. She had to run to keep up, toward the bridge and home. What should they have done, she wondered, for she did not doubt that they should not have let the hangmen kill the two. She had run through the streets and taken bread too. Now they were all hungry again.

The winter she turned fourteen, the winter of 1781, she remembered those deaths. It was bitterly cold. The Seine froze over. The wheat barges and the wood barges could not come in, and people died every night of the cold. Their bodies lay waiting to be picked up and stored for burial. The ice was filthy with offal and sewage and excrement. The sound of coughing filled the house. All the wood they could afford went into the fires in the shop. The price of bread soared. Beggars were everywhere. Dead babies lay on the steps of the church, foundlings who froze before they could be taken in.

Then in the middle of February, first Marie and then Maman came down with the grippe. Papa caught it but recovered, and Pauline never got it badly enough to take to the bed. She ached with fatigue, tending the shop with Papa and running back and forth. All the water had to be carried in. They were burning up and kept throwing the covers off. She took precious sous to buy them a remedy from an apothecary, but they could not keep it down. She felt frantic. She bought rosemary and sage to burn near the bed, to fight the infection. She poured vinegar on a shovel and heated it in the fireplace, piled with wood. Papa began spending time in the tavern. If they had depended on their neighbors for business, they would have starved; but chocolate was a luxury adored by the bourgeoisie and the aristocrats. Those people had plenty to spend this dreadful winter on hot chocolate and sweets. She tried hard to nurse her mother and sister. Never would she let them go to the Hotel Dieu or any other hospital, where the poor died stuffed six to a bed with strangers. Nobody got out whole. In the hospital, you did not get well; you got sicker and you died.

First Marie and then Maman died. Pauline wept and wept. She could not believe Maman was dead. She could not sleep without her sister curled into her. She was as tall now as Maman had been—not a big girl, but strong in her build. Quick. Used to working twelve hours or more with little rest. Now she had not only to take over Maman's tasks in the shop but to manage the household—cooking what she could, carrying the water in and throwing the waste out. Taking laundry to be washed when it could no longer be put off. Buying from the food peddlers as they came through, or running to their makeshift stalls against the Cordeliers church.

They often ate in the tavern, the Dancing Badger, because Pauline was just learning to cook and Papa was lonely. She made herself small and listened to the men talk. She liked best when they talked about politics; least when they discussed women. The tavern was a low-ceilinged smoky room with crude chairs and benches and stools crowded around long trestle tables. Old men played dominoes and piquet and bet on the lottery. Sometimes a woman who had been her mother's friend would take her to sit with the women and give her a little treat, bread dipped in wine. The women talked about hard times, the lack of bread, how to survive. Sometimes they too talked politics and sometimes they gossiped. She was used to the women being with women and the men with men: that was how it was. If you had a few hours off, it was saved for friends, often lifelong friends—always women if you were female. But she learned something from sitting with her father and playing mouse-in-the-hole. Maman had said it was no

business of women, worrying about the country and the King and his ministers, but Maman was dead. Someone in Versailles in the palace of the
King decided who lived and who died in Paris, who froze and who starved
and who was hanged for asking questions or demanding bread. So she
listened.

FIVE

Nicolas

(1775–1777)

MARIE Jean Nicolas Caritat, Marquis de Condorcet, stood patiently while his two best friends straightened his small-figured waistcoat and vest, adjusted the ruffles of his shirt at neck and wrists. His valet had of course turned him out presentable enough, he presumed, but as Julie de Lespinasse said, surveying him, "You can destroy your tailoring in five minutes of fiddling! And Nicolas, don't stoop. Your height is an advantage."

Nicolas was in revolt against the insistence of the aristocracy on the importance of petty details of appearance, of linens and style of perukes and powdering. Nicolas was the servant of reason. His father, killed right after Nicolas was born, had been a captain in the King's cavalry; his mother was a devout provincial lady innocent of ideas. His family almost disowned him when he refused to go into the army or the Church, becoming a mathematician. A marquis simply did not do that, for science was for tradesmen, except as a hobby. Nicolas for all his apparent meekness never did anything he was supposed to.

Now his friend and mentor Jean le Rond d'Alembert, named for the church on whose steps he had been exposed as a baby, and Jean's platonic love Julie were preparing him to answer the summons of another old friend, Turgot. According to the values of the class to which Nicolas had been born, Jean was nothing: illegitimate, poor, shabby, without wife or family. Jean had changed physics and mathematics almost single-handedly, although Nicolas himself had done as much for probability theory. Mathematics was beautiful. Nicolas would never be careless with a proof. He believed in thinking and writing clearly.

Nicolas had been taken in hand by Julie—also a bastard but the foremost intellectual hostess of Paris, who ran an important liberal salon. Nicolas lived in a web of important friendships. He had a gift for friendship, if not for romance. His friends included those much older than himself, like Jean and the great writer Voltaire; and younger men, like the liberal Marquis de Lafayette. He had replaced his family, in which he was viewed as a weird failure, with friends who cherished him, and for whom he would do anything.

"Turgot is my old friend," Nicolas said defensively. "He isn't sending for me to admire my waistcoat. He means to put me to work."

"So much rides on his shoulders," Jean said with a sigh. "If he can reform the government, we'll enter a new era. If he fails, France may be doomed to anarchy and decay."

Nicolas detached himself from their helpful primping and went into the salon, where Turgot was waiting. "Marquis," said Baron Turgot, motioning him to a seat. "Are you prepared to let your mathematical pursuits go, let go of the Science Academy and come to work with me? I'm a demanding task-master, and I have a great many tasks for you." Turgot was a heavyset stern man, a squat mountain of resolve. He had been appointed Chief Minister by the new King, not yet crowned, and was determined to reform the government and the economy. He operated out of the comptroller-general's office in Paris, reducing his own salary by half to set a good example to the court.

Turgot had begun to replace the entrenched bureaucracy with men steeped in new ideas. "You must move into the Mint. I want you to rationalize the money system and weights and measures. Every time a merchant crosses the border of a province, everything changes. It's absurd."

"Baron, I'm ready!" Nicolas wanted to embrace Turgot in gratitude, but confined himself to rising and bowing deeply.

The Mint was a great stone palace shining and new in the classical style on the left bank of the Seine near the Pont Neuf. Nicolas agreed to move, although he knew little about setting up housekeeping. He had always lived with married friends, because he liked being taken care of. "You're a perfect uncle," said Madame Suard, in whose house he had stayed for years enjoying an intense platonic bond. Everyone assumed that he would never marry, a bachelor at thirty-three. His one foray into love had been so disastrous, his female friends no longer tried to set up liaisons. He had fallen violently in love with a married woman. Marguerite de Meulun. For two years he had been besotted. If she had ordered him to go out in the street and fall upon his sword, he would have done it. In retrospect, she was an unimaginative flirt who liked to collect admirers. Finally he recovered, as from a long and virulent fever, slightly ashamed. Sometimes he thought his women friends viewed him as a gifted child. He was no Adonis. He was amiable looking, so he'd been told. The good Condorcet, Julie called him: a volcano covered with snow. Well, if he could not manage at love, he would have a go at government. He moved into the Mint and Turgot's ministry.

The reason he had become so involved in the new field of probability theory was because only statistical knowledge would make it possible to form intelligent proposals how to govern. It was a fine time to be alive and Nicolas wanted nothing better than to be useful. The air itself felt more lively. Ideas swarmed like midges in the rising sun of activity. Nicolas got himself appointed along with Jean to oversee canals and rivers. They were Plato's philosopher-kings.

Nicolas despised the bureaucrats he must supervise, but he determined to win through. Almost every evening he saw Turgot at one of the salons they frequented. Nicolas kept warning him about the pious camp at court, about enemies in Versailles, until Turgot, who liked to get on with everyone, told Nicolas he was a sheep in a passion, an enraged sheep. Turgot said, "Men in my family die at fifty. I'm forty-seven. My dear Marquis, that gives me three years to accomplish great things. Stop trying to rush me."

Nicolas found him slow-moving. Turgot deliberated; he pondered; he consulted too much. Turgot was friendly with Malesherbes, whom the new King recalled from the exile into which Louis XV had condemned him. Nicolas tried to warn Turgot against Malesherbes. "He's a cold and dangerous man who cares for no one. Do you remember the story of his marriage?"

"It always astonishes me, Marquis, how you can appear so benevolent and yet every bit of gossip you ever overheard is stored in your brain."

"I listen well. Malesherbes married into the upper bourgeoisie for money. No one saw his wife until the day she killed herself by tying a pistol to a tree with a ribbon attached to the trigger and blew out her guts with a single blast. Malesherbes never spoke of her again. You don't consider this significant?"

"No, I do not, Marquis. How a man behaves with women is none of my business. Nor yours, to be blunt."

"How men behave with those they have power over is a revelation of their character: how they behave when they can get away with it."

"What I personally care about is that Malesherbes censors with discretion. He warns writers he respects when they are to be arrested."

While most of their work was in Paris, Turgot had to travel frequently to Versailles. It was a rapid trip, for the best road in the country connected Versailles and Paris: the King's own road. Every time Nicolas made the trip, he fought despair over how impossible their task really was.

Versailles was a silly place where he felt awkward. While his family was noble for centuries, they were just country nobility never called to the King's court. He was comfortably off (though his family still had him on an allowance, in anger at his life choices), but his was not one of the great fortunes. He did not own four hundred suits of fine brocade and silk shot with silver or gold to change into several times a day and glitter as he walked.

He went to Versailles with Turgot reluctantly. None of his talents counted. No one cared about mathematics, social theory or philosophy. They treated him the way people behaved when served the new and nutritious vegetable, potatoes, earth apples. They stared at the objects on their plate and toyed with them. So the bored and haughty courtiers stared at him, an earth apple if they had ever seen one, and attempted to toy with him. Ladies of middle rank flirted. He could not flirt back. He hardly found them of the same species. A woman who took six hours to dress, whose hair loomed a foot over her head, who was painted bright gold with red splashes and artificial moles, who reeked of violets and attar of roses and was packed into a dress that stood out three feet on either side of her, inspired him with nothing but a kind of contemptuous fear. All the courtiers were ranked by absurd roles (the countess who handed the Queen's first lady of the bedchamber the royal petticoat; the comte who stood on the King's left as his shirt was buttoned) and their privileges, both formal (who could sit on a stool in the royal presence and who must stand) and informal (the marquis the Queen danced with last night; the lady she smiled at; who had made the King giggle).

Versailles was an unnecessary city, built on ostentation as if on sand. It was larger in land than all of Paris and enclosed by walls. The streets were lined with the houses of officials whose functions were frivolous, and storehouses that held too much of everything. One building housed two hundred seventeen royal coaches. In Turgot's coach as they made their way through the crowded streets, they passed the residences of men who cleaned the palace fountains, men who helped the King to hunt birds, who tended his packs of dogs, ten men in charge of crows, six of blackbirds. Scores of almoners, chaplains, confessors, clerics, choristers, the hundreds employed in the royal chapel or in providing sacred or profane music, clustered around the churches. Hairdressers alighted from carriages with the air of great generals, as heavily floured as bakers. The amount of flour consumed in a day in Versailles to powder the court's hair could feed Paris.

Soldiers were everywhere, smartly dressed. Ten thousand were stationed here, light horsemen, infantry, Swiss Guards in ruffs and plumes, Grey and Black Musketeers. All wore splendid gilt-trimmed uniforms and strutted in the streets like lords. This place could be carried away in a tempest and the essential work of France could go on: the peasants would plant and harvest, bread would be made and sold, wine would ferment and be carried to market, ships would sail from Bordeaux and Marseille, textiles would be spun, mines would plunder the earth, scientists would discover laws of astronomy and physics, surgeons and physicians would heal, chefs would cook and dressmakers sew up costumes. Versailles was an empty head that interfered unnecessarily with trade, Nicolas passionately believed, as did Turgot. It collected huge taxes from those who could least afford it and spent that money on maintaining itself and fighting stupid and costly wars.

Turgot rarely saw the King; Louis did not like him and the Queen hated him. But as he said, he was in power to work, not to gossip with the King. Never had Nicolas felt so useful, buoyed up and energetic. Even his family was less furious at him than usual. He had more access to his inheritance.

In the palace, huge rooms led into huge rooms, with not an inch undecorated. Rooms had walls inlaid with twenty hues of the finest marble. Ceilings depicted gods and goddesses disporting, Hercules at his labors. The ceilings suggested that this was Olympus and that the visitor was in the presence of deities. Gilded walls of bas relief, walls upholstered in velvet and silk, sagged with paintings of more deities and portraits of the royal family and mistresses. It gave him indigestion of the eyes. It was someone screaming in his ear, HOW IMPORTANT I AM! Outside on the grand canal, courtiers flirted in gondolas and held mock fights with small galleys and frigates. Yet everything was filthy. Excrement had been ground into the carpets. Every corridor stank of stale urine, as did the bushes in the grand garden. Pigs were slaughtered and roasted in a courtyard. In summer, the smell of offal stifled him.

The best times were in Paris when Turgot and Nicolas engaged in mapping out reforms. Turgot was freeing the grain market from the controls that had kept the price of bread at a certain level. Grain could not be artificially sequestered from the rest of the economy. Free trade must reign. The price of grain immediately soared and the cost of bread rose. Turgot knew it would find a natural level once the laws of supply and demand came into play. More grain would be grown because it would prove profitable, and the more grain was grown, the lower would be the price of bread. The free economy was their bedrock.

The people did not agree. Bread riots broke out all through the Ile-de-France—the country around Paris. The price of bread had risen from four sous to thirteen. Turgot held firm. "There's no reason to pay attention to the people's complaints. They don't comprehend. We must force them to realize that the more they kick, fuss and riot, the firmer will be the containment. It's the price of reforming the economy. In the long run, it will benefit even those who cry out the loudest now." By the end of March, the price of a loaf in Paris was twenty-one sous. The price soared all through April. More riots. Even in Versailles the little people took to the streets and confronted the soldiers. The authorities gave in and lowered the price of bread, setting price controls. Turgot was furious. An example had to be made. When bread riots broke out in Paris, he ordered in the King's musketeers, because the city guard would not attack the hungry mobs. His orders were to make examples of whoever they could catch and hang them.

Nicolas knew little about the life of the people swarming in the streets, and in truth they frightened him. Still he knew enough of the judicial system from his work with Voltaire on the cases of poor wretches to take Turgot to task. "Our laws work fine for those presiding in the courts, and are reprehensible for those who go before them. It's judicial murder."

Turgot shrugged him off. "We must set an example. We can't back down before the people or the court. We must slash spending and revive trade."

Nicolas ground his teeth. "Look, if the government is so encrusted with debt, why not cancel the coronation? Let the Archbishop come to Paris and stick the crown on Louis' head in Notre Dame and pour oil on him as if he were a salad, and we'll save millions."

"My dear Marquis, the King would never agree to abrogate a thousand-year-old tradition. Louis would think it sacrilege to give up one jot of royal power or prestige. The people want a king properly crowned."

The way it is. The way it has always been done. The customary method. The privileges of the nobility. The rights of the clergy. The King's will. Yet as the year wore on, something was happening across the ocean in America. In August Louis sent an agent to see firsthand, on the principle that, if the uprising discommoded their enemy England, it must have some merit. Nicolas joined the Nine Sisters lodge of the Masonic Order, where all the talk was of the uprising against the British. Nicolas read every pamphlet that came to him. He was serving as science adviser. He figured out how to test a new device for desalinating ocean water; he advised on controlling a cattle plague. He revised manuscripts on artillery and naval science and printed them. He put a committee together to test Magellan's naval instruments. Finally Turgot began to move. He abolished forced labor on the roads, so hated by the peasants, and the entitlements of the guilds. He was preparing to attack that great sacred cow, the tax structure. People of privilege protested to the King. Turgot was summoned to Versailles. The King dismissed him. With the system in chaos—reforms launched, the old system partly dismantled—depression hit France. The King appointed the Swiss-born banker Necker, considered a reformer but financially solid. Louis could not really appoint Necker, a Protestant. Louis got round that by appointing a nonentity as minister in name. Nicolas submitted his resignation. So much for the great reforms.

Surprisingly, Necker asked him to stay on, insisting he was needed. With serious misgivings, Nicolas agreed. Still, he could not abandon his attempt to bring reason to the Mint just because Necker, whom he disliked, had become minister. At least he did not have a sixteenth-century mind, as Nicolas felt both Louis and Marie-Antoinette did. They lived in a fantasy land where divine right rose with the sun and never set.

Nicolas continued his labors, but he was no longer at the center of decision-making. Then, early in 1777, Nicolas met a man who seemed the embodiment of the values he cherished: freedom, rationality, liberalism, science, philosophy. The American envoy Benjamin Franklin arrived, dressed not like a courtier but like a Quaker in a plain black suit. Nicolas spent hours discussing the new Declaration of Independence with him. He studied it phrase by phrase. Even if Turgot had failed, a true revolution led by rational men was taking place across the ocean.

All of Paris was in love with Ben Franklin, who especially enjoyed the attention of ladies, although presumably he was too old to do more than enjoy their public attentions. Julie de Lespinasse died, leaving Jean d'Alembert in despair, for he discovered her passionate love affairs. Nicolas took care of his friend as best he could, making sure he was never alone. Jean in turn was trying to get Nicolas into the Académie Française, a battleground for the war between the philosophers and the devout parties. Nicolas was already secretary to the Science Academy—a nice stipend.

Paris was a pot always on the boil. Books were banned and burned weekly, writers were thrown into prison or fled into exile, atheism and new ideas were denounced from the pulpit. Nicolas found himself in a constant ferment of political struggle, new and old friendships, the lively dance of ideas. He went out every night. If he rattled around the Mint with his servants, he was seldom in his apartment except to be dressed and to sleep. He scarcely had time to be lonely, even though for the first time he was living alone, away from his friends, the Suards. He invited them to join him, but they declined.

He did his work, he attended his meetings, and he dreamed of change that never seemed to come. In Versailles the Queen gambled away fortunes while hundreds of courtiers danced the Quadrille and dressed in ever more outlandish styles till they resembled mechanical insects of gold. In the liberal salons of Paris, men and women discussed America, where reason and liberty were exalted, where people spoke plainly, dressed simply and fought to the death for something new and fine, a republic. Sometimes his friends day-dreamed aloud about moving to America, if the young nation won its war against its superior opponent. Sometimes he even spoke of that himself. A man needed some kind of dream.

SIX

Georges

❦

(1771–1784)

GEORGES-Jacques Danton grew up in Arcis in Champagne. The Aube River rushed through the village, olive green and swift, near their wooden house that overlooked the town square near the lumpy church. Besides a chateau and tower, most of Arcis was squat stone houses of the poor, simple as stables, cobbled streets that gave way to dusty roads among the fields. Pastures, fields, vineyards, wooded hills were his playground. It was paradise for a boy with freedom to wander, flat country where he could see for leagues. He followed the river in an old leaky boat and then fought his way back upstream. He fished below the mill at the rapids.

His mother, his sisters doted on him. His father had died when he was not quite three, yet he would call his childhood happy. His stepfather was an easygoing unsuccessful lawyer. Georges ran wild over the countryside leading a pack of boys, leaving right after breakfast and never coming back till dinner, then rushing out as soon as he was full. When he looked in the hall mirror at home, a rectangular gilt-framed monster that had been in his mother's family for almost a century, he saw his face scarred and grinning. He had been chased and mauled by a bull he had attempted to wrestle. He had been trampled by a herd of pigs. Then he had battled smallpox. His face—marred, tough, lopsided—grinned back at him. Finally his mother and stepfather sent him to school with the Oratorians at the market town of Troyes. The Fathers were supposed to tame him.

He liked Troyes with its half-timbered houses and its canals, bustling, much larger and richer than Arcis. It had a zest, an energy in the air. In old medieval streets buildings touched over his head and a young man could stand out of the rain. There were big plazas and fountains along the canals, all his to explore when he escaped school. There were streets of whores who called even to boys and open air markets selling pigs, cattle, horses, selling produce, roasted chickens and chickpeas, local wine.

At fourteen, he visited home in June for the funeral of a great-aunt. He was glad to be away from the fiendish discipline of the Oratorians—studying or praying from five in the morning till eight at night, with an emphasis on science, history and modern languages. The serving girl, Denise, was a couple of years older, almost as tall as Georges, with light brown hair and a lean, muscular body. "Do you want to?" Denise asked in the barn. The cattle were lying under a tree. She tended them.

"Of course," he said. "Just show me how." And she had, up in the hayloft. Every afternoon they met in the loft. Sex smelled like hay to him.

It was disappointing to leave her and go off to the Fathers again. He won an occasional prize, but mostly he was a middling student, not brilliant, not failing, just bumping along. He learned what excited him while he waited to be turned loose on the world. The next time he came home, Denise was gone. She had been sent off to be a maid in Reims. Families like Denise's could survive only by exporting their children to the cities to make a pittance necessary to their families and vital to their own futures, if they were ever to marry. Denise's younger brother was keeping the cattle. The family strips of land could not support them. Even the father had to hire himself out in planting and harvest seasons, and the mother made rope for a merchant. They had to work on the roads for free, to give a good part of what they managed to grow to the absent lord in Versailles, and a tenth to the Church. They had to pay the salt tax and other taxes levied only on the poor. So Denise had been shipped off where he could not get his hands on her.

In Troyes, studying with the Fathers but living in rooms his sixteenth year, he had other women. He was in love with a second cousin for a month or two, but sighing was not his metier. By the time he graduated, of his four adventures, he most fondly remembered Denise.

As Georges turned twenty in his native town of Arcis, a sense of stagnation irritated him. He loved his mother dearly, he was fond of his sisters and his mild ineffectual stepfather. But he could not see an opening. Sometimes the whole society felt stuck like a carriage in the mud. But some advanced. Those born to it. He had gone to school with them. The son of a local petty lord had bought a regiment; the Bishop's bastard was sent to Paris: a place in the higher court had been paid for, where he could practice law lucratively instead of going along settling the problems of peasants and shopkeepers and scrabbling for little cases like Georges' stepfather. The children of nobles, even the illegitimate children of clergy, rose like those new balloons, effortlessly, full of hot gas, while he stood with his feet in the dirt, gazing upward. Arcis and the surrounding area were thick with his kinfolk, but no one could give him a real position.

Times were poor. If he was going to make his way, he had to leave. He would make his fortune, come back and set up his family in high style. He would own a big fine house in parkland and beyond that a working farm, vineyards, fields of grain. But that was for when he was thirty, middle-aged. Now he was young and he wanted success so passionately it felt like hunger in his belly, gnawing at him. He had chosen the law, but he was blocked. He read of the Enlightenment, he read of change and progress and new manufactures, but here nothing changed. The philosophers wrote of merit, of free competition of men and ideas, but those were the stuff of schoolboy fantasies. Paris was where a man must go to make his fortune. The mail coach went to Paris once a week. Arcis was where he wanted to end his life, but first he had to live it.

The coach dumped him on the edge of Paris, in a slum festering under a black cloud of pestilent smoke. As he hiked through the narrow streets carrying his two portmanteaux, he choked from the stench of shit and rotten garbage. He was suffocated and deafened at once. In the perpetual twilight of the open sewers between dark houses sealing out the sky, every half block some poor soul was singing at the top of his lungs, bawdy songs, ballads of adventure and crime, topical songs, religious songs: all seeking sous from passersby and selling song sheets, scraping away on violins or banging on drums. Women carrying racks of old clothes pushed through the crowds. Swarms of beggars, crippled, blind, maimed, clutched at him. A man slammed into him. He watched his purse. Two men glared; he glared back. He elbowed his way along. Toughs looking into his scarred face saw someone who would readily fight. They let him pass.

He began using up his meager money at the Black Horse Inn, where people from Champagne stayed. But Georges had not been in Paris long when he got a job as a clerk with a solicitor named Vinot. He wasn't paid but got bed and board. He worked hard during the week. Sundays he would have liked to spend in cafes, but that was costly. He had already learned to like coffee. Mornings, women would stand on the street selling café au lait to workers hurrying past. That was cheap; cafes were not. Instead he went strolling in the Rue Melée near the Porte Saint Martin, one of the city gates. High and low prostitutes walked there, as did noble ladies and bourgeois families. Thieves and pickpockets frequented the crowd that thickened around knots of entertainment, acrobats, dancers, puppets, clowns, street theater, carts selling food and used clothing and the meager property of the dead. He liked the bustle, the liveliness. Most of the week he was stuck in a little cabinet copying documents and might as well have been six feet underground.

One afternoon as he was coming back from an errand, he saw a fresh-faced woman with curly light brown hair saying goodbye to a friend in the street. He had seen her before in the neighborhood. When her friend left, he spoke to her, smiling. "The voice of home. You're from Champagne too."

"Oh, where are you from?" They chatted, discovering they had acquaintances in common from his years in Troyes, where she had grown up and married. The next time he met Françoise, they took a stroll together and he bought her a lemonade. Françoise lived next door in the Rue de la Tissanderie. A year before, her much older husband had died, leaving her a comfortable widow. She promptly shocked her family by picking up and leaving for Paris, where she felt she could enjoy herself without censure. A widow was about the only woman in France who might have a little freedom.

It was an easy and accepted liaison, someone with whom he could share memories of Troyes, with whom he could explore the Paris that challenged and mesmerized him. He picked up an occasional job for ready cash, as he met other needy young men and well-established lawyers in the archaic maze of the court system. He began to organize a law degree. Back in Reims, they gave them out if you paid and showed up a couple of times a year, without requiring such superfluous activities as attending classes, passing exams or writing theses. He signed up. He had to travel to Reims from time to time, but that and the payment were all that was required to deliver him a graduate in law degree by 1784. Now he could take such cases as he could find.

He had a mistress, even if she contributed to his upkeep more than he to hers. He had his degree. He had learned how to dress as a Parisian lawyer, although he cared little about clothes. He learned to go to the theater sometimes and to talk as if he went oftener. He read the journals of the day in the cafes, the few that got through censorship, and played dominoes. He made friends with Camille Desmoulins who was employed in the office of another lawyer. Camille was a younger man with a stutter and literary ambitions who had gone to a very good school in Paris, Louis-le-Grand, but was even poorer than Georges. They were part of the motley horde of young men trying to make it in the law, without connections, without background, without family money. As much as Georges wanted to make money, Camille wanted to be famous. He was bright, verbally deft when he did not stutter, with a sly and salacious wit.

"I b-b-burn for a name that sh-shines! Who wants to die like a mouse and rot and b-b-be forgotten, Georges? If everyone would know me, I would d-d-die happy!" He had lank long hair. Sometimes he was comely in a young, almost defenseless way; other times, he was gawky and storklike. He was always hungry. "We have a ch-choice of hack writing, writing pamphlets, writing p-p-pornography. Or starving nicely, sweetly."

"We're all desperate for a chance to climb out of the mud."

Georges had a natural gift for oratory, for persuasion in court and in private, and huge energy. He needed little sleep. He could walk at a brisk pace for miles through the Paris streets, over the rough pavement and through the gullies of muck, and arrive fresh and ready. Although he loved good drink and good food, he could get by on bread and café au lait, later a bit of cheese or sausage and cheap wine, like a peasant. He could only practice in the common courts, until he could buy his way into a better court. For that thousands of livres were needed. He could not finance the purchase of a legal office. Then he had a sad conversation with Françoise.

"Darling Georges, I have met a M. Huet de Paisy who is taken with me."

"Who wouldn't be, Françoise? I'm taken with you myself." He kissed her shoulder. They were in her bed, the hangings drawn making twilight.

"Ah, but dear sweet Georges, he is taken to the extent of wishing to set me up in style. He has money, houses, armies of servants, a carriage."

Georges felt it would be unfair to object, for he was fond of her but did not love her. They continued to have coffee from time to time or a glass of wine together, for the sake of their friendship, their nostalgia. Georges liked to hold on to his friends. They might be useful someday, and he was a warm and affectionate man. But now he had no mistress and little comfort.

He missed walking through the streets of Arcis and everybody knowing him. Above all he needed some way to scrabble up from the mob of indigent lawyers of whom he was merely one among hundreds, up to the level of making real money and a good reputation, one that would strike solidly like a gold louis rapped on a counter to display its soundness. He could take his knocks, but he was still a bottom dweller in the dark heavy seas of the law.

SEVEN

Manon

❧

(1779–1780)

MANON was twenty-five, late for a daughter of an artisan to marry. Peasants married late. They had to amass a dowry before they could afford to marry. The richer people were, the younger they married. Often girls of the nobility were married before they had begun to menstruate. But no one was about to arrange a marriage for her. All those who might have taken an interest were dead, her mother, her grandmother, her wet nurse. Her mother's death had driven her into a crevice of despair, where she crouched for months. She was left with her father, who only cared that she keep house frugally behind the engraver's shop, so he had money enough for his demanding mistress and his speculations. She had to bring in an accountant to go over his books, because he was sinking. The news was desperate. He had lost her mother's dowry, supposed to be inviolate. Occasionally they had a senseless shouting match about the cost of getting the door fixed or feeding the apprentices. Usually he did not sleep in the brick house on the Quai de l'Horloge. When they must waste an evening together, they played endless games of piquet.

She was tidying his chest of drawers when she found bottles of sassafras powder, tincture of mercury. She called her elderly maid Mignonne and read her the bottles. "What does this say to you?"

Mignonne crossed herself. "The pox."

Her father had syphilis. She tried not to despise him worse than she did. The only being who understood what she was going through was Mignonne, who said, "I'm scared we'll both end up in the street. He'll bankrupt the business. You could be forced into service yourself. I'm too old to find another job." Manon should have rebuked her for speaking familiarly, but she did not. Mignonne was right.

Life rushed by in the street outside. Manon engaged in long friendships and flirtations, usually with older intellectual men, but nothing came of it. She had to be married for love, because she had no money, no property. Her father was capable of marrying again at any time, even of wedding his newest greedy mistress. She had only her intellect, her will, her virtue. She was regarded as pretty, but she was not seductive. She approached everything with a blunt frontal assault. Ever since her adventure with the apprentice, young men frightened her. She toyed with the offer of a marriage blanc from an elderly admirer, but in the end, he had doddered off in trepidation before even that much commitment.

She had sunk into a flirtation through the mail with a man twenty years her senior, a government bureaucrat, honest, austere, something of an intellectual—never married. There had been meetings, fervent exchanges, deep discussions, books lent, notes passed, once a furtive goodbye kiss. Yet Jean Roland de la Platière did not propose marriage. He did nothing improper, he did not touch her again, except a brushing of the hands. Obviously he was terrified to tell his widowed mother that he was considering marrying a dowryless fiancée. His large family lived in Beaujolais. His four brothers were priests. He was to carry on the family, but there seemed no urgency in him. She wanted everything honest, open, two intelligent souls communicating their thoughts and feelings. Instead by his hesitations and cowardice, she was driven to playing him like a fish she must land to survive. Often she grew too depressed to continue. Let him suffocate in his scruples and doubts!

Jean needed her. He was not popular with his superiors, this inspector of the textile industry in Amiens (where broadcloth, linen, wool were manufactured), because he was too honest and too serious. He believed in science, the newest machines and the best techniques. He wore himself out. He needed a wife to assist him. She could learn about the industries under his jurisdiction. It was a rational marriage, one that would open to her a share of a useful and virtuous life. But he did not ask her. She admired his reasoning, his conversation, his serious demeanor, his accomplishments, his very dryness. She felt safe and stimulated at once. But the courtship idled: a visit when she felt their souls mingle; a quarrel, a misunderstanding; a rapprochement. In wide lazy circles they floated. It was four years since he had first shown interest in her. If she did not marry, there was simply no place for her.

Mignonne brought her a letter. "It's from M. de la Platière." She stood waiting while Manon skimmed the letter. After all, there was nothing between them to keep from Mignonne—only from her father, who would try to scuttle any possible marriage. She dropped the letter on her desk. "Nothing. He has a cold. He's tired. He's reading Diderot."

She had to get out of the flat. She had slept poorly the night before, for a gang of beggars had beaten another beggar to death, for encroaching on their territory on the quai. What could she do? Within her room and her mind, she was Joan of Arc, every heroine she had ever read about; yet here she was picking through produce and mending sheets, alone, untouched, wasted. What a chasm between the fire in her brain and the laundry of her life. She began a letter to Sophie Carnet, her friend from the convent. To Sophie she confessed she had lost her faith, despised religion, detested intolerance. But she could not sit still. She would go and visit the painter Greuze, who was married and respectable. Jean was not pleased by her friendship with Greuze. The last time she had seen Jean, he said, "Greuze specializes in sentimental, slyly erotic paintings supposed to be moral and edifying." She found Jean's judgement wanting in sensibility, but she was pleased he showed a flash of jealousy. She thought the paintings uplifting, for they did not depict naked goddesses or court ladies but ordinary people, always a story implied or a moral. His most famous painting was of his wife, when she was much younger: the broken pitcher—a study of youthful indiscretion and regret. Her pitcher was fortunately intact. She crossed the Pont Neuf and turned toward the Louvre where Greuze lived, just along the Seine. She carried a scented handkerchief, since they had no carriage and she must walk through the filthy streets.

The royalty of France had deserted the old palace for Versailles the century before. Now it was full of painters, sculptors, artisans who had gradually taken it over. It was a squalid but lively scene, fun to visit. Depressed and desperate as she was, she knew how to be gay in public—and it was not an act, because when she was with even somewhat interesting people, she did not think of herself. She loved to talk about ideas, to forget her sad female situation. The Louvre was subdivided into tiny apartments, odd-shaped flats. Families had started gardens on the roof and in the courtyard. Babies squalled, kids chased each other around the halls, little girls rolled hoops and boys played ball, pulled each other on straw sleds. Models padded around in dressing gowns. In the courtyards, women cooked on open fires. She stayed as long as she dared, before returning to her tiny room in the flat.

When Jean came to see her that Sunday, again she wavered. He was tall and skinny and yellowish in complexion, from the jaundice that sometimes afflicted him. His hair was thinning and his manner, stiff. But he was husband material, hand cut for her. One month he was dropping hints about marriage and the next he disappeared back into his work at Amiens. She heard he was seeing someone more suitable. This Sunday, their conversation was interesting, about America, but he said nothing of a personal nature.

Then Mignonne began to cough violently, all night, began to cough blood.

Manon called a physician. The man was annoyed to be called to treat a maid. "She's dying. There's nothing to be done. I would like my fee now."

Manon sat beside Mignonne's narrow pallet, holding her withered grey hand. "The doctor says you just need rest and you'll regain your strength. Let us pray to the Virgin." Pious lies. Finally Mignonne sank into unconsciousness. Death came almost imperceptibly. Manon wept as much as she had for her mother. Now she was utterly alone with her hopeless and uncaring father. She was going to end up a servant like Mignonne in some nasty family.

The week after she buried Mignonne, while she was sitting in her old black mourning dress counting sous in the household drawer, Jean appeared. "I have been seriously reconsidering my life. Manon, I have reached a decision as to the new course it should take."

He sounded so remote, she was terrified. He was going to emigrate to America; he was going to join a monastery like his brother. "Oh? What have you decided, then?"

"I wish you to become my wife." He managed a thin smile and held out his hand.

She did not hesitate. She took it and he winced. She realized she had grabbed his hand too hard and immediately loosened her grip. "I accept."

"I informed my mother and my brothers by letter. They are not enthusiastic, but they will raise no objections."

They would, but she did not care. "I'll try to win them over."

"I'm sure your charm will have that desired effect. . . . I do have two conditions." He folded his arms across his chest.

Why was she not surprised? "What would those be, Jean?"

"I don't want you to see your father again. You may write to him occasionally, but that is all. He's a spendthrift and an immoral sponger. I don't want him trying to squeeze me for money to squander."

She hesitated only a moment. Her father had not offered even perfunctory condolences on the death of Mignonne. "I accept your condition. He will never bother you, I promise."

"Excellent." He rubbed his hands together and then rose to kiss her lightly on the mouth. "Now that we are engaged, I would like to get the marriage under way without delay. My other condition is we not make a great fuss. I don't want to waste time or money, but to get on with our lives."

"As soon as you wish." She meant that fully: soon, immediately, before his family could raise difficulties, before her father managed to ruin things. "I need no more than a day or two to prepare."

After he left, she paced through the flat, then began to pack. They would be married in three days. She owned little but books, a few frocks, shawls and cloaks, tiny mementos like a perfume flask and earrings from her mother. As she packed, she stopped to dip into her old journals. Hope and despair flashed from them. At last she was beyond despair. She would be the wife of a man with important work to do in the world. Her life was finally about to begin.

EIGHT

Claire

❧

(1783–1784)

CLAIRE joined the theater company led by Jean Collot d'Herbois. Every little toady who had pretensions stuck a "de" in the middle of his name to imply he had land, was noble or practically so, the lord of whatever particular dungheap he was claiming. Every manager she had worked for was "de" something. Collot took it less seriously than most. He did not pose as noble, boasting about his rough times on the streets of Paris.

She was the primary ingenue in his company, since Yvonne had got knocked up and gone off to have her bastard. Yvonne had seduced an innkeeper, a widower. He offered her a room in back and said if it was a boy, he'd marry her. Nobody need know she was an actress. Otherwise the Church wouldn't marry them. Actresses were lower than prostitutes and forbidden the Church's rites. "So he doesn't wear silk and laces. He eats well. He sleeps in a warm room in a feather bed. I'm twenty-seven," Yvonne, officially eighteen, confided. "This is the best I can do."

So Claire moved up to main ingenue. She really was eighteen. Three years after she had run away from home, this was her fourth company. She had been hired away from the first group within six months, when they had been performing at a fete in Orleans. The women had never warmed to her. She had let the head of the company fuck her but she did not like him. She had not thought she had a choice. Since then she had learned she was in demand as an actress, for her striking looks, her loud voice, her carriage, the fact that she actually could assume roles, learn the lines and give some semblance of emotion. Nowadays she did not feel she had to oblige.

This was the best company so far. They played real theaters in every town—no more putting up a rough stage in a town square or screaming over the heads of drunken louts at a fair. They had costumes and scenery and written-down plays. They got paid regularly. One of the roustabouts who traveled with the company stood guard at the dressing rooms and did not let just anything with two sous in his pocket bother them.

Sometimes the boss himself, Collot, wrote plays for them, like a spectacle he had slapped together to celebrate the birth of the Dauphin, the heir to the throne. It featured a huge fountain surmounted by a dolphin, played by Claire, who had to sing in the fish outfit, when she had been at the bottom of the company hierarchy. She was glad when audiences showed they didn't like the play any longer. The Queen was growing unpopular, regularly referred to as "the Austrian bitch." She was also called Madame Deficit, spending money faster than it could be soaked from the poor. Collot had scribbled a new pageant, that featured a balloon taking off—pulled up by wires. Claire, in a costume of feathers, sang about going up, up in the clouds. The Montgolfier brothers had recently flown a hot air balloon at Versailles. Balloons were all the rage. Rich ladies wore big gondola balloons in their hairdos. It was good that ladies sat in boxes, because nobody behind could have seen through their elaborate hairdos, full of frigates in full sail, shepherdesses (the Queen liked to play shepherdess at her private palace Petit Trianon), forests, towers and vases of fresh flowers. Claire had hair down to the top of her buttocks, dark chestnut, black in lamplight. In one romantic comedy, she was discovered sitting by a river combing her hair, apparently naked but for those tresses, although of course she was wearing a flesh-colored shift. That always went over big with the gentlemen. Claire was not modest. They did a couple of pantomimes in which she was almost nude. She had the body for it, so why should she care if people looked?

When some lout with more money than manners tried to strongarm her into bed, Collot backed her up. She had left her previous company in Lyon, when the manager insisted she fuck the silk merchant who was the angel of the tragedy they were performing. Collot encouraged her to refuse. "They think we're dirt," he said. "We have four times the talent and brains of these pigs, but they relegate us to the gutter." He slammed his fist on the table. Platters and goblets rattled, and his wife, Madame, laughed nervously.

Collot had a pretty, weak-willed wife who did everything he told her and more. She kept the books, sewed costumes, filled in minor roles, carried the programs to the printers and picked them up. She soothed ruffled feelings, calmed roiled nerves, sat up with the sick and drunken, provided remedies to the hung-over. Collot was an unusual manager in that he was bright and faithful to his wife, although he treated Madame as he might a servant. That was considered by all (except Claire) a good marriage. He yelled at them, but that was to be expected. She didn't have to lie down next to him after he called her seventeen foul names for slut and told her she had the talent of a rotten melon. The company was successful, whether they were putting on pantomimes about current events, melodramas of virtuous bourgeois maidens pursued by wicked lords and rescued by equally virtuous men of their own class—the so-called Third Estate—or the occasional tragedy or farce. They were a good all-around troupe who gave audiences what they wanted.

Collot had come up from the streets of Paris by wits and hard work, fueled by a rage that never vanished. It gave edge to his acting. He played villain's roles, saying they were more fun. When she was older, she would do the bad women.

They ate together before the evening performance, around a big table in the inn where they were staying, everyone except Juliette, who had a merchant who was keeping her in her own small rooms. Juliette did the wicked women now; she had been the ingenue before Yvonne. Collot sat at the head of the table and Madame at the foot. Madame was slender, blond and wispy. She could make her voice carry onstage, but offstage, she whispered. It was hard to engage her in eye contact. Sometimes actors forgot she was in the room.

Not so Collot. Nobody could overlook him. He was a tall slender man with regular features, large striking dark eyes, hair even darker than her own that he kept long and loose on his neck or in a pigtail. He wore a wig on stage and when he was dealing with gentry. He looked better with his own dark hair around his face dominated by his striking and powerful gaze. His body was hard and whiplike, a waist almost as slender as hers. There was a fierce smouldering energy to Collot that worked well on stage.

Even though he stuck the stupid pretentious "de" in his name, he did not pretend to be a gentleman. His father had been an unsuccessful goldsmith on the Rue Saint Jacques in Paris. He had gotten to know the regulars at the Pont Neuf, where it was said that if a person wanted to find anybody in Paris, they had only to stand there for a day. He had befriended acrobats, fire eaters, jugglers, mimes, peddlers of quack cures and love potions. By twenty, he was part of a traveling company making their way in crude wagons across France.

"When you're an actor, nobody's your friend except other actors," he said in his sonorous voice. He always seemed to be addressing the last row in the upper balcony. "Every little prick with a shop that does a hundred livres of business a year looks on you as scum. They won't claim you as a friend in public. In private, they love you, but don't ask for help."

She could understand Collot's anger, although she did not have his drive for recognition. He felt insulted, kept down. He lusted after position and power forever closed to him. She felt as if her life was so much better than it was supposed to have been, that if she dropped dead tomorrow, she would have stolen three years of good living. She ate regularly, better food than her family had ever seen. She often had meat or fowl. While she was with the first company, she had been hit often and beaten for bleeding on a costume once, but since then, nobody had struck her. She had more clothes than her entire family put together. She slept in a bed with only one other woman, Lucie de Fontanelle, who did the heroines and had a fine soprano voice, better trained than her own loud uncertain contralto. Lucie could not dance as well as Claire and she had not as statuesque a body. She had the same delicacy of features and coloring as Madame, although with a flirtatious manner she could summon or drop like opening and closing a box lid. Lucie was sharp, although she concealed it behind that arch manner, a woman who held a fan before her face while she surveyed the world with a cold eye. Admitting to twenty-five now, she had been born in Bordeaux, in a shopkeeper's family with too many girls. "My papa sold me to a company that was passing through. When I went to leave them, they told me I couldn't, that they had bought me. I said, sue me. I walked out the door."

Claire admired Lucie because she got good roles, because she did not belong to anybody, because she was clever and unimpressed with the niceties and the furbelows that other women thought important. "Put some money by," Lucie said. "How long will the men want to look at you? Buy a little house, buy land. That's all that matters."

Claire did not make enough to save much, and she sent money home to her grandmother. She did not want land. She wanted to be free to roam all over France, beholden to no one.

Around the table in Caen, in the inn where they were staying, the women talked together, except Madame, about the sort of men they fancied. Claire had little to say. Every so often she saw a man she wanted, and she went to bed with him. A midwife had told her once when she was worried she had an infection, that she had a tipped womb and it would be hard for her to conceive. She hoped so. She picked up a spinner, she picked up a dock worker, she picked up a monk, she picked up a captain of artillery who claimed to be a nobleman and might have been. She tried them all for fun and was done with them. What mattered the most was that *she* chose.

"I don't think I'll ever marry," she said to the women.

"La, you're an idiot," Lucie said. "You need someone to ride out the hard times with. Just pick a man who can make a living and has the gumption to work hard. A man with some property."

"I don't see it's better," Claire said stubbornly. "I have no father. Nobody owns me. Why should I give myself to a man?"

"An unmarried woman is at risk," Juliette said in her know-it-all manner.

"A nun doesn't need to be married, because she has Christ for a bridegroom and the Church will protect her. But you're no nun. A woman needs a man as protector."

"I never noticed men protecting any of you," Claire said. "We can be carried off to prison for saying the wrong thing. We can be accused of picking pockets or blasphemy or indecency. We can be accused of stealing a handkerchief from the room of some man we spent the night with. Who'll believe us? We're at risk, but a husband won't keep off the law."

"Pregnancy does," Lucie said. "If you're ever in serious trouble, get pregnant fast or fake it. They never hang a pregnant woman."

"Nobody stays pregnant for long," Claire said.

"You won't say that the first time you're pregnant," Mme Abiel said. She was the oldest in the company and did the odd jobs Madame missed. "It'll seem like forever. But don't get pregnant, girls. It's the end of you."

"It wasn't the end of Yvonne," Juliette said.

"That's not my idea of how I want to quit," Claire said.

"Do you want to quit?" Lucie asked.

"Never," Claire said. "I like this company. Collot blows off at us, but he knows what he's doing. We always get paid. I like the life."

"You're young," Juliette said.

"I'm not young, am I?" Mme Abiel said. "I still relish the life. Once bit, always bit. There's always another play, another town."

Madame tapped on her door the next afternoon. "Claire, this letter came for you."

It was from her sister Yvette.

I have to tell you that things are very bad here. The last two harvests failed and nobody has money to spend on laundry. Grandmère died of a bloody flux two months ago, but it was the hunger that really killed her. Maman was sick for two weeks and last Sunday she died too. The money arrived too late to help. We were thrown out of the house. Pierre went off to Toulouse to look for work as a servant. The nuns are going to take me in as a laundress. At least I could have Maman buried in holy ground in spite of her refusing the last rites. I persuaded the priest she was out of her mind with fever.

I know you are damned forever for your sins, but I am your loving sister. Here is the address of the convent. Please send money. Everyone is starving. There are no babies or old folks left. People go around dragging like horses that have been worked to death. But the nuns have food in the convent, fish and chicken and fresh figs and even white bread. The kitchen staff look so pink and plump, my mouth waters when I look at them. I have not eaten more than weeds boiled into soup in weeks, but tomorrow I go to the convent. I'll pray for your sins.

Claire wept so hard she had to wash her face in alum water to take the swelling down for the evening performance. She should have stayed with them. But what could she have done? Grandmère dying without Claire to hold her hand and close her eyes. Grandmère gone, Maman gone. Dying of lack of bread while she had more than she could eat.

Collot talked to Claire more than to the other actresses. He said she had more brains, but he also told her she was a fool, for not getting what she could out of her admirers. "How long do you think your looks will last? You see anybody lining up to fuck Madame Abiel? Take what you can get while the getting is good. You should put the squeeze on all of them."

"I don't care what a man desires. It's whether I want him that matters. I'll never sell myself."

"We all sell ourselves. We sell passion and beauty and lechery and fear and pity. We sell everything we've got, Claire, and you're an empty-headed goose if you think anything else is going on."

Collot played a brigand, leader of a robber band, in a play about a kidnapped baker's daughter, who converted them to virtue by her sterling example. Claire played the heroine, but the lines almost broke her up. Collot said as long as she showed enough bosom and leg, it didn't matter what she thought. The strange thing was that while Collot was playing the leader of the gang, she found him attractive—this man she often resented, her boss who had reduced his wife to a timorous nonentity, who regularly insulted her. As soon as he became king of the robbers, he radiated sexual significance that he could never possess in life. She would never let him glimpse her reaction, but it put an edge on what would otherwise be a vacuous performance.

Men available to her often inspired her contempt. They were taken in by poses on the stage, by paint and flimsy costumes. They wanted to bed an image that in the darkened theater smelling of many bodies titillated them. Some were young lawyers who thought an actress a suitable object of lust, a prestigious mistress. Some were older men who longed for their youth and thought a woman desired by other men might magically restore it. For some she was a trophy. If she was occasionally moved by a broad set of shoulders, a flashing smile, a witty line, then she acted on her lust before it vanished.

The other actresses called her fickle, but she did not want more from those backstage and back alley admirers than a quick touch of sensual pleasure for a night or two. The less seriously she took those men, the more they wanted to hurl jewelry and other trinkets at her feet and the more they pledged undying love, as if they had any notion who she was, where she came from, what interested her. However, she liked the jewelry. Nobody in her family ever had jewelry. It could be sold in a pinch. Gold was gold.

She imagined a man who could move her. Her daydreams were absurd, but sometimes as they trundled along in rough terrain bounding and jouncing in a stagecoach on the way between relays and cities, from one flea-infested inn to the next, she would imagine a robber gang blocking the road. She imagined herself being carried off like the fainting heroine she played, but willingly. She could imagine being wildly and passionately attracted to a man who defied the law of the land, who placed himself outside society (as she was outside).

Her ability to read had greatly improved. She enjoyed reading novels, Gothic tales full of randy evil monks and lecherous uncles plotting incest in ancient castles. She read Rousseau, like everybody else. There was a man who dared to bare his soul. She read Diderot and Voltaire. She would have liked to read the *Encyclopedia*, but she could only carry slim volumes that fit into her pockets or her muff.

She read little paperbound books meant for peasant women and servants, but she also read books meant for the bourgeoisie. It satisfied a hunger that even the traveling didn't sate, the hunger to understand the world, to know why things were as they were, how they got that way, how it was in other lands and times. She read about Joan of Arc. There was a woman who strapped on armor and went to battle, out-generaling the men. She read about hot air balloons, electricity, mesmerism, animal magnetism, the war with the English, the new world, how the Americans had with the help of Lafayette overthrown the British and made themselves free. She read about Catherine the Great and how she ruled Russia as what Diderot called an Enlightened Despot. She wondered if the peasants considered Catherine enlightened. It was interesting to hear about a woman wielding power.

The other women sometimes read romantic novels. Mme Abiel read the lives of saints, full of gory illustrations. But everyone in the company, women and men, thought it was peculiar of her to read serious books meant for men. Collot told her she would cook her brains. She would lose her beauty and her female nature if she overused her naturally weak brain, he explained kindly. She didn't bother arguing. She simply bought books and read them.

Sometimes she imagined being involved with one of her intellectual heroes. Voltaire and Diderot had gone to prison for what they had written, but they were dead or dying. Abbé Raynal had written bravely and been sent into exile, but he was an old man. What she would like would be a man just her age as smart and iconoclastic as those Encyclopedists. Maybe he would write plays about justice and freedom, and she would act in them. That would be far more interesting than fainting in the arms of Collot the robber chief. Then she would say the lines with real passion. She imagined plays that would speak to ordinary people—like herself—but plays that dealt with real trouble and real pain and real anger would be censored. Still, she could imagine such a theater, even if she would never act in it.

NINE

Max

❦

(1782–1787)

AUGUSTIN entered into Louis-le-Grand on the same Bishop's scholarship, while Max returned to his hometown to set up housekeeping with his surviving sister Charlotte. They lived modestly, circumscribed by their lack of money. It was a humble choice to return to this stuffy town where he had always been viewed as a demi-bastard of dubious family, but he saw no way to advance in Paris. He had a duty to his surviving family and something to prove.

"Max," Charlotte said, "they will all come to respect and admire you. They have to! You'll win over the town fathers. In the meantime, what would you like for supper?" She beamed at him hopefully, tugging on her apron.

He shrugged. "Something simple. Soup and bread."

He loved his routine. Never had his life been under his own control. Since his mother died and his father fled, he had lived on the sufferance, the charity of others. Now he could set his hours, the way everything was arranged, the food. He liked to eat lightly. He was addicted to coffee and morning chocolate, for both clarified his mind. Otherwise he drank watered wine and ate mostly fruit and bread. With his sister as housekeeper he could get away with reading at the table. Often he had no idea what he had eaten, only that it was soup and not obnoxious.

He had control of his appearance too. No more shabby clothes worn until they rotted. He acquired a wardrobe suitable to his new station. He believed in being clean, crisp, elegant in an understated and never ostentatious way: he cared deeply that everything should be correct. It gave him confidence, visible credentials in the form of a silk suit, a striped vest, a fine shirt with lace ruffles, silk stockings. He had the hairdresser in every morning he went to court to comb, curl and powder his hair. It took an hour, for he was fastidious that no one should feel superior to him on the grounds of appearance. His manners were meticulous. When he looked in the mirror, he was reassured. It was not that he was vain about his face or body, but he was comforted by the totally unobjectionable appearance he created.

He took daily walks. They socialized with other young bourgeois. He belonged to the local literary society that dined together and read their poetry. He entered essay contests, as did all ambitious young men trying to make a name. That was how his hero Jean-Jacques Rousseau had first made his mark. He wrote poetry to young women with whom he dutifully flirted at social gatherings. Women liked him as a dance partner, since he was deft and did not tread on their feet. It was less work than making conversation.

Charlotte pouted. "That Mademoiselle Laporte was making eyes at you."

"I didn't notice."

"You'll marry her or one of those other hussies and I'll be alone."

"Charlotte, I'm in no hurry to marry, I assure you." People seemed to assume he would marry, and he supposed he would, although he thought Charlotte was fine as his housekeeper. She was not bright and she was prone to be possessive, but it did not take a great deal of brain power to shop in the market for apples and pears, to get soup on the table, to have his shirts washed and pressed. He left it up to her to find herself a husband or not, for he could not yet afford a dowry. Some women of good families seemed to find him attractive. He liked one, then another, but none well enough to do more than compose verse about their beauty and kindness, send them copies of his more interesting legal briefs, dance and carry on the decorous and tedious flirtation they expected.

He worked over his briefs again and again. He was aware that sometimes the other advocates thought he overprepared, but he believed in doing the best job possible for every client. It was a matter of respect, for himself, for the clients who depended on him to assuage wrongs or set them free. He was delighted to be an adult finally, although sometimes he felt as if he were pretending, and he would be caught and sent back to the Fathers at Louis-le-Grand. The more he established rules and patterns and habits, the safer he felt in their little house. An anger both hot and cold gripped him when he felt an edge of contempt from his peers, when he watched what happened to poor people the courts rolled over. What could he do except work ever harder and more meticulously?

There was one law for the nobles and the rich and another for the poor. When the poor came into court, punishment was automatic. They would die or go to the galleys, for the crime of being accused. It was a matter of making an example of someone who did not count, so it did not matter if the wretch was guilty or innocent. One of the worst felonies was banding together to commit any crime, even the theft of a shirt. That meant a painful lingering death in public. The wheel. The courts were terrified that peasants would organize into gangs and attack, not each other, but the local lord. Although it had not happened in a century and a half, that fear never dissipated.

He observed his society but kept his ideas to himself. With whom would he share them? Perhaps with Augustin, when he finished school. Max entertained a pleasing fantasy that he and his younger brother would set up practice together, sharing cases and ideas.

His first really interesting case involved a retired lawyer, who had built himself a lightning rod after the one invented by Benjamin Franklin, and then been forced by his neighbors and the town to remove it out of superstitious fear it would bring the lightning down. It was Max's first chance to make a name, and he played it to the hilt. He was no orator. His voice tended to rise shrilly at the end of sentences he had been told were overly long. Still, he reasoned densely and passionately, and people paid attention. So did the judges, for he won handily. The case was written up in the Paris papers. He sent his brief to Benjamin Franklin in Paris. The local intellectuals made a fuss about him. He was invited to speak here and there.

Then a monk, treasurer of the Abbey, accused a carpenter of stealing money. Max discovered that the man's sister Clementine, a laundress at the Abbey, had repulsed the advances of the monk. This case was bitterly fought. The monk was represented by a lawyer who had recommended Max to the local bar. Max worried that he might annoy his former sponsor; nonetheless he was glad to demonstrate his independence, as much to himself as to anyone else. He did not like to think he was a man who could be bought for a little patronage. Besides, the monk was guilty and his client was not; justice had to be done. Clementine was a good woman and should be protected. It was pleasant to play her protector.

Thus over the next few years, he marched along, sometimes having more cases and sometimes less. He was regarded as a fine pleader, but he did not attract wealthy or important clients. He was not accepted into the upper ranks of Arras society. Would he always be trying to make himself heard not so much in a vacuum as in a great pillow stuffed with dusty old goose down? Arras was conservative, petty, mean. No amount of talent displayed in the courts would make up for his lack of family. The people who looked to him were the little people, whose champion he had become. Perhaps he would have to marry into one of the established professional families to improve his position.

One local belle, Mlle Deshorties, a distant cousin, seemed pleasant. He would not mind marrying her. He paid her court, not assiduously but competently. They reached a sort of understanding, but nothing was signed. She was hoping he would do better financially before they agreed. She had a sweet singing voice, was undemanding as a partner in conversation. She liked animals and children. He thought that a sign of virtue in a woman. She had copious brown hair, large nearsighted aquamarine eyes that were her most striking feature. She could make him a satisfactory wife.

He met an interesting army man, an engineer by the name of Carnot, who asked him to take on the case of an old servant woman who was being bilked. Max won the case. He and Carnot remained friendly. They discussed the American revolution and the rights of man. Then a group of peasants came to him with a grievance against their landlord, the Bishop of Arras—his benefactor.

Max hesitated. He did not want to offend the Bishop, but he could not turn back from justice because the case was not in his own best interest. He would despise himself if he allowed his personal advantage to get in the way of his moral decision. The Bishop was behaving badly. He was using his power to mistreat peasants and force them off land they had a right to, having farmed it for generations. Moreover, they could not survive without that land. The Bishop was in the wrong. Max would prove it. He took the case.

TEN

Pauline

❦

(1787)

PAULINE usually liked fall. The streets stank less. Like most common people, she and Papa bought river water, and in the summer, it was dirty and sometimes had an odor. In fall, everything felt cleaner. The air began to smell of wood smoke. Everywhere sawyers were working, loosing the scent of oak and pine. Carts were dumping wood in the narrow streets. They took the right of way and everybody must watch out for them.

That was how the catastrophe happened. Her father was delivering chocolate to a customer who was very particular about his breakfast cocoa and must have the sugar pulverized into the powdered chocolate so that he need only add hot water. Papa was carrying a great jar full of the mixture and several boxes of made-up bonbons he was delivering as gifts from gentlemen to ladies. He had turned into a little street in the Marais and was looking at a building facade when a carter backed up and discharged a load of wood without looking. Her father was struck in the head and killed instantly. It was after dark and she was worrying what had happened to him when a constable came and told her to fetch the body.

Papa's funeral was large. He had been popular in the neighborhood, and people wanted to show respect. Her boyfriend Henri sat beside her and put his arm around her shoulders, to comfort her and to stake a claim. She was on her own now, proprietor of the business. She was twenty and could get married anytime. Henri was apprenticed to a hat maker, so he wasn't supposed to marry until he served out his time with his master, who lived four streets over. Now Henri had to decide whether to continue with the hat maker or to take over the chocolate business. She would prefer he came in with her. It was hard to run the business alone. She would have to hire someone to help. She missed Papa all the time in the shop. She was sleeping alone in the big double bed. Henri and she made love in that bed, but he could not sleep there. He had to be back at his master's for the night.

She sold off her father's few clothes to Victoire, the old-clothes woman, except for a shirt she gave Henri. It was tight on him but in good shape. She was an orphan now. She prayed fervently for the souls of her parents. She knelt trying to pray for Papa's soul, and all she could imagine was a bird like the stained glass window with the pigeon they said was the Holy Ghost. The church was damp. She could smell the chocolate on herself. Henri said it made him feel he could eat her up.

Henri she had known her whole life, but they had only become sweethearts the year she turned eighteen. His family had always lived across the street on the third floor of the building with the crooked door. One Sunday afternoon in May she had gone with a crowd from the neighborhood out along the river to Port Bernard to eat fish stew, drink cheap country wine and dance. Suddenly they had been dancing only with each other and suddenly they had looked into each other's eyes and then they were kissing by the river. They went out in a little boat and sang silly songs together. She had been as happy as if she was drunk.

They had been lovers for a year. The first time had been bad. She had not wanted to, but he had been out of control. It had happened in the shop while her father was making a big delivery. He had taken her on the floor, with an old rug under them. She cried afterward. He apologized and told her he loved her again and again. Then she had got used to it and began to like what they did. Papa had accepted Henri as her fiancé. If he weren't apprenticed, he could marry her right away, but as it was, they had to wait.

She said to her girlfriend Babette, "When I'm married, I'll have to cook and keep his clothes clean. It's a lot of work!"

"Of course you'll get married to Henri, but what's the hurry?" Babette rolled her eyes. "In the meantime, let's have a little fun. Now you have the pleasure of him and none of the labor."

Henri and she strolled out to the suburbs every Sunday or walked along the Seine. Making plans was fun, but neither was in a hurry to put them into practice. They were careful. He pulled out of her before he came and she washed herself inside. If she got pregnant, then they would have to figure out very fast what to do, but she got thinner instead, with all the extra work. She began to wish that Henri would make up his mind. She had a boy helping, but he was only eleven and could not lift anything nearly as heavy as she could. He was fast with the deliveries but could not carry much.

Henri was a hand taller than Pauline and stoutly built, with broad shoulders and big knuckled hands. He could lift and bear heavy loads. His back and shoulders were muscular. He had dark grey-blue eyes, fine light brown hair. His features were all slightly squared, his chin, his nose, the line of his brows, his mouth, as if he had been built by a carpenter with a good level. The touch of his hands was surprisingly deft. He had a light tread for such a sturdy man. She could always recognize his step.

She got lonely with just her little helper for company. She had grown up in a family business, and now she had no family. She had two particular pals, Aimée, who was married, a year older than Pauline, with one little boy. Aimée made coffee and sold it on a street corner every morning and noon. She had a station near the Pont Neuf, highly desirable because of the traffic. Babette was unmarried and exactly her age. Babette worked in the tavern her parents owned, the Dancing Badger, just around the corner. Pauline was closest to Babette. Babette was not an orphan but she too had a boyfriend and they were sleeping together, going to be married, but who knew when. Aimée was no good to talk to, for she always said they should get married at once.

Henri's parents did not want him to quit the apprenticeship. They had paid his initial fee to his master. They thought making hats was a safer business than chocolate, which they considered a fashion of the wealthy that would pass and leave Pauline without a viable business.

Pauline had a fair amount of freedom. There was no one to boss her but the gossip of her neighbors and the opinion of the neighborhood. When she was dealing with anyone from outside her little sphere, she pretended to be married. It was unusual, illegal, for a young woman to run her own business. She was supposed to be overseen by some man—husband, father, uncle, brother. She told the cafes she delivered to and the private customers that she was a married woman whose husband had been injured. He kept the books, she told them, yes, her husband Henri Léon. While she longed to have Henri help her in the shop, she was aware that once he had moved in, her life would change radically. He would want to know why she was wasting time in the street talking about the price of bread and reading together a clandestine pamphlet that talked about freedom and cheap bread for all. Often by the light of a candle late in the shop, she consumed little romances and political tracts that peddlers sold, the way her women customers consumed chocolates. She did not want to be told she was wasting precious money or time on such trifles.

Every day she changed her mind. She was angry with herself for shifting her desires and annoyed with Henri because he was just as uncertain. She'd known him since they were four. She liked the love-making in the soft bed with its green hangings in the room behind the shop with the window and a mirror her mother had been proud of. Papa had bought it for Maman when they were married. Many times Henri and Pauline looked at themselves in it, posing together. It was set up to reflect the light from the window and make the room lighter. She wanted Henri, of course, of course, but marriage could wait a little longer.

Then the army lottery was announced on wall posters. Wars were the business of the nobles and the King. The common people had to fight them, if they got taken for the ships or the army. Otherwise, they didn't much care. King Louis sent ships and money to America, where they had beaten the British. People talked about America, because they had no kings or nobles there and everybody was equal, except the Blacks. And the women, Pauline thought. We're never equal except in the amount of work we do. Now there must be armies marching somewhere, because they had the lottery in Paris. People were furious about the lottery, the way they always were. Servants were excluded, as if they were somebody special. In fact anybody who had a noble on his side could get out of it. Henri had no such luck. He lost in the lottery. He would have to go and be a soldier for the King. Everybody in the neighborhood commiserated with him.

"I didn't even know there was a war," he said. "Off someplace like the Caribbean, wherever that is. Down south, I think. Why do kings have these wars nobody cares about?"

Even Pauline who read all the pamphlets had no idea where the fighting was. A few years ago it had been India. Nobody she knew ever went to these places and nobody who went there to fight, came back.

He frowned. "Let's get married. You can go with me."

She promised to think about it, and she thought about it long and hard. Henri might never return to her. It would be years. He might get killed. He might be wounded and need her to nurse him.

She talked to Babette and Aimée. Aimée surprised her. "If you were married, you'd go, naturally, a woman must go with her man. But you aren't married, and this is some totally fucked time to do it."

Babette was as blunt. "Give up the business to go chase after the army with ragtag prostitutes and washerwomen? You'd have to be an idiot. They die like flies of typhus in those camps. If he's wounded, he can send for you."

That argument got to her. To give up the business in order to be a camp follower? Abandon her home, her friends, her business, her life? "I'll wait for you," she promised. "But I told Papa I'd keep up the business. I swore I would. It's something for you to come back to."

He couldn't argue with that, because his master was never going to take him back. That was the end of being a hat maker. His parents were desolate. They ran about from government office to government office, but they were obvious common people and could not get past the gatekeepers. Henri must go and he might never return.

His father told him, "If it gets bad, just slip off. You know nobody in the neighborhood would rat on you. We hate the King's army. But if you do take off, bring your musket. I know somebody who buys that kind of thing. It's worth some money." In the tavern, everybody gave Henri advice.

Henri was depressed and drinking too much. Now he sat at the table in her kitchen glowering at the fire. "Everyone says it's hell in the army. They can flog you for anything. The officers are all noble shithooks who don't even think you're human and don't care how many of you die in a pile. But sometimes there's loot. And I can always desert, right?"

She wept all night after she saw him off. She wept but she did not change her mind. He would return or he would not. In the meantime, she had a business to run. Her life was here in the neighborhood and she wasn't ready to give it up, not for any man and certainly not for the sake of being married. In this neighborhood, she was somebody: Pauline who makes chocolate, the Léon girl.

ELEVEN

Nicolas

(1783–1788)

NICOLAS, permanent secretary of the Science Academy, was proposed by Jean d'Alembert for a vacancy on the Académie Française. Buffon, the naturalist, proposed the astronomer Bailly. A battle half to the death was fought between the factions; the victory of Jean d'Alembert and thus of Nicolas was credited to women of the salons, who had championed Nicolas. But his pleasure was short-lived as Jean became mortally ill and his kidneys failed. Jean refused an operation, saying he'd had enough pain. He died, leaving nothing but a request that two aged servants be taken care of. Nicolas obliged. There was a hole in his life, where his friend had been.

Nicolas still lived and worked in the Mint, a huge imposing palace on the left bank of the Seine across from the Louvre, attended the two academies sedulously, went to his favorite salons. He was a genial man. People enjoyed being around him, although they often liked to tease him. He was seen as a bit abstract, absentminded, lofty: a secular saint.

He was just bringing out his *Life of Turgot*, while he continued his ongoing edit of Voltaire's letters, making copious notes for a biography. Whenever anybody important in the arts or sciences died, he was expected to write an elegy. He did his share of certifying experiments as good or bad science, part of what the Science Academy paid him to do.

One Jean-Paul Marat, a doctor to society ladies and the soldiers of the Comte d'Artois, the King's brother, had been sucked into the morass of charlatanism that was the home of Mesmer. Mesmer and his cohorts claimed to cure epilepsy and nineteen other afflictions by the use of electricity and peculiar baths. No evidence supported Mesmer's claims, but he was howling repression and censorship and claimed the court was willfully keeping his cures from the populace. Marat demanded the academy certify his work with light and electricity, poorly designed experiments Nicolas felt proved nothing except

Marat's ambition. Marat had become passionately fixated on Nicolas whom he blamed for his failure to achieve scientific respectability.

Nicolas had lately become concerned with the lot of black slaves in the colonies. He had heard firsthand accounts of how the slaves were shipped, as tightly as pigs to market, and how many died horribly on the seas, what they called the Middle Passage. He helped launch a new society, Friends of the Blacks, to work toward the abolition of slavery. To make a profit on human flesh was barbaric. No one could own anyone else. It was an abomination. Every man was born free.

Not only every man, Nicolas was beginning to believe. He was almost alone in his new ideas, but he observed in the salons that educated women were as intelligent and able in argument, in pointed discourse, as any of the men, and often as witty. He could see no basis in his own experience for the universal belief that women were mental or emotional children. Some women no doubt were, since they were given little useful training and no real education; but then, a great many men were idiots or mental incompetents. Freedom was a universal right of all humans or an intellectual contradiction. If only some were born free, then freedom could not exist except as a greedy privilege.

Much was to be said, much was to be done. Therefore Nicolas had begun to write pamphlets. He went to the academies, the salons, the Masons, the Friends of the Blacks. Every night he dined out. Every morning he rose with the sun and wrote furiously. How could he be lonely? Yet he was. He felt a physical longing for someone in his bed. He wanted to love. D'Alembert had told Nicolas that they were alike, neither was capable of real love. But d'Alembert had loved Julie for years. They had briefly been lovers, but d'Alembert confessed he had not satisfied her. Would he himself be able to satisfy a woman? Could he ever inspire a woman's love? Women friends fussed over him, as they might a lapdog with brains. Nicolas felt he had much to offer, but to whom should he offer it? The years slid by in a blur of frenetic activity. At forty-two, he was never at a loss for a cause or for a meeting or for someone—individually or in groups or clubs—to discuss or dispute with. He was never without something he was supposed to have taken to the printers yesterday. It was a full life—almost.

His older friend du Paty recruited him to take on an injustice, just as Voltaire used to do. Du Paty had interested himself in the case of three peasants who had been sentenced, essentially without benefit of trial, without witnesses, without proof, to be broken on the wheel for robbery. They had never seen their accusers. They had never been given a chance to defend themselves. They had been rotting in prison for years waiting for death by torture. As punishment for his efforts, du Paty had been stripped of his judicial offices by the King. Nicolas took over the battle and seemed to be winning.

Broken on the wheel, judges said unctuously, but it made Nicolas shudder, since Voltaire had insisted he view an actual torture. "Put to the question," was the phrase. In the Palais de Justice, they sat the accused murderer, still swearing innocence, on the interrogation seat. Sanson blithely explained the details, pleased to show off his work to a nobleman. The man's legs were held by boards. Then Sanson's assistants, under his watchful eye, drove wedges with a sledgehammer blow by blow into the wretch's knees. He screamed and screamed. "Sounds like a cat in heat," Sanson said. "He's a tenor." Four wedges were pounded into ankles and knees. Nicolas would never forget the sound of the crunching of bones. Conduits carried away the blood.

"This is just the simple question," Sanson explained. "I'm sorry you can't see the extraordinary question, but we go by what the judges tell us, Marquis. We have little leeway."

The man finally confessed and passed out. Nicolas left while they were bringing him to. He would observe the wheel, as he had promised Voltaire. The crowd was extraordinary in the Place de Grève. People had brought ladders and high stools. The windows in all the surrounding houses had been rented. Nicolas sat with other minor nobility on a special platform, not as close as that for the highest-ranking ladies and gentlemen, but well above the mob. The accused could not walk of course. He was dragged to the Saint Andrew's cross and stripped to his shirt. His arms and mangled legs were placed into slots in the crossbars and he was tied down. Then the executioners began to pound his flesh and bones with iron bars. He was screaming his innocence again. Again and again they smashed him until all but the trunk was a mass of broken bone splinters and mangled flesh. Nicolas had not eaten but still tasted bile. He fought to keep himself from fainting. The gentleman on his left was smoking a long pipe, which did not help. The lady to his right was wearing heavy musk.

Finally they were done and what was left of the man was abandoned on the wheel, high up at the end of a pole. He was not to be burned alive, often the culmination, but simply left to moan and slowly, slowly die. Sometimes it took twelve hours, sometimes twenty-four, Sanson had told him. It was three days before Nicolas could sleep.

From that day, he worked twice as hard to free the innocent. From that day, he hated capital punishment. He was eager to help du Paty save the three peasants from the wheel. Since their families were destitute, he hired one of their sons as his valet. Du Paty invited Nicolas to visit him at his in-laws. Now that it was hot, Nicolas was pleased to escape the miasma of Paris. Villette was a fine house, northeast of Paris, gracious, big enough to absorb the twenty or so house guests. The father of the house was a cold and severe soldier; the mother was a pious woman, sweet but limited.

He met the older daughter, a lovely tall twenty-one-year-old who was taking care of her little cousin Charles. He had noticed her in passing, because she was hard to overlook. Then he discovered her reading the newest Diderot in the garden. "I have to read out here," she explained. "Maman is upset I've lost my faith. When I came home from the convent at Neuville, she burned all my books. So I carry books I care about outside to read."

Sophie was the protégée of her great-uncle, du Paty, who spoke enthusiastically of her intelligence and strong character. "Ah, you met her. Isn't she a jewel? I can talk about anything with her, anything." All those factors made Nicolas take notice of Sophie de Grouchy, who was called by her family Grouchette. She was so much younger, he took only a paternal interest in her reading, as he assumed du Paty had done. It was a pleasure to talk with her. She had several languages and read English as well as Nicolas, although she needed more practice in speaking.

It was a warm day in July and Sophie was out on the lawn with little Charles. Her aunt, her mother, several nieces were all lounging on the terrace up at the house fanning themselves and gossiping, drinking lemonade. Nicolas was sitting under a tree with du Paty, talking about the King convening a gathering of Notables, by invitation only, to consider the state of the kingdom. Neither were invited. Before them spread the garden in the fashionable formal mode of long vistas, low cookie-cutter hedges, conifers in the shape of balls and cones. The boy was sailing toy boats in the fountain and Sophie was reading in the shade, when suddenly a large dog came tearing out of the woods. Before anyone could react, the dog had thrown himself on the boy and was worrying him, growling like a wolf. Everyone froze. It was a tableau stopped in time except for the dog attacking the child. Then Sophie in white lawn threw herself across the grass and, seizing the dog by the nape of its neck, hurled it from the boy. The dog was so surprised it did not even bite her but flung through the air and landed with a thud that knocked the wind out of it. Then it ran off howling.

"He's bitten," she cried. "Charles!" The blood ran down his arm onto her summer dress of white sprigged with tiny roses.

Now Nicolas finally moved. "Are you all right? Are you injured?" He could not tell at first if the blood were hers too or only the boy's.

"I'm fine. But Charles is hurt. Help me get him to the house."

Now her Aunt Adelaide, the boy's mother, was bustling down. "Is the dog rabid? This is a tragedy! We must get him to the sea and wash him in seawater, or he may die."

"He won't die," Sophie said firmly, holding the boy to her breasts as he sobbed, shaking with a delayed reaction. "It was simply a vicious dog usually kept chained up. We must fetch the doctor to see to Charles' arm."

Nicolas volunteered to go for the doctor. He was on his way before he realized what the strange sensation in his chest was. He had fallen in love with Sophie de Grouchy. He had fallen utterly in love. Before him on the road danced the image of her charging the mauled boy and tossing the fierce dog through the air. Her white dress hung like a banner in his mind. Her thick dark hair was tangled about her like a storm cloud.

He saw her as an Amazon, fierce in love, competent, fearless, strong. She was bright. Learned. She brought no religious or superstitious baggage along. She was also beautiful. If she was tall, that was fine, for he was always stooping with people, because he was taller than most people found comfortable. They would match physically. If she would have him. If she could love him.

He had no clear idea how to court Sophie. The house was in an uproar and he could not open a dialogue with her until his next visit, although he thought about her a considerable portion of the time. Fortunately he had remarkable powers of concentration and could read or write under any circumstances. D'Alembert had said Nicolas could write a pamphlet while standing on his head.

The discrepancy in their ages troubled him. But a woman his age would be married, and he did not desire a mistress. He wanted someone to live with; he did not want someone, he wanted Sophie. He was exactly twice her age.

He came again to Villette as soon as he could get du Paty to invite him. He hardly knew where to begin, except to tell her about himself. "My mother is as pious as yours, and crazier. She didn't burn my books, but she dressed me in the clothing of a little girl until I was eight. I think it made me understand the difficulties women face in doing almost anything, from running down a flight of steps to crossing a muddy yard."

"My mentor Du Paty tells me you have a very high regard for women."

"I do. And that is not a front for taking advantage. I don't want to take advantage of you. I want to marry you."

She looked stunned. Her eyes—how large and very dark they were—widened and her long mouth slightly gaped. "What did you say?"

"I've fallen in love with you. I want to marry you."

She blinked several times. "You certainly get right to the point. You're a remarkable man. I might find it interesting to be married to you. Most of the lives I see available are incredibly boring. I don't want to spend my life thinking about gowns and wallpaper."

They were interrupted by Charles, coming to show her a frog he had found. She got him to put it back where he had found it. Nicolas waited impatiently for her to return. "Do you mind that I'm forty-two? Do you find me too old?"

"The man I've cared for most in my life is married to my grandmother's sister—my mentor. I never found him ancient. He's my best friend. He's older than you by more than a decade. He has a high opinion of your character—a rare recommendation. I can't recall hearing him talk of anyone with such respect and approval."

"Everything about you delights me. I promise to share with you whatever you wish to share—work, politics, philosophy, writing."

She put her hand on his. His hand grew suddenly hot. He felt he might spontaneously combust. He did not want to alarm her, but he seized her hand in both of his and held it against his mouth. She gazed at him with great curiosity. Her eyes were a luminous brown. "I see my mother looking at us. She is about to appear, so let my hand go and we'll discuss something neutral."

"May I speak to your father?"

"You should. I'd like to marry you—I think. But you understand the families will enter negotiations as if we were two dynasties merging."

"I don't care about dowries. I have enough for whatever we might want. I will tell your father I wish no dowry at all."

"That's sure to delight him. But how shocked everyone else will be. You may not care, I may not care. But we're the only ones who won't fight for the last clause and loophole. Speak to my father tonight. Otherwise we won't be married for years." She smiled at him. "And try to find some time when my mother isn't around to kiss me. I'd like to kiss you. I've never kissed anyone I wanted to kiss. . . . Do you have connections I should know about—mistresses, children you've acknowledged?"

"Nothing but friends. I fell in love once before but it wasn't returned. Perhaps that seems a considerable weakness to you—"

"No, I want to be loved alone, not in a list. . . ." She turned toward her mother who was puffing up, swishing her fan at them as if they were flies.

"Maman, you look quite warm. Are you feeling well? Perhaps we should go and sit in the house until you've recovered."

As Sophie went off arm in arm with her mother, who appeared to be scolding her—probably about staying so long alone with him—she managed to look back and smile. It was not a coquettish smile but a big smile of pleasure and good will. She did not love him yet as he loved her, but if he was very very lucky, she might.

TWELVE

Georges

❧

(1787)

GEORGES had a new hangout, even if he had little else new. Oh, he had a room on the Rue des Mauvaises Paroles—and how could he not enjoy an address on the Street of Bad Words? He was still scrabbling for small cases and small rewards. He needed money. But he liked to enjoy himself, and a living man couldn't spend all his time conniving and finagling and trying desperately to pry open doors the system and the gentry bolted in his face. Now and then he needed to relax, to chat, to watch the world saunter by, to pick up news and gossip. Given the few papers the government permitted through censorship, a man could learn a lot in conversation.

His new cafe was on the right bank just off the Pont Neuf, where everybody passed and everybody saw and was seen, high and low. He liked the mixture. He liked a taste of low life and he appreciated refinement and veneer. He had discovered a comfortable niche in the Cafe d'École (the sign said Parnasse, but no one called it that), a lively place where a young man could meet others who were trying to make their way and sometimes meet those who could help them do it.

He struck it off at once with the proprietor, François-Jérôme Charpentier. Charpentier, who came from Provence, had married an Italian woman, still good-looking. There was a warmth, a zest to both of them that Georges was right at home with. L'École coined money, for it was in a great spot. The light food they served was excellent, with a southern flavor that set it apart; the coffee was dark and rich; the beer and wine were good and relatively cheap, for Jérôme had connections in the wine trade, as perhaps in everything else that went on. He had bought into the tax collection agency—taxes were "farmed out." The collectors got whatever they could squeeze and then gave the King his due. The rest was theirs. It was highly profitable, little risk, good return. Jérôme had bought into it as one might buy shares in any other business.

Jérôme and Maria had a daughter, Gabrielle. She was twenty-five but looked younger. Under a mane of thick glossy black hair her face was oval and sweet. Her dark eyes shone on him. Her skin was olive and perfect. Her bust was large, her hips full, and she laughed not like a lady but like a peasant, from the bottoms of her feet. He genuinely liked her. She stirred him, not outrageously but generously. He would enjoy taking her to bed, but more he wanted to marry her family. They had a gold mine in the cafe and fine reliable income from the shares in tax farming.

He spoke honestly to Jérôme of his situation (no point trying to fool a prospective father-in-law he intended to borrow from) and passionately of his ambitions. He flattered the mother, but always he was looking at the daughter. He took to sitting near enough to the counter to keep her in his line of sight. Now when he walked in, she snapped to attention and her large dark eyes gleamed. He openly admired Gabrielle to her parents. He was allowed to sit with her, to talk, but nothing more. They were exceedingly careful of her virtue. He did not press her. She wore a perfume scented with lilacs and sometimes she smelled of cinnamon from the kitchen. She was ripe as a peach.

He was always looking out for a chance to move out of the common courts, where he could count his fees on his fingers. Camille Desmoulins was still scrabbling and scribbling. He had fallen in love with a married woman who was too virtuous to have him, although she entertained him regularly. Mme Duplessis, wife of a bureaucrat, liked Camille for his wit and the poetry he wrote her incessantly, but he had not got further than snatching a kiss. Georges thought the affair absurd, but it did have the advantage of getting Camille out of his truly depressing servant's room up on the sixth floor of a rundown building and feeding him good dinners three nights a week.

Georges was not short of friends, all poor, ambitious and discontented as he was. Fabre d'Églantine was another. Even his name was an invention, much as Georges had taken to signing his name d'Anton. Églantine referred to some poetry prize he had won in Toulouse. Fabre was a law clerk, a would-be litterateur, always entering some essay or poetry contest, and in the meantime, writing pornography and the occasional pamphlet attacking the government.

Louis had been dismissing ministers every year or so since he'd dumped Turgot and then Necker, each new one more hopeless and unpopular. The meeting of Notables had brought down Calonne, who had admitted the government was bankrupt and actually revealed the size of the national debt. In the meantime, the Queen was buying new palaces and had recently been caught in a spicy scandal involving a handsome prelate, Cardinal Rohan,

Bishop of Arras, and a diamond necklace that seemed to have disappeared after costing a fortune. Many political pamphlets were pornographic, because attacking the Queen's morals was the quickest way to attack the regime.

Camille said it was due to Louis' floppy prick. "He doesn't like sex, Georges. He's the first French king since Saint Louis who doesn't enjoy women—or boys. He likes to shoot birds and fix locks. French kings always had a foreign wife but a French mistress, the real female power. We want a Frenchwoman behind the throne, not the Austrian bitch. We don't think she has our interests at heart. She was born a Hapsburg and reports to her family."

"It's hard for me to imagine having all that power and all those gorgeous women fawning over you, and not wanting to enjoy them. Now if I had a sweet juicy wife . . ." The image of Gabrielle leaning on the counter, her eyes doting on him and her full breasts quivering in her blouse assaulted him. "I'd be true to her, at least eighty percent of the time. But all that temptation? Something's missing."

"Deficit downstairs, deficit upstairs. The man is stupid. He'd make a great peasant or a cart driver. But as a king, he's a joke on us."

They had to drink the cheapest beer or cider or wine, for they had barely enough between them for a tavern meal. But good company made it bearable to be nobody at twenty-seven, still nobody.

Friends were important, and he tried to preserve them, which is why he still had a good relationship with his first mistress in Paris, Françoise, now kept by a lawyer Huet de Paisy. She remarked to him that Huet was looking to sell his office as an advocate before the Council in the Palais de Justice, a civil court that took care of cases concerning wealthy and frequently noble clients. The workload was not irksome and the fees were high. However, Huet's asking price was eighty thousand livres. Georges could get his hands on five thousand. That left a bit of a gap.

He whipped his courtship into a gallop and made his case as powerfully and passionately as he could. He was wooing the father as much as the daughter. Gabrielle wanted him, clearly, and she was no weak-willed ninny. She made her desires felt in her family. But he must convince Jérôme that lending him money was a winning proposition. It was tied up together: the office he must buy, the wife who would help him buy that office, and the new style of life that would open to him. This was his golden chance. If he had ever been told he had a persuasive manner, a gift for oratory, a commanding presence, charm, now was the time for those attributes to raise him out of obscurity into the good life.

One noon, Jérôme told him to come back on Monday, the day they closed, and they would have a family dinner together and talk business. The business was the loan and the marriage. The marriage would occur immediately after he had the Council status in hand, and the loan of fifteen thousand would be his.

Françoise, who had been saving her money and trusted him to pay her back, lent him thirty-three thousand francs without the knowledge of her lover. He scraped up some from his family. Still, Françoise had to broker a deal, a mortgage on his family land in Arcis, whereby he would owe Huet twenty-two thousand, to be paid off over the next five years. Most offices were bought. The crown made money on them. Then those who bought the offices sold them when they were ready to cash in. By the second week in June, Danton had his official papers signed by the King confirming him in his new office.

The wedding occurred as fast as his relatives could arrive from Arcis. Gabrielle looked splendid, vibrant, and he was as happy as he ever had been—and he was a man who knew himself to have an immense capacity for simple earthy happiness. He had the wife he wanted. He had an office that should finally bring him not only status, but plenty of cash. If he was in debt, that didn't weigh him down, for he intended to repay everyone who had faith in him.

His father-in-law set them up in a fine apartment across the river, on the corner of the Cour de Commerce and the Rue des Cordeliers. It wasn't a fancy neighborhood, but it was a bustling one where he and Gabrielle would feel right at home, only a few blocks to her parents and to the Palais de Justice where he'd be doing most of his courtroom work. He inherited some cases from Huet. He hired Fabre as his clerk. Why not spread the bounty around? They did not bother with a honeymoon, except for two days they spent mostly in bed.

She was a virgin, as he had expected. Not that that meant a great deal to him, except she was after all his wife and he intended to start a family. She was a virgin but hardly virginal. She wanted him. She told him she had been wanting him for six months.

"I knew you were for me, Georges. I waited for you to know it, and soon you did. Then I waited for you to make it happen while I kept up a clamor to Papa and Mama. I talked till their ears were sore. I knew you were my husband, since the day you walked in, strong and proud as a bull into his field."

She was not coy, she did not hold back. Before she got into bed she prayed to the Virgin, but he did not mind. It might make her a better mother. She let her black hair loose falling in coils around her bare shoulders. If he were going to pray, he would pray to her, just as she was. Her body in bed with him was truly holy. Gabrielle was June in his arms, flowers and fruit and solid flesh, that scent of lilac and cinnamon, his. In their new apartment that still smelled of wallpaper paste and paint and echoed because they had so little furniture, they lay in the big matrimonial bed and made love until they both were sore. Then they sank into sleep together, wrapped legs into legs, her hair brushing his chest lightly as a warm wind.

THIRTEEN
Pauline

❧

(1789)

RIGHT after mass on Sunday, Pauline, Babette and Aimée went to a meeting of neighborhood women to discuss the Complaint Petition they were drawing up. "Our little father, good King Louis, is calling the Estates General," Mère Roget announced. "The flower sellers, the lingerie women, market women, fishwives are drawing up petitions. We have grievances too. We must make a petition."

They had problems enough. "We women who dig ditches are paid half what the men make. We do the same work, barrow load by barrow load." If a woman's husband was called for a soldier, if he grew sick or suffered an injury, if he abandoned her or dropped dead, then she could scarcely feed herself, let alone her children.

Nobody could get married till they could afford it, but couples who were betrothed could not wait years to go to bed. Were they made of wood? Like Pauline and her boyfriend, couples made love; then if the marriage didn't occur and the woman got pregnant, the Church landed on her. The neighborhood would stand behind a woman who left a man for good reason, but the Church would make her go back. There was no divorce. No wonder couples delayed marriage, not just to save money to buy a bed, but because there was no recourse if things went sour. Like Victoire, the old-clothes woman married to a man with a vicious temper, a woman was stuck.

"We shouldn't have to desert babies because we can't feed them." The woman speaking had left her own baby five years before on the church steps. When her husband recovered and the family business of button making was going, she looked for her daughter. Like most foundlings, the little girl had died.

"How about enough to feed ourselves?" Pauline asked. "The price of bread goes up and up and never comes down."

There was a throaty mutter of agreement. Of all their problems, this was the greatest, for everyone lived mostly on coarse dark bread, as much rye as wheat, pounds of it every day for every working person. Bread was life, but the price rose and rose and their wages and their earnings remained the same. They were being squeezed to death. It was bread before rent, bread before fuel, bread before medicine or shoes.

Taxes were next. How could they pay taxes when they couldn't even pay for water and wood? "Why shouldn't the fat ones pay their share? The richer a man is, the less he pays. Bloodsuckers, all of them!"

The women addressed the King familiarly. "Dear little father. Our friend Louis just doesn't know how we suffer. He's calling the Estates General to fix things, and he's asking us what we need."

Pauline knew better. Louis was calling for the Estates General because he'd been backed into a corner. She read all the pamphlets she could lay hands on and the illegal wall posters quickly torn down by the law. She listened in taverns. The King was bankrupt. The government had spent itself deep into debt. The King had tried to get the nobles to empty their pockets for him, but they squealed like pigs at the butcher. Louis was trying to make them pay by calling the Estates General, which hadn't met in a hundred fifty years. Representatives of all three Estates, the clergy, the nobles and the rest of them, would go into separate sessions at Versailles. All over the kingdom, little groups were meeting by town, by profession, by guild to draw up their complaints, their wish lists, for the King and the Estates to consider. Everywhere people gathered to work on letters, hoping to catch the King's eye. Would he read any petitions? It was like putting a prayer on the wind, inscribing it on the down of a dandelion and setting it adrift.

Believe in the King? It was like praying to some saint for intercession. Saints were in the business of listening; kings were not. She had seen a pamphlet last week by a woman, Olympe de Gouges. Pauline had been thrilled, although the men said that a woman could not have written it and some man had done it for her. Olympe described herself as a butcher's daughter, but there she was writing in public all about the Estates General and how we the common people must demand double representation, because we outnumbered the other two estates forty times. Pauline cherished her name as if she were a saint: Olympe, the butcher's daughter. What did she look like? Where did she live?

Pauline herself could not resist hope. Perhaps somebody at court would read these petitions of grief and longing for a more decent life.

The dawn showers and morning overcast had opened into a wispy blue sky between the tall houses. It was too late to go with a group of friends to the country, but too nice, too warm a May Sunday to spend inside. "Let's go to the Palais Royal." Babette took her arm. "Everybody talks about it."

The King's cousin, the duc d'Orléans, did not get along with the King. He had gone into the real estate business in Paris. Orléans had made over a palace he owned on the right bank, just inland from the Louvre and the Tuileries— an old palace the royal family never used. People said the Palais Royal was the liveliest spot in all Paris. Respectable women didn't go there, but Babette and Pauline weren't respectable. Poor women never counted as ladies. "Are you sure they'll admit us? We don't look fancy."

Off they went in their Sunday skirts, walking as fast as they could through the crowd over the Pont Neuf and across the river. People were dancing on the quai. Some men were fishing a body out with a long pole, the corpse of a woman, swollen and blackish. A fiddler was entertaining a small crowd. Pauline saw a pickpocket working the back row, but she didn't say anything. He had to make a living too. She wore her red pocket under her petticoat on a ribbon. Over her breasts she wore an almost new fichu trimmed with fine lace she had bought from Victoire.

The Palais was in the official style, light colored stone with arches giving on a colonnade on the ground floor. It was built around a huge courtyard jammed with gentlemen, bourgeois, lawyers, working people, prostitutes high and low, mimes, sword swallowers, pamphleteers, balladeers selling song sheets, musketeers, the town militia, puppeteers, dancers and actors. Around the courtyard were cafes with tables set out to fill much of the interior of trees and welltrampled grass. In the center of the enclosure was The Circus, about twothirds underground, where a cockfight attracted a noisy crowd of bettors. When somebody wanted to make a speech, he just climbed on a chair or up on the table and began to shout. People applauded and he continued; or people booed, and the orator got down in haste. Underground was a wax museum; whorehouses and sexual exhibition halls, more restaurants and cafes, a real theater run by the governess of the children of Orléans, who wrote very moral plays. Aboveground were shops selling fancy clothes and hats and jewelry and books and perfumes and powders and ointments.

Pauline caught her breath and grabbed Babette's arm, thinking she saw a huge nude woman, but it was a statue of rosy wax. When there was trouble, someone would scream "Scipio! This whore is shouting foul!" or "Aladdin! The grenadiers are fighting the sailors!" The managers would come unhurriedly, two of the blackest men she had ever seen and over six feet tall. Calmly they would separate the offenders and impose order.

The brightly striped Italian Cafe was crowded with men jabbering Italian and drinking coffee and aperitifs. The Cafe of the Thousand Columns was studded with mirrors, creating illusions. The Mechanical Cafe had strange contraptions that made food and liquid appear and disappear. The Cafe Tortoni offered ices and frozen desserts. She felt dazzled. She felt as if her nerves were burning in her flesh. She had never seen so many colors, lights, vistas, images, illusions; never heard so many sounds of strange and familiar music, voices, speeches, declamations, screeching; never smelled such a stew of humanity, cook and drink. It was a place where things shrieked and danced.

She wanted, she wanted—what? She was not used to passionately wanting objects that fleeted by her gaze. This place was a web of sensations that pricked her mind as well as her flesh. It made her want things she had never known existed and certainly would not care about tomorrow. She could spend her week's earnings on multiflavored ices that shone like cathedral glass. It was as if the entire scene were entering her sexually, moving in her, bringing her to a torment of desire—but for what? She was not used to novelty. She tried to gain control. She would not spend her money. She would not desire what she had no reason truly to want, what she would never want if she were back in the chocolate shop or in her own bed.

The linden trees were just opening. A small band was playing a catchy new tune and people were dancing. Two men came up to Pauline and Babette and asked them to dance. "Where are you from, darling?" her partner asked.

"From over the river, the Cordeliers section. I run a chocolate shop—I'm not a whore, so you won't get anything from me."

He laughed. "I'm from Faubourg Saint Marcel. We're the roughest guys in Paris. I know what you are—just a working fool like me. I work at the Gobelins tapestry factory. You don't have to worry about me, I won't try to hustle you. Do you come here a lot?" He had light eyes and lighter hair.

"Never till today. Babette—that's my friend dancing with your friend— wanted to come. Her boyfriend keeps talking about this place, but he won't take her, so we came to see for ourselves what the fuss is about."

"There's a lot of freedom because it's under the protection of Orléans, and he's royal blood. People say whatever they want here. It's like Carnival every day. Don't you have a boyfriend of your own? Or is he too cheap to bring you?" He grinned, showing a chipped front tooth.

"He's in the army. He got taken in the lottery."

He clucked. "Rough luck. Think you'll ever see him again?"

"I pray for him. I'm ready to wait."

"You're a good girl. The right kind." At the end of the dance, he bought her a lemonade. While she was still drinking it, Babette came up breathlessly and he quietly left.

"I told you it's fun here. Oh, can I have a sip? I'm dying of thirst."

"Take half." Pauline believed in sharing. "Only half. No fair. Look how that girl does her hair."

"She's no girl, she's a whore," Babette said.

"She's like us, Babette, just trying to make her way. I like her hair up in that swoop. I bet I could do that."

"How do you know it's not some whorish style, and if you did your hair like that, men would think you were for sale."

"Look around. Do you see other whores like that? I'm going to try it when I go home. Let's walk around and listen to the speakers. That's free."

One skinny guy dressed like a lawyer was giving a speech about balloons and how they would transport people all over, never mind bad roads and highway robbers. Two guys were debating who should have a vote in the Estates General. One idiot dressed in fancy clothes was arguing about how the grain trade should be freed of regulation. He was hissed off his chair. One type was reciting an obscene poem about the Queen and the notorious diamond necklace and the Bishop of Arras who was fucking her. A woman just a few years older than Pauline sang a ballad about a woman in Normandy who had run an outlaw band, robbed merchants and helped her neighbors. Pauline had never heard of a woman leading a gang.

A man was warbling about the lives of the saints, but they were not popular here. Pauline was partial to Sainte Geneviève, the patron saint of Paris and special to working women. Geneviève was always evoked in times of rising bread prices and famines. Pauline burned a candle to Geneviève every week, because she felt Geneviève cared for the poor women of Paris and maybe, who knows, she could do them some good. Every woman needed a saint.

They watched a short comic play about a shopkeeper cuckolded by his apprentice and they listened to speeches about land reform, about free speech, about suppressing the Masons, about the healthy effects of electricity on the brain, about the need for better sewage disposal. "I can go for that," Pauline said to Babette, winking. When the wind blew from the wrong direction, all Paris stifled in the fumes of rotting garbage and shit.

Arm in arm, they straggled home, eating a hot roll they split. They peed in an alley, each standing cover for the other, each taking care not to get any on their good skirts. Both had two skirts, one for every day and one for Sundays, and they were proud of that. Many young women had only one skirt. Pauline's good skirt had been her mother's but it was still pretty and only worn in the hem.

Finally they were back in the neighborhood, telling friends where they had gone and what they had seen. Even though they had walked only twenty blocks, it was another world, and everybody wanted to know. Pauline was astonished how sleepy she was. She felt as if her eyes, her ears, her very nerves were burned out and could not absorb anything more. She could barely digest what she had experienced, and yet she could think of nothing else. Long after she had eaten some bread and a little leftover gruel, she lay in her bed and all the bright images exploded on the inside of her eyes. She had undergone something entirely new, entirely strange and intensely disturbing. There was Pauline before, who seemed to her inexperienced and naive, and Pauline now, who had been dipped from toes to brain in some new vivid dye. This new Pauline felt vastly experienced and sophisticated by comparison, although she was not sure why.

FOURTEEN
Manon

(1781–1786)

SHORTLY after Manon became pregnant, she and Jean moved into a house in Amiens, larger than they needed but because it had been deserted some years, cheap. The house was cold and damp and overlooked a cemetery. Jean had a placid grey horse he stabled behind the house. On it he went his endless rounds from town to town, factory to factory. She found a good maid, Marguerite Fleury, a sturdy widow her own age. She was less lonely after acquiring Fleury. Manon was also helping Jean with his encyclopedia of manufactures, a vast job that was to appear in many volumes and cover . . . everything. She was always researching some dull aspect of the wool trade or the manufacture of barrels. In the fall, her daughter Eudora was born. She had feared Jean might want to resume the conjugal relations she found tedious, but he did not seem to think of it.

"But Madame de la Platière," the doctor intoned in horror, "breastfeeding? You've had a gentle upbringing. Only peasants . . . do that."

"Jean-Jacques Rousseau says nursing bonds mother and child and produces healthy babies." From the window of her bedroom where the doctor was examining her, she could see the cemetery, the rows of tiny stones for infants.

"Madame, if you grow too attached to an infant . . ."

"I was one of seven. Only I survived the wet nurse when most infants die." She clutched Eudora to her, feeling the little heart beat. Eudora would survive!

She was trying to form Eudora's mind early, to provide that stimulation necessary to bring out the natural goodness and intelligence of a baby, according to Rousseau. It was reasonable to assume that Eudora would be like her, serious, intellectual, precocious. Manon took Eudora into the garden out back as soon as she dared. Fleury tried to talk her into swaddling Eudora, but that would impede freedom of movement. Eudora must enjoy nature early.

Manon was terrified Eudora would suddenly die. She hovered over her daughter and fattened her up.

Amiens was bleak and grey. Over the next three years, she did not grow to love it. She was not sorry to have an excuse to go to Paris on Jean's behalf to try to get his family confirmed as noble, as that would give them numerous social and financial advantages. It would also cost a great deal. Proving nobility was arduous to the petitioner and profitable to the government.

After a month in Paris, traveling through the morass of the vast bureaucracy with frequent trips to Versailles, she gradually realized that she would not succeed, because Jean was not liked by his superiors. She had a glorious time with friends in Paris including Dr. Lanthénas, a liberal interested in the political situation, whom she called "little brother," and Bosc, a dear young botanist, already elected to the Science Academy. While she was waiting to see some bureaucrat, finagling to have herself invited to the tea or garden party of the wife of an official, they attended lectures in botany together and public demonstrations of scientific theory.

She did not feel guilty running around Paris, with three-year-old Eudora and Jean tucked away in grey Amiens, for she was here at her husband's behest, trying to advance his family. She had additional help by now, so she took Fleury. Then she had a letter from Jean. "Why do you prefer the company of young men to your familial duties? This is not the behavior of a virtuous woman."

She wrote back with indignation and a wry touch of humor, poking sly fun at Bosc's shy bachelor ways and Dr. Lanthénas' intellectual pretensions. She did not take Jean's jealousy seriously, for she was a virtuous woman who would never prefer a moment's pleasure, if sex was pleasure, to the serenity of her conscience. She reminded him of the days spent cultivating dull bureaucrats.

After three months, she could not secure her husband's nobility, but she could get him a promotion. Her charm and diligence were worth that much. Jean was offered the inspectorship in Lyon, near his family home. They took a small flat in Lyon for the winter, but they lived most of the year in Clos de la Platière in the heart of Beaujolais. This was nature as she had never experienced it. The steep hills of the countryside were thick with low vines. The soil was red, and the local stone, of which most houses were built, was a deep gold. These were houses of the south, with rounded red-roof tiles and thick walls. They turned inward to their courtyards, roses spilling over, often a cat on the wall.

Clos de la Platière was old and pleasant, built low of whitewashed stone. Through a square arch of golden stone, an allée of plane trees led to the front door. Pavilions and barns formed a courtyard, private, charming. It was a working farm and vineyard. In the walled garden near the house were cherry and peach trees. Manon vastly preferred spending time at the Clos to the more elegant town house nearby in Ville-Franche, where his mother ruled. That house was grander but life meaner. Maman's passions were cards, gossip and trying to run the lives of her sons. Dominique, a canon, lived at home, as did Laurent. All except Jean had gone into the Church. Manon knew the family had opposed Jean's marrying her, wanting an heiress.

To please the family, she went to church every Sunday, riding a donkey up the steep hill through rich red and green countryside to Thiezé, one of the golden towns. Old women in black peasant clothes greenish with age squatted on the church steps begging. Fleury said, "They're too old to work and their families can't afford to feed them. Begging here is their right."

She greeted them, learning their names, and gave each a small coin. In turn they blessed her by name. One Sunday after mass, one of them, Jeannot, seized her arm. "Madame Fleury says you made her well when she had the flux. Please! It's my son. If he dies, we'll all perish of hunger. He's a good man! Madame, you must come and look at him."

After explaining for ten minutes she was no doctor, to which Jeannot only nodded fervently, she decided it was easier to go along than to argue. She set off on her donkey, with Jeannot hobbling at her side, up and down the steep hills past the rows of vines leafing out. The "house" of Jeannot's family was a hovel of old wood, rubble, plaster and an occasional stone. There was only one room, with a slat partition separating the sleeping-cooking area from the cow's stall. The floor was earth, the bed, a pile of dirty straw on a wooden frame. The stench was incredible, but Manon was not about to let her disgust show.

"You must feed him eggs. I saw hens outside."

Jeannot shook her head wildly. "We have to sell eggs. It's all we have for rent and taxes. He can't work. He'll miss the harvest and we'll starve."

It was clear to her that Jeannot's son had probably eaten something that poisoned him, something spoiled of which there was certainly an abundance, if of nothing else. Right outside the door was a great heap of dung and rotting vegetable scraps. Every scrap of manure was precious. She returned after supper with a broth made from beef and sage, with a little white bread. It was eaten as if it were holy. Jeannot's son recovered two days later. Whenever Jeannot saw her now, she kissed the hem of Manon's dress, embarrassing her.

Without meaning to, she became well known and popular among the peasants, because she knew something of herbs and medicine. Disease was rampant in the one-room hovels shared by up to twenty people. They were just work animals to those who had power over them. They lived on gruel made from grain, turnips, hedgerow greens. By thirty, they were toothless and arthritic. She came to know close to two hundred peasants by name. In winter, they brought what they cherished most, a cow perhaps, inside to keep both the cow and themselves warm. Without the cow, they would starve. A dying animal was mourned more than a dying child. A child could be replaced; a cow or a goat or an ox could not. Here was fertile country with everything to please and nourish, and those closest to its ocher-red earth lived worse than its pale cattle.

At Clos de la Platière, she began to make pies and put up fruit. Of all the treatises on the various manufacturing arts she studied for Jean's work, the information about making jams and drying fruit interested her the most. She was the Rousseau woman: warm, natural, caring for and educating her child, embedded in the countryside. Reluctantly she followed Jean to Lyon in November.

In Lyon that winter of 1786, the weavers began to agitate. Jean explained at breakfast. "Their lives are harsh. They work an eighteen-hour day, six days a week usually in one or two rooms, masters and men together. The weavers sell their cloth piecemeal to the big jobbers, who pay them less than it costs to produce. They're hungry; they're getting hungrier."

She had plenty of opportunity to observe them as she took Eudora and Fleury for their daily walks, or took Eudora to play in a park. They worked themselves into an early grave and their children begged in the streets. Sundays they got drunk on crude red wine in the taverns along the rivers. Lyon was built on the confluence of two great rivers, the Rhone and the Saône. The Rolands lived near a big hospital, at one end of the peninsula, and most weavers lived at the high end. Some lived in steep hillside warrens above the houses of the wealthy across the Saône. Through all the old areas ran hidden passageways, the traboules, unmarked and known only to locals, that led clear through buildings, making it possible to pass around the city invisibly. The workers used these to communicate, to meet. Traboules were vaulted passageways leading from doors on the street up, down from building to building, already old, dimly lit, secret.

The weavers were uncouth and filthy, but from an appropriate distance, she sympathized. Their lot was unceasing labor and growing debt. The mothers worked, the daughters worked, sometimes as whores, the sons worked, the children worked. They had no childhood like Eudora's. From the time they could use their hands, they were set at looms. Often they were blind by thirty-five. They turned out taffeta, fine silks, brocades, passementarie, all the fabrics adorning the nobility and the higher clergy.

Now Marie-Antoinette introduced fashions influenced by Rousseau. Ladies wanted to dress like idealized shepherdesses, in muslin, in cotton, in lawn instead of silk. The merchants set the prices the masters could pay the journeymen and the apprentices, and wages were forcibly kept low. A journeyman could not buy enough bread to fill his belly on twenty sous a day. Of course he lived with his master in the same stuffy room, with the master and the master's wife and four children and aged father and crippled uncle, along with the journeymen and the apprentices. No wonder they all smelled so strongly she would sometimes cross the street to escape the stench.

Now they were striking for an increase in wages and the price paid for piece goods: masters, journeymen, apprentices and their families. Strikes were illegal, but the weavers no longer cared. They saw the regal mansions of the merchants. They saw them dress like lords, traveling in carriages painted with gold leaf behind matched horses, with liveried footmen running before.

The weavers gathered across the Rhone in overgrown rocky fields. There they could mill around away from the armed militia hired by the rich merchants. Around campfires they listened to orators and debated and reached a decision by rough consensus. Then they marched back into Lyon, across a bridge of boats. Jean insisted on going to see what was happening. Manon went with him, wrapped in her cloak. She left Eudora in Fleury's care. The weavers gathered in the Place de Terreaux and threw rocks and yelled at the house of the most important official, the intendant, a huge stone palace. Manon was amused to find herself shouting too. "Manon!" Jean barked, appalled. "Behave yourself. You're the wife of a government official!" She was too excited to keep quiet. She found something wild in herself that wanted to riot with the weavers. Finally the intendant agreed to receive a delegation. Their best speakers went to the intendant to explain their grievances. The weavers milled around, waiting. Manon sat yawning on the plinth of a statue of Neptune. She bought hot chocolate from a vendor and urged some on Jean, who was arguing with some artisan he knew. Two hours passed. She was glad she had left supper for Eudora.

The delegates returned waving their arms for attention. The square quieted. "The intendant has promised us prices we can live on. Piecework prices will be raised a sous. We will survive!"

A great murmur of joy went through the crowd. Manon found herself roughly embraced by a bony woman in a tattered blue skirt. "See how easy it is when you just explain what you need!" she cried into Manon's ear. The weavers dispersed, cheering the intendant, praising the Virgin, singing and kissing each other.

While the weavers were still celebrating, the militia struck. They rounded up spokesmen and the merchants judged them. The next day, the strike leaders were slowly executed in the Place de Terreaux after appropriate torture. The town fathers decreed the bodies must hang till they rotted. That was the end of the strike. Manon avoided the Place de Terreaux and its rotting corpses.

Manon disliked the louts who shambled along in the street drunk every Sunday, but she disliked even more the rich merchants who believed it their right to crush the poor like lemons for lemonade. Lyon was a handsome city of elegant old houses, beautifully situated and with a fine tradition of the best cooking in France along with superior wine, with far more promise of a real political and social life than Amiens had offered, but it was in the hands of rich brutes. She preferred to retire to Clos de la Platière and live an honorable country life.

FIFTEEN

Max

❦

(Winter 1788–Spring 1789)

MAX felt around him the glass coffin that was Arras, a neat prosperous town with the stepped facades of the north, flat green fields to the horizon. He had thought that returning with his degree, working hard within the court system and the social hierarchy, he would soon have a respected place. He was still the almost-bastard of a forced mésalliance whose father had deserted him after killing his mother with too many babies too fast: that judgement was always there, like the limestone caves under the town. He smothered his anger, but it grew within him year by year until it was indistinguishable from his strength.

He had done the responsible thing. He had returned from Paris and set up housekeeping with Charlotte in a small but respectable house of brick decorated with stone around the windows, near the theater and close to the Abbey where he had been a student. He sent Augustin through Louis-le-Grand. He practiced law, he sat as a judge in the episcopal court. Then, when it came time to sign a death sentence, he could not do it. He could not murder a man judicially. He could not kill a man for the Church or the King.

He sat at their interminable dinners pretending interest in petty social obligations. He belonged to clubs, droned verse in praise of wine and women, he who drank his wine watered and kept his distance from women. He even contemplated marrying Mlle Deshorties with her simper and her hypocrisy. Yet all the time his anger and his intelligence, which were one and the same, glowed inside him. The Church went on lovingly about mortifying the flesh. His flesh was not demanding. But he had been mortifying his spirit and his intellect—except for those pure exalted moments when he was defending a client who had been wronged, who was being broken by the laws and the power of the rich and well placed, who was in mortal danger because of class rather than any deed one had committed or left undone. Then Max felt his power. Then his silly weak voice took on an edge and became a tool of justice.

His colleagues did not doubt his ability, but they felt superior to him because he took cases on their merit and not on their potential for money; and because he lost his temper in court and let his sarcasm show. Several times he had been rebuked for the way he spoke to judges.

He had tried hard to be the good father he never had. But Charlotte was vain and empty-headed. Those years in the convent for poor girls had ruined her mind. He had not the money to buy a husband for an opinionated spinster. Being his sister did not help her marriage prospects. Although she was perfectly capable of flirting, she would turn on the poor man half an hour later and rebuke him loudly for some fancied snub. She was loyal to him, jealous of any woman she thought he might take an interest in. She need not have worried. Sometimes when he was defending a client, he felt protective and almost attracted, but it would have been improper to take advantage of such a situation, and the women were often peasants or the daughters of poor artisans. His father had stooped to conquer and ruined his mother's life.

The Estates General election caught Max's interest. He helped the poor people of Arras and the surrounding area draw up petitions. The cobblers came to him and asked him to make their petition too. That inspired him to write a pamphlet in which he decided for the first time to be honest and direct in print. It would shock the gentlemen who were his colleagues at the bar, with whom he sat in the literary society, with whom he attended dances and weddings and funerals and mass. He was not writing for them. He was writing for the people who worked hard and got little. The people who fell into the law as off a cliff and perished miserably. The people whose children died in infancy and childhood, who had to send their daughters and sons off into service and often got back a corpse. Who worked hard till they were old and then begged through the streets, camped at the church door crying for alms, shoved into the poorhouse to end their days diseased. He felt as if gauze had been ripped off his mind. He wrote, yes, not the elegantly turned stillborn poems, the stiff little speeches with coy erudite references designed to create an illusion of high culture. For the common people he wrote simply, feeling the power of his words. This winter of '88–'89 was the coldest he could remember. He was often ill, but he did not care. He wrote through his colds and chills, he wrote as if he were galloping through the long night of the winter in Artois. He was launching his election campaign. He was going to run for the Estates General, to represent the Third Estate from Arras.

The pamphlet *To the Nation of Workers* was printed at his own expense and gained immediate success. He heard that some of his colleagues wanted him arrested for sedition. But the common people bought it. The first printing sold out in two weeks, when he had to go back to the printer for more copies.

The Estates General was to meet in Versailles in May. The King wanted it to operate under the old rules. The clergy would elect representatives and meet as the First Estate. The nobility was to elect representatives as the Second Estate. Everybody else, the remaining ninety-five percent of the population, would meet as the Third Estate. Max had heard that over eight hundred petitions had gone to Louis asking that the Third Estate representation be doubled. That would not give them a majority commensurate with their numbers, but it would mean that the clergy and the nobility could not outvote them every time.

The people would choose electors who would then pick deputies to the Estates, a cumbersome system designed to cause delays and to keep ordinary people far from making important decisions. He wanted to win. Things were going to happen when the Estates gathered. There was a deep sense of fury and exasperation among the people. The more impassioned and angry his speeches, the louder they applauded, but his voice was still weak.

He walked out onto the frozen fields and practiced public speaking. He denounced injustice to the crows. A neighbor's dog accompanied him, staring into his face. His voice seemed to vanish into the wind and the icy furrows. He came home with a sore throat, coughing. The next time he spoke, his voice did not break. He practiced projecting his voice, returning accompanied by the dog to the flat endless fields. The common people wanted to hear him. When he stood up in a meeting, they murmured approval.

He stood before groups in their rough clothes, men come from the shops, the fields, the quarries, the factories, women who worked as hard as any man in the dirt of farming and manufacture, men and women blinded by their work, coughing up the dust from cloth-making. They were loud and boisterous. They shoved each other and guffawed. They did not have the manners of his colleagues and their ladies, their tepid smiles, their empty compliments. The common people smelled of drink, manure and woodsmoke. They were poorly dressed and wore clogs or jabots, the heavy wooden shoes. Their hair was matted and wild. They were on the verge always of taking to their fists, both men and women, and punching somebody they had been having a friendly chat with ten minutes before. Yet he could make them fall silent and listen to him and mumble agreement. He could bring them to their feet cheering. He was for them, and they knew it.

He won the first round. He was one of forty-nine electors chosen to pick the real deputies from among themselves. The campaign was hard fought and bitter. Spring finally came and the storks appeared, but he had no time for long walks across the fields, no time to admire wildflowers in the hedges. He wrote more pamphlets, he gave speeches, he talked one on one to every elector.

Elections took months, but finally he won his place. The deputies from Arras were going to be late getting to Versailles. A married woman who admired him lent him money to travel on and a trunk in which to load his few clothes and books. A quarryman carried his trunk to the coach stop. Max was exhilarated. He spoke to his impromptu porter. "I won't forget you, l'Anquilette. You'll be mayor here someday, I promise you."

"I don't need to be mayor, my friend. I'd carry you and the trunk to Versailles to fight for us. Don't forget us!" He plucked a flame-red poppy just opening and put it into Max's lapel.

"Never!" Max promised, wringing the man's hand as he stood waiting to board the coach with the other deputies.

"Max never forgets anything," Charlotte said, dabbing at her eyes with a lacy kerchief. "Except to eat. Who'll remind you to eat in Versailles? You're too thin already. You're a bunch of bones in a silk coat."

"Don't cry. I'll be back when the Estates finish," he said, but he did not mean it. There was no going back. Once in the coach, he discarded the poppy that was already withering.

SIXTEEN

Claire

❧

(Winter 1788–Spring 1789)

COLLOT'S company was resident in Bordeaux for the winter of '88–'89, when Claire took an official lover. She was tired of being importuned by men and equally tired of the jibes of the other women in the cast that she was flighty and immoral as a cat in heat. She should be taking men to bed for love or for money or for protection—not for the simple transient pleasure of sex. Now she was getting truly involved with a man who owned several ships engaged in exporting textiles, and her little theatrical family was more upset than ever. Her colleagues did not know she had been raised as an outcast Protestant, a heretic on sufferance not to be burned alive. However, everyone knew exactly what Mendès Herrera was: a man with no rights, no legal status, hardly viewed as human: a Jew.

Most Jews in France lived in poverty, some in small squalid villages, others in ghettos where tenements were so tall and so close no light fell on the narrow stinking streets. But some Jews in Bordeaux had managed to make their way in commerce. Father Herrera had established himself in the export trade.

Mendès wore a beard—a peculiarity she found sensual. She had never before been with a bearded man. It felt animal. The beard itself was silky and dark brown, softer than the hair of his head. Otherwise he did not look like the Jews she had seen in Alsace. They spoke barbaric German and dressed all in black, foreign and raggedy. He was not like the Jews from her childhood in Langue d'Oc, the horse dealers who came to fairs with their cattle, their oxen and above all their horses, curried and with combed manes. They were leathery men, scorched by the sun, wiry, talking to the horses in a language she had not heard since, a crazy Provençal dialect called Suadet. Those Jews could make any horse look good. They could leap on and off the horses and make them run in circles. They could doctor sick animals. Like the Gypsies who traveled through, they were deeply mistrusted.

The same peasant who begged them to sell him a calf at a price he could afford or to cure his sick mule, would make the sign against the evil eye and spit when they passed.

Except for the beard, Mendès might have been any prosperous young merchant, sowing his wild oats, taking an actress for a mistress, going to meetings of philosophical societies and writing bad poetry praising love and liberty and reason. Yet there was a difference that attracted her. Oh, he was fine-looking. She had grown up among men of the Mediterranean south, and he was that type, bred into her from childhood as what a man should be. His hair was black, thick, glossy. But the eyes in his olive-skinned face were grey. Because they were so startlingly light, they dominated his face. His nose was aquiline, his mouth full. Against the dark beard, his lips looked red. He was stocky, compactly built and strong. His hands were not the hands of a gentleman. It was the custom in his family for the sons to work in the business, and he had shipped to the New World and down the coast of Africa. He had been to Turkey. He had been in storms and becalmed for three weeks in the doldrums. He had been shipwrecked near the mouth of the Amazon. Now he was thirty. His father had died of smallpox. His uncle and his older brother were running the business, and he was in the office and on the docks these days, no more roving.

She loved his stories, even when she did not believe them. Savages who went naked but for leaves on their private parts. Huge pink birds with red beaks. Alligators big as seven men with jaws that could eat a horse, swarming in the rivers so wide you could not see across. Huge snakes as big around as a cow that squeezed the life from their prey in powerful coils. Monkeys in the trees common as crows. Fish with breasts. Sea unicorns. Fish so plentiful you could cross to dry land on the backs of their schools.

She loved his stories as she had loved those her father had told her when she was a little girl as they all huddled around the hearth. Her father had been a wanderer too. He had practiced his craft as bricklayer down France from the Loire to Toulouse. She had outdone her father already, but she doubted she would ever get a chance to equal the wanderings of Mendès.

The moment she had first melted had been when she felt his hands on her back, on her hips, and they were not the hands of a gentleman. She was used now to men with soft hands, hands that had never done anything more difficult than turn a page or dip a quill in ink. The men who prided themselves on swordsmanship might have tiny calluses or a little nick on the back. Mendès' palms were thickened with hard work. The end of the little finger on his left hand had been nipped off in a shipboard accident. There were odd stains and scars. His hands excited her.

At twenty he had married a woman he loved. They had four children. The smallpox epidemic that had removed his father had killed his wife and two of the children. The remaining boy and girl were being raised by his mother. He said he had no desire to marry again. "I've provided heirs. I'm the younger son. Why have more to quarrel over the inheritance? Why bring in a wife to meddle with the lives of my children? I had a good wife. I don't need another." While speaking, he had the habit of stroking his beard, exploringly, as she had often noticed ladies stroking a small dog or a Persian cat.

It was not only the adventurer in him that attracted her, but the way he had of looking at things. He did not take much for granted. His position in society was precarious. "My family lived in Granada since Roman times. We were more Spanish than the Spanish. We had lived under the Visigoths, under the Moors, under the Christians. Who expected anything but an occasional bad decade? To be uprooted, sent into exile, stripped of everything in a place we had lived since before the country existed, it was unthinkable. Yet it happened."

"That was 1492. This is 1789. Three hundred years and you talk about it as if it happened last week."

"Nobody among the Sephardim—what you call Spanish and Portuguese Jews—will ever take for granted that we belong in a country. No matter how much at home you are, how accepted you imagine yourself to be—in come a couple of fanatics like Isabella and Ferdinand. Then you're lighting up the night like the new streetlamps, burned alive in the square for the edification of crowds, you instead of fireworks—cheaper and more entertaining."

"My great-grandfather was burned as a heretic," Claire said. "In the town where I was born, people still talk about the crusade that wiped out our religion, our rulers, our independence—as if it happened to them personally."

"Some peoples have sharp memories of what has been done to them. Others don't know how they came to be where they are. I met Indians in the New World who have a record in beads going back hundreds of years. I belong to the people of the Book, but those Indians found their own way of keeping the past."

"My grandmother told stories. When I was still little enough to sit in her lap, she impressed upon me there's truth in the tallest tale. Like how you saw fish in the sea with breasts and milk coming out for their young."

"Claire, I swear to you that was true and I did see it. You ought to believe me always. I'm a very truthful guy." He smiled like a great cat.

"There's no such thing."

"You're a cynic, Claire. If we don't believe in larger things than ourselves, we'll be in despair."

"What do you believe in? Really. Not what you give lip service to."

He was silent. "I believe in wind and water and the power of them. I believe in history. I believe the earth moves and time moves and things change. Sometimes they change for the better and sometimes they change for the worse, but always, always they change. And if you push hard, maybe you can change them the way you'd like them to go."

"If the Jews could send representatives to Versailles for the Estates General meeting, would you run for election? Would you, Mendès?"

"You see into me. Yes. I would."

"I wish we all could. But actors aren't people either. And women aren't."

"Actually, in some towns, women have been voting. They've just done it, joined in the discussion and voted."

"I'd vote for you. I think you'd be fair to me and mine. You're straight and level."

"I was raised to be just in my dealings. My father was famous for that. When you're a Jew in business in Bordeaux, you have to be twice as honest to be credited with half of it."

Sex came easily to Claire. After the first few men, she had learned how to move so that she got the contact she needed. She learned what she liked, how to get it. But sex with Mendès was sensual. His beard excited her. His hands with their rough surfaces, their strength, gave her pleasure. He used a kind of sheath so that he would not make her pregnant.

She was amused how upset her colleagues were. "But you said I should have a regular lover. You're never satisfied, even when I follow your advice."

Juliette made a gagging sound. "How can you? A dirty Jew."

"Actually he takes a bath every Friday. A complete bath."

"He'll die of the pleurisy," Madame said softly. "Bathing weakens you."

Lucie, who played heroines, said in her buttery voice, "I know for a fact that they cut off part of their pricks and grow tails instead."

Claire laughed until she spilled her soup. "Go on believing that. Absolutely! Leave the field to me."

Juliette looked thoughtful, putting her finger to her nose. "He does give you nice presents. You could pawn that necklace for a good price."

"When I need to, I will," Claire said. Someday times would be hard again. She would not have her looks forever. In the meantime, life was amusing. She enjoyed Mendès and she enjoyed annoying her colleagues. A lover who could please her and displease them had many virtues.

SEVENTEEN
Nicolas

❧

(Spring 1788–Spring 1789)

NICOLAS found he had a natural talent for being married to Sophie. His father had died too young for him to have any impression of how his parents had behaved but he understood his father to have been as stern and withdrawn as his mother was pious and interfering. He would never forget dragging about in girl's clothes for his first eight years; if he had been able to forget, there was a portrait of him at five to remind him, with an inscription from his mother bidding him to be as innocent before the Virgin in his adult life as she had consecrated him to be in his infancy. Sophie made it disappear. He did not ask her what she had done with it, his childhood repression in a gilt frame.

His marriage was nothing like those of his friends. He intended to be faithful and he meant to be open with her, as he urged her to be with him. Sophie expected to enjoy sex. His understanding was mostly theoretical, but he genuinely loved her body as well as her mind. She was not a small woman but built on a statuesque scale, so he did not fear hurting her with his weight or his occasional clumsiness, although that was passing as they got better at pleasing each other. Her size put him at ease. When they kissed, he had only to bow his head slightly to reach her. When he held her, her body touched all of his. They were a matched pair.

Her time in a convent had not inhibited her, as it was a convent designed to polish the daughters of the wealthy before marriage, not to turn them into nuns. There was more dancing than praying. It was mostly a legal scam designed to enable fathers to arrange for daughters to inherit. Sophie had gotten away from her mother and read books forbidden at home. For Sophie as for Nicolas, the Church was a problem rather than a solution, and the deity a superfluous construct that could comfort only the ignorant.

"I've never seen a marriage of equals," he confided, "but I want us to have one."

"Can we really be equal with you out in the world making interesting things happen and discussing serious ideas with intelligent men of action and intellect, while I putter around in our flat, attending an occasional lecture?"

Early the next year, she launched a salon. Every Tuesday she had the circle of which he had been a part for years, the surviving philosophers and younger men and women who showed promise, who had perhaps written something of interest. Salons were something Sophie seemed to understand intuitively. She attended several, including that of Mme Helvétius, out in the suburb of Auteuil. Mme Helvétius, widow of a philosopher, had adopted Dr. Cabanis who was courting Sophie's sister. They were all good friends.

First the hostess must set the tone and create an interesting and lively mix. Salons were the place where the liberal aristocracy mingled with intellectuals, with men successful in law or business or science or medicine as could never happen at court, where a bourgeois, no matter how bright or renowned, would never be received. Second, she must have both clever women and attractive women, to leaven the discussion, to keep the men at their best and to provide a mating pool. Marriages were conceived in salons and affairs were sparked. The court nobility fulminated against them, for they encouraged the mixing of classes and the rule of women, the devout said.

Reputations were made and unmade, literary, theatrical, political, scientific. Appointments were campaigned for and against. Fashions were created and banished. Of gossip there was some, but mostly there were discussions, flights, repartee, arguments, theses put forward and rebutted. The buffet that Sophie spread was excellent. She circulated constantly. Each hostess had her own method of running her salon: some sat in one place and watched openly or clandestinely. Sophie preferred to wander the room, dipping into conversations, making necessary introductions and nudging people towards or away from each other. She had a gift for nuances of personal interaction.

She read a great deal, went out with him to public and private theaters, to other salons, to dinner at this or that great or interesting house. She painted miniatures. He knew the gossip that attended his marriage, the ribald jokes about his discovery of sex at forty-two, how soon he would be cuckolded. His hearing was exceptional, so he often caught comments others had not intended he intercept. Some of his academic colleagues were shocked at his marriage; they feared he would prove to be in his dotage. They would never understand that Sophie was as intellectually stimulating as they were. He was deeply in love with her, but not besotted. He could see her clearly. She had a temper. She hated to be proved wrong, even in small things. She was careless with her books and her personal effects, leaving open volumes in the oddest places. He could no longer sit in any chair without looking first. She lost gloves and kerchiefs at an alarming rate. She was truthful with him, but beware being on her bad side. Having had plenty of practice lying to her mother, she showed a distressing talent for fabricating stories. "But I don't enjoy lying. A tyrant demands lies, because truth is punished unless it conforms to his wishes. Therefore a tyrant creates liars as the sun creates shadows."

"Then I must never in the smallest way tyrannize over you."

"Exactly!" She grinned.

"Nicolas," she said late in 1788, as the first puddles were freezing and the muddy streets turning to icy ruts, "we should start a school for adults. I want to study mathematics and science, and I suspect many women and men would like to learn more than their haphazard educations provided them."

They called it the Lycée and held it in a building across from the Palais Royal. Nicolas taught mathematics. She was one of his students, as she had promised, but she also did much of the organizing and daily administration. It was another node in the web of connections among the people who liked reason above tradition. The court was increasingly irrelevant; Paris was the heart and brain.

Nicolas had been going since November to the house of a wealthy magistrate and member of the Parlement of Paris, Adrien Duport. Duport had called together influential liberals to meet quietly at his house, to avoid exciting the King or the government. They called themselves the Committee of Thirty, but they soon rose to fifty. It was by invitation only.

One regular visitor was Lafayette, ginger-haired and lanky, a marquis like Nicolas but far more apt to style himself a general of the American army—an army which had appreciated and promoted him far more generously than his own. Nicolas and Lafayette had been friends for years. In spite of being younger than Nicolas, Lafayette had married much earlier, at fifteen. Lafayette had stood up for Nicolas at his wedding to Sophie. Frequently Nicolas and Sophie dined at his house Mondays, when he held his American dinners. Any representatives of the American government currently in Paris, from Jefferson to Franklin, came, and everybody spoke English and talked of events past and present in America the free, the democratic. Jefferson and the British economist Adam Smith were taken with Sophie and began coming not only to her salon but to the Mint for dinners and evenings of conversation. Sophie's conversational English had rapidly improved, catching up with her fluency in reading and writing. She was discussing with Adam Smith translating one of his works into French.

Another important member of the Committee of Thirty was the skinny, dour Abbé Sieyès. He had plunged into fame by writing a pamphlet that Nicolas, along with half the country, much admired. It began boldly. "What is the third estate? Everything. What has it been up until now in the political order? Nothing. What does it want to be? Something!" Yes! said all common readers.

Most members of the Committee of Thirty were wealthy, so they raised money among themselves to print and distribute pamphlets putting forth what they called a patriotic line. "A patriot," was the highest praise they could bestow. It was a new catchword among those who wanted change. The country first, the King second: the people are the country. Nicolas had been turning out pamphlets on every political subject. The Committee was producing sample Petitions of Complaint, so that towns and guilds all over the country would know how to draw one up—also to give them ideas on what to ask for.

The King had been forced to call the Estates General. Louis imagined it would set in stone his desires and those of the ministers he appointed and fired at will. Louis thought that he was Louis XIV and could nod and it would be so. But the world had moved on. People were more educated, more enlightened. A man had only to look at America to see how rebellion could pay off. It was an electrifying time to be alive.

When Nicolas looked around the salon that Sophie was running in their sumptuous apartments in the Mint, when he circulated among friends and allies at the house of Duport, when he debated republican forms with Benjamin Franklin at Lafayette's house, he felt at the center of everything vital. He stood on the point Archimedes had spoken about, when he said that if he had somewhere to stand, with a fulcrum he could move the world. They were going to move the world forward, out of the darkness of superstition and privilege and violence, into rational equality and sunny tolerance. They were good men, his friends, his colleagues, who knew what had to be done. They had only to explain it clearly for ordinary people to grasp the way forward.

His allies were the hub of a wheel, and as they turned in the center of Paris, the rim spun round. Important men in the Church came, successful bankers and businessmen, noblemen who had known each other for years. They could trust one another. They could delegate responsibility, knowing that each was capable and had the resources to put that capacity into action.

For years Nicolas had been writing about what had to be done in order to save France from itself, to end the deadlock of privilege, to rationalize a decrepit system, to ease the burden on the poor and give them a chance to raise themselves out of misery, to make education universal, to end all kinds of slavery. Now he was beginning to see how liberal men of influence might together bring about profound changes that had seemed a daydream. He had interested himself in the improvement of society, but since Turgot fell, it had felt like self-indulgent fantasizing. Now he came together with other enlightened men and women, ineffectual no more. Everything would be changed, and soon.

EIGHTEEN
Georges

❧

(1788)

GEORGES found he had been right all along. All he had needed was a foot up. Only a fool could have held the position he had purchased so expensively and not made cartloads of livres. He would have no trouble paying off his debts in the period promised. His card and his door now read "Monsieur d'Anton." One of his new specialities was helping bourgeois gentlemen who had made piles of money prove they were noble. He became accomplished at fiddling around with genealogies and faking connections. It was lucrative, and he was successful often enough for his clients to spread the word that this d'Anton could trick the system and get it to cough up a title.

After years of counting sous, nursing one coffee and borrowing a newspaper, alternating his two suits and his four shirts, eating at the cheapest tavern he could find, now he sat down to superb dinners. Gabrielle could really cook and she delighted in doing so, with the assistance of the maid of all work they had hired. Now that Gabrielle was settled, the Charpentiers had sold the cafe and moved to a pleasant holding outside Paris. It was close enough for Gabrielle and Georges to visit every Sunday.

He liked looking at his wife, with her opulent dark beauty growing riper every day, now that she was pregnant. He liked eating the savory food she knew how to prepare. He liked going out with her on his arm, pressed against him and making soft comments for his ears. Oh, she was no meek dove. When a tradesman crossed her or the maid disobeyed, her voice could ring out, harsh with contempt and anger. But him she wanted to spoil. Their bed rocked like a happy skiff on the river. She had begun to fear no one would suit both her father and herself. She had wanted a husband and children, and here he was. She had a way of folding her hands across her belly, still visibly the same, and looking as if she were counting gold. "You have given me a child," she said to him every morning, as if he had made her some grand present. Marriage was highly agreeable, no question about it. He had chosen wisely and was amply rewarded.

He would never stop looking at other women, he would never stop mentally stripping off their skirts and imagining how they might be in bed, but he was satiated. When he felt women eying him, he only smiled. He was under no illusions that he would be faithful to Gabrielle, but why bother with what he did not yet need? She was still full of surprises. He called her his lioness, and she purred.

She proved to have a sharp eye for how things should be arranged domestically, how the rooms of a young upward-climbing counselor should display to best advantage his taste, his acumen, his (so far nonexistent) wealth. She bargained fiercely. Her peasant's hands would pinch and prod, poke at the seams and joints. Her eyes would narrow and spark with scorn. Her voice would crack with indignation. What did they take her for? She knew the value of a livre. She knew all the tricks. Even as they fought near-mortal battles, tradesmen admired her. She knew her sofas, her tables and chairs, her linens, her china. One use to which she had put the years of waiting for the right husband to appear, was to learn everything about proper domestic existence. He had married a professional. His life was soon comfortably, even sumptuously arranged, on a budget.

Their bedroom was done in straw yellow, with the bed in an alcove lined with darker yellow and red tapestries. Gabrielle used an escritoire decorated with marquetry. In the drawing room, where he had clients wait, there was a sofa and six armchairs. Ten lyre-back chairs stood around a dining table for guests. Otherwise, they ate privately at a table in their bedroom. His study she had done in masterful red. What was supposed to be the dining room turned into an office for his clerks. He was proud of the impression the rooms made.

In court he was an excellent pleader. He had good help. He had hired some of his old penniless friends. Fabre d'Églantine and his pal from school, Paré, were his clerks. Camille Desmoulins did odd jobs for him. Camille was to be found at the Palais Royal most evenings, listening to inflammatory speeches and occasionally mounting a chair to make one. He was trying to overcome his stammer. He practiced speaking with pebbles in his mouth, like Demosthenes.

Camille had given up on his long seduction of Mme Duplessis and decided to fall in love with her daughter, Lucile, only sixteen but madly in love with him. "How can you go from courting the mother to courting the daughter?" Georges asked, swatting him on the back. "That seems a little coarse. Doesn't Madame object?"

"They all object, except Lucile, who's having the t-t-time of her life. She would run away with me. She st-st-starves herself, she f-faints, she throws fits. She wants me, she must have me."

"I notice you're not hanging around there any longer."

"I've been shown the door. It's one thing to be courting the virtuous mother, year after year. But to marry the daughter, they want money, position. As if they don't have enough themselves to share some with me. But I love the whole family, Georges, that's what it is."

"I know what you mean. I courted Jérôme Charpentier as hard as I courted Gabrielle."

"I love the Duplessis clan, one and all. My own father is impossible to please. He has a way of smiling that makes me feel like horse droppings. Monsieur is such a dear bureaucratic fudge. He knows everything someone in his position should know, and nothing he shouldn't. He respects everything he's supposed to respect, but he doesn't meddle in the family. His wife and daughter dance rings around him." Camille tossed his long lank hair. Sometimes Camille was not so much handsome as almost beautiful, like a young girl. Other times he was gawky, weird-looking, a stooping stork, at twenty-seven still a boy. A schoolboy's girlishness. A fragility that perhaps would appeal to a headstrong young girl, bored at home and full of romantic notions from novels and bad poetry. Always rumors swirled around Camille. He never had money from home and little from his work. Yet there were periods when he seemed flush, when he could treat Fabre and Georges to dinner out. Some of it came from women, and some if it seemed to come from older men. Camille was a bit of a whore.

"She doesn't mind your stammer then, this Lucile."

"I never st-st-stammer with women, Georges. Only with men. Don't you think I've gotten b-better?"

Actually he had. When Georges first met Camille, the boy could hardly force out a sentence. Now his stammer came and went. When he was flustered or nervous, it returned. When he was calm or passionate, it vanished. "How can you marry a woman whose family has shown you the door?"

"Lucile is determined. She'll make it happen. Then, like you, my in-laws will set me up. They're better off than yours. They'll have to take me whether they want me or not—and decidedly, they don't."

"You told me that Madame was your muse. Have you started writing poems to the daughter?"

"Actually I've stopped writing love poems altogether. Lucile found her mother's diary, and she's blackmailing her. My love poems were tucked in it.

Lucile is using the poems I wrote in an attempt to seduce her mother to force Madame's support for our marrying. Now there's a woman after my own heart. Devious, passionate, crazy. I must have her."

Georges was making money, Camille was trying to marry, and all about them, Paris was bubbling with a cauldron of hot fat, sizzling and spewing. On saints' days, statuettes of Benjamin Franklin, Voltaire, and Rousseau were more popular than the traditional little figures of the King and Queen and the saints themselves—and this was among the people, who were supposed to be stupid as the mud that clogged the streets.

Georges had never despised working people. He soon knew half his neighborhood. When he walked through the streets, he greeted everybody by name, asked after the husband or the wife, the kids or the parents, their bum leg or their arthritis. The Cordeliers neighborhood was rough and mixed. He felt at home. Everybody knew he was doing well, but nobody seemed to mind. He was comfortable with men and women of all classes, he knew how to tell the right joke and who to kiss upon meeting and who to slap on the shoulder and who wanted a slight bow. He went off to court and helped manufacturers and bankers and dealers in export-import cook up patents of nobility for themselves, and he got on with his clients. They felt he genuinely liked them, as he often did.

But he did not like his wealthy clients as well as the fellows in the taverns of the Cordeliers district. He enjoyed their open talk, their laughter, their solidarity. He respected people who worked with their hands. He liked to sit in the Cafe Procope across the square, where Voltaire had been a patron and the coffee was superb and the decor, quietly elegant, but he liked also to drink rough Montmartre wine in the Monk's Belly down the street. Unlike Camille, who believed passionately in the cause of the poor but could not sit at a trestle table in a tavern and trade jibes and buy drinks all around, Georges knew he had a peasant body and in some ways a peasant disposition. He would never take his law business seriously. It was a ploy to make money. It was a joke on the system. He did it well because he had a good strong voice and a gift for oratory and the ability to think on his feet. He could make people like him. He could make people want to be on his side. He could charm the stiff judges and he could charm his clients and their wives. People would look at his ugly face and draw back. Then he would start working on them, smiling, joking, setting them at ease with his voice that Gabrielle called rich as oxtail soup flowing over them. Pretty soon they would be edging closer, touching him. He observed it constantly, even while he wondered what he had that drew people. He saw it in animals. Other dogs trotted after the top dog down the street. Other cats gave way before the dominant tom. He would have more fun as a defense lawyer, but there was no money in that. Most people never saw a lawyer before they were condemned. No, he had bought his way into a level of the legal system that turned dull law books into gold coins. He was satisfied, and he would make sure his clients were satisfied too.

NINETEEN
Pauline

(Spring 1789)

"PAULINE! Pauline!" It was Aimée. "Martin is beating Victoire again. He's drunk as a monk and beating her with a big stick!"

Madeleine on the third floor back stuck her head out from the landing. "Lead the way, Pauline. Let's get him."

Pauline ran upstairs to get Catherine Fosse, who had not heard the racket because her children were making too much noise. Then the four of them went, carrying brooms and sticks, to defend Victoire, the old-clothes woman. Everyone said a man had the right to beat his wife if she had done wrong, but to beat her bloody for no reason but his drunken rage, that was not done. The women had a right to interfere. Everybody in the neighborhood knew everybody's business—how could they not? They lived against each other, doors to the stairways open, business carried on in the street, in the taverns or shops.

"Martin, come out here. We have a bone to pick with you!" Pauline shouted. "Eh, Martin. You put down that stick and come see us."

The screams inside stopped. A moment later Victoire, bruised and bleeding from her nose and mouth, came running down the steps. Aimée held her. "You poor thing. He's at it again. What a mess he's made of you." Victoire was only four years older than Pauline, but it was hard to tell half the time that she was still pretty with her face bruised and her eyes blackened.

"Martin, you come down here."

"I'm not coming down for a bunch of cunts. Go home where you belong." He scowled out the window but did not pursue his wife.

"Martin, are you scared of us? Maybe you use a stick because you can't use what else you've got. Everybody says you can't cut it with your wife and that's why you knock her around—because you can't knock her up." Pauline had grown up speaking the language of the streets. Everybody began laughing.

"Listen to chocolate mouth giving it to him. Hey, Pauline, you tell him. Tell him you women are going to hang him from the lantern."

Aimée led Victoire off. They were cousins, and she would take Victoire in for the night, just pack her into their family bed. The women yelled for a while before dispersing. Martin was barricaded in his room.

Ever since they had drawn up their Petition of Complaint, Pauline found her position in the neighborhood changed. She was seen as a strong and just woman to whom other women could go for help. She was considered politically astute, because she read the papers. She read the wall posters aloud. Only the government was allowed to paste up announcements, but clandestine posters were slathered up every dawn. In the tavern she read to others the pamphlets and papers smuggled in from Holland, where the press was freer.

It had been a hard, hard winter, as bad as the one when her mother and sister died. The Seine was frozen for leagues. No fuel, no grain came in. The price of bread rose every week. The cook's assistant around the corner from whom her parents had always bought leftovers raised his prices to the sky. Kitchen servants in the houses of the nobility and the rich bourgeoisie sold extra food to poor people.

In Paris nothing whatsoever went to waste. The clothes of the wealthy moved down the levels of society until they were rags worn by beggars. Any piece of wood would eventually be burned. Any scrap of food would be eaten. Any lump of shit would end up on a field in the suburbs somewhere. If a woman was filled with despair and threw herself off a bridge into the Seine, her body would be stripped of usable clothing before the authorities ever saw it. No corpse of the common people was buried with shoes on. Even buttons and candle ends were recirculated and used till nothing was left. Servants sold off everything from bits of soap to worn quills, cracked and chipped dishes, food and wine not finished. Servants lived better than other workers, unless their employers had little money. Then they would go hungry and sometimes be worked to death. But servants of the wealthy spent their days waiting at attention in anterooms, down in the kitchen listening for a bell to summon them. They had plenty of time to think up ways to skim off profit.

She had a cousin Nanette who worked as a scullery maid for a bourgeois family in the suburb of Auteuil. The family had been in furniture making, but now they speculated in suburban real estate. Pauline went to see if she could work out a deal for leftover food. Nanette saw her in the kitchen.

It was a big room, very warm. Pauline could not believe how warm it was. She could have sat there all Sunday afternoon, but Nanette obviously did not want her to stick around. She acted ashamed of Pauline. Nanette was in the old-clothes chain in the house and got decent dresses before they wore out. Nanette gave her a bowl of beef soup while they were talking and some white bread. Pauline was used to the dark bread that everyone ate, half rye, half wheat. This was like cake, light and all wheat. Pauline could have eaten a whole loaf easily, but Nanette only gave her two heels.

Nanette did agree to sell her some roast chicken and some of the rich soup she had just eaten. She carried her containers home along with a bag of heels from the white bread. Nanette had given her a decent price on the lot. The trouble was it was too far to go. She would have to find another servant in her own neighborhood. Aimée had heard of a lawyer's cook selling food in the Rue des Cordeliers. Pauline would ask around.

You had to be careful that servants did not cheat you and give you food that had spoiled, that would lay you up with terrible pains in the belly. She always smelled the food before she bought it, but strong spices could cover up rotting meat. You had to trust each other, so you needed to establish a regular relationship for used meals.

Nobody poor had kitchens like that at Nanette's house. Women just cooked in the fireplace, so no wonder they bought ready-made food when they could. Women worked, so who had time for anything fussy? Most people owned two pots, one for heating water. She was better off because she had chocolate-making pans and kettles and a little coal stove she cooked chocolate on, but she seldom bothered cooking for herself. If she were less popular, she would be mistrusted. Women simply did not live by themselves.

She had got used to sleeping alone, but she would never say that to anyone, for it would seem bizarre. It was considered unhealthy. Who would keep you warm? Commonly people slept up to seven in a bed. With no heat, she could freeze to death some night. But the shop stayed warm from all the cooking of the day. Only Sunday night was cold. She needed a Sunday night lover. She had been faithful to Henri. She had not looked at another man, paying no heed to flirtatious words or glances or young men falling into step beside her as she went off to the tavern or mass.

All the talk in the tavern was of politics and bread, as the iron winter relented into a hungry spring. The price of bread kept rising. Jokes, pornographic cartoons and pamphlets about the Queen were everywhere. The Austrian bitch was bankrupting France. She had bought another castle. How many did she own? How many houses could one woman occupy?

They had elections for the Estates General, but it looked like they were going to be screwed again. The rich people wanted everything to stay the same, only they wanted the court to spend less and they did not want to pay any taxes at all, thank you, let the poor people take care of that. Still, who wouldn't be excited? All the women gabbed about Versailles as they sat around a rough trestle table in the tavern. Only the fishwives had ever been there. A delegation of fishwives had the job of being present during any royal birth to verify it. That was their privilege from time immemorial. They marched into the Queen's bedroom when the time came. They watched the Queen's cunt and they saw what came out, so nobody could fool them. Versailles was fairyland, the golden land in the clouds where people wore gold, slept in golden beds, sat in golden chairs, ate off golden plates and pissed in golden pots. Who could believe it really existed not far away?

Aimée's husband came over to the table. "Hey, you women, when are you going to do something about bread? Get off your asses. Show them the business end of a pike."

"Maybe we will," Aimée said. "That's for us to decide." The women traditionally started the bread riots. They had to keep the government in line on anything to do with feeding their families.

"I hear they're rioting upriver. Seizing grain shipments. They're taking over bakeries," Aimée's husband said before he ambled off to join a game of dominoes.

Babette's father called out, "Guess the women up there care about their husbands and their kids being hungry."

"We'll take care of our business," Babette said, as she put down beers for them. They all liked wine better, but in hard times, they drank beer. It was cheaper. "Get off our backs. We'll do what we have to."

"He's right," Pauline said quietly. "We have to act. We need to send somebody to talk to women in other neighborhoods and the suburbs. Maybe we should go out on Sunday? We should ask the other women what they're doing."

Babette said, "We can send out word. I'll go to Faubourg Saint Marcel and ask my cousin."

Pauline said, "I'll talk to the fishwives and the market women." So this was how things started, just her and a bunch of other women at a table in the tavern. It didn't seem real. It didn't seem like anything could happen just from them gabbing. If she really thought a demonstration would result, she would be scared. Women could die or get arrested.

Within forty-eight hours, with no way to get in touch except conversations in the markets and at the river and the Pont Neuf, with no organization and no external discipline, the women were ready to take to the streets. It was a matter of making the government more scared of the people of Paris than they were of their own bureaucrats, who wanted free trade in grain. Suddenly every woman was talking about marching in the streets, all at once as if they were a flock of geese deciding to fly south. Pauline wasn't sure they could put a scare into the government, the way they'd punished Martin for beating Victoire too often. But they had to try. It was the women's duty.

TWENTY

Max

❧

(May–June 1789)

MAX felt that the delegates from Arras came to Versailles with open minds. After all, the King had called the Estates General. They knew that many, many Petitions of Complaint had been submitted. Obviously they were summoned to Versailles to set things right. Each delegate brought serious ideas on how to make France governable again and how to solve the fiscal crisis—and the crisis of bread. They were a somber but hopeful group.

But the very first day, the Third Estate delegates were slapped in the face. At the opening ceremonies, the clergy were received in a large hall by the King and greeted individually; next, the nobility were received with full pomp. Again the King spoke to each one. All this time the Third Estate were kept standing in an antechamber, hour after hour. The King grew weary. At four he retired to his bedchamber, opened one door and greeted them in mass in the Hall of Mirrors as they were herded along between barricades at a trot.

The next day they were to march in procession. The nobility were dolled up in lace and silks, resplendent, surrounded by musicians. The upper clergy gleamed in purple and gold and red, magnificent enough to blind the eyes. The lower clergy were a bit dusty in their cassocks, and the parade marshall stuck a marching band between the upper and lower clergy, since the bishops and abbots complained that the plebeian parish priests embarrassed them.

The Third Estate were told to dress all in black. They looked like a bunch of mummers from a bad play, in black mourning broadcloth and three-cornered black hats. They scurried along, sulking. Max was always aware of what kind of figure he cut. These were not poor people. He was probably one of the poorest. There were scientists, astronomers, bankers, doctors, financiers, successful lawyers, men of business, men of importance.

The duc d'Orléans tried to march with the Third Estate to show his political sympathy, but the parade marshall escorted him none too gently to march in his proper place with the Prince de Condé, the Comtes d'Artois and Provence, the King's relatives, of whom Orléans was the least favored. But Orléans was popular with the people, who shouted for him. He was greeted more enthusiastically than the King or the Queen, a fact that escaped nobody's attention.

Then came the interminable church service at which the Third Estate was once again kept standing. Max's lower back ached. Some delegates complained they had to piss. Some forced their way into corners. Finally on May eighth, the King addressed them. Once again the Third Estate was shoved to the back and kept standing. The King discoursed interminably in a high whine about the dangers of an unseemly zest for innovation, commending humility and patience. The King was dressed in cloth of gold with a huge diamond winking on his hat. The Queen wore silver, with a heron's plume in her hair, her entire person encrusted with jewels so that she glittered and clanked. All the princes of the blood sat on elaborate footstools, bedecked with forty pounds of golden finery apiece. Necker, once again the King's chief minister, then gave a three-hour drone on the state of the economy (deplorable) and the treasury (even worse), so detailed, so boring and so lacking in even a suggestion of a viable remedy, that he did not bother to read it all himself, but gave long sections of it to his deputy to mumble inaudibly. The King sat under a golden tent. The floor was covered with purple carpets flashing gold fleur de lis. Everywhere Max looked, thousands of livres of ostentatious waste met his eyes.

On the day they finally started deliberating, Max could feel their resentment, the raw pride, the determination. The King had insulted them, and they would look to him no further. Because of their numbers, they got the largest assembly room in the Hall of Small Pleasures, an echoey ramshackle warehouse where the King's costumes and props for plays and masques were stored. The clergy and the nobility were meeting in the same building, in smaller rooms. The storage area cleared for the Third Estate was spacious; they promptly invited the other two orders to join them, to deliberate together.

The galleries were so roomy that the public began to attend. Common people, market women, interested and increasingly noisy observers cheered or booed the speeches. The deputies had no idea how to run their meetings. Such an assembly was a novelty. It wasn't a court with judges and laws and traditional rules. They were improvising. A couple of Englishmen came by and commented that such unruliness, such a loud gallery, everyone on the floor talking at once, no agenda, would never be permitted in the British

Parliament. Some delegates asked the Englishmen how Parliament conducted itself. Max did not bother. He was not an impassioned admirer of things British. They would work out their own way.

He made his first speech about a plan to get the clergy to join them. Hardly anyone bothered to listen. That evening as he was going back to his inn, he ran into a journalist who hailed him by name, then seeing Max's puzzlement, identified himself. "Ca-Camille. Camille Desmoulins. From Louis-le-Grand."

"Of course. How are you?" Obviously from the looks of him, no more prosperous than Max himself. He should have recognized Camille, for he had not changed drastically in eleven years, the same animated boy with scraggly hair. They shared a frugal dinner at Max's inn—the Sign of the Fox on Rue Sainte Elisabeth, where people from Artois without money to waste usually stayed.

Camille was effervescent. He was writing illicit pamphlets for a printer who ran them off on a press behind a laundry. He was in love, he was sure he was going to get married any day, for the girl would not give up—she adored him. Camille reminisced about Max's saving him from a group of older boys he had irritated with his sharp tongue. Max was smaller than any of the other boys, but he could shame them. Camille had never forgotten. Now that Max was reminded, he felt warmly toward Camille. They had shared a passion for Roman history.

"What did you think of my speech today? Honestly? I ask, because I could see I wasn't being listened to."

Camille ran his hand through his long brown hair. His sharp almost girlish features contorted. "What do you m-mean by 'honestly'? How honest?"

"Your real opinion."

Camille sighed. "What you said was to the p-point, but you might as well not have b-bothered. Max, you sound like a country priest—that nasal singsong. Nobody's ever going to listen to a word as long as you sound like Father Mule Ears."

Max was silent so long Camille began to squirm. "I have to work on delivery. Do I need to get rid of my accent?"

"Not if you speak more forcefully. You put an audience to sleep."

"I must strengthen my delivery. Thank you." Max grasped his hand. "I won't forget this, Camille. If I once helped you, now you've paid me back."

"By insulting you?" Camille giggled.

"By taking the risk of telling me what no one else would. Let me pay for your dinner." Max could scarcely afford this gesture, but he could always skip a meal tomorrow. Camille did not demur.

That night Max practiced before the mirror in his room. He had to keep his voice down, but he watched his gestures and his mannerisms. Was there anyone he could model himself on? When Comte de Mirabeau spoke, every-body shut up. He was a nobleman, but he had been imprisoned and had chosen to run as a delegate for the Third Estate. He was a hideous man with a lascivious reputation, but he spoke well. His voice thundered out. He was forceful, direct. When Mirabeau was not speaking, he was everywhere, buttonholing other delegates, talking to journalists, haranguing, arguing, joking, telling stories. Max watched which delegates Mirabeau bothered to work on.

Some of the more radical deputies had begun meeting. They were called the Breton Club, because some came from Brittany. Several Parisian delegates joined the Breton Club, as Max did. After he had been to a few meetings, he was no longer invisible. He was identified with the radicals. At least some people listened when he spoke. Every morning he got up at dawn and walked into the formal gardens to practice. The area was so vast, he could shout and no one would hear him. It was what he had done during the elections in Arras, but now it counted more. He did not have a commanding presence like Mirabeau, but he could master his voice so that it did not squeak or sound nasal. He got rid of the sing-song. He studied the delivery of their president Bailly, the astronomer. He spoke with somber dignity as if measuring every word.

After five weeks the delegates decided to declare themselves a National Assembly. Max gave a speech to the clergy urging them to show compassion for the poor by coming to join those who represented them. He fiercely denounced the luxury in which the wealthy clergy lived. It was his first speech received with attention and applauded by the gallery. He was playing with pauses. Pauses could make things sound more ominous or important. A steady trickle of parish priests began to join the Third Estate. A slow inclination toward victory. They set up committees to deal with hunger in Paris, with taxa-tion, with the national debt. But the nobles would not budge and protested to the King, asking him to dissolve the Estates General.

The King responded by calling a royal session of the Estates to be held on June twenty-second. Max arrived early at the Hall on the morning of June twentieth. It had begun to rain hard during the night, so he had curtailed his morning practice in the garden. Delegates were already milling around the muddy street. They found the doors of the Hall of Small Pleasures barricaded. Inside, scaffolding was up and workmen were hammering and sawing and car-rying out rubble from a knocked-down wall. Louis had made the hall uninhab-itable. "It's all over," a tall wizened lawyer from Limoges mumbled. "He's cut us off."

"We represent the people. We can't let them down," Max said loudly over the downpour. They were getting soaked.

Dr. Guillotin spoke up. "I saw a big building a couple of days ago that looked as if we'd all fit inside. The tennis courts. It wasn't locked. The King likes to play tennis at odd times and so does his brother."

Bailly put a notice on the door. Then they followed Dr. Guillotin to the tennis courts. This was an even bigger space than the Hall of Small Pleasures, but it was all one room, with bare, bleak walls. Anybody who wanted to meet here would have to meet together, which was exactly what the Third Estate wanted. They filed in dripping and bedraggled. A deputy from Lyon built a fire in the stove so they could dry their clothes. There were no chairs, so they stood. The onlookers, the public, must fend for themselves. Some scrambled up the wooden latticework on the sides and perched there. The room was chilly and dank.

Max said to Camille, who was making notes, "Do you think the King will send his guards to disperse us?"

"He's not known for quick reactions. I'll bet he doesn't move against you until tomorrow."

Bailly began the session at once. They were here, so here was the National Assembly. "The place does not, gentlemen, make the Assembly. Rather the Assembly makes the place. We are the Assembly, even if we meet in the street."

Some King's guards appeared. They seemed surprised by the orderly show of the meeting and stood around at the door, uncertain how to proceed. Bailly ignored them and moved business with his usual dignity. He recognized Jean Mounier, who proposed they all take an oath, so that none of them could be singled out for punishment, to affirm their commitment to the people who had elected them and to the job they had come to do. "The King has sent for troops. He has forty thousand surrounding Versailles right now. We must take an oath to hold our ground, not to waver or retreat." Mounier took his pen and began to write. Others made suggestions. Within half an hour, they had an oath. Max was taut with excitement. If the guards did fire and killed some of them, it would actually strengthen their position. Sometimes martyrdom was power. He would prefer not to be a martyr so soon, but he would not back down. The hastily written oath was read out and then prepared for their signatures:

"The National Assembly has been called upon to create a constitution, to revive public order, to maintain the true principles of the monarchy. Nothing can prevent its deliberations in whatever place it may be obliged to meet. Wherever its members are gathered, there is the National Assembly constituted. Be it resolved that all members take a solemn oath never to separate but to meet any place they must until a constitution is established on a firm foundation."

"This is like the Declaration of Independence," Max said.

They lined up patiently. The room smelled of mold and sweat and wet cloth. Everybody signed except one delegate from Castlenaudry. Mirabeau was reluctant, for he said they were creating a conspiracy, but he announced he would sign because none of them would trust him if he didn't.

The next day the Comte d'Artois, the King's brother, had booked the tennis court all day. The National Assembly marched to the Church of Saint Louis, where a sympathetic vicar let them in. Max was beginning to enjoy this shuffling about. It showed their determination. He did not care if they ended up meeting in the King's stables.

On the twenty-third, a day later than promised, the King held his session in the Hall of Little Pleasures. He kept them standing in the rain for two hours first, while the two higher orders were seated. Max was not impressed with Louis' ability to change tactics. The King seemed unable to observe that when he was rude to the Third Estate, their anger made them more stubborn. The roads were lined with guards and musketeers, armed and at attention in the rain. The King addressed the delegates sternly, as disobedient children. They were to cease and desist from insisting they were anything more than his little Estates General, they were to do what he told them and no more, and they were to stop meeting with anyone from other orders, was that clear? They could not discuss feudal privilege. They could not discuss the privileges or properties of the Church. The public could no longer attend. "We have reached our decisions, and you shall hear them," he kept saying along with the threat to send them home by force if they were bad children. Max looked at the King, his antagonist. Max was standing so far back he could not make out details. This husky man in gold and jewels that would feed Paris for months speaking in a high whine, what was he? A relic with an army. "We order you to separate immediately and resume tomorrow in the rooms to which you have been assigned."

Louis left, followed by the nobility and the higher clergy. Max milled around with the other delegates. Mirabeau got on a chair and shouted at the guards standing at the doors, "We're here by the will of the people and we will only be removed by the force of your bayonets!"

Bailly went up to the head of the room, to the minister's table, and banged for order. "The nation did not assemble to receive an order to disperse. Let us proceed."

The Abbé Sieyès spoke. "We are today exactly what we were yesterday. Let us deliberate. Monsieur le President, do we have committees ready to report?"

They sat down and resumed where they had left off. Max was aware of the soldiers fully armed waiting for the King's order. They might die here. They might end up in various royal prisons, like the Bastille, to rot in chains as long as the King so pleased. But they would not willingly obey an unjust and arbitrary King. They were making history today, just as the Americans had. This was their Declaration. They would not be moved.

TWENTY-ONE
Nicolas

❧

(June 1789)

NICOLAS found love-making in the morning and then breakfast in bed marvelously stimulated his mind. He loved to start the day with Sophie in his arms, his lanky body twined with hers. Satisfaction did not make him drowsy but wakened him. Among the bric-a-brac of breakfast coffee cups, tea-spoons and brioche crumbs, the taste of strawberry jam, they discussed the day.

"What does the King really know?" Nicolas asked rhetorically. "Is it that he doesn't want to know, or is he too stupid to govern? Even in religion he prefers propriety. He wants everything in its place, including God."

"Well, Nico, he's rather well served by the way things are."

"His only real passion is hunting. He keeps lists of everything he kills. So many red deer, so many roe deer, so many boar, so many grouse, so many swallows."

"My father hunts. It's something gentlemen do in hierarchial packs attended by dozens of beaters and fetchers and masters and men of hounds. Like an army taking the field against a bunch of birds. It's what they do instead of war-fare. They get to use weapons and see blood."

"I hunted when I was young," he said apologetically.

"I can't imagine you on horseback chasing something." She was sitting up in a heap of pillows, flushed and rosy. Her peignoir was pale blue and printed with irises, a filmy light silk. Her skin glistened.

"It was the only thing I could find to do with my uncles, who rather despised me. I was a decent shot. But one day in the fall, we were hunting red deer. It came to me as the poor stag thrashed to death while the hounds tore at it that this was a disgusting pleasure."

"So what did you do?" She nodded. The maid removed the trays.

"I announced my decision in my usual serious manner—and lost the last scrap of respect of my uncles." He sighed ruefully. Thinking of his day's work, he said, "I'm trying to write for ordinary people. But I don't speak the same language as the woman who sells old clothes. We barely understand each other."

"It might be easier for you to learn to mimic her idiom and write simply, than for her to rise to your level of command."

"But to reason, she must have the tools for analysis. She must have a mastery of language in which she can do more than curse and buy and sell. She must have language adequate to discuss ideas and analyze politics."

"It might be easier to educate her children, Nico."

"We still have the problem of communicating with her here and now. . . ." He tangled a lock of her hair in his fingers. "Language is the great tool by which we manipulate each other socially and are manipulated. Poverty of life goes with poverty of mind. What we can't speak about, we can't think about."

"Doesn't music communicate with us? Don't paintings? If I'm walking and I meet a strange dog, I can tell whether it's friendly or hostile. How does a mother cat teach her kittens? Through example. Through example, Nico, we can communicate to others even if they lack the language of philosophy. We can demonstrate the good."

Nicolas was happy. He had found a way to engage at last in the important work of his time, engage with a woman, engage at once with familial and national history. He had finally become a full adult.

Nicolas was writing far more pamphlets than mathematical proofs these days. At the Committee of Thirty—long since swollen to more like sixty of the most intelligent and able liberals in Paris—Lafayette said to him, "Marquis, you are the only surviving Encyclopedist, the sole remaining philosopher of that generation that brought enlightenment to France, to Europe, to the world. We are the children of your intellect."

Nicolas did not want to be a relic. His wife was younger than Lafayette. "I'm not quite so ancient, Marquis. I have many more battles to fight." Lafayette was no longer one of his favorite people, vain, arrogant, sure no one was as brave or as bright or as fit to be a leader. He sought his image in every mirror he passed, and there was a kind of smile he had upon viewing himself that made Nicolas sigh. He had no illusions about his own charismatic abilities. No one would follow him into more than an intellectual squabble or a parliamentary debate. When he wore a sword, it was because a gentleman had to, a part of his costume like powdered hair. Nicolas kept his sword blunt. He could never dash or shine. Nicolas was listened to when he spoke, nonetheless. His opinion was sought. Lafayette was invaluable, an experienced military commander they could count on; yet after fifteen years of close association, Nicolas no longer completely trusted him.

A few of the Thirty were in the Estates General, including Abbé Sieyès, and Lafayette, who sat with the nobles. Lafayette was jealous of Comte de Mirabeau, who had been elected as a commoner and was making a name for himself. The Thirty were meeting three times a week, as the news from Versailles reached them. Never had Paris been so trained on another city. Even though Versailles was only twelve miles away and joined to Paris by the best road in the kingdom, all Paris experienced a famine of information. Messengers, travelers, journalists, pamphleteers, the curious rushed there and back with news and gossip and rumor. The coach schedule had been increased threefold. Private carriages clogged the roads. Men on horseback. People on foot. An occasional country clergyman on a mule.

Sophie and Nicolas had gone to Versailles the week before. The three Estates were meeting separately, but the Third Estate had invited the clergy and the nobility to meet with it to enact the future of France. The astronomer Bailly, once Nicolas' rival for admission to the Academy, was emerging as an important leader in the Third Estate. Louis was trying to be a good king, but he had no idea what was going on. The court nobility had too much influence. Those making fortunes out of the way things were had his ear. He would change with reluctance, but it was the work of Nicolas—and his cohorts, including Lafayette and the Abbé Sieyès, and even his old enemy Bailly—to make sure that the pressure for change was unrelenting.

"There's a definite split in the First Estate," Abbé Sieyès addressed the Committee. "The parish priests are getting fed up with the intransigence of the bishops. An increasing number of the poor clergy realize they have more in common with the Third Estate than with their superiors. I have reason to believe some may come over to sit with the Third Estate."

The situation was clear. The clergy had two hundred ninety-one deputies, the nobles, two hundred seventy; five hundred seventy-eight represented ninety-five per cent of the country. If the Estates voted separately, then nobles and clergy could block reforms. The King was immovable. As it has been, so should it ever be. That was how it was in the fifteenth century, and that was damned well how it was going to be today.

"Sophie and I had some hopeful conversations last week. There's a split between court and country nobility. There's a gap between a great lord at court, and a gentleman with fifty acres, a drafty leaking house and hardly enough income to keep his children in clothes, let alone buy them into the military or the Church. We must play on these differences."

That enlightened nobility could work with the bourgeois was revealed by this Committee. They divided up tasks each time they met and then reported back. Nicolas was to write a pamphlet explaining representative government.

Abbé Sieyès was to bring clergy over to the Third Estate. The bankers were to line up the financial community.

"There are moments in history we must seize or lose our way." Lafayette said sententiously. "We can see the constitutional monarchy we want on the horizon. Louis is obstructing with all his powers, but he underestimates us."

Nicolas wondered how many of the delegates in Versailles had any notion what was happening all over France. The Committee of Thirty could put it together; their intelligence gathering was more accurate than that of the King, which habitually told him what he wished to hear. People were blocking grain shipments, refusing to pay taxes or pay their lords. Troops balked at firing on crowds. The situation was approaching anarchy. The Estates General must pull together and act, for the good of all.

TWENTY-TWO

Manon

(1788–1789)

MANON'S winters were spent in Lyon, where she held receptions and attended those of other well-placed wives. This was the most trying aspect of her life, carried out expertly for the sake of Jean and his career. Manon prided herself that she could draw interesting men toward her and bring out Jean's best characteristics in small social gatherings. There were enlightened souls in Lyon with whom they could chat about ideas that mattered. Anyone with pretensions to philosophical or progressive interests passing through Lyon must visit the Rolands or journey out to the house at Clos de la Platière.

That gawky young doctor from Paris, Lanthénas, who had a crush on her, came often and filled them in on political doings. A young journalist of advanced opinions and great talent named Brissot began corresponding with them, having admired Jean's articles. Brissot had already written remarkable political pamphlets, for one of which he had been imprisoned in the Bastille.

As the years passed and Eudora grew, Manon still spent a lot of time educating her daughter. Manon had assumed that Eudora would be herself in miniature. "Eudora. Today we will discuss subtraction."

Eudora went on dressing her china-faced doll. "Do we have to?"

"You must master elementary mathematics, Eudora, to understand your own finances." When Manon came back with the text they were using, Eudora had vanished. She found her outside chasing the chickens. Manon called her in a loud stern voice. Well, at least Eudora was sturdy. She had one talent Manon had discovered. Like her mother, she liked to dance.

The peasants had dances when they married, when the various harvests came in, whenever anything could reasonably be celebrated. They asked her and out of politeness the first time, she went. She discovered that she liked to dance with the peasants, she liked the vigorous dances they did far better than the polite minuets and promenades Grandmère had taught her. Mme Roland did not think Manon's dancing with the peasants appropriate. Manon ignored her objections. She drank the good Beaujolais, she ate her own pies. If she did not walk every day, she would become fat. She did gain weight, but she looked better than ever. Her skin glowed. Friends liked to come and visit. As the years passed, they got to know other liberals, nearby or distant.

Manon's life here was more sensual than she had thought herself capable of. It was not her relationship with Jean that made the difference, for theirs was not a physical bond. They were truly married, for they shared their child, their ideas and their work. She had plenty of intellectual labor to perform on Jean's reports, his encyclopedia, his occasional papers for learned societies. He was elected to several, a mark of great distinction. She did not mind that he got the credit for her writing, because it was appropriate that he should be the public figurehead. It would be immodest for her to claim authorship. The Rousseau woman was nurturing, in accord with her inborn nature. She cared for her child, she served her husband and made him happy. Didn't she make Jean happy? He was pampered in every way. She took his notes and jottings, his old rambling dull letters, and turned them into good prose. When he had to make a speech, she wrote it. He was not the world's best speaker, but people respected his productivity and his dignity. He was a man of stern demeanor, simply dressed in black after the fashion of Ben Franklin, a Quakerly style he had adopted.

Roland did not stand for election to the Estates General the winter of 1789, saying he was too busy with his inspectorship. She would have liked to go to Versailles, but she knew he was hardly a charismatic figure. He lacked rapport with those beneath him socially. She did not know how to speak to the workers of Lyon, but her long loving relationship with her wet nurse had given her ease with the peasants. She helped them compose their Petition of Complaint. As she was walking with Jeannot to the church where they were meeting, Chevalier de la Chaise passed in his coach, making them scramble into the hedgerow. Jeannot spat. "Sir Paunch banging along. May his wheel fall off and break his greasy neck and splatter his guts for the vultures."

Manon had always imagined peasants to be awed by the nobility. When they began to curse them in front of her, she understood that she had been accepted, that they were showing her the underside of obsequious silence: brutal hatred. They had names for the local gentry, Old Rusty Rod, Lady Shit in her Shoe. That suppressed fury was invisible to those who were its target, because what could the peasants in their rickety stinking hovels do to those who passed in their carriages or rode through their fields trampling the grain that was life itself in order to chase a hare or a fox or a panting deer? Yet the anger was always present as the dirt under everyone's feet.

"No, I'm not idealizing them. Jean, they have political ideas, believe me. Marie the Stout reads pamphlets to half the village."

"Marie the Stout? Who are you talking about?" Although Jean had grown up here, he did not know any peasants. They were part of the landscape, like the vines on the steep green hills, but they were not real to him as the workers in the textile industry were.

"You've seen her hundreds of times. The wife of Barbière."

"Who's Barbière?" Jean looked mildly annoyed.

"She's uncommonly tall for a peasant, with a streak of shocking white in her dark hair. Her voice could curdle milk. The animal midwife. She has a talent with difficult deliveries of sheep and cows. Everybody knows her." Manon was fascinated. As the workers in the streets of Lyon all looked the same to her, dirty, unkempt, menacing although cowed, so all peasants seemed uniform to Jean. To her, each was individual, drawn in bright or drab colors, sharply etched. "Jean, they're not as simple as we imagined. A surprising number have some notion of progressive ideas. Those who can read consume cheap books that give them watered-down ideas of the Enlightenment, of Voltaire and Rousseau. Those who can't read are read to."

"But what can they understand? They can barely grunt."

"With each other, they're hardly taciturn or inarticulate. Helping them prepare their Petition taught me what they really think. They think the aristocrats should get off their backs. They want an end to the salt tax and unpaid labor for the lord and on the roads. They grow the food of France, and their bellies are empty, they say, these creatures we've viewed as stolid and wordless as rocks by the side of the road."

Brissot went off to America. On his return, he came to see them and she held a big reception for him in Lyon, so that those who shared liberal views could hear him speak about America and discuss the new ideas of government and law. She was thrilled by the response. Then the three of them retired to the country for more intense discussions. Brissot liked her but did not flirt. He was straightforward and intensely ambitious and daring. He had a long face in which everything seemed a little stretched out. He had a thin mouth, thin brows and a prominent straight long nose. He spoke well and firmly, as if he knew exactly how things were. Brissot planned to launch a newspaper in Paris.

Her mother-in-law's death removed a minor annoyance. Manon was delighted to assume the role of matriarch of the remaining Rolands. She was in the barnyards with the hens and rabbits, she was out in the vineyards supervising the harvest, she was among the peasants doctoring their sick. Up and down the steep hills past the golden stone houses and the ruddy earth she went striding or mounted on her donkey. Then she retired to her study and worked on Jean's manuscripts, read books and periodicals, wrote letters and articles, listened to Eudora's lessons.

After the Estates started meeting and then turned themselves into the National Assembly, Manon and Jean tried to follow events. Fortunately Brissot's new paper came to them regularly. Manon could not endure the sense of being utterly cut off from what mattered, the real events of the world. Her life of jam making and nursing peasants, all that had consumed her pleasantly began to feel frivolous. A woman was supposed to be fulfilled by this life. She was confused by her own reactions. She wanted desperately to be in Paris, where history was being forged. She wanted Jean to assume a position of importance and to work for the new order. Now when she carried out tasks that used to nourish her, she was fretting about events she had to read about instead of experiencing.

Censorship seemed to have vanished with the Bastille. After years of hunger for real information, for intelligent political opinion, Manon found herself drowning in a flood of pamphlets, newspapers, journals that she subscribed to and then could not speed through quickly enough. There were twenty presses churning out printed matter in Lyon. In Paris, there must be five hundred. Opinions she would only have dared whisper to Jean in bed were now published in bold type and read aloud in the clubs and reading rooms that were starting up everywhere—or spouted on street corners.

She never saw those sullen silk workers without papers under their arms. Those who could not read seemed to buy papers anyhow and demand others read to them. She was so accustomed to the lower classes looking down when they passed someone "respectable," that she could not at first understand what was disturbing in the demeanor of workmen. Then she realized they no longer lowered their gaze from her. As she passed lowly taverns that reeked of cheap wine and urine, she would hear a voice declaiming the words of some politician or journalist. She would never have believed that those tough closed faces had any interest in affairs in Paris or cared what the new National Assembly debated. But they cared passionately. They were hungry for knowledge. She would not forget that again. They needed enlightened pamphlets in language they could understand. She would pursue that topic when she saw Brissot face to face.

"We should go to Paris," she said to Jean.

"I hate Paris," he replied shortly.

"But my husband, your talents are needed. The government is reorganizing. Jean Roland de la Platière is needed."

"I have no time. I have to work doubly hard because one of my assistants fled to Austria, convinced he was going to be strung up on a lamppost."

Jean simply would not see that advancement lay in Paris, with the government changing and opportunities opening up for a liberal hard-working man knowledgeable about administration. How many of these eager young orators had Jean's experience with actually running anything? How many knew how things were manufactured or how to get the country moving economically?

Even in Lyon, things were changing. The city was still in the hands of aristocrats and wealthy silk merchants, but groups of enlightened men were beginning to meet. She started a Thursday night salon at their Lyon flat. Jean was pleased to hold forth, warmed by the attention. Afterward, she gave him her sizing up of each man, his opinions, his character, his usefulness to their cause. She listened to everything, sitting quietly in a corner doing her needlework or writing to Brissot. He had asked her to be Lyon correspondent for his journal *The French Patriot*. She agreed, so long as her name was not used. She did not want to embarrass her good husband by doing something public, as if she had no modesty. She wrote dispatches under the name Citizeness of Lyon. She picked up a great deal at her Thursdays, and besides, men liked to talk to her. If they sometimes seemed more interested in peering at her charms than in discussing ideas, she never gave them encouragement. Those who did not value intelligent discussion found someone more pliable to flirt with. It was pleasant to see her words in Brissot's fine newspaper. A few men guessed it was she writing the dispatches, but she smiled and changed the topic.

Finally it was too hot and unhealthy to stay in Lyon, and they left for Beaujolais. Brissot had planned to visit them in late July. One day she received a note that events were moving so quickly he could not get away. Manon carried the note to her room and flung herself on the curtained bed weeping with disappointment. It was not that she had personal feelings for Brissot, but he was so involved politically that sharing a room with him was like being in the presence of what people were beginning to call the Revolution. How she longed to peer over the walls of her marriage.

TWENTY-THREE
Pauline

(July 1789)

PAULINE could smell anxiety and excitement like a tang of acid in the air. Summer was upon them. Paris was cooking. After the long and terrible winter, everybody wanted to be in the streets, by the river, in the country. The people, who followed every word, every gesture of the delegates in the Estates General—that is, the Third Estate, their folks—were nervous. "They have balls," Babette's father said. "They stood up to those aristocrats and they said, you're nobody next to us. Join us or get out of our way. But the King won't budge."

The women demonstrated in support of the Estates General. Some days, a procession to the Church of Sainte Geneviève—their own saint. Some days, a meeting in the Place de Grève in front of City Hall. Sometimes a lot of women came out; sometimes, both women and men; sometimes just a few. They kept at it so the King would not think the people of Paris were asleep. Every dawn, posters went up and newspapers published. The government could not suppress the papers fast enough. The delegates sent back daily dispatches read aloud in every section. The electors of Paris were still meeting, discussing what the National Assembly—as it called itself now—should do. If interesting speeches had been printed by the Assembly, as was the custom, those were read aloud too. They had new heroes. People from the neighborhood went as if on holiday to Versailles to watch the proceedings and report back. Even though the King had tried to kick the people out and forbid them to watch their delegates, the people continued shoving into the gallery.

Pauline and Babette traveled there on a Saturday, getting a ride with Armand the carter, along with the family of Simon the pig butcher. At five-thirty, they started. They all sat in the cart drinking wine and eating leftovers from the tavern. They sang, they told jokes, they commented on the people they passed on the road, who made comments back at them.

In the gallery, they listened to the speeches and let the men know what they thought. If they liked a speech, they shouted approval and pounded their heels on the floor so the room shook. A couple of women had flowers they threw down. If they didn't like a speech, people made a louder uproar. Some people brought rotten fruit or vegetables. Up with them were the journalists, madly scribbling. Pauline never wanted to go home. Mirabeau was an ugly man with a face like a wild boar, but he was on their side, even though he was a count. A little man in a threadbare coat spoke up for the poor as if he really knew what he was talking about. The women with the flowers threw them down for him. "That's Robert Speer," one said. "Something like that. He's our man."

They slept in a stable. A bribe of some wine and bacon to the manager, and it was theirs for the night. In the morning, the church was too full to go to mass, so they headed back to Paris, stopping along the way to eat in a guinguette, a wine garden where everything was cheap and the roses were in mad lush bloom. Breathing their perfume made her giddy.

"It's stupid to have the Assembly meet in Versailles," Pauline said, her head propped on her hand as she half drowsed in the heat. "They should meet in Paris where we can keep an eye on them. We're the real capital."

"Did you see all those soldiers? They say the King is calling in new troops." Babette frowned, chewing on a thumbnail.

On the way into the city, they saw more soldiers setting up camp. "Those are the Swiss. They don't give a shit about us," Armand said. "They fight for money, and they don't care who they kill."

The sight of all those musketeers sobered them. Paris was being encircled. The King had tried to dismiss the Assembly already. "The King has bad ministers and bad advice. The Queen's a Hapsburg." Simon the pig butcher said, "She don't give a damn about France. Always the kings married foreign brood mares. But Louis XIV, Louis XV, they had French mistresses."

"Like du Barry, who spent as much as Marie," Pauline said. "No thanks."

"What's the advantage to being ruled by a French whore instead of an Austrian bitch?" Armand asked, giving the reins a jerk the old horses ignored. Nothing would compel them above a sedate walk.

"We're going to be ruled by bayonets and muskets before the week is out," Pauline said. "Look. There's ones in different uniforms. Germans."

On Thursday the word went through the quarter that ten French Guards—the King's own—had been thrown into l'Abbaye Prison for refusing to carry out police duties against the people of Paris. By the end of the day, the men and the women in the taverns could talk of nothing else but the guards locked up for being on their side. "Can we allow this to happen to such patriotic men?" Pauline read aloud. "Patriotic" was the new word for being on the side of the Assembly, not the King and the aristocrats. One of the new papers was her favorite, *The Friend of the People*. It was written by a doctor named Marat and full of letters from ordinary men and women in trouble, facing injustice, really fucked by the government or the aristocrats. Marat said the King was preparing to dissolve the Assembly by force. He said the loyal French Guards should be freed at once, for the people had to show their gratitude to get other guards on their side too. It was up to the people to act.

Word went from one quarter to the next. In the Cordeliers neighborhood, the electors began to arm local guys for a militia. A local lawyer named Danton marched them through their paces. The whole neighborhood was seething, one big informal meeting. Friday morning the impromptu militia accompanied by sixty neighborhood women marched off to meet at the Place de Grève with other militia. Men who were suddenly militia and women who were used to demonstrating about bread milled around listening to whoever would urge them on to l'Abbaye Prison. Pauline did not go, as she had taken last Saturday off and had orders to fill. But she heard that four thousand demonstrators surrounded l'Abbaye and freed the French Guards.

The King continued bringing in more troops, many of them his German mercenaries who would not think twice about firing on Parisians. The National Assembly asked him to disperse the troops, but he insisted they were necessary to restore order. If the Assembly feared disturbances, it should go home or else meet in some nice remote place he would provide them.

News came to the neighborhood: the King had dismissed Necker, whom the people liked because he tried to control the price of bread. That had made him a hero by contrast to Louis' other ministers and favorites. His dismissal meant the King was going to scrap reforms. "He's going to fuck us," the men said loudly. Six months ago, a man whispering such a thing would be turned in by a police spy and rotting in some prison before anybody knew what had happened to him. His family would not see him again, unless at an execution.

Now people shouted their anger in the streets. They placarded it on walls. They marched screaming slogans of anger. They got up on stoops and tables and church steps and bellowed their anger. They printed and bought newspapers proclaiming their anger in large type. They sang songs of rage. They began looking for weapons. Any ironworks, any blacksmith was besieged with orders for daggers, for swords, above all for the humble weapon of the poor, the pike.

Necker was sent into exile in Switzerland. In his place the King had stuck an old court louse de Breteuil. The Queen's party was triumphant. The King was saying loudly, "There will be no change! As it is, so shall it be." That meant: You can starve in the streets.

The bread was foul. It was black and full of clay and made her throat raw till she gagged. People said it was poisoned, but the bakers claimed the grain was spoiled and that was all the government was giving them. They couldn't make bread out of bricks. Armand had heard that less and less food was coming into Paris through the barricades. The customs officials were stopping food at the barriers, people said, for the King planned to starve them into silence.

The weather got hotter and the water began to stink. Paris smelled like a shithouse. There was little to eat, and most of that foul. Nobody was working anyhow, except the undertakers. They were busy and sang while they worked. They carted the bodies off and more bodies took their places. The winter had weakened them, and now they were being starved in the summer.

Sunday Pauline, Babette and half the neighborhood went off to the Palais Royal, because everybody knew that was the place to hear the freshest news— and the ripest rumors. So many were crowded into the Palais that people climbed trees like monkeys. It was bawdy, noisy, with shouting matches and fistfights breaking out. One novelty of the Palais Royal was tables set out under the plane trees in the big courtyard. It was a favorite place to eat and drink in warm weather, but today, the tables were platforms for speakers. There were the usual bevies of whores around, but they were indistinguishable from other working girls, for instead of plying their trade, they were listening to the speakers and shouting comments with the rest.

Pauline was so wrought up, she could not even feel her hunger, although she had had nothing to eat but a crust of stale bread soaked in watered wine, foul bread with which she had scraped the remains of the chocolate in her pots. She was agitated beyond control. It felt as if they—the poor people of Paris—had been given something wonderful and splendid and their own, their Assembly to talk for them—and now that was going to be taken away. That made the pain and longing and hunger worse. She could not remember why she feared the police or the aristocrats or the soldiers of the King. They could only kill her.

A sudden thunderstorm forced everybody to crowd under shelter. It was over as quickly as it started. Paris felt just as sultry. Steam rose from the paving stones. She had expected the rain to disperse the crowd, but more people kept pushing their way in.

A gawky young man got up on a table. He started speaking passionately and people were cheering him. He was waving his arms and thrusting his head back. He was dressed bourgeois but shabby. He looked as if he got a decent feed as seldom as she did. She wriggled through the crowd, determined to hear him.

"I've just come from Versailles, and if we don't act, the Assembly will be dismissed or imprisoned. Louis has sent for his Germans, he has sent for his Austrians, he has sent for his Swiss, his killers for hire, and they're surrounding Paris in a noose of steel. They've tossed out Necker, they've crushed hope underfoot. We must rise up or be slaughtered. We must arm ourselves and fight for our freedom! Not tomorrow. Not next week. Now!"

"Who is he?" she asked a burly man dressed like a porter.

"Camille Desmoulins. He used to stammer, but now he's an orator."

She recognized his name. "He writes about the Assembly."

Desmoulins pulled two pistols out of his shabby waistcoat and waved them. "To arms! Take up arms! Let's go, people. What are you waiting for? A German boot on your neck? A bayonet through your guts? Take up arms and follow me!"

He leapt down from the table into the crowd, who caught him. As he did, he grabbed a big leaf off a plane tree and stuck it in his hat. "Green for hope! Green for love! Green for the future! Let's go!"

The crowd stormed out of the Palais Royal as if they had only been waiting for someone to tell them to go. As they went, they broke into the wax museum and took out busts of Necker and duc d'Orléans. They boiled down the street and closed the theaters. Crowds from the theaters joined them. People poured out of taverns, out of restaurants and cafes.

When she looked back, the street was crowded as far as the eye could see. People had improvised green banners, as Desmoulins had suggested, but just as many had black banners to symbolize mourning for Necker and the dismissed government of reform. People were grabbing at ironwork, anything that could be used as a club or an improvised pike. She wished she had something to carry. At the Place Vendôme, they met a company of dragoons who ordered them to halt. The people just laughed and kept going. The dragoons stood aside.

They poured into the Tuileries gardens, where people like her were only let in once a year. As folks were wandering through the gardens, curious about what they'd been kept from all these years, they saw horsemen in front of them coming hard in a cloud of dust. It was the Royal German Horse charging with bayonets fixed, led by the Prince de Lambesc. Pauline scrambled up a tree, joined by Babette and a kid. They saw people go down, women screaming as they were bayonetted and fell under the horses' hooves. The horsemen were taking their time, picking out individuals to kill, going after them among the clipped bushes and the statuary of gods and nymphs. One hefty lieutenant with a bristly blond moustache looked up into the tree and swung his sabre at Babette, slicing through her skirt and cutting her leg superficially as she scrambled higher. He laughed and rode on. Then demonstrators began to fight back. They piled up chairs for barricades. Scattered shots rang out and two of the horsemen and one of the horses went down. People began to throw stones. They were using stones from the pathways, they were tearing down walls. The stones pelted through the air till the horsemen began to retreat.

When they cleared the garden, there were bodies of six horsemen, two horses, one dead and one flailing that a man shot in mercy; there were also the bodies of nineteen men, fourteen women and five children, including a baby who fell when his mother was hit. He had been trampled by a horse.

By dusk, the people controlled the right bank of the Seine, but the soldiers still held much of the left bank. Several French Guards crossed over to the people. The militia from the sections began to show up. Groups broke into gunsmith shops and blacksmith shops to find weapons. Pauline hadn't the faintest idea what to do with a gun. Except for men who had been in the army, few of them did. When guns were found, they were passed hand to hand until someone got hold of a pistol who knew how to use it. Then it became his. People broke off branches to use as clubs or improvised pikes out of railings and metal ornaments. "We fought back, and the soldiers ran away," Pauline said to Babette. "Next time, I'm not going to hide in a tree." It felt wonderful to be moving through the city as if they owned it at last, their Paris, to be part of a huge crowd of one mind, one emotion. It was as if her own feelings were enlarged until they filled not just her chest but the streets, the earth, the sky.

Word was passed along the street that other groups were attacking the customs barriers, so that food could pass freely into Paris. The walls of the city were being torn down from within. The troops on the left bank began to withdraw toward the Champ de Mars, the large open field near the military school. French soldiers were deserting. Sometimes they abandoned their weapons; usually they brought them along.

As night came on, the crowd thinned. It was dangerous running around the streets in the dark. Pauline and Babette crossed the bridge wearily. "My feet hurt," Pauline admitted. "We must have run for miles."

"My feet hurt and that bastard cut my leg. But it was fun."

"It was exciting," Pauline said slowly. When she lay down in her bed alone, hearing the snores of the Louvet family from above her, she wondered if she would get up tomorrow and everything would be as it always had been. Would the world be changed? Or would all the iron walls be back in place? Would the people calm down like a drunk after a spree, or would they remember how it felt to fight back? She could not imagine how it would be, tomorrow.

TWENTY-FOUR
Georges

❦

(July 13–14, 1789)

GEORGES stared at Camille, who was stabbing the air with his fist. "I spoke and lit a fuse. They exploded. Who'd believe that anybody would pay attention like that? Words are power, Georges."

"The right words at the right time." Georges envied Camille that moment standing on the table waving two unloaded pistols and inciting the crowd. The power of rhetoric in a court of law was strictly fenced in by custom, regulation, the tolerance of the judge. Rhetoric in the streets was power unleashed. Could he command that power? Camille seemed an unlikely leader of men, sallow, skinny, a waist like a girl's, a twig that could be snapped in his hand.

It was Monday but no one had gone to work. All Paris seemed to be in the streets. He recognized gunfire in the distance. The tocsin was ringing. That ringing of the bell very fast in the parish church was a call to arms, the call to come out and be ready to fight: the popular signal for revolt. Georges sent for the newly organized militia. Getting his men in line took more than an hour. They were not used to being a company yet. Only six had muskets. His own military experience was confined to meeting with these men. He had gone hunting with his stepfather and his uncles: that was his whole expertise with weapons.

Two women came running down the street heavily laden with bottles and cheeses. "We've broken into Saint Lazare. It's true what the posters said about the monks. We found hundreds of casks of wine, huge wheels of cheese, all the food you can eat for a month. Cartloads of wheat, kegs of melted butter, more hams than you can count. What a feast!"

His company looked about to take off in search of loot. "Men, we can't go barging around like mad jackasses," Georges bellowed. "If we stop and loot, then the soldiers will come and take the city. We need weapons."

A runner came. "Patriots have occupied City Hall. The electors have set up a commune to run Paris. They're calling for all militia to report. They've got some guns and some powder—what they've been able to find. They want you to march there now."

When they got to the Place de Grève, the paving was crowded with bales of cloth, sacks of wheat, kegs of oil and wine, nails, a load of kindling wood, timber, cabbages, all piled neatly. Since the customs barricades had been torn down, produce and products were freely entering Paris. The carters were told to leave some voluntary tax in objects at City Hall, and they were happily complying. As time passed, citizens were taking what they needed. In City Hall, women were sewing cockades for the militia, since they had no uniforms. The cockades were little simplified flowers, sometimes just concentric circles. They had given up on green and were sewing the old colors of Paris, red and blue. Militia were already lined up for cockades. Georges saw that his men got their share of the muskets and powder in short supply.

From all over impromptu militiamen were arriving. More men were coming to sign up. Their names were being taken at long tables in the Place. Another messenger came to say that the King had the Assembly locked up in Versailles and would not let them send a delegation to Paris, even to cool things down. "That doesn't bode well," Georges said to another improvised leader of improvised militia. "The King thinks he can crush this. We have to arm ourselves."

That's what everybody was saying, milling around City Hall, where the new government, just as improvised as the militia, was meeting in continuous session. Georges put his men to work building barricades to protect City Hall. He realized he was enjoying himself. It was much more fun to be a leader of men than a lawyer in the King's court. It was exciting. It was absorbing. He liked being out in the open air, instead of in dark and stuffy courts. He liked telling men what to do and having them obey him, not sullenly but willingly. He liked the way women looked at him with open admiration. He liked the swagger he permitted himself. He adjusted his cockade and grinned.

When night fell, City Hall seemed somewhat better defended. Everywhere they marched on their way back to the neighborhood, people were putting up barricades. "March" was a relative term. Georges saw no reason to imitate the mechanical precision of real troops. The sound of gunfire came sporadically from all sides. Rumors of pitched battles ran through the crowds.

Nobody slept much that night. "What does it all mean?" Gabrielle asked him. "It feels like Carnival, everybody in the streets, the world turned upside down. What will happen to us?"

"I have no idea," Georges said truthfully. "But we have to defend ourselves. And I'll tell you, Gabrielle, the world is changing while we lie here. The world is changing faster than any of us imagined possible. There's power to be seized.

Money to be made. Freedom is coming—opportunities for gain and disaster beyond anything I dreamed at my most ambitious."

"I'm scared," she said, but she did not curl into a ball or weep. She reached for him in a rage of passion and they made love half the night.

By dawn people were out in the streets. The tocsin was ringing. The word came by runner from City Hall, from militia to militia, that they were all to go to the Invalides to get muskets. Without firepower, the King's German and Swiss soldiers would slaughter them. The home for crippled old soldiers was also an arsenal.

The wind was from the south and the clouds were heavy. They dropped into the stinking streets like exudations of sweat. They felt like fear and tension turned into sky. He saw all Paris moving toward the Invalides, thousands and thousands of men and women armed with everything from kitchen knives to clubs made from chairs or firewood to improvised pikes and an occasional sword or pistol. With them came the militia, who looked exactly like everybody else except that they wore red and blue cockades, attempted a soldierly march and one in ten had a musket.

A runner, a kitchen boy pressed into service, came from the Invalides. The general in charge of Paris ordered the governor of the Invalides, where thirty thousand muskets were stored, to have the crippled soldiers dismantle the muskets. The inmates sent out word of what was happening and that they would be sure to have a great deal of trouble taking the muskets apart with their aged hands. In fact, if the people hurried, they would manage to have almost no guns pulled apart before the crowd arrived. These were old guys who had never had two sous to rub together, and they weren't going out of their way for the rich and high-living governor or for the King who'd had their arms and legs and youth. When the crowd assembled at the Invalides, the governor had the gates opened to address them. The minute the gates swung wide, the crowd surged forward and swept into the courtyard, carrying the governor along like a paper in the wind. Gladly the old veterans handed over the muskets. In six hours they had taken apart only twenty. The columns lined up for guns and headed back snakelike over the river. The veterans told them that the gunpowder was stored in the Bastille. So they had guns but nothing to fire. Obviously they had to go where the powder had gone: to the Bastille, the fort that had never fallen.

Camille turned up on the march. "This is a suicide mission," he said.

"Well, you were so proud of starting this insurrection. Do you think there are prisoners inside the Bastille who might revolt?"

"Only a handful. They've been gradually putting it out of operation as a prison. Still, it's a place we might end up if they don't blow our heads off first.

You don't have a trial. Just a letter from the King and bang, the doors slam. Goodbye. Of course, if you're rich, you can have your cook, your valet, your bed and your mistress shipped in. The poor don't survive the first winter."

"Maybe we can share a cell and eat cockroaches together." Georges turned to his men, putting on a bluff hearty manner. "Let's roll! Time to knock down tyranny's walls and get that gunpowder. Thirty thousand pounds!"

By noon they were assembled around the Bastille's thick walls, towering like rock cliffs above them. Georges had passed it a hundred times since he had been in Paris, but never had it looked so vast, so impressive or menacing, its eight towers that bulged out halfway up so they couldn't be scaled, its massive walls, its height like a mountain. It was a motley army he saw, men, women, old people, children, whole families as well as thousands of the new militiamen, distinguished only by cockades. Georges saw the thirty formidable cannons of the fort trained on them, ready to blow them to bite-sized pieces. Cannon peering over the crenelations, mounted on the towers.

"Are they going to shoot into the crowd?" Georges wondered aside to Camille. "Will they do that?"

"Your guess." Camille said. "Voltaire would say, it depends what they ate for lunch and how well they digested it."

Georges had his men draw up and wait to see what would happen. A delegation went inside to parlay for the powder. An hour passed. They had disappeared. People were getting restless. They said their delegation must be in the dungeon now, hung in chains.

"The walls can't be breached. It's too damned thick. Think of it. Voltaire was imprisoned here twice. The Marquis de Sade. The Man in the Iron Mask. What a great spot to enter history." Camille grinned. "I did want to marry first. Perhaps reproduce a little Desmoulins—an heir to nothing."

"Enough of dying. We got into the Invalides without a shot being fired, no casualties—not even a bruised knee. Our luck may hold."

They were standing with thousands of others, more crowding in all the time before a massive rectangle with eight towers as high as any building in Paris. There were two courtyards inside the moats and drawbridges. It had been built to be impregnable, a fortress-prison into which people disappeared. It was doom in the form of a great box.

Finally the delegates came out. De Launay, the governor of the prison, would not surrender or let them have powder. He would defend the Bastille. The crowd had now been milling around for over two hours. A party scaled the roof of a perfumer's shop that leaned against the outer wall, scrambled up and over into the outer courtyard. In a moment the drawbridge to the outer court banged down, crushing a man standing too close. The crowd surged forward into the outer yard. Danton tried to keep his company together in an orderly advance, but the crowd swept forward like a giant undertow carrying all before it. They came to an abrupt halt at the inner walls.

The Swiss began firing through holes in the raised second drawbridge, methodically picking off the vanguard. They were shooting into the crowd trapped in the court, every shot finding a victim. Soon close to a hundred people lay dead in the courtyard. The crowd wanted to retreat, but people outside were still pushing in. Georges tried to give an order to his men, but they could not hear him over the screaming and the shots. Gunsmoke drifted in clouds. Bizarrely, the smell made him think of fireworks. The dead, the wounded were trampled. People tried to lift them but when they raised a wounded man, he was picked off at once. Georges pulled his men aside so that two wagons of hay could cross the drawbridge, having the men pass on the order one by one, speaking into each other's ears to be heard over the screaming. He could not see what was happening, but soon clouds of smoke rose from the burning hay, blinding the defenders. Now nobody could see well enough to hit anyone. Finally they could get the bodies out. Women were weeping and shrieking over the corpses. Georges had lost no men, but one of his men had his arm partly crushed against a wall in the surging panic of the crowd. Two of the neighborhood women saw to him, a tavern keeper and her pretty daughter. He said some encouraging words and then pushed his way back to his men. He said to Camille, now that they could hear each other again, "How the hell are we ever going to breach the walls?"

About three-thirty, sixty soldiers arrived dragging four cannons and a mortar. Accompanying them were a few hundred armed civilians. The leader was a French Guard Camille identified as the director of the Queen's laundry.

"A general of sheets," Georges said. "I hope he knows a cannon from a washboard." He noticed that more and more French Guards were joining the crowd in the bloody siege. A new delegation under improvised white flags—more sheets; this was proving a day of laundry—went timidly forward to parlay. The Swiss Guards were either nervous or under orders to fire, because they shot the three delegates, their sheets falling over their bodies, turning red. One sheet bucked for several minutes, but no one could reach the fallen.

The crowd was furious. "Let's take it. Let's tear the fucking Bastille down." The Queen's chief laundryman had the cannons and the mortar pulled into position for a serious assault. Then through one of the holes the Swiss had used for firing, a white handkerchief waved and a piece of paper fell to the ground. Under covering fire the Queen's laundryman ran to retrieve it. "They've surrendered. Under condition no one inside is hurt. They're surrendering!"

"That's beyond luck." Georges wiped his forehead. "Why surrender?"

"Nobody's fired on us but the Swiss. The rest of the staff are French, vet-erans like at the Invalides." As a journalist, Camille either knew or pretended he did, which made him useful to Georges. "They don't want to fight half of Paris. They probably agree with the crowd."

Slowly the assault parties filed across the second drawbridge. Between two of the inner towers was a clock chiming five, a clock with huge figures in chains dragging themselves across its face. The staff greeted the people enthu-siastically. A lot of them were crippled veterans, as Camille had said. Soon the people were on the roof, eating vegetables from de Launay's private garden, drinking his stock of fine wine and waving improvised flags. The staff, the guards and the invaders were drinking together.

But the families of the hundred people shot down in the courtyard were out for revenge. The Guards tried to take de Launay and the Swiss who had done the firing to City Hall, where they could be held. The relatives were furious. "They killed my husband!" "That was my only son you shot down, you butcher!" "You let us in and then you murdered my wife in cold blood. She didn't even have a stick in her hand."

The crowd swarmed over de Launay. He went down and a moment later Georges saw his head hoisted on a pike and carried off. Five Swiss Guards were slaughtered on the spot. The Guards managed to get the others away.

Georges walked through the Bastille with Camille. His men were frater-nizing with the old vets, asking for stories of the prison. "They always brought new prisoners in a curtained carriage and we had to stand at attention with backs turned, so we couldn't see who it was."

"The stones are saturated with three hundred years of pain, Georges," Camille said softly, running his hands over the walls. They came away smeared with lampblack. It smelled like death in here, death and mold and backed up sewers. Even in July, it was cold. The cells were gloomy caves of despair, where men were stored to sicken and die. The torture implements turned his stomach, although they looked rusty with disuse.

"I can't believe how easily we took it. If all the soldiers inside were like the Swiss, they could have killed thousands of us and held out till the King's troops came to their rescue," Georges said.

"The regime is made of straw and paper, Georges. Don't you see? They aren't governing France. It's falling apart of its own rotten weight."

Georges climbed to the ramparts with those of his men not too drunk to navigate the winding stairs. They looked down on Paris, spread out like a map. This must be what the world looked like from those hot air balloons. Far away smoke was rising. More customs barriers going up in flames? People were moving off to City Hall, but Georges decided to lead his troops home. They had taken the Bastille, and now it was time to eat.

"I never had dinner today. No wonder I'm starving."

"Can I come home with you?" Camille made a pitiful face. "I'm just a waif without a wife. A supperless soldier of liberty. Gabrielle sets the best table I know."

"All right, come along. But don't hang about all evening. This has been an exciting day. I want to fuck my wife."

"Georges, you're a gross pig. No wonder your men adore you. I'm ready to march behind you—on to supper."

When they crossed the second drawbridge they had to go single file, as several workmen were standing taking measurements, while officials from the new city government waited. "I say we can tear it down in a week. But it won't be cheap," the work boss said, pulling a pad from his leather apron.

"We want it leveled to the ground. As fast as possible." The official spat. "Not a stone standing."

"I can put together a crew by seven A.M. tomorrow. My men are good and careful and fast. No accidents, no trouble. Let's sit down at a cafe and I'll draw you up an estimate."

"You know, Camille," Georges said softly as he led his men straggling toward the river, "fortunes are being made under our noses. Everything is turning over, and a man has to watch for the main chance. We both need money. We should keep alert."

TWENTY-FIVE

Max

❦

(July–August 1789)

MAX was beginning to be respected. Comte de Mirabeau noticed him, calling him the stalwart Robespierre. Camille, who now put out his own paper, told Max that Mirabeau liked to collect rising young delegates and others he thought might be politically important. He had approached Camille, giving him a fine cravat, taking him out to lavish suppers. Max took care not to be collected. Mirabeau's reputation as an insatiable womanizer put him off, lives left in disarray. A woman who had left her husband for him had killed herself. Numerous sources insisted he had committed incest with his sister. He was tricky, close to the court at the same time that he claimed to represent the people. Max watched him carefully—from a distance. He was pretentious and overblown, extravagantly dressed and lavish in his gestures.

The Breton Club was growing more interesting. The efforts of the radical deputies were no longer directed at securing the continuance of the Estates General. It was now the National Assembly and did not recognize the right of the King to dismiss it. The King had been behaving himself since the uprising in Paris. It was a fait accompli that Paris ruled itself now. Lafayette set up a National Guard other cities were emulating.

After the July insurrection, the King had to recognize the crisis. Too many of his generals told him the troops would not fire on the people. He had insufficient foreign mercenaries. Therefore the King went to Paris to accept or pretend to accept the new Paris commune. He was accompanied by fifty deputies, chosen by the Assembly. Max was one. The cockade the Parisians wore added white, the King's color, so it became a tricolor of red, blue and white. Improvised banners were everywhere in the jammed streets near City Hall.

When the King put on the cockade of the Revolution, the people cheered. They threw caps and hats in the air, they shouted till they were hoarse. He saw many women and some men weeping, transported with joy. The illusion of the King as father had power over them, as opposed to the shortsighted pudgy narrowminded fool Max saw. The King had not changed his mind. He had been raised for absolute power. Max watched the charade. Louis was biding his time, dismissing his new repressive ministers, summoning Necker back.

In a ripple effect, other cities had risen. A deputation from Arras presented Max with a piece of the Bastille suitably mounted and ready to sit on a desk or hang on a wall. He thanked them politely. It could have been any piece of street pried up. He did not care for holy relics. He would give it to someone else, as a token of esteem. Perhaps Camille would enjoy it. Austerity pleased him both morally and aesthetically. He did not like physical clutter any more than emotional or intellectual. The virtue of the people was inherent in their direct simplicity. Their representative should be the same.

He could not help but view himself as something to work on, like a project in the Assembly, a piece of unfinished legislation. He practiced his voice projection at dawn. People in the gallery were beginning to trust him. They looked for him, they called his name. They all seemed to know he liked fruit, so women brought him peaches or a bunch of grapes in a handkerchief. He wanted to be worthy of their trust, for whom had they to depend upon? Who cared how hard their lives were? When deputies of the right upheld the King and the nobility, when other deputies waffled, the gallery threw rotten fruit. But to him the people brought the best they could find, pick or steal.

From all over the country, stories came of peasant revolts. What nobody had believed possible was now happening, not once, not in isolated pockets, but in hundreds of villages. The peasants were marching on their lords and burning manor houses. Sometimes they simply burned the papers that gave the lord claim to their land and their services. They burned the tax rolls. They burned the lord's deeds and legal records. They scared the nobles rather than killing them—but that did happen. That occasional violence was multiplied in the minds of the elite, because they did not understand the peasants.

If he had not gone back to Arras after school, he would be as ignorant as the rest. But he had come to know the peasants he defended. They were not, as the delegates muttered, violent by nature. On the contrary, they had put up with violence against them all their lives. The aristocrats and even the bourgeoisie saw them as savages, half animal in nature; but the intelligence of their revolt, aimed at the legal basis of their oppression and the records that condemned them to servitude, showed that they understood quite well.

The delegates did not talk about the peasants. Instead the knowledge of their revolt threw a giant shadow on the walls of the hall where they met. Even middle-of-the-road delegates came to feel they must act, authoritatively, decisively. They had an audience waiting to see what they would do, and the time had come to prove themselves on the people's side. Max could feel that mood building and did what he could to encourage it.

Still August fourth caught him by surprise. It started like any other day, at nine A.M. The Assembly was to discuss feudal privileges. The Breton Club had worked overtime preparing a strategy. A liberal nobleman was to rise and offer a plan to abolish hereditary privilege. He would be immediately seconded by a deputy from the provinces—not from Paris. They had written the first six speeches of the morning, although they could not control whom Bailly would call on. Everybody was urged to be prepared. The time was ripe, Max was convinced. The peasant uprisings had shaken the delegates. The insurrection in Paris had proved to the Assembly that far from being in the vanguard, they were running to keep up with the populace. If they did not speed up their deliberations, they would be left in a back closet of history. These were educated men, used to considering themselves an elite. They did not enjoy chasing after the crowd, which had proved ready to force changes the Assembly had not even discussed.

It was hot in Versailles in August. Max, whose nose was more sensitive than was convenient, wished he could defer breathing for a day. Not only did the room reek of lavender and musk and all the thousand varieties of toilet water bestowed upon each gentleman by his barber that morning when his hair was being done, the tons of powder on their heads, the smell of horses that wafted in from the stables, but they were all sweating and had been for days. The humidity was visible in the wilting stocks and cuffs, the crumpling linen, the fine film on every forehead, the pages that hung limp as overcooked greens. Even the King's hideously ostentatious fountains in the gardens, full of gold frogs and twining nymphs, looked inviting. Max had never before appreciated the beauty of simple water rising and drifting its mist across grass. They must all wish they were out of this room and under the sky. But once he took his place, he dismissed any thought of discomfort. It was not appropriate to think of one's own ease while the people waited.

Bailly began the proceedings with minutiae. A committee must give its endless report. Objections, amendments, discussions of amendments, corrections. For all the planning of the radical deputies, nothing could be accomplished in the day session. They were to meet again at eight P.M. As soon as that session opened, the duc de Noailles rose to propose that in the interests of restoring peace in the countryside, the Assembly should remove the special privileges enjoyed by the aristocratic, the wealthy and certain towns. Everyone should be taxed equally according to income. Then every citizen would have an interest in public order, and none would feel unduly and unfairly burdened. Servitude to the lord would be ended (where peasants had not already forcibly ended such demands, he did not add) and feudal privileges terminated, with appropriate compensation.

The seconding speech by another noble went off smoothly. The first four speeches the Breton Club had set up were called upon in order, setting a tone for the debate they had hoped would be successful in abolishing as much of feudalism as they could get away with. But something strange and wild happened. Delegates began jumping up and proposing wider and wider reductions of privilege. It was an avalanche, and the Club, which had prided itself on its preparation, saw events plummeting of their own weight and momentum. The nobility themselves seemed to have been moved to a bonfire of privilege, demanding to be stripped of rights, incomes, honors they alone enjoyed. Some deputies no doubt were being sarcastic or hoped that by going too far, they would undermine the process. But some aristocrats and most of the bourgeois deputies were saying what they'd secretly thought for a long time. Let's blow all this trash away.

Max finally got to give the speech he had prepared, already wishing it were twice as strong. What had got into the men? Max was sure that the King himself had caused much of this, with his damned feudal opening of the Estates, all cloth of gold and contempt. Versailles burned money as if it were a mighty furnace stoked with livres, and they were stuck in the midst of it. The deputies were sick of bankrupting the nation to support a court that did little but amuse itself at public expense. The Queen was known to lose several hundred thousand in a night playing cards—money supplied by the public.

The right of the lord to have his own court, to be his own judge and jury was abolished. Hunting rights were abrogated. No more would the lord have the right to ride through the peasant's wheat at any season in pursuit of a hare. No more would the lord's doves eat the peasant's grain while his family watched, seeing their living go down birds' gullets. Serfdom was ended with a voice vote. Applause greeted every new proposal. A wild enthusiasm swept along most deputies, while those of the right muttered and passed notes to end the session. They tried to move adjournment and were shouted down. No more would military or judicial offices be sold. The Crown could look elsewhere for cash. Tithes were abolished. Every Church office, every military rank, every governmental position was to be open to all qualified regardless of birth. Priests could no longer hold many benefices, only one. Accounts of pensions and salaries should be open to the Assembly, so it could decide who was being overpaid and find out where the government's money was going. Passed, passed, passed, passed, passed.

The deputies staggered out into false dawn exhausted and emotionally drained, nine-tenths of them unsure what had been done. They only knew that they had changed France forever. Max, who kept a running tab of the motions, knew exactly what they had done and not done. It was not as much as the nobles, muttering about the utter ruin of France, believed had been wrought. The respect for property that was an article of religious faith for almost all of them had kept the estates of the nobility intact. But in truth it was far more than he or anybody in the Breton Club had hoped for twenty-four hours earlier when they had planned their strategy.

He walked home under a heavy humid sky, satisfied with a night's work. Camille trotted beside him, chattering. Camille was talking as if they had made a revolution, which Max was well aware was barely begun. The people would be pleased but not satisfied. They were his masters, not the other deputies. The main task of the next days was to keep those who had been carried away by enthusiasm from backsliding. They had gone only a short way forward, but that journey had changed the landscape. The sun that was rising shrouded in ruddy clouds over the formal gardens was no longer the sun of Louis XIV, founder of absolute monarchy. No, it was the sun that Benjamin Franklin had pointed to on a carved chair at the Constitutional Convention in America, asking if it were rising or setting. It had been rising there, and now it was rising here.

TWENTY-SIX

Claire

❧

(September 1789)

CLAIRE was fitted for a costume that was mostly a pseudo-Grecian drapery, and not much of that. Suddenly everything had to be Greek. She was Marianne, the symbol of France, leading the attack on the Bastille, which the heroes would tear apart on stage, throwing the paper stones through the air while backstage the stagehand made appropriate crashing noises.

"Shouldn't I have a pistol? Or a musket? Or at least a pike?"

"It wouldn't be appropriate," Collot said disdainfully. "It isn't done for women to bear arms."

"It's better to lead a charge on a fortress in a couple of gauze curtains with my tits flapping?"

"You're a symbol."

A symbol of unpreparedness, she thought. Collot had thrown together *The Heroes of France Storm the Bastille*. It was a huge success, six evening performances and two matinees. Some people came back twice or even three times. Claire could not comprehend the appeal, as it had little plot, much assuming of grand postures and heroic speeches, a couple of big crowd scenes; it was more pageant than play. Their aristocratic audience had fallen away, but the bourgeois ate it up and even some of the common people who had a few coins to spare came and loudly approved. Collot knew exactly what his audience wanted: melodramas, sentimental plays, spectacles. Collot knew how to hit them where they could feel it.

She continued seeing Mendès. She actually liked him, she enjoyed being with him. The sex was good, and she still liked the conversation. It astounded her, that she could be faithful and interested in a man for five months already. She was not about to take up with anyone else, not because she feared his jealousy—although that would probably show itself unpleasantly—but because no one seemed comparable. The other men she met seemed pallid.

Every night she took enormous dancing leaps across the stage, carrying high a banner of red, blue and white that was supposed to stream over her head as if in a wind, only the fabric was too heavy to stream properly. Her arm tired waving it around, but fortunately, she had not lost her peasant strength. Costumes made for her often revealed her breasts, her shoulders, her legs, but covered her upper arms. Her upper arms were muscular, and women were not supposed to have muscles. Her arms were considered unfeminine, but they were damned useful when hauling a cow's-weight of cloth around the stage. None of the other women could lift it longer than a minute.

Collot was getting edgy. He had gone into the provinces because it was much harder to succeed in the theater in Paris. Theaters chartered by the King, like the Comédie-Française, had an advantage. Everything was expensive. Audiences were more critical. There was fierce competition, for aristocrats had private theaters in their mansions that were prestigious to attend.

At supper he fussed over events in Paris. Among them, the theater company bought twenty-five papers of all political complexions from lily white to flaming red. Collot was a self-pronounced radical. He was fuming that so much was happening while he was stuck in Bordeaux, but she thought that rather a lot was happening here too. A man from Paris would never quite believe in the importance, even the ultimate reality, of actions in the rest of the country. All over France, people were seizing arms, peasants were rising and overthrowing their lords, militia were forming and marching, people in the towns were forcibly removing old officials or just ignoring them and starting parallel governments that simply took over. Bordeaux was in the hands of a new patriotic government that had developed from the electors who had chosen deputies. After all, electors were the first representatives that people had ever voted for. Their authority came from being chosen by free election.

Bordeaux had a new militia that was training seriously. "I'm going to volunteer for the National Guard," Mendès told her. That was what they were calling the militia.

"They won't let you in. You know that."

"No, I don't—not anymore. They passed a Declaration of the Rights of Man. I was a man last time I looked. I'm going to try."

She was astonished when they accepted him into the Bordeaux Guard. She thought he was secretly just as surprised. He was not a legal citizen, but now he began to think that perhaps he soon might be. The Jews of Bordeaux were actively raising the issue. The supreme virtue of a Jew in Bordeaux had been to be inconspicuous. "Don't be noticed," was their constant motto. If a Jew was visible, only disaster could result.

But now they were lobbying the local patriotic government and the deputies to the National Assembly. They wanted to be citizens. They wanted to be treated like other Frenchmen. The community wasn't of one political opinion. Some supported the King; most were patriots. The talk about rights and equality stirred Mendès. He wanted to believe they could mean him too. But he was wary. So often things seemed to be offered and then were snatched back. He had been issued a tricolor cockade and a musket with a bayonet. The Guards were hoping to have real uniforms soon. She hefted his musket where it stood in the corner of his bedroom. Lately he had her come to his house, instead of always coming to her room. If Marianne carried a musket, her charge would make sense. Claire brooded about her future. If Collot broke up the company and went back to Paris, what would she do? She had few illusions about the life of an actress.

"You needn't worry about starving," Mendès said. "I can set you up."

Set her up as what? Being a part-time lover was one thing; being a kept mistress dependent on a man, even one she perhaps loved, was quite another. Men got tired of women. She would not be able to exercise her own will, but rather depend on him for a place to live, money in her pocket. "That would put a strain on what we have," she said honestly. "I'm sure I can get a position with another company. I've always been in demand."

A letter came from Yvette.

It is wonderful here at the convent. I wish I could become a nun, but I just work in the kitchen and I can't persuade the sisters I have a vocation. I bet I could be a perfectly good nun. What do I care about men, anyhow? We had enough of our brothers to last me a lifetime! Who needs that kind of trouble?

We have plenty to eat every day, and even Lent is just lovely. I hate to leave the convent to run errands for the sisters, it is so safe and comfortable here. I could spend my whole life here and never miss our old home. Nuns have the best life of anyone!

At least Yvette was doing well. Once a month, Claire sent her some money.

Men acted a certain way when they met an actress. She was a public woman. That made her highly desirable and yet just next door to a prostitute. It was assumed that her favors could be purchased. On the other hand, actors made a fuss about what they did. They spoke of it as art. She was not sure she had such a high opinion of her job. She had started out with the group that had performed in squares, at fairs, putting on simple plays on a few planks. Her current job paid much better, yet it was all of a piece. They were taking people's money and giving them sensations. They sold them pity, they sold them a sense of being compassionate and superior, they sold them excitement. Even Collot thought they were pursuing some higher calling. She alone in the company did not. In a way she thought what they did was worse than a sword swallower at a fair or a lady who read minds. In many plays, the audience was allowed to feel smug, to feel that bourgeois folks just like them had some prior claim on virtue, honor, compassion, now patriotism. She did not like the way weeping a few tears for virtue in danger made both men and women in the audience feel they were extraordinarily sensitive. They would go home and beat their servants and demand the beggars be cleared from the streets.

Six nights a week she ran across the stage whipping the tricolor banner through the air shouting for liberty and equality. Six nights a week she led the attack on the Bastille. Unarmed. She would have to be an idiot to charge without a single weapon, and it bothered her more, not less, as she repeatedly led her troops into mock battle. What would it be like to be a part of such a demonstration in real life? If her nightly gallop left her cold, would the reality stir her? She had seen pieces of the Bastille for sale just yesterday. There was a peddler in the square who had bits of stone mounted as bookends. Mendès practiced marching and shooting with the Guard. It turned out he had used a pistol, for the merchant ships went armed in fear of pirates. One early October day he took her out in the woods. He was supposed to be hunting for grouse, but he promised to teach her to use a pistol. If she had been weaker, she could not have held it steady before her. The retort made her ears ring. She had to learn not to flinch when she fired. She quickly got over flinching. She wanted to shoot the pistol so badly that she would have endured anything. Mendès was patient with her. He seemed more amused than alarmed that she wanted to learn. "This way you can protect yourself if you ever need to. These days, it doesn't hurt to have a little something extra you can count on."

Unlike Collot, he did not seem to think it broke some heavenly law for a woman to take up shooting. After they had gone practicing several Sunday afternoons, he presented her with a pistol of her own. It was lighter than his, inlaid with silver but just as real, just as deadly. Afterward, she made love to Mendès with a passion that had little to do with her own pleasure. She fucked him in gratitude until he slept, exhausted. She wanted to be the best lover he had ever had or might ever have. In her own room, she slept with the pistol under her bed. She felt she had grown six inches. She had been a tall woman since puberty, but now she was taller. Marianne might have only a banner, but Claire Lacombe had a pistol.

TWENTY-SEVEN
Pauline

❦

(October 1789)

PAULINE had to wait in line an hour and a half to get bread. Bread was expensive, thirteen sous, and scarce. It was said that the harvest had been good, but where was the grain? Aristocrats were fleeing, taking with them half the money in the country. There was even a shortage of coins. She saw their heavy laden carriages trundling out. Good riddance, but their flight had thrown servants out of work, hairdressers, workers in the luxury trades. Some of them went back to their villages, but others hung around, ready to make trouble.

The aristocrats would be back soon enough if the King had his way. He had refused to sign the Declaration of the Rights of Man the Assembly had passed. Nor had he signed the decrees abolishing feudalism. But the people had a real National Guard. Men had to buy their own uniforms, which meant that ordinary working guys couldn't afford to be in the Guard. They were still the people's soldiers. Often when the women held demonstrations of support or protest, the Guard marched with them. The women were marching a lot these days, to protest the scarcity of food, the price of bread, to keep the high and mighty aware that the people had not gone back to sleep, that they were armed and powerful. People said the King meant well but he was weak, under the influence of his Austrian Queen, his reactionary brothers, the court. A pamphlet was going from hand to hand, being read aloud. It was called *The Lamppost Speaks to the People*, written by the guy whose speech had started the taking of the Bastille, a skinny guy with long hair named Camille Desmoulins. He told the people to remember they could take direct action again.

Babette had thrown over her old boyfriend for a National Guardsman in his uniform. He looked handsome, certainly. Pauline wished she had a uniform to march around in. It set a person off as official. If he was standing someplace, he looked on guard. If he was marching along, people got out of the way. The Guards took their new status seriously. They kept their muskets and bayonets clean and their boots polished. They had a prouder stance than the troops used to, not that air of swaggering dogs in livery. She wished that Henri were back in Paris in the Guard instead of the King's army. Her worst nightmare was that he would be with troops ordered to attack the Guard and the people. Rumors were circulating, flying wildly from person to person, repeated in the papers, enlarged and repeated again, that the King was once again summoning his dependable troops to Versailles. The people were jittery as September rolled to a hot close.

The butchers went out on strike. So did the apothecaries' assistants, the tailors and the shoemakers. Strikes were still illegal, but nobody was about to throw strikers in prison. Things were too tense. The authorities were nervous. There had been little wind, little rain. The water tasted as if something had died in it. Only the wine and the beer were safe to drink. People were thirsty and they drank what they could.

Her business was slow. Nobody wanted chocolate in the heat. She let the boy who worked for her go, hoping to hire him back later on. She did not stand around idle. The women had the interests of their families, their neighborhoods to look out for. Food was their business. Food was their problem. When there was not enough food, not enough bread, then the women rioted. So it always had been, and so it was right now. The women must act.

There was always a time before an action when discussion raged in the streets and markets and taverns like the buzzing of the flies that were everywhere in the heat. The women had to reach a critical boil of anger and intent. Marat's paper, *The Friend of the People*, reported that the King had sent for troops not influenced by revolutionary ideas. The Flanders regiment arrived in Versailles the first day of October. On the fourth, the papers were full of a party some called an orgy, given the night before in the opera house at Versailles, a party thrown by the King's bodyguards for the Flanders regiment. At this party the black of Austria and the white of the Bourbons had been raised and the tricolor cockade of the Revolution, trampled underfoot. Toasts underscored by regimental trumpets had rung out to the King, the Queen, but not to the Revolution or to the people, who had been cursed. In Paris it was felt as a direct challenge.

Now angry women filled the streets. Louis must be made to sign the Declaration and the Acts, he must sign at once. He could not hide in Versailles behind a wall of troops. Tomorrow first thing, came the word, tomorrow before dawn. We'll go see Louis and that bitch and we'll tell him what we

want and he'd better listen. Arm yourself as best you can and be prepared
to walk.

During the night the rain began. Pauline had a pike she had made from the
spear point of a railing on a house a marquis had deserted for his country mansion. The fishwives of the central markets were already marching to their own
drummer, going to City Hall. There women would assemble before they set off
on the twelve-mile march to Versailles. The women of the Cordeliers district
milled around getting into formation. They had been in so many protest
marches already, they had a well-worked-out line of march. Pauline was
always in front with Babette on one side, Victoire on the other. The Guard
from their neighborhood got into line with them. A boy named Albert was
their drummer. There were market women, shop women, women who made
hats or books, who worked in furs and in leather, who sold flowers and peddled
old clothes, like Victoire. There were servants and bourgeois women in nice
dresses, several with real swords. Occasionally a woman was mounted on a
horse. The wives of coachmen could always lay hands on horses and so could
the carters.

In the Place de Grève, thousands of women were gathering. Babette's boyfriend hastened over. The Guards had a few cannons. The women pushed
their way into City Hall past the officials to the armory. Enough women had
been in and out of City Hall since the fall of the Bastille so they knew the
layout down to where the extra paper was stored. They passed out arms in an
orderly way. None of the men on duty made more than a perfunctory protest.
Pauline assumed they understood it was time for the women to act. The men
always looked nervous when the women took to the streets, as if they might go
too far. Well, they intended to go far today. Pauline was told to get her women
in marching order. As they marched out of the Place de Grève, led by Mail-
lard, a hero of the Bastille, new and old songs were going around. The market
women sang how they were going to explain to Louis what the women
needed.

> Oh, papa, little papa,
> you're silly and blue.
> You need a smart woman
> tell you what to do.
>
> Oh, papa, little papa,
> up there in Versailles
> no one to teach you
> how we live or die.

> Oh, papa, little papa
> don't shiver and moan
> we're coming to fetch you
> we're bringing you home.

The procession was cheerful in the rain, for it was cooler. All the women except the occasional wife of a lawyer were used to getting wet. The Guard marched with them. Lafayette galloped past to put himself in front. The Commune had finally agreed to back the march, since it was going to happen anyhow. Up ahead Pauline could see a woman on a horse, dressed in men's clothing, wearing a long red scarf and waving a sword. "Who's that? She's pretty."

"That's Théroigne de Méricourt," Babette said. "My boyfriend told me. She's a peasant girl who became a rich whore. But she never forgot where she came from, and she's on our side. She gave the Guard money for arms."

Pauline carried her pike in a determined way, trying to keep her women in order so that no one would laugh at them as they marched to Versailles. It took them seven hours and a bit. The rain slacked off and the sky lightened.

When they got there, passing through the outer gates and then up the long allées to the great gardens and the huge palace that was the biggest building she had ever seen, a musketeer told them the King was off hunting but the Assembly was in session. They were all pissed at the deputies. They had done a good job in August, but since then they just sat around gabbing. The women poured into the galleries and took over the floor. The men looked aghast, shocked, a few of them amused. "Look, honey," said a big fishwife with a fourteen-inch fileting knife at her waist. "We need the grain to move into Paris. We need the prices fixed for bread. Our bellies are empty, and our patience has run dry too."

Deputies tried to shoo them out. The women laughed. They hadn't walked twelve miles in the rain to be scared of some men in waistcoats. A little guy with green eyes, spectacles pushed up on his head, took the floor. He was neat as a fancy woman, powdered like a dandy. But he did not look at them as if they were scum. He said in a shrill ringing voice, "These are women of Paris. They are telling us what they need. They walked here to talk to us, and we should heed them. These are working women. They know what they want, and we must listen well and be ready to act." She remembered him from the last time she had been here. After that, the delegates let the women speak.

The women were lounging around, they were not acting respectfully and respectably, as if they all picked up how to behave to scare the men. They were not being ladylike or meek. They were being raunchy and loud. They were sitting in the deputies' chairs or on the tables, their legs swinging. They were letting the deputies know that if they didn't mind what the people wanted, this hall could be torn down. They too could hang from a lamppost. These guys thought they'd done their job by making up some fine phrases, but nothing had changed. Not where it counted, the belly.

As soon as they heard the King was back, around five, the women sent a delegation to the immense palace. The King received them, but they got only vague promises. He would make things better for them, oh, sure. The session ran on and on. Women went out for food. They discovered there was plenty of bread in Versailles, white bread such as they had rarely seen. The women pic- nicked in the hall. The Assembly did not adjourn until three A.M., by which time the King had finally signed the Declaration of the Rights of Man. So far, so good.

Some women slept in the hall, others in stables, in doorways, in coaches they commandeered. Some Guards took over a barracks, and some shared the hall with the women. Most Guards and quite a few women spent the night in the gardens keeping warm around huge fires they built. Pauline wandered off with Babette, Victoire, Aimée, a group from the neighborhood. After they strolled by torchlight through the woods, they came on something they couldn't quite believe. It was a pretend village. It was an imitation of a country village but clean and cute with thatched roofs and a spotless mill. It was like an adult-sized child's toy—the toy of a very rich child. Nearby were pens of baby farm animals, washed and beribboned. Everything was tidy and smaller than real—except the rooms, which were well furnished with uphol- stered chairs and gilded beds, perfumed and hung with silk draperies. Someone played here, someone who could command any fantasy and have it built to order.

Victoire was infuriated. "This is obscene! I grew up in a village in Beaujolais and I know what peasant homes are like. Who had roses tumbling over the door and six rooms, all with glass windows and nice straight doors? Who had neat clipped hedges and everything clean, flowers in pots all the way up the steps to the mill! Who made this toy? It's a mockery of all of us who grew up poor. This belongs to the Austrian bitch."

They slept in the tidy beds in the little houses, on real linen. Babette and her Guardsman were making love in the next room. Pauline pulled the goose feather bed over her ears. At dawn, they were up. The sky had cleared. The sun rose golden over the city of gold and gilt. They had only concluded half their business. It was time to empty out this place of display, this jeweled mirror in which the court studied itself. They would bring the King and the Assembly back to Paris, where they could make sure they did the people's business.

The palace was locked up tight but always there were servants, there were soldiers who sympathized with the people, who knew they were the people too. Someone had just accidentally left a gate unlocked, and in went the crowd, rushing into forbidden areas. No one like them had ever trodden the slabs of these courtyards, the parquet and marble floors, the Persian carpets. Waving their pikes, their axes, their muskets, their knives, their improvised banners, they roared on into the white and gold and crystal world with rooms wider than streets, the spun-sugar world, whooping and yelling. The King's bodyguard met them on the stairs and began to fire into the crowd. It all happened so suddenly Pauline stood still, paralyzed. One moment they were surging along yelling, the next they were dying around her. Women fell bleeding. Mère Roget was struck in the shoulder and carried out to the courtyard by Aimée and Babette. But momentum from behind shoved Pauline forward. The crowd flooded on to surround the bodyguards. When they stopped to reload, they were hacked to pieces. The carpet was already slippery with blood. More and more people were crowding into the palace. The crowd broke into the Queen's bedchamber, but she was gone. The word came she had run to the King.

Pauline looked around as the crowd pushed on. The bed, behind a golden balustrade, was huge and painted with scenes of gods and goddesses. Over the damask hangings, the ceiling was thickly encrusted with gilded cherubs. The carpeting on the floor was as thick as needles in a pine forest. The bed hangings of gold embroidery were set with jewels. They passed into another bedroom behind this one, not as huge but equally luxurious. Why did the Queen need two beds? On the vanity table were pots and bottles shaped like angels and doves and flowers. She picked up one and smelled the stopper. Lilies of the valley. She touched the stopper to her forehead, to her arms.

Near the bed was a clock in the form of a shepherdess. As the hour of eight struck, it began to play a melody, It is raining, shepherdess, it is raining. One of the women raised her pike and smashed it and smashed even the little pieces on the Oriental carpet. "They hanged my husband for stealing a piece of beef," she said softly. "May they all rot in hell. I'll use the Queen's guts to tie up bunches of flowers."

A woman dressed like a fishwife picked up a gold-backed brush and stuffed it in her apron. "None of that," a bourgeois woman in a velvet hat said. "We're here to make a point."

"My point is, I paid for all this in taxes, and I want a piece."

The women were pulling at things, throwing them down, stomping on them. More women came piling in to see what was there. One woman was standing on the bed pissing. Another was tearing at the draperies.

Lafayette pushed past with his grenadiers, Lafayette's own boys, loyal to him. He drew up his grenadiers in the anteroom to the King's bedchamber, their weapons cocked to guard the King and the surviving bodyguards. Since Pauline could not get any further, she went down to join the crowd in the courtyard yelling for the King and Queen to show themselves on the balcony. First the King came out. Then the Queen and the kids. She looked scared shitless. The crowd was calling for her head, but when she curtseyed to them and stood there alone, the howls of rage began to abate. Lafayette came out on the balcony, bowed and kissed her hand and tried to lead a cheer for her. The people began to calm down. Pauline wondered if they had won. People were murmuring in satisfaction. If the little King and the little Queen would behave themselves, the people would bow to them and cheer all they wanted. Lafayette stood on the balcony with the Queen. The crowd was yelling, "To Paris! To Paris!"

"My children," Louis said in his weak voice. It carried from the balcony because everybody shut up to hear what he would say. "You want me to go to Paris? All right, my children, I will go, but together with my wife and children. I will not be separated from my family."

The crowd cheered. It was a sunny day, and they were ready to go home. Just about noon, the King got into the carriage with his family and Lafayette. Pauline balanced on the rim of a fountain watching. The coach started off in the midst of a procession of women and National Guardsmen. Some Guards and two women had the heads of bodyguards on pikes. They had commandeered flour and bread. Many of the marchers had loaves of bread stuck on bayonets or pikes. They had wagons of flour, wagons of foodstuffs. The women were singing songs about how they were bringing the baker, the baker's wife and the baker's apprentice back to Paris, and nobody would be hungry any longer. Pauline's group had got flour and bread too, in a cart, and they fell into line.

It was a cheerful, relaxed and bawdy crowd that went home. They were proud of themselves. They were really bringing the King to Paris, which Louis XIV had deserted so many years before to build Versailles. Now Versailles would be abandoned and the King would be accountable to his people.

The Queen would not play shepherdess any longer in her toy village. Pauline was exhausted but satisfied, walking hand in hand with Aimée and Victoire more slowly than they had come, just behind Babette riding with her Guardsman on a roan horse they had commandeered, pulling a cart with Mère Roget lying in it. Pauline had done her duty. They were bringing bread and power to Paris. Once again the people had taken the world in their hands and changed it.

TWENTY-EIGHT

Nicolas

(October 1789)

SOPHIE held her salon as she had for three years, but the visitors changed. There were fewer aristocrats and many young revolutionaries, like Nicholas Bonneville who had found a way to bring grain into Paris. "Revolution" was the word they used now. "We haven't the words for half of what's happening," Nicolas said to Sophie. On this grey October morning, they sat at a small table with the French doors open on the Seine. They no longer took their breakfast in bed, for Sophie needed to eat sitting up. She was queasy in this, her third month of pregnancy.

"I always thought," Sophie said smiling at him, "that revolution meant a complete turn of the wheel, so that all would end up in the same position as before. We've made revolution mean the opposite."

"All sorts of new words are being coined, or old ones yoked to strange new meanings. The working people of Paris are calling themselves sans-culottes— without breeches. It's a word of powerful emotional resonance to them, but to me it sounds silly. The breech-less. As if politics wore clothes."

"You wear culottes to your knees and they wear trousers to the ground. I always thought gentlemen wore culottes to show off their fine calves in silk stockings. Wearing trousers means a man does manual work."

"Now whether someone wears the tricolor cockade is a matter worth coming to blows about. All these arbitrary symbols have a life of their own and run about the streets and council chambers wielding broad swords. Suddenly lampposts have sinister significance. A picture of a lamppost is a threat of hanging. That rabble-rouser Desmoulins is called the Lamppost Lawyer."

"How can we tell what a lamppost or these other objects mean to the common people? We know very little about how most of Paris lives, Nico. We don't know how they feed themselves, how they feel about each other, how they raise their young. Deer have been more studied than the poor of Paris."

"One of the important tasks facing us is to communicate with these people.

To educate them and to learn more about their problems, so that we can begin to solve them. I think some of the younger patriots know more about the common people than we do."

"Perhaps, Nico, but most of them are lawyers, not tradesmen and certainly not carpenters."

"Sophie, I want to start having the sort of dinners Lafayette used to for the Americans. I want these young men I've been meeting to come, with their wives. One advantage of living in the Mint is that we certainly have room to entertain. I want you to look these men over and tell me honestly which of them you trust. Your judgement is often shrewder than mine." He was too busy at work governing Paris to spend a lot of time brooding over anything. He was in the ad hoc government set up during the Bastille days.

His old rival Jean Bailly was the mayor. Bailly, who was doing no more astronomy these days than Nicolas was doing mathematics, would never forgive him for winning "his" seat on the Académie Française. Bailly was far more conservative than Nicolas. He wanted to be a strong mayor, to hold executive power and the initiative to introduce legislation. He distrusted the assembly of electors that called itself the Commune and functioned as a city council, of which Nicolas was a member. At the same time, districts of the city were clamoring to rule themselves. They wanted to vote on everything. They wanted to keep power in the neighborhoods. In between both extremes was a group Nicolas found himself allied with. Unlike Bailly and himself, they had scrabbled for a living before the Revolution, small lawyers, journalists. One of their leaders was Brissot, who had been shut in the Bastille for his journalism and had a great admiration for the American experiment. Another was Abbé Fauchet, a revolutionary priest and their most charismatic speaker.

Many of these men had known each other for years. They spoke of other friends politically close to them, the Rolands in Lyon, for instance. Nicolas was one of the newer members of the group, for he was drifting away from his old friends. He no longer went to Lafayette's Mondays. Lafayette and Bailly were in total agreement. They both considered the Revolution completed, perhaps having gone a bit too far. They wanted a constitutional monarchy, society pretty much as it was, with a compliant king.

Back in the Committee of Thirty, they had all seemed of one mind. They were the liberal elite who were going to pry the country out of its long wallow in the muddy sty of tradition. They were the heirs of the Enlightenment about to bring that light into the darkness of outmoded absolutism. But he remembered how Voltaire had admired Catherine of Russia, who had been Diderot's benefactor; how both had called Frederick of Prussia friend. They had believed in enlightened despots as a way to drag a country into rational order;

ɛ did not. The ultimate meaning of the Enlightenment was recognition of the inborn intelligence of each individual and his or her right to make decisions and express them freely—not just those born to money or privilege, not just those who had a law degree, not just those dressed like gentlemen.

His old colleagues were horrified by the women's march yesterday. He heard them trying to explain it away. "It was men in women's clothes," they said to each other. "It was paid for by the duc d'Orléans." "It was rabble from Faubourg Saint Antoine, the out-of-work laborers wearing skirts." The women were on the road back with the King and royal family, while already those who did not like this piece of history were revising it.

Mobs in the streets were as frightening to him as to Lafayette, who had put himself at the head of the line of march when he could not stop them. But Nicolas understood that people denied the vote, denied an education in making governmental choices, and, indeed, with no way to make their will felt, had little choice but to riot. Because they could not vote their will, they picked up pikes and hatchets and paving stones.

About seven, the women and the Guardsmen brought the royal coach to City Hall, where Nicolas was one of the dignitaries nominated five minutes before to greet them. He had never been presented at court, so could not officially meet the King, but the elaborate minuet of court etiquette seemed to have dropped by the wayside during the trek from Versailles. The King was clearly tired and wanted to get to his dilapidated and almost empty palace. But the dignitaries must greet him and make speeches. Nicolas declined to make one. He felt there were quite enough speeches.

He was asked to accompany the royal family to the abandoned palace of the Tuileries, joined on the river side to the old Louvre, but with gardens between. No one had been allowed to enter the King's presence who had not been summoned and who had not three hundred years of noble quartering. Now everybody was pushing along into the palace, women who had not yet gone home to their dark slums, lawyers, politicians, journalists, Guardsmen, a fishwife or two, including one old lady who insisted on telling Louis how she had seen him born, his red face coming out of his mother's cunt. She probably had.

The palace was thick with dust and cobwebs. It smelled musty. What furniture remained was hidden under old grey coverings. Women were wandering around lifting the dropcloths randomly. Guardsmen were setting up their duty rosters. Everyone was clamoring what had to be done next, while the royal governess attempted to settle the children. Nicolas stood at the top of the coil of staircase marveling at the bustle and chaos. The King, who had never been spoken to since he had ascended the throne in any terms but the most dulcet and flattering, who had been raised to believe himself semi-divine, had been this day packed up and trundled off against his will by a pack of working women whose clothes were muddy and whose manners were exceedingly direct. Since his coronation, Louis had scarcely left Versailles except to hunt. Now he was a citizen of Paris, a city he feared and disliked. The people had picked him up, dusted him off like a china figurine from a mantelpiece and set him down right in the middle of their lives. It remained to be seen, Nicolas thought, how Louis would cope with his new role. He was a good family man, much as Nicolas aimed to be. Perhaps he could adjust to being a good constitutional monarch, like William and Mary whom the British had installed after they chopped off Charles' head and then dumped James. He could be a homely down-to-earth king, if he chose.

The Queen, whom he had never viewed closer than a block away, now stood halfway up the staircase waving her arms and throwing a tantrum. Her train was filthy, her hair had lost its powder and its curl, the hem of her long white robe was trampled upon. She had a long horsy face but a fine complexion, visible since the rain had washed off the customary heavy golden powder and magenta rouge. She saw him looking and glared. He dropped his gaze.

It was time for him to slip out and hasten back to Sophie. He would see if she could tolerate something light for supper, perhaps fish. He had ordered a clear but nourishing soup for her earlier. He had never been around children much. They had decided to stop using contraception in May, the sheath he had always worn with her, and to let nature take its course. Still, he had been surprised when she announced her pregnancy one morning, after throwing up. He had been more taken aback than overjoyed. He supposed they should have a child. It was an experience he could not deny her, however much he might secretly prefer to retain all her attention. He had a great theoretical interest in education, but now he would have to conduct practical experiments. He was a little daunted at the prospect, for he had no models of the good father to draw on. He had never known his father. His uncles were nasty and tyrannical with minds of granite. He would have to improvise. Well, he might be father, but he would not be king in his house. They would be a little democracy of three. He hoped the King would abdicate absolute power as willingly.

TWENTY-NINE

Georges

❧

(November–December 1789)

GEORGES' fellow lawyers in the high court were frantic with worry. If the King lost his powers, what use was the King's court? Suddenly nobody was trying to prove patents of nobility. If offices were no longer bought and sold, how would they ever recoup what they had paid? Georges was in debt over his eyebrows but far less anxious. He found the new situation promising. He told Gabrielle, pregnant again after losing the first son, "Everything's looser. We'll land on our feet. There's always something an able and energetic man can do."

Mirabeau had noticed him already. They got on. Unlike most noblemen, Mirabeau did not expect to be groveled to. He had endured hard times. He had been decapitated in effigy, publicly condemned, pursued by vigilantes and angry fathers (including his own), shut up in prison. When Mirabeau had walked into the Estates General representing the Third Estate because the nobility would not have him, Georges heard that everyone moved away from him as if he had a communicable disease. Soon delegates were seeking him out, because he became important.

He was, like Georges, a physically ugly man who did not give a damn. They were both men who liked women and whom women found attractive. Georges thought that with himself, it was energy, virility coming through. Sometimes women seemed to scent him and turn, as if he were a tomcat leaving his mark.

Mirabeau wanted a constitutional monarchy, and he wanted to be the intermediary between the National Assembly and the royal power. Mirabeau told Georges honestly that the court did not trust him but could not do without him. He was a good orator. When he spoke to a point, people listened. His speeches were often quoted. He was an interestingly ambiguous figure, revolutionary and mistrusted courtier at once.

Georges sat in the galleries of the National Assembly a few times, after the Assembly followed the King to Paris and set up in the former royal riding school. Georges did not meet Mirabeau at the Assembly. He always saw him at the Palais Royal. That was why he made his way there tonight with Camille. Camille enjoyed the notoriety, the cheer that went up when he was recognized, the way respectable people drew away from him. The orator of the lamppost. Ten minutes after they entered the crowded courtyard, where the early November moon was just a sliver above the lanterns, Camille forgot Georges, and he was free to slip away. He left Camille wobbling on a table, shouting.

There were many restaurants among the theaters, whorehouses and shops on the level below ground. Mirabeau met Georges in one restaurant, the Black Rose, whose private rooms were often used by higher-priced courtesans. Georges thought Mirabeau's choice of locale for their meetings not inappropriate, since he was certainly being courted with an eye to being bought.

Mirabeau was clearly at home in the Palais Royal for he did not arrive, as did Georges, through the public entrance, but appeared in the room by some private passage through the bowels of the Palais. Mirabeau had a fat purse to influence and bribe. All things considered, Georges thought that Mirabeau was acting for the duc d'Orléans, master and founder of this weird emporium of sex, food, theater and politics. All forms of entertainment in Orléans' opinion? Orléans was ambitious. He felt he would make a much better king than his cousin. He had placed himself far to the left of the royal family, but he was unmistakably royal. Red in opinions, blue of blood: the liberals who wanted a constitutional monarchy must eye Orléans with interest. Georges had an open mind. He would go for that which offered the most freedom to the most people; otherwise, he would ride along and listen, reserving the right to make his own decision.

Mirabeau always wined and dined him lavishly. He was an ostentatious dresser, big jewels and bright silks and satins. His head was extraordinarily large. Like Georges, he had been marked by smallpox. His eyes were bulging, commanding. Georges found him stimulating company. He told stories well and he knew the gossip about everybody.

"The Queen is bored, so she gambles harder than ever and flirts with the noble Swede Axel Fersen and her old favorite, the Comtesse de Polignac. Polignac had been thrown over for a new intimate, but Princess Lamballe fled to Germany. Marie abandoned her old wardrobe in Versailles. Now she buys and buys dresses and jewels. She's defiant. Her Hapsburg blood is up."

"Doesn't she know how angry the people are?"

"Danton, she's seen nothing of France but the cathedral at Reims, the palaces of Versailles and now the Tuileries. That's her entire France."

They were still feeling each other out, but Mirabeau was a shade more aggressive. Georges suspected he wanted to land his fish tonight. Georges was in no hurry. He would betray no eagerness because he felt none. He enjoyed his meal, from the oysters on through the sole and the venison, accompanied by fine Bordeaux. Georges gave his opinions when asked, not shading them to please Mirabeau. Mirabeau collected able men. He would have to take Georges as he was.

"Congratulations. I hear you have a new child on the way. But children can be expensive. You want to give him a good start in the world."

"He's not born yet. It's a little early to start looking for a regiment or a match."

"Never too early to consider how to provide for your family. Your expenses have been high. Your debts must worry you, perhaps distract you from giving your full energy to the crisis our city, our country finds itself in."

"I land on my feet."

"Like a cat."

"I'm probably more of a bulldog. Or a bull."

"So I hear. You have a man's needs. We like to help men of talent who lack means. Consider it patronage to those who will serve the country."

"What you see is what you get. I won't turn into someone else."

"What we've seen is what we want." Mirabeau put a book on the table. *The Adventures of Casanova.* "You might find this quite stimulating. Don't read it now—that wouldn't be polite. Read it when you're alone."

Georges looked at the leather-bound gilded container, which he was sure held some quantity of livres. It would be interesting to see what Mirabeau judged him worth at this point. It was his first bribe. He would be losing his cherry. He considered it on the table, making no move to touch it. "I will not take instruction. I will listen to you with interest, but finally I will make up my own mind. I hope you understand my position."

Mirabeau nudged the book a little closer. "Oh, I believe I understand your position quite well. Enjoy the book. You might as well. If any of your friends ever discover our quiet meetings, you might as well have taken it."

"But if you publicized them, that would end my potential usefulness." Georges did not care for dueling with weapons, considering it foolish vanity. But he could enjoy a verbal duel.

"Excellent observation." Mirabeau helped himself to a pastry from the platter the discreet and silent waiter had left.

Georges felt he had played the scene for as much as he could get from it. Except the money, except the money, which he did desperately need. He would never allow that eagerness to show. He was doing Mirabeau a favor by agreeing to take his patronage, that was what his bearing was intended to convey. He hoped he was succeeding. He picked up the book.

Georges left first, as always. Mirabeau remained seated. He was there before Georges, so that Georges never saw the route by which Mirabeau entered the little red-velvet-hung room with its atmosphere of a well-appointed brothel. Georges stopped to listen to orators, greeted acquaintances in the crowd. Was Mirabeau reporting even now to Orléans? Or did Orléans just give him money and trust Mirabeau to know what best to do with it? Or was it not even Mirabeau's money but the court's? That was as likely.

"What did you think of my speech?"

"I'm sorry, Cam. I was getting laid. A dish I couldn't pass up."

Georges was putting much effort into the Cordeliers district, whose president he had become. His neighborhood was seething. Camille had finally got his prospective in-laws to permit him to court Lucile. Georges told him when they married, they could move into his building, owned by old friends of Gabrielle's family. It would work out famously. They would dine together, discuss everything. Georges had a direct line into Camille's newspaper, *The Revolutions of France and Brabant*, which was catching on. Camille was famous, but Georges was becoming known too, after being elected president of the Cordeliers.

It was a turbulent district assembly. He had already survived several attempts at unseating him. When he stood up before the district, instead of feeling cowed or intimidated by the rowdy crowd, he felt enlarged. He could raise his voice and fill the room till it reverberated. He could get people out of their seats cheering or shouting. He could give voice to what they wanted, what they hungered to hear said.

Yes, the King's law court might be gone, but municipal politics had its charms and plenty of openings. He aimed for power, for he believed that a man in power could always make money. He was gathering a group of men around him in the Cordeliers district, radicals able and eager. He could speak to the working people, who were beginning to call themselves "sans-culottes," he could speak to the shopkeepers and the printers. He could also command loyalty from men he had previously known, Fabre d'Églantine, Camille, Paré, another former lawyer Panis who was also in the district, to all of whom he had thrown work. Around him were many young men with careers to make, who had liberal ideas but also well-honed ambition and great needs. They were his kind. They admired him. They listened to him: men he could count on.

Marat, the foremost radical journalist, had recently taken refuge nearby to escape the police. Lafayette hated Marat and kept trying to lock him up. His presses were regularly destroyed. He had a good woman, Simonne Évrard, who took care of him as well as anybody could, but his life was that of a hunted animal. He would not trim his rhetoric. He denounced what he hated, and the people loved him for his anger. Georges admired Marat but would never emulate him. Martyrdom was not his metier. He had a family to support in what he intended to be considerable style. Gabrielle must not lose this child. They both desperately wanted children. Neither could be complete without them.

He liked his neighborhood, he liked his political allies, he liked leading the troops and making speeches, he liked feeling himself push on the world and make an imprint. He had only begun. And if on the way, some sucker who thought himself far cleverer than Georges wanted to shower money on him, he was not too coy to let it fall in his lap.

At home he waited until he was alone with Gabrielle before opening the book. She was the only person in the world he trusted to know exactly what was going on. Their love was powerful, as solid as the table between them, after two and a half years of marriage. She had her peasant shrewdness and her bourgeois respect for hard cash. Whatever he did was right in her eyes. "A thousand livres," she said. "My only worry is what he expects for this!"

"It doesn't matter what he expects. It only matters that I do what I want to, and he can't ask for it back. Money has its own color. It doesn't wear livery. And neither do I."

THIRTY
Claire

(Winter 1789–Spring 1790)

CLAIRE had been happier in Bordeaux than ever before in her life. It felt almost unnatural. Joy in her childhood had been rare and usually followed by catastrophe. Now she had been in Collot's safe and prosperous company for four years. Few actors left Collot. He had a cruel streak, a temper that could light up an auditorium, contempt for women that Claire was always aware of: but he took care of them. Thus it was like the sky breaking open and the darkness and hail pouring through when Collot called them together still in make-up and costume, just after a performance one Sunday in November.

"I have an announcement to make. I'm going to Paris. If one of you wants to take over the company and run it, be my guest."

"Are you going on the stage in Paris?" Juliette asked him.

He shrugged. "I've had offers, but I'll decide when I get there. Momentous things are happening, and I can't sit out here. I want to be part of the Revolution."

"There's a lot going on in Bordeaux," François said defensively. "This is a very revolutionary place."

"I need to be back where I belong. If you want the company, old man, it's yours." Collot put his tricorn hat on and strode off. At the edge of the stage he paused. "We'll split up the take evenly, like good revolutionaries. See you on the ruins of the Bastille, and I'll dance a jig with you all."

Claire didn't know what to do. François decided he would try to keep the company together, but Claire found him lacking in business sense. Bordeaux had been good to her. She was known, highly thought of as an actress. She wouldn't have anything if she left in Collot's wake. Then there was Mendès. She found that relationship a heavy anchor. She loved to be with him. He still interested her, after all these months. But Mendès had his own announcement to make.

"You can go to Paris with me. I'm off in ten days, as soon as I can wind things up here. The Jewish council has asked me to observe the National Assembly and present a petition to be recognized for full citizenship. We hear that the issue is going to be raised in the next month."

"All right, I'll go." She decided on the spot. She didn't see anything to hold her. She could look over the scene, and when Mendès was ready to return, she could make up her mind. She had never been to Paris. She got Collot to write her a letter before he left about what a good actress she was.

"Claire," he said. "Nobody is going to hire you because I say you can act. They'll take you for your looks. You think any Parisian snob cares what a provincial company director says about an actress? Just stick your tits out and smile. You'll do all right in Paris. You'll have a job before me."

Still, he wrote the letter. She was packed for six days before Mendès could tear loose. Once she had decided to go, she was already gone in her mind and endless reiterated farewells made everything stale.

They put up in inns on the road, much like the ones her company had stayed in all over France. But in Paris, Mendès took her to one inn and then set off for another. He said he would be staying in a place for Jewish travelers, where she would not want to accompany him. He was not about to bring her there. She was slightly offended. This was going to work out less well than she had imagined.

From her room that opened onto the street she could hear the roar of Paris, the clatter of hooves, the rolling of wheels on uneven stones, the cries of peddlars, pigeons, dogs, children screeching, horses neighing, the bray of a donkey, the clatter of a bucket being winched up. The stench was strong. The innkeeper said that when the wind blew from the great dumping ground of garbage and human waste outside the city, that smell was the result. Mendès had told her to stay in the inn and he would come as soon as he could. She ignored that, running downstairs as soon as she unpacked. She hoped he was not under the illusion she planned to sit like a poodle in a window and wait to be taken for a walk. She had a city to learn, a job to find.

By the following Friday, she got a role in a boulevard theater that put on pageants and pantomimes. She was Columbine in a low-cut red-and-blue dress. It was a comedown from Collot's plays, but she would eat. And she would not be dependent on Mendès. She spoke to the other women, wanting to make friends. They were suspicious, aloof, disdainful. "Girls from the provinces don't last around here," one said to her.

"We'll see who lasts. I'm not worried."

She did not see a lot of Mendès. He was staying twenty blocks away. He was busy with his politicking, and she was working. The National Assembly was debating extending rights to Jews. On two occasions, she sat with him in the gallery of the former riding school to observe. A scent of horses and their urine still seeped from the walls. Many clerical representatives were violently opposed. So were liberals influenced by Voltaire, who had written anti-Semitic diatribes. But some on the left were strongly in favor. A delegate named Robespierre argued for rights. "Let us remember," he said at the rostrum, "it can never be politic, it can never be wise, to condemn a multitude living among us to oppression and degradation. That diminishes all our rights." He spoke with a kind of cold intense precision she thought persuasive. The biggest stir was made by Camille Desmoulins, however, who was not even in the Assembly. He ridiculed the notion of denying rights to Jews by saying that a man would have to take his pants down to vote. It was amazing how politically useful it was to make people laugh. Desmoulins' joke was repeated all over town.

"We're only seeking rights for the Sephardim. The eastern Jews are another story," Mendès said. "They have representatives here too. They're a backward people, disgraceful. They speak a debased guttural German. They're poor and ignorant. We have nothing in common."

A woman at work befriended her. Hélène had been born in a village ten leagues outside Paris and worked in this theater for two years. She was tiny with bright red hair and brown eyes. Her figure was voluptuous on miniature lines. Hélène was quick, bawdy and sensible. Claire felt at ease with her. "I'll show you the ropes. You'll need all the help you can get around here. Stay on the good side of the boss or he'll fire you with one minute's notice."

"Does he insist on fucking us?"

"No, he does the boys, not us. You don't have to worry changing in front of him. He couldn't be bothered."

"Hélène, I need a place to live. Got any ideas?"

"You're in luck. A family just pulled a midnight flit in my building. . . ." Seeing Claire's blank stare, Hélène explained. "They couldn't pay the rent, so they took off. The room's on the fourth floor front. It's reasonable and the building is pretty good."

It was in a mixed neighborhood near City Hall, lots of working people and some professionals, mostly lawyers. The ground floor was an apothecary. The parlor floor, the best lodgings in the house, were occupied by a down-and-out lady with aristocratic pretensions and two daughters. Hélène was just under Claire. Across the hall another theatrical couple lived. Above her were two unmarried brothers who worked as carters. Their horses were stabled in the yard behind the house.

Hélène's room was intensely hers. She had a drapery on the window that matched her bed hangings. On a delicate chest of drawers only a little battered and painted with a scene of swans and maidens, Hélène had set up her make-up and scents. It had never occurred to Claire to decorate a room or do more than inhabit it. No one in her family did such things. On a little shelf was a bust of a scowling man. "That's Marat," Hélène said reverently. "He's my hero."

Claire let Hélène tell stories about him while she unpacked. "I figured you for a patriot." When Claire assured her she was, Hélène said doubtfully, "How come you don't know about Marat then? He's the people's friend."

"I've been out in the provinces."

"He was a doctor, but he lives in poverty, to be near us. The government is always after him. He can't be bought. He can't be scared off. He's our watchdog. He doesn't mince any words. He doesn't bow down to anybody. Come on, let's go to the Palais Royal and see what's doing."

The streets were swarming with beggars, but incredible equipages went galloping past, matched pairs or fours pulling gilded, carved, painted coaches. The aristocracy was far more visible here than in the provinces, their wealth flashing out. A funeral was the occasion for as conspicuous a display as a wedding or christening. Ladies alighting for the theater or going to a ball were dressed outrageously with hats as large as bushes and huge hair. The men dripped jewels. At the Palais Royal, they had Turkish coffee and Viennese pastries, while men ogled them and tried to pick them up.

Mariette, the woman who had predicted she would not last, was always talking about what kind of jewels women were wearing, what kind of furs, how much dresses cost. Mariette intended to have nice things. She was playing off two lawyers and a banker against each other. Claire was not impressed. She had never wanted anything from Mendès except that pistol she still had. Over the course of nine months, he had given her a necklace of garnets, a gold bracelet, a brooch in the form of a lion with eyes of tiny diamonds.

Once he gave her a bolt of silk to have made into a dress, for it had come to him at the docks and he had no use for it. She had a fancy dress made up, which she had worn exactly once, when the theater company was invited to a ball en masse by a young man more interested in shocking local society than in honoring them. Mendès insisted it would come in handy on social occasions when they could appear together. Actually that happened several times a week now, while he was wining and dining deputies. Her role was to be beautiful and keep quiet, he said. She imagined she was on stage playing a mute. These deputies were men like any others, no wiser, no less venal. They looked sideways at her bosom, stuck out in the low-cut dress, and they lost the train of their argument. Mendès did his best to charm them. She was a prop.

The only one who behaved differently was the small man Robespierre, who was courteous to her but otherwise indifferent. He ate little, drank little and observed Mendès with sharp intelligent attention. He asked many questions about the Jews of Bordeaux and about the different cultures of the three different groups of Jews inside France. He also asked about the political factions in Bordeaux. There were two types of questioners: those who actually listened to answers and those who did not bother. She suspected that Robespierre would file every answer in his organized brain.

He spoke frankly about the Assembly. "In Paris, the people won't let the delegates forget that the Revolution is still going on. Many of the delegates would like to believe it's all over but for commemorative tablets. They already see their grand moments sculpted in bronze. David, a radical painter whom I find congenial, is doing a portrait of the Tennis Court Oath—already."

"Do you think we'll get our rights?"

"I will do my best. I try to be a representative not just of Arras but of all those who desperately need representation. But the Assembly is preoccupied with finances. The government is hugely in debt, and the only place we can see to raise money is by annexing Church properties. Then we can sell them off, put some into the hands of the landless, get them onto the tax rolls. It's a huge battle and everyone's preoccupied with that question."

She found him icy but impressive. He had little physical presence, unlike Mendès, who exuded strength, but he had another kind of presence that made him formidable. As he studied Mendès, she studied him. There were all sorts of new types making themselves felt in Paris these days. Collot was right: things were happening here. If a man could make things happen, perhaps a woman could too. When Mendès went back to Bordeaux, she would not go with him.

THIRTY-ONE

Nicolas

(*Spring 1790*)

S OPHIE was visibly pregnant. Dr. Cabanis came by to check on her every
week. Cabanis was the adopted son of Mme Helvétius, whose salon they
both attended Tuesdays even though she lived a bit out of Paris in Auteuil.
Cabanis, a patriot and a friend, was courting Sophie's younger sister. Sophie
and Nicolas had been looking at houses near Mme Helvétius, to have a place
to get out of Paris in warm weather, especially after the baby was born.

Sophie was carrying off her pregnancy with style and élan. It was perhaps
easier for a big woman to lumber about at the fulsome end of gravidity;
nonetheless he admired her stamina. She would not take to her bed or even to
her chaise longue. The translation of Adam Smith proceeded, as did her
labors at the Lycée.

He had nightmares about the birth, which he kept from her. He felt guilty
to have taken her lithe firm body and made it swell. He could not bear to lose
her, and he wondered why they had not simply gone on together perfectly
contented, without a child in the way. Had he been proving his manhood?
Had he been concerned with bringing into the next turbulent century the
dubious blood of his undistinguished ancestors? Did he crave the impossible
duplication people sought in children? He felt that her pregnancy was a lapse
on his part. Oh, he knew she wanted a child; but he also knew that she was
deeply committed to pleasing him, and he could have talked her out of it.
Now he had put her in danger, and for what?

It was late to indulge these doubts, so he kept them to himself, with the
murky sense that this was the first thing he had kept from her since they married. She seemed content, stoical about the discomforts of late pregnancy, a
vast monument to fecundity. He noticed with disgust how men and women
who would never dare touch her with familiarity in normal times, now felt
they could pat her belly, an amazingly intimate gesture that brought to his
mind violent images of drawing the sword he had never used. Men and

women spoke to Sophie differently, as if pregnancy had emptied her mind and rendered her simple and pliant, instead of the stubborn, brilliant intellectual she was. He was embarrassed, humiliated, indignant for her. Her giving over to maternity made others insolent. The more she was a woman, the less she was considered an adult.

As Nicolas was about to have lunch one spring day, he spread out the news-papers he had sent his valet Henri to purchase. He was sipping a glass of white Burgundy and waiting for Sophie to finish her correspondence and join him. Then he began to find bits of nastiness. "It is obvious that the beauteous Sophie, wife of the Marquis de Condorcet, formerly Sophie de Grouchy, is expecting a blessed event, but for who is this event truly blessed? Surely not the husband, with whom the very young lady, half the age of the philosopher, is said to enjoy a marriage blanc. Then who is the black knight who has taken the white queen?" The monarchist papers were the worst. He could feel the gossip seething through learned and fashionable society.

He rang the bell and told his secretary Cardot to dispose of the papers.

Sophie came in, looking flushed. "I'm always warm lately. Instead of a child, I may be carrying a brazier. Where are the papers?"

"I thought we might do without them today."

"Oh, the gossip. Nico, I'm ashamed of you. You mustn't care what the idiots say. You know me and I know you."

Her pregnancy made him a more avid defender of women than he had been; he spoke about women's rights, women's wrongs, the need for suffrage. A Dutch woman, Etta Palm d'Aelders, addressed the club. She was concerned with divorce, with abolishing primogeniture so all sons and daughters could inherit equally, protection against wife beating, the right to divorce. Sophie had befriended Etta, and soon they were close.

He had recently delivered a speech in favor of extending the vote to women. His speech had not been booed, as had another by a younger man, but the attitude seemed to be, good old Condorcet, that's his hobby horse. The general assumption was that to be in favor of women's rights was to be less of a man, and thus unable to father the child Sophie was carrying. It annoyed him. "It's simply unpleasant to be talked about."

"Come now, you have friends who'd shoot themselves on the Pont Neuf at noon if they thought that would get them sufficiently talked about!"

She was always feet to the earth. He smiled for the first time since he had sat down. "Nonetheless, when the baby is born, I would prefer that he or she look like you. It might set the tongues to rest if it resembled me, but it would be far better if the child were beautiful like his mother than big and shambling and homely, like his silly father."

They had never hung on each other in public, and they did not do so now. Those who did not understand their intimacy could live on in ignorance. Most of the men and women who gossiped around him could not imagine a relationship in which everything relevant could be discussed, in which no tricks were needed to pique or keep interest, jealousy was not a useful tool of intimacy, and trust was the environment. Yet he admitted to himself that he was offended. He did not view himself as a great lover, a ready cocksman, a Casanova. He had fallen in love only twice, loved passionately only Sophie. How could they imagine he did not have the wit or the energy to satisfy her? As if only people who abused each other could inspire love.

It made him recall that scandalous novel that had come out and been suppressed without daunting its success, *Les Liaisons Dangereuses*, written by an ex-army officer Laclos, secretary of the duc d'Orléans. Laclos had recently joined the Jacobin Club and begun a newspaper to correspond with the other Jacobin Clubs springing up in the provinces. In that novel, sex was a war. Seduction was victory. Fidelity was only an obstacle to overcome by stealth, by lies and false promises, by coercion, by force if necessary. He could not imagine deriving pleasure from such intercourse.

The funniest part of the reaction of other men to his support of women, was that none of them seemed to realize that if he were in search of ladies to seduce, he could hardly do anything that would have rendered him more popular. Women were always cornering him and telling him how wonderful he was. Even at his wife's salon, she had to rescue him. They gave him bouquets. They wrote him love letters, some amazingly explicit about their charms. Women liked men whom they perceived to be on their side: why not? It made sense, even if the manifestations were bizarre. Sophie did not like women pursuing him, especially during her pregnancy. In reality, she was far more jealous of him than he had ever had occasion to be of her.

Gossip was annoying, like a cloud of mosquitoes or the stench of the city as spring advanced. But gossip could also be dangerous. With the royal family in Paris, curiosity about the details of their life intensified. Since Louis XIV had invented the elaborate rigmarole, the dense gold-encrusted dance of courtly etiquette and ceremony where even getting dressed in the morning for the Queen or the King could involve fifty courtiers, the royal family had been set like gods above the people. Every item from shaving to eating soup was a prescribed ritual involving written and unwritten rules and hundreds of courtiers and servants. Now they had been brought down to earth with a thump, and the people in their ongoing affection wanted contact, knowledge, specifics. But it felt to Nicolas as if the more intimate details were printed about the King and Queen, the less they were admired, even respected. The court etiquette, described in newspapers, sounded farcical. Gossip about Axel Fersen, reputed to be the Queen's lover, was unending. He was frequently seen leaving her quarters late at night. But the worst blow to royal prestige came from finances.

The court and the royal family used up money at a terrifying rate. As the Assembly was struggling with the budget and arranging the sale of confiscated Church properties, it was inevitable that the King for the first time be called to account. Louis controlled vast sums never tallied or monitored. He received secret funds to spend as he chose. This struck the deputies as a ridiculous way to run a country or a business.

After great protest and procrastination, the royal accounts (called the red book) were finally published in the newspapers. It was one thing to imagine the jolly good King on high ruling. It was another to read how much money had gone down the drain on gambling, partying, clothing, royal entertainments. How many millions of livres were rained upon the King's brothers who had fled the country at the first successes of the Revolution and were now plotting abroad. How many millions had been showered upon the Queen's favorites, male and female. These figures printed in the newspapers inflamed some people and disgruntled others, but among no one did they render the royal family more beloved. Not even the former nobility viewed the red book with complacence, because most were country squires in Provence or Auvergne. No king had given them sinecures, offices or tithes. There it all was in rows of numbers. The day the papers published the King's accounting, Nicolas saw people studying the figures in cafes, in restaurants, in taverns as he walked about the city. The commonest sight in Paris that week was someone silently scanning those columns and frowning, or someone reading them aloud to a group, who began to mutter. "You know how many people it takes to roast the man a damned duck?" "And then she gave her girlfriend Princess Lamballe another twenty thousand livres?" "Marie must be the worst cardplayer in France to lose that much. The woman must be an idiot." "A thousand livres a day for flowers? What do they do, pave the roads with them?"

Even the Communal Assembly could talk of little else. Most of the members were businessmen or lawyers, who had always had to account for every penny. They were gossiping about the royal family, so perhaps they would forget Sophie and himself. When he walked into City Hall, he wondered as he was greeted from all sides who among these men thought him cuckolded. The town government seemed to run on gossip and factionalism. They were engaged in a war with three sides. On one side was his old academic rival, Mayor Bailly, representing Lafayette's faction who wanted a strong central authority, restricted citizenship, and order above all. On the other side were the districts, wanting to vote on everything, the most democracy possible. Sometimes his faction made common cause with them. His group of colleagues were sometimes called Brissotins for Brissot. They were closer to the districts than they were to Bailly. Personal animosity between Nicolas and Bailly stretched back fifteen years, but now there was internecine warfare between the Mayor and Nicolas' colleagues in the Communal Assembly.

Finally his group decided to legitimate themselves as a formal organization. They named themselves the Social Circle, a bland enough name and in reality what they had all along been, a group of friends with similar ideas and interests. They rented an office and started a paper. On the door they put a box with a metal lion's head called the Iron Mouth, and invited anybody who wanted to air their views to put a message inside. The most interesting would be published in the newspaper Nicholas Bonneville would edit.

The idea caught on, and many, many messages and letters and notes were shoved through the lion's mouth, littering the floor within. Some were written on weighty, imposing stationery with a well-trimmed quill. Others were crudely printed with many misspellings and not a few of the obscenities that filled popular speech, on the back of pages torn from pamphlets, in ink made of charcoal. Nicolas spent many afternoons in the office. He was comfortable around books and papers, newspapers and pamphlets, education and propaganda. It was his contribution to the Revolution. He could persuade and he could explain. Not the worst duties he could assume.

Sophie went into labor attended by Dr. Cabanis and her mother, who had arrived over Sophie's protests the week before. Nicolas refused to leave the Mint. He sat at his desk trying to work. Then he gave up and paced. He began to understand the appeal of knitting for women, of embroidery, or anything at all, perhaps whittling. Men were allowed to whittle.

He tried singing to himself, but he had never been musical. Sophie was the artistic one; she painted exquisitely. It was her relaxation. She had done a series of portraits of him. She liked to paint flowers and still lifes. She said that no lily or pumpkin had ever gotten restless as it posed. Sophie, Sophie! She did not cry out. She would bite through a pillow sooner than alarm him by screaming. This was taking hours. Shouldn't it be over by now?

He imagined all of them on a lawn like the one where he had fallen in love with Sophie. The child—sexless, vague—Sophie, slim again, and he stood in a garden in full bloom. It was healthier for children out of the fetid city. He had done a lot for the Revolution; perhaps it was time to retire and live comfortably and quietly. To, as Voltaire urged, cultivate his garden.

Finally Dr. Cabanis appeared. "You have a daughter, Marquis."

"Titles have been abolished," he said automatically. "How is Sophie?"

"She's resting. But this was an easy, short labor, and she's healthy and strong. It was quite simple."

Easy. She had been in labor for almost nine hours. Cabanis was his good friend, but at the moment, he could have torn his head off. "Thank you," Nicolas said coldly. "I'm glad you found it easy."

The child was perfectly formed with a single swirl of fine brown hair on the crown. Sophie sat up in bed looking pleased with herself and pale, the child in the crook of her arm and the new nanny hovering while her own maid combed her hair. Her mother was lying in the armchair with her eyes closed, as if she had been the one giving birth.

"Conceived with the Revolution," Nicolas said, gazing at his child. "May both of them thrive together. Is it too much to wish for her liberty, equality and brotherhood?"

"Not too much," Sophie said so softly he had to lean close to hear her. There was still a scent of blood. "Just enough."

THIRTY-TWO
Manon

❧

(1790)

MANON was frightened when Jean came home from one of those exhausting trips with a high fever, his skin loose and grey, his gaze bleary. The doctor, when he finally arrived, pronounced him in mortal danger from a fever she had never heard of. The doctor bled Jean, gave him an enema, prescribed some vile salts and sent a stiff bill. She set about to cure Jean with bed rest, nutritious soups, good herbs from her garden and the fields. She had nursed scores of peasants through their illnesses, and she had a better record of patient survival than the doctor. She rearranged the house to give Jean a room near the kitchen where he would be warm. At first he slipped in and out of sleep, near delirium. After the second week he began to have coherent interludes. He apologized profusely and tediously for being ill. He was weak and needed help for all his functions. She learned he had been ill for much of his journey but had insisted on continuing his rounds.

Her days settled into a new pattern. Every dawn, she drank strong coffee and walked. Sometimes it was the only time she escaped the house all day. She walked two miles down the road and two miles back, unless the rain was heavy. Sometimes she rode the donkey. The bushes were leafing out, the currants, the gooseberries. The vines were fuzzy, then green. The days grew warmer. Now she had to keep him cool. She moved him to an airier room.

By midsummer, he got up sometimes, but he was still weak. In the meantime, news came that his post had been abolished. How ironical for a liberal like Jean to have survived all the King's bureaucrats could throw at him, and then to be dismissed by the Revolution he had longed for, only a year after it had come to power. No matter. Once he was well, she would secure him another post. They had friends in Paris, and now Paris—not Versailles—was the center of power.

She doubted she had ever had romantic feelings for her husband. She was not entirely sure what romantic feelings were. She knew the sublime from viewing the grandeur of the Alps, the somber power of storms lashing the hills. She had wondered how any woman could talk herself into feeling such awe or excitement about a man. She loved her husband and honored him. She accepted her role in life, to serve him, to second him, to succor him. But it was disconcerting to feel toward her much older husband as if he were a balky and whining child. He really was far more difficult than Eudora. In the early weeks, she had kept Eudora away from him, but now the girl seemed a good companion for Jean in his bored and bedridden state.

When Eudora had taken her nipple, she had experienced a rich sensual pleasure and a powerful connection. She had felt much closer to Eudora as a babe in her arms than she did now, with the little lady daydreaming over her sums and making eyes at the vintner's boy. How could an eight-year-old flirt? Well, Eudora could. She reminded Manon of the silliest girls in the convent, the ones who called her a bookworm. Eudora loved clothes and sweets. Her worst deceptions concerned whether she had stolen an extra slice of tart from the counter or finished a box of bonbons. These were petty sins to be annoyed by, but their very pettiness embarrassed. She did not want her daughter to care passionately about furbelows and bonbons. How had she failed to awaken Eudora intellectually? She had spent years trying to shape Eudora's mind—but it was shapeless.

All summer, she nursed Jean faithfully. When Jean's brother the priest arrived, she was smitten with happiness as if he were a first-rate intellect to converse with. If she was summoned by one of the peasant families for some emergency—a swollen infected foot, a sudden fever in an infant—she could not fight her own pleasure at having a good excuse to escape. When she walked back into her house after one of these visits, she was struck by the smell. Peasant houses stank, of course. The pile of manure and garbage ends outside the door gave its odor to the whole house in warm weather. They had almost no change of clothes. Sometimes they dipped in the river in summer to get cool, the extent of their bathing for the year. But her own home smelled unpleasantly medicinal and musty. It smelled like what it was, a sickroom expanded till Jean's needs and routines and demands filled the entire house, sinking in the stucco and wood and stone. The stable had a pleasanter odor.

She rode on horseback to Lyon from time to time, on some excuse of family business. She went in for the great fete of May thirtieth, a patriotic festival on the banks of the Rhone and the biggest crowd she had ever seen. An official told her there were sixty thousand National Guards, all in uniform, auxiliaries of various sorts including women with pikes who made her wince with scorn, and what the official estimated was two hundred thousand ordinary people celebrating. She was half terrified, half exhilarated. The crowd was a vast ruminating animal, making a sound she had never heard, an endless soughing, murmuring, muttering. It produced its own heat. Here and there people were playing fiddles or flutes and dancing. She even danced with a group of strangers.

A huge artificial rock had been built near the river with a statue of Liberty on top wearing a Phrygian cap, the red cap taken from the galley slaves that some revolutionaries had been affecting lately. Between Liberty's feet was erected an altar to the nation. There were speeches and songs and parades and more dancing. When she got home the next day, she wrote an account for Brissot's paper. She described the joyful camaraderie of troops and populace, swearing fidelity and celebrating together.

He wrote back that her article was a tremendous success and he had to print up sixty thousand more copies of his paper with her long description of the fete. Desmoulins had picked it up and reprinted it. "If you signed your articles, Manon," he wrote, "you would be as famous as Desmoulins."

The happiest times were the few visits from the outside world. Henri Bancal came for a day. He had just bought a piece of Church property and was full of plans for all his friends, including the Rolands, to live there together. Manon loved the idea. She would not be lonely and bored then.

In August, Bancal returned for a month. She was grateful for his company. By that time, Jean was up occasionally, but he tired quickly. The more time he spent in bed, the weaker he was, and therefore it seemed to her, the more time he spent in bed. At times she despaired that he would ever go about like a normal adult again. Bancal was a welcome contrast. He shared her love of walking and climbing in the hills around them. She felt a true meeting of minds with him. He was a very political man, who had been a lawyer but given up his practice for the Revolution. He was closer to her in age than to Jean. He had grown up in Clermont-Ferrand and had the air of a country man more than a Parisian, perhaps because he was husky and muscular. He always seemed to be straining his silk waistcoats and fine linen. He seemed happiest in country boots, striding along at her side.

Then one evening, he clasped her hands in his and told her he was in love with her. "No," she said, "you're mistaken."

"I know what I feel, Manon, and I hope you feel something for me!" He began kissing her passionately, holding her in a tight grip. She controlled her panic and finally thrust him away with sufficient force that he left off.

"I mean, it's impossible. I'm a married woman, as you well know."

"What has that got to do with love?"

Very little in a way, to be sure. "It has to do with virtue, my friend. How I behave matters very much to me. We cannot permit ourselves impurities and venalities when we are trying to make a better world—can we?"

She was moved by his wooing, though not as he wished. She had tender feelings toward him, but none that could not be controlled. When he left, they continued to correspond about politics. He seemed willing to forget the aborted romance. She did not exactly forget. If she did not long for Bancal, his passion had touched some hidden place in her that said, There's something we have never known, Manon. Never known.

She kept these seditious thoughts to herself. To Jean she spoke encouragement. Sometimes she caught herself speaking to him in that sweet simple way one spoke to children, senile old men, village idiots and dogs. Yet he basked in her care. He liked to be fussed over, in spite of his telling her constantly not to bother. He wanted her to insist on doing for him. It was a tedious game they played. She experienced at times a sharp desire to back out. "Oh, let me make you some fresh soup." "Oh, don't bother. I'll have the old soup. What does it matter?" Then she imagined saying, "Fine, if it's the same to you."

But she couldn't. She knew her duty as a good wife. After all, he needn't have married her. She could still be stuck back on the Quai de l'Horloge with her dissolute father watching age wither her. No, she had a husband, even if he was taking an impossibly long time to get back on his feet; she had a healthy pretty daughter, even if her mind was second rate. She had a lovely house, even if it wasn't in Paris. She had a woman's life, and for that she owed him, including nursing him month after month.

He read voluminously. He read learned journals and liberal newspapers and technical reports. He worked on revisions to his encyclopedia of industry. He wrote an occasional article on textiles or politics. That is, he scrawled a draft and she wrote it, their modus operandi. She was pleased when he did anything that got him up at least as far as his writing desk. But his eyes tired. Much of the time he had her read to him. Sometimes she dozed off while she was reading some report on mining or harvesting machinery, and she would wake with her head fallen on her chest and his plaintive voice saying, "Manon? Manon? What then?" as if it were some Gothic melodrama.

Losing his position had sapped his energy. He needed to be in harness. Without work, he did not know what to do with himself. If she ever wanted to get him out of bed, she must provide him with an overweaning purpose, something that would fulfil the same desire to be useful as his abolished position as inspector of textile manufacture.

On her trips to Lyon, she approached men they knew and began feeling them out for Jean. She wrote letters that strongly hinted at what he needed to well-connected friends in Paris, Lanthénas, Brissot, men they had known for years and who were now in or near power and influence. There was a group of them, many of which she had entertained over the years or with whom she had carried on a lengthy correspondence. They were calling themselves the Social Circle. They had just lost the Paris elections. Now they were setting up a publishing house to propagandize for their views and educate the public.

One of them had to come through for her. Hadn't she spent an enormous amount of time listening to them, nodding, smiling, offering suggestions, now and then writing a little something they needed. Half of them at one time or another had claimed to be in love with her. Let them show their devotion now. Let them produce some kind of position that would rouse Jean from his far too comfortable invalid stupor.

But it was the patriots she had cultivated and entertained in Lyon who saved them. In the fall, two of the men who frequented her little salon approached to sound her out. Jean must run for municipal council. He was needed. He was well enough known in a field of men whom no one had ever heard of. In spite of or because of his radical reputation, they assured her he would win. Within two days, Jean was out of bed. The idea of running for office galvanized him. He would be someone of importance again.

THIRTY-THREE
Pauline

❧

(June–July 1790)

PAULINE was busy making chocolates. Bonbons shaped like the Bastille and National Guardsmen proved very popular. Half the neighborhood had gone off to the Champ de Mars to work. Before the Festival of the Federation to commemorate the anniversary of the fall of the Bastille, an enormous amount of hauling of earth and building had to go on. It was all done by volunteers, every day and by torchlight into the night. These were the long pale nights of June when she had fallen in love with Henri, who had disappeared as if down a hole. She kept expecting him to appear. Many soldiers had deserted.

She went to the Champ de Mars several times. Women were hauling and pushing wheelbarrows too. It was to be a great festival of unity, showing that everybody was together behind the Revolution and the new Constitution. Lafayette was organizing the program. An enormous triumphal arch with three entrances had been erected. A large earthen amphitheater was being constructed for spectators. In the center they were creating a raised area from which the speakers could address everyone, with an altar to the nation to be the focus of public thanksgiving. The King would sit there, right in the center of his people where all could see him.

It would be grand. Each time she went there, the scene was frenzied and more structures were being built. Nothing like this event had ever been. From all over the nation, National Guardsmen would come. To take so seriously being French was new. She had not grown up with that. The nation felt as if it were a huge hungry baby only one year old. Before that, you lived in a neighborhood, in a town or village, you lived in a province. You were a Limousin, a Breton, an Alsatian. Now you were first and foremost French. France had been born and must be fed and could, if they were not careful, receive a mortal wound and die.

On the great day, a year after she had fought at the Bastille, at dawn she rose and dressed in her best—including an almost new salmon-colored bodice from Victoire—and went off with Aimée, Babette and her mother, Otile, to walk to the Champ de Mars. Until the Assembly had decided to hold the Feast of the Federation there, it had just been a large dusty field in front of the École Militaire, where soldiers could drill and not trip over each other.

It was raining just as hard as it had been the day she marched to Versailles. By the time their hike was rewarded by the sight of the earthworks and the triumphal arches, they were bedraggled, soaked, and the streets were running streams smelling of human and horse waste. It took forever to get to the arches, for half of France seemed to be converging right there. She was scared as the crowd tightened around her. She was borne along.

Men in uniform were everyplace. When she finally passed under the arches, they were covered with people who had climbed on them for a better view. They headed for the left embankment, although it meant sitting in the mud. Pauline had brought a small rug, which she stretched out. All the seats were already occupied, so they sat in front of the first row. Spectators had umbrellas of every color opening like flowers in the rain.

At one end she could see the grandstand crowded with dignitaries. While they were waiting for the fete to begin, Pauline read off the words on the triumphal arch. "With the defense of the Constitution, no poor man need fear any longer that he will be robbed by his oppressor!"

"That's beautiful," Otile said. "I wish I could read. I never minded before, but now I miss too much. It makes me ashamed."

Aimée said, "Pauline, we should start a little class for women of the neighborhood who want to learn their letters. We could do it Sundays after church. Do you think women would like that?"

"I'd go," Otile said, blowing her nose on her kerchief. "Patriots should be able to read the papers, I know it."

First the cavalry charged in, to the accompaniment of salvos of guns. They galloped around and around the huge field, their horses all groomed and shiny. Then came the grenadiers, row upon row upon row. "There are enough soldiers to start a war here," Babette said. "I love their uniforms."

"You like any uniform," Otile said. "It's the same old equipment in a fancy package."

"Look, here comes the Assembly marching." Babette pointed. "Who are the old guys?"

"Veterans from the Invalides. They wouldn't take the muskets apart when we were attacking the Bastille. Give them a cheer." Pauline was proud of herself for knowing. "Here come the electors of Paris. Look, there's our Danton with the presidents from the districts."

The King and the Queen had been brought out to the raised area in the center where they could review the marchers. The flag bearers from the National Guard lined up with their companies to file past the royal family. More battalions marched by, including their own. The crowd was cheering itself hoarse. Everybody was screaming and waving whatever they had to wave.

"Here come the fédérés!" Babette yelled, carried away completely, jumping up and down. "Ain first. They came from all over, just to be here."

The procession went on for hours. The rain stopped and the sun came out dimly. The women went behind the earthworks to pee, then bought lemonade. When they slipped back, still the fédérés were passing. Then came more soldiers and sailors. It was halfway through the afternoon before the marching was over and the Archbishop of Autun, a patriot clergyman, cele-brated High Mass and blessed every banner and flag, thousands of them.

The King and Queen seemed to be blessing everybody too. It felt great, everybody pulling together for a change. It was like the best mass she had ever attended, better than a wedding or a grand funeral. Then all the guns went off, deafening her. She pressed her hands over her ears and waited for the ground to stop shaking. She could feel the cannons in her bones.

Lafayette in his tricolor sash got up where the King and Queen were and everybody shut up. Faintly they could hear him taking an oath in the name of the National Guard and all the soldiers and sailors to remain faithful to the nation, the law and the King. Then the fédérés swore the oath, as if they were all getting married. Pauline found herself moved so that tears swelled in her eyes. Oh, come on, she told herself, it's just old Lafayette. He has contempt for us. But she could not help it. She wanted to believe in the King swearing the oath and the Queen, holding up the Dauphin as the tricolored plumes on her enormous hat swayed in the breeze.

She wanted to believe as she cheered in her failing voice: she wanted des-perately to believe. The King had taken the oath to uphold the Constitution, the same oath taken by the fédérés, the National Guard, the soldiers and sailors. But she could see the King. He looked bored. Men were always swearing something or other: I'll love you forever; I'll always be true; if you let me put it in, I won't come. In their minds they had their fingers crossed. Who wouldn't want to stay King?

The fédérés meant it. They were shouting with a passion that found its equal in her own. About the other soldiers, she wasn't so sure. When push came to shove, would they fire on the people or join them? And those deputies from the Assembly, they had done great things but they were backpedaling.

At six the fete was over, although it took them an hour to get out through the enormous crush. "What do you want to do now?" Aimée asked them.

"I'm going home, I'm all used up. My feet, my butt, my throat are sore. But you girls should go to the Bastille Ball. If I was your age I'd go hop up and down where the Bastille stood." Otile winked.

Aimée shook her head. "My old man has had the kids all afternoon."

"We have to stop in my shop and dry off first," Pauline said. Two minutes ago she had been exhausted and a little downcast. Now she was full of excitement and energy again. "The Bastille Ball! I'm going. Babette? Please go with me."

"Of course! I wonder if those gorgeous grenadiers will be there."

To party on the place of the Bastille, what a lovely turn life had taken. Pauline was hungry but she did not care. She wanted to dance all night on the Bastille. What was the use having a Revolution if they could not have fun?

THIRTY-FOUR
Georges

❦

(Spring–Summer 1790)

LAFAYETTE had a grudge against Marat. Georges could imagine how Marat rubbed a patrician gentleman of ancient blood, family riches and great personal glory, and above it all, towering arrogance, not only the wrong way, but into a fury. Here was Marat, who had been a society doctor, a physician to a royal regiment, gone far to the left. Lafayette pursued him from refuge to refuge, driving him into the sewers where he lived like a rat and still put out his newspaper. Sometimes Marat hid in the cellars of old monasteries. Sometimes an admirer put him up for a few days or weeks. Sometimes he camped in the quarries of Montmartre.

Marat was said to have been a ladies man. Now he wore shabby workmen's clothes. He had a good woman, Simonne Évrard, who supported him in poverty, made sure he ate, tried to care for his ailments. He was wearing himself out, she said, in the service of the Revolution. Marat would never compromise because he wanted nothing at all but revolution. Lafayette and Bailly had the power in Paris, controlled the police and City Hall, but Lafayette was not enjoying power as much as he must have expected to.

Again and again Lafayette had the Châtelet issue warrants for Marat's arrest. The Châtelet was an ancient fort at the Pont au Change, but the name referred to the King's old star chamber which had the right to arrest political prisoners and lose them in the dungeons underneath. Now Lafayette controlled it. Lafayette was always sending out squads to break up or confiscate Marat's presses.

Georges found Marat foulmouthed. He had no inner checks or censors. He said what he felt, never diluting it out of politeness, fear, desire to please. Georges admired that, at the same time that he would not emulate him—or care to stand too close downwind. The poor workingmen and women of Paris, the sans-culottes, worshipped Marat. Georges, who also craved their admiration and support, understood Marat's appeal to the poor and the desperate. He would not sell them out. Marat was a verbal juggernaut who could not be reasoned with, bought off, led astray or seduced. Many of the new political men viewed him as a rabid dog, but Georges respected his power. If he could, he meant to stay on the good side of Marat, although he doubted that personal support would win him anything from Marat beyond a moment's nod for having done the right thing.

Marat had moved his newspaper, *The Friend of the People*, into the Cordeliers neighborhood, seeking protection. Georges took that appeal seriously. A Guardsman came to warn Marat and the district that Lafayette was on the move again. To arrest Marat, Lafayette arrived with two cannon and three thousand men in arms, all in their new National Guard uniforms.

Georges got enough people into the streets to slow them down. Then he stood in the street in front of Lafayette on horseback, reading the warrant line by line. He put his training as a lawyer to work and found a flaw in their warrant. While three thousand National Guardsmen stood around twiddling their thumbs and a messenger ran to get the warrant corrected at the Châtelet, one of Georges' men—he had a whole group by now fiercely loyal and ready to follow his orders—got Marat out of the neighborhood. Marat would be safe until Lafayette cooled down. Thus when Georges said, "Oh, be my guest, your papers are in order, you may arrest Marat," Marat was long gone.

In March Lafayette attacked again. This time his target was Georges. His friend Panis came to warn him that Lafayette was demanding his arrest in the National Assembly. He doubted if Lafayette was skillful enough at discerning differences in what he considered the lower orders to tell Marat's politics from his own. To Lafayette, they were both jackals. The Cordeliers district protested to the Assembly. Both Lafayette's warrant of arrest and the petition of protest languished in committee. Nobody came to arrest Georges. He was more amused than frightened. It was good publicity. In a society just beginning to have elections, nobody had any practice running for office. They were studying at being politicians, a new career line. Georges had already figured out one thing: if nobody has heard of you, they aren't going to vote for you.

In May Bailly and Lafayette persuaded the Assembly to abolish the districts, which had been so uppity, so independent, so able to summon the people into the streets. Instead Paris was to be "rationally" divided into forty-eight sections, with only citizens owning sufficient property able to vote. Cartoons in the right-wing press showed the dragon of Paris cut into little pieces by a Saint George who looked like Lafayette. Lafayette was now their hero.

Georges, Camille and the Roberts, husband and wife who ran a revolutionary paper, sat at the Danton family table. Gabrielle, eight months pregnant, waddled to and fro overseeing the service of supper and then gateau caramel and coffee. On a map of the city Camille plotted out how their district had been redrawn. They now ran down to the Seine. The limitations on the powers of the old district assemblies, as they were forcibly metamorphosed into the new section assemblies, meant they would be weak and ineffectual.

"We can't give up our power base," Georges said bluntly. "We are the Cordeliers. That's a name to reckon with in Paris. Now they call us the Théâtre-Français section, as if we were a bunch of actors in costumes."

"Most of the new blocks they've given us are sans-culottes," Madame Robert said. "They're good people, but they can't vote."

"We need some way to reach them," Camille said. "We need face-to-face organization. The Jacobins have a club. Lafayette and company just broke away and started the Society of '89. We'll be the Cordeliers Club."

Georges stood, yanked Camille upright and embraced him. "That's a brilliant idea."

"Why Georges, do you adore my idea, or is it just that Gabrielle is out of combat these days?"

Camille would try to disconcert him but always fail. Georges could not be embarrassed sexually. That was his turf. He slapped Camille on the backside and dropped him into his seat. "The Cordeliers Club. With cheap membership. Dues the sans-culottes can afford. Not only let them in, welcome them! Make them comfortable. We are their political home. Be sure to look them over carefully, pick some new guys to groom and give them offices to make them loyal. Lafayette and Bailly think they skewered us, but they just gave us a bigger power base. They'll live to regret this game."

Thus the district became the Club, and the Club was more militant and better organized than the district had been. Nobody referred to them as Théâtre-Français. They were still called by everyone in Paris the Cordeliers. Now there were more of them.

It was a sultry June night, a reddish moon hanging like a slice of country sausage over the steamy streets. Gabrielle's mother had arrived for her confinement, and he was ordered out of the flat. After things at the Club petered out, he sat in the Cafe Procope, nervously sipping eau de vie. "You're out late tonight," his old friend Fabre said, sitting down at his table. "I thought you were very much the married man these days."

"My wife is in labor. Why aren't you worrying about your play? Didn't it just open?"

"To applause and fury. I have written the first great revolutionary drama. If

I'd known you were at liberty this evening, I would have insisted on taking you." Fabre still dressed as a fop, an enormous cravat setting off his long homely face with its somewhat receding chin.

"I hope you have a huge success."

"There's another revolutionary playwright in the neighborhood. An actor-manager who used to have his own company touring the provinces. I'll have to introduce you, my dear Georges. Collot d'Herbois. A very political as well as dreadfully handsome young man—tall, dark. We should recruit him for the Cordeliers. He's a firebrand with a big carrying voice."

Twice Georges went home and twice he was turned away. Finally Mme Charpentier let him sleep on the sofa. At four-thirty he was awakened. He was permitted in briefly by Madame and the midwife to view his new red squalling son and sweat-soaked Gabrielle, who had fallen into a sleep of exhaustion with the baby in the crook of her arm.

They named the baby Antoine. Some of the militant revolutionaries were withdrawing from religious activities, but he had his son christened. It would have upset the grandparents to neglect that; it would have upset Gabrielle. It was polite to follow custom and it did not matter to him. Why mark the boy with the prejudice of a moment? Governments changed.

"Are you happy now?" Gabrielle asked as they walked back from church. "O paterfamilias."

"You've made me happy." And he was: a son at last, a good woman.

The Cordeliers were growing weekly, meeting in the old monastery that had given its name to the neighborhood. It wasn't a fancy building, just an oval inside with wooden benches, a raised platform for the president and another for the speaker of the moment. The Declaration of the Rights of Man was pinned to the wall with crossed daggers. The only other decoration was a row of plaster busts of Mirabeau, Rousseau and William Tell. It was always dusty and often the mud of the street was tracked in. He also joined the Jacobin Club, which had much grander quarters. It was moving left. It had garnered power and prestige. Everyone in France had heard of the Jacobin Club; chapters were being organized in every provincial city and town. It was time to get his foot in the door, but the Cordeliers were his base.

Lafayette and Bailly had stolen the power from the districts, turning them into impotent sections. Well, if push came to shove, he could show them how potent these sections could be. They might be surprised down at City Hall how fast the Cordeliers could call out the troops.

His section chose him late that summer to represent them at City Hall; but each of the one hundred forty-four delegates had to be approved by all the sections. He was the only delegate to be voted down. It was a bit of a shock to his ego. He was outrageously popular in his section. He had obviously become known in Paris; but among the citizens with property enough to vote, he was not acceptable. He was conflated with Marat. That helped him at home, but obviously hurt him in greater Paris.

It was an obstacle, but hardly insurmountable. Either more citizens had to be given the vote or he had to make a better name. He began working toward both those ends. An election was coming for the Departmental Council—far less powerful than the Paris Commune, but something. They were all learning this election business on their feet. He was beginning to vary his speeches once he had judged the audience, to talk one way to sans-culottes and differently to a bourgeois audience. This time he was successful. It was almost an empty office, but he had proved he could win.

The National Guard in his old district voted him their commander. That was a power base too. He kept on top of the Cordeliers. He went regularly to the Jacobins and made a speech from time to time. He watched everything and ran for every office that became vacant. He was getting proficient at campaigning. The Departmental Council was his, but boring and far from the center of power. No, he wanted into the Commune. They had to pry control of the city away from Lafayette and Bailly, and he had to be part of that effort.

The King's court had been abolished and he had no more income from the law. He still had debts. He took a bribe from time to time, but the problem of how to live well hung on his neck. The situation was promising, he maintained to Gabrielle, now breastfeeding his handsome baby son. But he had to figure out how to work it. In the meantime, he had lots of supporters and a group of loyal allies who were his to command. He had to maintain his base in the neighborhood and break out into the city; and eventually, the country. A newspaper like Marat and Camille had used to make themselves known was not for him. He rarely bothered writing down his speeches except for jotting a few ideas; he improvised. He would have to improvise himself a career.

THIRTY-FIVE
Max

❧

(Late 1790–April 1791)

WHEN the Assembly reluctantly followed the King to Paris, Max did not choose to live near the Tuileries. He found inexpensive lodgings in the Marais. Some blocks of the Marais held aristocratic town houses favored by bankers, investors, industrialists, minor aristocracy. But near the river were old narrow streets of leaning houses, where he rented three rooms. An elderly widow came in to cook and clean for him. When she was not about, he just ate fruit and chocolate or coffee with milk.

He was paid as a deputy, but he was supporting Charlotte and Augustin, back in Arras. Augustin wasn't doing well at the law. Being the brother of a man who had become notorious did not help. As head of family, Max felt guilty at having escaped Arras. True, he had not run off with a mistress or to make his fortune in Brazil, but he had abandoned his family for politics. He sent them every bit he could and still they always needed more. Unscrupulous operators tried to bribe him occasionally. He knew how to freeze a man who was trying to slip him something, hinting at some advantage to be gained by trimming his principles or his vote to their interests. No one was fool enough to try it twice.

Max worked hard to stay abreast of important issues and speak to them. Aside from the galleries, few deputies listened. "They see you as a dangerous radical," Camille said as they sat in a bright cafe near the Assembly. Camille read aloud from a monarchist paper: "This Rattle-spear wants to give the vote to artisans and peasants and then, no doubt, to barnyard animals too."

"They think I'm a joke," Max said bitterly. "But I'll laugh last."

"You have a following on the streets of Paris. The little people light candles to you." Camille made a gesture of praying.

"Many of these deputies are provincial lawyers like me, but they think if they've secured a place as full and equal pigs at the trough, then the aims of the Revolution are achieved. They're already retreating from the grand and fair claims of the Rights of Man. Now they're granting full citizenship only to men with an ample income. Most citizens were called passive and expected to be so, without a vote. It's a sickening reversal of the democratic ideals of August."

"You've improved as an orator. I heard your speech yesterday."

"You alone did, then. When I speak, the delegates pass notes. They chat. They slip out to relieve themselves. Only the gallery listens. And a few friends from the Breton Club."

"I'm praising your speech in my paper. And everyone calls the Club the Jacobins now, as if you'd all become monks!"

"I'm the only monk." He smiled wryly. The Club had moved into an old monastery near the Assembly, further along on the Rue Saint Honoré. That was an even longer hike from his lodgings, but he walked briskly, carrying a stick, and most of the street people knew him by sight. Just as the Cordeliers were named for the building where they met, his club was now called the Jacobins. When he spoke there, he was far more respectfully heard than in the Assembly.

On December thirtieth, 1790, Max stood as best man to Camille as he finally married his sweetheart Lucile in the big, rather bland church of Saint Sulpice, near the empty Luxembourg palace. Outside in the square, it was poultry market day around the fountain. The shouts of buyers and sellers drifted in. Max was moved for Camille. It was given to few men to achieve their heart's desire, and this appeared a true marriage of affection to which he could give full approval. "You've sometimes been wild and unconsidered in your actions, but now you can devote your best efforts to the Revolution." He straightened Camille's cravat.

It had been hard to find a priest. Camille had made fun of the Church often enough. He was strongly supporting the confiscation of Church property in his newspaper, and what was called the Civil Constitution of the Clergy, which meant all were paid by the government and swore an oath to the Constitution. Priest after priest refused to marry the couple, until Camille was joking about getting an American medicine man. Finally Max spoke to a man who had taught them at Louis-le-Grand. Camille mouthed a few transparently false promises of recantation, which the father did not believe but would be useful to him with his own superiors. He was a good-natured man pleased, like Max, to see his mischievous student finally married.

As Max stood through the ceremony, attentive, serious, he knew he could not hope for anything similar. He felt dizzy with relief that the Estates General had been called in time to keep him from marrying the cousin whose face he could not clearly recall. He would neglect a wife the way he used to walk off and leave Charlotte in the street, forgetting she was there. He had no right to children. Even if he did not die before he did what he must, he would have only his political legacy. He could dream of a woman who would see clearly his aims, his ideals, but what then? He had nothing to offer. He watched Camille kiss his bride and tears briefly burned his eyes. Soon, he thought, I will not even remember I imagined being held and cherished. Lucile wore pale pink. She shone, as only a very young bride who desperately wanted to be married to her husband and him alone, can gleam. To look into her face hurt his eyes. Gravely he kissed her cheek, inhaling lavender perfume and the scent of her body. A throb of sexual reaction touched him and he grimaced. He did not have a strong sensual nature, fortunately, and his body troubled him little. What vexed him sometimes was the desire to be in a warm relationship. He imagined a simple dignified domesticity, the physical manifestation of a spiritual and political harmony.

Max wished they lived nearer to him. He liked to be around happily married people. But they set up in the same building as the politician who had recently been coming to the Jacobin Club, Danton. Danton had an unruly aspect but good politics. He had a streak of the demagogue, but his voice was usually raised on the correct side, and Max could hardly fault him for vehemence in good causes.

Max was deeply concerned for the Revolution. Everywhere the forces of reaction were rising. In Aix-en-Provence, a former lawyer of the Parlement and two noblemen were persuaded by the King's cousin the Prince de Condé to plot an uprising against the revolutionary town government. In Perpignan, the local Jacobin Club had a shooting war with a royalist club. In February, a royalist group armed themselves and attempted to seize the Tuileries and liberate the King. Every day new plots broke out. The Revolution was far, far from being won, and yet the fools in the Assembly could not see the danger.

In March the Prince de Condé began to organize an army. In Worms across the Rhine, he recruited soldiers to invade France. The King's brother, the Comte d'Artois, was gathering an army at Coblenz. Mirabeau's younger brother, the drunkard called Barrel, had his deathshead hussars at Colmar. All these armies were heavy on generals and captains and weak on privates, but Max knew that the poor could always be conscripted. Economic necessity made soldiers of farmhands. The poor of Germany and Austria would march off to invade France the way the French had always marched at the King's bidding. Max hated war. It was organized slaughter in the interest of those who organized it. There was no such thing as glory for a poor boy gut-wounded and dying like a stuck pig.

The royalist armies were unprepared. Still it was criminal folly to forget the enemies within and the enemies without. These military aristocrats did not mealymouth the way the King did. They were open about their intention to hang every last member of the Assembly and all the journalists of Paris. They wanted to crush the peasant uprisings and the workers, as they had so many times. They wanted exactly what they had enjoyed, every privilege, every sous, every scrap of land, every feudal right. They wanted the ancien régime back, but more so. The King had dishonored himself by promising to sign the Constitution. He would be replaced by his brother, Artois, who was ready to lead an army that would vindicate divine right and smash the Revolution.

Max noticed how ghastly Mirabeau looked when he spoke in the Assembly. Mirabeau was forty-three, older than most delegates. In April, he died. Rumors were repeated in wall posters and newspapers that he had been poisoned. The public prosecutor ordered an autopsy. Just an inflamed liver from overindulgence. Max was asked to deliver one of the many eulogies. Whatever personal reservations he had about Mirabeau, the man had been a strong force for the Revolution, indispensable in the early days of the Assembly. Mirabeau was buried as a hero of the Revolution in the unfinished Pantheon.

Max was in a minority of radicals in the Assembly. He had learned to be more vehement, more passionate in an icy controlled way. He was finding a way to speak that the galleries loved, even if the Assembly often tried to shout him down. When he volunteered for a committee, it was as if he had not spoken. He was shut out from the work of government.

When Max walked in the streets, people cheered him. He was embarrassed to see crude replicas of himself made of clay, wood, even porcelain on sale. He was always seeing his likeness hung in humble shops and taverns and workshops, little factories. Men and women alike wanted to touch him. Women brought him their babies to bless and named them for him. It seemed as if the less power and influence he had in the Assembly, the more he was revered by the people. Their increasing adoration made him feel like a fraud. What have I done for you? he wanted to ask. He managed to shame the Assembly into voting that they could not succeed themselves in the next elections. They were increasingly conservative.

But he had not been able to secure for ordinary people the right to vote. He had not abolished black slavery. Slowly he was working toward rights for the Jews of Alsace and Lorraine. He had not been able to protect the rights or even the lives of soldiers who revolted against unjust conditions and lack of pay. He had not been able to abolish capital punishment.

The day after the King finally signed the Constitution, people in the streets unhitched the horses of a cab that he and Pétion had just climbed into. They began to draw the cab themselves. Max jumped out. "You're not horses, people. Don't act like draft animals. You're free Frenchmen! Don't make idols!" He railed at them, trying to make them understand that they should not adulate anyone. The more he tried to order them not to exalt him, the louder they cheered and cried out his name.

He did not know where to turn for advice. When he spoke of his new fame to Camille, Camille teased him as a new popular saint. It was not fitting for people who worked so hard for so little to adore anyone. They desperately wanted defenders and heroes, and certainly he was their defender and would die for them. But this uncontrollable worship of public men could bring the unscrupulous to power. At the same time, he recognized as he examined himself and his behavior meticulously, that it did salve the wounds to his pride delivered daily by his fellow delegates. If his speeches were addressed now more to the galleries than to the floor, that was because the galleries listened. The words no one in the Assembly bothered to heed were published at once in the radical papers and repeated as gospel in taverns and workshops. Every day he was more famous among the little people and more infamous among the big people. He could see what had to be done, and yet he could not make those with power do what was needed to save the Revolution. In spite of the adulation and his friendship with Camille, he felt bitterly alone.

THIRTY-SIX
Claire

❦

(January 1791)

A YEAR had passed since Claire said goodbye to Mendès. He had returned to Bordeaux, his mission accomplished and with fervent plans to organize young Jews into the National Guard. She thought of him more often than any man she had been with, but less as the year went on. She did not replace him with a new lover. She had no time to waste.

The theater on the boulevard where she worked was putting on a big pageant in the new year of 1791. As usual she would be almost nude, the centerpiece of a tableau called *France Is Reborn*. Flesh-colored tights and a tricolor shawl completed her costume. She was looking for a better job, but actresses were commoner than horses. On her side were her looks that men always seemed to end up staring at, even with twenty other women on the stage. She exuded something. She fulfilled some wish. She had no idea what it was, and she didn't take it seriously. It was a matter of a few years at best, and then she would be a middle-aged woman sagging around like her mother: her mother who died in Pamiers and whom she had never seen again once she ran away. Sometimes she wondered if anyone was left of her family, except for Yvette in the convent.

She had a letter from Yvette just a week after she had been brooding about her. It had a Toulouse address.

Dear sister,

I am to be married next month. The revolution broke up the convent and I had to look for work. I was hired by a lawyer in Toulouse. There I met Pierre, who was the valet of a nobleman until the coward ran away and left all his servants to fend for themselves. But Pierre saved his money and he is buying a restaurant. He says that people have to eat, no matter what government is in power. I am very happy. He is older than me but his two children are dead. So there is no problem. His wife is dead too I forgot to say. I have been saving my money, so we have a real nest egg. We are looking for a good property. Every Sunday we look at possible restaurants. I am terribly happy and I wish you were a good woman and could get married too. Please send me whatever you can at once as we are going to need every sous we can scrape together.

Your loving sister,
Yvette.
P.S. Pierre does not want you to come to the wedding, but I know he won't mind if you visit us after a while. I will work on him.

"So!" Hélène wrinkled her snub nose, "Are you jealous of your sister?"

"Just suspicious. I can't imagine a man willing to marry her."

"They say for every man, there's a woman, if you believe that stuff."

"I don't think I could trust a man enough to give up and marry him."

"What do you mean, give up?"

"Give up the freedom I have."

"Freedom!" Hélène laughed bitterly, pushing her hair from her eyes. "Some great freedom . . ." She wrung her hands. "Claire, I'm caught."

"Are you sure?"

"I haven't had my time for three months. My breasts are sore and swollen. I remember my mother. She had eight kids, Claire. We women can get pregnant from thinking about it. The Virgin Mary has nothing on us."

"Who's the papa?"

"How do I know?"

Claire laughed and put her arm around Hélène. "Well, who have you been thinking about?"

"You remember that masked ball in October we were all invited to? You walked out early."

"I don't like pigs in masks pinching me."

"I was with this guy. I don't know who he was. It was very romantic, Claire, he was like a hero out of a play—"

"Hélène, how could you? You know what crap we put on."

"A girl likes to believe in something above the ordinary. I felt carried off. It was like a dream. We danced and danced and he kept kissing me. He gave me a gold bracelet. It turned out to be fake."

Claire took her hard by the shoulders. "Hélène, what are you going to do? Anatole will fire you. You can't raise a bastard by yourself. Will your mother take it?"

"My father threw me out when I was sixteen and he caught me with my boyfriend. I was on the streets for four months before I got a job in a pantomime. I can't go home. . . . I'm going to a woman tomorrow. They say she's a wise woman and she can get rid of it."

"Do you want me to go with you?"

"Would you? Please. I'm scared. I've heard of girls dying that way."

"You've heard of dozens of women dying in childbirth too. What doesn't kill you, makes you stronger, right? We'll both go."

The wise woman lived in the Faubourg Saint Marcel near the Gobelins tapestry factory, one of the most revolutionary sections. They went down the steep Rue Mouffetard. They passed the Salpêtrière, where they shut up whores and women punished for transgressions of morality. Hélène said wryly, "That's where if somebody does you wrong, they jail you so you can feel really rotten. It's supposed to be one of the worst prisons in Paris." Women shouted to them through the gates in the heavy walls and they waved back. On Sunday visitors were streaming in and out and peddlers of all sorts. They could smell chicken cooking and backed-up drains.

Claire knew why Hélène was staring at the walls of Salpêtrière prison. If an unmarried woman got pregnant, she was obliged by the law to report it at once. She could go to prison for being pregnant and not reporting it. She could go to prison for trying to get rid of the baby. She could go to the workhouse if she had the baby, unmarried.

"As the Revolution moves along, as the people get more power, we'll open the doors of Salpêtrière and free the women. We know why women are whores. Because it pays. Because it's a job like any other. We'll fix things, Hélène. You wait and see. I believe in this revolution."

"So do I. But the men don't understand what we need. They don't care about the same things."

"We'll do it ourselves then. You're walking slower and slower." She grasped Hélène by the elbow, muscling her along and craning her neck to look for the address. Things were more spread out here. Houses did not loom over the narrow street, as in their neighborhood, but the streets were wider and often houses had gardens in back and rabbit hutches, a shed. The people had no more money—many hovels were patched together out of trash—but they could spread out a bit, grow beans, raise chickens for eggs. The snow from last week was yellow with horse piss. Today it was above freezing. Dirty heaps of old snow wept into the street, making going sloppy. They were standing in a street that seemed to be the right one, both looking around, when a woman hailed them. "By the looks of you, you want Auntie Michelle. Just turn at the corner and her door is the blue one. She's two stories up."

"How did she know?" Hélène muttered. "Do I look pregnant already?"

"Because when two women come together to this street obviously lost, they're nine times out of ten looking for the wise woman. Come on."

It took an hour. Claire had to hold Hélène down and keep the gag in. The blood ran everywhere. Claire felt faint and nauseated with the stench of blood, the awful blood running from Hélène. It was not right for Hélène to be lying there naked from the waist down bleeding profusely. But they had to take off her skirt for fear she would stain it. A skirt was not something Hélène could do without.

Hélène was weak afterward from the pain and the loss of blood and still bleeding. Claire was afraid the woman would throw them out, but she let Hélène rest until it was beginning to get dark. "Now you better go, girls. It's not too safe to be hanging around at night."

Hélène had to stop frequently. The bleeding continued. It was much harder to climb the Rue Mouffetard than it had been to descend it. The night was still relatively mild and at least the puddles did not freeze. Slowly they made their way home, Hélène leaning more and more on her. Instead of taking Hélène home, Claire put her in her own bed. Slowly the bleeding ebbed to a slow regular flow.

The next day Hélène could not go to work. On the way home, Claire got soup at the corner tavern. Hélène took an hour to eat a bowl of soup, she was so weak. Claire was scared for her.

"You'll stay here, with me. You're going to get better. You're going to eat up the soup and drink this wine and you're going to feel better. I'm going to ask the apothecary for something to build up your blood. My grandmother said liver." She went to the butcher's for a piece of liver. Grandmère knew. She had always known what to do for burns and bruises, strains, cuts and lacerations.

The next few days were frightening. Hélène stayed weak and seemed feverish and then lethargic. Her red hair hung lank, no curl left. Her face was without color. Then slowly her strength returned. Claire fed her a potion from the apothecary supposed to restore vigor. She bought brandy. Nothing was too good for Hélène. Claire marveled at herself, how she did not mind taking care. Once she got over the fear that Hélène would die in her bed, she rather liked playing mother. She felt closer to Hélène after a week had passed than she had to anyone since her grandmother. Hélène was her friend and her project.

By the time Hélène was well enough to return to work, she had been replaced. Unable to afford rent, Hélène moved in with Claire. After all, she had a big double bed all to herself. She wasn't about to move some guy in. Hélène needed a respite. She would look for work soon. She was a working girl. Either she'd get a job in the theater or in a shop or in a factory or she'd go on the streets or into a house for a while, if she really had to. But Hélène would work. Claire did not worry about that. They were the same kind. They could trust each other. For neither of them was there any safety, anything to fall back on if their health or wits or job failed. But they could help each other. She slept with her arm around Hélène, who felt thin and fragile, as if she were made of tiny sticks. She was soft in places, brittle in other places, but under it all, she was strong enough. They both were. Strong enough.

THIRTY-SEVEN
Nicolas

❧

(February–June 1791)

NICOLAS saw rather more of the royal family than he enjoyed. Louis was obviously displeased with the progress of events. He did not want a Constitution; he did not want a Legislative Assembly; he did not want a clergy loyal to the Constitution and huge Church properties sold off. His wife liked it even less: no Hapsburg relinquished power. Divine right was spoon-fed them from babyhood. Marie was far more arrogant than Louis, but they were both equally stubborn and, as far as Nicolas could see, equally blind to the larger picture. They were surrounded by intriguers who echoed their views. They both found the Tuileries inadequate, insultingly threadbare.

Mirabeau had tried to act as liaison between the National Assembly and the royal family, but Louis would not listen. Lafayette was the only revolutionary leader they might have accepted, for he alone had blue enough blood to have been received at court. The Queen had even danced with him at court balls. He might have bridged the gap. But they hated him. He was their Antichrist.

Nicolas would not do; his was a lower nobility. He was simply under-minister material, suspect by virtue of his association with the Encyclopedists. If Louis found the *Encyclopedia*—the great product of eighteenth-century Enlightenment and the conscious attempt to provide a summary of science and philosophy—heretical and far too modern, what chance was there of his becoming the compliant British constitutional monarch the middle-of-the-road delegates dreamed of? The more Nicolas watched the King, the less likely he found it that Louis would ever adapt.

There were other candidates for king: to the right the Comte d'Artois with his army in exile; to the left, the duc d'Orléans. His secretary, the novelist Choderlos de Laclos, constantly schemed for Orléans at the Jacobin Club. Gradually Nicolas relinquished the notion of a king. Could any man be entrusted with such power over others? A king if elected was not a king; if not elected, on what did his power base itself, except despotism?

Whenever Nicolas walked into the Tuileries, he smelled intrigue like smoke in the air. Louis brooded, then stumbled into action. He tried to leave with his family to hear mass outside Paris on Easter, with an illegal priest who had come out against the Revolution. Lafayette's guards feared he meant to escape and stopped his coach. Louis still had the option, as Nicolas told Sophie repeatedly, of embracing the Constitution and going forward as the first constitutional monarch of France. After all, the British had a limited monarchy and their kings did not seem to feel utterly degraded. Louis's other choice was to abdicate. The Americans managed quite well without a king, and Nicolas suspected, so would the French.

The informal group of liberals to which he belonged had given themselves a name, the Social Circle. Their first public meeting drew four thousand people, eager to discuss issues facing the Revolution. They met in The Circus (it had gone out of business) of the Palais Royal. At the second meeting, the audience doubled. He addressed the Club frequently. They did not have the clout or fame of the Jacobin Club, and nobody started other little Social Circles the way Jacobin Clubs were springing up in every town. Their aim was education. Clubs were suddenly important in politics. The French did not have parties, unlike the British or Americans; what they had were clubs.

He had grown close to Tom Paine, who had been thrown out of England for supporting the French Revolution. Tom was English-born, but had been an important pamphleteer in the American revolution, also serving in the army. Tom dined with them often and made a point of coming to Sophie's salon. When Tom needed a place to live, for he was not a wealthy man, the Condorcets invited him to move in. After all, they had the room.

Eliza was a year old. She had learned to walk slowly and awkwardly but had begun to talk early. Mostly she babbled. Nicolas never spoke baby talk to her but addressed her as a small, innocent but intelligent being. She fixed him with brown eyes that looked enormous and seemed to take in every word. Nicolas thought Sophie an ideal mother, concerned and loving, but not consumed. The nanny and another new maid took care of most of Eliza's physical needs. Sophie was as busy as he was. Time flowed by, and every time he looked at Eliza, she was noticeably bigger and, he thought, increasingly bright. Sophie was right, as always. Having a child had been the right thing to do. They made love now almost as often as they had.

On a hot day in late June Sophie was playing with Eliza. Tom Paine had already gone off to the *Iron Mouth* office. Nicolas and Sophie liked to take the morning together. It was the summer solstice and Paris was muggy. The maid had just sponged Sophie's face, hands and feet. She was still in her negligee. Nicolas in his striped damask robe was eating ripe cherries from a silver bowl that still held some coolness, as he read the latest journals. Suddenly Tom Paine rushed in, highly excited, his face flushed with sweat.

"The King's fled," Tom said in English. "He's cut and run."

Nicolas dropped his paper. "How could he get past Lafayette's guards? Is there collusion?"

"Apparently they slipped out in the night, at the time the courtiers and visitors leave the palace. In disguise."

"Who's gone?" Sophie asked. Tom was a close enough friend for her to receive him in dishabille.

"The King, the Queen, the children, the children's governess and the King's sister, Elisabeth—Mademoiselle, I think she's called?"

Nicolas whistled. "The whole royal family. So it's a real decampment. Do you think he's gone off to the Germans to join one of the royalist armies gathered on the border?"

"No one has any idea. But Fersen is gone also—the Queen's lover." They were still speaking English. They almost always spoke English with Tom. His French remained childish, and it was good practice for them.

"I hate the gossip that surrounds her, as if it mattered if she bedded half the court," Sophie made a sour face. "I don't care if the Swede is the Queen's lover; I only care if he was her coachman."

"Rumor has it that he was." Tom ruffled his often unruly hair till it stood on end. "Nico, shouldn't you and I head for the Assembly to see what must be done?"

"Ask Henri to give you some lunch, and I'll dress and have my hair powdered. I'll be with you in an hour." He rang for his valet and his barber.

The news had obviously spread in the streets, for people everywhere were muttering, listening to speeches. They were frightened—would the foreign armies invade them with the King at their head? Above all, they were angry. "Louis betrayed us," Nicolas heard again and again. "He lied and ran off to our enemies. He's gone over to the other side."

"If he headed for the Rhine, this could mean an invasion, then," Nicolas said to Tom as they rushed toward the old Riding Academy where the Assembly met. The Assembly was in session, the galleries already jammed. There was no room even for standing. If they pressed near, they could hear that Artois lawyer Robespierre's thin high voice denouncing the King and demanding his removal, a condemnation in icy lightning. He was playing to the galleries.

"No point standing out here straining to catch an odd word. Let's go to the

Iron Mouth office. Bonneville may know something. Brissot may. We must figure out how to respond to this flight. We must get a paper out," Tom said.

The *Iron Mouth* had its offices where Nicholas Bonneville lived, by the Cordeliers Club. The office was in an uproar. Brissot had just come from the Assembly with the news that the King and family had run in the direction of Germany, as feared. Would they be able to recapture Louis? Would he lead the Rhine armies on an invasion of France?

That evening Nicolas and Sophie discussed the King's flight over supper. Although it was ten-thirty, the Seine was still silvery lavender and the sky was not yet dark. They ate in front of the large windows flung open onto the balcony. At this late hour, there was still considerable river traffic and music came from the Pont Neuf, where people were dancing. A barge passed, lit by torches, and they could hear a woman singing Gluck. It seemed peaceful, almost idyllic. Yet he did not feel at ease.

"Tomorrow we'll look at the house Mme Helvétius has found us in Auteuil. It would be good for Eliza to grow up at least partly in the country—and it's only a short carriage ride from Paris." The image he had clung to during the birth of the three of them in a green and healthy setting continued to obsess him. He would make it happen. He must. It was more important now.

"You're worried, Nico. About what?"

"War may be coming." Across the table they held hands in the twilight.

THIRTY-EIGHT
Manon

❦

(Spring 1791)

A S soon as Jean was elected to the municipal council, he was appointed to the finance committee, to find a way out of Lyon's budgetary doldrums. Lyon owed thirty-nine million livres in debts incurred under the ancien régime. If the city was ever to function again, they must have a loan or forgiveness of debts. In 1791, Jean was sent on a mission to Paris.

That meant going for some time; as far as Manon was concerned, it meant moving to Paris. "Holding on to our Lyon flat while we spend months in Paris is foolish. No doubt we'll return by early summer, when we can go into the country as we always do. Why waste money on a flat we don't adore? When we return . . ." silently she added to herself, *if* we return, "so many wealthy citizens have fled, we should have no trouble finding something less gloomy."

She also persuaded him that Eudora should remain behind. Manon put her with the nuns of Ville-Franche. She had a convent education, why not Eudora? She would learn to get on with other girls her age and she would learn discipline. Manon was going to be running all over politicking for a position for Jean. If things changed, she could always send for her daughter.

As for Paris, she did not care if they moved into a room under the roof. She would be back where she belonged, in the heart of things. Brissot, Bosc, Lanthénas, their old friends were so involved in making the Revolution, that they simply could not remember Jean. But when she was face to face with them they would remember. Jean would be given a position worthy of his talents.

She felt pleased with Jean once again. She no longer doubted he had needed his long convalescence, for hadn't he risen from his sickbed to become a councillor of Lyon? Within four months, hadn't he been chosen for an important mission in Paris? What more could she ask of him?

She packed with dispatch. Her maid Fleury said, "Madame, I've never seen you so full of joy." Manon did not dread the long stagecoach ride jolting over the hideous roads. It was entrance to paradise, the heaven of ideas, of political discourse, of men who shaped the events that shaped an era.

Their journey was in pouring rain, day after day, and yet she did not despair. She kept Jean and the other passengers smiling. She told stories, she got everyone talking, she had them sing. She would crawl to Paris on her knees in the mud. What did she care if the coach got stuck twice and everyone must pile out into the slough of clay and push? Each push, each mishap, each jolt that pounded the joints and made the kidneys throb, brought them closer. She had discovered that when she was happy, she could charm almost every man and a great many women too. It was an almost palpable thing, that warm spell she could cast that made a man feel she was fascinated by his ideas, by his way of thinking and speaking, and that she could take those ideas and put a polish on them and hand them back improved, given a luster that could only delight the recipient. It was one of her gifts, the feminine talent of a bright and perceptive handmaiden.

She had a sickening fear of being seen as unwomanly, as thrusting herself forward past Jean. Then she would feel naked in public, dishonored. But working in Jean's behalf was permitted a good wife. She was skillful at it, as he would see once they had their place in Paris.

Bosc found them a furnished flat in the Hotel Britannique, on the left bank close to the Pont Neuf where she had grown up. The rooms in the Britannique were not grand but pleasant enough. She could entertain there, and she fully intended to. At once she went to see her old friend Lanthénas, who was involved in a group called the Social Circle. He was passionate against primogeniture and seemed to be the local expert on its pernicious effects. Within two hours, they were back on the old footing: she once again called him Fratello, little brother, and he called her Sorella, little sister. He opened up and gossiped about everyone she knew and wanted to know—and some people she definitely did not want to meet.

Most of the wives of the Social Circle men seemed of no importance. Only the former nobleman Condorcet had an intellectual wife, who ran a salon and published translations from the English. She was said to be beautiful, but she had just had a baby and should not represent a threat to Manon's plans. Condorcet seemed moderately important. Somebody named Bonneville was important also and edited their paper. Then there was Brissot, who sounded like the most influential of all this faction.

Lanthénas told her about a women's group affiliated with the Social Circle, but she had no interest. What would talking to other women accomplish? She was not about to start educating the wives of tradesmen. Surely there were plenty of born schoolteachers who would take on that unrewarding task.

She pumped Lanthénas thoroughly and then invited him to supper the following Tuesday. She urged him to bring his friends. Before the week was out, she must encounter Brissot. Lanthénas told her she should go to the Assembly, which Brissot covered for his newspaper. When she got home, Jean was still out. She went into their bedroom and stood before the mirror. She had to form an accurate assessment of herself before she marched into battle. Lanthénas was easy. Brissot, so long her editor, might not prove as easy to charm, but obviously he was one of those who moved the great wheel of the Revolution.

She looked herself square in the eyes. Her complexion was still excellent and rosy, satiny and highly colored. Her skin showed no age. She had not a wrinkle. The years spent mostly in the countryside had been kind to her skin and her figure. Her mouth was generous, large, and when she smiled at herself, she understood why men liked it so much when she smiled at them. She had a smile that made people feel like smiling back and made them think her far prettier than she was. Her eyes were large and greyish brown. Her face was not an insipid mask like those of many women considered beautiful, but it was expressive. Her arms and shoulders were shapely, she had a fine bosom, even better since breastfeeding Eudora. Her hair was silky and brown. She still looked young. That would certainly help in what she intended to do: create *the* salon where the most important political movers of the revolutionary movement would meet and discuss their ideas.

The next morning, she went out to buy flowers, showing Fleury exactly what she wanted so that her maid could carry out that task every week. She arranged and rearranged the room. The food would be simple. She felt plain republican cuisine would better represent Jean's position than an attempt to emulate a noble banquet, a superfluity of dishes under heavy sauces. She set up her delicate writing desk in one corner of the salon. She would sit modestly there, out of the way. She would not interfere in the arguments, but she would observe, she would listen, and then privately, she could express her opinions—to Jean, of course, but also to others if they sought her out.

She carefully observed what bourgeois women were wearing. Fashions had changed, and she must put Fleury and a dressmaker to work at once. Women were wearing dresses either white (white she knew very well Marie-Antoinette had brought in, but nobody seemed to remember that) or bright colors, particularly red or blue. Over the dresses, they wore light shawls draped over bodices. Stripes were still in fashion. The striped dresses she had would do. Jewelry had political themes and everybody was wearing red, blue and white cockades in their hair or pinned to their bosoms. Sashes were prominent, often tricolored. Almost no one was powdering their hair, but wearing their natural hair colors. Hair had ceased towering. Even wealthy ladies could pass through doors easily, for skirts and dresses draped or hung naturally. One of the most fashionable styles was the redingote, a coatdress in one piece requiring a minimum of corseting.

She did not care for jewelry or other frippery. A few simple dresses with white linen or lace collars would do. Jean, bless him, was said to dress like a Quaker, for he always wore a plain black suit, the plainest and most serviceable of shoes or boots and a round hat. She would not permit him to leave the house if he looked shabby, but he dressed in an unadorned and homely way, proclaiming his honesty and lack of pretension.

Finally she was ready to see Brissot. One new dress was ready, and she wore it. She did not want to remind him she had spent the last nine years in the provinces. When she reached the Assembly, she found him talking to a delegate. He still looked young. He was a short amiable man with rather elongated features who carried himself with great assurance, walking through the crowd nodding here and there as if everyone in the world must know him. Indeed, everyone seemed to. His voice was clear and carrying. She waited till she caught his eye. He smiled at her, as at an admirer. Brissot was married to some inconsequential woman, but he was obviously used to female attention. Then he did a double take and bowed, recognizing her finally.

Waiting for an opportunity to speak with him, she studied the Assembly room, long and heated by a porcelain stove in the shape of the Bastille. The floor had been a racing oval when this was the riding school. The only light—and presumably in warm weather the only air—came from windows just below the roof. Six rows of seats for delegates canted sharply up from the floor. The hall was divided in two by a speaker's podium on one side and the elevated chair of the President on the other. The delegates faced each other across the narrow aisle. They were crowded together, but not as crowded as the gallery above. The atmosphere was disappointing. In her mind's eye, she had seen the Assembly like the noble Romans in paintings, dignified, speaking in rounded sentences aphorisms of wisdom. Instead the place smelled like a sty and was as noisy as a barnyard. The delegates freely cheered and booed and whistled and stamped their feet. They were out of their seats half the time chattering, having conversations shouted up to the gallery. The level of discourse was low and quarrelsome.

She waved to Bancal. He seemed pleased to see her but restrained in his greeting, perhaps embarrassed at remembering how he had pursued her. She finally saw Brissot approaching. "Ah, my literary citizeness from Lyon, your person is as pretty as your writing. What a great pleasure. Is your husband in Paris also?"

"Jean has been sent by the city of Lyon as an emissary to the Assembly. But perhaps it's time we were in Paris, where so much is being done for the greater good of our country. . . . Doesn't anyone say 'vous' any more? Even the flower sellers address me as 'tu'—it took me aback."

"That's our friend Bonneville's doing. He decided in the *Iron Mouth* that using 'vous' was an aristocratic hangover. You 'voused' those above you and used the familiar 'tu' with those below you. The use of 'tu' with everyone reflects social equality, that we're all brothers—and sisters too." He leaned close. "It still startles me sometimes. But you'll get used to it."

She changed the subject to the day's debate on setting up workshops for the unemployed. Before she left, she invited him to her Tuesday. There was something about him, the way he moved through the crowd, the way he spoke, that made her understand why Brissot was mentioned so often. He was a natural leader. He had not seemed so when he had visited them before the Revolution; had he changed, or only her perception of him?

Bancal said at her elbow, watching with her the progress of Brissot through the gallery, "Brissot admires your writing. That's a great advantage to you."

Manon pretended she had not heard. "Now who is that very young man haranguing a group in the hall? The one Brissot was speaking to just before he came over." She did not describe him as handsome, although he certainly was, on a small and almost delicate scale.

"Buzot. He may be young, but he's reliable. He's a true revolutionary. He's in the Jacobin Club. Just last week Robespierre praised him."

"Who's Robespierre?"

"If you stay for the whole day, you're bound to see him. Nobody in the Assembly thinks much of him, but he's the darling of the sans-culottes—that's the new term for what we used to call the little people, but they don't want to be called little any longer."

She invited Bancal to her Tuesday, and then got him to take her over to Buzot to invite him. She was starting to collect her salon.

The gallery was full of rowdy low-life women, half of whom she suspected were prostitutes. At one point a tall woman strode in wearing men's trousers, with a pistol stuck in her belt. A great stir went through the crowd, and even some delegates turned to bow or wave. "Théroigne de Méricourt," Bancal said. "The heroine of the Women's March on Versailles. She wants to organize a battalion of Amazons to defend the Revolution."

"She does not look like a respectable woman."

"She was a high-class courtesan before the Revolution. She sold all her jewelry and gave the money to the Assembly."

"I assume de Méricourt is not her real name."

Bancal grinned. "She was a peasant. I'm sure she concealed that fact before, but now it's a proud boast. People used to scurry to produce noble ancestors, but now they'd just as soon shove them back in the closet."

Manon would not be comfortable with most of the women of the gallery, but she suspected there would always be a friend or two to sit with. It was important to attend the Assembly assiduously for the next month, until she had learned more of the players and more of the play. So far no one had turned down her invitation. She suspected she was meeting a need, someplace liberals could get together informally and discuss and debate, away from the public. Make connections. Feel out each other's positions on legislation pending and future. She had learned that Sophie Condorcet's salon was full of women as well as men. Hers would be strictly for working politicians, journalists, political philosophers. The only woman present would be herself, discreetly after supper in a corner at her writing desk. All as it should be.

THIRTY-NINE

Georges

❦

(June–July 1791)

L OUIS was as inept a fugitive as he was a king. He barely bothered to disguise himself, and a postmaster recognized him. How did the postmaster recognize the King? Georges did an imitation for the benefit of Gabrielle, Camille and Lucile, all gathered around Gabrielle's plentiful table for supper. Georges crept up on Camille, peering at him as if incredulous. Then he groped in his pocket, pulling out a louis. He held up the coin and stared at Camille, his mouth dropping open. "A perfect match! It's the King!"

Everybody wildly applauded. The two couples living in the same house shared many meals. Lucile took care of the baby when Gabrielle ran errands. The women were so different, Georges was amazed they got along. Lucile was the overeducated pretentious daughter of a literary mama. If she had been a shade less pretty, Georges would have found her affectations unendurable. Gabrielle was of the earth: ripe, voluptuous, skilled in kitchen and bed, robust and watchful for his good. She was exactly what he wanted. He would eye Lucile with pleasure, but she was no mate for him. And what would Gabrielle do with Camille with his girlish looks, his occasional stammer, his inability to earn a living, his willingness to offend for the sake of a witticism, his spendthrift habits and his tendency to talk all night?

Gabrielle saw that Lucile was far too in love with Camille to look at Georges, a lack that amused Georges more than it annoyed him. Plenty of women looked at him and plenty of women made overtures. Now and then he went to bed with one of them, just for the moment's pleasure, out of curiosity, out of sensuality. Gabrielle was what he wanted in his bed evening after evening, morning after morning. She had the body of summer. This marriage suited him, even if he strayed now and then. He made sure Gabrielle never knew—for he had no desire for a stiletto in his side, ice instead of fire under him. She was the woman he loved, no other, and he loved his son. He was a family man, who did what he could for his mother, who kept on good terms with his in-laws. One thing he liked about having the Desmoulins in his house was that they too became family. Camille was at odds with his own family, who wanted nothing to do with him. Camille had made Georges into an older brother.

Over the next couple of days, the King and the royal family were brought back, far more slowly than they had fled. Crowds lined the road, but not to cheer. No man removed his hat in respect. People shouted threats. It was a procession of shame. In a matter of months, Louis had managed to dispose of the love and now even the respect of his people.

The monarchists in the Assembly were determined to salvage Louis; once they had a new Constitution, they would offer him a chance to support it. They were putting out the fiction that Louis had been kidnapped. The King was prepared to go along with any far-fetched tale the right wing of the Assembly tacked together.

In the Jacobin Club there was war. Robespierre led the left wing, who wanted to depose the King, who did not want to pretend he had merely been taking a little ride to see the countryside but rather to admit he been on his way to lead the armies across the Rhine. The right wing had exactly the same ideas as the Assembly monarchists; there was overlapping personnel. Georges supported Robespierre loudly and long.

Now there was a funny little man. He was half Georges' weight and Georges could have picked him up under one arm and carried him about like a child. But he did not dare even touch him. Once he had slapped Robespierre on the back. He could still remember how the little man had turned and fixed him with those cold green eyes. Georges felt his heart catch in his chest. One did not treat Robespierre without respect. One never touched him.

When they stood side by side leading this fight, they must look amusing: Georges was tall and robust, strong as a wrestler. He could lift a heavy table over his head. Maximilien Robespierre was short, slight and often ill. He was delicate and approached his food gingerly and his drink abstemiously. Georges was a mighty trencherman. Gabrielle had won him with her cherry duck as much as with her peach breasts. Robespierre seemed equally leery of food and women. Yet women chased after him. Georges was amused to watch beauties he had ogled traipsing after Robespierre, who paid them no more attention than he did other constituents. He seemed impervious. The people had given him a nickname, the Incorruptible. He could not be bought. Georges knew he himself could not be bought either, so he freely accepted money. But Robespierre seemed to need no more than bread and coffee.

Georges was called a natural orator: true to a degree, although he had watched other orators for years, observing what worked and what didn't. He was a pragmatist; Robespierre was not. Georges had a rich voice, strong, pulsating, a trumpet that moved people almost in and of itself. When he was speaking, he was always conscious of how much of his energy, his volume, his force, he needed and how much he should hold in reserve. Robespierre had a high thin voice like a fine drill. Robespierre should have been a bit ludicrous, standing at the podium like a dried up ancien régime dandy curled and powdered and wearing a silk coat, speaking in his squeaky voice, a stick of a man. Yet there was power in his delivery. Nor was Robespierre much of a butt for jokes. Georges was fascinated by the paradox. He could not define for himself where Robespierre's power came from. This was not a manly man. Yet he was far more popular than Georges himself or any politician except Marat. People loved him. He was their saint. At least Marat had a woman. Georges did not like Marat, but he understood him. Robespierre he could only admire and observe and sometimes dread. A man without pleasures. A man without vices. A man alone. Why should Georges sometimes experience a jolt of fear?

Georges managed to charm him now and then, but it was hard work. Camille was far more familiar with Robespierre, who seemed to care for Camille as he cared for few others. They had been schoolboys together. Robespierre liked calling on the young couple. He was brotherly with Lucile, brotherly with Camille. Come to think of it, Camille seemed proficient in providing himself with useful and diligent older brothers, didn't he? That was Camille. Always on the lookout for how to get himself taken care of.

"The Assembly's gone belly up," Camille said at the Cordeliers Club. "They're going to pretend nothing really happened."

"For now," Georges said. "But Louis will never govern again."

Camille was dashing off incendiary pamphlets. The Cordeliers were working on a petition to depose the King. They carried the idea to the Social Circle, where it caught on. Both clubs decided to call a demonstration on the Champ de Mars, where the celebration of taking the Bastille occurred every July. Crowds would sign the petition publicly and then present it to the Assembly.

The three radical clubs were close to each other, the Cordeliers, the Jacobins and the Social Circle. Each had a different constituency. The Cordeliers were the closest to the common people, the cheapest to join. The Jacobins had lots of delegates and lawyers. The Circle drew both men and women of the educated classes. Camille and Georges went to the Jacobins and their own Cordeliers regularly; sometimes they attended meetings at the Circle. Georges could barely remember when he had not had eleven or twelve meetings a week on his agenda. He could dimly recall days when he sat yawning in his office preparing paralyzingly dull briefs on some bloated grocer's desire to prove himself noble back to the time of Charlemagne. Elections were approaching for the next assembly, which Robespierre had succeeded in assuring would have no one from the current National Assembly. Thus Robespierre was not eligible; but Georges was. He meant to run.

On Friday, July fifteenth, there was a huge meeting in The Circus at the Palais Royal to organize the petition signing. People were enormously excited. The general consensus was that the King must not be put back on the throne. They didn't need Louis, who had only been obstructing the Assembly. It was time for a republic. The petition drawn up rebuked the Assembly for refusing to debate the King's guilt. The Assembly had been cutting back on the freedom of the people, refusing even the right for petitions such as this one. It was time for a massive show of strength.

When the meeting broke up, many were too excited to go home. About four thousand marched to the Jacobins, just along the Rue Saint Honoré a few blocks. The Jacobins were debating what to do about the King. The argument went on for two more hours. This was a night without sleep, for who could sleep with so much happening? Robespierre looked pale and weary, but his voice did not give way. He thundered condemnation. Robespierre always believed every damned word that flew out of his mouth. Georges found that amazing.

Finally a committee representing all three groups was set up, consisting of the duc d'Orléans' secretary Laclos, Brissot and Lanthénas from the Social Circle, Sergent from the Cordeliers, and Georges. They went off to a side room, some monk's cell when this had been a monastery, and sat down with their quills and paper and went to it. Head to head till it was growing light outside. They ended up with a statement they all found acceptable.

In the morning Bonneville said he would publish the petition and people could come to his *Iron Mouth* offices to sign it, or they could sign it next day at the Champ de Mars. Several forms of the petition were floating around, for Laclos had rewritten a version favorable to Orléans' desire to be King. In the meantime, the Jacobins decided the demonstration was illegal. That left the Cordeliers and the Circle calling out the people without the Jacobins.

Georges convened a meeting of what he considered the unofficial board of Cordeliers directors the morning of the seventeenth. The demonstration was scheduled for that afternoon. They were arguing strategy when the butcher Legendre ran in with a message from the Lameth brothers, who were close to Lafayette, but with whom Georges had a history. They laid some money on him from time to time. Legendre was breathless. "Bailly and Lafayette are going to use this as an excuse. They say the petition and the demonstration are both illegal. They're going to arrest you all on the spot. They may even shoot you down. Lafayette's arming his guards now. The Lameth brothers say you should get out of the city and stay out till things cool down."

Gabrielle had heard. She stood in the door of the salon hands on hips staring at him and making sure he met her gaze. "Get packed," Georges said. "Camille, I think a few days in the country are on our calendar. This damned petition has been so fucked up by now, six different versions circulating and nobody ever satisfied. We need to stay out of prison. Go get Lucile, throw some stuff in a hamper. We're off to visit my in-laws. Any of you who want to come along, you have exactly half an hour to get ready."

He had no taste for martyrdom. Behind walls, he would be where Lafayette wanted him, where he could do no harm and no good. He did not bother thanking the Lameths. There was no love lost. They had inherited him from Mirabeau and sometimes they paid him and sometimes they didn't. Mirabeau had said about him that the court was not getting their money's worth bribing him, and no doubt Mirabeau had been right.

Gabrielle was ready in half an hour. Lucile was not. But within the hour, both families were on their way in a hired coach. Their mood was more jolly than fearful. He did not expect Lafayette to pursue him the way he pursued Marat, through the sewers of Paris. It was sweltering in the city. In the country, they would have a nice holiday.

"Soon we must all go down to my new property near Arcis. Gabrielle hasn't laid eyes on it yet. Eventually, Camille, I'm planning to retire and become a country squire on the English model. Keep horses and sheep and cows and a vineyard. Make my own wine. That's how I plan to spend the second half of my life. Once I've made a bit of a fortune, of course, and done the work given us. When we've set the country right, then I plan to live high and long. The good life, Camille, it's not in the city."

"Perish the thought. Why go to the theater when you can lie down with hogs and contemplate mud? Why bother with salons and cafes, when you can commune with cows? Absolutely, Georges, I see it all now."

Gabrielle was setting out a light picnic on the tray she balanced between herself and Lucile, who held the baby. In low tones, they were discussing pregnancy. Lucile thought she might be expecting. She came to Gabrielle rather than her mother for advice.

"Camille, you don't know true relaxation and pleasure. I'm going to teach you how to enjoy the country. You don't have enough respect for pigs. Some of my scars are wounds from battles with pigs."

"Oh, now we're to be wrestling pigs. Something to look forward to."

Georges felt his heart expanding as the filthy air of Paris gave way to the sunshine of July in the fields. "We're going to organize the pigs into political clubs. They can't be more backward than the Jacobins."

FORTY

Pauline

❧

(July 17, 1791)

PAULINE was trying to round up her women to go to the Champ de Mars. She had taken a whole group over to the *Iron Mouth* offices earlier, the mothers who couldn't get away, the shopkeepers who couldn't afford to close their shops or who were working in someone else's, Babette who could not escape the tavern. Everybody could fit in a short trot to the newspaper office and a quick scrawl on the petition. But she wanted to make a good showing at the protest meeting too. It was a matter of pride, that they were the most revolutionary neighborhood, the most patriotic, always turning out, like Faubourg Saint Antoine and Faubourg Saint Marcel, when it was time for a show of force.

It was hot today. Aimée and Victoire walked on either side of her. They marched along with another thirty women beside the river, for the breeze. Some men bathing in the Seine shouted obscene invitations. The women shouted back equally obscene suggestions about what the men could do to themselves and each other. The women marched on: that is, they proceeded smartly together, attempting to look military so that no one would think they were out for a stroll, so that everyone would know they were on revolutionary business.

Other groups, some marching under banners from their section or their club, were heading in the same direction. Pauline felt festive. It was a good day for a demonstration under the fierce lion sun of July. Vendors of lemonade and ices peddled their wares along the embankment. Aimée and Pauline treated themselves to an orange ice. "They say that the Incorruptible loves oranges," Pauline said.

"You're crazy about him," Aimée said.

"I admire him! That's all. He's for us."

"You're crazy about him."

"Well, if I am, what harm is it? All I ever said to him was hello once at the Assembly when I was going up to the gallery."

"I bet you blushed."

"Did not. I don't blush."

"You're blushing right now!"

"Aimée, sometimes I hate you!" Pauline walked very quickly until she pulled away. Aimée was insufferable when she got into her older-woman, always-knows-better routine. As if being one year older and married to a useless numbskull made her an expert on love.

She did adore Robespierre. He was like a cat, lean and elegant, always clean and precise in his movements, never loud or bumptious or overweening. There was nothing gross or piggish about him. Even his eyes were a cat's eyes, green and mysterious-looking. Mostly she adored him because she knew he was fighting for people like her. He spoke in very long sentences sometimes that made her feel lost, but at the end it all made perfect sense.

At the last fair of Sainte Geneviève, she had bought a little bust of him that she kept on the shelf beside her bed. Henri was never coming back. She no longer missed him. She was used to living alone. She scarcely knew another woman who lived alone, free and at ease. She need take care of no one but herself. She ran her own business, she kept her own books. She lived and ate as she pleased. The sex she remembered with Henri was mostly his heavy urgent body driving into her. She supposed women got married because they wanted children, but she didn't desire a baby yet. If Henri had not been conscripted, they would long ago have married. She did not like to think of him dead or even married, but she also did not want him to come for her.

She vastly preferred adoring Robespierre from the galleries and going home to her little room. She did not imagine the Incorruptible helping her make chocolate or climbing into her bed. He was a focus for her adoration, worthy of all she could offer up to the little icon of his bust or pour into applause from the gallery when he spoke in the Assembly and the monarchists scorned him. But she did not like to be teased about her feelings.

The group closed up as they approached the Champ de Mars and the crowds around them thickened. It was not a huge crowd, as it had been at the celebration of July fourteenth, but large enough. A woman told them that two peeping toms had been caught under the altar of the nation, looking up women's skirts. Only prostitutes wore underwear, so they must have seen quite a bit. The crowd had been furious, hauling them off and lynching them. Pauline could see their bodies swinging from lampposts along the edge of the field.

The altar to the nation was still set up in the middle of the old drill ground, just as it had been for July fourteenth last year and for the July fourteenth celebration three days ago. The crowds were forming a long queue to sign the petition at the altar. Pauline got her group into line. She was still angry with Aimée and hung back, preferring to walk beside Victoire. They chatted about neighbors as the line edged along. Victoire had a fresh bruise on her cheek, but Pauline pretended not to notice.

They had been in line for about an hour and some when they heard shouting. Pauline, who had mounted to the first turn of the ramp that led up to the altar, could see the National Guard arriving with horses and cannon and many, many men in uniform carrying guns. On the edge of the crowd, a lot of jostling and shoving was going on. "That's Lafayette on the horse," she said to the women. "I bet he's here to try to keep us from signing the petition."

"Not today he won't," Aimée shouted from the turn above. "I haven't stood for two hours just to go home again. If he doesn't like the petition, he doesn't have to sign it."

The shoving was getting worse. Everyone was yelling. The Guards were telling people to disperse and the people were refusing. It was a pushing and screaming match. Then the Guards fired in the air. Nobody was impressed. After all, they weren't about to shoot the people. Not one person climbed down from the line snaking around the altar. Lafayette could not arrest all of them, and they were unarmed. He could fume all day, but the only people leaving were those who'd already signed. Just below on the next turn were a lady and gentleman, from their ages maybe a father and daughter. She didn't see them giving up.

Pauline and the women around her turned contemptuously from the Guards, who had pushed the crowd back almost to the bottom of the altar. They were simply ignoring the Guards, continuing to hold their place in line, when more shots rang out. Pauline swung around. Just above, a young man screamed and fell, clapping his hand to his shoulder. The Guards were firing into the crowd, firing and firing.

"The Guards are shooting," the lady below cried. "Nicolas, get down!" In her fancy white lawn dress she threw herself down off the altar, dragging the gentleman with her. They both went tumbling.

Pauline threw herself down where she stood. She heard a woman shriek very close, an awful desperate sound. She turned, to see who had cried out. Aimée was lying on her back with her head twisted in a funny way, way to the side.

Pauline crawled upwards to her, reaching out. "Aimée! Are you hurt?"

Aimée did not answer. Pauline knelt beside her. There was a hole in Aimée's head. A large ragged hole. Blood was still running out, slowly now, ever more slowly. She could see brains too. Aimée was dead. She could not be. She could not be dead in an instant! It was like her father, except right in front of her. Alive one moment and a minute later, no more. She rose in rage and screamed at the soldiers, "Pig bastards, you killed an unarmed woman! You sons of shit!"

A woman pulled her down with surprising strength, thrust her off the altar as more shots rang out. They both fell into the crowd panicking below. Pauline was bruised. She took an elbow in her midsection. Victoire screamed, above where Pauline had been standing. Pauline yelled, "Get down off the altar! Get down! They're killing us. You make perfect targets."

Victoire threw herself down, her arm bleeding. Pauline took a quick look, tearing the jacket back. "It's shallow. Get out of here fast."

The woman who had saved her now tugged on her. "Come on! They'll kill us all if we don't run for it. This way!"

"Women!" Pauline shouted, trying to fight loose. "Follow me! We have to get out of here!"

The Guards were still shooting into the crowd. Pauline could not pull free so she began to run with the woman. Together, followed by the neighborhood women who had managed to save themselves, they ran at dead heat through the crowd, jumping bodies, over the wounded and the dying and the dead while still the Guard fired. She saw a little boy with his arm running blood, his father dead on the ground before him. She saw an old woman shot in the belly, moaning as dark blood bubbled from her mouth. A dog was barking hysterically while a wife tried to bind up her husband's thigh wound with her torn skirt. Everywhere those who could flee were running for their lives. The shots rang out again and again and she saw a horse rear. A woman was sitting on the ground holding her baby, who looked as if he had been crushed, keening. They could hear her wailing behind them. Then a shot ended it.

Finally they were off the killing field and into the streets. Pauline had a stitch in her side. She should not have let Aimée get above her on the altar. It was her fault. They should have been together. She should have been there to save Aimée. She stared at the woman who had saved her. She was much taller than Pauline. She had dark hair, a vivid highly colored complexion, a voluptuous figure and long, long legs. She could run like a colt, and she had dragged Pauline halfway across the Champ de Mars by brute strength. "Who are you?"

"Claire Lacombe. I've seen you at the Cordeliers Club. You're Pauline Léon. You lead the women's section."

"I'm just a neighborhood busybody." Pauline found tears blinding her and scrubbed them back with her hand. "She was my friend, the first woman who was shot. Aimée. And I was angry at her."

"Why?"

"She was teasing me."

"Pauline, I lose my temper all the time. I'm sure she didn't think anything of it."

Pauline shook her head. "I was angry at her and now she's dead."

"You didn't kill her. Lafayette and his fucking Guards did."

"We should have weapons too. We should be able to fight back."

"I can shoot," Claire said. "A guy in Bordeaux taught me. If we had muskets or pistols, I could teach the women how to use them."

"I know a lot of women who'd want to learn. If we can get weapons."

"We'd better stay in the back streets and avoid the river." Claire gestured to the right. Where the street opened onto the quai, Guardsmen were pursuing groups of fleeing petitioners. More gunshots, more shrieks.

"It's a crackdown. The right is trying to stop the Revolution." Pauline tried to sound tough and knowing, but she could not stop crying. Her eyes would not obey her. "I have to go back and find Aimée's body."

"That's a bad idea," Claire said. "They're arresting everybody they can catch. The bodies will be laid out at the morgue tonight."

They came upon a man carrying a wounded child. He was weeping. The child was unconscious, his head hanging. "Citizen," Pauline said. "We won't forget today. We'll get ours back at the bastards."

"I want to see Lafayette's head on a pike," the man said. "My son is dying. I won't forget. I'll never forget!"

They walked on. "Thank you for pulling me out of the line of fire."

"You were an obvious target, up on the altar." Claire gave Pauline's shoulder a squeeze. "You smell better than any woman in Paris. You smell like a bonbon."

"I make chocolate. If I cleaned sewers, I'd smell like shit." Pauline found her kerchief and blew her nose. She imagined Aimée lying in the mud like something discarded, as if no one cared.

"I'm an actress. I just opened in a new play, the *Patriotic Family*. You know Collot d'Herbois? He's a dark handsome guy who goes to the Cordeliers and speaks in a sonorous voice like God just gave him the word? It's his play. I used to act in his company in the provinces."

Pauline was surprised how normal Claire seemed, considering she was an actress. With her body, every man on the street looked at her as they passed, looked again, kept looking. Sometimes men followed them, but Claire ignored them, or if they were too persistent, cursed them out. She could take care of herself. Pauline had an idea. She wanted somebody to share the leadership. Someone to help decide things, so she wouldn't make mistakes that would kill more women. Someone who would help her keep every remaining woman alive. "Even if we can't start arming," Pauline said slowly, "I think we should meet tomorrow to discuss what happened. And raise money for Aimée's kids."

"Afternoons are best for me. Before I have to go to the theater. In the meantime, we should try to find out what's going on," Claire said.

She sounded clear, just like her name. Maybe they could work together. At the next block they parted to go their different ways. Now she must find Aimée's husband and tell him and then her mother. Guilt sat in her chest like a crow on a nest. She had asked Aimée to come, she had insisted. All she had thought of was how important it was to make a good showing for the neighborhood, for the Revolution. She had not considered Aimée's safety or her children. Now who would love them and care for them? It was her fault, because she was the leader and she was supposed to lead her women safely. She was supposed to know what was happening and to make good plans. Including retreat, obviously. What should she have done? She was not sure, but she knew she had failed Aimée. Victoire was slightly wounded, Pauline was only bruised and everybody else had got out safely. But her friend Aimée, whom she had known since they were little and used to sit giggling on the stoop sharing a straw doll, Aimée was dead.

FORTY-ONE

Max

❦

(July 18, 1791)

MAX was furious at the Cordeliers for going ahead with their petition after the Jacobins withdrew theirs. They should have known that Lafayette was spoiling for an excuse to declare martial law and crack down. It was clear that the right was as much their enemy as the old regime ever had been, and even more dangerous: the old regime had toppled with few casualties, rotten from within. These pretend-revolutionaries had support, had arms, had organization, had the Guard, were in firm control of Paris.

Rumors were flying everywhere. A clerk from City Hall came to see him early in the morning. "Citizen, you're in danger. I saw the warrant for your arrest myself. They're going to shut you up in prison."

"Citizen, I thank you. I can see no advantage to being taken."

The right had a network of spies; he had only the good will of strangers to rely upon. He packed a bag rapidly. He could not go to the Assembly. They would expect him there. Did he dare go to the Jacobin Club? He was carrying his bag over his shoulder and walking slowly, wondering if he should head for the stagecoach north and flee to Charlotte and Augustin.

A burly man hailed him. "Citizen Robespierre, we hear there's a warrant out for you." He was dressed in trousers, sawdust powdering his short jacket.

"Who are you and where did you hear that?"

"I'm Duplay, a carpenter. I heard it at the Jacobin Club when I stopped by an hour ago. Citizen, do you have friends who can safely shelter you? Because if you don't, you come home with me. The wife and me will make you comfortable. We'll hide you till the traitors get tired of looking."

Once again a stranger had intervened. Max believed in God, perhaps as history, a Supreme Being who held his destiny in eternal hands. Here was a man of the people offering him safety. "Citizen, I accept your hospitality with deep thanks. Perhaps I won't have to be a burden to you long."

"You're no burden. My wife will be overjoyed. I have three daughters, all good patriotic girls. I live right near the Jacobins, so once this matter is cleared up, you'll be much closer to the Club and the Assembly than you are now. You'll see how much at home we can make you."

They walked quickly now, Duplay insisting on toting Max's bag. The carpenter lived quite near the Club on the Rue Saint Honoré, in a wooden house with a courtyard where workers were making beds and cupboards and repairing furniture. It was a larger house than Robespierre had expected, with a narrow two-story section in the middle and two wings that created the yard. Mme Duplay met them at the door with exclamations of astonishment. "I'll make a room ready for you at once. In the meantime, I bet you didn't have a chance to eat."

"Just some coffee with milk, if you can, and perhaps a little fruit."

"Peaches and apricots, it's my pleasure."

He thanked Madame and sat at the dining room table. It was a cozy room, all the furniture probably made by Duplay, nicely turned sturdy pieces with much less decoration than was fashionable. There was a watercolor of himself and one of those embarrassing busts they sold in the streets at popular festivals. It was a pleasant light airy room, with a breeze from windows on both sides. There were also oil paintings he recognized as influenced by David, heroic scenes of Roman tableaux, the taking of the Bastille, a portrait of Monsieur and Madame Duplay. The tablecloth was green damask with posies in a bowl.

"This is Vivienne, my youngest. She helps me with the house. She's going to move a few things around to make ready for you."

"You shouldn't go to any trouble. I need little."

"It's no trouble," Vivienne said. She was a plain no-nonsense girl wearing an apron damp from the kitchen. She smelled like soup. She smiled shyly and ran off. While he was eating, the middle daughter Elisabeth came in. She was vibrant, pretty, told him she went to the Jacobin Club regularly. He did not recognize her, but then he seldom looked at the galleries where the women sat, and he was nearsighted in any case.

"I see you looking at the portraits. Eléanore, our oldest, did that. She's a real painter. She's studying with Regnault. Have you heard of him?" Mme Duplay seemed to want his approval for her daughter's apprenticeship.

"I have. She has a worthy master."

Madame beamed. She was a woman in her late forties, still handsome, probably five years younger than her husband. She had strong hands. All of them had the hands of artisans who did real work. It was time for him to do something useful also. In case he might soon be back in public, he set to work on a speech about education and how important it was to make it available to everyone. Obviously in this house, they believed in educating daughters.

Around noon, Vivienne came in. "The room is prepared for you, Monsieur, I mean Citizen."

If he was going to live here, he should put them more at ease. They were tiptoeing around him as if he might break at a loud noise. "You must all call me Max. We can't have so much formality."

Vivienne said, "Here's Papa for his dinner."

Just behind him came the last daughter. She saw him at once, and her dark eyes grew very wide. He supposed that she would not be considered as pretty as Elisabeth, yet she carried herself with dignity and an authority that was surprising in a young woman. She could be no more than twenty-four or twenty-five. "Citizen," she said in a low gentle voice. "It is an honor to see you here. All Paris is turned upside down. I hope we have the pleasure of giving you sanctuary while this madness endures."

"What have you heard?" he asked her.

Madame said hastily, "This is Eléanore. You may have seen her at the Jacobins too. She's also a member of the Tricolor Brushes, who make paintings and engravings of patriotic scenes for the education of the people."

"I've been admiring your work."

He could see she had trouble not curtseying. She kept her eyes on him as she sat at the table, some distance away. He motioned her closer, and slowly, she obeyed. "Again, what have you heard?"

"There are warrants out for many patriotic leaders. Etta Palm d'Aelders has been put in prison for saying that women should have rights. The Social Circle has been forbidden to have public meetings. The *Iron Mouth* has been shut down. Marat is in danger again and like yourself, has had to seek shelter with friends. Danton and Desmoulins have disappeared, arrested or in hiding. Half the newspapers of Paris have been suppressed. Bailly has declared martial law." She spoke quickly but firmly, reporting without emotion or rhetoric. Clearly she could be relied on as an observer. She could be useful to him while he was in hiding. He could have her keep an eye on the Jacobin Club until he could return.

"Everything has happened in a matter of hours. Clearly, they were waiting and prepared for this opportunity to close us all down," he said.

"You should clear my room for Citizen Robespierre," Eléanore said.

Vivienne piped up. "I already cleared Elisabeth's, and moved her in with me."

"You need room for your paintings, child," Madame said.

"I need very little," he said, as before. He smiled at Vivienne. He did not bother smiling at Eléanore, for he felt it was not necessary.

The meal was more than he desired, but they allowed him to pick and choose. It was a good family atmosphere here, almost the ideal family he had fantasized since childhood. Then he thought it would be with his own sisters and brother. But in truth these people were far more agreeable and politically savvy than his sister. Augustin he knew little about, for it had been years since they spent time together.

When he rose, Eléanore jumped up as if on command and followed him upstairs. "I'll help you unpack," she said.

"Will your mother mind?"

"Oh, no. We all want to make your stay pleasant." She did not blush, she did not flirt. She unpacked his clothes efficiently, handling each item with a cool reverence. When he was ready to work, he dismissed her, and she went without a backward glance.

He had the strangest feeling with her, from the first moment, almost as if he remembered her. It was as if he had recovered a lost inheritance, something that belonged to him that had been estranged or forgotten. After supper, he summoned her and gave her instructions for the Jacobin Club. He told her to report to him at once when she returned, no matter at what hour. She nodded, asked a few questions about how specific her notes were to be. Then she went off.

When she came in, the older Duplays and her sisters had retired. She came into his room without coquettishness or hesitation and began at once to report on what had been an extremely long and stormy session, full of recriminations. He questioned her closely, taking notes on her notes. He corrected the spelling of some names.

It was after midnight. She was alone with him in his room, yet no one in the house seemed to question his right or her duty. She was utterly matter-of-fact in her deportment. She did not touch him, she did not lean forward or brush against him or give him melting looks. He looked at her openly, admiring her and studying her. On one level, there was no hint of sex or anything muddy or murky. On a deeper level, he understood that she was utterly his. She had already given herself over to him absolutely, although they scarcely knew each other.

Lafayette and Bailly and their gang of traitors had given him quite by accident what he had never expected to enjoy. After less than twenty-four hours he knew what he had found. He now had a family, in all ways superior to his own. He had a living situation where he could work without a thought for expense, for they had made clear they would accept nothing from him except his presence, where he would be cared for and protected and even coddled. And he had been given the only woman he had ever met with whom he could have some kind of relationship, what kind he did not know: only that whatever he wanted from Eléanore, she would give him without blinking, without hesitation, without terms. Whether he ever touched her, whether he ever spoke one word of courtship or affection or not, she was his.

FORTY-TWO

Nicolas

❦

(Late July 1791)

NO doubt his houseguest, Tom Paine, had influenced his thinking. Nicolas liked and respected Tom, who had the benefit of having been involved in the American revolution, giving him in the eyes of Nicolas an authority far beyond his own. They started from similar premises and arrived at similar conclusions, in spite of differences of birth and class. Nicolas was becoming an out-and-out republican at a time when the conservative faction—Lafayette, Bailly, the Lameths—were determined to hold on to the King. Some parties were intriguing for Orléans. Other faint-hearted souls would take any nincompoop, so long as the blood was blue and he could look regal in robes.

Nicolas was driven to write a proposal for a new king. The Assembly should order a large golden marionette which the properly elected government could manipulate as appropriate. The marionette would put its signature to all laws passed by the legislature, unlike Monsieur Veto, the present king. It would preside over assemblies, religious occasions, parades, receptions, and be able to raise its arm to receive the salute of troops in review. It would be present when required and otherwise stored in a closet. This, he proposed, would be the perfect king for a constitutional monarchy, and a great economy besides. He read the piece aloud to Sophie, who, as usual, had concrete suggestions for making it sharper. Then he gave it to the press at Social Circle headquarters to be published. They still were forbidden to hold public meetings, but they had resumed as a publishing house.

The government was hunting what they considered agitators. He had not been bothered. It was probably a holdover from his days as a marquis, but while his former colleagues from the Committee of Thirty denounced him as a turncoat and sometimes snubbed him, he was not only noble but the last of the Encyclopedists. Therefore they could not bring themselves, he surmised, to throw him in prison or rough him up. They called him ineffective and sneered.

They laughed at him when he proposed freedom for Blacks, and with Brissot, worked in the Friends of the Blacks club. They had told him black people were docile, childlike, mere domestic animals, that he was a sentimental idealist to imagine that Blacks were interested in freedom. Well, the sheep had turned to wolves. On the island of Saint Domingue in the Caribbean, the countryside was burning. The slaves were in armed revolt. The freedom that could have been peaceably granted a few months before would now be taken after bloody massacres and savage reprisals. But once a people had a notion of freedom, it was only a matter of time and persistence—and endless brutality and pain and death—before they got it.

Sophie urged him, "Go to see Bailly. See Lafayette. It's a disgrace that Etta Palm is in prison, an absolute disgrace. What danger to the State is Etta? Does her call for abolishing wife beating threaten order? She's holding up reasonably well, but her imprisonment is without reason!" Sophie was in high-colored indignation, angry and helpless.

"I doubt if they'll listen to me. But I'll try. I'll see Lafayette first. At least he used to be my friend. Bailly and I have detested each other for a decade."

Lafayette received him at his grand town house in Saint Germain de Près, where a great many fine houses were going up, in a parlor adorned with portraits of himself, usually in military garb on a white horse. The walls were crowded with mementos of his glorious service in the American cause and objects recalling his dear friend and almost-father, George Washington.

"Why are you so interested in that harridan?" Lafayette asked him, standing at the windows as if looking out. He was a tall man, just as tall as Nicolas and leaner. His hair was still reddish. After all, he was considerably younger. His manner was as imperial as ever.

"Etta is a friend and colleague of mine. I respect her ideas. She is hardly a street-corner orator stirring up mobs to storm palaces."

"She's been stirring the women up. That's trouble enough."

"She may cause domestic turmoil, but surely we can leave that to individual husbands and fathers. It's no crime to discuss the problems that primogeniture causes."

"It is a crime, it is seditious, to attack the Assembly the way she has, denouncing our policies." Lafayette finally turned his profile from the window. Nicolas could see his anger. "This unbridled anarchy must stop."

"It's a long way from citizens running through the streets with pikes to Etta delivering speeches on women's rights and the improvement of the family. What are you afraid of? Not that your wife will finally object to something." Nicolas knew, as everyone did, that Lafayette's arranged and very useful marriage was one of love on only one side.

Now Lafayette turned fully around to glare. "Some say you brought the Palm woman a bed. A strange present unless you're her lover."

"I have the extreme peculiarity of being interested only in my wife. I bought Etta a bed because the one she was furnished with in prison was not fit for the mice that infested it. Sophie and Etta are friends and share many ideas. Are you planning to toss Sophie into prison?"

"We will put however many people in prison we need to, to preserve order. . . . Bailly is resigning as Mayor this summer, you know."

"I'd heard," Nicolas said guardedly. "Is the job of running Paris getting on his nerves?"

"He's tired of the constant struggle to do the simplest thing, without your confrères at the *Iron Mouth* clawing at him, or that thug Danton inciting to riot, or Pétion from the Jacobins impugning his patriotism. Not to mention Marat calling for all of us to be strung up like common pickpockets. The man incites to murder daily. He speaks of eating our livers."

"So there'll be an election," Nicolas said blandly, smiling.

"Some people think I should run."

Nicolas opened his eyes wide. "How intriguing. Do they say why?"

Lafayette drew himself up. Nicolas would not have imagined he could stand even straighter, but he did. "Obviously, they think I would govern Paris wisely. That I would be able to take authority and exercise it."

"Exercising a bit too much authority over people has gotten other men in trouble," Nicolas said, "my dear Marquis." He intentionally used the old and now obsolete title. "I'm surprised you'd consider giving up your National Guards. They're your creation." There was a short spiky silence. Nicolas waited with his head cocked, an expression of benign interest on his face.

"Are you referring to the incident in the Champ de Mars?"

"Actually I wasn't. But since you mention it, don't you think that might have made you a little less popular in Paris than you have been? Sophie and I were there, by the way. It was not a pretty spectacle."

"Respectable people want order, not chaos. You should avoid unlawful public gatherings where violence easily erupts. Laws must apply to everyone. My men showed great restraint in the face of disorder."

"It is said a hundred people were shot down. I could not loiter to count them, being under fire myself."

"We counted no more than a few dozen bodies afterwards. And the men are loyal to me, yes. That is neither here nor there. I want to know if I can count on your support."

"Surely it's a little premature to think seriously about who should be Mayor, when Bailly is still in office and I have no idea who may run. But I'll certainly keep you in mind. I'd have more time to contemplate the coming election if carrying fresh food to Etta and trying to keep her spirits up in prison was not taking such a large portion of my time and energy."

"I see," Lafayette murmured. "Not that it's my decision. Have you talked to Bailly?"

"He wouldn't give me the time if he could avoid it. But if I must, I'll entreat him. I've been to the Conciergerie and to the Châtelet. I have sat in some very dingy and dreary waiting rooms for Etta, and I dare say, I'll cool my heels in a few more. Friendship, Gilbert, we must put ourselves out for our friends, don't you think?"

"That shrew is no friend of mine. I can't imagine what you can find to talk about with her. But then you have some peculiar friends these days. That British agitator you've taken in. Thrown out of England for sedition. Now causing trouble here."

Nicolas decided not to defend Tom Paine. He was being baited to distract him. There was a general tendency among his former colleagues from the Committee of Thirty to assume he had become simple, because he believed in outlandish things like rights for Blacks and women.

Lafayette suddenly sank into his favorite armchair, rather like a gilded throne. Finally he motioned Nicolas to a seat also. "We've got to get things under control, surely you can see that. The country was going to pieces, but we've reorganized. We'll have the new constitution in place soon. We have to pull together, those of us who have some perspective on the problems of the nation, to bring order and harmony again."

"A new constitution with a monarch who's already tried to get away once. What will you do when he tries again?"

"He'll behave himself," Lafayette said. He frowned slightly, his sky blue eyes opaque. "I don't understand why Louis and Marie-Antoinette can't perceive me as their protector. I am protecting them. But they persist in viewing me as a traitor to our class."

"Very few people think of you as that any more," Nicolas said mildly. He rose. "Please do something about Etta. She doesn't belong in prison."

"I'll look into it," Lafayette said noncommittally. "Are you going to support me?"

"I told you, it's premature to say," Nicolas answered softly. "You must ask me again as the election nears."

Lafayette remained seated, folding his arms. "You ask a great deal, but you do not give much."

"I observe how people act, as well as how they talk. I offer my honest opinion, Gilbert. Formerly, you thought that a sign of respect."

FORTY-THREE
Claire

❧

(September 1791)

CLAIRE read Olympe de Gouges' *Declaration of the Rights of Women and Citizens* with Pauline and Hélène as they shared supper in the tavern. All around them, families were eating, men were arguing over the news, kids were playing dominoes. It was dim but Pauline had brought a candle. They read aloud to each other and debated every page. Pauline was upset that the pamphlet was dedicated to Marie-Antoinette. "How can she care for the Austrian bitch, who doesn't give one tiny damn about us except to grind us under?"

Hélène said tentatively, "I've heard some women say that we all have the same problems, that all women are less than citizens—ladies or peasants."

"We don't have the same problems," Pauline said. "My main problem is getting enough to eat. Surviving." She patted her flat stomach.

"Anyhow," Claire said, wanting to move them on, "maybe the printer put it on. They say she's illiterate and has to dictate everything." Claire continued reading, "All women are born free and equal to men in their rights. The aim of political association is the preservation of the natural and inalienable rights of men and women. The nation is a union of women and men. Law is an expression of the general will. All female and male citizens have the right to participate personally, or through representatives, in its formation."

Pauline was mollified. "Well, she makes sense once she gets moving."

They had to stop for a while because a fight broke out and they could not hear. It was just guys brawling over one calling the other a pig's shithole. The women kept out of the way, snuffing the candle till the fight was over. None of them took fistfights seriously. Ordinary people were likely to get mad and try to punch each other, men or women alike, but it meant little. It was just blowing off tension.

Claire was feeling generous. She liked living with Hélène. They shared food, clothing, the bed, their ideas, the past and desired future. She had not been so close to anyone since she had left her grandmother's side. Further, the play she was acting in for Collot had been challenging. But the run was ending.

She liked Pauline, her best friend after Hélène. They worked well together. Hélène was not as political, but went along. She had a good heart. It just never would occur to her to do more than feel a lack, to get angry, then wait for some man to do something. Hélène was working now, in another pantomime, but hadn't moved out. They were content as they were.

Claire admired Pauline, but Pauline did not need Claire the way Hélène did. There was a softness in Hélène that Claire did not admire but depended upon. Claire saw Pauline as the complete tough Parisian sans-culotte woman. Pauline knew how to get anything cheap. She always had connections. Everybody in her section knew her. Her errands around the neighborhood were a procession. Women brought their problems to her. They stopped her to tell her what was going on that shouldn't be happening. They asked for advice. They asked her what to do about issues from prisons to schooling.

Pauline would never be considered beautiful, for her nose was too sharp, her teeth gapped. But she had a good figure and she was strong for her size. She could lift a crate by herself. She was cute, pert. She had an infectious laugh and a fine clear speaking voice. She could talk quietly enough, her voice caressing. Her voice could also carry over a crowd. Claire had heard her in the women's meetings and even in the Cordeliers. Women were not supposed to be members, but they acted as if they were, speaking out when they had something to say. Pauline was regarded as a strong local leader who could be depended upon to bring out the women. Yes, Pauline was vital, a spark. But Claire doubted they would ever giggle together half the night telling secrets from their childhoods, that they would admit they were blue and hold each other.

When Claire heard that Olympe de Gouges was going to have a play put on in a private theater, she was determined to audition. She was no longer having trouble getting jobs. Her reputation wasn't exactly pristine. She had not had a role in Paris in which she remained fully clothed. She was becoming known as a rabid revolutionary. With some people that helped; others immediately labeled her a whore. She said to Hélène, "Have you ever noticed how when the right is putting down women on the left, they call them whores? To work for people without money means you're a whore, while to fight for people with money or sit on your bum and do nothing is virtuous."

Hélène shook her head. "Whenever men insult any woman, whether she's a mother superior or a midwife or a peasant mother of ten, they call her a whore. So don't get fancy about it. I've heard you refer to Marie-Antoinette that way fifty times."

"You're right," Claire said slowly, embarrassed. "We have to hate with intelligence and love with intelligence."

Hélène laughed bitterly. "Is that conceivable? Love is the opposite of intelligence."

"Is it? I love you. I use my brain and see you clearly and I use my heart and care for you."

"Oh . . ." Hélène dismissed that with a wave of her hand. "Women are different. Just being friends, that can be with open eyes."

"Then maybe it's a better sort of love."

"Probably," Hélène said without conviction. "What shall we do for dinner?"

Claire found out where Olympe was casting. The theater was in the mansion of a marquis in exile, now owned by a wholesaler and his wife, who was attempting to make a reputation as patroness of the arts. Olympe was a tall woman, almost as tall as Claire but much older. Her hair was her own, brown streaked with grey and shoved up in a chignon and topped with a gauze headdress supposed to cover her hair, but constantly slipping. She wore a bedraggled white muslin chemise dress that had seen better days, a while ago. So had her cashmere mantilla. But her voice was strong. "Say it as if you mean it," she ordered the actor on stage. "I don't care whether you do or not. Just sound as if you have a couple of convictions rattling around in your skull."

Claire had heard that Olympe was illiterate and had to dictate her plays. Yet she was putting on and taking off a pair of Ben Franklin spectacles, obviously following the script in her lap. One more rumor turned out to be trash. Olympe had probably been a beauty, but she did not have the manners of a grand coquette. She was loud, straightforward, direct as a bludgeon. Claire had also heard that Olympe was a butcher's daughter from Montaubon. That she did believe. Olympe was no aristocrat, with her loud direct manner. Watching her, Claire felt that she did not even think how she looked most of the time, she was not pinned by the regard of the men around her. She aimed to dominate the moment and the project: not a feminine program of behavior. Olympe would be interesting to work for, interesting to observe.

Olympe was not the only woman playwright, just the predominant woman radical playwright. The play was *The Necessity of Divorce*, about unhappy marriages. Claire desperately wanted the part. These were not first-rate actors or actresses coming out for Olympe, but most of them were from legitimate theater. They were used to the kind of declaiming this play would require—something Claire had only done in the early days. When Olympe gave them direction, some of them argued with her, unwilling to take orders or even advice from a woman—even a woman who had written and planned to direct the play for which they were auditioning.

When Claire's turn came, she went up, took her position and said as preamble her experience. An actress who had boasted she had been in the Comédie-Française for three years, tittered audibly. "Pantomimes!"

Olympe grimaced. "This isn't a pantomime, young lady. This requires acting. I would prefer classical training, frankly."

"I'd like to try. It would be a great honor to work for the author of the *Declaration of the Rights of Women and Citizens*. My friends and I have read it through countless times." That was the truth, but it was also flattery; she doubted anyone else there knew what key to press.

When Olympe smiled, her face looked years younger. The marks of penury and strain eased. "Let me hear you then, Citizeness. Can you read the part?"

"Yes, Madame, I can." She used the more honorific title intentionally, and Olympe did not correct her. Claire was reading Herminie, the selfless heroine. High declamation was not her forte, but she had heard enough of it to have a good idea how she should deliver her speeches. She had the carriage for a queen, as she had often been told, and she moved about the stage as she read the script. Okay, she had no classical training, she was hardly an actress from the Comédie-Française like that bitch, but she could carry it off.

When she finished, Olympe was frowning. There was a silence in the theater, that smelled of tallow and sweat and dust. Olympe nodded then, abruptly. "The auditions for the part of Herminie are closed. This one—Citizeness Lacombe—will do. I will now be auditioning for Constance."

Claire came bubbling home to tell Hélène, who was not as pleased as Claire had expected. "But everybody says she's illiterate and a butcher's daughter and a scandal."

"I'm the daughter of a laundress and a bricklayer. You're the daughter of people who made and sold candles. I saw her read. And speaking for myself, do you think I'm not a scandal?"

"But will you really get paid?"

"She has backing. She has a theater. I like the idea of a woman writing and directing a play. I bet I get to keep my clothes on in this one."

FORTY-FOUR

Manon

(Summer–Fall 1791)

MANON and Jean had gone to the Champ de Mars to sign the petition against the King. To avoid standing in the hot sun for hours, they arrived on the late side. The line was still snaking around the altar to the nation and in wide lazy loops across the training field. Manon was walking on Jean's arm looking for the end of the line when Lafayette and his men arrived. She assumed they had come to keep order, but Jean pulled her out of the throng. She could not believe what she was seeing, troops shooting into the unarmed crowd, people falling. She started forward to try to stop the Guards, but Jean held her forcibly and hastened her away.

She was grateful for his cool head, but she could not stop sobbing afterward. She could not sleep. Weeks passed before she was free of it, the image of an old woman struck in the belly, sitting with her legs spread and blood seeping through her fingers, a boy lying dead across his dead father. They appeared before her as she was brushing her hair, as she was shopping for a new fichu, as she was writing to a friend.

One pleasure Manon revisited was to write regularly to Sophie Carnet. When she had married, Jean insisted she break off her friendship with Sophie. He had separated Manon from her closest women friends, and she never stopped missing that warmth. Finally in Paris, he lifted his ban. At once Manon got back in touch. Sophie had married a very old man and worn herself out nursing him. Now she suffered from weak lungs. With her maid Fleury, Manon had a daily intimacy, a sharing of the life of the family and the household. But they were not equal. Sophie was not her intellectual equal, but they had known each other through adolescence and early womanhood. Manon did not tend to find the company of other women interesting, but her dear old friend was an exception. She had missed her desperately. There was no one else to whom she could speak with any degree of frankness about her marriage and her life.

She wrote Sophie how terrified the massacre had left her. She had pitied the innocents struck down, but she had also been afraid for herself. It had not occurred to her that she might die for the Revolution. It had been a matter of writing letters or articles, of discussing ideas with men in her salon, of arguing now and again. She had not thought of mortal danger until she saw the bodies, their blood turning the soil into mud. "I begin to think," she wrote, "that freedom may have a higher price than I had guessed."

Manon's salon was in full sail. The Assembly usually adjourned in late afternoon, and the Jacobin Club did not open till evening. In between, favored politicians gathered at her flat. The food was spartan—usually one course. Men were not encouraged to flirt with her. Other women were seldom present. It was a great convenience for the members of the liberal group to have a place to review the day, analyze, discuss, refute, plot. Sometimes she went along afterward to the Jacobins. She felt an immediate admiration for Robespierre and tried to attract him to her salon. Occasionally he came, but he said little and sat in a corner, observing. She wished she could draw him out as she did so many of the other men. He seemed deeply shy, a very private sort of man. She sensed in him a kindred soul, a true man of ideals who would never waver from what he believed, who would never compromise what should not be compromised. She wondered if he had not had some terrible disappointment, a lover who died tragically or proved perfidious.

"Citizen Robespierre, what do you think of the new Legislative Assembly?"

"Not much," he said. "They do little for me to consider." But he did not ask what she thought or let the conversation develop. She could not charm him as she did Brissot, Pétion, the young Buzot, Louvet. She had trouble with Condorcet also, although he was talkative enough. His wife ran a rival salon and was said to share his ridiculous ideas about women's suffrage. Condorcet came occasionally to her salon. He had a turgid overly formal approach and a tendency to go on. She had trouble taking him seriously, but he was active in the Assembly. They kept giving him posts—posts Roland could have done wonders with. She was aware he tried to avoid her dinners and simply drop in for the conversation. She supposed his much-gossiped-about wife set an elaborate aristocratic table. That was a marriage superficially like her own, with a twenty-year difference between them. The resemblance ended there. Condorcet was polite, always remembering to ask her opinion, but he showed no partiality, no sense that he recognized she was not an ordinary woman, but one with a masculine intellect.

An increasing number of liberals sought out her opinion on issues and proposed legislation. They loved to use her as a sounding board for their ideas, running speeches by her. She saw their faults all too clearly. Brissot was an incorrigible optimist, shallow, although he was personable, a good speaker, a true patriot. Buzot was young and had so far done little of note. Pétion was an overgrown child. Lanthénas was languid and lacking in drive. Her own Jean was too dry. He expected others to agree simply because the facts supported his position. He could sound smug and self-righteous. He assumed the facts spoke for themselves and despised rhetoric.

It was disillusioning to see how many human faults these patriots had. Instead of rising to the great occasion of history before them, standing tall in the pursuit of their ideals, they fiddled around, they temporized, they womanized, they lined their pockets, they worried about their own personal safety, they longed to be popular with the masses or the well-to-do. They were all currying favor with someone. All except Robespierre, and she could not attract his focused attention.

From Lyon, how noble all these posturing men had seemed. She had thought them figures of grandeur, like the ancient Romans she adored in Plutarch and Tacitus. Close up, they had axes to grind and resentments. They had mistresses and expensive households. They had a weakness for flattery and adulation. They did things halfway and hoped the slapped-together mess would hold. The Assembly was a great disappointment to her, not at all the great theater of ideas and republican virtue she had imagined. These were far smaller men than they should have been to stand in the sun of history and cast such long shadows. She was wasting her energies trying to set them on course.

She had forgotten how humid Parisian summer could be. In August she was ill with stomach cramps for two weeks. She had not seen Eudora in months and began to think of her daughter fondly. Jean was always wanting to go home. She had not managed to secure him a position in the government. Their friends were well known, sometimes able to be elected to office, but they had no patronage to bestow. She began to feel restive.

Jean complained. "You're not well, I feel ill, and who knows how things are going at home? No one but ourselves can be trusted to oversee the harvest and make sure the wine is correctly made and laid down. Do you want to lose the whole year's vintage? My brother writes that it should be a good one in Beaujolais, if the weather holds."

Jean persuaded the rump end of the Assembly to reduce the debt of Lyon by more than half. Suddenly he had succeeded in the mission that to her had been only an excuse to reach Paris. There was nothing to detain them.

They left Paris on September thirtieth, just in time for the harvest. In Beaujolais, this was the most beautiful season of all its beautiful seasons, a time as golden as the stones. Eudora was nine years old and seemed to have learned at least manners and deportment from the nuns of the Visitation at Ville-

Franche. Manon collected her and brought her home. Her daughter did seem more obedient. Manon resolved to love her better. She was surprised how glad she felt to be in the country. The peasants began trooping to see her, full of minor and major complaints. Within a week of arrival, she was regularly doctoring them again, making her rounds. Here she lived surrounded by steep green hills of vines instead of narrow dark streets reeking of sewage. There was everything to do—pears ripening, table grapes to be dried—and she was satisfied to immerse herself in country chores, to forget for a while the Revolution and their political friends in Paris. But not forever.

FORTY-FIVE
Georges

(Fall 1791)

GEORGES stayed in the country till fall. He had bought an estate near his old home, and now they had time to fix it up. He got to know the men who worked for him, fired one and hired a couple more. He discussed each day's work with his head man. You had to let country people know at once that you were not a lawyer from the city who had never shoveled manure or seen a grapevine pruned, that you were in for the long haul.

The house was ample enough; would do for the family they planned. The vines had been left to run wild, but in a couple of years, he would have his own wine. Pears grew on a hill along with an apple orchard. Both needed work. He and his uncle Robert attended an auction and got a few cows and two roan horses. A local man had been haying on the meadows. Now he would keep his own hay.

Gabrielle flourished. Even though she missed seeing her parents every Sunday, she was happy. She took to the country life, supervising the servants and the kitchen, raising chickens, preserving wild and cultivated fruit. She turned brown from the sun. Their son ran about in the courtyard underfoot, brown too and suddenly sure on his sturdy short legs. At fifteen months, he was already the size of most two-year-olds. His hair was bleached by the sun far lighter than either of his parents'. Gabrielle was pregnant again.

Georges almost let her talk him into staying, but he had to make a better name for himself, he had to make money. He needed a profitable office. He had been recruiting supporters for two years. Camille, who had returned to Paris, wrote him weekly of the Cordeliers, of the Jacobins, where Robespierre was remaking the Club stronger than ever. Robespierre was emerging as the number-one man there. Camille reported that their section had made Danton an elector for choosing delegates for the Legislative Assembly.

"I'm going to have to return for the meeting of the electors. I have to show my face, or people are going to forget me or start thinking I'm afraid."

Since he only expected to be in the city a fortnight, Gabrielle stayed on the farm. He took a coach and arrived in Paris just in time. The electors were meeting in City Hall. He had just finished his first speech when a man called Damien came and shoved a rumpled parchment in his face. "You're under arrest, Georges Danton!" he shouted. "When I came to your section for Marat, you tried to humiliate me. Let's see how you like some time in a cell."

"How dare you interrupt the proceedings of the electors of Paris, you little worm who kisses the bums of aristocrats. Still doing Bailly and Lafayette's dirty work for them!"

The electors were outraged that Damien came in with an old and politically motivated warrant to interrupt their deliberations. Instead of Georges being arrested, Damien was removed by the bailiffs. Georges appealed at once to the old Assembly, and Damien did the same. It was great publicity. Georges could not have hired better press. Two hours after he returned to Paris, he was the center of a controversy emphasizing his revolutionary credentials. Robespierre defended him at the Jacobins. The Assembly released Damien and left Georges alone. They would be out of office in no time, replaced by the new Legislative Assembly, and none of them could see an advantage in picking up such a hot rock.

In the wake of the King's acceptance of the Constitution, the Assembly voted a general amnesty, so Georges was free to forget the old warrants. But he had not been nominated for the Legislative Assembly. A new prosecutor for Paris was about to be elected, along with a new mayor. It was too late to run for mayor. After his country sojourn, he was not in the minds of those who usually pressed money upon him. He got a stipend from Orléans, but the court had not been slipping him money. He had expenses. The country felt distant and irrelevant. He sent for Gabrielle and his son. She was to close up the house for the winter, leave the men their instructions and come to Paris. It was time for Georges to get into office. He would run for prosecutor.

Since he had no home life for the moment, he went out every night, to the Cordeliers, to the Jacobins, to the theater, to meetings of other clubs and societies. He saw the new plays. He even went to the one most reviled and discussed, a play by an illiterate butcher's daughter. It was a perfectly workable play full of nonsense about women. What he liked about it was the heroine, a big gorgeous woman with dark cascading hair, a voice that the crowd could hear in the back row, a commanding presence and the body of a goddess.

Afterward he went backstage. She recognized him at once. "Oh, I go to the Cordeliers when I can. I'm one of those women who are always marching around shouting at the Assembly." She grinned at him.

Close up, in ordinary street clothes and with her make-up cleaned off, she was just as impressive. Beautiful skin. Flawless. Like a piece of perfect ripe fruit. Gradually the other admirers left the room. He daunted them. He could usually dominate other men. The two of them studied each other. He wondered if she was used to presents, jewels, whatever. He was not about to do that. Best to be clear from the start.

"Claire," he said, using her first name intentionally now that they were alone, "I find you irresistible. Is there any reason to resist you? Let's go have some supper and then some pleasure."

"You get right to the point."

"I'm a revolutionary, Claire. I'm no marquis to pave the way to bed with gold or diamonds. If you like me, then we'll have a good time tonight."

"I like you," she said, shaking her hair back. "I'm hungry for some supper. But aren't you a married man?"

"My wife's in the country. I won't tell you she doesn't understand me, because she does. I adore her. But I'm here on my own for a few weeks. You're the best thing I've laid eyes on since I got back to Paris."

She explained she shared lodgings. After supper in a cafe, he simply brought her back to his flat. If Camille or Lucile noticed, they would not say anything to Gabrielle. Ultimately, they were loyal to him.

She was as beautiful naked as she had been on the stage. Further, she had been well schooled. She was sensual without being jaded, accomplished without a hint of whorishness. But she did not admire him as he liked to be admired. He sensed that she was looking around carefully, watching him. She had a critical eye he disliked in a woman. "You live very well," she said at one point. He did not like to be observed. She was good at sex, but he did not think she would be good at loving. She lay under him, but he did not have the feeling of entering an open city. She was still defended.

She left early in the morning, not lingering for breakfast or expecting a present. He had been correct in his assessment. She was not an amateur whore. She was also not as much a woman of the south as he had imagined, not as languid or as generous as Gabrielle. Once again, the encounter with another woman refreshed him—although neither had gotten much sleep—but made him appreciate his wife anew. He did not imagine Gabrielle would forgive him if she ever found out, but she would not; he knew his occasional forays did nothing but confirm the strength of his marriage.

He had used the opportunity to question Claire about the politics of the theater. He did not think he would bed her again, but he might consult her as a good source on neighborhood women and theatrical folk. That critical intelligence he disliked in an intimate encounter was useful when he was gathering political information. Claire Lacombe seemed a reliable source.

Most days and evenings were spent politicking. He was running for prosecutor in a full field of candidates. His primary opponent was a playwright also active in the Cordeliers, Collot d'Herbois. He had asked Claire and she knew him well. Perhaps he had been her lover. Collot was a fine speaker, although not as forceful as Georges. He was a handsome actor. He had revolutionary credentials from the Cordeliers Club and from his political plays, written with a popular touch. Georges learned that Claire had been in several. She seemed highly regarded. He hoped he hadn't gotten into anything sticky. He had not realized how integrated into local politics she was.

The next time he saw her, at the Cordeliers, Gabrielle was back in town and he felt rooted again. He was nervous, avoiding eye contact. She was with a group of the sans-culottes women who were always marching around screaming their heads off. She sat with a cute redhead and Pauline Léon, the bulldog of the neighborhood women, their leader and a real fire eater. He realized why he had not recognized Claire on stage, although he must have seen her at the Cordeliers numerous times. She did not seem glamorous offstage. She did not dress like an imitation lady or a whore. She dressed like the other women of the neighborhood, somewhat cleaner, a bit more style to the cut of her apron or the way she pinned the cockade, but he would not have guessed she was an actress. Like the Léon girl, she was in the thick of the neighborhood brigade. She smiled at him briefly but did not approach him or pay him more attention than anyone else speaking that night. He was intensely relieved. Obviously, she did not regard their night as the beginning of a heavy liaison. He was amused to notice he was also a little piqued that she could so easily dismiss him. Even in an old striped skirt and a tricolor shawl, she was certainly lovely.

The race for prosecutor was hotly contested. There were always rumors about him, that he took bribes, that he lived too well, that he had just bought a big estate. He would deal with them head-on. Bull on through. He spoke till he was hoarse, talked with every little subgroup and guild and organization, everyone he ran into on the street. On the night of the election, he and Camille drank themselves silly.

It took two days to count the ballots. He was ahead, he was behind, he was defeated. Finally, when he had resigned himself to losing, he was told he had won election as deputy prosecutor. Manuel was the real prosecutor, but it gave Georges a foot in the door of the Paris Commune and a base from which to operate. His acceptance speech was improvised, but he had decided beforehand to paint himself as a self-made man, the opposite of those born to wealth and privilege. He depicted himself as rough-hewn, vigorous, the working man's champion, the people's pugilist. He took on the rumors. He mentioned his house near the village where he was born, which he described as a sort of comfortable peasant holding. He knew what it was like to be persecuted wrongly. He was a down-to-earth man and he would continue to be who he was—more of a sow's ear than a silk purse, but one hundred percent there for the people he was proud to represent—because he was one of them. He would never have made a monk. But he would fight hard for the Commune and the people's Revolution.

The crowd at City Hall liked the speech. He had begun to shape his public persona, not exactly a mask or a fiction, but more of a cartoon, a simplified Danton for general consumption. Camille saw clearly what he was doing and teased him in private. "You better hide your library," Camille said. "It gives away that agile brain and broad education you're bound to conceal these days. You and Marat are outdoing each other with the common touch. How about belching contests?"

"You're just jealous because you could never bring it off."

"Too true. I am a fop to the very bones of my elegant, refined and utterly irresistible body."

Camille understood the stakes. He was seen as a loose cannon, still the lamppost lawyer who had raised the mob to storm the Bastille. His paper was popular and sold well, but he wanted office too. They were young married men making their way across volcanic country, with no maps and no guides but their wits and the help of their friends.

FORTY-SIX

Max

❦

(Fall 1791–Winter 1792)

WHEN the Assembly held its last meeting, the people seized Pétion and Max as they were leaving and made an embarrassing fuss. They crowned Max with oak leaves, they read him bad poetry, they kissed him and pelted him with flowers. He endured it, because it was genuine. Now, because of his own motion that former deputies could not serve in the Legislative Assembly, his time as a delegate was over. The Jacobin Club needed his full attention.

Max had much work to do after the more conservative members of the Jacobin Club walked out and started the Feuillants—so named for the former monastery where they began to hold rival meetings. Without monasteries and convents, what would the Revolution do for public buildings? The Feuillants met just down the street from the Jacobins. The conservative city administration allowed the warrant on him to run out. He knew the reason: Lafayette and Bailly feared repercussions in the streets. Even though they had cowed people with the Champ de Mars massacre, they were not about to forget that passivity could erupt into violence if provoked.

Or perhaps they thought that by walking out of the Jacobins, they had destroyed the Club, and he was no longer to be feared. But they had walked out dramatically, a poor way to accomplish such a move. They had left the membership rolls, the addresses of contacts at the daughter clubs. Even before he dared resurface, he sent Eléanore for the addresses. After he had written to every one of the hundreds of Jacobin clubs with her help and that of her younger sister Elisabeth—most clubs thrilled to receive a personal note from the Incorruptible himself—only four clubs defected to the Feuillants. How he hated that appellation, "the Incorruptible": as if not to be bought and sold was such an unusual characteristic as to warrant public note.

Most members attended now and then, when there was a good speech coming or a controversial stand being debated or they had something they wanted to propose. He went every night. He arrived in a timely manner, sat at the back or leaned against the wall and listened. He did not speak unless he had something to say. Then he prepared a speech. He preferred to write his speeches beforehand, although most members spoke extemporaneously. Some, like Danton, were best that way. Others were not, but never seemed to learn. He let his eyes half shut and followed without seeming to pay attention. He knew others were always watching him for his reactions, so he had learned to produce a slightly bored and impervious facade to protect himself from their curiosity.

Nothing escaped his notice. He involved himself in the daily running of the Club, in correspondence, in the minutes. Many politicians had joined the Jacobins and then left. No one had been with it from the beginning and stayed the way he did. It was the place he could always get the floor, always receive a respectful and most times enthusiastic hearing.

Lately his life felt calmer. In the Duplays' cozy home with the hammering in the courtyard, the smell of sawdust, the scent of good simple cooking, the voices of the women of the household, he was close to happy. Even when meetings ran long into the night, Eléanore would be sitting up to open the gate for him. If Eléanore stayed late at the Club, Madame or Elisabeth would wait.

Couthon, a wheelchair-bound cripple who was braver than any whole man, came to see him often. He relied upon Couthon for reports on the newly elected Legislative Assembly. Couthon followed his lead. Max also enjoyed the company of the painter David. He had never entertained before, but the Duplays encouraged him to invite friends and colleagues. The Duplays provided a core group for singing, readings, excursions, walks. Eléanore would sketch his friends and of course himself. David thought she had talent. Max was pleased by this evidence that she was a genuine artist, but more pleased that whatever she was doing, she would stop when he needed something.

In October he returned to Arras for the first time since he had been elected to the Estates General. A few leagues outside the city, he was met by a contingent of National Guard. When he entered his home town, candles were lit in every window, an illumination in his honor. However, he learned quickly he was the bête noire of the local Feuillants and royalists. No rumor was too vile to be repeated and believed.

Charlotte was fussy and demanding, combining overacted submission with an insistence on unremitting appreciation. Augustin had grown into a full political man with strong character, but practicing law halfheartedly. Augustin seemed someone he could depend upon. Augustin was a hand taller, but Max was still head of the household. He felt guilty for his neglect. Perhaps

Augustin would find a political career in Paris; perhaps Charlotte would find a husband. He wrote to the Duplays, to see if they had room.

The local authorities had prepared a banquet for him where he was presented with a civic crown. Speeches were made, unctuous and endless. Some of his old friends were delighted, but he could feel the envy, the mistrust, even the hatred of others. If this was a triumphant homecoming of the outcast semibastard orphan, he could taste a hidden menace. Speeches praised the Revolution, but among the worthies of the town, he felt little genuine commitment. The tradesmen, workers and peasants who had sent him to the Estates General had his picture on their walls. They shouted when they saw him. They had begun naming their babies Maximilien.

One day when he was walking with Augustin outside of Arras, they met a bricklayer with a Great Dane. It was a magnificent animal, friendly but dignified. Max got down on his knees to stroke the fine head.

"He's a proud papa," the bricklayer said. "Back at home, my bitch had pups. If you like dogs, sir, I'd be happy, I'd be honored to give you one."

"You shouldn't call me 'sir.' " Max considered the offer. "Can we see your pups?"

Thus he acquired Blount, a two-month-old Great Dane who went home with him that day and slept on the foot of his bed at night. Since he had been out of the legislature and living just down the street from the Jacobins, he had not been walking nearly enough. Blount would fix that.

A reply came from the Duplays: they had a small apartment in the north wing that could be fixed up for Augustin and Charlotte. By all means, Max should bring his families together. He told them to pack up. They would retain the house in Arras in case things did not work out. Charlotte fussed and wrung her hands, but Augustin was delighted.

Blount immediately chased Felicia, the calico cat who was mother of all cats in residence, and got his nose scraped. Vivienne took an immediate liking to Blount and had to be ordered not to spoil him. Augustin and Charlotte moved into the apartment. It opened directly on the street instead of into the courtyard, but also connected internally through a corridor. Charlotte was displeased by the furniture, displeased by the arrangement, displeased by the decoration. He told her to fix it as she chose, as long as she did not spend much. He had little money but needed almost nothing for himself. The Duplays took care of everything.

Upon his return, he was disturbed to notice how much war was talked of. Some Jacobins were forming a war party, touting how the armies of the Revolution could crush their enemies, unite the nation behind the flag, liberate neighboring countries from their kings and nobles. Their leader was Brissot.

Max considered his position carefully. Finally in December, he made his first speech opposing war. The émigrés presented no real danger. They played at war across the Rhine and talked big but could do little without armies to back them up.

The dangerous enemies were the King and those around him, former nobles and powerful foes all over France who tried to undermine and defeat the Revolution. France was not prepared for war. To go into war with the King commanding armies against his own brother and cousin was insane; to expect Louis to spearhead an effort to liberate other countries from their kings was idiocy. Further, people seldom appreciated an invasion, even one aimed at liberating them. They could not expect neighboring countries, with a traditional mistrust of French armies, to greet them as liberators. Finally he argued that a war might unite the nation, as Brissot expected, but could lead to dictatorship. A successful general could march on Paris.

In January Marat came to see him at the Duplays'. It was clandestine, because Marat was pursued by the government. He had been chased out of the country, taking refuge in England. Now he was back, forced to hide in the sewers where he contracted a skin disease that tortured him and gave him an odor that made Max feel slightly faint in the close room. For once Charlotte was tactful and silently opened a casement just behind Marat's back.

Max had often seen him across a room, but they had never sat down face to face. Marat had praised him in his paper, *The Friend of the People*. Max suspected that Marat and he had hung back from meeting because both of them preferred a certain distance. They agreed in much but their styles were discordant. Max found distasteful Marat's gutter rhetoric and constant references to slitting throats. He suspected Marat found him too formal. "Why do you write with such violence? Your paper is extremely popular and you make so many excellent points, why mar it by posturing like a criminal?"

"Posturing? The language I use is mild as mothers' milk next to how I feel. I feel a rage I can never put into words against those who have power and use it to destroy the common people. All words fall short of the fury I know."

Marat was little taller than Max, but broader built. He dressed in old filthy clothes and wore a stained kerchief around his head. He looked as if he had just escaped from the galleys. He had been hunted like the British ran a fox, and he had developed the cunning and the cornered ferocity of a beast. Max spoke gently to him. Marat roared back. "We have to slaughter them before they fuck up the Revolution. Every scheming lying priest, the aristocrats who have dined on the liver of the nation so long and so well. If they had one head, I'd chop it off. They want to freeze society the way it is, with the people getting nothing, nothing at all!"

Marat had scraggly brown air, uncombed, caked with some salve he was using. His hands were covered with running sores. He wore a brace of pistols in his belt. Max never carried a weapon and had no idea how to use one. He had never learned to wave a sword around.

"You're a wise man," Marat said to him, "but you lack the belly for the hard tasks we must carry out. A man of action needs a taste for blood. Your politics are as good as they get, but your rage is insufficient. You need to strop your anger to an edge that can cut flesh."

Max was a little sickened by the conversation, although he tried not to show his squeamishness.

"When a man lacks everything, he has a right to what another has too much of," Marat was saying. "Instead of starving, he has an inborn right to cut a rich man's throat and eat him whole."

"You love the people, but you don't respect them," Max said. "You talk of them as vengeful beasts or as children. You've been arguing for a dictatorship. If the people are ruled by a dictator, they have no more freedom than they do ruled by a king or priests."

"It depends entirely on who the dictator is. I think you and I could do a pretty good job for the sans-culottes. Don't you think you perceive far more clearly what needs to be done than the man in the street?"

"I think freedom is more important than being absolutely right." Max could sense how prissy he must look to Marat, his clothes immaculate, his hair precisely curled and powdered, his green-tinted glasses perched on his head. It had got back to him that someone had said he looked like a tailor of the ancien régime. Then this was a meeting of the pirate and the tailor.

They were not alone in the room. Charlotte and Eléanore were the silent spectators, along with Simonne Évrard. Marat had not bothered with a legal ceremony, but everybody considered Simonne his wife. How did Marat dare take a wife? Marat and he would be killed in the Revolution; they would both be martyred. One of Max's chief fears if he married or had children was that they would be put to death because of him. Yet Marat had not hesitated to take Simonne. He would have liked to discuss that choice with Marat, but doubted if Marat would appreciate the inquiry. Further he was not about to bring up the matter in front of his own women. Charlotte was already jealous of Eléanore and told him every two days Eléanore was trying to trap him into marriage: as if he wouldn't have married her quite willingly, married her whole family, if he dared. He could not imagine how Marat, who had lived as a hunted felon, had risked taking Simonne for his own. Simonne was Max's idea of a good woman. Probably he liked her rather better than he liked Marat.

When he approached his concern obliquely, Marat burst out, "Martyrdom?

I want to win! I want their heads to fall. I'd trade mine for that pleasure. You fuss too much about virtue—especially your own. We're fighting to win, not to set a good example to the angels."

The meeting ended with the two men as they had been: they shared a common politics and a commitment to work for the good of ordinary people. They shared a mistrust of the conservatives. They believed the enemies within France far more dangerous than the enemies without. Neither of them expected to survive the work they had given themselves to. Neither could be bought or swayed or moved from what they considered correct. Neither sought power or wealth or personal benefits. But they differed in their ways of talking and acting and living. They would respect each other with reservations, and they would continue to make common cause most of the time. But each would never cease to believe that the other should be more like himself.

FORTY-SEVEN

Nicolas

(Late Fall 1791)

NICOLAS was not surprised that Lafayette was defeated by Pétion in the '91 election, although he knew Lafayette was. He had not publicly supported either candidate, but he had voted for Pétion. The people of Paris hated Lafayette, and even those few who had been given the franchise would not forgive shooting unarmed citizens, including children, on the Champ de Mars.

At the elections for the Legislative Assembly, Nicolas was voted in. When he took his seat, he was quickly chosen as secretary, which involved more speech-making than he liked. Sophie always told him to talk more to the point and then sit down. He went on too long. He feared not being thorough. He explained and explained, unable to stop trying to educate.

Since the Declaration of Pilnitz, most of his friends had been talking war. The Declaration was a direct threat to France from Prussia and Austria, demanding that France restore the King fully to his powers, dissolve the Assembly and give German princes their old feudal rights over the people and lands of Alsace. No invasion had yet followed. He had no enthusiasm for war. He believed no nation was justified in attacking another to conquer land or resources. However, if a war had to be fought to preserve the Revolution, he would support it.

The Social Circle's press cranked out a great deal of propaganda on the subject. He wrote copiously. He had never understood making a fuss about style, any more than he greatly cared what he wore, as long as he did not look ridiculous or too out of date. He left his clothes to Sophie, who had an innate sense of aesthetics. He was always writing and it was always wanted yesterday or the day before. It was one in a queue of articles or pamphlets crying to be gotten out to people.

One reason Nicolas believed they would have war was that he had been watching the court. The Austrian emperor had died and been replaced by one of Marie-Antoinette's brothers. Marie expected much from her brother and might get it. Nicolas suspected that the King and Queen dreamed of restoring their power with a little help from the Austrians, the Prussians and probably the Spanish. France would be fighting a two-front war, on the seas too if the British got involved. The French generals were more the King's men than the country's. This France much sung-about now was something that he and a bunch of others had invented two and a half years ago. Out of a feudal mess of little states almost mutually incomprehensible in language and customs, they were building a nation, in haste and desperation and high hope.

His daughter Eliza had been taught she was French. Not an aristocrat—for aristocrats frequently had no real country. They might hold titles and lands in feudal right in various domains and kingdoms. The willingness of the aristocracy to leave France rather than submit to a change of government revealed that their real country was their class. But not his.

Sophie went along partway. "As a philosopher, you have an international identity. Voltaire served several kingdoms. Diderot owed loyalty to Catherine of Russia. Of what country am I as a woman a citizen? Even the America you admire so much will not allow me the full rights I was born to demand."

"I want Eliza to feel herself a citizen of France. Perhaps by the time she's of age, she'll have the rights we want for her."

They both looked at their daughter, playing with a black kitten and a red, blue and white ball. Even the kitten wore a tricolor on its neck. Eliza sat down hard on her behind and grinned at them. "I want another ball. A bigger ball," she said. "I want a ball as big as Inky."

"Then Inky won't be able to play with it," Sophie said. She was a fine mother, patient but uncondescending.

"Inky gets bigger every day," Eliza argued quite reasonably. "So do I. I want a bigger ball."

"I'll see to it," Nicolas said. How pretty she was and how bright. The latter was far more important, but he could not resist enjoying her resemblance to his wife. Unfortunately she had his nose. Perhaps she would grow into it.

On the whole, he liked fatherhood, although he was aware he sometimes resented sharing Sophie with anyone, including his child. Of course there was a nursemaid. Sophie learned not to flinch and run whenever Eliza cried. Sophie had not given over to motherhood, but continued her translations, her studies, her painting. If anything, she painted more seriously. She preferred to catch Eliza in watercolors or in pencil sketches. She said oils were too slow to do justice to their ever-changing child.

Lately she had been doing portraits of Tom Paine, Bonneville and Henriette, a set to be presented to them. Tom Paine had moved in with the Bonnevilles, a subject of much speculation and gossip.

"Sophie, do you ever imagine living like that? With me and perhaps a younger man?"

"Nico, don't be silly. You take a great deal of looking after. If I had two husbands, I'd never finish Adam Smith. I'd have no time to myself."

He was silent a moment, contemplating the three portraits ranged against the wall. She came to stand just behind him. He could feel the heat of her body and smell her personal scent that always worked on him. She was so beautiful, sometimes he felt like a large floppy animal, a sheep dog, shaggy and wagging, sprawled over her. He loved her so much that from time to time, he was frightened. Then he wondered if she wished for a younger, handsome mate.

Tom Paine brought over a new board game called the Game of the Revolution. It was clever but years beyond Eliza. The successful end of the game was the passage of the Constitution, the one already outdated by events. Still, the game was an engaging way to carry out political education. It went round in a large spiral with places that held penalties (the courts, the prisons) and places that enabled the player to leap ahead, like the Tennis Court Oath and the Taking of the Bastille. There were little colored portraits of the King and Queen, Mirabeau, Lafayette, Robespierre, Bailly. Not himself, of course. Did he long to have his face on a game board?

When he walked into the Assembly the next day, delegates were attacking the current administration, the King's ministers. Even previous supporters denounced them. Reports from deputies who had gone into the field insisted that Austria and Prussia were making military preparations on a scale that the administration had been concealing. "It's treason," they were shouting. "They're selling us out to the Austrians." "They're hiding the truth." "They're loyal to the King only." Brissot craned back his neck to address Nicolas, who at once took a seat so they would be on the same level. Brissot was more than a foot shorter than Nicolas. "The government must resign. The King will have to appoint new ministers. Do you want to be in the government?"

Nicolas said fervently, "No, thank you. I think I'm more useful writing propaganda and working in the Assembly."

"I have a feeling Louis is going to have to turn to us to continue to govern. I think we're ready! It's our time, Condorcet. It's our time."

He felt a quiet satisfaction, smiling at Brissot, although he could wish Brissot and his friends were a little less eager to go to war. They thought it would unite the country. Some were convinced that as soon as the French armies appeared, the subjugated masses would rise and throw off their masters. Perhaps. Or perhaps not. They would all find out soon. He did not know if war would make or ruin their future.

"Things certainly change quickly, almost too quickly for us to see what's happening before it's past," Nicolas said, but Brissot was already on his feet and off to buttonhole Louvet.

FORTY-EIGHT

Manon

❦

(February–June 1792)

JEAN'S pension was suppressed, so Manon and Jean returned to Paris to petition the new Assembly to restore it. They signed a lease for a small flat on the Rue de Harpe. She set about visiting their friends. It was immediately evident she should not have left Paris. Brissot and Louvet and everyone else seemed a little distant, as if they had forgotten her and Jean. She did not like to think of herself as someone who could be so easily dismissed. Brissot was in the Assembly, chair of the diplomatic committee. Pétion was Mayor. Condorcet was one of the secretaries of the Assembly. The only one who seemed exactly the same as when she had left was Robespierre, who appeared isolated over the war issue. He greeted her as if he had seen her the day before, accepted her invitation to dinner, then issued a warning about Brissot and her other friends, whom he called the "war party." He described the recent sugar riots, when the women and pastry cooks had taken to the streets. The sansculottes, he said, were incensed with the policies of the King's ministers.

At the Jacobins, Bosc got Jean on the committee of correspondence that kept up with hundreds of daughter clubs all over the country. Jean was secretary, which meant Manon did the work. Robespierre served on the same committee, so they were colleagues. That pleased Manon. She still preferred him to other politicians, for he was a man of ideals. She felt they had a certain sympathy, an understanding.

Then in one evening on March twenty-third, their life changed. She had just had a long chat with Condorcet, whom she disliked but cultivated. He briefed her on the total incompetence of the present ministers. The nation was about to be attacked, yet nothing had been done to defend its borders or mobilize a functional army. The King must appoint ministers with popular support. One could only imagine that this set of Feuillant ministers were doing their best to do nothing whatsoever and would probably welcome the Austrians.

Condorcet left and Jean was dozing with a dozen newspapers littered around the chaise longue where he lay under a woolen throw. She was startled by a sudden knock. He rose abruptly, straightened himself and his area. She repinned her white fichu to make sure she was not showing too much décolleté and nodded at Fleury to answer.

General Dumouriez and Brissot came in, highly excited. "Congratulations, old friend," Brissot said far more warmly than he had greeted Jean when they arrived in Paris. "You've been drafted for the new government."

Jean could not keep himself from looking astonished. His hands clasped and unclasped. "Well, well," he said lamely. "Could you explain?"

Dumouriez bowed over her hand, kissing it. She eyed his elegant manners with mistrust. He would have been far more comfortable with Versailles than with the new constitutional government. Still, he was by all reports an able and talented general, and for that, apparently, there was a dire need.

General Dumouriez said, "The King has appointed me Minister for Foreign Affairs. He has agreed to appoint you as his Minister of the Interior. It is important for all of us and for the Revolution that you accept."

Jean met her gaze and she imperceptibly nodded. This was a signal opportunity for him to show his ability. Besides, it would end their financial difficulties. Jean brightened and said slowly, "Well, then, my friends, I'll do as you ask. I'll accept the great honor you offer me."

"It'll be far more work than honor," Brissot said. "I'm glad you're taking the portfolio. None of us in the Assembly can serve as ministers, thanks to that ridiculous measure passed by the last Assembly. Now if we repeal it, we'll seem self-serving. Servan will take over the war ministry."

As the general prepared to leave, he turned to Manon. "Madame, you should prepare your household. As soon as the formalities are over, you are expected to move into the Ministry residence. I believe you'll find it . . . comfortable, one of the pleasanter aspects of being a minister's wife."

"I am indifferent to my abode, as you can tell from this simple flat. But we will comply willingly with all obligations."

After Dumouriez left, Brissot remained. Manon paced, her hands clasped before her. "I suspect Louis' motives. Three ministers from our group. No other Jacobins. Most of the previous government preserved intact to quarrel with us and undermine us. I think we're meant to fail."

"That may be," Brissot rubbed his chin, "but that doesn't mean we will. I have great faith in Citizen Roland to seize control of his department and knock it into shape."

"I certainly have ideas," Jean said. "This will be most interesting. An opportunity to govern, instead of criticizing."

"Jacques-Pierre," she said to Brissot. "Could this be a clever trap? To discredit us by drawing us too close to the court? It happened to Mirabeau."

"I doubt it. Do you think Louis has the brains to plan that?" Brissot was ever the optimist, as she had noticed before.

"Louis is a man of mediocre intelligence, with a good memory and as stubborn as any two-year-old," she said slowly. "He's able to use people and lie endlessly. I would not trust him, ever."

"Well, I suppose I shall be meeting him soon enough," Jean said. "They say when one door closes, another opens. I was lamenting the end of my position as inspector of manufactures, and now I'll be Minister of the entire department. That ought to shock my old superiors out of their lethargy."

"You're finally getting some of the attention and the respect you richly deserve." Manon rested a hand on his bony shoulder. "At last, you'll have a position of real power where you can affect the course of the country. I'm extremely proud of you."

As Brissot was leaving, she walked him to the door. She said quietly, "I know you're responsible for this. I won't forget. I will be a true supporter and a true friend to you until the grave, Jacques-Pierre."

"Your friendship's a formidable gift. The King thinks Jean's an obscure bureaucrat. He'll find out differently. And . . ." he clasped her hand, "we all know how much enjoyment we'll get from his well-written crisp memos, like so many daggers." He winked and left.

Jean told her about his first presentation to the King, but she heard a much better version of it from General Dumouriez, who presented him. Jean went off that day as he did every day in his black Quakerly suit, wearing his ordinary shoes and simple round hat. Apparently the lackeys and the courtiers threw fits. They stared at Jean. They gaped at his clothing. The Master of Ceremonies finally approached Dumouriez. "General, this is not done!"

"No," said Dumouriez, "it is in process. What do you want?"

"Sir! This is terrible!" The Master of Ceremonies pointed to Jean's shoes with horror. "Sir, he has no buckles on his shoes."

Dumouriez threw up his hands. "All is lost! Whatever shall we do?" Then he took Jean by the hand and swept past the Master of Ceremonies. The King was going to see Jean as he was. Hearing the story, Manon was amused.

The move into the new house was a shock. It was immense and ornate. It was, fortunately for them, lavishly furnished. They had nothing suitable, except for the pianoforte she had been thinking of selling when the ministerial appointment saved them. This residence had been built for the Comte de

Lionne and had housed Mme Necker in her day. A magnificent coil of marble staircase led to a huge salon with crystal chandeliers, Venetian mirrors, ormolu inlay. At the focal point of the salon was a twice-life-size portrait of Louis XIV being crowned by Victory. Bergères and sofas were covered with tapestries of scenes of cupidons. The draperies were red velvet.

The bedroom was scarcely less imposing. The bed was vast and canopied with ostrich feathers. The ceiling was painted with gods and goddesses disporting their unwrapped flesh in diverse arrangements. She would like to whitewash it, but it was the property of the nation, and she must learn to live with Louis and sleep under Venus and Mars. There were the same overdone frescoes in half the rooms and corridors. Room upon room sat there. However, they did not remain empty long. Mondays and Fridays, she provided supper for all the ministers. Mme Brissot was permitted to attend, as an exception. She was not talkative and she was bright, if homely.

Manon continued, on the Sèvres plate decorated with nymphs and satyrs provided with the house, to serve up simple fare, just one course and sugar water, sometimes watered wine. The actual eating was quickly accomplished and they adjourned to the immense salon to politick. On Tuesdays she had a general salon for old friends, who were beginning to be called Brissotins or Girondins (since some came from Bordeaux, on the Gironde River). Robespierre never attended. He was annoyed at Jean for joining the government. He did not trust Dumouriez or Brissot. He did not want the war that was inevitable and would save the country and make its borders secure. She was disappointed in him. He was becoming more partisan every week. He was not the disinterested patriot she had supposed. He attacked Roland for compromising with the King.

A war of liberation is not a war of conquest; she had written an essay for the Chronicle on that subject. She was writing regularly. Either the work went out signed by Jean or else it was published anonymously. Everyone knew who wrote Jean's trenchant essays, letters, reports to the Assembly.

She depended on Jean for news of the Council. Meetings with the King were frustrating. Louis would not allow a policy discussion to go forward, but was always bringing up trivia, trying to keep them from taking action. In other words, he was blocking them, as he continued to block the work of the Assembly by vetoing every substantive measure.

Robespierre was ever more isolated. Brissot had gained the advantage by a huge majority. On April twentieth, he had the King sign a declaration of war against Austria which the Assembly approved almost unanimously. Robespierre alone denounced the new ministers as tools of the King, playing into the hands of the counter-revolution. She was dismayed by the violence of his attacks and wrote him a letter asking him to come and see her. She missed him at her gatherings. She appealed to him to be tolerant and stop treating patriots as if they were enemies of the state just because he differed with them.

She waited for an answer. When she mentioned, as if casually to Brissot, that she had written a note to Robespierre, he treated it as a joke. "No one listens to him. An impotent little man."

Robespierre never answered her appeal. He ignored it as if she did not matter, but she did. It was he who no longer mattered. He was envy personified, a furious spirit of fanaticism in a lost cause who would do and say any violent thing to arouse the ignorant rabble of the city. If he continued to attack her husband, she would attack him in turn. She had offered him true friendship and understanding; he had responded with silence and scorn.

Things were not going smoothly for the new ministers. The government was composed mostly of old hacks who did not want change. The King vetoed every important measure the Assembly passed. It was a stalemate. Louis really thought if he fooled around long enough, events would magically undo themselves and he would be back on top of the world. The army was not ready; the army was not equipped. On the northern front, the soldiers had no rifles and no food. They killed their own general in fury. When the men did march into battle, they were soundly defeated. This halfway reform, halfway reactionary coalition government was a nightmare. Those idiots in the Cordeliers, the few fanatical adherents Robespierre still controlled in the Jacobin Club and that savage anarchist Marat were attacking Jean, Servan and Dumouriez, as if they weren't killing themselves to try to save the nation.

Late in May, Brissot denounced Lafayette in the Assembly, for secret negotiations with the Austrians. Lafayette in turn wrote an insulting letter to Jean, saying that he did not recognize the validity of a government containing Brissotins. The Assembly voted to set up a military camp near Paris, to protect the city. Louis promptly vetoed the measure.

Something had to be done. They were being stymied at every turn. On June tenth, Manon sat down at her desk and wrote a letter to Louis, to be signed by her husband. She wrote sternly, clearly, without the usual equivocation and flattery with which Louis had always been addressed. "Sir, the present crisis of France cannot long endure. The French have adopted a Constitution; some are dissatisfied and rebellious, but the overwhelming majority wish to uphold the Constitution, swear to defend it with their lives and gladly accept war as a means of defending that Constitution.

"Your majesty grew up with great privileges which you were trained to believe were the rights of royalty. You cannot have witnessed the suppression of these privileges with pleasure. These sentiments, while natural in the human heart, have encouraged enemies of the Revolution. Your behavior has created mistrust in the nation. Your majesty is thus faced with two alternatives: you can yield to your childhood training and your natural preference for retaining all your privileges and powers, or you can make the sacrifices dictated by wisdom and demanded by necessity."

The result of her letter was that the King lost his temper and took the opportunity to dismiss ministers he disliked anyhow. Jean and she were ordered to vacate the mansion. However, her letter was much reprinted and cheered in the Assembly. The Rolands were once again private citizens.

FORTY-NINE
Claire

❦

(June 20, 1792)

CLAIRE spent the whole week arguing with Hélène. "I'd be much happier if you'd stay home. You're no street fighter."

"And you are? There's a difference between playing Marianne waving a banner and being shot at by the National Guard."

"Hélène, I'm a big strong peasant. I know how to use a pistol. I want to be in the action, and I don't want to be worrying about you."

"Who asked you to worry about me? I've been taking care of myself since my folks threw me out."

Claire felt like shaking Hélène until her teeth popped out, but she would never lay a rough hand on her friend. "Hélène . . . please! For me. Just let me know you're safe. . . ."

Hélène tossed her head, looking petulant. "I'll think about it."

Claire kissed her on the mouth, quickly. Hélène let herself be kissed but said, "Don't try to get around me. You just want to go off with Pauline."

"Pauline's one of the best in demonstrations. All the women follow her lead. But you know she could never be my special friend, the way you are."

Everyone was talking about the demonstration called for the twentieth of June, the anniversary of the Tennis Court Oath. They were furious at the King and sick of waiting for the Legislative Assembly to do something about the war and the King's vetoes. The clubs and sections had been meeting in almost continuous sessions. The official reason was to present petitions to the Assembly and the King and plant a liberty tree at the former Feuillants monastery right by the Assembly—and very close to the Tuileries.

Pauline always knew what was going on. "The Girondins—the right-wing Jacobins—want their ministers recalled to power. They want to take over the government. Robespierre says we should wait till the fédérés arrive from Marseille, because they're radical soldiers. They'd protect us. But Marat says we should march now and so do Santerre and Danton. We'll put the fear of the people into Louis and show him he can't keep trying to break us. And we'll remind the Assembly we put them in and we can take them out."

So it was to be mostly pageant. Everybody would go armed who had arms to bear, but mostly they would carry flowers and ears of corn and the boughs of trees and banners—all the things they were used to carrying in religious processions. They even had busts of martyrs to carry.

The night of the nineteenth, the section met and met. Messengers went running through the dark streets bearing contradictory messages. The remnants of the old regime kept issuing decrees to the sections not to march. Claire was too excited to leave the Cordeliers, until Hélène fell asleep on her shoulder. Finally at two A.M., Claire shuffled off with sleepy Hélène to get a few hours in bed. It was a hot night. Claire sat up again and again from a fitful sleep with her heart pounding and her breath catching in her throat. She remembered the slaughter at the Champ de Mars. She remembered it too well.

At five A.M. Faubourg Saint Antoine and Faubourg Saint Marcel were gathering, but her section wasn't supposed to start until eight A.M., to give the faubourgs time to arrive. At seven she rose quietly, not to wake Hélène, who was sprawled like a child on her stomach. Claire threw on her skirt and apron and chemise, strapped on her pistol, picked up her sign THE CONSTITUTION NOW OR DEATH and tiptoed down the steps. She ran across the bridge toward the Cordeliers.

Legendre the butcher had a calf's heart on a pike bearing the sign THIS IS THE HEART OF AN ARISTOCRAT. They formed up into squadrons with drummers and piccolo players, with banners and placards and great sheafs of red and pink roses and mock orange. Some were waving boughs of linden trees. A local priest carried the Virgin before them. Babette's father brought his fiddle. One old veteran pounded a big bass drum. They looked at each other and they were proud.

Claire had never before belonged. In her own town, she was a fatherless child, a suspected Protestant. She was poor and neglected and had no dowry. Here she had dozens of friends. Pauline had taken her into the bosom of the neighborhood, and the women did not hold it against her that she was an actress. They marched beside her and joked with her the same as anybody else. They were to rendezvous with the two faubourgs at the site of the demolished Bastille. Off they went, in good order, singing the "Ça Ira," It Will Go On, a popular song this year. Pauline was everywhere, at the head, at the rear, urging her women on. She wore a tricolor sash across her bosom and she carried the pike that had gone to Versailles. "We went all that way to fetch the King, and we got no good of him. We might as well have left him there and burned the place down."

Both Pauline and Claire were wearing the red bonnets that were all the rage for patriots. Even among the poor people, everybody must have a red bonnet or cap. The cockade was fine, but even ladies getting out of carriages pinned it on nowadays. The cap said, we mean it, we mean blood. It was modeled after the red wool cap that galley slaves had been forced to wear.

The Pont Neuf was closed by soldiers, so they simply marched down to the next bridges and crossed through the Ile Saint Louis. Far downstream, they could see another group crossing. She could hear singing and drums from every side. The square where the Bastille had stood was already jammed. There were grenadiers, fusiliers, Guardsmen, old invalids in uniform on canes and crutches and being pushed along in wheelbarrows. There were charcoal burners, market women, fishwives. There were bakers and Savoyard chimney sweeps, women of the flower market, horse dealers mounted. Cannons had been dragged from the various sections. It was a mammoth orchestra out of synch, every drummer and musician setting a different rhythm. Sunlight glinted off the muskets and the bayonets and the pikes, lit the banners and flags. Some were carrying hatchets, axes, kitchen knives, butchers' cleavers and blacksmiths' tools. A tavern keeper had taken the spit of his barbecue. Others had old swords, pitchforks, scythes bound to short poles.

Thousands and thousands of them set off to march on the Assembly and to the King, to present their petition—and to scare them with the threat of popular violence. Still it felt like a holiday as they marched along, singing full throat almost in step with the drums, the sun brightening their banners, fallen flowers underfoot, everyone beaming at each other as if they were indeed one large family. There were so many of them, they felt invincible, Claire imagined, safe because they were such a great crowd. At the head of the procession were the sappers and cannoneers, Santerre—the Faubourg Saint Antoine brewer—on a horse, men bearing the tables of the Rights of Man, imitated after stained glass windows of the Ten Commandments. Behind them came a wagon with a liberty tree and buckets of water. Claire sang until she was hoarse. A vendor was giving away lemonade and she got one of the last drinks before he ran out.

Hope was the most intoxicating brandy. Despair and grief and trouble were the lot of most of the people most of the time. Hope they had almost never known. Now they swept through the streets like a summer wind, blowing all before them hoping they too could have dignity and a future. That each of them was someone who counted. People who had spent their whole lives limping from crisis to crisis, just trying to get through another day, to save a sick child or a starving mother, now saw a way forward. For the first time they were experiencing imagination in their own lives, that all need not continue as it had been. The future had been something only the religious contemplated, death and reward beyond that opaque barrier. The idea of a future that could be shaped was a new intoxication. If the demonstration was dangerous, so was daily life. They would make the King and the Assembly pay attention: they would command the regard of those with power and position, to whom they had never been more than ants running across the pavement. Many insisted on carrying their weapons, not because they wanted to use them, but because gentlemen with swords had always represented the right to command. Now they had their own makeshift swords to flourish. As they marched toward the Assembly and the Tuileries, passersby joined them. Shopkeepers put up their shutters and marched along. Women waved from windows, then came running down. Their pace slowed as the crowd clogged the narrow streets.

As they reached the Rue Saint Honoré, Pauline pushed to her side. "Robespierre lives on this street," she announced breathlessly. The area between the gardens of the Tuileries palace and the street where they stood was occupied by the old Feuillants monastery. In between the Tuileries and the Feuillants stood the Assembly building. At one-thirty a delegation went inside to ask the Assembly to receive them.

At last the great doors opened and the crowd began to march through the Assembly. They went in with weapons at attention, muskets, pikes, hatchets, sheafs of flowers, banners, placards, as they sang the "Ça Ira" and filed through with great pride. They all felt ten feet tall, Claire thought, waiting her turn. Some sections had petitions. The women pushed Claire forward to present theirs. They thought she was the best person when it was a matter of standing up and being seen, because she was tall and considered beautiful. It took the people an hour and a half to pass through.

As people exited, they were caught against the closed gates to the palace gardens. The press grew worse and worse. She was having trouble catching her breath as she was jammed against the man next to her and he was pushed into the metal fence. Pauline shouted, "There are cannons in the Tuileries pointed right at us."

Suddenly she found herself carried forward. The gates to the garden were forced and the procession began to move along the terrace above the river. They trotted the length of the palace where guards were standing in a double row with bayonets fixed. The crowd was good-natured, although taunts were shouted as they passed under the King's windows. They were still singing and shouting slogans, waving their wilted flowers and banners. The line of march entered the Place du Carrousel, where people turned and began to try to enter the closed gates to the palace. No one gave orders. It was as if the crowd had one brain that had decided they were not leaving without presenting their petitions to the King.

For an hour, the crowd pushed and the soldiers pushed back. The guards fixed bayonets to charge and then stood down. The cannoneers from Saint Marcel said they had come to get something done. They dragged their cannon up to the gates. Suddenly the gates opened and Claire was swept forward. She heard some officer yelling "Fire!" but nobody obeyed. The soldiers just got out of the way. Some waved happily, no longer pretending they were guarding what they did not want to guard.

Inside the crowd kept going, across the courtyards, through the inner gates. In the palace one of the cannons got stuck in a doorway. People climbed over it and went around it through other passageways. She hoped somebody knew where they were going. The rooms were huge with high ceilings and paneled walls painted with pastoral scenes. It was too jammed to see much. "It's not as fancy as Versailles," Pauline said.

Claire laughed. "You're turning into a connoisseur of palaces."

The guards were yelling at them, "Don't touch anything! Don't take anything!" Almost everyone obeyed. They were here for a purpose. If someone did try to help themselves to a gold clock or a fancy dish, the people around them took it and put it back. "None of that," she heard an old woman say. "We're the people. This here is our palace. It belongs to the nation."

"Here's Louis," someone was shouting down. Pauline dashed up the steps, waving her pike. The gendarmes, the soldiers, the guards stood to the side or walked away. Many shouted encouragement. Claire, borne upward in the press, heard the sound of a great door crashing down. It was the Oeil de Boeuf room. A man in gold damask and maroon velvet stood in an alcove flanked by a few National Guardsmen, looking very nervous. With him was a woman in court attire whose paniers stood out two feet on either side of her pinched-in waist. Claire wriggled through to Pauline. "Is that Marie?"

"No, that's Madame Elisabeth, the King's sister." Pauline was staring at the King. Claire and Pauline were pressed against the wall just inside the big room. "He looks like he could do an honest day's work if he wanted to. But he has guts anyhow. He must be afraid we'll tear him limb from limb."

For the first time, Claire felt apart from the crowd. Hungry, tired, she leaned against the wall. Anything could happen. Indeed, if a leader emerged who grabbed the King, he could be killed. He had lost his mystique; his person was no longer sacred. Men who never expected to lay eyes on him, women who had blessed him in their prayers, automatically listing him among the saints, now looked at him as part symbol and part obstacle and part ordinary man. Maybe they had a little goodwill left over, but only a little. He looked at them with resignation and puzzlement.

Everyone was shouting at once, Pauline with them. "Down with the veto!" "Bring back the good ministers!" "Out with the bad priests!" On and on. Claire was tired of shouting. She simply lay against the wall, held up by the crowd. It was hot, with more people trying to force their way in, screaming and chanting outside in the hall. For an hour the people yelled and the King moved his mouth. Nobody could hear. Finally leaders with petitions made their way in and gave the petitions to the King. In the tumult, Claire was carried away from Pauline, away from the safety of the wall and across the room in the wake of the petitioners. She ended up too near the King for comfort. He was standing on a green and gold striped brocade chair, trying to make himself heard. His gold damask waistcoat was stained with sweat. She could see the gossamer lace at his throat and his cuffs, but she was struck by his shoes, leather as thin as silk but inlaid with what she assumed were jewels. His stockings were heavy with gold embroidery. He was wearing far too many layers for the heat. His hands were laden with heavy rings with more big winking jewels. A man turned and grinned at Claire. "Give me your cap."

"Sure," she said, too hot and sweaty to care. Who needed a wool hat on a day like this?

He took it, and sticking it on the end of his pike, began battering his way toward the King. "Here, Louis. You need this."

Louis took the cap and put it on his head. A bald guy laughed, made as if to clap him on the back. A guard started to go for his pistol, but another restrained his arm. The guy handed the King a wine skin. "Drink to the nation, Louis."

The King stood there in the hat he must have hated and drank the wine he must have found loathsome and nodded and smiled and tried to save his life; and Claire saw that he was succeeding. Santerre had finally made his way in and now he mounted a table. "You've given your petitions to the King and he has heard you. Now it's time to move along so that your neighbors can meet the King too. Don't be pigs. Move along and give your neighbors a chance."

In good humor, the crowd began to shuffle out of the end of the Oeil de Boeuf chamber, giving the folks who had been screaming in the hall opportunity to enter. Claire left with her contingent. By the time she got downstairs, it was clear that Santerre had managed to set up a receiving line for the King.

Mayor Pétion was running up and down the staircase, trying to move the crowd along, trying to make sure that those who had already seen the King left the palace promptly.

Mostly people were tired and satisfied. They had been marching since dawn, and they were ready to go home. So was she.

FIFTY

Max

MAX had lost much of his popularity because of his harsh criticism of the war. Now he was subjected to a war at home. Charlotte had taken a dislike to all the Duplays except Elisabeth, with whom she went about everywhere arm in arm. Charlotte particularly resented Mme Duplay and Eléanore. "I can't believe how she invades your privacy. The girl is shameless."

"She goes nowhere I do not wish her to go."

"Max, she comes into your bedroom as if she were your mistress!"

"She's in my confidence. She acts on my behalf. She carries messages for me and reports back."

"It's not proper."

"Would you prefer I marry her, Charlotte? Would that make Eléanore's working with me proper in your eyes?"

"Max, don't joke! You can't marry a carpenter's daughter. Really!"

"I should think marrying the daughter of an honest artisan would be most appropriate. Unless you think people would suspect I was marrying her for money. After all, they're much better off than we are."

"Max, you can't marry her! And as for money, if you wanted to make money now, I know you could do it. For instance—"

"Enough!" He glared at her. She was carefully dressed, yet somehow her appearance always slightly annoyed him. There was a family resemblance. He was careful about his own appearance, but seeing his fussiness and his fastidiousness writ large in Charlotte and turned into open and foundationless vanity was not a boost to his self-esteem. He wanted to thunder at her to shut up, but she would weep. "Charlotte, I am not about to marry anyone. You can rest easy on that count. I can't afford a wife, financially or morally. I am wedded to the Revolution."

"You could make a dozen advantageous matches. I see how the women look at you. Even the rich ladies. They make eyes at you."

"I'm not a plate of hors d'oeuvres. Have you nothing better to think about? Why don't you assist Madame Duplay with the preserving of peaches? I love peach conserve."

It was no gift he was inflicting on Mme Duplay, but he had to get Charlotte out of his hair in order to do any work. How happy he had been in the house of the Duplays before he imported Charlotte. Augustin, however, was a true brother. They went to the Jacobins together. Augustin attended the Cordeliers several times a week and kept Max up-to-date.

Things were moving rapidly from both the left and the right. Lafayette returned to Paris without warning and attempted a coup in the Assembly, where he expected a majority to support him. Runners came to Max telling him that Lafayette planned to march on the Jacobins and crush them by force. Lafayette could not find support to carry out his plan. In a huff, he withdrew to his troops at the front. The wildest suspicions of counter-revolution that Max harbored were seldom equal to reality. He was stunned how quickly events had come to crisis and been resolved, while he sat working on a paper about freedom for Blacks. He must snap to and take an active part again. Even if he wasn't in the Assembly, he could still have some effect on the rapid slide of events. He began spending even more time at the Jacobins.

Something massive was brewing. Unlike the June twentieth demonstration, this one did not have Mme Roland's salon behind it. He no longer trusted her. A touch of power had changed her ideas about war. Couldn't she imagine the actual bloody deaths of the peasants she claimed to hold so dear? Everything to her was a drama, starring none other than Manon. Perhaps he saw himself in that intense self-scrutiny, but he did not like it in a woman. She was a schemer like Charlotte, but more dangerous than his silly sister, because more intelligent.

The armies were losing every battle, when they bothered to fight at all instead of just surrendering or fleeing. It was possible that the army's plans were being leaked to the enemy, for the enemy's intelligence always proved superior to theirs; the Austrians and Germans seemed to know exactly where the French armies were preparing to strike and the weak points in their lines. The generals might be betraying them. Or the Queen might be sending information to the Austrians. He hated the war, but if they were in it, they must not lose. They must make peace or win.

The Assembly was a bird with a broken wing. The deputies were too conservative. The people were being asked to fight a war when they could not vote for representatives to speak for them. They needed universal manhood suffrage now. They needed a real elected body to govern France, and this time, he would run again.

He had not wanted a demonstration on June twentieth. For one thing, he did not support the Girondin ministers, and wouldn't waste five minutes getting them back into office. People should risk their lives to make Roland a minister again? But now the Marseillais fédérés had arrived to defend Paris: superb fighting men who marched to a new song that everyone was learning, "The Marseillaise."

He sat in on planning sessions. All over Paris and its suburbs, people were hammering out tactics for the coming demonstration, this time a serious attack. He disliked depending on armed rebellion in the streets. For one thing, the outcome was uncertain. The King had been badly frightened by the twentieth of June and had moved his most reliable foreign troops, the Swiss, into the palace. Louis had ordered the defenses thoroughly overhauled. He was fortifying the Tuileries to withstand a siege. Further, violent demonstrations encouraged the worst elements in the lower classes. Finally, it cost lives. But to get to a republic, it seemed that violence would be necessary.

He was as out of place in a demonstration as a Persian cat. He had never mastered a single weapon except his political skills and his tongue. He could not imagine himself physically injuring anyone. He was feared because of his integrity, not because he could pick up a truncheon and bash some stranger's head in. He could not inspire troops. He was too fastidious to rush along in a crowd screaming. Yet he was helping to make this insurrection happen, and happen effectively. He saw no other choice.

They must have a republic. He could not rest with the patched system they were suffering under. The Revolution would be destroyed if it was not completed, for the government could neither win the war they had insisted on starting, nor give the people the rights they had been promised and passionately wanted right now. He spoke nightly at the Jacobins, standing at the high rostrum in front of the slab of black marble that had been a memorial and created a dramatic backdrop he appreciated. The Jacobins held fifteen hundred spectators in seats canted sharply up to the vaulted ceiling. Every night it was mobbed. "The State must be saved by whatever means. Nothing is unconstitutional except what can lead to ruin!" He argued for the right to insurrection, knowing it was planned for the fifth of August.

Then on the first of August the Duke of Brunswick, who had been winning easy victories against the disorganized and ill-armed French troops, issued a manifesto. Although his name sounded British, he led Austrian and Prussian troops against the French armies of the Rhine. Brunswick said he was fighting to restore the power of the King and the Church. He threatened to lay waste to France in punishment for the Revolution and to execute the entire population of Paris if the royal family was threatened again. The proclamation was in every paper. People could talk of nothing else. Max could feel a fury seething in the streets. Everywhere knots of people were letting anger take them over. Their fear for themselves and their families translated quickly into an anger that demanded an outlet. The Duke of Brunswick had just enlarged the size of the coming demonstration by half.

The insurrection was postponed till the tenth. It must be successful. The sections of Paris issued an ultimatum—which Max helped hammer out—that the Assembly must remove the King from power, or the people would do so themselves; they gave the legislature five days to quit waffling. Five days, or the people would act.

FIFTY-ONE
Pauline

❦

(August 9–10, 1792)

PAULINE could not stop talking about that bastard the Duke of Brunswick who was going to level Paris and kill them all. "Well, he has to take the city before he can burn it down and shoot us. Sitting over there with those rotten aristocrats who ran off as soon as they lost a few privileges."

"We aren't winning," Claire said. "The government tries to pretend everything is jolly, but you can tell if you read the papers carefully, the war's a mess. Maybe Robespierre was right."

"Our soldiers are as good as anybody's. They're guys just like in the neighborhood. It's the damned aristo officers, betraying them. It's the Queen sending the army's plans to her brother."

"Marat says they don't have boots and they don't have muskets and they don't have ammunition and they don't have food," Claire said. "Imagine if we had to go to the big demonstration barefoot."

"This won't be a walkover like last time," Pauline said, pacing in the basement of the Cordeliers Club where their women's group would be meeting in half an hour. "We didn't face any resistance. Now we'll be going up against Swiss Guards who hate us."

After the women met, they went upstairs. The ultimatum ran out at midnight. The sections were in session, the elected reps of the neighborhoods and ordinary people. The children who had come with their parents were cranky and whining and hungry. Babies were crying and then cried themselves to sleep and still the sections met. When she had to use the latrine in the hall, its stench was worse than usual. People had diarrhea from fear. The Cordeliers hall stank of fear. Could it be a giant mistake? Just as on the night of June twentieth, messengers ran back and forth between City Hall and the sections, to the faubourgs, back again. The Assembly was still in session, but the followers of Brissot were holding the line against revolt. They were negotiating with the King.

As far as she was concerned, the King had no right to form or dismiss a government. He was just a gold hole down which they were expected to pour money. She had looked the royals right in the face in June as the people confronted them in the Tuileries. When she remembered how she had called Louis her father, she felt ashamed. How could she have been so stupid? She had a real father who had died in the street.

Midnight came and the Assembly had not dismissed the King and the King had not abdicated. It was time. The tocsin, that bell of alarm in the churches, began to sound. Come, come, come, come, to arms, to arms. "This is it," she said to Claire and Babette. "We stand or fall tonight. If they crush us, then we've had it. We can eat sawdust and remember our glorious adventures while we starve." She did not add that they might well die.

Danton was speaking. He was a fine speaker, but Pauline looked at him differently since Claire had fucked him. "How was he?" she asked Claire. Anything to get her mind off what was coming.

"Very vigorous. He can do it all night."

"So he was the best?"

"No. Some men are good lovers because they have so much drive that you get satisfied. But the very best know your body as you do. My Jew was like that. He could just reach out and put his hands in the right places. That's a knack few men have."

She could not understand how Claire could size up a man and decide if she wanted him. For Pauline, attraction was slow, gradual, rare. If she died in the morning in the battle that was to be, she would have had only one lover, Henri. At least she would not die a virgin. She had never experienced love as the songs and plays depicted it. Maybe she was too practical. She knew herself to be affectionate with her friends. Even her little apprentice was always telling her he loved her. But a great passion, even a middle-sized one, she would die without having known. Oh, she had her adoration of Robespierre, but that was like a special devotion to a saint. She could adore him for years and never lose sleep. She was one of an army of women who revered that small neat passionate man whose voice moved her almost to tears, who was the voice of the Revolution and its conscience. He knew this battle was necessary. So did she.

Babette's mother threw open the Dancing Badger and fed everyone free. "You can't go to battle on empty stomachs. This is my gift to the Revolution. We'll eat till the food runs out, and then we'll march."

None of them went to bed. They might be dead in a few hours. The streets were simmering. Torches were lit and the darkness pushed back. People were everywhere, as if it were noon. The rallying points for the two pincers that would converge on the palace were the Faubourg Saint Antoine and their own neighborhood, by the Cordeliers Club. Guardsmen, gendarmes, soldiers, men and women were marching in companies, armed with everything they could lay hands on from muskets and pistols to pikes and hatchets, saws, kitchen knives, cudgels, the spikes from railings mounted on broom handles. This time they did not carry flowers. They had drums and some had flags and banners, but this was not a peaceful demonstration. They were not going to educate the King, to rebuke or instruct him. They were marching to bring him down. They were marching for a republic. The Marseillais fédérés, patriots all, had been billeted at the Cordeliers Club and formed up smartly. They were a real citizen army. Maybe they could fight the professional soldiers, the Swiss.

Dawn came up brilliant and red above the slate roofs and chimney pots. "Is that a sign of blood or victory?" Claire wondered. "My grandmère always said it meant that there would be a storm later. I guess that's sure."

Runners came to the Cordeliers every few minutes. Word came that Danton had led a successful coup: an insurrectionary commune had taken City Hall and was now the authority in Paris. Danton had sent to the palace for Mandat, the commander of the National Guard.

"He won't obey us," Claire said. "He doesn't respect the people."

Pauline grimaced. "Danton has to get Santerre to take over the Guard. Then instead of attacking us, the Guard will march with us."

Finally, with City Hall secured and their own people in power, they began to move out. The latest news was that the Tuileries and even the old palace of the Louvre at the east end of the gardens were heavily defended. All the palace gates were reported to be sealed and guarded. Artillery was placed to defend the Place du Carrousel, where the people had entered on June twentieth. The King had been seen reviewing his troops just after dawn. He had been greeted enthusiastically by the Swiss and his noble guards, but the National Guards posted there booed him. The King was believed to have between four and five thousand troops, maybe more. The frontier between palace and city was closed.

A vast underarmed and raggedy army was crossing the river in the hazy morning light. Over on the right bank Théroigne de Méricourt with a sword and a pistol in a dashing version of a military outfit was leading the women's club from the Faubourg Saint Antoine. The National Guard had been ordered by Mandat to prevent them from crossing the Seine, but the Guard stood aside. Some joined the marchers. She saw the Marseillais crossing the next bridge. They congregated on the right bank and waited two hours till everyone made the crossing.

The forces drew up before the palace. Claire, Babette, Hélène, Victoire, Babette's mother and father and all Pauline's friends were near but not in the front ranks. The troops inside looked at them and they looked at the troops inside. The troops wore blue uniforms with red revers, crisp and elegant, hung with cartridges enough to blow them all to hell. Section leaders went to parlay. Pauline had not eaten since three in the morning and she was hungry. A man fiddling with his musket discharged it by accident and everyone started yelling and pushing. Rumors of deals and betrayals ran through the crowd. She shifted her pike yawning. Claire and Hélène were arguing in low private voices. The sun was beginning to heat up. Ten, said Notre Dame and the bells of the former monasteries answered, ten.

Suddenly the crowd started moving. Someone had opened the gates. People were entering quickly but peaceably. The Marseillais soldiers had taken the lead. They were marching across the courtyard while the people poured in behind them. They shouted to the Swiss to join them, to share camaraderie. "We're all soldiers. Why should we kill each other?" Once again the forces supposed to be against them had proved to be on their side.

From ahead came the word, "We're in the palace. The Swiss are throwing down their weapons and cartridges. They're going to come over to us!"

More and more people crowded in. It was a repeat of the last time they had stormed the palace. But as the Cordeliers contingent was entering the court-yard, they heard from ahead the sudden bark of muskets and then screaming. "The Swiss fired!" "They trapped us." "It's an ambush!"

They surged forward, but now blood puddled on the stones underfoot. They tripped over the dying and dead. Bullets rained down from above where the Swiss had taken up strong positions. Then came a wave of those ahead of them running back, wounded, panicked. The Swiss were firing at will into the crowd in the courtyard, hitting a target every time. They could not miss, with people packed so tightly. No one could fire back. No one could stand or take a position. There was no cover. All around her people went down. The wounded were either picked up and carried away, or they were trampled underfoot. It was turning into a rout. Pauline could not even lift her pike in the crush.

"Stand and fight!" someone was yelling, but bullets continued to smash into random flesh. People screamed and fell. Hélène fled with her hands over her ears. Claire was cursing. As they ran, the Swiss followed, shooting methodically into their backs. Pauline turned as they were forced through the narrow gates, more going down all the time, and saw some of the Swiss dragging away cannons the National Guard had abandoned. Swiss artillerymen were pulling the cannons into the palace. They had won. Every movement exuded confidence. More Swiss trotted forward toward the gates the crowd was squeezing through, bayonets fixed and spearing at will into back after back.

The captain of the Marseillais climbed on the fence. He berated his men. He bellowed at them to be brave. Finally, he told them to sing. The drummer boy was hoisted up beside him and began the tatoo. The fédérés gathered into a ragged mass and began, "To arms, you citizens!" More and more of them sang. Then they turned and started back.

"No retreat!" Their commander was yelling. "Advance or die! No retreat!" The Marseillais went charging through the gates, carrying the remainder of the fleeing crowd with them. People began to scream their anger as they pushed forward. Everyone was rushing back into the court. Bodies lay everywhere. As Pauline ran forward, her pike fixed at last for use, she saw several of the Swiss musketeers finishing off the wounded. They were caught by surprise and gunned down as they stood over the dying and mangled.

The Swiss kept shooting from cover, deliberately, every shot bringing down a body, but there were hundreds now charging forward, there were thousands. The railings crashed flat. The court was open to the street. People were racing across into the line of fire. The shooting became more sporadic as the Swiss fell back into the palace. So many people were flooding into the courtyard that Pauline saw a Marseillais carried on with the crowd, although he had been shot in the eye and was dead.

Claire at her side, Pauline entered, her pike fixed for action. They could hear Théroigne's loud husky voice exhorting the soldiers ahead. A Swiss Guard behind a column shot and the bullet flew past Pauline close enough to make her cry out before it hit Babette's father. He went down without a word. Claire stepped forward and fired her pistol as the musketeer was reloading. She shot him in the shoulder and he fell. There was no time to think. A man in silk culottes swinging a sabre was coming at Pauline. She speared him with her pike and then could not pull it back, for he had fallen on it. Blood gushed out of him. He was dying on her foot. Feeling sick, she left her pike and backed away. She had killed him, some unknown man. She began to cry, rubbing at her eyes in shame. As she stood there, a Cordelier pulled her pike free and charged forward into the melee.

At the foot of the grand staircase, the Swiss were firing down. "Shit!" Claire said. "Shit!" She fell on her knees. She had taken a bullet through the flesh of her left arm, and blood was pouring down on her clothes.

They found shelter behind a pillar. "You should get out of here," Pauline said.

"Just bandage me up. Tear off part of my petticoat. The bullet went through, thank God." She leaned against the pillar, eyes closed. "Take my pistol."

"I don't know how to use it." Pauline hefted it uncertainly. Hélène began to cry. Between them they tied a tight bandage and stopped the heavy bleeding. Claire lay back against the pillar. A Guardsman handed them a flask and she drank the brandy.

More and more people were pouring in, National Guard, men and women, all the ragged army of the morning. They were charging into the fire from the Swiss and knocking them off one by one, stabbing them, shooting, bludgeoning them. The line of the Swiss broke under the sheer numbers. The stairs had been cleared and there was hand-to-hand fighting all over the palace, wherever Pauline looked, pikes against sabers, improvised weapons against pistols. Many bodies of Marseillais lay on the marble floor and on the grand staircase, but up above were bodies of the Swiss. Babette had found her father and was keening over him. People were kicking the dead Swiss in their smart uniforms. "The bastards tricked us. They invited us in. Then they slaughtered us."

Babette began to move through the palace with a butcher's knife in her hand. When she found a living Swiss or nobleman, she stabbed him through the heart. She tried to hack off a head, but she was not strong enough. "You tricked my father. You killed him with muskets against his little knife. How do you like this little knife?"

With Claire weak from loss of blood leaning on her and Hélène, Pauline led them wandering through the rooms. Corpses were everyplace, the attackers, the defenders and any inhabitants of the palace who had not fled. Blood stained the silk and tapestry seats of the sofas, the armchairs, the bergères. A mirror the size of a wall had been shattered by bullets, turned into a glass spiderweb. Someone had bayonetted a big portrait of Louis XVI. A woman in court dress with paniers had been shot and stuffed into the works of a clavichord, the immense hoop of her skirt sticking up, holding the lid. No one could find the King or the Queen. The palace was theirs, for although an occasional shot or scream rang out, they had won. Claire collapsed on a blue silk sofa in a room all blue and white. "I feel very weak."

"Rest." Hélène wiped Claire's forehead. "Soon we'll go home."

Pauline wondered why she felt only numb.

FIFTY-TWO

Georges

(August 3–17, 1792)

GEORGES went to Arcis the week before the insurrection. He wanted to fix a pension on his old nurse and make sure his mother would get her share of the estate he was leaving mostly to Gabrielle. He was fully aware of the troops the King had brought into the Tuileries. The revolutionaries were going up against real soldiers with a mob from the sections, ill-armed, dependent more on enthusiasm and anger than on military know-how. The fédérés, on whom so much hope was pinned, had learned to march and sing and carry their muskets properly, but none had been in a skirmish. Georges was settling his affairs, in case he did not survive.

He came back to Paris calmer. He had tried to mediate, he had procrastinated, he had made militant speeches with conciliatory endings, but the time had come to change the government into one that could pursue the war with real commitment, with full mobilization. Otherwise the Austrians would march into the city, and he would be hanging on the end of a rope.

The Queen still imagined if she could buy off a few leaders, the Revolution would vanish. She simply could not believe in any players of note who were not in the old court nobility. She hated Lafayette, who had been trying to save the royal family, far more than she hated the populace that was about to overthrow her. Nothing that had happened could persuade the Queen that the Revolution was anything but the plot of a few dissatisfied and jealous courtiers who felt they had not received sufficient royal favor.

The time had come to sweep the whole mess away. Gabrielle wept in his arms, but he had committed to an action from which there was no turning aside. August ninth, the section met all night. He made a good rousing speech and then met with Camille and men he could depend on, who were fiercely and personally loyal to him. Then he went home, made love to Gabrielle and slept.

Finally it was time. They were to meet with whatever desperate men the other sections had sent, and they were going to take City Hall and put in their new Commune. They would seize the city or be shot down in the attempt. When Camille took up his musket, Lucile burst into tears and clutched him. Then she turned to Georges with huge baleful eyes. "Promise me you'll take care of him! Promise me you won't let harm come to him."

"In God's hands," he said, but that wasn't the answer she wanted. Finally to shut her up, he promised. Camille would return with not a hair mussed. They took their weapons and went off in the grey predawn. As they crossed the Seine, they could see the red sun rising. "A morning of blood," Georges said, staring at the ruddy sky.

"Let it be theirs," Camille said fervently. "Georges, this is really bizarre. It's just us, you know, you and me. Only we're not off to pick up a whore or cause a little trouble or rattle some windows. We're actually proposing to take over the government. We're going off to seize power. I feel like an imposter. Don't you?"

"No," Georges said frankly. "I know what to do with power. Those fools have not used their power well. I can rule. I know what people want."

"Maybe I'll have to lead a revolution against you next month."

"Nonsense. If we win today, you'll be in the government too. I'll see to that. You can use the money."

"Papa Duplessis is tired of subsidizing us. It would lighten the atmosphere marvelously if I made a few sous, a little something toward supporting Lucile. She does like to spend money. You must admit she has exquisite taste—but exquisite objects have the most exquisite prices."

"Everything costs," Georges said. "Children, wives, houses, families, and today we gamble for power with our lives for chips."

"Power is not real to me," Camille murmured. He had slowed his pace, wearing that dreamy introspective look that made him appear all of eighteen. "Power exercised upon me, I know that. My father, the domestic tyrant. The Fathers at school. Bosses—"

"Keep up your pace. We aren't taking a Sunday stroll. We shouldn't be the last to arrive. If you're tempted to dawdle, remember what the Duke of Brunswick promised us. Summary execution. The city leveled. Our families condemned. Troops turned loose on civilians. Move it!"

At six A.M, they walked into chaos. The Insurrectionary Commune was attempting to disperse the old machinery. They were armed; few of the old officials had weapons, but there were scuffles. One bureaucrat of the old city council, who had a pistol in his belt, shot an insurgent in the thigh and was himself shot down. One police official was stabbed. An insurgent was pushed down the stairs. Another was hit by a chair. Danton stood at the head of the stairway and bellowed, "Your resistance is illegal. The people put you in. The people have removed you. You are no longer wanted or needed here! The city is in arms. Fight with us or get out of the way, or die like slaughtered pigs. You can't block the armed people." The fighting stopped. Officers of the old government began to leave.

Pétion was hovering. His sympathies were with the Revolution, but he was Mayor. Georges decided to simplify things for him. He issued an order to two of his men. "Put the Mayor under house arrest for the next twenty-four hours. Take him home."

Pétion could scarcely suppress his relief. "As you wish, Danton," he said. "I cooperate." The man was overjoyed. "Citizens," he addressed his supposed captors. "I am your prisoner!"

The next problem was Mandat, for the head of the National Guard intended to defend the King. The lines of authority over the Guard were confused. It was not clear what governmental body had the authority to call them out, but clearly, their general did. One of the Guard commandants from Croix Rouge showed Danton an order signed by Mandat ordering the Guards to march with the sections and then fire on them from the rear when they attacked the Tuileries, thus catching the people between fire from the palace and fire from behind. It would be a massacre. Georges dispatched a message, using Pétion's seal, summoning Mandat to City Hall for an emergency meeting to discuss defense. He thought Mandat would come, and indeed, Mandat arrived just ten minutes after the return of the messenger. He was arrested at once.

Georges ordered a Cordelier to take Mandat to prison. The man made a slashing sign at his throat and Georges nodded. Mandat would shoot no one in the back. Santerre, the revolutionary brewer, took command of the Guard. Now they would join the insurrection or sit it out. That improved the odds.

By eight A.M., the insurrectionaries had taken over City Hall. Representatives to the Insurrectionary Commune trickled in erratically but in growing numbers. Eighty-odd representatives elected by the sections were on the job. The popular government of Paris was in session. They sat around a big oval table in City Hall and divided tasks. Now they could hear gunfire. It was already hot. The day was sultry. There was an odor of shit and smoke in the air. Runners came regularly with news of the battle beginning at the Tuileries twelve blocks away.

Georges occupied the former comptroller's office temporarily and sent Fabre d'Églantine to Brissot stating that he thought the people would take the palace that day, and the King would fall. What was Brissot prepared to do? They must discuss the new cabinet that would be set up. He signed himself,

"Danton, representing the Insurrectionary Commune of Paris." He was not quite sure whether to use the Commune as his new power base or whether he could move into the national government. His negotiations with Brissot were aimed at getting a good ministerial portfolio.

They could hear a lot more gunfire now and cannonballs landing some-where. Runners told them the insurrectionary forces had been driven from the palace with great casualties. Danton debated rushing over to take part. Then a messenger came to say that the Marseillais were leading the charge back into the palace. Hundreds were dying on both sides. It was a real battle. In the meantime, Fabre came back from Brissot with a note. "Let's have a discussion. I don't want to go to City Hall at the moment. Please come by my flat around four."

Wise man. Someone in the Commune might find Brissot tempting to remove. "Fabre, I don't think we should meet with Brissot on his territory. Tell him we'll meet him in the Palais Royal—the Italian Cafe at four. Camille and you should be there too."

Four was a good hour to meet, because the Tuileries had fallen. The King had escaped while his Swiss Guards were being slaughtered and dismem-bered in the palace and then on the streets. They had shot down too many people to survive. Each Parisian slain had a dozen family and friends to avenge them, and they did. The bodies were stripped for practical reasons: the poor needed every scrap of fabric they could lay hands on. Weapons were even more precious. But the people were enraged, because they had been tricked.

On the way to the Palais Royal, Georges passed among the women at their grisly task of vengeance on the dead. He understood: the death of a bread-winner could mean the death of the whole family next winter. Camille was sick behind a bush. Fabre pretended to be amused at the grislier mutilations, to judge them according to aesthetic criteria. Georges kept his party moving.

They ran into Santerre, who told them casualties on both sides probably amounted to twelve, thirteen hundred dead. There were more dead on the King's side, more wounded on the popular side. Now it was over except for the crowds milling around in the palace and hunting down the Swiss. Santerre walked along with them. "The King and the rest of the royal family hid in the Assembly. By the way, only half of the delegates had the balls to show up today. When the Swiss started shooting, the King had already run to cover. They weren't defending him but an empty palace. What a piece of work he is—ordering them to fight and then bolting."

"What's the Assembly doing now?"

"The people are confronting them. The Assembly's debating suspending the King and calling for a National Convention to replace themselves. They're scared to the point of wetting their culottes—for good reason."

By the next day, Georges was Minister of Justice in the new government. All the rest of the ministers were from Brissot's group. Georges' position was awkward, as the only representative of the left in the government the people had put into power through insurrection. He might be able to close the gap between the two factions.

In the meantime he was the liaison between the new Commune and the new cabinet. The Commune demanded the King and the royal family be handed over to them. The Assembly would not risk their own necks to protect the King. The royal prisoners were taken to the Temple—once the stronghold of the Knights Templar in Paris. It was not what Georges would call a pleasant hotel, grim, with a grim history. It looked medieval, high crenelated turrets with slits of window.

Georges held court in his new office in the Tuileries. "Camille, you and Fabre will both be my secretaries. Good pay." He put the printer Robert in charge of his staff. He appointed other Cordeliers, including his old law clerk Paré and Billaud-Varenne, to the Council of Justice. He offered a place on the Council to Robespierre, who declined: he would not be compromised by entering a government controlled by Girondins. Fine, thought Georges, I get credit for asking, and somebody else will owe me. I spread the favors around.

The patronage was considerable. Within a week, Camille got a letter from a cousin who wanted a job. "Why not?" Camille said. "It will drive my father crazy." So Fouquier-Tinville was appointed to the special court trying those the Commune accused. Camille knew little about him, but it was amusing to give largesse to a cousin. Fouquier-Tinville's politics seemed properly militant. Why not?

Dozens of emissaries were sent out to the provinces to present the new government's official story about August tenth. Georges managed to send several Cordeliers on the road. They all had political careers to make.

Ten days later they had a party, Camille, Lucile, Robert and his wife Louise, Fabre, everybody. They ate and sang and danced till two in the morning. Gabrielle had outdone herself with a goose and a ham, a huge tricolor cake. The next day he got up early. He would not slack at his new job. He would set the ministry staff on fire. They would learn that someone with a strong hand was in charge. He was making a handsome salary and he controlled a great deal of ministry money. He finally paid off his old mistress for the position he had bought years ago. He was clear and free of debts. The future was coming up brisk and sunny. He felt his blood surging in his veins. He felt strong enough to wrestle a bull again.

"Camille!" He clapped his friend on the back. "We're young, we have good wives to fuck, we have a great life before us. Now we're in the saddle. This is a horse we're riding to victory. What could be better? This is what I was born to do. This is what I'm made for."

"How can you be so loud at this hour of the morning? I was born to sleep late. You drag me to work and I'm still hung over."

"I think I can bring the factions back together. I'll start working on the Rolands. She's the key."

"Oh, the virtuous Manon, the aging almost virgin."

"She has a gorgeous bosom. Nice arms. Nice eyes. Her husband doesn't fuck her, I can tell. I'll get her on our side. She used to have a crush on Robespierre. Now it's my turn. Then I'll use her to turn the Girondins around. We'll show the Austrians and the Prussians a solid front. It can be done, Camille, and I can do it. You'll see."

FIFTY-THREE

Nicolas

❧

(August 10, 1792)

A T times during the past two years, Nicolas had thought the people a rabble who did not have enough education to govern themselves; at times, he had felt humbled before their courage as they had seemed ready to decide their own destinies. Since he had swung over to a republic, he had tended to cling to the latter position, the power and dignity of the people.

He still belonged to the loose assortment of friends, colleagues, political men and women who thought if not alike, then somehow reasoning from the same premises—a collection others purported to see as a faction, a party. Robespierre even referred to them in the ludicrous terms of a conspiracy. Some called them Brissotins, as if they all followed Brissot's lead. Brissot was an able politician, as he had been a competent journalist, but there was no sense in which he was their leader. Others called them Girondins, because some came from the department of the Gironde. Nicolas voted his conscience. Nor did the so-called Girondins always support him. He had spent a great deal of time on a program of universal education. But when he had brought it to the floor of the Assembly, it had been pushed aside in war hysteria, led by his allies.

He lacked the enthusiasm for this war that Brissot and Roland showed, but he recognized the difference between a war of defense and a war of offense. Austrian and Prussian armies had invaded France and were advancing on Paris. In Brunswick's manifesto he heard not ponderous Germanic threats, but the sly and nasty hand of court émigrés, congregating in towns across the Rhine and dreaming of getting all their old riches and entitlements back. It was the émigrés who wanted to hang all reformers and revolutionaries, including himself. It was the émigrés who wanted to burn Paris to the ground to punish the city for refusing them their ancient privileges. He suspected that Marie-Antoinette had encouraged those threats. She had never grasped the anger or the resolve of the ordinary people of Paris.

On August ninth, he spent the night at the Assembly. Delegates were slipping out. By morning, there were less than two hundred left. They were afraid. He had been present during the tumult on June twentieth; he did not see why this should be different, except that his friends and colleagues had very much wanted that demonstration, and they very much did not want this one. Brissot had moved toward supporting the King, whom a few months ago he had wanted to topple. Nicolas did not agree that they needed a King—an anachronism without purpose.

The delegates milling around in the Assembly had little idea what was happening outside. Nobody wanted to go see, but the doors swung open occasionally and people came to tell them. A battle was being fought for the Tuileries. They heard gunfire. Twice cannonballs shook the walls. Nicolas was not a military man. He had no desire to stick his nose into the fray. But neither would he leave. Perhaps it was pride, not to show fear. He had a sense that, having been elected, he had a duty here. The Assembly had failed to remove the King. Finally the sections had asked the Assembly to dissolve itself so that a National Convention could be elected by true popular vote. He did not disagree.

The sounds of musketry grew more intense. Smoke floated into the former riding school. The acrid stench of gunpowder, a sour smell of something rotting lay on the fetid heat. They were all sweating. The room was close and smoky. He sat fanning himself with a distributed speech no one bothered to look at.

Then the doors burst open. "The King's coming!"

Several delegates rushed to greet the royal party. Nicolas stayed near the door. The King stumbled in. He wore a silk suit of violet, the royal color of mourning, rumpled as if he had slept in it. His hair was untidy and only half-powdered and his visage, drawn and pale. Nicolas was struck by how furious the Queen looked, among the others who seemed terrified. She had aged in the months since their unsuccessful flight. Her hair had turned grey. Her features were sharper. She looked more than ever a Hapsburg.

Roederer, who had been thrust into charge of defending the Tuileries after Mandat was called away, seized upon Nicolas and poured out his troubles. "I tried to talk the King into going to the Assembly at once, but he wouldn't budge. He gave the order to resist force with force. Then he sat down in a chair and wouldn't talk. He just sulked for hours.

"I kept begging him to avoid bloodshed. The Queen insisted she'd rather be nailed to the palace wall than retreat. He kept wringing his hands. The mob was attacking and we were all waiting on him. The more we insisted, the angrier the Queen got. She said, 'Don't you dare raise your voice with me!' We could hear shooting. Finally he said, 'Let's go.' We went across the gardens to the Riding School. The King took off his plumed hat and handed it to a Guard. 'Put it on,' the King ordered. The Guard thought he was crazy, then he realized why the King didn't want to be visible and snatched the hat off his head.

"We crossed the gardens. It's been so hot and dry this summer, there were already leaves over the paths and they hadn't been raked. The Dauphin was playing in the leaves and kicking them up. The King turned and said solemnly, 'The leaves are falling early this year. We shall have an early autumn.' It seemed so sad." Roederer held Nicolas' hand in his, his eyes moist. "What will happen now?"

Delegates fussed about what to do with the King, since it was against the Constitution for the King to be in the Assembly while it was in session. Some objected. Others insisted they must protect him. Finally they led the royal party to the logographie, a box behind the rostrum where the legislative reporters took down speeches. It was separated from the Assembly by an iron grill, which the deputies, the Guards and the King himself helped to remove. The space was tight. The royal party was crammed shoulder to shoulder. The children began to fret and cry.

So now they had a king on their hands. It was proposed he be moved to the abandoned Luxembourg palace. Others objected that the Luxembourg, like the Tuileries, had extensive underground passages. What was to keep the King from taking off as he had to Varennes?

Brissot appeared at Nicolas' elbow. "We have to talk. This bunch is just chasing their tails. We need to set up a new government. The Commune is already running Paris. They'll take over the country if we don't act at once. Do you want the foreign ministry?"

"I'd rather stay in the legislature," Nicolas said. He would support the war, but he had no intention of waging it. "You're going to have to bring in some of those who planned this. You have to give them something."

"I won't have Robespierre in my cabinet," Brissot said.

"I dislike the man too," Nicolas said honestly. "A small fierce mind, like a ferret. Besides, he's not at the crest of his popularity any longer. How about Danton? He can be reasoned with, and he has the popular touch."

Brissot hesitated. "Do you think we can work with him?"

"His rhetoric is bloody, but his mind isn't. He's a pragmatist, not a fanatic. He might serve as a link between us and the Commune."

"I'll check with the Rolands, but time is running out. I want to put a government together today. I'll stay in the Assembly too. I want Servan at War again and Roland back in the Interior. What would we give Danton?"

"Justice. Wasn't he a public prosecutor?"

"Fine. If the Rolands don't object. By tomorrow, I want a new government in place. This is wartime, and we can't risk anarchy and indecision."

"I'll go with you to see them."

At seven P.M., they walked in the direction of the Tuileries. The smoke still hung in the air, but they heard only an occasional shot. As they passed the courtyard, women were kneeling and stripping the bodies of the Swiss Guards.

"What are you doing?" Brissot called, shocked.

"Getting clothes, what do you think I'm doing?"

"They're mutilating the bodies! Dear God." Nicolas could not bring himself to say, castrating. He felt sick to his stomach. He put out a hand to the iron grating, but it came away sticky with blood. There were gobbets of something impaled there. Gorge rose in his throat, burning and acid.

"Let's get out of here." Brissot shuddered and began to walk very fast. Nicolas noticed that they both were walking with their hands down around their groins.

"I suppose when you're dead, it doesn't matter what's done to your corpse," Nicolas said, trying to find a philosophically detached position. Brissot did not answer, walking with his head bowed. Everywhere were naked bodies, many decapitated. On the iron spikes of the fence, heads and penises were impaled. Finally Nicolas was sick in the gutter. As soon as he began to heave, so did Brissot.

"Look at the gentlemen losing their dinners!" a woman yelled. "Gets you right there, don't it, gents?"

They trotted along the street. Nicolas was soon short of breath, his side stabbing him, but he did not dare slow down. Out of what dregs did such women arise? Were they women? Vultures? He was seriously shaken. Were these the people he was championing? They must be criminals who came out as darkness fell, like rats. "You go on to the Rolands' alone. Sophie will be frantic with worry. I should go directly home and make peace with her."

"I wish I could go home," Brissot said fervently. "These people terrify me. We must take over and keep order. Look what's waiting to rise up from the gutters!"

FIFTY-FOUR

Manon

❧

(August–November 1792)

MANON was pleased to be back in the quarters allotted to the Minister of the Interior. She had never really unpacked into the small flat. The city felt out of control, cooking around them. They had not wanted this uprising. Although her friends had been responsible for bringing the fédérés from Marseille, Robespierre had appropriated them. He had befriended the men and Danton put them up at the Cordeliers Club. They had been indoctrinated with the violent fanaticism of that faction centered on the Cordeliers, the Jacobins and the new Paris Commune.

She did not like Danton in the Ministry. He began inviting himself to her dinners. He would show up with Fabre d'Églantine and take over the room, holding forth. She was upset when she saw how good men seemed seduced by him. They hung on his loud words. Even if she knew they disliked him and talked against him, in his presence they acted like hens around a cock.

She could hardly bear to look at him. His face was exactly the mirror of his character: sensual, arrogant, deformed, powerful in every dangerous way. Several times he put his huge hot hands on her shoulder, her arm. Once he dared touch her posterior, giving her a pat as if she were a pack animal. She almost slapped him, but political considerations and her need to avoid an open scandal prevented her. Instead she glared and he withdrew at once, looking, she would swear, slightly puzzled.

Other women seemed to swoon in front of him, sunflowers to his torrid sun. It was depressing. He did not even pretend to principles. He said often enough, Whatever works. Men of deep convictions, like Brissot and her husband, had come into prominence, but she was beginning to understand that a revolution, in stirring up society, also brought to the surface villains and thugs. Danton was such a man in whose face she could see vices and reckless sensuality writ large.

He enjoyed shocking her. He would grin and say he did not understand why anyone would hesitate to take a bribe—after all, it wasn't a contract, and only a dolt thought he had bought a man just because he had given him a present. It was like buying a woman supper and thinking you had bought her sexual favors. She might or might not think so too, and if she didn't consider it a bargain, you were proved a fool. She heard rumors that he had taken bribes. She found him deeply disturbing. He dominated gatherings as if everyone should be enamored with his words. He also listened; she had to give him that. He was truly interested in each man's position and how they had come to it. With him in the government and forming their liaison with the unruly and dangerous Commune, she could scarcely ask him to leave. She had to endure him and his lackey Fabre whenever he felt like inviting himself.

The Commune had demanded a special tribunal to punish those they held responsible for the ambush they believed the Swiss Guards had laid. The man in the street seemed convinced aristocrats were plotting against him and that the armies were being defeated because of right-wing conspiracy. More aristocrats were fleeing. Their carriage horses had been confiscated for the army, and that proved the last blow. They were not about to walk or hail a cab. Manon was not sorry to see them decamp, but she did not like the reason they were leaving: fear of the violence of the little people, as they called them, who hated them and wanted them dead.

She admitted to herself that she was reasonably happy. Jean had a position of importance in the government, befitting his talents. They had filled the ministries with people who thought as they did. Except for Danton, they gave not an inch to the left. She was surrounded by intelligent high-minded men who believed firmly and thoroughly in the Revolution but were not scoundrels or opportunists. They were men of principle. They were friends.

The Assembly had agreed to capitulate to the common people of Paris by dissolving itself and letting a National Convention be elected. Campaigning was under way. The Convention would be different from the Assembly: it would rule. It would draw up a new Constitution for a republic, and it would act as the government until a Constitution was accepted. Condorcet was excited about the Convention, imagining it on the American model. He wanted to write the new Constitution for France. He was indefatigable. She saw him as a large sheep pulling a plow. She could never take him wholly seriously.

Still, for the Social Circle Press, he was irreplaceable. Jean controlled a great deal of money as Minister of the Interior, some earmarked for popular education and propaganda. They had been shifting that money over to their Social Circle Press. The press churned out periodicals for audiences with different degrees of sophistication, works on government and the economy, marriage and divorce, education and primogeniture. Divorce had just become legal. The common people had demanded it, along with a civil registry of births, deaths and marriages. She was startled how many more women than men were asking for divorces. She would have expected it to be the other way round. The most common complaint was wife beating.

Her group must retain power and steer the Revolution on a sane and responsible course. Would-be tyrants of the left like Robespierre and Marat kept sniping at them. Marat particularly reviled her. He made up sexual libels, as if she had done anything shameful ever. They hated her partly because she was a woman, hence all the filthy innuendo; they hated her partly because she was effective politically and she was now in power. Marat dared to write that she had seduced all the men who came to her salon and that she used her sexual favors to control the Girondins.

In the meantime, just when her friends thought that the populace had finally quieted down, news came that the Austrians and the Prussians were advancing into France, winning victory after victory and aiming for Paris. Longwy and Verdun had fallen. Lafayette had deserted and gone over to the Austrians, who promptly arrested him. Danton was making speeches to get the common people to enlist, which fortunately they were doing in large numbers. Then the people went crazy and broke into the prisons to massacre refractory priests and aristocrats and common criminals alike. It was a bloodbath, for which she personally held the Commune, Marat, Robespierre and Danton responsible. The violence was incredible. When Lanthénas and Bosc started to tell her, she made them stop. It was a scene of animalistic slaughter, men and women hacked limb from limb.

A style of journalism had arisen that promoted violence. Hébert, a squat man who had been a ticket taker in a theater, was putting out a journal called *Père Duchesne*, after a rough folk figure who made stoves. Hébert used consciously foul language. These fucking asshole aristocrats, we should cut off their pricks and stuff them down their throats. It was disgusting and vulgar, and it stirred up the people to a dangerous extent. Marat was just as bad and he had been at it longer. He was always screaming traitor and calling for somebody's head, frequently hers.

She considered sending Eudora back to the country, but decided it was a bad idea for the child to be separated from them. She hired a governess instead. There was plenty of room in the mansion. Their old friend Lanthénas, her "little brother," moved in. When Buzot won his seat in the Convention, she invited him to remain until he had arranged lodging. After all, they had room upon room upon room. She might as well treat the mansion as a lodging house for colleagues.

Jean had been elected to the Convention and wanted to resign the ministry, but Brissot and Buzot insisted he remain at Interior. Of all the delegates to the Convention, she soon felt closest to Buzot. He admired her openly and respectfully. She began working on his speeches. Buzot was young but far more serious than most men around her. He took nothing lightly. He was fiery, emotional, a man of true principles. Physically and in character, he was the polar opposite of Danton: neat, principled, a slender small man who often chose to remain in the background while others held forth, a man of honorable and intense emotions.

"You're the best, the finest, the most attractive woman I have ever met," he said to her in her little office.

"François, I'm six years older than you."

"My wife is thirteen years older. We've never had anything in common. I don't think she's ever met an idea she liked. It was an arranged marriage. At the time I had no notion that there could be loving communication between a man and a woman, that we could share a universe of discourse."

He came from a nasty provincial town in Normandy, the oldest son of a bourgeois family. He had early formed an attachment to Plutarch and other Roman writers and then, as she had, found Rousseau. He was gentle-spoken, always impeccable, with large luminous eyes and a direct gaze.

"Don't you think he looks a little like Robespierre?" Lanthénas asked.

"Don't be absurd. You can't compare that savage little weasel with the loyal and good Buzot, with his generous great heart."

"You're very partial to him," Lanthénas said sourly.

"I respect each according to his virtue and his ability."

"He's a good orator but his arguments lack cohesion and edge."

"Perhaps his speeches will improve. Let us hope so."

She refused to take Lanthénas' jealousy seriously. After all, she was doing nothing wrong. Quite simply, Buzot and she understood each other. It was a joy to work with him. He did not dismiss her suggestions nor take her labors for granted, as her husband did. He made her feel supremely appreciated. For her to feel a precious fondness in return was only natural. To talk about François, even with someone as insensitive to his true nature as Lanthénas, was a deep, almost embarrassing pleasure. Sometimes even hearing his name unexpectedly sent pulses of warmth through her.

"The Revolution needs new men and new women," François said, "yet in order to make a revolution of virtue, we must be renewed ourselves. It seems an impossibility, Manon, a circular thesis, that we must already be what we must become in order to accomplish our goals."

"The impossible is what is not yet possible, François. When we do it, it is no longer impossible. Only difficult."

Using given names was a small but permissible sign of intimacy. It was the new fashion, for the aristocratic manner of greeting people by title was mistrusted. It was a little caress to say François, to hear him say Manon.

The salon that week could discuss nothing but the revolt that had broken out in the Vendée in support of the King and the Church. These were dangerous times. Still, when she sat at her frugal but beautifully set table looking around at fifteen or sixteen men whom she trusted and who were now the government of France (providing that Danton had not invited himself and that worm Fabre along), she felt a glow of accomplishment and pride. This was the center of decision, the brain and heart of the Revolution. Jean presided at the head of the table between Brissot and Louvet. She sat at the foot, François on her right hand, Lanthénas on her left. There were always flowers. She would have felt the table was undressed without flowers. She provided the place and the time and the atmosphere, and afterward she would open her mind to whichever of them sought her out to discuss the issues. She was a good woman, a good wife, a good revolutionary. If she had a private tender understanding with François, how did that impact anything else, including Jean—who did not even notice?

FIFTY-FIVE
Claire

❦

(Fall 1792)

CLAIRE and Hélène walked arm in arm, with Pauline and Babette just ahead, all of them stealing an afternoon for a half-holiday. Now Claire was out of work and Hélène had a job in a patriotic musical. She was the wicked aristocratic vamp who seduced the patriot from his truehearted girl-friend and tried to get him to betray his country. She wore a wonderful purple silk dress with a farthingale, the bodice cut most of the way toward her waist. Hélène had recovered her full health, glowing again, her hair a little bonfire.

Last night the women of the quarter had celebrated the passage of the divorce law they had urged on the men. Since its passage, already ten women of the section had gone to court. Primogeniture had been abolished at the same time. Now all children would inherit. Almost everybody had something to leave, if only a bed or coat or tools or a chest of drawers. Always the oldest son had gotten it all, the way her mother's house had been earmarked for Pierre. Claire thought, I will live to be an old woman, and I'll still be angry at my mother because she could not cherish me as she loved her sons. It was more than ten years since she had run away from home to join the traveling players, and still she had that sore spot just under her heart. She felt a little ashamed. She had not been sent out crippled to facilitate begging. She had not been starved, she had not been abandoned, her maidenhead had not been sold.

Jacques Roux, a radical priest who had become her friend, talked often of the plight of children. He had a heart as big as the Champ de Mars, and he cared about the children of the poor, he cared about women, he cared about the old and the infirm and those who had worked themselves nearly to death. He felt that a revolution that left people poor and half-starving was no revolution. "Jacques is a good soul," Claire said. "As good as they grow them."

"He makes me nervous," Hélène said. "He's so intense."

"I'd go to his church if it wasn't such a long walk." Jacques Roux lived in the Gravelliers section, one of the poorest.

"I want a striped petticoat like that one," Hélène said. She was changing the subject deliberately. Claire had not realized how uncomfortable Jacques made Hélène. Now that she thought about it, Hélène usually found an excuse to go shopping when the priest came by. She had assumed Hélène was being tactful and letting them discuss politics.

"Tell Victoire. She's all over the place lately." Victoire was the first local woman to get a divorce. Her husband's beatings had caused her to miscarry twice. Now she was on her own, singing the praises of the Revolution at the top of her lungs. She looked five years younger.

They sat on the balustrade of the bridge swinging their legs and watching people go by. It was a free show, though nowadays it was regular people looking at each other instead of footmen running ahead of the matched horses drawing fancy carriages and more footmen running behind. Workmen were demolishing a statue of Henri IV. Statues and metalwork were being melted down for the army, where most of the horses had gone. Hélène was prattling about the petticoat. Claire nodded and made appropriate noises, but she was actually listening to the story Babette was telling Pauline.

After Babette's father was killed, her older brother Baptiste turned up and tried to take over the Dancing Badger. He told his mother to get out from behind the counter and work in the kitchen and he told Babette to go find other work and clear out. He was planning to install his wife as waitress and bar maid. Babette protested to the section, and they upheld her. The eldest son could no longer take everything. They must all share the Dancing Badger. Now there was daily war between the two factions, but at least Babette had not been turned out on the streets.

Suddenly Pauline said, "There's Victoire. You wanted her. She's in the street with her rack."

They had to go to her, because the bridge wasn't her territory. She stood on their bank, waiting for them.

"I love fall. It makes my blood run faster." Victoire had hair almost as dark as Claire's own, and her face was freckled from being out in the streets so much. Her eyes were a clear light brown, huge against her skin and dark hair. Claire had always thought of her as a quiet, somber woman, but now she was talkative and grinning all the time. "I'm a free woman, Claire, just like you. I've always admired you for that. Now, why did you call to me?"

"For me," Hélène said, standing on one foot and looking from under her lashes as if she had to flirt to do business. "I want one of those shiny striped petticoats."

Victoire reached into her pile and pulled out one striped yellow and green and white and black. "How's this?"

Hélène fingered it, frowning. "I don't know. . . ."

"This is brighter." It was even shinier, green, red and blue.

"I like it better." Hélène pinched the fabric, shook out the petticoat to go over it inch by inch. "It's not bad."

They began to haggle. Claire and Pauline strolled back on the bridge to wait, while Babette looked at bodices. A boy was hawking the newest *Friend of the People*, and Claire bought one. The Commune Tribunal had a new prosecutor, one Fouquier-Tinville, who was trying traitors briskly. "What a weird name the new prosecutor has," Pauline said, reading over Claire's shoulder. "But they say he gets the trials over in half the time."

"Austrians still advancing . . ." Claire handed Pauline the paper, her mood dampened. "What will happen to us if Paris falls? It could be brutal beyond belief."

"We'll fight them ourselves if it comes to that," Pauline said stoutly. "They'll never take Paris."

Hélène and Babette finished their purchases and Victoire went off pushing her cart laden with old clothes, the better ones set up on a wobbly rack. She had to be her own horse, like most street merchants. The other women went off across the bridge, Hélène and Claire bringing up the rear.

The guillotine was set up in the Place du Carrousel, in front of the Tuileries, but there was talk of moving it. Refurbishing the Tuileries was taking forever, because the workmen would rather watch the executions. Claire had seen public executions at home, of course. A Protestant had been burned in the square when she was little. Her grandmother stood and prayed for him defiantly. A horse thief had been hanged along with his young son. Thieves and robbers, arsonists and murderers, all had hung on the end of a rope and slowly, slowly died. Sometimes they were broken on the wheel first. Sometimes their flesh was torn open or they were tortured with hot pokers or rods. Once a noble had been beheaded for rape and abduction, but it was done in effigy. Only the straw head rolled. He was in seclusion under a lettre de cachet, the King's arrest warrant. She tried not to bring her old horror of executions to this event, because this was ordered by the Commune. It was just and fair. They were executing an officer of the Swiss Guards, a counterfeiter, two aristocrats accused of smuggling information to Austria, a rapist and a former naval captain who had flogged his men to death.

The guillotine stood high in the center of the square. There was a crowd, but they could see pretty well, because it was elevated on a big wooden platform. It looked plain and ordinary and serviceable, not particularly frightening. It was like a big window with a blade at the top. A window to quick death. While they were still trying to find a good place to stand, a prisoner was executed, snick, snack, just like that.

Down it came and a head rolled into a basket. The executioner looked bored. Pauline said it was the same royal executioner Sanson, who missed the good old days when he got to do fancy public torturing. Now he just fitted them into the mechanism. They lay facedown on their bellies with their throat extended. Down came the blade with a whomp. That was it. After the first few, the air smelled of blood as in the squares where butchers worked.

The people around them cheered when a head rolled. Pauline and Babette cheered, even Hélène clapped, but Claire could not. She could not applaud death. She knew they were getting the justice they deserved. It wasn't like the old executions. There was no prolonged suffering to witness, no torture. Very efficient, they said, almost painless—you couldn't feel a thing. But people were still dying, and she felt like a traitor because she could not cheer. It was certainly fast: the last man had just been executed and the crowd began to stir and drift away.

Sometimes she thought her childhood had warped her, that she was apart from everyone else and could not enjoy what they did, that she always had doubts. This was no entertainment for her. On one edge of the place, a musician was playing the fiddle, a woman was beating a drum and people were dancing the carmagnole. The dance was named for a jacket worn by the working men of Paris. Hélène held out her hand and pulled Claire into the circle of dancers. At last Claire felt united with the others. It was a perfect golden and blue afternoon despite the news of enemy victories and the approach of troops whose general had sworn to put the city to fire and sword. To turn them into a monstrous pile of corpses to show what happened when a people arrested their king.

After the dancing stopped, they stood watching the crowd. "It's an exciting time to be alive," she said to Hélène. "Now the Tuileries is ours." She pointed at its vast bulk. "What shall we do with it? If the Convention moves into the theater, that still leaves the whole palace. We should put orphans in here. Orphans and the elderly who have no one to care for them. Prostitutes thrown out of work by the Revolution will take care of them, and the rest of the time, teachers will give them their letters and a useful trade."

"In a palace? You've gone crazy."

"Ah, Hélène, the real revolution is just beginning. Women can divorce now, women can inherit just like their brothers. Soon we'll vote too. We'll run our own businesses. No more kings, no more nobles. Justice, Hélène, justice!" She felt as if she were flying. Her blood still fizzed from dancing and her mind felt incandescent. Everything was being made new. Jacques Roux was right. The poor need not suffer any longer. No one need lie down in freezing cold and wake to hunger. It might be fall, but it was the spring of the world—unless the Austrians and Prussians came and burned it down.

Babette and Pauline wanted to attend the new Convention, but Hélène insisted on the Palais Royal. "It's my holiday too," Hélène said, sulking, so Claire said goodbye to her friends. The Palais Royal was as crowded as ever, still the center of hot politics and fashion. At first they stood and watched the crowd, Hélène pointing out interesting clothes. Women of style were wearing their dresses looser, with less boning, less pain and strain. Big floppy bonnets covered with lace and flowers and ribbons were in vogue. The new cottons were popular, whites mingling with primary colors. Coatdresses without over-skirts showed up, often with military trim and buttons. The Palais Royal was no longer only for prostitutes and poor women; bourgeois women had started going there, as bourgeois men always had. No one here seemed worried that the Austrians might slaughter them next week. Maybe it was only in the poor neighborhoods that people took the threat seriously and felt it was meant for them.

Then they came to the Cafe Italien and Claire learned why Hélène had so much wanted to come. Several men and women from her musical were enjoying ices there and gossiping. Claire sat down with them and joined in, but she watched bleakly as Hélène began flirting with a tall young man with hair down to his shoulders and a Roman profile he kept showing off, turning his head to the side to be admired. As he kissed Hélène's hand and held it, Claire began not to enjoy the sunny afternoon.

FIFTY-SIX

Max

❦

(Fall 1792)

MAX returned to Arras to help with Augustin's campaign, so he could be elected to the Convention along with Max. A vicious smear campaign did not prevent Augustin from winning, but it reaffirmed for Max how strong and entrenched the counter-revolutionaries still were.

Charlotte took this opportunity to make her demands known. She adored Elisabeth and went everywhere with her, but she detested Mme Duplay and Eléanore. She insisted that now both brothers were elected to the Convention, they should live according to their class and be able to entertain properly. Max couldn't see anything wrong with the way he entertained now, chez Duplay. But Charlotte hounded him. "You went off and left us in Arras all these years. I devoted my life to you. Who'll ever want to marry me now? I'm forced to live as a guest in another woman's house. I want to make you happy, Max, I want us to live together as a family—not as lodgers in the house of a carpenter and his scheming daughter!"

Max let himself be dragged off to an apartment with Charlotte and Augustin in the Rue Saint Florentine. At once he began to miss the Duplays. He liked having the Duplay women around him. They saw to his every need quietly, unlike Charlotte who trumpeted everything she did. He missed Eléanore's sleek, dark presence, her eyes upon him, her surprisingly strong hands kneading his shoulders when he was tense, rubbing his temples when his head ached. He could not bear to be touched—except by her. Her touch soothed him. Her touch drew the tension from him. He could not say that to Charlotte, who was always shocked when she discovered Eléanore in his room.

Now he never saw Eléanore except from a distance at the Jacobin Club. At least there he escaped his sister. Eléanore would be in the gallery and when a speaker bored him, not as infrequent an event as he could have wished, he tilted his chair slightly so that he could see her. He loved Augustin, his tall handsome brother who could charm as he never could, who was loyal and goodhearted and thoroughly dependable and honest. Augustin got on easily with other men. He had that rough common touch, a gift for friendship. Max trusted his back to Augustin. But Charlotte was another matter. She was his sister, his responsibility (which he had shirked). Of course he loved her; but he did not much like her, and he did not wholly trust her. She had too little insight, too little politics, too much of an injured sense of her own martyrdom. He wished she had married in Arras. He was half-convinced that any man who showed interest in her now would be attempting to get close to him. He had allowed her to force him into moving, but he did not have to like the new arrangements. Blount missed the Duplays too and spent too much time sleeping by the hearth, head on his paws.

The Convention was not the ineffectual Legislative Assembly that had crept round in timid circles. This was a different cast of characters, far readier to act, but the Girondins, in control, seemed to have inherited the old support of the King and status quo defense of the previous right, whom they used to oppose. The Revolution created its own opposition as it went, those for whom it had "gone too far"; those who had traveled a way on its road and now wanted to settle down and build a fine mansion on newly acquired land. The Girondins had gained power from the August tenth uprising, but they would not keep it. He, for one, would see to that. They had taken only Danton from the left into their government. He was doing the jobs of Minister of Justice and also Minister of War. He alone seemed to have energy and vision. Now that they were hip deep in this foreign war, desperate measures were needed to save the country. Only Danton seemed willing to take those measures. Max did not understand the man. He hated the sexual jokes and innuendoes that Danton was given to, but it was more important to save the Revolution than his own ears. Augustin teased him about his prudery, but Max liked a certain dignity of discourse. Camille was close to Danton, which did recommend the man. Max had begun writing down observations, overheard stories and comments, analysis in a notebook devoted specifically to Danton. Thus did he hope eventually to figure out the man.

Max had allies. The radical Jacobin group in the Convention was called the Mountain, because they sat up on the high benches on the left, almost to the ceiling. If they were the Mountain, and delegates committed to neither faction were called the Plain, then, Camille said, the Girondins must be the Pit: the Pit down which revolutionary ideas had disappeared and into which the Revolution itself would fall if it was not prevented.

Max had many new comrades around him who gave him their loyalty. He could count on them in the Convention, in the Jacobin Club, sent out on missions. A certain power was beginning to accrue to him from persisting. If he was in the minority in the Convention, it was a vocal, organized minority that sometimes won support of the Plain: a minority prepared to take power when the chance came.

Valmy, the first victory of the war, came right after the Convention opened, declared the Republic and instituted a new calendar. This was to be Year I of the French Republic. He felt energized. He could remember how depressed he had been after the Champ de Mars massacre, when the forces of reaction had triumphed and driven most of the true leaders underground. Now all things seemed possible. Marat was out of hiding and in the Convention, the focus of Girondin hatred. Marat had a private war going with the Rolands. Max maintained an uneasy alliance with Marat. They often found themselves holding the same position but would never communicate easily.

Camille was in the Convention and at the Jacobins too, as close as ever, the only person who could always make Max laugh. Camille could be annoying and precious and endearing—like a puppy. He could not remain angry at Camille. Their son looked like Lucile, all curls and pouts and emotions bigger than he was. Max liked to get down on the floor and play with him. He had long ago dismissed ever having a child of his own, but he adored Horace and, when Danton's boys were there, he romped with all of them, letting them ride his back and tickling them till they wept with laughter.

A charming and politically dependable young man had become friends with Augustin and himself, Philippe Lebas. Max liked him. But the most important of his new colleagues was Saint-Just, who had written a scurrilous anti-government poem that had been suppressed. He had also written intelligent and admiring letters to Max over the last two years. Although he was the youngest deputy in the Convention, he was already important. From the moment Saint-Just walked in, everyone noticed him. He was tall and cold, sculpturally handsome. His manner, Max would admit, was touched with arrogance. He would bow to no one. He would court no one—except Max. In his first letter, Saint-Just had written, "You sustain the fatherland, staggering under the flood of despotism and intrigue. You are not merely the representative of a province, but of all humanity and of the republic." Max still remembered those words. Max always answered letters he received from ordinary people, unless they were hostile. He felt a responsibility to people everywhere who turned to him.

Max was taken with Saint-Just from the first time they sat down to talk. He was like a perfect gleaming sword. He did not hesitate. He did not waver. There was no corruption in him. His mind glinted. His words were lapidary.

"I have something inside me that triumphs with this age. Because I am young, not in spite of it, I am closer to the spirit of the times. I have despised my own weakness and abandoned it. I pursue the truth with absolute zeal and I proclaim it without regard for the consequences." Saint-Just offered Max perfect loyalty, but also a constant critical regard. He was not a humble follower. He did not hesitate to criticize, to exhort, to insist. He made his judgement known with authority. When my will fails, Max thought, as it sometimes does, this youth will force me to pursue our difficult and dangerous path. He will keep me from hesitations and weakness.

Always now, in the Jacobin Club, in the Convention, at the Commune, there was Augustin on his left side and Saint-Just on his right. He was never unattended. Couthon, crippled in body but robust in will, rugged in politics, was dependable as ever, a warrior in a wheelchair. Lebas had given Max unconditional support. His popularity with the sans-culottes was high again. Max had been accustomed to loneliness, to isolation, to believing himself correct when everyone about him considered him foolish. He had always believed he was destined for a difficult and lonely fate. He and Saint-Just alone shared an awareness of themselves as actors in history. "The future will know of us," Saint-Just said, and Max added, "We will have a nation of descendants as Abraham was promised."

The most important nongovernmental political institution in the country was his. He was in full control of the Jacobin Club after years of patient work and painstaking committee building. He no longer had to hide in his room brooding, trying to figure a way to be effective in his isolation. He had only to suggest something for someone to rush to do it. He was never free of the sense of time running out, but now he had allies, colleagues. He had a base. If he did not succeed in toppling the Girondins from power and establishing a true revolutionary republic, he had only himself to blame. He had a mission and nothing else finally mattered. Friendships warmed him, who was always chilled to the bone, but finally he must do what he was destined to, no matter how difficult or dangerous.

One afternoon when the Convention was briefly in recess, Saint-Just and he walked by the river where the laundresses were scrubbing on their barges. Blount trotted ahead of them. Max said, "The Girondins are the primary problem now. Louis is dangerous so long as he's alive, but he's safely stowed in the Temple. Roland and company mean to keep the Revolution from proceeding. Again you have a faction saying, Halt. This is as far as we go. We have what we need. Go back to your slums and be hungry quietly now that we don't need you in the streets."

Saint-Just did not demur. He saw clearly, icily, without sentiment or shading. "How shall we topple them?"

"We attack when we can. We slowly win over the deputies of the Plain. We keep our base among the people. We never forget where the Revolution must go and we keep saying it to the people again and again."

"And what do the Girondins do?" Saint-Just paused to toss a stick.

"They attack. They try to isolate us. They try to put us in prison. They may try to execute me. But they're cozy now. They've gone from revolutionaries to being an eating club. They fear the people instead of listening to them. They dream of moving the government out of Paris and away from possible insurrection. That will bring them down."

Saint-Just folded his arms. He had a habit of raising his chin and gazing as if he could see valleys and valleys from his mountain. "Halfhearted revolutionaries are more dangerous than counter-revolutionaries, because they sound plausible, but they destroy."

Brissot and the others had been Max's colleagues in the Jacobin Club. They had fought on the same side for years. He had a debilitating tendency to remember those battles; Saint-Just had no such qualms. Those who were their enemies now had never been his friends. Mme Roland had once courted Max with a regard as flattering as Saint-Just's, but power had corrupted her. She was a woman who played at compliance but always had her own agenda. A more intelligent version of Charlotte. He shuddered.

Max knew the Girondins feared and hated him as they did Marat, and that they were preparing an attack. He was ready. They would provide him an opportunity to explicate to the Plain exactly how he differed from the Girondins. Yes, his enemies would think they had built a scaffold, but they would give him the best pulpit of all: the theater of the unjustly accused.

FIFTY-SEVEN
Georges

❦

(Fall 1792)

GEORGES liked being a minister, although he knew he had only been brought in as a sop to the Commune and the radicals. He tried to unite the two factions, the Girondins and the Mountain, the right and the left. He found he could sway most of his ministerial colleagues, except for Roland. Roland looked down his thin nose at Georges, and his distaste was like an odor of vinegar and sanctity.

He knew how to reach Roland: through the brains of the family, Madame. But Manon would not let him charm her. She began to irritate him. She was judgemental beyond endurance. She operated in a blur of self-righteousness. He found himself enjoying his ability to shock her, so she would blush and clench her fists as if to strike him. All through August he went to her dreadful dinners of watery stew or one stringy lamb chop and a mound of dry rice, a heap of beans and a thin pat of butter, watered wine and the conversation of the sages of the Gironde. He made Fabre go with him. Afterward, when they stopped at a cafe for a real supper, Fabre would do imitations of each in turn.

The war was going disastrously. The Prussians were advancing on Paris. They took the forts of Longwy and Verdun, which should have held them for months. The generals were not winning, the officers were waffling, and the men were ill-equipped, hungry and badly trained. If he and his colleagues were not to be strung up or shot by firing squads, somebody must stop the enemy advance. It did not seem to be in the repertoire of the Girondin ministers to rouse themselves to the desperate measures required to pursue the war they had passionately craved. Fools. He would have to take over the war.

He sent Fabre and Billaud-Varenne, trusted Cordeliers, off to keep an eye on General Dumouriez's negotiations with the Prussians. Georges intended to bribe the Prussians out of their uneasy alliance with Austria. Austria was determined to fight for Hapsburg right, but Prussia could be moved. He found out where the crown jewels were stored and arranged with some deft

Cordeliers to burgle a few of the best. He was acting as foreign minister in the secret negotiations, offering Frederick William not only a separate peace, some sapphires and rubies, but a French alliance in place of the Austrian. He sent a colleague to England to see what was needed to keep the British out of the war. He sent emissaries to the royalists who were thinking of starting a revolt in Brittany. He would rather negotiate than fight. But if he had to fight, then he would fight to win.

At the Rolands' frugal table that night, Roland said in his dry voice, "The Prussian advance endangers the government. We should take the King and remove to Blois during this emergency. A disruption in the government could prove fatal to the survival of the Revolution."

Servan, the peaceful Minister of War, seconded him. "Blois's a good choice. We can use the palace. It's central. Good roads."

Georges looked at Fabre, who looked back at him. A setup. Roland and Servan had discussed this earlier, obviously. He was expected to agree. Georges let his eyelid droop slightly, a wink no one else could catch.

Clavière, the finance minister, chimed in. "It should teach the population of Paris a good lesson. That the government is able to function out of Paris. Let's see how well Paris functions without the government they keep criticizing and complaining about."

"Gentlemen," Georges said, putting his elbows on the table. "I just brought my mother and my two living sons to Paris, so that we can share the jeopardy of the people. Personally I will torch this city rather than surrender it to the Prussians."

"We weren't talking surrender," Servan said hastily. "A strategic retreat is necessary to avoid capture."

"How many citizens of Paris will you take on this strategic retreat?" Georges grinned at them, an intentionally mirthless grin he was sure looked tigerish. "I wouldn't, my dear Roland, talk too loudly about flight to Blois with the government. If the sans-culottes and the sections catch wind of this, I can see how your plan might be misinterpreted as offering up Paris to the enemy. If I were leaving, I would leave quickly, and I would take no baggage—certainly not anything that belongs to the people, such as the government. Otherwise they might be tempted to come and take it back."

A long and deadly silence fell on the dinner table, set with the finest linen and silver of the Ministry of the Interior, every plate cleaned down to the painting of nymphs. "I really must be going," Servan said. "I'm sorry to rush off, but we're burning the midnight oil at the Ministry these days."

Manon glared at Georges. She had been quietly advocating removal of the government to get away from the Commune, the sections, the active and tempestuous population who wanted direct democracy. It was no doubt her idea to take advantage of the military emergency to effect a move to the provinces, where most Girondin support was located. He had just stuck a large spoke in those wheels. His threat had been immediately understood. This government was going nowhere.

Rumors leaked out that the Girondins wanted to flee. He did not know if Fabre was responsible, or if Girondins had talked too freely. He heard from the Commune that delegates were applying for passports under assumed names. The Commune responded by locking the gates of the city and posting guards. The city was close to panic. He could feel it. If the panic could be turned into zeal, maybe he could save Paris and France. It would be tricky. It was necessary to be open about the danger, without increasing panic. "Citizens," he wrote in a proclamation the other ministers signed without a whimper, "your only choice is between victory and death. Citizens, no nation on earth has ever won its freedom without a fight. There are traitors among you; without them the struggle would soon be won. Keep up your unity and stay calm. If we defend ourselves with vigor, victory will be ours."

He proposed raising troops to reinforce the army at the front. He also urged house-to-house searches to confiscate weapons for the soldiers. He recommended rounding up those suspected of counter-revolutionary activity. That would give the panic a focus, turning it into anger on one hand and patriotic fervor on the other. All his proposals passed at once and began to be carried out within the hour.

But panic increased. Men were joining up by the thousands, but they said, "Who will defend Paris once we are gone? Who will watch over our families?" They feared the counter-revolutionaries, the refractory priests, the aristocrats would make common cause with the criminals to break out of prison. The makeshift jails were targets of popular anger. People were calling them powder kegs. The crowded prisons were scapegoats, but the fear was real. People circulated in and out of the prisons all day. Hardly anyone was locked in a cell except at night. Those who had money lived far better in prison than the people without money outside the walls. People in the neighborhoods watched wagonloads of hams and barrels of wine trucked in and repeated stories of orgies and balls. People suspected the prisoners had weapons hidden. If the prisoners revolted, they could take over their prisons easily, overcome their few guards and sally forth, an informal army of chaos.

The city was going to blow, he could feel it. He tried to talk to Servan and Roland, but they thought he was coming around to their way of viewing what they called the rabble of the sections. He could not get them to understand what was happening, so they were irrelevant. If he had to let Paris explode, he must control the explosion. If it cost the lives of a few hundred prisoners, then so be it. If Paris fell, tens of thousands would die. If the Girondins would not act to save Paris, he would.

He had a big war map on the wall of his office at the Ministry. He was in touch with Dumouriez whose army was to the north and Kellermann whose army was to the south. He sent messengers several times a day so that he could tell whether they were managing to bring the two armies together before the Prussians could advance between them. He would have liked to head for the front, but he could not leave Paris with the crisis at hand.

On the day the volunteers were to gather for the new army of defense, he gave a speech. If the Rolands called him a rabble-rouser, let them see how well he could rouse the people. "The tocsin will ring tonight in all the sections, but not as a signal of alarm. It is the signal to march for the new army of Paris. The tocsin sounds the charge against the enemies of our nation. To conquer them, citizens, we must have courage, more courage, always courage, and then France will be saved!"

Marat had been calling for the massacre of counter-revolutionaries held in the overcrowded old jails and the even more overcrowded prisons improvised from nunneries, hotels, the houses of aristocrats who had fled. Georges knew that such a slaughter was likely, but he could not urge men to join the army and march out when the tocsin rang, and also hold the people back from what they considered vital to protect themselves while their men were gone. He knew something was going to happen that night. How bad it would be, he had no idea. He was not involved in whatever plotting was going on in the sections, but he could smell the fear, the anger, the odor of conspiracy.

Robespierre and Billaud-Varenne were both calling for the arrest of the Girondins, insisting they were not prosecuting the war with zeal, that they were scheming to put the King back in. Georges was not going to permit that infighting. When the Commune sent a warrant of arrest for Roland to him, he tore it up. He had no love for Roland, but he did not think he deserved to die for providing lousy suppers and sanctimonious self-congratulatory conversation. Georges helped whomever he could. He sent private messages to monarchist former deputies to get out while flight was still possible. He would do nothing to prevent the massacre Marat was insisting upon, but he would save anybody within his arm's reach.

Marat caught wind of what he was doing and stormed into his office like a shit heap on fire. Georges would not back down. "I won't stop what we both know is going to happen. But I won't push anyone in the way of the mob. I save whoever I can. You can't scare me, Marat. I have as big a mouth as you do and plenty of followers."

"You're a sentimental fool. Every enemy you save will raise twenty more against you. You have fun playing God—I save you, I save you—but in the end, we all croak, Danton, and you'll lose your head like your friends. You're on one side or the other, or you'll get cut in half."

Georges tried to jolly Marat. "We have common enemies and a common cause. If we differ about a few minor players, what does it matter?" Marat did not reply, stalking off, his head bandage crooked and pistols visible in the waistband of his long dirty trousers.

When the tocsin rang, the volunteers began to gather and the prisons were attacked. Groups of men and women rushed the gates of the prisons with muskets, with hatchets, with pikes and knives and scythes and all the makeshift weaponry they used in the streets. They set up tribunals and on the spot they either released the prisoners, kissing them, applauding, welcoming them back to society, or they slaughtered them. Georges tried to regularize the instant trials. He appointed judges. He urged the impromptu courts to consider evidence. But he had to support the people, because he understood their fury. By the end of the second day, it was all over.

The Rolands and Brissot were running around wringing their hands and calling him a murderer. They imagined you could take people, brutalize them all the days of their life, let them see their fellows tortured and hung for stealing a loaf of bread or a cloak to keep warm, a piece of wood to burn, you could give them executions as the only public entertainment, you could starve their daughters into prostitution or work them to death, you could walk over them with boots, and then be astonished when they seemed to enjoy killing those they blamed for their misery. He did not relish slaughter, but then he had enjoyed a happy childhood in a middling bourgeois family. Everybody had needs. He wanted money. The poor wanted revenge. Who was he to say they could not have it? So he stood up before the Girondins who were crying Savages, Murderers, Butchers, Fiends, and said, "The people did what they had to. They're sending their men out to save the country. It was swift and dirty justice, but it was justice." He cast his lot.

He read the gruesome reports and went into the prisons. They had been emptied. Over half the prisoners had been tried and released. The rest had been cut down on the spot. Record-keeping was so sloppy that no one really knew how many had been shut up, how many had been let go and how many had been killed. The Queen's old favorite, the Princess Lamballe, had been slaughtered, hideously dismembered, cut up like a chicken, and her head carried on a pike under Marie-Antoinette's window. It was said that Louis warned her not to look down. Mostly the invaders had killed aristocrats and priests, but they had also executed common criminals they thought dangerous.

Reports of the bloodbath made him wince, but he could not back down. It had happened, and it was over. A better mechanism of administering justice quickly must be set up, so this would never be repeated. They needed to give more authority to the court of the Commune where Camille's cousin was prosecutor, to move fast and decisively, condemn or let go.

Georges had been elected to the new Convention. They still had that old rule that a member of the legislature could not be a minister, although they tried to get Roland granted an exemption. The Girondins weren't about to do that for *him*. His ministry was over. When Manon saw him in the corridor, she drew aside her skirts as if he could contaminate her. "Madame Roland," he said, "do not fear. Unfortunately, common sense is not contagious." Fools, all of them. They would never believe he had saved them.

The next day he learned that his efforts to rouse the army had not failed. The Duke of Brunswick was defeated at Valmy. It was not a ferocious battle—casualties on both sides were less than at the Tuileries—but the French army held. Astonishingly, the Prussian army then withdrew, marching across country to the frontier and out of France. His secret negotiations had worked. The French army did not harass the Prussians, only following them, as agreed. But the Prussians had a worse enemy than the French. Bodies littered the roadside. Bloated corpses awaited the French troops. The Prussians had dysentery. They were dying and they were done. Now was a precious opportunity for the French army to be trained properly and given guns, ammunition, clothes and boots. Time to integrate the new troops he had recruited. Paris was safe. The war was beginning to go well. The Girondins were happy and shone with confidence.

Now, he thought, would be an opportunity also for reconciliation and reunification of the factions of the Revolution. No better time would ever come. But no overtures were tendered from the Rolands, Vergniaud, Louvet, Buzot, Brissot. Instead they turned and began a fresh attack on him, on Robespierre, on Marat, on the Mountain and the left. Since he had saved their war from disaster, they had declared another war, on him.

FIFTY-EIGHT
Pauline

❦

(Fall 1792)

PAULINE studied the life of her neighborhood. On one hand, nothing had improved. The Convention would not control the price of bread. When the sections asked for price controls, the Girondins refused. They had never gone hungry, men with flowing hair and grand postures who kept talking about the noble Romans. Damn them all. She and her people were just as poor and just as ragged and just as hungry as they ever had been—as Marat said. Hélène was always quoting from *The Friend of the People*. Pauline was having a hard time making a living, because the high price of sugar meant that she had to charge too much for chocolate.

On the other hand, life was livelier. Nobody lay around depressed. Fewer men and women sat drinking till they fell asleep at the table or slipped down on the floor. She did not know anyone who had killed herself in the last two years. There was less wife beating since divorce became legal. Claire and Victoire had been running a school for the women who wanted to learn to read and write. Most women could sign their names and spell out wall posters, but some could not do that; and many wanted to read books. It was a popular thing to go to reading and writing class Sunday mornings instead of mass. It felt patriotic to dismiss the Church. Pauline missed Sainte Geneviève, that sense of connection with her own saint, but otherwise, Church passed out of her life and the time closed in and filled up and she never thought, I should be there.

When she tried to decide what was better, it was how people felt about themselves. If they were hungry, as they usually were, they weren't lying on their backs suffering in silence. They were out in the streets letting the Convention know just how they felt about their hunger. What they had, they might be more apt to share, because they felt a common cause with each other instead of divided into striving competitive families.

Every day there were sectional meetings and meetings of the women and meetings of this or that committee of vigilance, of justice, of making bandages or collecting iron or saltpeter for the army. There were committees of propaganda and education. Any time of the day and sometimes all through the night, there were meetings and discussions, speeches and votes. Instead of a hundred saints' days, they had anniversaries of victories, defeats, remembrances. The calendar was jammed.

The Convention was theirs. They—the sans-culottes, what the rich had called rabble—were the watchdogs of freedom. They were the soldiers of the Revolution. They had changed the government twice. They could do it again. All their lives, the aristocrats had been telling them they were dirt underfoot. Nothing ever truly belonged to them, not even their bodies that might be coerced and starved, beaten, torn in pieces to make an example to frighten other nobodies. Under a low grey sky, they had been mice in their dirty rooms.

Now they knew anything could change. Whatever they desired was possible, if they took action and made it happen. Hadn't they discovered their power? They must never let up the pressure on the Convention to make the laws they desperately needed. They wanted victory, they wanted justice. Everyone was human, the King too. He had been sacred, he had been all-powerful and all-wise, he had been the sun: now he was just Louis Capet, whose every move in the Temple was printed in the papers. There were rumors that he was a traitor, that incriminating papers had been discovered in the Tuileries.

A lot of people said that so long as the corrupt and the secret sympathizers remained in Paris, in power or able to influence the government and buy favors, the people would never be safe. Always they would be in danger of the Duke of Brunswick who had sworn to burn down the city and kill them all. Always they would be in danger from within. Marat said they had to kill a hundred thousand to be safe. She could not imagine a hundred thousand people alive, let alone lying in dead piles.

But there must be a conspiracy for real. The proof came when Robespierre was attacked in the Convention. They had mounted a plot against him, those Girondins with their big words and their small deeds, their secret connections to the court and the King. The papers said that Roland had attacked the Commune and Robespierre, accusing them of terrorism. He said more massacres like the prison massacres of September were being planned. He accused Robespierre of working to make himself dictator.

She went at once to the Convention. Enough women in the crowded gallery knew her for her to be passed in and to squeeze through the crowd to a good place. Some women saw her the way she saw Robespierre, as a hero of the Revolution, someone truly and entirely on their side. She never had to wait in line. Always another woman would start calling her name, "Pauline! Pauline!" and others would take up the cry. It embarrassed her. But there were those who glared when they realized who she was. If she was a heroine to some women, she was a villain to many men. She heard herself described as a dangerous demagogue and had to ask Claire what the word meant.

She was mainly a leader in the sense of being willing to do organizational work. If the women wanted to petition the Convention, it was, "Pauline, take this petition to the Convention. And would you rewrite it clear and get more people to sign it, please?" Demagogue? Drudge was more like it. She was a maid of all work to the Revolution.

Now, Robespierre, there was someone who could set a crowd on fire. They'd see what they had stirred up, those windy do-nothings. It was so cold in the Assembly, she was glad it was overcrowded in the gallery, to keep warm. The only heat in the whole drafty place was a porcelain stove down on the floor, in the shape of the Bastille. It was only October twenty-ninth, but today a cold wind was blowing from the north. There had been a frost. She peered down at the ranks of the deputies. The two sides of the hall faced each other across a narrow aisle. They were always passing notes and murmuring and sometimes loudly arguing, whatever was going on.

A small thin balding man, Louvet of the Girondins, was attacking Robespierre. People said Louvet was the lapdog of Mme Roland. He had been famous before the Revolution for writing a novel—*The Adventures of the Chevalier de Faublas*—which she had actually read. It was racy and her girlfriends had passed it around, the ones who could read. She was ashamed of how much she had liked it. His speech was full of references she had trouble figuring out, Cicero and Brutus and the Capitoline Hills and the Sibyl and Plutarch. Lots of delegates were nodding away like their heads were on strings he was pulling.

"You say who dares accuse you? I dare accuse you." He was off and running. "You are the leader of a longstanding and vile conspiracy. Your aim is nothing less than to destroy those who now try to govern fairly and in the name of the people, my colleagues. Your aim is nothing less than our complete destruction and your own assumption of total power. You are guilty, Maximilien Robespierre, of arrogance. You have fostered, you have nurtured a personal cult bordering on a religion among the poor and ignorant, a cult of which you are the saint. You provoke their adoration and you hope to ride to power on it. You have taken over the Jacobin Club one denunciation at a time and turned it into your personal tool for power. You have driven out every man who could stand against you. You purged and purged until it's only a shrine to your ego-tism, your vanity and your lust for power.

"On August tenth, where were you? Where are you ever? Cowering at home plotting how to use the violence for your own ends. On August eleventh, you began to take over the Commune. You used the Commune and the threat of mass violence to control the Assembly, and you are planning to use it to con-trol the Convention. You try to impose your will with the bodies of the slum dwellers armed with pikes and hatchets.

"You, I accuse, and your henchmen Marat and Danton. You are the tri-umvirate attempting to subvert the Revolution to bring yourself into power. You and Marat work in tandem. He arouses the rabble to blood lust and rampage, and then you coldly step in and take over the machinery of power. The blood of helpless prisoners is on your hands as well as on Marat's and dripping from the hands of Danton. Is there anyone you would not kill to seize power? You want our blood to run on the streets. We have in our hands a secret police report which says you intended that we all be shut up in prison and then murdered by the mob. We escaped you then, but you will not escape our justice now! I call you a would-be tyrant. I call you a man conspiring to seize power and rule as dictator. I dare to accuse you, to stand up to you and send you back into the obscurity from whence you crawled. I demand the immediate arrest of Marat and establishment today of a com-mission to investigate the conduct of Robespierre with the aim of indicting him."

Many delegates wildly cheered Louvet, but the galleries were still. Finally Robespierre got the floor, shouted down until Danton intervened and in his huge booming voice insisted Robespierre be heard. He looked so alone there, small, neat, intense, the focus of the hatred and scorn of all those men who thought themselves better than her and better than him. "Many serious charges have been leveled against me. In my respect for the Convention, I wish to answer carefully. To do so I will need to consult the records of the Assembly and the Convention and my own notes. I ask the Convention for eight days to prepare, after which I will come before you ready to answer each of these charges fully. I too could rant as my accuser has, but I prefer to deal with these accusations not with empty words but with full account-ability and disclosure. I therefore ask you to accord me a hearing in eight days."

After haggling, finally the Convention agreed. Pauline got up to leave. She had to get to work. On November fifth, she would be back. That night as she climbed into her old bed in the back of the chocolate shop, she envied the women all around her who had company, a warm backside against them, someone to care what happened. Sometimes she felt twice as vulnerable as the other women, because she was completely alone. Would she ever marry? Would she ever have a family? She began to doubt it. She would die in one of the increasingly dangerous demonstrations and in five years, no one would remember she had ever lived. Even her fame was two-edged, making her more visible to her enemies and frightening off men who might have liked her.

She returned the night of November fourth, because there was going to be an all-night line waiting. She brought a blanket, but gentler weather had returned. The women huddled together around a few braziers and bonfires. Bottles were passed around and bread. It was a long night but they sang revolutionary songs and told stories. The hardier dozed on the pavement. At dawn, a coffee seller came to them with her tank of coffee on her back.

She got a good seat and waited, gnawing nervously on a bit of stale bread. Robespierre was one of the last to arrive, flanked by the lanky guy always with him lately. Saint-Just had a tall lean body and a handsome face, but she did not know any women who were crazy about him. He looked too cold and too perfect. She found him intimidating, although he was near her own age and a newcomer to Paris. He looked as if he could kill with a stare, disdainful when he wasn't coldly furious. Still, he was loyal to Robespierre and always at his elbow. Flanking his other side as he marched in was his younger brother. She liked Augustin. He was not awe-inspiring like Robespierre. Everybody called him by his first name. He looked approachable, as well as handsome. Would Robespierre silence his accusers? Or would they do him in?

He began with a careful refutation of the specific charges, first that he had threatened the Assembly with revolt. He read the minutes, proving he had actually rebuked the deputy who had made that threat. "If I wished to be a dictator, would I have called for the replacement of a weak Assembly with a strong Convention? Yet I was one of the citizens who first proposed a Convention, who tried to assure that it would represent all the people and not just some, that it would have broad powers. Why would I demand again and again that a Republic be proclaimed, if I wanted to be dictator?"

He was holding his speech before him. He spoke deliberately, as he always did, as if each word were a nail driven in. He spoke in long and rolling sentences that would probably move the people even if he were speaking a different language. He did not have a big sonorous trombone of a voice like Danton, but he spoke so intensely and with such controlled passion, it lifted them all and bore them along. He was speaking from his soul to her soul. He never spoke quickly. He paused for emphasis, he paused to look over his green-tinted glasses at the crowd, he paused as if to think, to ponder.

He had finished with his brief personal defense, and now he was defen. not himself but the Commune. He was speaking again for the people. That high intense voice with its long sentences moved them like a fierce wind, carrying them along. "The revolutionaries and the martyrs of the tenth of August saved France. I will freely admit that there may have been excesses in the heat of battle, but public safety must always and ever take precedence over the details of the criminal code. It has long been recognized that in self-defense violence is permissible, and the Revolution is our purer, our better self. Louvet has implied that the Commune acted illegally in overthrowing the monarchy. Yes, it did. Yes, we did. So did the people who stormed the Bastille—a great illegal act. Revolutionary acts are fully as illegal as liberty itself.

"As for the summary justice executed by the people in the prisons, no one regrets those deaths more than I do. But the people who carried them out did so out of a genuine fear of the counter-revolutionaries—who are more powerful, better financed, more numerous and better placed than we imagined. Our worst nightmares are constantly proven insufficient to the machinations of our enemies.

"Fellow deputies, Citizens, we must realize what we are doing. All revolutions are violent. It is their nature. We cannot celebrate the fall of the Bastille and condemn the fall of the monarchy. Both are the will of the sovereign people in arms. Citizens, what do you want, a revolution without a revolution? We must go forward or perish."

Enormous cheers went up as he finished. She was on her feet screaming. He had carried the Convention. Delegates were weeping. Of course they were always weeping, throwing their arms around each other and kissing and carrying on, then attempting to oust each other the next day. She did not take their blubbering seriously. But when Louvet wanted to speak, he was shouted down.

Robespierre had triumphed. For the moment, he and the Revolution were safe, if it was possible to distinguish between them. She went to the tavern hoarse from cheering, where she was promised a large bottle of hard cider if she would tell those who had not been able to get in, exactly what had happened.

Pauline took the bottle in one hand and climbed on a table. Babette was banging on the counter for order. Pauline told them as much of Robespierre's speech as she remembered. "He's our saint," Babette's mother said.

"He takes them all on," Henri's father said. "He shoves it down their throat. Damn right. No revolution without a revolution. They want a lace revolution, one for ladies and gents. We'll give them a revolution they'll choke on. Down with the mincing bastards."

Pauline was exhausted when she finished. Babette brought her mutton stew. She had not eaten anything but a crust of bread since the night before. She was happy to eat and then go home. When she got into bed, she beamed at the bust of Robespierre. "You showed them," she said to him. "You gave it back to them good. No one frightens you. Me, I get scared sometimes. But I try not to. I try to be as brave as you."

FIFTY-NINE

Max

❦

(Fall 1792)

MAX spoke carefully, watching each member of the Convention. It wasn't like the Jacobin Club, an assured friendly audience. The Plain was now with him and now against him, blown by the winds of rhetoric and political climate. The Girondins were his open enemies. They had attempted to finish him off, to put him in prison, and they had failed. They would find him a slow but implacable enemy. The Mountain was his, but they formed less than a quarter of the deputies. He needed to make converts from the Plain. When he paused in his speech and applause broke out, he ignored the gallery and watched carefully to see who in the Plain was with him. He would remember each face and attach a name to it. Some he had notes on already, if they had been in either Assembly. Most of the others had cut their teeth on local politics, provincial assemblies. Some had come out of Jacobin clubs in the provinces and were already his.

He watched the ones he did not yet know for possible supporters. More and more of them were applauding; he had them, at least temporarily. Even some of the Girondins were clapping, including Condorcet, who had always treated him with patronizing contempt. People did not know that almost everything they said about him would find its way back. "A narrow second-rate mind and a first-rate ambition," Condorcet had said. The former marquis thought himself above partisan politics. Max's strategy was briefly but definitively to refute specific charges, but then defend, not himself, but the Revolution, as if in attacking him they were attacking the Revolution itself.

Max finished and knew he had brought it off. The fools had given him a chance to stand before the Convention clad in the mantle of the Revolution and to become its foremost spokesman. They had thought to destroy him and they had increased his public stature. But he was exhausted. This was the most intense personal attack he had experienced. He knew he was hated, but never

had any group tried quite simply to destroy him. He saw through their machinations, for they were inept conspirators.]

A fine misty rain was falling when he went home to the Rue Saint Florentine, where there was little cheer and he must at once take Blount out for his
walk. Now it was raining harder. Man and dog attended to their business
quickly and went back to the apartment that always felt cold. Charlotte had
no gift for creating comfort. The very smells of this flat irritated him. He disliked Charlotte's perfume and the smell of polish that hung over the house.
His friends did not come by, for she made them uncomfortable. She was too
jealous to share him. He could not have his political allies in to discuss politics, as she made inappropriate remarks. The Duplays were politically sophisticated; Charlotte believed whatever she read in whatever rag she was buying.
She wanted things to be more pretentious. Her model of the good life was how
the provincial ladies of Arras had dressed, had behaved, had decorated their
houses when they were snubbing her as an impoverished orphan without
dowry.

The next morning he had a sore throat and his entire body ached. As the
day went on, his fever rose. Charlotte fussed over him, forcing upon him foul-
tasting teas which he promptly threw up. The next day he was sicker,
coughing a green phlegm. She brought a doctor, who said he had a raging
pleurisy.

He had been sick in bed for a week, his fever falling but his body as limp
and weak as a heap of string, when Mme Duplay arrived. "This is terrible," she
said. "This room is icy cold. I wonder you haven't died of pneumonia. There
aren't enough coverlets. There's a draft in here."

He could hear her confronting Charlotte. He drifted into sleep. When he
awoke, the women stood glaring across his bed at each other. "Max, tell this
woman that your sister is taking good care of you! That your health is none of
her business. Tell her to poke her nose out of my affairs."

"My dearest Max, you look terrible," Mme Duplay said, running a damp
warm cloth over his forehead. It smelled of lavender. He disliked strong musky
scents. Lavender was soothing. "You haven't been resting. Obviously you
haven't been eating enough."

"My speech," he croaked out. "Had to write my speech."

"Your political survival depends on your physical survival, son," Mme
Duplay said. "You need to come home. Then you'll be properly taken care of."
She turned to Charlotte. "I'm going to take care of him until he's on his feet.
You can see that with so many of us to share nursing duty, he can't help but
get well much faster. Poor dear, you look exhausted yourself."

Max let himself be borne off by cab to the Duplays. His room was just as he had left it. He crawled into bed, Madame helping him undress. Soon he was sound asleep with the smell of sawdust and good cooking lulling him. He slept fourteen hours. When he awoke, he knew instantly where he was. He felt weak but complete. Charlotte was a leech: he must not allow her to suck away his energy with her constant complaints, her egotistical maundering. He looked around the little blue room with the white dimity curtains that Mme Duplay had sewn. He looked at the drawings on the walls that Eléanore had made of him speaking at the Jacobin Club, relaxing at the Duplay table, the oil painting of him with Blount at his feet. He had not taken all his books when he left. Secretly he had determined to come back. He was not here for a week or to recover his health. Too bad Augustin couldn't move out too. Max could not give up his life to his sister. He would happily support her. But he would not live with her again.

He had dressed and was sitting at his desk drinking coffee and studying his notes on the Convention delegates, when he heard Eléanore's light step running upstairs. Then he heard her pause outside his door. For about two minutes nothing happened. He smiled. She was trying to guess if he was awake. He moved a few papers and let his chair creak. She responded with a tap on the door.

"Come," he said. He had not seen her except in the gallery of the Jacobin Club. She had not come to visit on the Rue Saint Florentine, and all of them knew the reason: Charlotte hated her.

She came in swiftly and paused in the middle of the room. Then she swept forward and knelt before him, putting her hand lightly on his knee. "Will you stay?"

He nodded.

Her face tightened into a grimace and then went stoical. Finally she let herself smile. Another woman would have wept. Her eyes, dark, enormous, fixed on him. They gleamed. Her adoration was powerful but controlled.

She said, "I don't want to be separated from you again."

"That is not always under my control. But I won't voluntarily leave you."

"Are you very weak?"

"I'm almost back to normal. Tomorrow I'll return to the Convention."

She rose and stood before him. "I want to be yours." She was gazing at the floor, then made herself meet his gaze. She grew visibly pink. Her hands clenched before her.

He was silent. He felt a clutch of fear. Yet he also felt calm. He had already accepted her gift of self. He understood that the Duplays regarded Eléanore as belonging to him. "I can't marry you."

She nodded. "Your family doesn't approve."

"I don't care what Charlotte thinks, and Augustin likes you. I'm the head of my lame family. That is not the determining factor." He rose and walked to the window. Outside in the courtyard Blount was barking at the saw. "By the way, have you noticed that your sister and Philippe Lebas have fallen in love? They should marry. I just defeated an organized attempt to destroy me. There will be many such attempts. One will succeed. I'll be assassinated or I'll fall to a better laid conspiracy. I will never see forty. Do you understand?"

"Yes. I see. I understand. I want to share your fate."

"If I marry you, you certainly will. But I don't want to die like an Eastern tyrant, surrounded by my dog and my wife and my friends, all lying on the same pyre. I want you to survive me. I want you all to survive me. Tell the truth about me when I'm gone. But when I'm taken, when they finally manage to kill me, I want to die alone. I don't want to pull anybody down with me. That would make it unendurable."

"I don't want to survive you."

"Eléanore, obey me. I want you to live. I want to leave you all in this house intact as I found you."

"I will never be as you found me. I wasn't fully alive then." She put her hands on his shoulders, nervously but with strength. Her face was close to his. "My life *is* yours. I would give it up to you in an instant."

"As my wife, as my widow, you'd be vulnerable. You'd die because you bore my name. So I can't give you my name. And I can't have offspring. I can't have a son to carry on my name that so many will curse."

"I can promise you that I will not bear children."

"You say that now. But I won't change my mind. I couldn't endure putting a woman I care for through that. My mother died ... that way. Her screams echoed through the house for three days. I can't."

"I promise you, if you will let me love you, I won't bear you any children. I know what to do. I've asked. Do you think I don't know how you feel? I know what you feel as soon as you do."

"You always do." He smiled slightly. "Suppose you should become pregnant in spite of these precautions which you and I would take?"

"You'd never know it. No one would ever know." She moved closer. She wore a flower perfume, almost herbal. Lemon verbena. It was slightly astringent, like Eléanore. He had been with only two women in his life, and they had been far more experienced than he. He was sure Eléanore was not. He seemed to be agreeing to go to bed with her, without having a clear idea how he would set about doing so. He put his hands on her upper arms. She felt firm. She was used to doing housework and hauling her canvases through the streets. At his touch, she surged forward against him. Her mouth pressed against his. He felt himself stir. He was almost surprised, but then, this was Eléanore who belonged to him already.

She led him to the bed, and he realized as she undressed him that she did not expect passion from him. She would provide that. She was inexperienced, as he had suspected, but eager. She ran her hands over his body, she adored him. Her touch was pleasant. He never minded her touching him, he who could not endure the touch of anyone else. He lay with his eyes lightly closed as she caressed his body, experimenting, judging from his breath what pleased him.

He sat up and turned her on her back, spreading her legs. She was thin but womanly. He was glad she was not fleshy. As he placed his member against her, he said, "This may hurt." He hesitated.

"No. I've been stretching myself. I knew you would be upset by blood."

He thrust into her with a great sigh. "No, I don't like blood." It was very easy with her. He could tell she was a little frightened but also happy. He withdrew just before he came. He would tell Madame and Monsieur that he and Eléanore were engaged. That would satisfy them. And he had placed Eléanore's body squarely between Charlotte and himself. She could not use guilt on him again to make him set up gloomy housekeeping with her. He had provided himself with an obligation. It would be his secret, but as far as he was concerned, Eléanore was his wife. He was married to the whole Duplay family through her flesh. He anticipated that it would be a satisfying marriage.

SIXTY

Manon

❧

(Fall 1792)

MANON was busy. The care of Eudora and her education occupied a portion of every day, dealing with the governess as well as her daughter. The grand house that came with Jean's being Minister of the Interior required constant attention. Besides Fleury, as much friend as servant, she had a staff to direct. It would not do to pass on this residence that belonged to the Republic in worse condition than they had received it.

She had a small office in the house where she screened petitioners, saving Jean time and inconvenience. Sometimes they did not need to see Jean, for she could take care of the matter. He was often exhausted. The Ministry of the Interior was a vast operation that should have been subdivided into several bureaus, but it was just as well that someone as staunch and wise as Jean should oversee it all. She wrote his speeches and Buzot's for the Convention—and every day she stole some time to see François.

Her dinners continued. They finally got rid of Danton, ousted from his ministry. The hostility was in the open. He attacked her in the Convention. When it was a question of Jean being reappointed, he had been vicious, insisting it was a double appointment. He said he had been alone in his ministry, while Roland shared his with her. Jean counterattacked, demanding Danton give an accounting of the finances of the Ministry of Justice when he had headed it. Presumably he had used some money to bribe the Prussians, but it was likely that he had helped himself. He was corrupt through and through. Then he had the nerve to attack Jean about the monies for Interior that they were using for propaganda. He claimed they were using money of the Republic to finance journals that supported their faction.

She lay awake at night feeling a fury consume her against those who carped and conspired against them. She considered herself a warm-hearted soul, but she had certainly been schooled in how to hate. Danton, Marat and Robespierre, those would-be dictators were her worst enemies. They were dangerous men, ambitious, bloodthirsty, without scruples. Danton was lustful, half animal, but the other two lusted only for power, which made them more dangerous in the long run.

The Girondins, as people called them, had thought to discredit Robespierre, but he had outwitted Louvet. They attacked Marat then, bringing charges against him, but the court would not convict. All charges were dismissed and he was free to return to his lair, to stir up violence. Marat was the most frightening, because he published vile sexual slanders against her daily. The other two had dined at her table. She had their measure. Marat was a savage she could imagine drinking blood and rending the flesh of those he hated.

If it were not for François, she would have felt herself perishing in an emotional desert, blasted by sandstorms of intrigue. Every day she managed to see him briefly. It was important they not spend too much time alone. François swore he absolutely respected her virtue, but she suspected that he would give way to passion if she let him. She permitted him to embrace her and to kiss her, that was all. Even friends did that. From time to time he would push a little.

"Don't you think passion too has its rights? That love as great as ours is entitled to full expression?" He put his hand on her thigh.

"François," she said. His full name was François Nicolas Léonard Buzot. She said it to herself when she was carrying out household tasks. "The despicable women of the old regime married as a matter of property arrangements. They never hesitated to commit adultery. We're not of that breed. I chose to marry Jean. No one coerced me. My father did not approve of the match."

"Did he think Roland too old for you?"

"I don't know, as I didn't listen. As I would never listen to anyone who slandered my husband." She looked down at his hand.

"I have the utmost respect for my colleague, Minister Roland. No one has his grasp of the economy."

"I respect him deeply, François, and I could never cause him pain."

"I understand." He removed his hand. "You're the whole world to me, Manon. I could never offend you. You have the keys to lock and to loose. I know how much you do for me. There's no woman like you. I'm hardly able to believe you care for me, that you chose me."

How could she not cherish him? He was only a little taller and heavier than she. He was neat, handsome without flourish or self-consciousness, a pleasant well-turned-out man. And he loved her. That was the gift she carried against her heart. She was not ashamed to be loved and to love him, because she never deviated from the path of virtue. She was a true wife to Jean.

Still, as they lay under the canopy at night, Jean to her right, she on the left side of the ornate bed with cupidons and cornucopias on the head and foot and writhing grapes on the posts, she thought of François. He lay with his much older wife, as she lay with her older husband. Of course it was not really the same. Jean was a minister, a superb administrator with, as François had said, a keen grasp of the economy equaled by no other politician. François' wife was a silly woman who had brought him an ample dowry but little else. There was nothing to be jealous of. Yet sometimes Manon felt a scalding of jealousy when she imagined the intimate moments they shared.

François assured her they had not made love in years, as she assured him she had not been intimate with Jean. It was almost true. Jean asked for her wifely submission perhaps once or twice a month. She always obliged, unless she was truly indisposed. It was a meaningless scuffle in the dark. She could not understand why a woman would risk life and reputation for such dumb grappling. Yet occasionally when François touched her, when he kissed her, she felt something unexpected and wild in her. She turned her mind elsewhere.

There was plenty to concern her. The war was going well. General Dumouriez, whom she had never quite trusted, was nonetheless proving to be a most competent, in fact a talented general. He had been racking up victories. It helped their cause immensely with the people and with the Convention. A victory in the field assured them a good vote in the Convention.

Not only were the invaders driven from French soil, but the war had been carried across the border in the north. French armies were liberating the low countries, just as Brissot had predicted. Robespierre had claimed the French armies would not be welcomed by the common people. Perhaps he had feared a war would lessen his chances to seize power. He was too crafty to admit his ambition to be dictator; whereas when Marat was accused, he said, Why not? He claimed that a triumvirate of Danton, Robespierre and himself would rule much better than the Girondins. Those three dangerous men were highly popular with the volatile rabble of Paris. Their effigies were everywhere. Their faces—Danton's crooked leer, Marat's scrofulous countenance with its dirty bandages, Robespierre's pinched little cat face peering out—adorned mugs, lamps, candlesticks, broaches, rings, plates. Portraits were sold on linen or silk. Little statuettes, the sort that used to be sold of the King, were peddled through the streets. She wondered if the ignorant prayed to them.

One day in late November, a locksmith named Gamaine appeared in Roland's office along with the architect Heurtier. Gamaine had just gone to Heurtier, who was in charge of the renovations at the Tuileries, and recounted that Louis had him make a secret safe in the wall shortly after the King and Queen had been forced by the women to move there.

"Could you find this safe?" Roland asked Gamaine.

"Of course! How many times does a king ask you to install a secret safe? I can take you right to it. A good job I did too of hiding it."

As soon as Gamaine opened the safe, Jean saw that these were dangerous papers. He was appalled. As he said to Manon in bed that night, "Louis was a fool not to burn them. The Mountain and the Commune have been calling for Louis' head since September. Now he's doomed. He was plotting with Austria. He was sending money to the émigrés to invade. The Queen was sending messages to her brother in Austria detailing our plans for battles. The idiots!"

Jean brought the papers to the Convention, but the Mountain immediately attacked. They said he should have opened the safe in the presence of official witnesses. Since the papers contained information that several members of the Legislative Assembly had been bribed by the King, they accused her husband of removing papers that would implicate Girondins. Reputations were tumbling. Mirabeau was revealed as having been in the King's pay. His ashes were removed from the Pantheon. His bust was smashed at the Jacobin Club. These revelations made the madmen of the Commune and the Mountain madder than ever. They suspected everyone, even Jean, even her, saying they were in league with the royalists, in the pay of London. It was so absurd she could not imagine that even the men who wrote these libels daily could actually believe them. She hoped that the papers would incriminate the leaders of the Mountain, especially Danton, but he was lucky. He was in the clear, whereas her husband, who had just been doing his duty, was under suspicion of destroying evidence.

A cry for the King to be tried went up, far stronger than in August. Now even the moderates of the Plain were calling for a trial. It was a question how long Brissot could stave it off. The war was going well. Louis was harmless now. They feared only Robespierre and Marat and Danton. Brissot still controlled the Convention; the men of the Plain usually voted with them; the presidents of the Convention were still drawn from their ranks. The president determined the agenda, the order of speakers, settled questions of procedure and appointed committees—from their own men.

But the people were always demonstrating about something. Lately they were complaining incessantly about bread and demanding price controls, something neither Brissot nor Roland would ever stomach, for they believed passionately in free trade and a free marketplace. Price controls were anathema to them.

She had fun the next week, writing a letter to the Pope demanding the release of two young French artists who had been studying in Rome; they had been thrown in prison as revolutionaries. She gave him a history lesson in the same tone she had adopted for her famous letter to Louis. Of course this one too would be signed by her husband, but she shared it first with François. The personal attacks on her continued. When she was feeling especially vulnerable and shamed, she took refuge with François. He held her, stroking her hair. They kissed and kissed till she had to run from him and hide herself away, so that she would not lose control. When she left him, sometimes she wept with frustration and keyed-up emotion.

She was summoned peremptorily to the bar of the Convention to answer the trumped-up charges. She dressed carefully, spending two hours on her toilette with Fleury's help. She was booed when she came in. But by the time she had spoken for half an hour, she was applauded. Robespierre wasn't the only speaker who could carry a crowd. As a respectable woman, she never had the opportunity to speak in public. Oh, some of the harridans of the Paris slums would raise their shrill voices. That chocolate maker and that actress were always jumping up and declaiming. She never would put herself forward unless forced to.

She could see her enemies scowling and the men of the Plain applauding her warmly. Afterwards, they voted not a censure but complete vindication. Men pressed from their seats to embrace her. It was hard for her not to turn and flee, but she made herself smile and smile. When she came home that night and Fleury helped her change, she thought, I could have been as good a speaker as Vergniaud, the Girondins' best orator. I would have been an effective politician (better than Jean) if I had been born a man. It was out of the question. Only academic fools like Condorcet wanted women voting and running for office; what other women would she trust doing that? No, it was enough that she could defend herself and her husband when she must. It was only a pity she could not be with François tonight, to share her triumph with him. But tomorrow they would steal an hour together. Tomorrow.

SIXTY-ONE

Nicolas

❦

(December 1792–January 1793)

NICOLAS found the Convention more difficult than the Legislative Assembly, where he had felt at home. In his earlier days of admiring the Americans and dreaming of a republic, he had imagined an austere and rather formal chamber where cultivated men of a philosophical bent debated at whatever length was necessary the issues and laws that came before them. The old Committee of Thirty had resembled his ideal legislative body. They were all men of a certain level of education, a certain class, of course. He could chide himself now for naivete: events developed their own momentum.

His circle of enlightened gentlemen had been sure they were the center of whatever might happen. They imagined a revolution that would be vigorous but polite, a matter of making speeches and passing laws and perhaps a referendum or two. They had never imagined that people who waited on them in stores and made boots for them, who carted off their waste and brought them water, would come to rule. Had it occurred to any of them that the ordinary people they walked among like grass in the field, with no more attention to their individuality, would overthrow their authority so quickly after they had assumed it? Would say, no, gents, we prefer our own leaders. We like our rhetoric direct and profane. We know what we want. Get out of the way!

The Convention was loud and disorderly, and always there was a sense of the mob outside waiting to charge in if they did something the populace disliked. A royal veto no longer hung over them. Now they had thousands of vetoes armed with pikes and hatchets and wearing the red wool cap of liberty. These delegates screamed, they booed, they shouted each other down. They belonged to factions and slandered each other. Some still dressed like old regime gentlemen. Others looked like highway robbers. Marat resembled a lunatic loosed from an asylum, where Nicolas would like to put him. Others looked like the butcher or the baker. So-called Girondins mostly wore their hair long and assumed poses as if they were in heroic plays about their own

with them, he often voted with them, but he sometimes
fools.

ncompetent. They would neither rule nor step aside. They put
on into faction fighting instead of running the government and
solving problems. The Rolands were the worst. Anyone disloyal to them personally was an enemy of the state. Manon was the brightest of the lot but
unbalanced in her judgements, too romantic, too vehement, too personal.
Nicolas wished Danton were still in the government. Danton was a powerful
speaker. Nicolas could not help admiring that attribute, because when he rose
to speak, within five minutes the delegates were chatting, eating lunch,
having a nip, snoozing, sneaking out. Danton's rhetoric often seemed to say
one thing when his intention was far more moderate. "Let the bastards croak
in their blood! Let the enemies of the Revolution tremble in their gilded
shoes," he would thunder, then end with a proposal to vote a censure. Danton
was more humane and reasonable than he let on.

The man saved Paris and roused the people to incredible efforts. He had
been running half the government before he was sacked: because the Rolands
hated him. Danton was scarcely a gentleman and seemed to be doing suspiciously well out of the Revolution. Certainly funds disappeared from the Justice Ministry under his tenure. But he was a man you could reason with, a man
who could straddle the widening gulf between Convention and Commune.
He had a good brain under all that hair and attitude. He was widely read.
When Nicolas talked with him, he was often surprised. So many of these men
seemed to have read one author, Rousseau, and to have built an entire world
view on his maundering.

Nicolas simply could not manage the popular rhetoric of the Convention
with its self-dramatizing and self-aggrandizing gestures. Even Robespierre
seemed to confuse himself with the Revolution. He was incessantly martyred.
This style offended Nicolas' sense of decorum. It produced a kind of emotional
and intellectual hysteria. It confused self-pity with righteousness. It carried on
about its own virtue and forgot logic and temperance.

"What you want," Sophie said, "is a republic of Condorcets, my dear."

"I wouldn't want a republic without a Sophie for every Nicolas."

"Ah, but you're not including Sophies in your republic." Sophie tapped the
papers on his desk.

Nicolas had been appointed by the Convention along with Tom Paine and
Abbé Sieyès, to draw up the Constitution for the new republic. They had
decided upon universal male suffrage. "Sophie, I can't even make the other
committee members grant the vote to women. In the Convention, we have no
chance."

It was the culmination of his entire life's work, this Constitution of which he was the primary author. It was extremely long, for he had been brooding about these matters for twenty-five years. Here was a chance to put all his best thoughts into usable form, to set his imprint on the new government, once the Convention was done with the problem of the King. Over them all hung the question of Louis. The Commune grew increasingly impatient for resolution. They wanted Louis' head, especially since the affair of the iron safe. They might never have found the safe in the wall of the palace, so well hidden, if it had not been for a stomach ache. The locksmith who had installed it had eaten in the palace and was violently sick. He believed he had been poisoned.

Nicolas had been elected from Aisne, along with a strikingly handsome young man always at Robespierre's side. He dressed as formally as his idol but in black. He carried his large magnificent head in which all the features were bigger than usual—his eyes, his mouth, his chin—stiffly on an oversized white cravat he tied just so. About Saint-Just Nicolas knew little, except that he had gotten in trouble for stealing silver from his mother and running off to Paris, that he was the author of a radical and pornographic long poem. When he began to deliver his maiden speech in favor of the King's death, delegates paid no attention at first; then they all shut up.

He spoke in a clear harsh voice that was electrifying, crisp, laconic. He used no flowery language—exactly the opposite of Barère, who was regarded as one of the finest speakers, far different from the emotional self-regarding tone many of the delegates affected. He spoke as if from the tables of the law. There was something inexorable about him. Nicolas was impressed and discomforted as Saint-Just demanded death for the deposed King.

Brissot was delaying. The enemy, he insisted, was not their hostage Louis, but Robespierre. Nicolas felt that deposing the King should have ended the matter. He knew Danton was negotiating secretly with the British to save Louis if it would keep Britain neutral; but the British government was not interested. "If we judge Louis, he's dead," Danton said privately. He was never enthusiastic about executions, although he backed them publicly. Nicolas knew he had been right about Danton, and Brissot and the Rolands were wrong; Danton was a working politician, a new breed, master of compromise. Nicolas was fascinated, as if a startlingly novel animal had come into being overnight. Saint-Just, Danton were no one he had met under the old regime. Even though the times were increasingly dangerous, he was pleased to observe these exotic new human types.

Saint-Just and Robespierre were arguing for immediate execution. The people had rendered their judgement. "There is no way to rule innocently," Saint-Just said. To try the King, Robespierre argued, would be to put the

Revolution on trial. Louis had already been found guilty. But the overwhelming opinion of the delegates was that they weren't accepting a version of history where Louis was tried by the people of Paris; no, they were going to try him themselves. A radical, Robert Lindet, was chosen to prepare the case for the prosecution.

December tenth, Lindet's accusation was presented. Nicolas shuddered as he listened. It was compelling, thorough and quite damning. Louis had run the government way into debt and summoned the Estates General to solve his money problems. When the Estates had insisted on real reform, he attempted to intimidate them, to send them home. He called up his troops. Only the attack on the Bastille and the women's march had forestalled his plans. In Paris, he thwarted the will of the legislature. He conspired with France's enemies. He sent money to encourage armies to invade France. He bribed legislators. He funded counter-revolution. He massed troops at the Tuileries in August, commanded them to defend an empty palace and left them to die.

The galleries were watching; the Commune was watching; the people with their pikes and muskets were watching. The convention voted to bring Louis to them the next day to hear the accusations. They spent two hours debating stringent security precautions. If Louis escaped, the Commune would kill them all. They decided to send a small army. Louis would come to the Convention in the Mayor's coach, surrounded by soldiers, cannons before and behind, a detachment of cavalry guarding him.

The next morning, streets around the Convention were blocked by armed citizens. The people of Paris were taking no chances. Chambon, the new Mayor of Paris, was dispatched to fetch the King. Nicolas heard that when Chambon addressed him as Louis Capet, Louis refused to answer.

Louis was brought in wearing an olive silk coat, simply but elegantly dressed and without a wig, his hair curled. A chair had been set up for him in the center of the Convention. The president was Barère, who tried to be nobody's enemy. "Louis Capet, the French nation accuses you. You will hear the accusation. You may be seated."

Louis proceeded to deny everything, with unflagging dignity. "It was the ministers. I did what they asked of me. I am not responsible for my brothers. I am innocent. I know nothing of these papers. That isn't my signature. I never saw these papers before in my life." He was ordered to find a lawyer of his choosing and prepare his defense.

All during the rather dull trial, Nicolas had nightmares. Sophie held him, but he slept little and woke abruptly, dreaming of blood. Then his Girondin colleagues came up with a new ploy to save Louis. The judgement on Louis should be submitted to the forty-five thousand primary assemblies of France.

That would certainly delay matters up to a year or more. It sounded democratic and it would take forever.

The Mountain began attacking immediately, first Saint-Just, then Robespierre. The referendum would tie up the Convention and the government. It would use up endless man-hours while they were at war. How could each of the forty-five thousand assemblies judge Louis without evidence, and how could the evidence be trucked around to every town? If they were true representatives of the people, they could not dodge this issue. Clearly voting for a referendum was voting to reprieve Louis.

The Convention went on waffling for days. Finally on January fourth, a surprising hero emerged. The greatest waffler of them all, Barère rose, dressed in a red waistcoat. He was handsome and vain. He had belonged to the minor nobility outside Toulouse. Barère was generally regarded as master of the ornate and flowery style. This time however, his hand on his hip and his long brown hair flowing, he spoke to the point. The trial had been fair, he argued. Everything had been done openly. Now by a roll call they would establish his guilt or innocence. "In the midst of all these passions and quarrels, a single voice has a right to be heard, that of liberty. Let us unite to save the Republic. Before the entire world, it is with our careful judgement on the last king of France that we shall enter history. Let us be worthy of the moment."

It would have been the new year under the old calendar, now Nivôse, the snowy month. The endless speeches went on endlessly. Everybody wanted to go on record. Great speeches, dull speeches, long speeches, longer speeches. Finally the day came when they must vote. First, was Louis guilty? Second, should the sentence be appealed by referendum? Third, his punishment. The moderates wanted a secret ballot; the Mountain wanted open balloting. Let everyone's vote be recorded before the people. They won.

Twenty-six were absent, and six hundred ninety-three voted for guilt. No one voted not guilty. The first question was settled quickly.

Then came the tricky one: should the judgement on Louis be submitted to the primary assemblies? As he sat waiting, he realized he could not vote for it. He hated to admit that Robespierre and Saint-Just were right, but this was a delaying tactic that would tie up the government for months. There would be no possibility of getting to his Constitution. If Louis were not found guilty, what would happen to him? Would Louis be stuck back on the toppled throne? Nicolas could not support the appeal. He voted against it. His own friends glared at him. The appeal lost by a wide margin. Many changed their minds, as he had, wanting the business over. Tomorrow came the decision on punishment.

Since they had run late into the night, the session began at ten-thirty. It began with trifling daily business, communiqués from representatives on mission, reports of minor committees, petitions. Nicolas looked around. Nobody was paying attention. They were whispering together. Brissot said to him, "The city is going to rise. It's August tenth all over again, but this time they're coming after us."

The current Minister of Justice was sent to the Commune. He reported back within the hour that nothing was happening. Paris was going about its daily business. Mayor Chambon came in person to assure the Convention that he had taken every precaution to assure tranquillity. The delegates remained nervous. When a book fell to the floor, half of them flinched.

The newest ploy from his Girondin colleagues was to propose that a two-thirds majority be required to vote death. The Mountain responded that Louis had been found guilty of treason. It was superfluous to vote; they need only open a law book and read the penalty. Danton took the floor. He had been off in Belgium with the armies. "We proclaimed the Republic by a simple majority. Do you really think the fate of Louis is more important than the fate of the entire country?"

The Convention agreed to require only a majority. It was now ten at night and they had been at this for nearly twelve hours. Torches had been lit in the hall, casting a flickering uneasy light over the pallid faces. Outside it was dreary and overcast, no moonlight. The air reeked of torches and the sweat of their weary bodies. The galleries were still packed. The spectators ate and drank and began to keep count as the delegates got up one by one to vote. The handsome little orator Buzot told him there was betting on the outcome in the cafes. The odds on Louis' survival had been dropping for three days.

Even some Girondins were voting for death now. People were shifting sides from fear, fury, boredom and exhaustion. He could not vote for death. He had never approved of the death penalty. By midnight they had reached only the eleventh delegation. Nicolas was so tired he wanted to weep, he wanted to throw himself on the floor.

When the roll call reached Paris, it was morning although still dark in the hall. The former duc d'Orléans, the King's cousin now known as Philippe Égalité, voted for death. He was hissed. "Call yourself Phil Turncoat," someone yelled. At noon the Aisne delegation voted, Nicolas against death.

Finally the new president Vergniaud announced that the vote was narrowly for death. At ten-thirty at night they went home, after having met for thirty-six hours straight. Nicolas could scarcely walk. He imagined he must appear drunk as he staggered through the streets. Sophie was waiting. "Death," he said. His voice sounded slurred. She took hold of him, rang for his valet. Between them, they carried him off to bed. Despite voting no, he was implicated in an execution. He felt years older and feeble.

SIXTY-TWO

Claire

❧

(January 21, 1793)

CLAIRE rarely found Hélène in their shared room, for she had taken up with a man in her musical. She went only occasionally to the Cordeliers and to the women's meetings. Her new lover seemed mostly to care about dining well and dressing up. Hélène was in love, although Claire could not figure out with what. A dressmaker's mannequin would have as much force of character. Hélène told her she was jealous and should find a man of her own. Finally, just after what used to be New Year's, Hélène moved out.

Claire's room was used so often for informal meetings that she decided she would not bother with a roommate. If she did not have the rent money, she would just pass the hat. Jacques Roux, the priest of the Gravilliers section, came often. Sometimes he just sat silently in a chair and brooded or poured out his soul to her. He hated speculators, hoarders, middlemen, the rich, all those who lived off the poor and ate them down to the bone, as he put it. His gaunt ascetic presence radiated no sexuality. He met her mind to mind. Lately he had been bringing a young army officer, Théophile Leclerc with him. They were close politically. Théophile was darkly tanned, slender but well built.

Jacques cared about nothing but the poor. He was their shepherd. The first shall be last and the last shall be first, he preached in his harsh impassioned voice. He lived no better than his parishioners. People gossiped about his going to her room. The opposition papers spoke of her as a whore who received aristocrats (she knew absolutely none) and priests of dubious reputation. They pretended to think she and Jacques were lovers.

She missed Hélène in the mornings, when she woke alone in the old double bed, when Hélène would hum as she brushed out her red hair till it crackled as if it were the bonfire it made her think of. She missed the intimate conversations after meetings, after the theater, the dissection, the easy gossip. It was not that she was lonely, for she was seldom alone. She was with Pauline, with Victoire, with a dozen other friends. Sometimes she helped Victoire with her old-clothes business, especially the buying. She was at meetings day and evening and sometimes all night. But she had grown used to living with another woman, and she missed that soft intimacy, that sisterly presence unlike her real sister. She went to visit Hélène twice, but her lover hovered, mistrustful.

On the twenty-first of January, Pauline, Victoire and Claire went before dawn to the Place de la Revolution, where the guillotine had recently been moved, to see Louis Capet executed. In the darkness, the square was already filling up. Some had been there since the night before. During the night, a dusting of snow had fallen. The temperature had not risen above freezing, but many feet had trampled it to a damp smear except on the roofs. The crowd, standing in the dark morning when the sun seemed reluctant to rise, was at once jolly and solemn. They sensed they were consciously making history. They assented in his death, Claire thought, but they were not giddy. She was of two minds herself. She had seen the guillotine in action three times. It did not give her the same pleasure it gave many citizens, who felt safety, retribution in the drop of its blade. It was a merciful death, certainly. She had seen Protestants burnt alive. She had seen hangings where the poor wretch flopped and flopped like a dying fish.

But death was death, and she could not rejoice in it as Pauline honestly did. She would always be an outsider, the way Mendès had been, for as a Protestant she had not been born into the body politic. In the presence of the guillotine, she was insecure. Her friends viewed it as their own. It belonged to the people. It was a tool of justice. But she, alarmed at how she was attacked in the Girondin papers as a whore of the Revolution, felt vulnerable in the presence of the high scaffold. It was necessary to view the death of the man who had been king; but it made her silently and secretly nervous.

She bought coffee from a woman peddler with a tank on her back and shared it with Victoire. Victoire was shorter than she was, sturdily built. A real peasant body, Victoire said about herself, born to push a cart. Lately she had been dressing more brightly, no longer ashamed of herself, no longer hiding bruises. She was only ten months older than Claire, but only recently had that seemed true. "You're jumpy," Victoire said softly, so no one else could hear.

"Why do you say that?" Claire was scared to be thought unpatriotic.

A royalist sympathizer. Olympe de Gouges had offered to defend Louis. Everyone was against her now. She was considered a turncoat. She had always been a royalist by sentiment, as well as a genuine revolutionary.

"Shhh. It's all right. I can tell. I understand."

Sanson the executioner appeared, bowing to the crowd. He had begun under Louis XV. He had no more politics than a butcher slicing up a steer. He would decapitate Louis as he had torn apart limb by limb and organ by organ Damiens, the would-be assassin of Louis XV. His son was with him; they nodded at each other and passed little jokes as they got ready. Death was the family business. He had a wife he went home to, with whom he had made the son who would succeed him soon. Sanson was fashionably dressed, his hair in perfect order. He nodded to acquaintances, a star about to perform. He was spry and deliberate in spite of his age.

Finally at ten-fifteen a closed carriage made its way through the crowd. A big man lumbered out. "That's Santerre the brewer," Pauline said. "I met him when we took the Bastille. He's a born general."

More gingerly, Louis Capet descended. He was wearing grey culottes, grey stockings, a pink waistcoat and a brown silk coat, all pastels. His hair was carefully coiffed, but it had been cut off in the back. He looked older and somewhat fatter than when she had seen him in the Tuileries. He seemed calm. It was important to die well, everyone knew that. A priest was following him, praying from a breviary. Louis crossed himself, his lips moving. Then he ascended the high platform. He seemed to be arguing with Sanson. Finally he pulled off his coat, then his embroidered waistcoat, waving his hands, frowning. A murmur passed through the crowd, everybody telling those behind them what was happening. "He doesn't want his hands tied. Sanson says he must do it."

Until last June, she had never seen the King except on gold coins. His face was stamped on the money that passed across her palm, a remote figure, a myth. In June he had become a dumpy man with reserves of dignity. She had seen him sweat. Now she would see him die.

The argument was continuing, Louis beating the air with his hands, Sanson drawn up to his full height and scowling. The confessor came forward and whispered in Louis' ear. Louis nodded and let his hands be tied. He started to speak to the crowd. "My people, I die an innocent man," he cried. Santerre signaled to the drummers and they drowned him out with a tattoo. His lips were moving, but no one could hear him. Santerre didn't want anybody being moved to a last-ditch rescue attempt.

It struck her how new was this sense they all had of being actors in history, seeing themselves in a painting by David as the event was still occurring. People had not used to think that way. History had become a daily thing, something they could almost grasp in their hands. Louis was still trying to speak and the drums were beating and the crowd was waving and yelling to get on with it. Quietly, invisibly in the crowd, Victoire took her hand and held it.

Sanson and his son clutched Louis and laid him on his stomach in a big wicker basket with his neck in the guillotine's lunette. The voices of the crowd rose in a furious insectlike buzzing and then dropped almost to silence. Sanson stepped back and signaled his son. The blade dropped. A roar rose from those who could see. Louis' head fell into a small basket placed to catch it. Sanson drew out the head, holding it aloft by the hair to show the crowd. The roar grew louder until it seemed to vibrate through all the bones of her body. The ex-King was dead and there would be no more kings. They were truly a republic now, no going back.

People rushed forward to the scaffold to dip handkerchiefs and scraps of paper in the blood. Some of his effects were auctioned off on the spot, the executioner's privilege. Immediately both parts of the corpse were carried down, loaded and driven off in the same closed carriage. Usually remains went to the cemetery heaped in an open wagon.

"What will they do with him?" Claire asked.

Pauline knew. "They're taking him to Sainte Marguerite cemetery to be buried. Right next to the mass grave of the Swiss killed in the Tuileries after he ran away."

Of course, Claire thought, it had all been thought out with an eye to history and the fitting gesture.

Everyone stood around the plaza, looking at the empty guillotine. Sanson and his son Henri rode off waving to the crowd. The Commune should have had Danton or Robespierre or Barère give a speech to mark the occasion. Now they all felt at a loss. The crowd had lost its energy. The death was so quick that they were still standing there waiting, looking at nothing.

"Well," said Pauline, practical as always, "time to go back to work. So much for Louis Capet. May all those fucking Girondins die the same way so we can stop starving. I haven't had my belly full for three months."

Victoire grinned. "At least you can eat chocolate."

"If I eat my wares, what will I live on?" Pauline shrugged. "We need price controls on bread and sugar. The bastards won't give it to us. Free trade, free trade, as if starving were a god-given right. Damn them all."

"Amen," Victoire said. Arm in arm, the women crossed the Pont Neuf. They were cold, they were hungry, and like most of Paris, they would stay that way. The Revolution marched on, Claire thought, but their lives were still as hard as they ever had been.

SIXTY-THREE

Manon

❦

(Winter–Spring 1793)

MANON'S "little brother" Lanthénas was jealous. He was furious that she had fallen in love, although she explained that François was not her lover. After ten years of platonic friendship, Lanthénas had thought her impervious, a saint. If only he were not still living in the Ministry house, she might have had some rest, but she never knew at what hour he would pop out ranting and throwing a tantrum. Now he was flirting with the Mountain to punish her. Even Jean noticed that Lanthénas was acting strangely. He asked her what was wrong. She put him off, feeling guilty. She was not in the habit of lying. She suspected Lanthénas of telling Marat about François: somebody had.

"I can't stand what Marat says about us." François took her face between his hands. "I should kill him for you."

"Really, you don't imagine he's about to fight a duel with you. The man is confined to a medicinal bath most of the time."

"He scarcely attends the Convention. He's literally rotting. When he does drag himself there, even his fellow thugs from the Mountain won't sit near him. Some say it's syphilis."

"This is the man who calls me immoral." She paced to and fro, clutching her elbows. "According to him, I've seduced half the Convention at my luxurious and decadent dinner parties. He calls my little office my boudoir. He's afflicted with sexual fantasies, but why must he attach them to me?"

François threw his arms around her and held her close. "When a woman becomes well known, it arouses the filth in men. The scum rises to the surface of the boiling pot."

She thought his metaphor a bit off the mark, but she was comforted in his embrace. She let herself relax against him. "Lanthénas is a nuisance."

"He keeps glaring at me in the Convention." François tilted her face up and kissed her.

Hearing someone in the hall, she jumped away from him. "No one takes him seriously any longer. He's compromised himself, changing sides and yet continuing to sponge off us."

Her situation was becoming impossible. The Mountain had picked out Jean as vulnerable and attacked him daily about the funds he had spent for propaganda. The most disturbing aspect was the lack of support among the other Girondins. Jean and she had pushed hard for a government modeled on America, with strong states as well as an elected central authority. They wanted to move the capital out of Paris, as the Americans had moved it to a new city—away from the Paris mobs. That well-reasoned position had been turned into treason by the Mountain and the Commune.

Finally Jean had enough. "I want out," he said. "I cannot endure these accusations. I've never deviated from a righteous path for one day in office. I can account for every penny. I want to resign and demand an investigation into the finances of the Ministry of the Interior. I know I'll be cleared."

They were both worn down. In February, she wrote a letter of resignation for him and he submitted it. He expected his fellow Girondins to argue him into staying on, but no one did. It was shocking.

They moved out of the mansion and back to their little flat. At least that got rid of Lanthénas as well as the hordes of petitioners and job seekers. In fact it got rid of just about everybody. All attention was on the King's execution and the war. Only a few good friends like Bosc came around and of course François. Even Jean remarked that Buzot was faithful. It was awkward. Jean was always at home. It was hard to steal time for François. In the mansion the rush of people had not impeded their privacy but guarded it. Now François' presence was terribly obvious.

When they did snatch a private moment, François was desperate. He seized her. "Jean's no longer in office. He doesn't need you the way he did."

"He always needs me, François. His health is fragile. He's depressed."

"I need you more than he does, and I'm in the Convention. We can both get divorces and marry each other."

"I told you I will never hurt or betray him."

"Manon, our lives are passing. We have to seize the time to be together." He kissed her passionately. His hand closed on her breast.

She was shocked at his ardor but more shocked at her own. Desire passed through her like a hot bar of iron. She had never known desire. She had denied its power and felt superior to those it swayed, like that animal Danton, but she had not known what she was scorning. She pulled from him and ran to shut herself in the kitchen with Fleury, weeping on her shoulder.

She realized she must talk to Jean. She had been balancing her wifely role and her love for François for months, but she no longer trusted her own control. She must force herself to remain virtuous. That night as they prepared for bed, she summoned up her courage. "Jean, there is something important I must speak to you about."

"What's important now except clearing my name? I fume when I consider how those scoundrels dare accuse me of impropriety, when I've always put my own interests aside in the service of the State. Always."

"Jean, I must tell you that I have strong feelings of affection for Buzot. I have been faithful to you and I'll always be faithful to you. I am your wife. He is not my lover. But I do . . . love him."

"What are you saying?" Jean turned grey. Now she understood what was meant when someone was described as ashen. He sank on the bed's edge staring at her, haggard, clutching his belly.

She tried to explain but all he could say was, "You love another man. You love Buzot. I want to die!"

"I love you too," she kept saying, but he repeated, "My wife loves another man." From that moment, things changed between them. Jean went about with his chin sunk on his chest. He caught a cold two days later, followed by vague fevers and chills for three weeks. She wore herself out nursing him. Remembering the last time, she wondered if she faced months of his weakness and inertia.

They received death warnings in every post. Sometimes they were threatened on the street. Marat's campaign against her had not stopped with Jean's resignation. People were furious at the Girondins. People shouted that they were starving and it was the fault of the government. Manon knew it would make sense to leave for Le Clos, but it was winter and dreary there, and she could not bring herself to leave François. He was her heart and soul. Instead she sent Eudora off with her governess, writing to Dominique, Jean's brother, to watch over them.

Now France was at war with England and Spain as well as Prussia and Austria, battles on land and sea. The war that had started almost lightly as an exercise in patriotism to bring the country together had turned into an interminable campaign on too many fronts. It was draining the country. Had the war been a mistake? She and Jean had strongly supported Brissot. Sometimes she could not remember why. Brissot was no longer calling on them. He was embroiled, fighting for his political life in the Convention.

Jean glared at her across a deep abyss of resentment. They slept in the same bed, they ate their meals at the same sad table, but they were prisoners sharing a cell. Jean was never well, and in mid-March, she herself began to run a high fever. She coughed until she choked. Her linen had to be changed twice a night. Fleury cared for her, bedding her down in Eudora's room so she would not infect Jean. It was a relief to sleep alone. She was tired of hearing him sigh for dramatic effect, keeping her awake. She could not seem to make him understand that she had been entirely virtuous. With the fuss he was making, she might as well have gone to bed with François.

All the energy had drained from her. She got their passports in order so that they could leave for Le Clos, but she had not the strength to pack. François came to see her daily. He brought flowers, he brought books. Whenever François arrived, Jean shut himself in what had been their bedroom, slamming the door. Sometimes he seemed to be moving furniture in there.

One afternoon when Jean was at his old ministry to look for papers he was sure would clear his name, she napped in Eudora's bed. When François found her there, he lay beside her and embraced her the full length of their bodies. As he held her, she fell into a feverish sleep. When she awoke, he was gone. The lemon and smoky scent of the cologne he favored clung to her pillow along with the rich scent of his body. How could she leave Paris? How could she leave him?

SIXTY-FOUR

Georges

(Winter–Spring 1793)

GEORGES was greatly relieved that his name did not turn up with Mirabeau's in the King's iron safe. He had never been paid directly. His most recent contact with the court had been through Talon, whom he had allowed to escape by sending him on a mission to England. He had promised to help the King if he could, but that became problematic after the affair of the safe. He would always save whomever he could, without too great risk to himself.

Manon Roland would have been far better off making eyes at him instead of that naive idiot Buzot, who couldn't be trusted to argue a motion that was already sure to pass. She had rejected Georges even as a friend. He might have been able to save her husband's job if they had worked together. Now she could reap the nasty consequences. The foul mouth of Marat plus accusations of misuse of funds and wanting to move the government from Paris, brought the Rolands down; but it was also Roland's boring the deputies to death with the recitation of his own virtues, and Manon's incessant infighting. People were always getting on the Rolands' bad side. After a while, they had few friends and few supporters. Purity bred its own problems. He had never been able to resist shocking her, once he had learned he could not charm her. It was fun to act the bandit chieftain in her presence. For a revolutionary, she was easily appalled. He saw her as a plump-breasted bird, quite the queen of her barnyard but confounded by an unexpected movement or loud noise.

He got himself appointed to the commission sent to General Dumouriez to check into irregularities in supplying the troops. He wanted to stay out of Paris during the King's trial. He found the troops ill fed, the hospitals primitive, desertions common and the army bogged down. The situation of the army inside Belgium was precarious and unclear: were they liberators, occupiers, annexers? How did they get provisions? Buy them (with what) or take them?

It was a mess. He brought Fabre in to furnish boots, and cut himself in as a quiet partner.

By January Gabrielle was begging him to return. The problems in Belgium dragged on. Antoine was almost three; François-Georges was eleven months old. This new pregnancy was proving difficult. Gabrielle feared the child would be born prematurely, and she wanted him with her. In addition to two maids, Gabrielle had Lucile nearby (although unlikely to be much help) and the Gélys upstairs, mother and daughter, with whom she had become close. The daughter Louise was excellent with the boys. Gabrielle trusted Louise, but nothing would replace having her husband at hand for her confinement. Georges arranged to come.

When he returned to Paris, a former minister living in England attempted to bribe him into saving Louis. But the English did not produce the money. He realized he must take a stand in favor of Louis' death. He had his reputation to consider: he could not afford to seem in the royalist camp. Life was always precarious, and he had scandal and rumor clinging to him like mud to his shoes.

After the King's trial, an old royal bodyguard went gunning for the duc d'Orléans for voting to execute his cousin. He could not find Philippe at the Palais Royal, so he settled for the representative Lepeletier, best known for his plan to reform education and bring it to every French child. Lepeletier was shot in the courtyard of the Palais Royal. The murder scared the Convention.

The Convention sent Georges back to Belgium on the last day of January. Gabrielle was upset, but the situation was acute, and the baby would no longer be premature enough to be in danger. Dumouriez was furious at the King's execution. The Belgians were unhappy with the occupation. The men were discontented with their provisions. Everybody was at each other's throats. He had to smooth it all over. He rushed around Belgium from Dumouriez to the camps, from Brussels to Liège. He was having supper one night in mid-February when a messenger arrived to speak to him privately.

He knew what it was. "My wife has had her baby? Is it a girl?" That's what they had hoped for. Gabrielle would be angry at him for not returning in time, but so it went.

"Citizen Danton, I bring you good and bad news. You have a son—"

"What do you mean, bad news?"

"Your wife died in childbirth, Citizen. We all grieve with you."

He felt stunned, like a bull about to be slaughtered. "Gabrielle, dead? That can't be. She's a healthy woman. She had babies before. She can't be dead. There's some mistake!"

He summoned a coach and left at once, traveling all night. When he finally got to Paris six days after Gabrielle had died, he felt numb. How could he live without her? She had been his strength. Only the two maids were in his flat. Gabrielle's parents had come to Paris for her accouchement and taken the children. She was already buried. She had vanished, but there were her jams in the kitchen, clothes still smelling of her ripe and beautiful body. Her perfume, her rouge, her scarves. The jewelry he had given her. The whole flat said wife. He had lost his wife as if he had somehow misplaced her and she was gone into smoke and air. Only the scent and clothing remained to mock him.

He felt crazed. How could he move? How could he act? A letter from Robespierre was handed to him. "If during the only kind of misfortune which can shake a spirit as strong as yours, you can find any consolation in the knowledge you have a tender and devoted friend, I want you to know that I love you as your true friend. I love you more than ever, until death. We two are one self."

Georges was moved to tears. He had not thought Robespierre had it in him to respond so tenderly to his loss. He was astonished that Robespierre could understand loss, especially of a woman. Some people said that Robespierre had a fiancée, one of the Duplay girls, but Georges had never believed it. He had always thought the man cold through and through, except with children or animals.

He could not sleep. He kept feeling her in the bed with him, her sweet lush breasts, her hip pressing into him, the way they slept sometimes like spoons fitted together. He kept smelling her. He kept hearing her in the kitchen or in the bedroom. She had been stolen from him.

He went to the cemetery and insisted they exhume her. He had a savage fight with the authorities and with her family, but he would not give in. He must say goodbye to her. He must see her body, or he would never be rid of the feeling that she was hiding just in the next room, that one of his enemies had kidnapped her. The smell was strong but so was his stomach. He knelt and kissed her goodbye and had a sculptor make a death mask for him before he would allow them to close the coffin. Then, finally, he permitted her to be put back in the cold earth. Now he knew she was dead and his life was empty.

He summoned a family council and gave his father-in-law a deputy guardian status and Gabrielle's brother power of attorney. The last born son was still surviving, but weakly. Georges had no idea if the boy would thrive, but he had two to care for. He signed the papers, put his affairs roughly in order and took a coach for Belgium and the army.

The Belgians were in revolt against the occupying army and had killed French soldiers. They were sick of the army they had welcomed as liberators. The French had gone in a few months from saviors to oppressors. Scandal about provisioning the army was growing, although he had done his best to squash it. The damned radical crew that had wrestled the war office from Girondin control were trying to make sure nobody made a cent, as if you could run a business that way. Fabre was minting money, from none-too-good boots. Dumouriez, Fabre, himself had all made a bundle, so they must cover for each other. It was how things got done, in war and in peace and no doubt everywhere but the kingdom of heaven. When he had first arrived, the men were hungry and cold. If the materiel cost more than it might have, at least the soldiers were fed and clothed and outfitted, boots and bullets.

It was back and forth, back and forth all winter and early spring. There were defeats after defeats and troubles after troubles. He had to raise more battalions in Paris by appealing for volunteers among the sections. This time he would not let the people slaughter the prisoners before the men left Paris. He argued for the creation of a Revolutionary Tribunal to mete out swift justice to traitors, in order to prevent the people from rising again and attacking the prisons. This would persuade the people they didn't need to kill potentially dangerous prisoners. It would be a kind of pacifying theater, justice every day. This proposal was his, but Robespierre, Marat, Camille, everybody from the Mountain and a huge number of Plain deputies leaped on it. It passed overwhelmingly. He felt frantic, exhausted, rushing from one crisis to another, delivering ringing speeches he scarcely listened to, words and phrases rolling out of his mouth.

Dumouriez was getting harder to control and finally Georges lost his big fish, the general who had won sufficient battles to keep them all in business. Dumouriez went over to the Austrians. Luckily Georges was in Paris reporting to the Convention. Some of the scandal stuck to him, but mostly it was the problem of the Girondins, who had put Dumouriez in power, who had feted and fussed over him. He was not surprised that Dumouriez had defected, but the timing caught him off guard.

Too bad for Philippe Égalité. His son, an aide to Dumouriez, deserted to the Austrians along with the general. Philippe was arrested. Georges had put a fair amount of distance between himself and the Orléans faction in recent years. He should be all right. If only he were not so lonely. Whenever he sat down chez Desmoulins, he found himself melancholy. He was not sleeping well. He took his children back into his flat and got the girl upstairs, Louise Gély, to care for them. Louise told him that Gabrielle had made her promise on her deathbed that she would take over the children. The baby died, quietly. The other two boys cried a lot, but they were used to Louise and began to flourish. She had cared for them through Gabrielle's difficult pregnancy. The Gélys were old friends of Gabrielle's family.

Things were not going well for anybody. The Vendée region, one of the most backward of France, was in armed revolt against the government, so now they had a civil war for the improvised French army to fight, as well as the wars on their frontiers. The peasants in the Vendée had been roused by the Church to fight a holy war, and nobles had come back from exile to join them. Dumouriez's treason had shaken the Girondins' hold on the government. Gradually they were losing their grip. Now the Convention recognized it was in jeopardy. The nation was in grave danger from within and without. At Marat's instigation, a Committee of Public Safety was organized to oversee the government, to consist of nine members from the Convention and have broad sweeping powers. It had more scope than the most powerful of the standing committees, Security, which oversaw police and prisons. He understood at once he must get himself appointed.

The infighting in the Convention was growing more partisan and violent. The Girondins tried to impeach Marat and everybody was threatening everybody else with death. Georges made several rousing speeches in the Convention, trying to direct their attention toward winning the war, the one they had entered so blithely and were now losing on every front. But the Girondins were still in control of the government and not about to resign. The bureaucracy was the old royalist engine that preferred spinning idly to doing anything productive. Many of the bureaucrats presided over operations they wanted to see fail. It was a mess that ground round and round in the mire of politics. He was at home there, compromising, finding allies, greasing the wheels, pulling a little here and pushing a little there, trading favors and insults. But he knew they were at crisis.

He tried to make a coalition with the Girondins, talking up a common revolutionary front that would exclude fanatics and extremists (leaving out Marat and Robespierre in other words but including strong representation from the Mountain). Let bygones be bygones, he said to Vergniaud.

Vergniaud's reply was to threaten him. "Let there be war. Let one side perish."

"You want war, do you, Vergniaud? You'll get it! In your teeth, then."

In the Convention, Danton rose. "Citizens of the Mountain, I begin by paying you homage. You were right and I was wrong about Dumouriez and about the Girondin faction. You're the only true friends of the people. No truce is possible between the Mountain, who voted the King's death, and those who slandered you up and down the country trying to save his neck." If they wanted war, they'd have war. Let's see if they had more stomach for winning this one than the big one. The Girondins were threatening Paris with rousing the provinces to revolt, with moving the government away, anyplace but Paris.

When he went to the Cordeliers, he found talk of insurrection against the Girondin government. Lacking a constitution, there was no legal way to remove a government that was not functioning except to overthrow it. All over Paris, preparations were under way to do just that. He had cast his lot with the Mountain just in the nick of time. His luck, the great Danton ability to land on his feet, was still fully in play.

SIXTY-FIVE

Max

❦

(May 1793)

MAX was delighted. Elisabeth Duplay and Philippe Lebas had fallen in love. They'd met at the Convention, where Charlotte and Elisabeth were sitting in the gallery. Charlotte was still living with Augustin, and Elisabeth was still her only friend. Charlotte was barely speaking to Max, sulking. She had tried to play Cupid. The romance proceeded into a tangle of wounded feelings and misunderstood gestures, until Max had stepped in and straightened everyone out. Now Elisabeth and Lebas were engaged. When Max had time off on Sunday, often the new couple and Eléanore and he went to the country together, or at least stole a couple of hours to sing and relax.

Elisabeth was fairer than Eléanore, conventionally pretty and not as intense or as bright. She would make Lebas an excellent wife. Lebas was a reliable Jacobin, often sent on mission by the Convention because of his common sense, his ability to get along with a wide variety of people and his innate honesty. Max liked to attend the weddings of his friends. He was well settled himself, cared for in the Duplay household, with Eléanore, with his dog Blount. He had a strong and secure domestic scene as his grounding.

Poor Danton had not recovered from the death of his wife. He was increasingly unkempt. Rumors went around about his wild life, but Max doubted that Danton had time for revelry, what with going back and forth to the army, trying to raise his two sons alone, and now serving on the great Committee of Public Safety. Danton was one of those men who required a wife to maintain him in order, to see to his upkeep. Max felt pity tinged gently with contempt for a man who simply could not manage alone.

When young revolutionaries came to Paris, they tried to see Max. Always they seemed shocked that he was not on the Committee, that he had never had a government post. Because of the Jacobin clubs in every town, he was the best known of the men the Revolution had thrown into prominence. But the only power he wielded was that of an ordinary representative or the influence people accorded his words.

All through April, while Lebas and Elisabeth were falling in love, the drama of Marat was going on. The Girondins, who would not relinquish governing, had failed to destroy Max and failed in their attempt to discredit Danton. Now they had turned on Marat, thinking him more vulnerable. The skirmish had got off to a roaring start when Marat called for the extermination of traitors: the Girondins. The next day, Pétion, one of them now, attacked Marat in the Convention as a scoundrel who was trying to overthrow the government and introduce despotism. The Girondins still had sufficient sway over the Convention, where Marat was disliked, to vote his arraignment.

At first Marat simply did not appear before the Revolutionary Tribunal. After all, he had plenty of experience as a fugitive. Suddenly, a week later, he stormed into the Revolutionary Tribunal, demanding to be heard.

Fouquier-Tinville, the public prosecutor, did not attempt to conceal that he was on Marat's side. "This is no guilty criminal who stands before us," he thundered, "but the apostle and the martyr of liberty!" Max nodded when he heard that. Marat was safe. There was no need for Max to take action. The Revolutionary Tribunal not only refused to convict Marat, they congratulated him for his uncompromising work on behalf of the poor people of France. Fouquier-Tinville was a cousin of Camille's, who had politicked for him out of family feeling. Max did not like the prosecutor. He had a nasty streak entirely suitable to his job, but not endearing. Still, a useful man. Augustin called Fouquier "The Owl" because he had round eyes and a beaky pockmarked nose. He even looked like a prosecutor, viewing the world with mocking distaste, as if it were shoddy goods.

The Girondins tried to destroy Max first, then Danton, now Marat, and had succeeded only in making them heroes and discrediting themselves. Max judged them fools to have tried to imprison or execute Marat. Marat was half man and half icon. There was no distraction in him, no being tempted from the path of duty. He went ahead like an engine. His sickness, his sense of having little time left, only honed his commitment. The pleasant and well-spoken gentlemen of the Gironde looked at Marat and saw a stinking man dressed like a rag picker with a foul mouth and a fouler newspaper. They did not see what Max saw: a man who had given everything to the Revolution, a man who could raise Paris, a man whom the common people trusted with their lives.

Max frowned, making lists of Girondins. They were inept at governing, too little able to manipulate events or people and too given to believing that manipulating words was enough. All was in preparation to get them out of the way before they brought the Republic down with them. They were dangerous as long as they had power and would not use it justly, effectively. The women were organizing and marching. The sections were getting ready. He supposed that a quarter of the citizens of Paris were arming to get rid of the Girondins by the only method that had been proven to work.

But the Girondins were not prepared to yield. They formed a Court of Twelve with extraordinary powers to protect the government. They were issuing threats hourly. "If Paris attempts to use force against the legal government, then Paris will be wiped from the face of the earth!" Hébert, the publisher of the popular, far-left and scurrilous paper *Père Duchesne*, had been arrested. Several popular agitators from the sections called by their enemies the Enragés, the *mad dogs*, had been picked up too. The Enragés: Varlet, the red priest Jacques Roux, a hotheaded youngster from the army Théophile Leclerc, and those women who had lately organized themselves into something part political club and part battalion led by the actress Lacombe, they were all potentially dangerous to public order but also extremely useful. They had enormous support among the sans-culottes. They could pull thousands of people from the sections into the streets. They had the courage and numbers to storm barricades and take over the city. Brissot and the Rolands were quite right to fear the people of Paris, because the people of Paris were going to bring them down. The situation was desperate. They were running out of time. The Revolution would be lost; the war would be lost. He reluctantly decided that violence was the only tool that could do the job.

The Girondins were threatening everything from the destruction of Paris to raising armies of revolt in the countryside if they were ousted from power. Their Court of Twelve was arresting the left. It demanded a list of the membership of revolutionary organizations in Paris. The Girondins claimed they could start civil wars and rebellions all over the country.

"The forces in the Vendée are winning their civil war," Saint-Just announced. "The poorest peasants in France led by the most reactionary priests who promise them paradise if they fall in battle. This is a holy war against us." They were meeting at the Duplays. The section leaders were meeting at the same time in the Bishopric to plan the uprising.

"Since the Girondins will not move, they must be gotten out of the road," Max said calmly. "The people will remove them."

"This could be quite bloody," Camille said. "Can we depend on the National Guard? Whose side will they be on?"

"They will be on the people's side," Max said. "We're getting Hanriot appointed as commander."

"Who the hell is Hanriot?" Camille asked.

Danton answered him, "He's a little guy, fiery. A battalion leader. The men like him. He's always in the front. We can trust him."

Max nodded. "At midnight tonight, the tocsin will ring. The Insurrectionary Committee will meet at City Hall. We must be at the Convention before six A.M. The galleries will be jammed with our supporters. The streets around the Convention will fill. It's time to act. The Court of Twelve has issued warrants for the arrest of every man in this room. I assure you, I have seen them. They mean to kill us, but they're clumsy. We are not. Because our arm is the people in motion."

Saint-Just rose to his full height, towering over them. "Don't be afraid of a little blood," he addressed Camille. "Our blood will be required by the people sooner or later, but now the people want to see the color of the blood of traitors—the secret royalists who led us into a war they have proceeded to lose, squandering the lives of common soldiers. Who permit the priests and the aristocrats to raise an army in the Vendée and prepare to march on Paris. Who are promoting revolts in every corner of the country. So long as they live, the Revolution is in danger of dying."

"As of course are we," Camille said softly but audibly. He and Saint-Just glared at each other.

Saint-Just began, "It is demanded of us that we rise above ourselves—"

"While we're assuming heroic attitudes, let's never forget that it's the people who are carrying the pikes—men of the sections and their formidable wives. They do the fighting for us and for themselves," Danton said with a smile, trying to defuse the tension between Camille and Saint-Just.

Max did not like Camille and Saint-Just to quarrel. They were both dear to him. Camille he was fond of; Saint-Just was fierce strength personified. He stood like a marble statue of Brutus poised to cry Death to the Tyrants! He looked, Max often thought, exactly as a leader should, with his perfect firm chin and his piercing huge eyes and his noble head and carriage. How well Saint-Just was named, the spirit of revolutionary justice incarnate. Max felt like a father whose sons were quarreling. He felt fatherly toward Camille, even though Camille was only two years younger; at school that had seemed a great gap in age and experience, and it still did, for Camille was a schoolboy at heart, thumbing his nose, writing witty aphorisms about the teachers or the Girondins. Abroad among the émigrés and royalists, he was reviled as the attorney of the lamppost: poor Camille, who along with Lucile, often seemed scarcely more mature than their little boy. Camille was forever speaking without thinking, unlike Saint-Just who rarely spoke an unconsidered word. Sometimes they fought for his attention like jealous siblings. They were temperamentally at odds, Camille the joker and Saint-Just the judge.

He realized that everyone in the room was waiting for him. He was their leader, all of them, even Danton who would never acknowledge the leadership of another man. "We must be each at our posts today and we must keep communications open with the Insurrectionary Committee. We have planned, we have spoken, we have plotted. Now the issue is in the hands of the people and of the Supreme Being. The people's way to justice is a blunt one, but finally the only road. The people have suffered. We'll give them price controls so they no longer fear starving. We'll give them justice. It's time!" He made a chopping motion with his hand and stood. "It's dawn, friends. Let us go offer our lives to the Revolution."

"Of course he only offers his life in a committee room," Danton said softly to Camille, but Max heard. He gave no sign but felt the gibe in his stomach. He would record it in the notebook he kept on Danton, with all the other careless comments that fell from his big mouth. Max had a duty to understand the man, as he must study all his colleagues on this long and dangerous and bloody road. History would judge them, but in the meantime, he had to measure and remeasure each man himself.

SIXTY-SIX
Pauline

❧

(May–June 2, 1793)

PAULINE was always busy, since she and Claire had organized their new club, the Revolutionary Republican Women. They decided on casual uniforms, the red cap and the tricolor. Most of the women wore pants and jackets, so they could fight better. They had been having lessons and they were beginning to get a reputation as street fighters.

"Of course, it's just for show," Claire said as they were sitting with Victoire and Babette drinking in the Dancing Badger. "The men are terrified because they think we're unnatural. They see us as fearsome Amazons."

"But we are serious," Pauline said. "We're deadly serious."

Claire took her hand. "My dear friend, do you really think if a platoon of the regular army attacked, we'd last five minutes?"

"If we had muskets. If your friend will go on training us."

"We're good street fighters. But we're no Amazon army," Claire said.

Claire had a new boyfriend, Théo Leclerc. He was younger than Claire, just Pauline's age, and adorable. Pauline was so used to Claire being on her own or picking up men for a night, she was shocked to walk into Claire's and find this guy sitting on her old double bed with his boots halfway under and his army coat hanging on the door. Clearly he was moved in. She did not know if she was jealous because she was used to Claire always being available, or because Théo was so attractive. She wanted to plunge her hands through his curly hair.

Théo had been in the army and he was willing to train the women. Oh, he was for real, not one of those blowhards who drank in the taverns and claimed to have taken the Bastille single-handedly. In Martinique he fought supporting the Blacks who were revolting against their colonial masters. He had been in prison three times for revolutionary activities. Without patronizing the women, he taught them marksmanship out in the Faubourgs on Sunday afternoons. They shot wine bottles and straw men.

He had them practice with the pike too. Théo was a real find. It wasn't that she had any objection to his being around. He was crazy about Claire. Claire was so beautiful, all men wanted her. Obviously Théo was the one madly in love, but Claire liked him better than any lover since Pauline had met her. The one who did not like him was Victoire.

Pauline had little time to brood over Théo. The RRW core group thought they could pull out a couple of thousand women for the great day coming, when they were going to surround the Convention, put fear of the people into the lazy deputies and make them act. No more long speeches full of long words and no action. The men were being led into death by generals who couldn't wait to desert to the Austrians, because the Revolution had not really come to the army yet and those generals were aristocrats.

"Every man who voted for sending the King's trial to the little assemblies, every man who voted to save dirty Louis' fat neck, he should go through the little window now!" Babette's mother said, pouring them more beer and giving them each a dose of watery brown soup. "They need a public haircut."

Parisian slang was full of a hundred pet names for the guillotine. The people felt it was their tool, their arm coming down. It showed their power. Get out of our way, or zip! There you go.

People differed mainly on how many members of the Convention should get shortened. Some wanted all the Girondins to stick their necks out, some wanted only the top guys, some had particular enemies or scapegoats. Pauline just wanted to be rid of the Girondins. She didn't even know what that name meant. It was some river. That's what they were, wet and flowing and mud on the bottom, running toward some other country soon enough.

The Mountain was counting on them, the Commune was counting on them. Brissot's Court of Twelve had declared the Commune abolished and started arresting sans-culotte leaders. The sections all knew what they had to do and so did the women. The Guard would march with them. Paris would rise and march on the Convention to say, Let's have a real constitution and power to knock down hoarders, the rich guys who are still screwing us to the wall. The damned remaining aristocrats, bob their shoulders. Give them a fast trim. Teach them the second dance you do lying down. The mood of the sections was grim but strangely jolly. They were about to do their own dance in the streets round and round the Convention until the walls fell down.

It had been a bad winter. Pauline led two bread riots. They had made a revolution; why didn't they have enough to eat? Why were they always hungry? Someone must pay for the hunger and the cold. Pay for going to bed hungry and getting up hungrier still and dragging through the day dreaming of food, dreaming of bread, dreaming of soup and meat, for once enough!

On Sunday, June second, Pauline woke at the first light of dawn, after three hours' sleep. Her belly was empty. Her trick of kneading her belly or remembering old meals did not work. She found a crust of stale bread and heated water to make gruel. She heard mice in the walls. What could they be living on? If there was anything a mouse could eat, she would eat it first.

At seven, Claire arrived with Théo. Théo was on the Insurrectionary Committee. He was a good speaker, although he had a tendency to get shrill. He was so passionate about his politics, he lost control of his voice. This uprising was carefully orchestrated, involving the Jacobin Club, the Cordeliers, the sections, the National Guard, the Revolutionary Republican Women. This time the Insurrectionary Committee had given orders directly to the women: Take over the Convention building, fill the gallery, block the corridors, stop the Girondins from leaving, pack the streets around the Convention, terrorize the delegates. "Go to it, girls," Danton shouted as he passed Claire and Pauline on the street. His massive hand fell heavily on Claire's shoulder. "We're counting on you to scare the hell out of those traitors."

"Are you going to the Convention?" Claire asked him.

"On my way. Remember, girls, no excessive force. We're just going to push them till they squeal and get out of the road."

Everyone was taking them seriously now. Pauline's heart felt as if it were bigger than the walls of her chest. Finally, women were beginning to be treated as equals. Olympe de Gouges' great manifesto would be true. There would be the Rights of Men and Women. She made herself not mind that Théo was marching with Claire. He had heard about the bullet she had taken at the Tuileries. No, she would not be jealous, for the great Danton had addressed her as a fellow soldier.

She saw Mimi at her window. "Aren't you coming?"

"My husband says it's enough you got his last wife Aimée killed. He says he can't afford to risk me too. After all, you're on your own. No husband, no kids, no parents. Nobody depends on you. I have to raise Aimée's kids and my own too—thanks to you."

Pauline felt her eyes sting and she gripped her pike hard. Aimée had been her friend, not Mimi's. She wished she could think of a reply that would make Mimi feel as bad as Mimi had made her feel.

Claire ran off to talk with Victoire. Théo was waiting for her, looking a little lost among the women. Pauline fell into step beside him. "I hope you'll address us about the colonial situation, about sugar and slaves and the rights of the Blacks," she said in her president-of-the-club style. Then she smiled and said, "I surely would like to hear your experiences. You were in prison out there, right?"

"My first time. They use old hulks as prison ships so you can't escape. Those waters swarm with sharks. If you try to swim for it, they'll eat you to the bone." Théo looked pleased to be asked. He stopped watching Claire and smiled at Pauline. "Are you frightened, little one?"

"Everybody is." She shrugged, but she could not help smiling back. "I fought in every great day of struggle since we took the Bastille. I led the neighborhood women to Versailles, when we went to fetch the King."

"You could use a pike with a shorter staff. There's a proper ratio for a person's height. I'll cut it down for you."

The women, several thousand strong, converged on the Convention. About three hundred were active members of the RRW, another thousand came sometimes, and the others were just women who agreed with their objectives and were ready to act. The RRW was the biggest, the strongest, the most militant of the women's organizations. Claire and she had set it up so no man belonged. What they did have was a lot of children. Pauline had strongly urged mothers to leave the kids home today, but not every woman could. They were marching to battle on the Convention with five-year-olds, ten-year-olds and babes in arms. An army of women often became an army of women with children.

A great crowd gathered, many armed. The National Guard was marching with sixty cannons, with Hanriot—a scrappy little guy who had fought on previous days of uprising—astride his horse to lead them. The women poured into the Convention. The Convention no longer met in the old riding school, where Pauline had often gone; it now used what had been the Tuileries theater, a bigger, more formal room. The deputies were not crowded together. The speakers were farther from the galleries. The women occupied the corridors, all the seats in the galleries and blocked the doors. "Justice and bread," they shouted. "Down with the Girondins! Down with the traitors!" The roar of the crowd outside penetrated the theater. It sounded vast and dangerous.

All their lives the women had been pushed around, by fathers and husbands and priests and every man who felt like it, landlords, shopkeepers, tax collectors, doctors, pharmacists, aristocrats and politicians. It was fun to stand in the doors in their red pants and red bonnets, with their pikes and some with daggers and pistols and even an occasional musket, and to push those scheming nitwits around. The Girondins were scared. It was astonishing, Pauline thought, how scared they actually were. These were gentlemen, lawyers, men of property. They were afraid of the women of the city streets. These were not ladies; these were not the sort of women they married or had as mothers. The women kept shouting and shoving. They would not let anybody else into the hall. They made a wall of their bodies.

The Convention refused to act against the Girondins. Hérault de Séchelles, currently presiding, led a walkout. Some of the women went and sat in the delegates' places, while Pauline led a charge after them. The men walked into the Carousel straight into a face-off with Hanriot and the Guard. Hanriot stayed on his horse, looking down. "The people have not come to listen to idle talk," Hanriot bellowed. "They demand the guilty be arrested. Gunners: to your cannons. Prepare to fire!"

The representatives ran around trying to escape. Marat climbed on a cannon to harangue them. "Delegates, to your duties! Don't run like cowards. Return to the posts you've abandoned and do the people's will!"

Théroigne de Méricourt suddenly appeared, in her usual tricolor uniform. Pauline assumed she had come to join them, but she stood with the Girondins. She marched out in front, between them and the cannons. "Protect the great leaders of the Revolution. Don't turn on them! These are good men!" she began in her carrying voice. "Don't forget what they've done for us—"

The women hurled themselves on her. Théroigne went down under a pile of women pummeling her. They did not use weapons but they used their fists, and it was thirty women on one. Pauline was furious at her for betraying them, she who had led the march on Versailles, who had killed an aristocrat at the Tuileries. Now she had joined the counter-revolutionaries.

Claire tried to stop them. "She's one of us. If she's got a Girondin boyfriend, forgive her. Don't kill her! She's fought on our side." Claire ran back and forth tugging at the women.

Marat was shouting too to spare Théroigne. Finally the women left off. They backed away from where she sprawled on the pavement. She lay almost naked, her clothes in rags and bleeding from her nose, her mouth, her breasts. She had lost consciousness. Marat told two men to carry her to safety before he swung back to glare at Hérault and the representatives.

Hérault de Séchelles was an ex-aristocrat who claimed to be a revolutionary. With little choice, he turned and led a retreat into the chamber. Reluctantly they filed back in, followed by the women and National Guard. They resumed their debate on the Girondin leaders.

In midafternoon the Convention voted the arrest of twenty-two Girondins including Brissot, the Rolands, Buzot, Vergniaud and Louvet, who had attacked Robespierre. The Mountain was triumphant. The government had fallen the only way it could: the people had toppled it. Now they would have what they wanted: bread and freedom and a new constitution. The Mountain would owe the women big.

As they made their weary way home, Pauline said to Claire, "Now we'll get what we want. We put them in and they know it, and they know we can pull them down too. We can't let them forget that."

Claire was walking with her gaze cast down. She didn't respond.

"Are you okay? Did you get hurt?"

"I feel bad about Théroigne," Claire said. "She gave a lot to the Revolution."

"But she turned on us," Pauline said stubbornly. "She turned against us for those guys with their fancy cravats and their fancier talk. The women just gave her a whipping."

"They humiliated her," Claire said. "They hurt her badly."

"Forget about her," Pauline said, gripping Claire's arm. "We have to keep the organization going. We need to draw up petitions for laws that women need, like education for all the kids. We showed today how important we can be, and now we have to press our advantage. Justice and bread. Respect and a full belly, that's our demand."

SIXTY-SEVEN

Manon

❧

(May–June 1793)

MANON knew they should leave Paris. She was finally up, after more than a month of illness. Now that Jean was out of office and the Girondins were in peril, she found herself without energy to fight. She packed. She made arrangements. But she could not go. She imagined herself back in the house she used to love in Beaujolais, with her husband and his grey reproachful face. She had been sleeping in Eudora's childish room. The excuse was that she did not wish to infect Jean, but she was glad to escape that depressing marital bed. Leaving Jean would make a mockery of her principles; she would be reduced to the level of a courtesan of the old regime, trading in an old man for a young one. He was dependent on her. He did not write any of his letters or papers. His health was fragile. With what could she reproach him? He had done nothing wrong.

But she could not leave François either. She could not turn her back on the only passion she had ever felt. She loved François, and if she forced herself to hold that passion in check, it did not mean that she found abstinence easy or that she could bear months without seeing him. She simply could not abandon the comfort, the intensity, the fascination of his presence. She did not want to be shut up in Le Clos with Jean, full of sighs and dismal moans, while the fresh sweet face of François was leagues away. She could no longer do without him. So she remained suspended, a fly buzzing in a web of white silk, while events precipitated downhill. She hoped for a rising in the provinces to overwhelm the armed Parisians. She hoped for those good people who supported the Girondins to make themselves heard. She hoped for the Plain to rise against the Mountain and recall Jean to office.

At dawn when she awoke, drums were beating, the tocsin was ringing. She ran to the window. Armed citizens were gathering. Pikes glinted in the darkness between buildings. Something was happening, and it was not good. Was there an invasion? Was this another day of violence when blood would run in the streets?

A messenger came to report that all was uproar at the Convention. They must flee. Neither seemed able to act. Jean kept worrying how to clear his reputation. Uncertain what was happening, they told each other that the National Guard would defend the Convention against the mob. In the late afternoon, there was a knock on the door and several armed men tramped in. "Citizen Roland, I'm here to arrest you," a young man said nervously. "The Commune sent me."

Jean took the papers and glanced them over. "These are highly irregular. They are not properly made out or signed by the correct authority. I certainly will not go with you on an illegal warrant. You may go back to your Commune and tell them I await correct papers."

The young man seemed flustered. "Take him anyhow," one of the armed men snarled. "Don't be fooled."

"But he's right," the young man said, reading the papers himself. "It isn't correct. We have to go and get it fixed or we'll be in trouble."

Manon watched from the window as they marched off. They did not even post a guard. "Jean, you must go now! Your bag is packed. Go someplace safe and send for me. I'll join you."

"Get your valise and come with me," he said, staring at the street. A vein was throbbing in his forehead. His hands were knotted behind his back. "They mean to try me like a common criminal. They'll chop my head off. Come! At once!" He ran to get his suitcase and his coat.

"I'll slow you down. I'm too weak to travel quickly. They'll close the gates of Paris. Get out while you can. There's no warrant for my arrest."

Fleury hovered in the doorway, twisting her hands in her apron. "Monsieur, you must go! You must get out of here, now!"

He was too frightened to argue. "As soon as I reach a safe place, I'll send for you."

He kissed her dryly on the lips and then was gone, actually running down the steps. How would he manage without her? He would break down, become ill. She watched him trotting away. Then he turned the corner.

She sank back on the couch, putting her arms around Fleury, who began to sob. They held each other for comfort, rocking back and forth. Then Manon rose. "We must see to his papers. Let's build a little fire in the hearth. They'll be back soon enough. We should make sure there's nothing that can involve anyone else, people who've written to him."

It was dusk before the men returned. This time they had a properly executed warrant. "Where is Citizen Roland?"

"He told me he was going to the Commune to straighten this out."

"I'm sure," said the young man bitterly. "So he's flown away. You can take his place. Come with me."

"You can't take Madame. She's a mother," Fleury said. "She isn't a politician."

"Citizeness Roland, you are formally under arrest by order of the Commune," the young man said. "This time, no nonsense. Come along."

They did not touch her or jostle her. They simply surrounded her at a respectful distance and marched along through the streets. She considered it a sign of the chaos of the times that hardly anyone glanced at them. She was taken to the prison of l'Abbaye. No cell had been prepared for her, so the jailer's wife took her in. They spent the evening in the salon chatting. Manon could not eat, although the jailer's wife tried to press some chicken on her. Finally a small cell was ready. When she was locked in for the night, she lay down on the trestle bed and covered her face in her hands. She felt too weary and too desolate even to weep. She could hear coughing and sobbing, cursing and singing, night sounds of the prison. She felt utterly alone and abandoned. How long would she remain here?

She rose in the morning determined to exhibit stoic calm. At least Jean was safe. If he had been captured, she would have heard. But what had happened to François? Was he in danger? The jailer and his wife seemed civilized and friendly, probably sympathizers. She must set a good example to the other unfortunate women incarcerated in l'Abbaye.

By the end of the first week of captivity, the cell was full of flowers that Bosc picked in the Botanical Gardens and placed in vases Fleury carried to her. Her cloth covered the rickety table with its scars of previous prisoners (Here lay Marie the Poisoner, may God have mercy on my soul; Jean Forrestier, 1790, Innocent!). She sat in her little chair at her delicate desk. Her books, her coverlet, her linens were on hand. Soon they must release her. She looked forward to her interrogation. She would be composed and prepared.

In the meantime, she felt oddly free. She was reminded of her days in the convent. The convent too had been peaceful, full of women. She was not a mother here. Not her husband's amanuensis and counsel. She ran no salon and had no appointments. She neither shopped nor oversaw cooking. If she lacked something, a friend brought it.

Her gracious jailers permitted her unlimited visitors. During the day, the cells were unlocked and the women freely circulated. They chatted. Many entertained male friends. Others saw their families. How comfortable a prisoner was depended more on their resources, social and financial, the devotion of friends and family, than it did on what crime she was accused or convicted of.

What Manon had, she shared, except for precious paper and ink. Since she no longer had to write Jean's or François' speeches, she could write for herself for once. She began to set down her recollections of the Revolution and the men who had made it. She rose early and wrote all morning. Afternoons she received friends. Evenings she passed in the apartment of her jailer or with other prisoners, singing or telling stories, acting charades or playing whist or checkers. When a prisoner had a visit from her son or daughter, the other women including Manon, would gather and make a fuss over the child. It was like the convent, except that her life, instead of starting, was perhaps ending. There was always a niggling fear in the back of her mind that prison massacres could recur. If there were more military reverses, if Paris felt threatened, then the same murderers who had attacked the prisoners before could force their way in and slit their throats.

Bosc told her Girondins had raised an army in Normandy and were trying to start revolts in other provinces. She imagined the entire country in arms against Paris and the Convention, now controlled by the triumvirate of dangerous demagogues, Danton, Marat and Robespierre. They had produced some specious Constitution written in eight days by Hérault de Séchelles. She stayed reasonably well informed. Many Girondins had escaped, including Jean and François. She was told both were hiding in Normandy.

Finally armed men came for her. She was taken to the Palais de Justice. Her interrogator was the assistant prosecutor, not Fouquier-Tinville. They wanted to know where Roland was, where Buzot was, a dozen others. She learned that twenty-one Girondins had been arrested the same time as she. Some were held under house arrest; others were in prison. The Tribunal was determined to hunt down those who had escaped Paris. She was evasive and deft. She kept insisting that as a woman she really had no idea what the men intended. She had met them all while entertaining for her husband, but she had not taken part in their conversations, as any guest could verify. She did her needlework and attempted to make sure the guests were comfortable.

In three hours, they got nothing out of her. She was proud of her evasive skills. She did not lie. She did not refuse to answer. The next day when her jailer came to tell her she was being released, she was not surprised. She sent for Fleury and they packed. A few leftover items she distributed. It was a warm and humid day. It felt astonishing to be walking outside, at liberty, between the steaming sky and scorching pavement stones. She would stay in her apartment until she was sure she was not being watched. Then she must figure out where to go. She would have liked to join François, but could not: unless she failed to find Jean.

She had just taken off her bonnet and looked around at the dear familiar furniture in her flat—the cabinets and drawers still secured with the red sealing wax of the authorities—when she heard heavy feet on the stairs followed by knocking on the door. Fleury opened it cautiously.

"Citizeness Philipon, wife of Roland, I have a warrant for your arrest. Please come with me at once."

They took her, not back to l'Abbaye, but to Sainte Pélagie, to a narrow cell with a slit of window onto the courtyard. The whole charade had been to assure her arrest was legal, since she had been picked up the first time on her husband's warrant. Now she was properly arrested.

The jailer here was even kinder to her, since he had been appointed by Jean. She soon had her cell in Sainte Pélagie fixed up as cozy as her last. This time she was under no illusion she would be out soon. She must get on with her memoirs, all she could leave to her daughter, to posterity: a record of who she had been. Now there was no hiding behind Jean or François. These were the memoirs of Manon Roland, by herself, about herself. In the long run, she understood politics as well as Brissot, as well as Jean or François. Most memoirs she had read were marked by hypocrisy. She would tell the truth of her life with an openness and an honesty that must convince. She had seen little truthful written about girlhood. She remembered her own vividly but without sentimentality. She would include everything, including what would be considered in bad taste for a lady to discuss. This would be a memoir as honest as salt. Friends could sneak out the pages.

A letter from François was brought by a sympathizer. He was in Caen. There were revolts all over France, he said, in Marseille, in Toulon, in Normandy, in Lyon. They would soon be together and he would no longer allow her to keep them apart. This danger had taught him to value love above life. He would not allow her to sacrifice them to an outmoded notion of virtue.

She wrote him often, trusting the letters to friends. His letter she read and reread. She wrote him about life in Sainte Pélagie. She had been shocked to find herself thrown with prostitutes, madams, thieves, women accused of murdering an unwanted baby or their husbands or another woman of whom they had cause to be jealous. But none of them tried to hurt her and some became her friends.

Sophie came to see her. Their friendship, interrupted by Jean's jealousy, now grew as intimate as when they were seventeen. Sophie was a widow. Manon no longer felt like a married woman. She had no idea where Jean was. She wished him well, she wished him safe. She sent a couple of letters to him, urging him to be careful; her letters would be passed along until they reached someone who knew where Jean was. She did not spend much time thinking about him, outside the context of the memoirs she was writing as quickly as possible. No time for fancy language, no time for long philosophical discourses. She might be tried at any moment; she might be killed.

One afternoon she heard two women quarreling outside. They started slapping and punching each other and had to be separated.

"What's wrong? Was Marie flirting with Anatole?" she asked Berthe. Berthe was extremely jealous of her pimp.

"Some slut killed Marat, and this bitch says it's a fine thing. I want to kick the shit out of her. The friend of the people is like my father."

Some father, she thought, but tried to soothe Berthe. "Killing is always terrible. But we all have different heroes. If we don't respect each other, then we'll be at each other's throats. I'll talk to Marie for you."

To Marie she said, "It's reasonable to rejoice in the death of that butcher, but unwise to celebrate publicly. You'll get yourself beaten or worse. You can talk to me, but be careful what you say to the others."

Often the women came to her with disputes, with problems, with letters they had to read or write. She helped them prepare for interrogation. She had a social circle of women of the streets. Surprisingly many of them had dreams of a better, fuller life. It was odd to think of a prostitute as a good woman, but Berthe, in spite of her jealousy and her temper, was hardworking, a good mother, loyal to her friends, willing to share any extra food or drink she was given. She had a handsome son who, Manon felt secretly after she spoke with him, was much smarter than her own Eudora.

She had frightening news of Eudora. Her governess had gone to the Tribunal and offered to testify against the Rolands. She had submitted a formal accusation of counter-revolutionary activity. Manon begged Bosc to find out where Eudora was and to take care of her. He promised.

Fleury had been interrogated. Manon felt a noose of malice tightening. They meant to make an example of her. Did they mean to kill her? Some nights she lay awake, imagining her trial, her execution. She had never actually seen the guillotine, for she had avoided it. As if casually, she asked the other women what it was like, so that she would be prepared. But they must free her, they must, for she had done nothing wrong.

The woman who had stabbed Marat, Charlotte Corday, a Girondin from Normandy, had been shut up in her old cell at l'Abbaye. She wondered about Charlotte, a heroine to some, a murderess to others. Had she seen herself as Brutus? As Judith with the head of Holofernes? Manon was insatiably curious, but could learn little. Charlotte was said to be young and quite beautiful. Her portrait had been painted in Manon's old cell by an artist Charlotte sent for. Charlotte's trial was swift. The next day she was taken to be guillotined.

Marat's funeral was huge. The people mourned him wildly, but not Manon. He had tried to kill her. Posthumously, he still might succeed.

SIXTY-EIGHT
Georges

❧

(Summer 1793)

GEORGES had been noticing Louise Gély. She was, after all, around a great deal. Her parents lived in the same building—it was their building—and Gabrielle had entrusted his sons to Louise. Louise was excellent with the boys. They were not only used to her; they loved her. She was affectionate with them but kept discipline. Gradually she had taken over the job of ordering food and instructing the cook. She made a good wife, Georges thought, eyeing her body. She was fully developed for sixteen. He caught her looking at him too, sideways through her thick lashes.

She was dark, like Gabrielle, lighter of body and step. She was extremely pretty, as he paid more attention. She did not own many clothes and did not dress to show off her figure. She was a good girl, unfortunately, or he would have bedded her already. He caught her in his arms and kissed her. She did not pull away, but immediately afterwards, she ran out of the flat. She slipped a note under the door asking him please not to do that again, or she would find someone else to care for the darling boys.

If he wanted her, it was the same story as Gabrielle: he'd have to ask her parents for her. Well, he lacked a wife, and she could slide into that role. The boys liked her. She was attractive and full of sap and energy. He could hear her running up and down the steps, light and fast. The boys needed a mother. He had no time to court a lady who'd play games. He went to see the Gélys. They were reluctant. "Georges, you're twice her age."

"When I'm seventy, she'll be fifty-four. Is that so bad?"

Madame spoke up. She had been close to Gabrielle. He knew she was pious. Indeed, the flat where he was making his pitch was hung with crucifixes and lugubrious paintings of the saints. There was Saint Denis with his head under his arm dripping along, like a graduate of the guillotine. Some notion of interior decorating. Well, he wouldn't have to look at it, and once he married her, neither would Louise, who seemed a more cheerful type.

"We can't accept a civil ceremony," Madame said grimly. "It's not valid in the eyes of God. And we can't accept any but a real priest."

"What's a real priest?" Danton asked, although he suspected.

"What you call a nonjuring priest. Not one who swears allegiance to the government instead of the Pope. A real one."

"Henri IV said that Paris was worth a mass. So is your daughter."

Louise expressed no surprise that he wanted to marry her. The negotiations began in earnest. It was not that he didn't get laid from time to time. Women were always around in the cafes. He remembered fondly the night he had spent with that actress Claire, but she was either with that troop of wild women or with Leclerc, a young ultra-left hothead who wanted to kill all the aristocrats and half the bourgeoisie. Even if Claire had been free, a quick romp in some soft bed was no replacement for a good wife.

Finally Mme Gély, the chief negotiator, agreed he could marry Louise in a Catholic ceremony in the attic. Then they would be publicly married in a civil ceremony at City Hall, protecting both his revolutionary reputation and their religious sensibilities. Once the agreement had been drawn up, he saw no reason to dally. After the Girondins were tossed out, he was ready. One ceremony occurred June eleventh and the public one, the next day at noon. His colleagues congratulated him, a little stunned.

"How long do you think it will take him to wear this one out?" Camille told him what they said. They envied him a young and gorgeous wife. Most of them had married for money and had prunes for wives.

He had an instinct for women. This one was young and pious, but within a week, she began to enjoy love-making. Louise had a strong back and powerful thighs, from running up and down the steps all day, no doubt. "Ah, Louise, Louise, I'm crazy about you," he breathed into her wavy dark hair.

"Of course," she said. "That's how it should be."

Everyone was shocked he had married again so quickly, everyone but Louise. He had the impression that she thought he had been slow to figure out he should marry her. She seemed to have assumed their marriage since Gabrielle had told her that the boys were hers to care for. She took no interest in politics. She was conventionally pious but not a fanatic like her mother. She understood food and servants. She had been raised to be a good wife, and she performed above his expectations. He felt a certain reluctance to leave in the morning for the Convention, and he came hurrying home at night.

The asinine Girondins, thrown out of the Convention but in no real danger, did themselves in royally. They tried to drum up revolts all over the country. The rebellion in Normandy was put down immediately, as it had little public backing. But Marseille and Toulon were in revolt and so was Lyon, far more serious upheavals. A civil war was still raging in the Vendée.

His policy of accommodation was discredited and he was in trouble politically. Marat wrote a blistering piece, calling him the leader of the Committee of Public Loss. He was blamed for military failures and blamed for the Girondin uprisings, because he had tried to protect them. Then on July tenth, when the members of the great Committee of Public Safety came up for their monthly review, he was out on his ear. Let them grind along without him for a month. They'd beg him back soon enough.

He was still angry at Marat when a crazy girl from Caen, where the Girondins had been fomenting revolt, stabbed Marat in his bath. Georges was secretly relieved to have a wild card removed from the political scene, but he had protected Marat and been supported by him as often as he had quarreled with him. He did not like the man—a stinking fanatic—but he could be counted on to call out the people when they were needed. Marat had hated Manon, now rotting in prison; he had hated Marie-Antoinette. But when Théroigne de Méricourt was stripped and beaten by the women, he stepped in to save her. Marat had a soft spot for the flamboyant Théroigne. People said he had been her lover in the old days, when he was a society doctor and she, a fancy courtesan ruining counts and bankers, but Georges doubted it. Marat never had the kind of money that Théroigne had drawn before she quit the business. They simply liked each other. Now Théroigne was in the Salpêtrière, mad after her head injury, and Marat was dead, leaving a pauper's estate of twenty-five sous.

Charlotte Corday went to the guillotine, and after her would walk many Girondins because of her quick knife. After the revolts, after the murder of Marat, the Convention no longer discussed Girondins in respectful tones. They were traitors. They were the enemy as much as the Prussians or the English. She had been acting for the Girondins, and most people thought they had sent her.

Burying Marat was a full-time business. On the sixteenth of July, at five in the afternoon so people could come from work, the painter David arranged Marat's funeral. Marat lay on a fanciful huge bier a foot deep in flowers. He was already starting to rot, so the flowers helped. The bier was supported by a dozen men. None of the weight was Marat, skinny as a piece of paper. The cortege started at Marat's house. The hearse was followed by children in white throwing flowers. Then came the Convention in mourning. Then patriotic clubs and people in the thousands, under the banners of their sections. Every five minutes an artillery salute went off on the Pont Neuf.

Long after dark they ended up in the garden of the Cordeliers Club, where he was to be buried under a clump of trees in a tomb that had been hastily knocked out by the sculptor Martin. It was supposed to be a granite mountain symbolizing Marat's inflexible resolve. The coffin and two urns, one with his lungs and the other with his intestines, were placed inside. Then every orator got a chance to make a speech, himself included.

Two days later they did it all again, when the heart of Marat was placed ceremoniously on the old altar in the Cordeliers Club, in a vase carved out of a single chunk of agate and adorned with jewels—part of the royal hoard of Louis. Danton was amused that Marat's heart should end up inside such a casing.

In the following weeks, the cult got out of hand. Every corner was selling mementos of the fallen hero: Marat busts, Marat engravings, Marat pins, Marat scarves, Marat dishes, Marat mugs, Marat cravats. Little replicas of his bath were everywhere. Half the theaters in Paris were staging tableaus, plays, pantomimes, musicals on Marat's life and death. Songs were composed and hawked on the street corners. Danton got used to seeing depictions of the death scene on every other wall. He was reminded of the lugubrious paintings and artifacts that adorned the walls of his new in-laws. Marat was filling a niche that used to be occupied by the sacred heart of Jesus and the crucifixion. Ordinary people bought representations of the death of their saint and hung it over the matrimonial bed.

He fucked his new wife, ate the good meals she put on the table and dreamed of the countryside. In the midst of a rainy July, Robespierre was elected to Georges' old place on the Committee of Public Safety. Robespierre had finally succumbed to power. Now Georges would see if the Incorruptible could avoid being corrupted. Georges was careful to offer congratulations and vote approval. What would happen now that Robespierre had the great Committee and thus the government in his bony hands?

The government was cracking down. Marie-Antoinette was moved from the Temple to the Conciergerie, the jail in the same building as the Revolutionary Tribunal. The Dauphin was given to a cobbler to raise. This treatment felt unnecessarily cruel to Georges. Marie had been extravagant in the face of poverty, gilding her favorites. She was one of the stupid Hapsburgs; but that needn't be a lethal offense. It would be quite sufficient to lock her up in some unused palace until the war was over, then send her home to Austria.

They were gearing up to execute her. Maybe he was lucky to be out of the great Committee for a while. It was getting a little too bloody for his taste. He said to Camille as they walked to the Convention, "So if we were the ultimate high judges, couldn't we be more imaginative in our sentencing instead of death death chop chop chop."

"Robespierre has that gesture on the podium, have you ever noticed? He really shouldn't do that." Camille chopped with his hand.

"Marie is going to trial. So, we convict her. What should she be sentenced to?"

"That's easy." Camille tossed his hair. "Nursing wounded soldiers. Washing bloody bandages. Changing bedpans. That would teach her a few things about war and the common man. But death is the simplest way to solve any problem. The guillotine is so fast, it's like slapping a fly."

"Unless you're the fly."

Marseille was taken. The troops supposed to be supporting the Girondins deserted to the government. Toulon was another story. Late in August, the French admiral turned over the fleet at Toulon to the British. Georges felt that blow. When Barère read the dispatch to the Convention, a great groan went up and they all turned to each other. Never had such a thing happened. Robespierre rose to say this was proof that the worst enemies of France were within. The old commanders would sell them out like Dumouriez. New men who had risen from the ranks might not have the polish or military school background of the old officers, but they would not go over to the enemy.

Georges understood the problem because he read history. For centuries soldiers had been mercenaries. Generals and admirals were professionals who sold their services to the highest bidder. It was not treason for a general to be bought by the enemy and lead their troops. Spaniards commanded French troops; French generals commanded Austrian troops—all in the line of a good career.

The new soldiers were patriots. They were fighting for their country, their freedom. That's how it had been for the Americans. That's what the slaves in Dominique wanted. But an army of free Frenchmen needed officers who were patriots too, not career men who would lead them into death and then go over to the other side if they got a better offer.

"It's a mess," he told Louise as he was resting from his pleasant labors on her sweet body.

"I want to move to our house at Arcis. I love the country."

"So do I, Louise my peach. We'll do that before too long, I promise you. It's almost time for the good life for us. I've managed to put away a decent amount of money. When I retire from public life, we'll be comfortable. I know how to live, how to be happy—and so do you."

"Oh yes," Louise agreed, plucking at the hairs of his chest. "You should retire before you wear out. I'm younger than you, but I don't want to bury you. The boys would grow up healthier in Arcis."

"It would be a pleasure," Georges agreed. To be done with the daily battles.

Not to have to witness the execution of men he had worked with. The Girondins were going to the guillotine soon. Why not retire and enjoy what he had accumulated? He wished Robespierre joy in governing. Let him run himself into the ground and see how easy it was to criticize compromises from the outside. Let him figure out that in governing, everybody wanted from you, and whatever you did, nobody was satisfied. Let Robespierre find out how dismaying it was to shed real and not rhetorical blood. It was his turn.

SIXTY-NINE
Claire

❦

(Summer 1793)

CLAIRE liked living with Théo. Théophile Leclerc was certainly bright, but he was not broody. He did not waste time sorting through his motives or hesitating over what he wanted. His feelings were close to the surface and available. He did not have to figure out why he was angry or sad. There was an admirable simplicity in him of one who acted out of his inner impulses and followed them like a rock slung through the air.

She had noticed that early. Not the first time she had met him a year ago (he had been in Pairs pleading for some issue involving soldiers), but the second time, when the left had been defeated in Lyon and he returned. He had given her a beautiful silk tricolor scarf. Drawing the scarf about her shoulders, she asked, "Why give me this?"

"I want you to like me," he said. "I thought it might please you. It's a very fine silk chiffon. It's from Lyon."

"Why do you want me to like you, Citizen Leclerc?"

"Because I want you to call me Théo. Because I want you to love me. Because I want to make love to you."

Refreshingly direct. "Why not? Come home with me."

Within a week, he moved in. They had been together ever since—not stuck to each other's sides. They were both extremely busy. This time in Paris, he achieved sudden visibility. He'd already been arrested by the Girondins and held in jail for a week before they'd gotten together: not his first time in prison. Théo was an odd mixture. Like Mendès, he came from the middle class but he had been out in the rough world. Odd memories would flash out of him matter-of-factly that sent a chill through her. They were passing through Les Halles near the butchering stalls, and a butcher was flaying a calf. "I saw a man flayed once in the islands. A black slave they were making an example of. Except he wasn't dead. His widow lived to tear out the heart of the overseer who skinned him and feed it to her pigs." He smiled as if he were telling her a pleasant anecdote.

"It's not true," he would say, "that people always die of head wounds. I knew a man who had his head cut open with an ax and he lived for two months. Of course he was crazy all that time."

Or, arguing with Pauline about how merciful the guillotine actually was, "Listen, at Lyon when they were rounding up the patriots, when the Girondins won, they meant to make an example of Chalier, so the Girondins set up the guillotine. But the thug they picked was not a real executioner and didn't set it properly. So the blade kept coming down and hacking at the poor bastard Chalier, a real revolutionary that one, with the blood spurting out but still he could not die. Finally the butcher gave up and sawed off Chalier's head with a knife."

Yet Théo was gentle in bed. He liked her to mount him, which she enjoyed. It was easier for her to come in that position, but often men were afraid of it. Théo wasn't about to be scared of a woman on top. He had a fine lithe body, well muscled and tight. It was marred with scars. There he had taken a saber cut. That was the exit mark of a bullet. This was from being thrown against the bulkhead in a storm. That was from a flogging.

They did not have much of a domestic existence. Intimacy was haphazard. She was extremely busy with the Revolutionary Republican Women. They both went to the Jacobin Club and the Cordeliers, although she had recently been denounced at the Jacobins and Théo had been thrown out twice. They were called Mad Dogs, Enragés, by those they considered too fond of compromise. So was her good friend Jacques Roux, always in trouble with the authorities. Théo started a paper, taking over Marat's title, *The Friend of the People*. Robespierre persuaded Marat's widow to denounce Théo, but ordinary people seemed to like the paper, which increased its circulation every week.

She had a brief job that paid the rent, playing Simonne Évrard—ironically Marat's widow who was attacking her friends—in a play called *Marat Enters Olympus*. Then she had a role in a fete, Liberty embracing Marat. In that one, her right breast was hanging out. She had to slug the actor who played Marat and threaten to sic Théo on him so he'd keep his hands off.

The women had a festival to commemorate *The Friend of the People* in the Place du Carrousel, where an obelisk had been erected. Around the stone obelisk were displayed a bust of Marat, his bath, his lamp and his writing desk. She had trusted him, but she found the veneration hard to take.

There were more and more executions lately. She did not know if she could go to see Olympe de Gouges' execution. It was a sign of respect to go. To say goodbye if only with your eyes. But she did not want to see Olympe die. Olympe had got in trouble for refusing to renounce her adoration of the royal house. She was a revolutionary monarchist. That piety ran deep. Now it would cost her life. Claire kept her opinions to herself, because all around her everyone was calling for death to hoarders, to speculators, to the guys in the Convention who had not voted death for the King. Things were out of control, with generals going over to the enemy and the fleet given to the English and revolutionaries killed in Lyon and the Vendée. But the Mountain, now that they controlled the Convention—won with the aid of the women—was not honoring its promises.

The Mountain was trying to win over former supporters of the Girondins. The people had their own agenda. They wanted local democracy, direct recall of delegates who didn't do what they were supposed to, immediate execution of aristocrats and traitors who worked against the Revolution, execution of hoarders, speculators, those who starved them for a profit. They wanted price controls on bread and other necessities. They wanted higher taxes on the rich, the distribution of the property of exiles and traitors. It was a simple direct program and not about to dissipate in the new clemency and moderation of the Mountain. Claire made the people's program her own, although her heart was not in the call for executions. The poor had always cursed the rich, but now it seemed they could curse unto death.

Claire and Pauline moved the club out of the Jacobins. They were tired of the men trying to interfere. They began to meet in Saint Eustache, a church in Les Halles, the market district. It was big as a cathedral, plenty of the room they needed, for they were attracting more women every week. It was a light pleasant space, often with market smells wafting in.

When Claire arrived home late the last week in August, Théo had fallen asleep across the bed in his clothes, so that she could not climb in without waking him.

"I was so disappointed you weren't here. Where were you?"

"The meeting. We had a lot to settle, so we went on till midnight."

"You're going to have the husbands up in arms, Claire. They'll start denouncing you."

"Really. I'm glad I'm not married."

He was silent, rubbing his eyes. "Are you glad? I thought you might like to be married, to me. It's simpler that way."

"Death is the great simplifier. No, Théo, I don't want to be married to anyone. Not even to you." She was taken by surprise. Where was this coming from? She didn't want to be tied to any man by a legal cord. "Don't you think the kind of free union Marat and Simonne had is best?"

"They didn't have children. He was sick all the time. Suppose you get pregnant?"

"That's what wise women are for. But I doubt I will. I never have."

"But don't you want to some time?"

She looked at him, sprawled on her bed, and for the first time, she was not entirely pleased he was there. She liked him well enough, but she did not love him the way he wanted to be loved. She wondered if she had any romance in her. When she listened to other actresses, she felt not only years older but of different stuff. She wanted a lover who was first and foremost a friend. "Théo, I'm exhausted. I've been dealing with four hundred fractious women for four hours. I want sleep far more than I want anything else in the world. I can't even remember what we're supposed to be talking about."

Why couldn't they just be friends who fucked? He imagined himself in love with her, and she dutifully said the words. She could not act the part correctly because all the mooning and romantic glue seemed to her the stuff of bad plays she had acted in over the years. It wasn't real, like a good meal or a good fuck or a good glass of wine or a talk with a friend and a laugh in the cafe. The good things in life were simple and direct. They did not require talking yourself into wanting them. They did not require a suspension of judgement and common sense. Too many of her women friends who married for love were dealing with broken jaws and beatings a year later. It was the privilege of the Parisian poor to follow their feelings, but that seemed to lead the women mostly into trouble.

Fortunately they were both too frantically busy for the subject of marriage to arise often. Beyond anything else, she wanted the ordinary people who did the work of the world to make the important decisions about their own lives—especially the women. That was why they had to keep hammering at the Mountain. Too much compromise with the fat folks, and nothing good would happen. So they marched, they petitioned, they agitated, they made noise in the streets.

They were highly visible, the Revolutionary Republican Women in their dirty red caps and their red pantaloons and their tricolored shawls, they were far more visible than the men who always outnumbered them. They were scarier than they should have been. Most men saw them as bloodthirsty Amazons about to do something unspeakable. That they had seized the male prerogatives of weapons and bold demands seemed to scare the men the most, as if some enormous charade on which their power depended might topple. That was their most potent weapon: the perception of them as unnatural, out of control and therefore wild and dangerous. Everyone gave them a lot of credit for the overthrow of the Girondins and that lent their petitions clout. But it was male fear that gave them their edge. Too bad Théo knew her too well to be afraid.

SEVENTY
Nicolas

❦

(June–October 1793)

O N that terrible day in June when twenty-two of the Girondin delegates were outlawed and either thrown in prison or forced to become fugitives, Nicolas was surprised he was untouched. He was shocked that a mob could oust elected representatives. They no longer had a republic but rule by violence. He tried to protest, but the Convention was not the Legislative Assembly. In the Assembly, he had been prominent, and the delegates, reasonably polite. In the Convention, half the time when he tried to speak, he was booed or simply ignored. These men were young and rambunctious. Most had come up through the Revolution. They were used to shouting and arguing without polite formulae or indeed, without manners. They called each other names like aristocratic lackey and drinker of blood. The gallery applauded when they were rudest.

He was deeply wounded by what happened with his Constitution. It had been four-fifths his. Danton made some comments, the others had a pet clause or two. Tom Paine had worked most closely with him, but it was the child of all those years of studying society. It was as close to a perfect machine as he could create. It was long, certainly, because it attempted to spell out exactly how the government should be elected, run, monitored, changed. It was eighty-five pages of dense small printing. When it had been distributed to the Convention, he had expected cheers, but they groaned. They sounded like schoolboys. "How do you expect us to read all this?"

"One sentence at a time, gentlemen. It will be worth your while."

But most of them never bothered. For three months part of the business of every working day was haggling over some clause. Half the members left whenever the Constitution came up. Then after the Girondins had been driven from the Convention, Hérault de Séchelles dashed off a Constitution in a week. Abbé Sieyès said to Nicolas, "It's just a bad table of contents for a Constitution." But it was short. The delegates liked that.

"How could you hope to create a working Constitution in eight days?" Nicolas objected.

Hérault shrugged. "God made the world in six."

Nicolas wrote a pamphlet denouncing that ridiculous sketch for a Constitution. Chabot rose to demand Nicolas be arrested for sedition. Friends told him a warrant for his arrest had been issued. His brother-in-law Dr. Cabanis found a woman who would hide him, a widow who usually provided lodging to medical students. He was whisked out of his house, with barely time to kiss Sophie and his daughter Eliza goodbye.

Now he lived in a little room in Mme Vernet's apartment, on a narrow street between the Luxembourg palace (recently turned into a prison) and the church of Saint Sulpice, in the Latin Quarter. She was the widow of a painter. He could not go out for fear of being recognized. However, being idle had its own rewards. He had time to write, not pamphlets like the one that had got him in trouble, but a real book. If he had not been able to reach his countrymen by his speeches, he would reach them with his words on paper.

He was personally upset when Olympe de Gouges went to the guillotine, as if her *Declaration of the Rights of Women* and her plays constituted a threat. No decent government would fear such intelligent and reasoned dissent. She was not deeply cultivated like Sophie, but she was bright and original. One of a kind. Marat too was dead. Marat had been an important figure of the changes, no matter how much Nicolas personally disliked him. His world was being depopulated. It was embarrassing to find fanatics who called themselves Girondins, like the unhinged Charlotte Corday, posing for her portrait with every hair in place and a soulful look, in between stabbing Marat in his bathtub and marching with a martyred air to the guillotine.

In mid-October, he was condemned to death in absentia by the Revolutionary Tribunal. Dr. Cabanis slipped in to see him. "Pierre, could you get me a sure poison? Something to fall back on in case they catch me. I should not like to ride that tumbrel. I don't wish to die with a thousand people watching as if it were a balloon ascent."

"Sophie would never forgive me if I gave you poison."

"Sophie would never forgive you if I had to go through the humiliation of a public execution. Could you do that to her?"

Ten days later, Pierre gave him a small quantity of poison in a ring with a gaudy stone, hollowed out: a mixture of a nightshade derivative and opium. It would finish him off supposedly without pain. Since he intended to wear it constantly from now on, he wished the ring were not in such bad taste. It was insurance that he would control the time of his death, that he would not be made a spectacle, subject to a punishment he did not feel he deserved.

The first month he missed Sophie fiercely, a pain like a toothache. She could not come, for she was watched. The Committee of Security—the police committee—had hoped she would lead them to him. Finally they relaxed surveillance, and she could visit him occasionally. She was extremely careful. She never came directly and never went directly back. He wished she dared bring Eliza with her, for he had not seen her since he fled. Most of his assets and properties had been seized. Sophie was supporting him, Eliza and her own sister.

Mme Vernet always led Sophie straight to his room. She did not intrude or chat. He never knew when Sophie was coming, but of course, he was always there. At first they embraced stiffly. Then they sat down and had a glass of wine together. It took them a while to find their intimacy, with all the habits and rituals of their domesticity broken. They were shy with each other. He felt guilty about exposing her to risk. If he were braver, stronger, he would forbid her to come. But he needed to see her.

Sophie had opened a lingerie shop, which she was running. "Oh, our customers are courtesans, high-priced ones, and mistresses of men with money."

"Under the Revolution, I wouldn't think there'd be many of them."

"Think again. Your army contractor, your new millionaire who speculates in grain or assignats, your landlord who bought up three monasteries and turned them into estates, wants a good time. The deputies from the provinces, some brought their wives, and some didn't. None like to sleep alone. And there's old money lying low and living a little less ostentatiously. They let go their carriages, but they kept their diamonds and their servants and their mistresses."

"Sophie, I hope you aren't becoming a cynic."

"I'm never a cynic about you. You're a good man, and you don't deserve this . . . imprisonment. Your color is very pale."

"I can't go out. I'm not safe."

"I read the manuscript you've begun. Nico, it isn't worthy of you. You don't need to justify yourself to a bunch of fanatical nincompoops—most of whom would be taxed by anything weightier than *Père Duchesne*. This is your chance to create your vision. I want you to tackle something larger, something that sums up your philosophy. Not a petty series of anecdotes—I didn't do that and you did that to me, and then I said and he replied."

"I won't write a word more." He rolled over to face the wall, pouting.

"Nico, do something grand. You have the time. You've always had the vision. Never mind the circumstances of the shabby moment. Let yourself fly."

After she had left, he was sorry he had sulked. It was only that, seeing each other every two weeks, every second had to be filled with honey. But her criticism struck home. He had been answering carping attacks, instead of writing for the ages. He would show Sophie he could still fly.

Mme Vernet was a few years older than Nicolas, a round squirrellike woman with tiny bright blue eyes and a turned-up nose. She was a reasonable cook, better when Sophie had extra money to give her. Sophie was not only working in the lingerie shop but painting miniatures. That was more lucrative but chancier, four commissions one month and none the next. The shop paid more reliably. She was living out in Auteuil, in the house they had bought for weekends and summers; she traveled into the city almost daily. She was not allowed to sleep in Paris, being a fugitive's wife.

Mme Vernet and he spent their evenings sitting by her small fire. He read aloud to her from Voltaire or Abbé Raynal's *History of the Two Indies*. The French had been forced to loose their hold on the colonies. At least the slave trade had been stopped, not by the Revolution so much as by war. Robespierre would finish it off now that he was in power. Robespierre was a man of principle; only his principles were narrow and his means increasingly ferocious. Death solved all political problems.

Paris was becoming a huge theater. There was the theater of the Convention, where great speeches rumbled and demagogues clashed. There was the theater of the Revolutionary Tribunal, where that terrifying moron Fouquier-Tinville tried people in batches, as he called it, and in batches they went to the guillotine. The guillotine was another theater. How would this or that one die? Final words? The streets were yet another stage, of demonstrations, protests, marches. David regularly mounted mammoth festivals involving music and flowers and bright colors, banners, cannons. The death of Marat seemed to have generated public entertainment for two months. Shut up as he was, he had Mme Vernet bring him papers. He questioned Pierre and Sophie. He tried to understand the upheavals, the transformations, the volte-faces, the abrupt rises and more abrupt falls. People spoke of the Terror. Some evoked it with loathing, some with excitement, some with fanatical hope. "These are the times that try men's souls," his friend Tom Paine had written about the American revolution, but that seemed tepid by comparison. Some spoke about the Terror with admiration as if it were a great beast, a thing in itself, instead of a repressive policy instituted by the government. Some wrote of it with religious fervor, as if it would cleanse society, renewal through blood. Some saw it as the Antichrist.

He was writing a history of the human mind, of the perfectibility of society. He divided history into great ages that revealed a pattern. He decided to call it *A Sketch of the Intellectual Progress of Mankind*. When he gave Sophie a copy of the manuscript as far as he had gotten, she sent a message that she was overjoyed. This was the culmination of his life's work. He agreed. He had no idea how much time he had. He wrote on with intense concentration, a gift to his daughter so that she would understand her father. He would never embrace the royalists or the reaction. Calmly but swiftly he put his vision down on page after page. A great light seemed to fill him as he worked.

SEVENTY-ONE

Max

❦

(July–October 1793)

MAX had no time for anything superfluous. Everything light and pleasant and casual had burned away. He could not remember what it was like to walk in the sunlight, to dine with his adopted family, to talk with Eléanore, to sleep more than four hours. Often he was up all night and worked the next day. The Revolution was an engine that must be stoked. No one was indispensable, but no one was excused from doing the work placed before him at his full capacity. He found himself finally meshed into the place he was needed, his will the will of the people, himself the brain of a great organism, everything he could summon to give needed, used, combusted. Now he was truly and completely the representative of the people. He moved in a blur of action, yet his mind was clear.

He had come into office in disaster. The great Committee of Public Safety had been Danton's, but he preferred to play house with his adolescent wife. He had lost interest in governing. Max knew about Danton's secret religious marriage. An ex-priest told him in confidence, and he kept that confidence one might say religiously. Max smiled at his little joke as he entered that tidbit in his notebook on Danton. Danton was a puzzle: Now a worthy tool of the Revolution. Now a pig wallowing in his domestic sty. He had thought Danton had been ennobled by suffering when he lost his partner for life, Gabrielle, who was such a good mother. Max did not find her attractive—she was too full-bodied and overblown for his aesthetic appreciation—but as a madonna she had shone. Then after Max had opened his heart to Danton, offering him friendship, scarcely five months later, Danton married a child bride and acted as if he had just invented conjugal pleasure. Here was a man with much surface but little center.

He had disreputable friends, as did Camille. Camille was still friendly with the royalist Dillon; both of them dined with financiers, speculators, the underbelly of the rich class determined to make money from the Revolution. People gossiped about the settlement Danton had fixed on his new bride. He seemed to have bought her, and dearly. Lucile was surrounded by a cloud of scandal. She flirted with everyone. Max believed her faithful, but he did not believe that of Camille, who had always fallen into bed with anyone who crooked a finger at him. Max tried to ignore that sexual morass. Orgies and affairs were sordid but did little damage to the State. But financial chicanery was what the English relied upon to undermine the paper money, to wreck confidence in the fiscal stability of the revolutionary government. Money was a powerful lever to overthrow a government. He hoped that Camille and Danton were more honest than they appeared. Lucile spent money like water. She had none of the frugal virtues of the Duplays. She was elegant when she should have been simple. What was needed was a single will. Whatever did not cleave to the Revolution must be excised like a cancer. The internal enemies were no different from the armies at the borders or the English cutting them off at sea.

Some things had been accomplished. The Constitution had passed overwhelmingly, but they could not put it into effect in the present emergency. For the peasants, he had pushed land reform through the Convention: All feudal dues and obligations abolished without compensation, and land made available for collective purchase by communities.

Every morning he rose, breakfasted with the Duplays—often the only time he got to see them, and then went along the street toward the Tuileries. Sometimes he would run into Carnot, who lived nearby, and they would walk together.

Lazare Carnot was the military man on the Committee of Public Safety. Older than the rest and a talented engineer, he had come up as far as a commoner could under the ancien régime. Max had known him in Arras. He was a big man with a long sharp nose and deep-set eyes, a laconic manner. As they passed, children were already playing in the gardens. The Committee used the entrance from the courtyard. He climbed what had been called the Queen's Stairway. Every morning as he climbed that stairway, he was forced to think of Marie-Antoinette. The fury created by Charlotte Corday had spilt over onto Marie. Everyone agreed, women were getting out of control, running wild like mischievous children, like savages. That too must be put in order.

At the head of the steps was a series of connecting rooms crowded with messengers, functionaries, petitioners, clerks carrying papers to be signed, officers, sans-culottes with something urgent to say, couriers from all over the country, would-be contractors for the army or the battered navy. He passed through the midst. The last room housed the Committee, which had the right to meet in closed session. He no longer noticed Persian carpets or parquet floors, mirrors, chandeliers dripping crystal, dancing goddesses. He saw only the large oval table covered with green baize where the Committee met and the desks and tables scattered around the room. By Saint-Just's table was a camp bed where he often slept. Couthon was wheeled in by his wife. "Here am I, the Nimble One, who overslept ten minutes from dancing all night."

Barère was finishing up paperwork before heading for the Convention. Max did not trust him, handsome, florid, always seeming to pose for a portrait. Barère tacked to every wind. He was slippery and oily, indispensable at present because he was popular. He was the person who made little jokes as they worked late into the night around the green table. He made light of their quick suppers of dry bread and wine with a bit of sausage or an apple. He was even more important in dealing with the Convention. He took the day's victories and made them sing and dance across the floor of the theater where the Convention met. He made bad poetry of war, and the delegates adored him. Saint-Just would report that the men had broken ranks and been cut down by cannon fire. Barère would invent a heroic stand to the last man with the tricolor bravely fluttering, men dying with a last word for mother.

Carnot dealt with military matters and dealt firmly. Finally someone who knew about the army was giving orders and following up. No more boots whose soles fell off; no more bread rotten with weevils. No more blankets that rotted in the damp. Things were on an honest footing at last. Another entry in the notebook labeled DANTON. He had been in bed with the contractors. Fabre d'Églantine and Danton had much to answer for from their lucrative sojourn in Belgium.

Several of the Committee were always on mission, running all over France bringing the edicts of the Convention, making sure that the work of local government was just and revolutionary, that no demagogues got into power, the war effort was proceeding, the peasants were bringing their grain to market. Saint-Just went to the army often. He was tireless, not able to be bribed, moved, cajoled. Max also sent Augustin and Elisabeth's husband Philippe Lebas on a mission. Max was justly proud of his kid brother.

"You should be married like Philippe," he said one day as they grabbed a quick meal before heading off to the Jacobins. Max went regularly, no matter what the press of business. The Jacobins usually adjourned by ten, and he could still rush back to the Tuileries for a late meeting.

"None of us will marry," Augustin said. He was handsome, Max thought, an open masculine face. "Not me, not Charlotte, not you."

"I can't offer a wife anything but death. But you, Augustin, you'd make a wonderful father. Charlotte? She has no politics but vanity."

"We're all the children of our mother who died screaming, after that pig stuffed her full of too many babies and took off. I'm told he's in Germany."

"To me, he's dead," Max said. "That's all I want to hear on the subject."

Augustin shrugged. "Charlotte drives me crazy. Every time I get involved with a woman, she becomes insanely jealous. . . . I like a nice married woman who's separated from her husband. Or a widow. Really, why don't you marry Eléanore? Everybody knows about her."

"I have too little time, Bonbon. In two years, there won't be ten of us alive who made the Revolution."

"You need to get more sleep. Relax. Maybe we could steal a day in the country, while the weather's warm."

September came tramping in, crowds of sans-culottes in the streets again waving banners and pikes and shouting. The paper money kept falling in value. Efforts to provide a secure supply of bread at a reasonable price failed. There were long, long lines at the bakers, at the grocers. The people were sure that speculators, hoarders, middle men were forcing up the prices. The Mad Dogs stirred them up with violent rhetoric, claiming the mantle of Marat. Those young agitators infuriated him. They had no respect. Leclerc dared jump up in the Jacobins and scream, "If new men seem too passionate, that's because the old men are worn out. Only the young have the fire to carry the Revolution forward!"

Max had him thrown out. How dare they speak for the people, these loud-mouths? The so-called red priest Jacques Roux. That young idiot Leclerc. Billaud-Varenne and that actor, Collot d'Herbois. All of them in bed with those wild women of the RRW. Hébert's lewd rag had the largest circulation in France. Hébert was entrenched in the Commune and leading the Corde-liers Club, which had gotten away from Danton. Danton should have kept a grip on the Cordeliers, as Max never, never relaxed his vigilance over the Jacobins. You needed to keep your base. Hébert was building a base; Hébert was challenging him. The Mad Dogs were as dangerous as the right, because they could split the Revolution. The peasants were pleased by Max's land reform; the Vendée showed what happened when you didn't please the peas-ants. Now he must satisfy the sans-culottes.

Those Mad Dogs would lose the Revolution by scaring the middle class. The coalition of the poor and middle class had to be kept intact, the alliance on which the power of the Mountain rested. He must move against the Mad Dogs when he could, but for now he accumulated information. He would adopt enough of their program to cut the ground from under them.

He sat down at the green baize table, placing a notebook before him. "We must have price controls on foods here and in the provinces."

Barère said, "The shopkeepers, the market women, the distributors won't like that."

"We'll raise wages and then we'll put on controls. That will please the people. Marat said, 'Feed the poor before anything,' and we will."

"That demagogue Billaud-Varenne wants a revolutionary army," Carnot said. "Now the sections are demanding one. Utter chaos."

"Not necessarily. We'll send them to the Vendée. They'll be fighting peasants and priests."

Carnot frowned. "The Vendée peasants are great unconventional fighters. They know their country. They know how to attack and vanish."

"It's an experiment. If the revolutionary army doesn't work out, we'll disband them," Saint-Just said. "If they work, we'll fold them into the regular army." He did not add what he had said earlier to Max, that it they were wiped out, it would be easier to govern Paris.

"Excellent," Max said. "Now we must add to the Committee a couple of the agitators." He turned to Couthon. "Say we need more men to share the work of the Committee. Propose the men we want."

They settled on Billaud-Varenne and Collot d'Herbois. The people loved Billaud for demanding a revolutionary army of sans-culottes and proposing that any defeated general should be killed. He had a reputation for ruthlessness. Collot d'Herbois of the Cordeliers was close to the Mad Dogs, close to Hébert, close to that actress who led the RRW. People said they had been lovers. The Convention added Danton, who declined, pleading ill health. He asked for a leave of absence to retire to Arcis to regain his strength. Danton was withdrawing from politics. Max was amused that Danton knew the moment to step down.

To Eléanore in one of the precious moments they could be alone, lying face to face fully clothed on his bed, he said, "It's like being married to twelve men. A marriage of convenience. I would not choose them—"

"Except perhaps Saint-Just." Eléanore was sometimes jealous of him.

"Twelve men do not make a good marriage, but the volume of work forces us to march over our differences, to crash through what we dislike about each other. It doesn't matter I consider Billaud a cutthroat and Collot a demagogue and Barère a weathercock. We are the Committee. We must save France. Nothing else signifies. We'll die to save France as clearly as soldiers must."

She held him tightly, her face intense, her grip hard. "Won't you be disappointed if you survive this period of crisis, retire covered with glory and have to deal with me?"

"Then I'd dare to marry you. We'll move out of Paris. Trees and clean air, clear water, and many dogs. We'll take the stray dogs of Paris with us. Blount will be a patriarch." Blount, sprawled across the foot of the bed, wagged his tail at the mention of his name and eyed his master. Max hardly even got to walk Blount lately. Eléanore took care of him.

"I want to believe in that future."

"Danton is retiring to the country with his child bride."

"Good riddance. Max, I never told you this. But that time we all were in the country together, Danton tried to seduce Elisabeth. If you can call it that. He put his hands all over her. Elisabeth screamed and ran away—"

"Why did the two of you keep this from me? Does Philippe know?"

"I doubt it. Elisabeth made me promise not to tell. She was embarrassed. She was afraid she had somehow given him encouragement. I hate keeping secrets from you. Now that he's leaving Paris, I see no reason not to let you know."

"I wish you had told me at the time. I will not forgive this."

"It doesn't matter, Max. Nothing happened."

They rarely made love now. He was too exhausted. He assured her that he did not care for her less. He had nothing left inside.

At the Committee, they were dealing with economic problems, with the war that was going better against the Austrians than in the Vendée. Lyon, where the Girondins had massacred the Jacobins, was under siege. The Girondins had a lot to answer for.

Before he could move against the Girondins, the Revolutionary Tribunal summoned Marie-Antoinette, the focus of Hébert's rage. Max did not consider her dangerous, for she could not rule. Max stepped in when Hébert was pushing the charge of incest. That confused child, the Dauphin, had been taken from his mother. Then he was coerced into claiming Marie-Antoinette had seduced him. Rubbish! Max demanded they stop that nonsense.

The damage was done in the Tribunal and in Hébert's rag, before Max caught wind of the trumped-up farce. Max lost his temper, briefly, then he settled into a cold fury. Hébert was becoming dangerous. The ex-Queen went to her death, crowds heckling her all the way to the guillotine. Max thought the spectacle unnecessary. Billaud went to watch. No one else did. It was reported there was dancing in the streets. Hébert devoted a special issue of his paper to gloating. The Committee, along with their sometime rivals, the Committee of Security, took the Revolutionary Tribunal away from the Paris Commune. They wanted to control trials and executions.

Nothing could be done yet to Hébert, who controlled the Cordeliers and the Commune. But it was time to move against the Mad Dogs, Leclerc, Jacques Roux, the RRW women: Hébert's allies. Billaud and Collot liked their new power and would go along. Putting them on the great Committee had been a clever move. It was a long, exhausting and dangerous chess game he was playing against history and opponents who kept multiplying. But he held everything in his hands.

SEVENTY-TWO
Pauline

❦

(Fall 1793)

PAULINE felt personally betrayed by Robespierre. She had adored him. She had cheered him on. She had defended him in public and private, most recently to Jacques Roux. She risked her life in demonstrations Robespierre called (but never marched in). She had been content that he was the brain and she was one of many bodies. She felt a sense of unity with him, that he understood the people of the sections, that he would lead the way they passionately wanted to go. When he stood up in the Convention or the Jacobins, he spoke as the Revolution, with an icy passion that seemed empty of self-interest. Although he spoke often of himself, the self he spoke of belonged to the people, to her.

Now he was giving the people the price controls with one hand and taking away their power with the other. He turned on the women who had always come out for him. Suddenly he spoke of them with disgust. They were unnatural. They were dangerous. They were a threat to the Revolution—the Revolutionary Republican Women who put justice, bread and freedom before everything. She burned with betrayal. She felt scalded, a pain that did not diminish. Since September, when some of their program had been adopted by the Convention, everything had been going wrong. The RRW presented a petition for national homes for prostitutes, where they could learn a trade to support themselves and their families. Instead the Convention adopted a statute punishing prostitutes severely.

Théo's paper was suppressed. In the Jacobin Club, the RRW was condemned. "Those counter-revolutionary sluts cause bread riots. They make a revolution about coffee and sugar and soap, and they'll make others if we don't watch out!" Claire's room had been searched and weapons they had stored there, seized. Claire was far more the focus of the attacks than Pauline. For one thing, she was more visible because she was tall and beautiful. For another, she was living with Théo, whom Robespierre particularly disliked.

Robespierre did not understand Théo, a man of action. He had gone to be a soldier very young; he had lied to join up when he was still underage. Théo spoke before he thought. Claire stopped to shape her thoughts, but Pauline found that often words tumbled out, and that was when she moved women to action. Théo was the same way. He spoke and then he heard what he had said.

The Committee of Public Safety was cutting back the rights of the sections. They were doing just what the Girondins had done, curbing power at the local level. The people wanted government in their own hands. If they delegated power, they wanted to monitor its use and be ready to recall representatives. Here was Robespierre, carried in on the backs of the sans-culottes, and now he thought more about holding on to power than about respecting the people.

The RRW was being denounced from all sides. The men who had been scared of them stood up and screamed what ugly harpies they were and how they should be ashamed. The Convention, the Jacobin Club rang with speeches about the proper place of women. The revolutionary woman was home suckling her babies. The revolutionary woman did not go to meetings, but got her news from her husband, who always knew where she was. The revolutionary woman did whatever they told her to and not one thing more. The husbands who had been pissed off that their wives weren't making supper or waiting for them, they all cheered.

The RRW had been fighting with the market women. The market women had been for the Revolution till price controls. The fight was economic at its base, for the RRW represented the women who needed controls and the market women were those whose profits it would eat into; but blows started over costume. The RRW women wanted every woman to wear the cockade to show support for the Revolution. The fight was really not about cockades, but that was how it came down. At their new meeting place in Saint Eustache in Les Halles, the market women took to waiting to catch them alone or in small groups and beating them up.

One afternoon, they had just met and a few of them were straightening up the church afterward. Claire left, because she was late to the theater. Pauline was still putting things back in place when she heard screaming outside. She ran to the door. Claire was being attacked.

"Come on," Pauline shrieked. "They're killing Claire!" She launched herself at the market women, Babette and Victoire and Babette's mother Otile pitching in. But there were too many beating on Claire. Pauline punched and shoved. She remembered what had happened to Théroigne, who had never gotten out of the hospital. Claire was fighting back, but she was in the center of the mob. Her nose was bleeding and her blouse was torn.

bed beside him. He was already asleep. She felt confusion and turmoil. She could not sleep lying beside Théo. Was she in love with him? It was wrong to be in love with Claire's man. It was totally wrong. Suppose his head injury was like Théroigne's and he went crazy. Who would take care of him? She could not imagine Claire taking on that long-suffering role. But Pauline could. It was wrong to wish he would be injured seriously so she could nurse him.

What would become of them all? The RRW was disbanded. She had been a leader: now she was a severed head. She had seen how frightened even the most militant women were. They did not want to be taken from their families and stuffed into prison. They did not long to march to the guillotine. She admitted to herself she was scared. Surreptitiously she moved closer to Théo in the double bed, to share his warmth, to take comfort from his presence. He was ardent and extremely brave, but he had no power to protect himself or her.

When she rose in the morning, he was still sleeping. She went to buy from the water carrier, who came around just after dawn and then again in the late afternoon. She toted two buckets back. As quietly as she could, she stoked up the fires. Théo woke, confused. He stirred and groaned. She had to help him up so he could piss in the pot she would empty in the street.

"How did you ever get me here?" he asked, back in bed but sitting up with the pillows behind him.

"I couldn't leave you in the street."

"You were gentle with me, I remember. You were crying."

"I was afraid you were badly hurt."

His gaze stayed on her as she made cocoa for both of them. "I'll get bread. It will be a while. Drink the cocoa and stay in bed, please. Won't Claire be afraid since you didn't come home?"

"I doubt she'll worry too much," he said sourly. "Don't fret, I'll stay in bed. I don't have the strength for anything else. Every move I make hurts like hell. I feel like a sixty-year-old."

She ran to get in line at the baker's. When she returned, he woke again. She had some jam Babette's mother had made. They ate bread and jam with more cocoa. She was going to feed him in bed, but he insisted on sitting at the table with her. "You work alone? Don't you have family?"

She explained. Soon all the jam she had been saving would be gone, but she did not care. She kept looking at him. He was radiant, even in the bandages she had put on him clumsily, torn from an old petticoat.

He slept again afterward while she made batches of chocolate. Then he woke and watched her. "You seem surprisingly . . . domestic."

"I like my work," she said softly, staring at him. It seemed so unlikely that he was here in her bed.

"Don't you have a lover?"

"I did ... years ago. He was taken for the army before the Revolution began. For a long time I thought he would come back."

"And you were faithful to him?"

She nodded, too embarrassed to speak. Now he was staring at her. He kept watching her as she worked. She felt as if she danced in his gaze. Even if his gaze was all she ever had of him, she had the sense that his eyes touched her with respect and understanding. They talked about what was happening. The revolutionaries were fully in power for the first time, so why didn't they feel safe? It was their side who had won. Why were they in more danger now?

She knew she should run across the river to Claire's and tell her where Théo was and arrange to move him. But she did not. She told herself she had to take care of him till it was obvious how serious his injuries were. She brought supper back from the tavern, where she found that she did not want to tell Babette or anyone else what had happened. She pretended to herself she was afraid of police spies. She could not put Théo in danger while he was weak.

He got out of bed to eat, wearing her father's old dressing gown. She told him about her father. "You were close to your family," he said.

She nodded. "I loved them all dearly. I miss them still."

"I don't belong in my family. I'm a fox born to a family of geese."

"Claire isn't close to her family either."

But he did not pick up that cue to talk about Claire. "I'm feeling much better," he said. He made no move to dress himself or to leave. She went out for papers and they read them to each other. "Like an old married couple," he said. "Do you ever think of marrying?"

She knew she blushed. She could not look at him. "Perhaps," she said. "Should I go to the tavern for wine? We've drunk what I have."

"Let's go to bed. It's time."

She blew out the candles and lay down beside him. There was no place else to go. What was she doing? He reached for her and drew her into a firm embrace. He put his mouth on hers and began to kiss her. She had only kissed one other man, years and years before, and she did not think it had been like this. She felt as if she were falling into him.

"No," she said, pulling away. "You belong to Claire."

"Claire doesn't want me. But you do."

She could not speak. She felt consumed with shame, that he had read her desire. She felt like a fool. But she could not draw back when he pulled her close to him again. "Pauline, don't hide your face. I see who you are. You work so hard for everybody else, nobody sees you. The sweetness and the love in you. I see it. I want it. I want you."

"No, I can't do this. I can't hurt Claire. I can't just go to bed with someone like a whore."

"You're not a whore. Give yourself to me, Pauline. Willingly." He laughed softly against her hair. "It has to be more than willingly, because you're going to have to be gentle with me. I'm just a bag of bruises. You'll have to do most of the work."

"Why do you want to do this with me?"

"We're suited, Pauline. I just had a revelation. My parents will be a little shocked when they meet you, but you're exactly what I need. You failed to be a soldier's wife once, but the fates have it set in stone for you."

"I don't understand." But she put her arms tentatively around him. She wanted him, she could not help it. She loved him.

"Yes, you do." He put his hand into her bodice, closing it gently over her breast. She could feel his prick against her belly. She had never wanted Henri this fiercely, never. She could not have refused him if Claire had been standing in the kitchen with them. She moaned. Her mouth opened into his.

But when he spread her thighs, it was his hand, not his prick, he put under her petticoat to find her opening. With his fingers he rubbed and rubbed at her and stuck his finger into her. Something began to catch like a fire. A convulsion took her that she had never known. "Oh, I love you," she said.

Then he came into her and began to ride slowly. "Yes. We will love each other. Now and again and again."

When they lay quietly, she said, "We must tell Claire."

"All right. Tomorrow I'll get up, we'll tell Claire. Then we go straight to City Hall."

"Why?"

"Silly Pauline, to get married. Because deep down, you're a good girl. I'm a good bourgeois inside. And an officer. An officer needs a wife. We both want to be married. To each other."

SEVENTY-THREE

Manon

❧

(September–November 1793)

MANON wrote impassioned love letters to François, far beyond what she had allowed herself to say to him. Occasionally she wondered what she would do if they acquitted her. The situation remained impossible. She could not divorce Jean, who had done nothing wrong. Nor could she give up François. He was the only man she had ever loved passionately; it had not happened before and it could not happen again. She was inescapably pinned in place between the two men. Prison protected her from a fierce tug-of-war.

She finished her memoirs, smuggling them out in batches. Friends still dared visit her, including Sophie and Bosc. She had two letters from François, which she read and reread. She wrote to Robespierre, intending to beg his mercy. He could save her if he chose. She remembered when they had been friends. The letter emerged from her cold and full of bitter anger. It would be pointless to send it. She could not beg. She tore up the letter.

She stopped eating. She would starve herself and deny the Mountain the pleasure of seeing her die in public. Then her property would not belong to the State but would be inherited by her daughter. She asked Bosc to make sure her memoirs were published—when it was politically safe—so that Eudora might have the income. She permitted herself only water. As she grew weaker, she began to dream of eating. She could not sleep and then she slept and slept. Her jailers begged her to eat. Her fellow prisoners tried to tempt her with chicken and apples, late grapes.

The trial of the Girondins began. Some had been living under loose house arrest, entertaining their friends, plotting together, writing letters and petitions, trying to organize support. But the revolt in the provinces, the actions of their colleagues who had escaped, turned them from defeated politicians into traitors. A war was being fought at Lyon between Girondins and the revolutionary government. Twenty-one stood trial together, including Brissot and Vergniaud. As she followed the trial in the papers, she understood she had no chance. This was not a trial designed to establish guilt or innocence: it was a drama designed to demonstrate that the accused were guilty and to justify in advance the execution that would immediately follow, a trial to whip up popular enthusiasm for the spectacle of death.

Amar of the Committee of Security had drawn up the accusation, printing so many thousands of copies that she had no trouble getting hold of one. Half the charges did not apply to half the defendants. They were all deemed guilty of anything charged to one. The witnesses were their political opponents, who made long speeches about how dreadful the Girondins had been to disagree with them.

She managed to get a message to Brissot urging him to protest to the world. His reply came back, "They did it to us before we could do it to them. We failed; they didn't."

They were accused of a conspiracy against the Revolution. Against France. She was deeply grateful that neither Jean nor François had been caught. But if there was anything her friends were good at, making speeches was their forte. By the fifth day of the trial, it was clear that the Girondins could hold their own on the field of words. Fouquier-Tinville was chewing his nails. He appealed to the Convention, "Each witness gives his own history of the Revolution. The accused answer and the witnesses answer them and it turns into a debate that goes on as long as they desire. The trial will never end."

The Convention responded with a decree. After the third day of a trial, the judge might end it if the jury informed him they had enough evidence. At seven on the evening of day six, the jury so declared and retired to deliberate. The accused were marched in to hear their sentence three hours later. All and entirely guilty. Valèze stabbed himself on the spot with a knife he had concealed. The prisoners were seldom rigorously searched.

The last of October under the old calendar, they were taken to the guillotine. She heard the details the same day. Valèze's corpse was guillotined with the twenty live men. In the tumbrels, they sang "The Marseillaise." They died well. She was proud of them. Then she was informed her own trial was scheduled for next week. She broke her hunger strike at once. If they could die well, so could she. She could show the brutes how ably she could defend herself, that a woman with convictions could be brave.

She was transferred to the Conciergerie, the antechamber of death, not half a block from the house where she had grown up. She began writing her defense. Her new cell smelled like a sewer and was almost too dark to see the paper. Everything felt slimy. It was truly a tomb and for the first time in a while, she broke down and wept. She kept being interrupted by interrogations. They never touched her roughly but they questioned her again and again about the whereabouts of the fugitives. Some questions were outrageous. They seemed to imagine she had been the mistress of half the men who were fugitives and all those who had died last week. She managed to smuggle out a last letter to François. "I am still in this world. While there is any refuge for honor, stay alive to convict the unjust who have unfairly condemned you. But don't let yourself fall into their hands. Die free, as you have lived, following the generous impulses that have always endeared you to me."

It was a chilly morning of grey fog when the summons came. She dressed herself carefully. She wore a white muslin dress, perhaps a little summery for early November, representing her innocence. Around her shoulders she had a paisley shawl, and on her head a little white mob cap. Her hair was loose. The dampness made it curl. Her trial lasted only three hours. They would not allow her to deliver her defense. They seemed in a great hurry to get rid of her. When the death sentence was pronounced, she managed to speak for a moment. "You have pronounced me worthy to share the fate of great men you have already murdered. I thank you. I assure you that on my way to the guillotine, I'll try to display the same courage they did."

She was prepared for execution at once. Her hair was cut, her hands tied behind her back. She walked out with her spine held straight, to the tumbrel in the courtyard. She was to be executed with a man named Lamarque who was accused of forging paper money. He was sweating with fear. She smiled at him. "Courage, Citizen Lamarque. We have only a short ride and then a shorter trip. Don't worry. They say it doesn't hurt."

The tumbrel rattled over the stones, jarring her, but she was determined to remain upright. She sighed as she passed over the Seine, seeing the brick house where she had grown up on the Quai de l'Horloge. She was young to die, but her life felt long indeed. "Now, Lamarque, bear up." He was kneeling, weeping into her waist. She made soothing noises. It was a little late to worry about propriety. She saw her friend Sophie standing on the bridge, as she had promised. Sophie waved and Manon nodded, her hands still bound. She held herself straighter, letting the forger lean against her. Finally she saw the Place ahead, the guillotine on its scaffold near the enormous statue of Liberty. It was said that doves released at some festival had built nests in the folds of its plaster draperies. It was getting dark. There was always an audience for executions, but this was a modest crowd. It was a workday and time for the evening meal.

Lamarque was still blubbering. Fouquier-Tinville always gave Sanson a list of the order of the executions, but she argued with him, smiling into his face. "You must take him first. He'll become completely hysterical if he watches me die. I don't mind, you understand."

Sanson nodded. "I never do this, but for you, I will."

"Thank you. You're a man of feeling despite your profession," she said, remembering that when only the nobility had the privilege of being beheaded, some woman—Mary Queen of Scots?—had tipped the executioner to make sure the sword was sharp and her death would be swift.

Lamarque was carried up the steps to the platform and tied to the form. She was glad to see how it was done, so there would be no surprises. Snick, the blade descended. His body was unstrapped and tossed into the cart, where her own soon would lie. She mounted the steps without prompting. Over her the statue of Liberty loomed. "Ah liberty," she said loudly, "what crimes are committed in your name." There, she got to say one sentence from her defense. Then they strapped her to the form. She was aware of an unpleasant odor of stale blood. They should do a better job cleaning. She heard the sound of the release and a noise from the crowd. It was a pity she had not got to give her speech, but one of the prisoners would smuggle it out for her and

SEVENTY-FOUR

Georges

(November–December 1793)

GEORGES supervised the harvest, meddled happily in everything, lending a hand and his strength—thus endearing himself to the men who worked for him. The respectable people in town kept away: Danton, drinker of blood. But the peasants and the artisans, the laborers liked him. He bought another piece of property. He tramped over it with Louise, who had sturdy legs. At first his mother was shy with Louise, but she managed to charm his family. The boys loved Arcis, where he was available to them and his family spoiled them.

When he thought of Paris, it was with a shudder. He remembered a night in October, strolling with Camille along the Seine just at sunset. The trial of the twenty-one Girondin leaders had been announced. "The river is running blood," he said to Camille. "We have a lot to account for."

"It's gone far enough," Camille said. "It's not amusing anymore."

The next day Georges asked the Convention for a leave of absence. Now he was free. "Do you miss Paris? Do you miss power?" Louise asked him.

He put his hand on her breast. "This is enough power for me."

The leaves had fallen. The grasses were brown, the weeds frosted in the mornings. The sun set markedly earlier. He was in the big barn supervising the treatment of an ailing cow, when Camille suddenly appeared at the open barn door. Camille was dusty and looked exhausted. "Camille? Have you come for a country vacation? Is Lucile with you?"

Camille embraced him, leading him into the air out of earshot. "Georges, old goat, everything's going to hell. We're in danger. There's nothing but ambition biting ambition, the cupidity for money wrestling with the cupidity for power. It's raining shit, my dear, and we're getting covered."

Georges sat down on a stone fence and motioned Camille beside him. Camille was shivering. His flyaway hair was tangled and dirty. "The Committee—" That phrase without modification meant the Committee of Public

Safety, created by Georges but now Robespierre's—"arrested three of our friends. They're accused of using political influence to blackmail bankers and merchants. Of illegally changing the text of the decree terminating the East India Company." Camille drew his finger across his throat.

Georges let out his breath in a long sigh. "That's close to home. Are we both in trouble? Have they linked us to the stock?"

"It won't take them long to find out. Fabre is involved over his head, but they didn't arrest him. Max prevented it. He's protecting Fabre—and probably us. But he's in trouble himself. Hébert is attacking him daily. Chabot denounced us to the Committee of Security. He says we got rich in a plot led by royalists, with the intention of undermining the Convention and the government. He says you were bought by British gold."

Georges groaned. "A bloody mess. But it can still be headed off. We've been in trouble before and we'll live to cause more. How's Lucile?"

"Beautiful, scandalous and a little bored. She wanted to come with me, but I knew if I came hard, I could get here by sunset tonight."

"Come see my beauty, and we'll let her know there's one more for supper. How long can you stay?"

"I leave at dawn. Georges, things are closing in on us. It made me feel rotten, like a betrayer, to see the Girondins die. And Manon Roland."

"What a waste. Not that she used what she had."

"You don't think Buzot finally laid her? Sure he did. . . . Her husband and lover ran away, and she died in their place."

Georges paused. "Is it really vital I go to Paris? I'm in pig heaven here."

"You'll die in Paris if you don't go live there and fight."

"Dying is a last resort." Georges poked Camille. It took a lot to scare Camille, who never took much seriously. "All right, I'll pack it up here. I'll make my speeches and tame the Convention."

"Unless the Committee tames you first."

Georges stroked his ravaged cheek. "I'm a wise old bull."

It took Georges three days to set off, and he did not go flat-out as Camille had. He had his wife, children, clothing, toys, produce, wine, three servants and piles of valises to transport. He spent his first day in Paris just sitting and thinking. He dreaded plunging into the turbid muddy Convention and the windy wars of the Jacobin Club. He delayed, until he heard that Hébert had reported to the Jacobins that Danton returned to Paris but neglected to respect the Club by coming to answer the charges against him. He cursed and got dressed.

His old Cordeliers Club was lost to him, under the control of Hébert and the Mad Dogs. The important playing fields left were the Jacobin Club, where

Hébert was also a power, and the Convention. Hébert lacked support in the Convention but controlled the Commune. A lot of old players, both friends and antagonists, were gone, out the same narrow window: The duc d'Orléans, whose hospitality and purse he had often enjoyed, condemned by his son's defection to the Austrians. Bailly, the old mayor and astronomer, once the hero of the Third Estate in Versailles. Brissot, Vergniaud, Barnave had ridden the tumbrel of no return. Oddly, Condorcet, that mild academician, had successfully disappeared. Louvet had so far eluded pursuit. He had been poor for years and was used to living hand-to-mouth. He would fit into a city slum without anyone remarking on him. Georges wished the fugitives luck. The guillotine was busy enough.

He had always caught the mood of the populace. If he felt the Terror had gone too far, others must secretly harbor those thoughts. If he dared articulate moderation, that might be an act of courage, a way not only to survive, but to lead again. Camille had been thinking along similar lines. Who better to articulate a cry for moderation than the lamppost lawyer? They needed a vehicle. A paper for Camille to edit.

Camille agreed. They sat in Georges' study, with striped tricolor wallpaper and a wide selection of Paris periodicals overflowing the desk. Georges was reviewing the opposition. Camille said, his voice rising with passion, "Enough blood. It turns my stomach. They say people living near the Place de la Revolution can't stand the smell. Like a shambles where cattle are slaughtered."

"Never forget, my friend, where the Revolution kills twenty, the old regime killed a thousand, in the galleys, whipped to death, broken on the wheel, starved when the food they had grown was ripped from them. Never forget what we replaced. . . . But it's enough. What will you call your paper?"

"That's easy. Hébert and his henchmen make me sick. They've taken over what we built and turned it into a sty. I shall call the paper *The Old Cordelier*. That will make several points at once." On his long fingers that would have been elegant if not stained with ink, he ticked off his points. "One, we were here first. We made the fucking Revolution. Two, we stand for the values the Cordeliers once stood for, against a tyrannical Tribunal, against Hébert and his hogs. Third, it sounds nice and homely, just like his *Père Duchesne*. We're going to take Hébert on."

"We'll roast him on a public spit." His blood was zipping in his veins. There was nothing like a good fight to give him an appetite. "You know, he does look like a pig. A nice caricature, don't you think? Who can draw? David? *The Old Cordelier*. I like that. In the meantime, I need to carry the battle to him in the Convention—and at the Jacobins."

"I'll talk to Max. We have to detach him slowly from the Committee. From

Saint-Just, the rabid. Max adores Lucile and me and Horace. We do his living for him. We have to ally him with us. He hates the spilling of blood. He was only won to the Terror by his blathering fear of conspiracy. If we can seduce Max, we'll get our way."

"In the meantime, weaken the Commune and the Tribunal." Georges rose to pace. He found his energy surging back. The old bull was good for one more fight. "Strengthen the role of the Convention, and eventually take the great Committee back, pack it with moderates or abolish it. Every month it comes up and is reinstated, so we have a monthly shot at the Committee. That's my strategy. Carefully lay the groundwork for mercy. Test the waters for moderation. Aim to finally end the Terror."

They found Robespierre fuming over deChristianization. Hébert and his pals were behind a movement to get rid of what they saw as relics of superstition. "Two weeks ago, they had a festival of reason in Notre Dame," Robespierre said, entertaining them in the Duplays' dining room. A big plate of fresh fruit stood on the table. Robespierre was peeling an apple neatly, the long red skin unscrolling from the tiny silver knife. "A mostly naked woman on top of an artificial mountain. That RRW actress, can you believe it? Then two days ago, the Commune closed all the churches of Paris. This must stop! We just brought the peasants over to our side with land reform, and now these dangerous fanatics want to stir them up again by taking their Church away. One Vendée in revolt is not enough for them. Hébert wants twenty Vendées! Danton, you have a soft spot for religion. . . . Can't you mount some opposition to this outrage?"

It was an icepick in the chest. What did Robespierre mean? Did he know that Louise went regularly, secretly, to a priest loyal to Rome? He could not know. "I believe in tolerance, just as you do, Max. That's part of the Constitution, if we ever can bring it into play."

"We all look forward to that day. Because that will mean the war is over, the nation is saved and instead of fighting for the Revolution, we can build for it. . . . But deChristianization is splitting the populace. We promised religious freedom. That we can deliver if we control those fanatics."

Camille picked up the peel and strung it around his head, a crown of blood. "Do you believe in God, Max?"

"Yes. I do."

"You didn't toward the end at Louis-le-Grand."

"I simply didn't believe in the Christian God. I still don't. It seems narrow. But Camille, how can you be surprised that I believe?"

"Why do we need a divine rationale for good behavior? But I'm astonished by your vehemence."

"I experience God. God is virtue." Robespierre let the little silver knife drop onto his plate and rose. He looked exalted, his face paler than usual, his voice even more intense. "When we act in accordance with the higher part of our natures and when we act as one with the people, there is a sense of divinity that overwhelms me. It's not that I feel worthy. Whatever I do is never enough and never can be. There is a destiny that works through us. I am only a tool. But a conscious tool."

Camille and Georges glanced at each other surreptitiously. Robespierre caught the glance. He challenged Georges directly. "Don't you have a personal religion?"

"Fucking my wife, Max," Georges said truthfully. "That's as close as I come to God."

Robespierre glared at him and said nothing, nothing at all.

Camille hastened to change the subject, "I'm starting a paper to be called *The Old Cordelier—*"

"Ah, as opposed to the new dangerous kind." Max's voice dropped to a conversational level and he sat down, slicing his apple into fours to core it, then into neat segments he fanned out on his plate. "Hébert's crew."

"I want to show you the first number before it goes to press."

Thus implicating him in its genesis. Georges saw what Camille was up to.

"Would you have time to look it over now? Shall I read it to you to save your eyes?"

"I'd be delighted. Yes, read it to me." He called out to Mme Duplay for more coffee.

"Not for me, thanks." Georges rose. "I have work to do." Mme Duplay saw him out. Robespierre did not rise but went on talking with Camille. Georges supposed that he had offended the Incorruptible, but sometimes his prudery offered too inviting a target. God flowing through Robespierre, that was a rich one. The saddest thing was, he supposed Robespierre believed it. His answer had really been to the point: don't confuse thrills with religion. Robespierre hadn't got it. And yes, he did find sex as holy and powerful as Robespierre found virtue.

Thus began a power struggle acted out in the Convention, the Committee, the Commune, the clubs. Georges said to Camille, "The ultimate irony is that each of us feels we must win for the Revolution. You and I think the Terror has gone too far and we'll solidify the gains, make peace with the allies and strengthen the economy. Hébert thinks he's the next stage, power to the sections, terror stepped-up, a revolutionary army moving grain to Paris, the bottom on top. And Robespierre thinks he has a pipeline to God and he'll police the rest of us."

Commune, in City Hall. He kept her waiting. She read his paper, marshalling her arguments.

"Come in, my dear, come in." Hébert was a portly man who reminded her of a pigeon. "How are you? Those of us who've been in the theater have a special bond."

Hébert had been a ticket seller at the Opera before the Revolution. Even so, there was a camaraderie in the theater that extended to everyone who sewed a button on a costume, put up posters, guarded the stage door. Claire said, "The Convention crushed our group. That leaves us out in the cold politically, with no way to look out for the women's interests except by taking to the streets."

"That wouldn't be advisable right now. Not so soon after September. But it will happen again, never fear."

"Then we need our organizations—"

"It's not becoming, a bunch of women wearing red pantaloons and caps with daggers stuck in their belts and pistols in their teeth. It offends everyone. Now, you look dashing, but most of the Lacombe Amazons looked ridiculous." Was Hébert trying to flatter her? One of his best traits was his fidelity to his wife, who rather resembled him. They were a team. Indeed, he was talking about her now. "The way for a woman to be politically effective is to work through a man. Look at my wife. There isn't a stronger revolutionary in all Paris. But do you see her making speeches in front of men? Brandishing pistols? She's my right arm, but she keeps quiet in public, like a decent woman."

"So you won't support us."

"You haven't a chance. Robespierre is determined to suppress women's groups because he doesn't want you screaming about economic issues. Your violence, my dear, it makes him faint." Hébert giggled. "Now me, I go along with your demands. I think you could find a more effective way of presenting them. But if I was as powerful as Robespierre, you'd get what you want, believe me."

It was sad. She disliked the man personally, but she needed him. He really was a man of the sans-culottes. He saw the world as they did. Robespierre felt for the poor people, but he'd never lived among them. He knew the world of lawyers, of comfortable artisans like the carpenter he lived with. He didn't know life in a furnished room with five other people, pissing in the hall and sleeping all in the same bed. Hébert knew. He was doing well by the Revolution. He had made a bit of money on the side, but so what? Danton had made a lot more. She didn't mind if politicians put money in their pockets so long as they did the same for ordinary people. One great advantage of dealing with Hébert was that she could speak to him bluntly. "Hébert, what do you want from me?"

"We're putting on a festival of reason. . . ."

So there she was two weeks later, perched on an artificial, somewhat tipsy mountain with her breasts bare and the rest of her covered only by diaphanous chiffon, freezing for two hours while the choir sang and the children threw flowers and speeches were made and songs were sung en masse. At the end fireworks went off just outside the church doors.

Afterward, Pauline and Théo told her how beautiful she had looked, how moving the ceremony was. It was hard for her to imagine. Yet sometimes she loved the festivals. They were inventing their own holidays, their own rituals, their own symbols and icons. It was exciting to be part of that invention, even if the results ranged from striking to ludicrous. Spectacles affirmed popular beliefs, whether in Sainte Geneviève or the Revolution. They broke up the days of the poor and hard working. They brought people together in a common vision. It was considered an honor to have been the Goddess of Reason; Hébert's choice had caused controversy. She was considered too scandalous. But playing goddess said that someone valued her politically, that she had protection.

Lately when she had any chance to address a group, she concentrated on a few economic demands: taxing the rich, enforcing price controls, setting a limit to the size of the income and properties any individual could amass. But mostly she urged that the Constitution of '93 the entire country had ratified be put into effect. Men and women alike cheered her speeches, but when she looked into the audience, a man always sat in the second row. He had a pad on his lap and all the time she spoke, he scribbled. He was all grey: grey hair, grey complexion, a grey coat he kept on. She described him to Hébert. "He reports directly to the Committee of Security. He's Amar's man." Hébert grimaced in disgust.

A cold draft blew on her nape. She was under special surveillance. Her room had been searched twice. Amar was one of those responsible for squashing the women's groups. She still remembered his face that day in the Convention when he reminded women about the fates of Olympe de Gouges, Manon Roland, Marie-Antoinette and Louis XV's mistress du Barry, who had returned from exile to look after her properties. When women try to assume power, he said, thrusting themselves into the spotlight, this is what happens: he smiled when he described their deaths.

Hébert offered her some protection. Her old boss, Collot, had become one of the most powerful men in France, one of the twelve who ruled in the Committee of Public Safety. They were the government. Collot mocked the women but was friendly to her. Hébert had strong support in the poor sections. She suspected that he was going to try to move on the Committee of Public Safety and Robespierre soon.

She was coming from a surreptitious meeting with a small group of former RRW women, when she passed through the Palais Royal. It was a cold crisp day, the air metallic. The Palais was not as exciting a scene, for the Committee had closed down the sex shows. Robespierre did not appreciate them. Fewer people hung around the Palais and fewer speeches were made, from fear.

Danton hailed her from a table where he and Camille were drinking. She had observed Fabre d'Églantine with them earlier and pretended not to see them. She could not bring herself to be polite to that woman-hating pornographer. She despised his calendar. She imagined ninety percent of Paris going around saying, "Oh, the second of Frimaire" and then a blank look and the mental translation, let me see, they really mean seventeenth of February, oh. However Danton did not give her a chance to slip past. "Claire, come on over and we'll buy you a drink."

"Something hot," she said, slipping into the seat that was still warm from Fabre's behind. "One of those coffees with brandy in it. I'm freezing."

"And you looked so warm in the chilly cathedral," Camille said. "Quite the goddess." He was giving her a lascivious look from under long lashes. She was not interested in Camille in her bed. He had flirted with her before.

"You should watch out for Hébert and his crew. They're nipping Robespierre like terriers. The Jacobin government has huge popular support, and Hébert won't overthrow it. The Committee just needs to loosen up a bit."

Was everyone trying to recruit her? Perhaps it had been a mistake to play Reason for it seemed to have stirred up a little too much interest in her by both opposition factions. What was it about showing your tits in public that attracted men's attention? She drank the brandied coffee quickly and it went straight to her head. Danton ordered another. At least it made her warm. In fact she began to sweat, under her chemise. She sat there wanting to hide under the table. She felt vulnerable. Even Pauline had a husband now. She was out there alone, without her organization, without a job, with the fear she could be arrested tomorrow and trundled off to the guillotine. She could imagine herself ending up in bed with either, with both these men just because she felt so alone and because there was always the illusion that if you went to bed with a man, he might protect you.

They were both watching her with palpable sexual interest. Camille put his hand on her knee. "How could that Mad Dog Leclerc prefer the little troll Pauline Léon to you?"

She stood. "Thank you for the drinks, old Cordeliers. . . . Is it true that Robespierre is hopping mad at you for the last issue?"

"Oh, everyone gets mad at me sooner or later. I have that effect on people. But then I charm them around again. So it goes," Camille said. "Do consider if you wouldn't be better off under our big umbrella than with *Père Duchesne* or the Mad Dogs."

Danton smiled. He looked better than he had when she had seen him in September, before he went off on extended leave from the Convention. He was less bloated. His eyes were clear. "They call us the Indulgents. An actress should feel at home in such a group. Keep that in mind."

That evening, she sat on her bed in her cold room and fretted. She could not afford to buy wood to burn in the fireplace. She must find a job to pay her rent. Victoire came by while Claire was crouched on the bed brooding.

Victoire shook back her curly black hair. "So why don't I move in? I hate where I live. I can smell the tannery."

"Why not?" Claire said. "Théo's gone."

"He wasn't for you," Victoire touched her shoulder.

Claire shrugged. "Skip the attempts to make me feel better. What I need is money and a job and to get the police off my back."

Victoire looked around the room. "Let's see how we do keeping house together. My old-clothes business has picked up. So many people are going into prison, I keep getting clothes to sell."

"You know, there's some danger in living with me. I'm a little too interesting to the Committee of Security."

"I'll take that chance," Victoire said. "You're worth the risk."

Claire sighed. "Everyone's scared now, have you noticed? When did that happen? When did our people start to be afraid of each other? I don't understand how it came to be. We won, didn't we? And now we're worried for our lives."

general amnesty. Empty the prisons. Let's go forward with a clean slate for everyone and be one country."

"You're bubbling with optimism tonight. Me, I was just thinking when you came in I'd like to have another kid. Two isn't enough. Maybe a girl this time."

"How are the sections taking it?" Camille refilled their glasses. "*Père Duchesne* had quite a following."

"It's like their own heads are cut off. A lot of sullen sans-culottes are milling around, asking each other what the world has come to. More confusion than rage. Who should they believe? They trusted Hébert. But they've trusted Robespierre forever and Collot and Billaud stood with the Committee. For them it's like a sudden blow in the belly. The wind and the will to fight are knocked out of them."

Camille refused to be daunted. "Now comes the Republic we've been aiming for. The new heaven and new earth, or at least a well-washed version of the old one. Now comes dancing in the streets and a million opinions expressed every day, poetry on the walls, schools for every child."

George slapped his back. "We'll pave the streets with diamonds and live for five hundred years, always able to get it up twice a day."

A week later, shortly after Louise had gone to sleep and Georges had settled down to read, he had a visitor. His old friend Panis, whom he had helped to good positions in the government, burst in. "Georges, the Public Safety and the Security Committees met together. Saint-Just presented an accusation against you. Carnot and Lindet defended you, but the others won—"

"Robespierre?"

"I heard that his notes were all over Saint-Just's memorandum. That he corrected it himself to damn you absolutely. He added facts and dates and quotes from you. He's out to get you—"

"I'll tear his guts out and eat them. So he thinks he can take me on, that dickless pussycat."

"Georges, don't bluster. They're after your head." Panis rose and began to pace. "They're not going to wait. Saint-Just and Robespierre wanted to confront you in the Convention tomorrow morning. But Vadier argued that was too dangerous. He insisted you be arrested tonight."

"Tonight? I don't believe it. Who else?"

"Camille, Hérault, about a dozen others. Saint-Just accused Vadier of being afraid of you and insisted you be confronted in full session of the Convention. Robespierre wanted that too. But they lost. The Committees have closed ranks. Do you understand now?"

He felt weary. This was a bad play he had seen before. "Robespierre wouldn't dare. They would not dare."

"You can be out of Paris before they come for you. Get out and give your friends time to rally. You've done favors for everyone. I'm convinced the British would give you asylum. The Americans surely would."

"A man can't carry his country with him on the soles of his boots."

"Well, I'm bolting. A lot of your friends are going down with you if you fall, Georges. I won't be one of them."

Georges went up to warn Camille, rousing them from bed. When he left them, Camille was scrawling a hasty speech, and Lucile in her negligee was having hysterics. He considered waking Louise, but decided to let her sleep on. He sat back down, reading by a small oil lamp. He was rereading *The Lives of the Emperors*. He had known obscurity and he had known power. He had lived pretty much as he'd wanted to. He'd lent his strong back and his good right arm to the Revolution and his powerful voice like the wind of change itself. Finally he could not believe that the Convention would go along, that Paris would permit this outrage. Sure, everybody knew he'd cut some corners. He had waffled here and there, and money stuck to his palms. But he had never done anything that he considered detrimental to the nation. Saving a few lives, that was just being human. What good had blood ever done anyone? If people liked their lives better, they'd have less desire to see others lose theirs. Paris reeked of blood. To say that more had died hideously under the old regime was to beg the question of how many deaths he had been involved in. He had thrown himself into the fight for a general amnesty because he could not endure one more execution.

He heard the sound of boots and the clink of weapons in the street, the Cour de Commerce renamed for Marat, although everybody called it by its old name. Now he went to wake Louise, who sat up, lovely as always and at first grumpy. "Louise, they're coming to arrest me. Once they have taken me, dress the children and leave at once for Arcis. Ask my mother and stepfather for help. My will is made. They have a copy. Most of the property is in your name, so it can't be confiscated if I'm convicted."

Louise held him tight but stayed calm. She began to pack a bag for him. The guards were at the door. Already they had Camille who was wildly struggling. Lucile fell in a faint as he was torn from her and dragged out. Georges called back to Louise, "See to Lucile." Both his sons had wakened and were crying.

Camille and he were marched off to the Luxembourg. The first person Georges saw when the guards brought him in was Tom Paine, looking older

SEVENTY-EIGHT

Nicolas

❧

(March–April 1794)

NICOLAS expected the pressure would diminish, insanity would cease and those labeled Girondins would slowly return to their normal lives, out of power but out of danger also. They were all supporters of the Revolution, of the Republic. Their crimes were political. Such errors should be punished by a loss of office, a loss of control of the executive or the legislative branch. It was barbarous to defeat a faction, then put them to death.

Sophie could not come to him as often. She was watched. She had to begin divorce proceedings against him or lose their remaining property, which would be confiscated. She assured him the divorce was only a formality, but he suffered. The hard part was not to see his daughter, and especially not to see his wife except every three weeks or so. And to know she was no longer his wife. Every time he thought of the divorce, he felt as if he had been struck in the chest.

Finally Sophie was able to come. "Everyone is full of hope that the execution of Hébert and his cohorts means the Terror is over. They were pushing for more executions, and they seem to have gotten what they wanted. Everyone is whispering that Robespierre means to ease things now. Soon you may be able to come home."

"I never trusted that man. A narrow mind and great intensity. Sophie, I have something to give you today."

"You finished your book!" She embraced him.

"I believe I'm done, but you'll tell me if I'm right."

It was two and a half weeks before she could return, on a Sunday. "It's a true Sunday, a day of sunshine, when I see you," he said awkwardly. He was shyer with her, knowing she was no longer his wife.

She laughed. "Nobody calls it Sunday any longer, Nico. It's Seventh Day of the ten-day decade. You see people counting on their fingers. Now listen to me, this is your masterpiece. We have to get it published."

"There's no hurry. . . . Sophie, is it true that Danton and Desmoulins have been arrested?"

She nodded. "The Terror isn't over. It's stepping up. They just took Lucile Desmoulins and Hébert's wife, the ex-nun. They will all die. It's predetermined."

He took her face between his hands. It disturbed him to see signs of wear, of stress. She worked tremendously hard to support their child, him, her own sister. "Sophie, I won't survive this. Few of us who made the Revolution will. The people were not educated enough. But it will work itself out. We'll have republican institutions and an educated populace able to vote change, instead of picking up pikes and pistols and rioting—"

"The Terror can't last forever. Just sit tight. Stay hidden."

"What matters is that you must marry again. I want no widow's weeds, no black crepe. I lived a full and good life. I enjoyed my work, I effected some change, I loved and was loved. I had amazing friends, Voltaire, Tom Paine, Bonneville, Franklin, Turgot, d'Alembert. When I'm gone, you must make a new life full of joy and companionship."

"Nico, forgive me if I decline. I can't do it—No, don't shake your head at me. I'm not sentimental. But I've had an equal relationship with my husband. I've been treated with respect. We shared our minds, our bodies, our child. I can't marry someone who won't treat me as an equal. I don't believe the man is born who can do that, except you. You are unique. I've had you, and I won't settle for less. I want friends, I'd like to be more comfortable, I want a good education for Eliza. But I do not want an inferior marriage."

"I hope life surprises you, Sophie." He felt they were saying goodbye as they embraced, holding each other fiercely.

When she had left, he spoke to his landlady. "Mme Vernet, my presence endangers you. Those who shelter fugitives are going to the guillotine. I can't permit that to happen to you. What would become of your niece and your cat?"

"Sir, you may be outlawed by the government, but they can't outlaw you from my house. I know you're a good man. You stay right here." She set her niece to keep watch on him when she couldn't.

He waited for a slip in their surveillance. He had told Sophie to keep his manuscript safe. She said she would have it copied. He knew she meant she would do so herself—at night when she should be sleeping. He cut off his hair with a nail scissors, trying to look different. Danton's trial was going on as broad farce. He had always like Danton, a man willing to compromise and find the pragmatic way through. A good man on committees and in assemblies. Probably in a functioning republic, there would be many such politicians. People might scorn politicians and their willingness to negotiate and shift positions, but they were preferable to fanatics. People were more real to them than ideas. Desmoulins was different, brilliant but disturbed. They would be missed. The lion fell, the gazelle went down, and the lesser beasts remained, the rats, the ferrets, the nippers and biters who required a crowd to bring down their prey. He was being melodramatic. The Republic would continue when all of them were dead. He had finished his life's work with his *Progress*. He must not bring anyone down with him. So many of the Girondins were gone, to the guillotine or dead by their own hand: Roland had killed himself when the word came to him that Manon had been guillotined. Buzot had done the same.

One morning, a tablecloth hanging by the fire was set ablaze by a spark. Madame dunked it in a bucket immediately. The women were preoccupied fanning out the smoke. He took the small valise he had packed, put on a ragged red wool cap and rough jacket Cabanis had brought and walked out. The papers of the day proclaimed the death of Danton. He headed straight out of Paris.

He knew where the Suards had a house, the couple with whom he lived until he moved into the Mint. He had loved Amélie for years, platonically. They had disapproved of his marriage and his political career. But what did that matter? He needed them, and if they wanted to say that he had received his due, then he would bow his head and listen to reproaches. He reached them by nightfall and rapped on their door. "Antoine, it's me. I've been in hiding, but I had to leave."

Antoine was not pleased to see him. They gave him supper but made it clear they did not want him under their roof for the night. Amélie put bread and sausage in his pocket. Antoine lent him a Horace to read on the journey. They thrust him out the door. How afraid people were. Here was a fellow academician, and he would not even risk for one night what Mme Vernet, who had known nothing about him, had been willing to risk for nine months. His feet were sore. He had never been a great walker, and for months, he had scarcely left his room. His feet swelled. Blisters puffed and cracked open. He stumbled into an area of stone quarries, dangerous in the dark. He lay down shivering in a field and tried to sleep. It was bitter cold. The ground was wet with dew. He slept scarcely at all but rose at dawn, stiff, chilled, his nose running and with a bad cough.

He walked on, soon thoroughly lost. He should have a map: where would he get one? He had the vague idea of heading for Switzerland, but he could not tell in what direction he was walking. It was a cloudy day. It seemed the sun was rising that way, which must be east. Then he must head that way.

Soon he was back in the quarries again. He used up the little food the Suards had given him and spent the night in a shed.

A dog set upon him the next morning and ripped his leg open before he could fend the beast off with a stick. He staggered on. By now his clothes were torn and he could not walk farther on his raw and bloody feet. His boots were considered fine leather, but they were not made for walking all day. The soles were beginning to separate. Toward seven he came to an inn. He staggered inside. Fortunately, he had money.

"An omelette," he ordered. Food. That was what he needed more than anything. He had not had anything to eat in twenty-four hours. He had been drinking rainwater from puddles.

A couple of men came to stand over him. "Who are you?"

He had identification papers in the name of Pierre Simone, a carpenter. One of them took his right hand. "Soft. A gentleman's hand. You're no carpenter."

"How many eggs do you want in that omelette?" the innkeeper's wife called.

He had no idea. He had, of course, never made an omelette. He had never been in a kitchen in his life. But he was immensely hungry. "A dozen."

The room fell silent. Now all the men were rising and moving toward his table. The man who had seized his hand before now pulled him up out of his seat. "Nobody, nobody ever has an omelette with a dozen eggs. You're one of those fucking aristocrats, aren't you? You're one of them stealing our food and keeping us down and bringing in the enemy soldiers. Martin, let's take him to jail. The tribunal can deal with him in the morning."

"Look, he has a book in his pocket. In some foreign language. Who knows what it says? He could be a spy."

A tribunal met in the next town. They set out to march him there, but he could not walk. A peasant took pity and lent a donkey for him to ride to prison. The innkeeper's wife gave him a heel of bread and some onions and sausage, which he ate on the donkey. He had little doubt he would be sent to Paris, if not in the morning, then after a hasty examination here. In Paris he would be recognized. He would follow Hébert and Danton to the guillotine.

They turned him over to the local guards, who marched him to a freezing dank cell. It was late and they did not bother to search him. He considered writing a note to Sophie, but why compromise her? They had said their good-byes. He was spent. Every part of his body ached. If he were tried, the question of where he had been hiding would arise, condemning Mme Vernet, implicating Sophie. He could not risk a trial for the sake of Mme Vernet, Sophie and Eliza. Here they would have trouble finding out who he was. He checked that he had nothing on him that might establish his identity or involve anyone else.

He pried open his ring and drank the poison. Then he shoved the hideous ring into a crack in the wall, where it might never be found. He felt little as he slid into heaviness. Sophie had the manuscript. She would survive him. He saw her before him, beckoning in her negligee, smiling invitation. She was here with him, with him again as his wife. He reached out, murmuring her name. She gathered him in her warm strong arms, and he slept.

SEVENTY-NINE

Pauline

❦

(February–April 1794)

PAULINE and Théo lived in her shop. The bed at the back that had been her parents' became theirs. They ate at the table where she ground the beans and packaged the chocolate. Business had fallen way off, but she was trying to build it up again. Many old customers had gone into exile; others remained, living quietly. There was new money. Many suppliers, industrialists, middlemen, financiers, bankers had grown rich on the war. She despised them, but she wanted to sell them chocolate; she had to, to survive.

She saw her friends in the neighborhood, but she did not see Claire as often. Claire was less ebullient. Being arrested had frightened her, even though she was released a week later. She kept talking about the suicide of Jacques Roux. He had been in prison for months, sometimes briefly released. Finally in despair and sure they were going to guillotine him, he had killed himself. It had not been a tidy job. It had taken him days to die. Pauline could not help feeling responsible for Claire's unhappiness, because she had married Théo. They were still learning to live with each other. She was astonished how little Claire had taken him in hand and taught him anything. He explained, "We didn't so much live together as share a room and a bed."

He was not as untidy as Henri, perhaps because he was a soldier. Soon he must return to his regiment, now in the Vendée. The leave he had been granted to carry their grievances to the Convention had been extended, but no more. He did not think she should accompany him. "From all I hear, Pauline, the war in the Vendée is a dirty war. There's no real front line. I wouldn't feel you were safe. You stay here, tend your business, and I'll get back as soon as the Vendée is cleaned up. They say it's finally going well."

They ate sometimes in the tavern and sometimes she cooked on her stove. With price controls Robespierre had put in, people had enough bread. A strange passive depression pooled in the neighborhood, not unlike Claire's mood. People had not recovered from the execution of so many leaders, all in two weeks. It shocked and confused them. Yet the Jacobin government was not unpopular, because they brought the grain in and kept prices steady. Everybody ate well.

People whispered against the measures taken to restrain the sections, forbidding some groups like the women from meeting at all, trying to cut back the role of others. Ordinary men and women missed the sense of making things happen, of being vitally involved. Still, they could not fault the government for winning the inner and outer wars, and they had food. Once upon a time, not many years back, that had seemed everything, before they had tasted a little power, a sense they could make things happen, before they counted.

"Women are afraid to speak out. Babette's mother was arrested for complaining about the quality of meat." Pauline clutched Théo's hand. "Now everyone's going to vouch for her and we hope they release her. But she could go to the guillotine. When we demanded the Terror, we never meant for ordinary people to die. We just wanted aristos cleared out and the fat people who were standing on our bellies."

"Nobody called louder for the Terror than I did," Théo said. "Now it's the answer to any criticism, any opposition. Disagree with Robespierre and your head flies off."

No one in the tavern used pet names for the guillotine any longer. It had been turned against them. Nobody she knew had attended an execution in weeks. They kept their heads down and their noses clean. They feared police spies. You never knew who was working for the committees of vigilance, for Security, who might turn you in for a careless word, who might denounce you because of some fancied wrong you had done them and long since forgotten— but they had not.

Théo was her husband. She still could not believe that. She woke in the middle of the night to lean over him, his longish hair tousled on the pillow, the fine sweet bones of his face. His hands in spite of calluses and old abrasions were the hands of a gentleman. What did she mean by that? They were shapely and long fingered. They touched her with magic. It could not be natural to feel so open to him. It could not be natural that her heart began drumming as soon as he touched her arm.

She was used to the way things were in the neighborhood. A husband and a wife might be enemies, they might be allies, but they were not close in the sense that women friends were close. A husband was a necessity. You came together for sex, you had children and you stuck up for each other, mostly. But you relaxed and played and drank and politicked with women. They were the ones you turned to when you had troubles. Your husband might blame you, might even beat you.

Théo seemed to expect a kind of closeness he had not achieved with Claire. He wanted them to share their feelings and he wanted them to talk to each other. It felt almost indecent at times, what he wanted to talk about. He asked questions about intimate things that made her blush and hide her face in his shoulder. "How does it feel when I touch you there? Is it better if I do it harder?" But in many ways he was a man not unlike her father or Henri. He wanted his food when he wanted it; he wanted certain foods and not others, whether they were available or not. He thought his opinions on all subjects cast in gold and expected hers to be written in water. He could grow icily sarcastic or furious if she displeased him by getting distracted and burning a stew. On the whole, though, she had acquired a husband she could reasonably count on. When he returned from the Vendée, he said, she would meet his family.

After he left for his regiment, she scarcely knew what to do with herself. In spite of having lived alone for years, she had quickly grown used to Théo's presence. He had been gone two days and she was still weeping into the chocolate, when two of the Tribunal police marched in. "Pauline Léon, wife to Leclerc, I have a warrant for your arrest on charges of conspiring with the Hébertists to overthrow the revolutionary government."

She was terrified. She spilled the chocolate and burnt her arm. Then she was carried off, hustled between guards while her neighbors sullenly watched. As she was pushed past the tavern she called out, "Tell my husband I've been taken! Please send him word."

"He'll know soon enough," one guard said, grinning.

It was the new Law of Suspects. The prosecutor of the Revolutionary Tribunal could arrest anyone denounced by the authorities or even by a single citizen. A lot of men had grudges against the RRW. One of the market women she had fought in the streets near Saint Eustache might have denounced her. She had made plenty of enemies. She was taken to the Luxembourg, a piece of luck as it was one of the better prisons. There she saw Théo almost immediately. He was wearing a bloody head bandage. They embraced. "They jumped me on the road. So here we are. What are we charged with?"

"You haven't been charged with anything yet," the jailer said. "Come on. We'll put you lovebirds upstairs."

They had a room larger than at home, an old double bed with nothing but a worn mattress and a greasy wool blanket on it. Pauline sent word out to Babette and Claire to bring them bed linens, clothes and food. There was no difficulty sending messages out from the prison. Visitors came every day. The Luxembourg had been a palace, and while little remained of the furnishings, the rooms were large and airy and the corridors, decently lit. In the garden men and women gathered. An elaborate social life went on, much of it among aristocrats with whom they would have nothing to do, and who would not acknowledge them. They had set up a miniature ancien régime, addressing each other by their old titles, having tea, gossiping and gambling and playing cards, staging theatricals, dressing up elaborately in the afternoon and flirting.

Babette arrived the next day with a basket of food from the tavern. "Claire has been arrested too. She's in that awful dump Port Libre, in a cell about six by six. You two really have a pleasant niche compared to her."

It became clear they were not being formally charged. The longer it went, the better, because to be charged was the preliminary to being tried, which was the doorway to execution. Sometimes people in prison were forgotten. Théo and she kept quiet and made a little home. Some prisoners had started a garden. Théo was happy to dig in it. The aristocrats were disgusted, but the commoners were enthusiastic about growing lettuce and other greens.

They were issued bread and wine and beans. If they wanted more, it was their problem. All jails had people, sometimes staff, sometimes prisoners, who acted as caterers for those with money to spend. Théo and Pauline had enough friends so that they had fresh food brought. She told Babette where to find money, under the loose floorboard.

Some rooms in the Luxembourg were luxurious again, as if it were still a palace. Wealthy inmates brought in inlaid furniture, carpets, hangings, secretaries and chaise longues. Their own room remained spartan, but most of the day they were out in the garden or taking part in the social life of the commoners and the patriots. Newspapers were smuggled in, people shared news from letters. Théo and Pauline both read aloud from journals and popular novels and tracts passed around. Théo began teaching reading and math. She wondered who was responsible for them being put in the Luxembourg. Danton and his crew had been here. Tom Paine was still here. Aside from the aristocrats, it was a friendly society. People shared. But always the list was read out, the names were checked off. Suspects were called to trial and never came back. Death waited just through the door.

She wished she would get pregnant. If she was pregnant, she could not be executed. Who knew what would happen if they could hang on a few months? Affairs started easily in prison. Most of the women wouldn't mind getting pregnant. The scandal was nothing to fear if it kept them alive. This was a world apart. The common people played cards and gambled too, set up a little guingette under a grapevine and put tables there. They had singing and dancing almost every night. They told jokes and acted out little plays. One man did imitations of animals. Another did a Robespierre that broke them all up, but not when the warders could see.

The warders weren't bad. They watched the governments come and go and did their job. Those inside might be dead tomorrow or they might be in power. They took a few bribes, looked the other way when they could. Pauline taught the children of the prisoners and took care of a baby or two as needed. She hoped they could live to have children. Lately she had been dreaming of that, not just to save her life, but because she needed something to dream about. She could not imagine that she would again be a leader of women. She made no fuss and stuck close to Théo. Maybe she would abandon the attempt to run her business, which would be lost by the time she got out. Any empty store would be looted. She could go off with Théo as an army wife. At least he would be an officer. This time nothing would separate them. A few months ago, the Convention had decreed that women could no longer fight in the army, not even the women soldiers who had been decorated. But women followed the armies: wives, laundresses, prostitutes. She was a good wife now, and she would go.

EIGHTY

Claire

❦

(April 2–July 27, 1794)

CLAIRE was sure when they came to get her, that she would be taken straight to the Conciergerie to go on trial with a mixed lot of forgers, swindlers and royalists and then within twelve hours, to the guillotine. Instead she was in what had been a convent, Port Royale, now renamed Port Libre after the expulsion of the nuns. It wasn't far from where she had taken Hélène for her abortion. Claire was thrust into a dark cell with two other women and a bare trestle bed. Victoire found her quickly, bringing food, linens, a blanket, clothing, dish and spoon. Prisoners were not allowed to have forks or knives. Victoire hugged her. "They took your pistol and a bunch of papers. Also the sketch of Jacques Roux you had by the bed. Everybody thinks you were his mistress."

"People think what they like, Victoire. Jacques was celibate. He still had more respect for women than any man I've ever known."

"I miss you already. I had to let the room go. The landlady wanted me out, she was scared. I've taken another room for us just a block away."

"Did you talk to anyone? Am I going to be tried?"

"If you've fallen through a crack, we don't want them to suddenly remember they meant to try you." Victoire sat on the rough hard bed. They were alone, as Claire's cellmates were out in the courtyard. The only light came from a slit of window. The low ceiling was black with old tallow smoke.

"I know you'll be careful." She kissed Victoire and they held each other hard. She felt Victoire's tears on her shoulder.

The prison was relaxed inside. The cells were not even locked, although the high wall and the guards with dogs made it unlikely anyone could escape without armed help. The prisoners shared food. They were a mixed lot, from beggars to ex-noblemen and ex-clergy, men and women in equal numbers, but no children. They had a curé who played the harp skillfully, a fiddler and two women who sang. Every evening in the old chapel, they improvised entertainment or discussion. They called it the Salon of the Rejected. Someone had painted above the chapel door, "Man cherishes freedom even when he is in prison." Woman too, she thought. They had three poets, who recited their verses. One wrote a play, in which he asked Claire to play the Goddess of Fortune. He had seen her as Marat's wife. Another lady had performed in the plays of the mistress of the duc d'Orléans, in his private theater. He cast her as Juno.

It was a highly rhetorical play, poorly conceived, but better than nothing. She offered to put on a drama by Corneille. That infuriated the literary men. "How could a woman stage a play? That's absurd."

The other poet said, "It's like that illiterate woman, Olympe de Gouges, who pretended to write plays."

"Olympe was not illiterate. I knew her," Claire said. "She had an extremely tiny handwriting, from when she was forbidden by her husband to write. No one could read it, so she had to dictate her plays to a copyist. That's where the nonsense about her being illiterate got started."

They had prisoners who could whittle, who could embroider, who could make clothes or repair them, do fine calligraphy, paint portraits or do sketches or silhouettes, sing and dance and juggle. Except when the guards appeared to call out the names of prisoners who were going to trial, usually to death, it was less stressful inside prison than it had been outside. Everybody here treated each other as an equal, except for the war between the sexes. They did not use titles. Lisette, who had been the mistress of a British viscount, rattled off to Claire all the prisons she had been in. "This is one of the friendliest," she said. "There's a tone to each of them. In some, the rich hang together. I was just a commoner who bedded a British lord. I didn't have any political opinions, just a few good pieces of jewelry. Some prisons the political people run, or the old nobles. Here everybody pitches in to make it livable—while we live." So said Lisette.

Claire ran into Momoro's wife Marie the fifth week. Marie had been sick in bed after losing a baby. Her husband had been executed with Hébert. She was delighted to see Claire. They went off into a corner and compared notes. Robespierre, Saint-Just and Couthon were running things, as near as the women could figure out. The Committees were all-powerful. The Convention was cowed. Delegates were convinced if they raised any objections, they would follow Hébert and Danton and Desmoulins. Marie was lucky she had not been guillotined with Lucile Desmoulins and Mme Hébert. Like Claire, Marie was sure every time the guards came in with a list, she would be on it. "Sometimes I think you and I are the only women in here who are not in love or in lust with someone. The nearness of death does it. Why not have a last fling? I just can't imagine bothering at a time like this. Death does not excite me."

One prisoner kept a public calendar so everyone would know what day it was. When someone had a saint's day, they celebrated. Any excuse for a party. Nights were warm now. They wanted to sleep in the courtyard, but that idea made the warden nervous. The men and women could consort during the day, but they must sleep separately. "We can't have a scandal," the warden said. "Robespierre wants a Republic of Virtue, and we're supposed to be abiding by a high moral code. It's said affairs and dalliances are a rotten vestige of the aristocrats."

This caused a great deal of mirth, afterwards. Even in prison, no one laughed publicly at Robespierre. By the end of Prairial she had been in Port Libre for three months. That day, when the guards read the list, her name was called. The list of death. She had time to kiss Marie Momoro goodbye and ask her to send a message to Victoire, who came almost daily. The guards stuffed her into a carriage with five other women. They rattled across Paris jolting on the cobblestones. Two of the women were crying. One was saying a rosary. A fourth took snuff and sneezed into her kerchief. The last appeared in a stupor. They ranged in age from eighteen (she decided the weepers were mother and daughter) to a woman of sixty, the one saying the rosary. They arrived at the gates of the Conciergerie. This was it. She would be dead soon enough. She clutched her arms and breathed carefully, to calm herself. She had already lived better and longer than she had been fated to. She hoped Victoire could find her, so that they could say goodbye. She had never told Victoire she loved her, but she did. She trusted her even more than she had trusted Pauline. Since Pauline's marriage, she had disappeared into Théo's side, like Adam's rib restored. But Victoire was her support in every circumstance. Victoire was loyalty itself; they saw the world through the same eyes and they saw each other.

When she went to climb out, the guard grabbed her arm hard. "This isn't your stop. All the other citizenesses, out. Citizeness Lacombe, get back in and shut up." They tied her hands together. Then the carriage trundled off, just her inside. The blinds on the windows were down so she could not see, and her hands were now bound at the wrists. But she could tell when they crossed the Seine back to the left bank. She could smell the water.

When she was yanked out, she was in Sainte Pélagie, near the Botanical Gardens, a few clustered buildings that had housed arrested prostitutes. Now it held political prisoners, male and female. It had, she knew, imprisoned Mme Roland and Mme du Barry, before their respective executions.

Claire was not the only actress. A whole group of actresses from the

Comédie-Française were living in semi-luxury. Their admirers had brought in good furniture, rugs, mirrors, so many clothes that she rarely saw them in the same outfit. They looked down on her as a lesser being, but she did not greatly care. They were like hummingbirds, fragile, jeweled, light as paper.

It was noisier than Port Libre but had the same air of feverish gaiety and underneath it, fear. Whenever the guards marched in, everybody froze. Except for the actresses. As they became less unfriendly, one of them confided in Claire that they were safe. For the price of their favors, a bureaucrat had lost their files. They would never come to trial. When things cooled down, as the ingenue put it, they would be freed. She asked Claire if she would like to meet that bureaucrat, as she was sure he would prove accommodating to her also.

"I don't think so," Claire said. "I've always had this silly policy of never fucking anybody I didn't want. Not for parts, not for protection, not for money. It's just my way."

The young woman looked at her blankly. "Really?"

She found comrades there, several women who had been in the RRW, a man who had been associated with the Enragés. He drew her aside to whisper, "Your friends Pauline and Leclerc are in the Luxembourg. They haven't been charged either. Somebody's protecting you."

"I can't imagine who. So many of our people are dead."

"Some of our people and some of Hébert's are still in the Tribunal. They do what they can for us. They can't free us, but they can move us around so we kind of get lost. I've been in four different prisons. They try to keep us from entering the fatal process of being charged, tried and—" He clicked his tongue, making a slicing motion. "All these government agencies, they generate bales of paper. I was in the War Ministry. It snows paper over there. So what if a few sheets get lost?"

So some survived on sex, some survived on old political ties, and some bribed their way with gold or jewels. Thermidor arrived hot. Marie Momoro appeared one day, puzzled by her transfer. Everybody shuttled about and they became cellmates. "I'm thinking of going into the supply business here if we stay long enough," Claire told her. "We have good contacts to the outside. Not everyone in here does, but everybody has something to exchange. I'm thinking of becoming a sort of informal caterer and supply office."

"I can get groceries through friends in the trade. We could work out a deal with them."

The prison was filling up. They had to take another woman into their small cell. Some rooms were now dormitories, with beds side by side down both walls. Newspapers and journals were brought into Sainte Pélagie daily. There was a discussion of the meaning of the law of twenty-second Prairial. It enlarged the Revolutionary Tribunal and simplified the process of trial in a manner that terrified everyone. There were only two verdicts, acquittal or death. The jury need not call any witnesses. Defense counsel was abolished.

After Marie had a visitor, she told Claire, "A lot of the men in the Convention don't like it, but they voted it out of fear."

"If I were them, it's that law I'd be scared of. It eliminates their immunity—not that Danton and Desmoulins found that of any use."

More and more prisoners arrived. Now four were crammed in the cell. Prisoners were carried off to trial, to execution, sometimes more than once a day. Claire was boiling with nerves. They watched, from the courtyard or the windows, as the daily list of the damned marched out. Prisoners gave away possessions to friends, handed over messages, whispered last wishes. The worst was when a family was broken up and a mother or son dragged off.

It was a hot day in July, humid so that clothes sagged and everything felt damp and filthy, even the leaves on the trees in the courtyard. Marie pulled her aside. "Listen," she whispered, "the guards are talking. Something big is happening. I heard gunfire. The army has been winning lately, they've crushed all the revolts, so it must be an attempted coup."

Claire hugged herself. "It can't be our side. Our leaders are dead."

"I heard them mention Robespierre, but I couldn't hear more. I just hope it doesn't mean prison massacres."

That threat always hung over them. She could tell as they walked through the corridors that everybody had heard rumors. It was unnaturally quiet in Sainte Pélagie. Some hoped, some feared. The air felt thick with images of death. She could smell the reek of bodies. The sweat of anxiety seemed to coalesce into an almost visible yellow fog. Outside the high walls and the locked gates, the guards with their muskets and dogs, something played out that would seep down to them. Was it a day of uprising? A coup? Even worse repression? She did not know, she could only guess; but there was no chance she would not find out.

EIGHTY-ONE
Max

❦

(March–July 27, 1794)

MAX was exhausted. He had been working from eight to midnight every day. He had fought enemies outside and inside France, enemies to the right, to the left, enemies through cowardice, through greed, through false conviction, enemies through ambition or opportunism or vice. He was weary of forcing himself to repugnant acts. He could see with clarity the choice that must be made, but each act of blood left him closer to a dangerous apathy approaching quiescence; yet not to fight actively was to abandon the Revolution.

It was worse when Elisabeth had her baby. He was at ease with children and dogs. He knew that Saint-Just was correct in the utopia he had written (in who could imagine what spare time) where male children were taken from their mothers at age six and raised by the State. But in his heart, the ideal would always be the good hardworking artisan family. He would rather be raised in such a family than in Saint-Just's utopia, where children were never touched. Saint-Just had rather too much of a doting mother; but Max had not had enough. Now he was well mothered. Why, then, did the sight of Elisabeth nursing little Philippe sadden him? It could not be remembering Lucile, as Elisabeth was nothing at all like Lucile, nothing at all.

He was sick to his stomach, sick to his brain of the infighting. He had been married to eleven other men since July, and he hated them. He had reached the point where he wanted to throttle Barère for that smirk and his little jokes. Sitting in the room with Collot or Billaud made him feel he was sharing space with two murderers, one vain, one stinking. He respected Carnot but would never like him. Military men were trained not to virtue but to blind obedience. Carnot and Saint-Just were fighting about strategy. Carnot was the military man, but Saint-Just proved to have rapport with soldiers in the field and a head for planning battles.

Something had gone wrong in the Revolution. Something was rotten. He was sick and exhausted, yes, but he was also morally sore. He had been right to squash the deChristianizers. The peasants needed a Church. If someone was thoroughly persuaded there was no afterlife, would he behave with true altruism? Max believed in a force of virtue he called God, active in history, active in him, palpable as pain, a force that shaped his morality. Christianity had much to recommend it: in its origins, a concern with the wretched of the earth. But the Church was the enemy of the Revolution. Pius VI had proved intransigent. He was not interested in reaching a compromise with the new government of France but only in anathematizing them. It was becoming clear that people required a religion, a deity. That would bring soul and freshness back into the Revolution. It should be something grand and simple. He began working on a speech for the Convention, about worship of the Supreme Being. That was a formulation that should displease no one, except the atheists. With festivals at natural points in the year, an emphasis on nature, on behaving well, on virtue.

He knew he was defying some members of the Committee, but so be it. He was right, and they would give in or go down. He was going to take on the Committee of Security. They were furious at him because he oversaw the police closely. Security complained that people they arrested were let go by the Great Committee and that the Great Committee arrested people Security had released. Why should they have a second committee? Through Security's network of spies, they had a hand in everywhere. Vadier and Amar were old enemies, of Hébert's stripe. Cutting off the head did not always get rid of the active body. Lizards regenerated tails, but factions regenerated heads.

When he set out his plan for the Cult of the Supreme Being, the Convention met it with mixed reaction. They were blinded by their limited politics. People needed a sense of exaltation, of being joined in a vast harmony that spread out to the whole nation—that is, the nation of those who were worthy. This religion would bind the nation into one. The worst of Catholicism was the priesthood, the notion that a free man required some mediator between him and the eternal. And original sin. That was a travesty. "Man was born free, but everywhere he is in chains."

Some were moved, some eyed him with obvious cynicism, some were confused. But they passed his legislation. No one could call the Revolution atheistic now. He turned to David and instructed him to prepare a pageant for the first festival. David said it would take about a month to organize. Max wanted a day never to be forgotten.

The armies were winning; paper money had risen in value. Slowly the work of the Committee was paying off, yet the squabbling, the infighting, the jostling for position continued. Obviously the forces against the Revolution were bribing, undermining. The Terror must be stepped up. He could see no other way to move ahead except by eliminating those who obstructed. Soon, soon the way would be clear and the opposition silenced. They would reach harmony. This festival would lead the way.

On the great day, he dressed carefully in yellow and blue, because they were symbolic colors. Rousseau had shown the way of enlightened sentiment to Goethe, who had written about the soul of Werther. When Werther was going to his death, he dressed in the colors of sacrifice, which Max put on for this great day. They meant, to anyone who could read the costume, that far from the dictatorial ambitions his enemies ascribed to him, he was offering himself to the Revolution and to the people, to use, to use up, to martyr, if it came to that.

He walked alone before members of the Convention, carrying flowers, and the people cheered him. He felt the love of the people, and for once he was not embarrassed. He did not turn away but looked at them benignly. In praising him, they praised themselves, for he was their will personified. That was why they had always followed him, why the people cared for him and trusted him above all other politicians.

David had built a great mountain in the Place de la Revolution. The guillotine had been rolled away. No executions on the day of the festival. It was a vast procession. Half a million people, almost everyone in Paris attended, the people joined in ceremony as he had envisioned it. Bands played, choruses sang, women danced, flowers were heaped up and tossed down, doves were released. Children marched and danced and sang. Old men from Les Invalides, crippled and wounded soldiers, rode on wagons laden with banners and roses. Veterans of the Bastille, of all the great days of insurrection, marched with their pikes, their flags. He felt a sense of exaltation as he approached the great mountain David had erected, representing the Mountain itself, virtue, resolution. Strength. A mystical aspiring. He could never in his life be so happy again.

The next day he had Couthon move the laws that would speed up conviction of the guilty plotting against the Revolution. The prisons were getting too full. Trials must go faster, so that the vast cancer would be cut from the body of the country and health and peace would come. This prolongation of a painful process was an error. Terror should be swift, inexorable, exalting to the just. Get it over, get it done and leave it behind. The law of twenty-two Prairial stripped the process to the bone. The Convention passed it, but he could feel their reservations. If they were afraid, that showed they were guilty too, did it not?

There were two attempts on his life, clumsy but real. In one case, the man ended up attacking Collot thinking he was Robespierre; in the other, a young girl—a counter-revolutionary fanatic like Charlotte Corday—was caught trying to force her way into the Duplays' house armed with two knives. He could feel the forces of his enemies gathering. The Committee of Security had arrested a crazy woman Catherine Théot, who had been prophesying that Max was the messiah. They had got as much publicity for the poor woman's idiocy as they could, to discredit him. Members of the Convention were whispering that he wanted to be dictator, that he wanted to be a kind of Pope.

He began to skip Committee meetings. He mistrusted them all. Something else was needed. In the meantime, he simply could not make himself go to the Convention. His will had worn slack. He needed to find his way again. It was comfortable at home with the Duplays. Whatever had been causing him queasiness at the sight of Elisabeth with little Philippe had eased. Philippe was a jolly baby, fast growing, always hungry. He was a living answer to the ridiculous notion of original sin. He was original joy. Max always surprised people when they saw him holding a baby. There was no malice in babies. They were simple and good as dogs. Philippe senior was in a dark mood, even while holding his child. He spoke of plots, something underhanded going on in the Committee of Security, who kept sending him away on mission.

One Sunday late in Messidor—early July—Max went to the country with Philippe and Elisabeth, the Duplays. They picnicked near the Seine. Afterward he withdrew with Eléanore. It was cooler under the trees. He spread his jacket. They made love in nature for the first time. He was tempted to spend in her. He was tempted again to marry her. It would please the Duplays. If he managed to get through the next crisis, perhaps the government would be stable. He could withdraw. He spoke his fantasies aloud as they lay together, reluctant to leave this soothing grove.

"We'll live in the country. We'll have a small house," Eléanore promised him. "If you still don't want babies, we could adopt."

"We could adopt the orphan of a hero of the army or a murdered sansculotte." He could see them in a small clean house with roses growing around it, children studying under the arbor. Doves in a coop. Blount chasing rabbits. They would grow lettuce. Perhaps they could grow oranges under glass. Their fragrance was his favorite smell.

Monday afternoon, Saint-Just stormed in, back from the front. "Why aren't you going to the Committee and the Convention? Are you trying to commit public suicide? Don't you care what happens to the Revolution?"

"Of course I care. I've been to the Jacobins every night. I've been trying to see exactly what we must do." He was not about to admit to Saint-Just he was worn out, wanting to drift and be cared for. He had been hoping to recover the sense of swift inexorable justice that had sustained him through so many duels and battles. "We've lost our momentum."

"The Revolution is frozen. Everywhere petty bureaucrats squabble for minute advantages of position. There's a massive loss of faith. Everyone is full of mistrust and petty anger." Another man would have paced in agitation. Saint-Just stood still at the window, blocking the light. "We have agents on mission making fortunes—like Tallien did. We have agents on mission who terrify helpless populations like that butcher Collot did in Lyon. But when we recall them, they have friends who defend them, factions who conspire."

"Those are symptoms. The disease is vast and growing."

"How do you propose to stop it sitting in your room writing in your note-books? While you scribble and contemplate, France goes to hell. And our enemies plot."

Max rose. "Fortunately, our enemies have no ability to get along with each other. We have enemies to the right, the remaining Dantonists. We have enemies to the left, the surviving Hébertists. We have enemies whose hands we plucked out of the public till. But can you really imagine Collot combining with Tallien to fight us?"

"I can imagine anything." Saint-Just stood like a column of marble against the window. In the light from outside his hair ignited like a visible halo. "You've allowed your loathing to overcome your good sense. You like being outside the government better than being inside. Until recently, you were riding the wave. Now you've let yourself be sucked under."

Max glared at Saint-Just, towering over him so that he was sorry he had got to his feet. He took his seat as if casually. That restored the power balance. He did not like to be pushed, and he was irritated because he suspected Saint-Just was right: he had been staying away out of a great distaste.

He let Saint-Just bully him into going back to the Committee next day. Barère was all smiles, trying to tell everybody they adored each other. A puddle of lukewarm hypocrisy. Underneath, he could feel silent fury, ambitions writhing. He caught Collot looking at him with slitted menace.

Saint-Just was right. There was a plot against them. He could smell it. Saint-Just, Couthon and Philippe met with him that evening to work out a plan of attack. His brother Augustin would be back in a day. They had to purge the Great Committee. They would eliminate the Committee of Security and establish one Committee instead of two, to stop the intriguing.

On eight Thermidor, a sultry day under a copper sky, he went to the Convention. When he took the rostrum, he did not speak as a member of the Committee, but as himself. He was open about the divisions in the Committee. He spoke of the plotting of his enemies who were the enemies of the

Revolution. It was a long speech, aimed at preparing for the overthrow of the plotters. Saint-Just would follow up the next day, detailing the measures to be taken to bring both Committees into line. He named no names, for that might be premature. He wanted to give the plotters a chance to show their hands. Then he would pounce.

They breakfasted together at the Duplays': Couthon, Augustin, who was tanned from being on mission, Saint-Just, who remained pale no matter how much time he spent with the armies, Philippe and himself. They drew up a comprehensive enemies list, everyone they needed to take out in the first line of attack. Then they were ready. They would turn the Convention against the Committee today and overthrow it. Saint-Just would speak first.

Collot was president, which wasn't great luck but soon would not matter. Max took his seat and waited for Saint-Just to go to work. In early afternoon, Saint-Just mounted the platform. He had not said four sentences when Tallien interrupted with a false point of order about whether Saint-Just was speaking as a member of the Committee or personally. Max expected him to be silenced at once, but pandemonium broke out. Delegates were shouting that Max was a tyrant, that he was planning to seize absolute power. "It's a conspiracy," Augustin muttered. "They've rehearsed this. We have to get out of here."

Barère proposed their arrest. Collot ordered, "Seize the tyrant. Take Caesar into custody and save us all!"

Max could not make himself heard. They feared his voice so much that when he tried to speak, they howled, they screamed, they drowned him out, they pounded on the floor. That had happened before, yes, but then Danton had roared out and quieted them. Then a phalanx of guards marched in and grabbed him. He was arrested with Saint-Just, Augustin, Philippe and Couthon. There was chaos, jostling. A fistfight broke out between their supporters and the plotters. "Don't offer resistance," Max said firmly.

A delegate of the Plain shrieked at him, "You planned to murder us all, but now we've got you! We know you were going to slaughter us!"

They were shut up in rooms of the Committee of Security, in another wing of the palace. A line of guards stood outside the doors, under the windows. As they were eating supper, they heard a commotion in the hall. The guard serving them said Hanriot, head of the National Guard, had tried to free them and was arrested. As they ate, they made a collective list of those who had conspired against them, obviously in a carefully orchestrated plot. Most of the Committee of Public Safety; the Committee of Security; large numbers of the Plain in the Convention. Max would not forget a name. He memorized them. Then he destroyed the list.

Around seven, guards marched into the room. They were taken out one by one, each to a different prison. He was delivered to Luxembourg.

The warden called his own guards. "We've had word from the Commune that dirty business is going on. How can anyone arrest the Incorruptible?" He dressed down the escort, humiliating them. Then he had his men accompany Max as bodyguards to City Hall, where the Commune was in session. Much relieved, Max went off with them. Now he would sit down and figure out how to retaliate. The next move.

EIGHTY-TWO
Max

❧

(July 27–28, 1794)

MAX was tortured by indecision. He did not know what had happened to his brother, Saint-Just, Philippe and Couthon. Guards were dispatched from City Hall to the various prisons to find them. The Commune of Paris went into emergency session. They were backing him.

Armed men began to assemble outside. It had not occurred to Max that the sections might rise, but now he began to think that the only answer. He had been outraged by his arrest, but he did not take it as a mortal wound. He had followers. Now it seemed he might have to encourage an uprising against the Convention. He had always supported the uprisings, when he thought they had a chance of succeeding, but he had never been the man to call the people out. That was more Danton's line of work, Desmoulins', Marat's. The Enragés and Hébertists had roused the people to pour into the streets with their pikes and pistols, their makeshift weapons, and to put themselves in danger to push the government in a particular direction, or if necessary, to topple it. Of course, those leaders were gone. Max disliked the random clashing of blind forces determining the future. But it might come to that tonight.

It had begun to rain on the troops gathering outside. He could see by the light of the campfires before the rain put them out several artillery pieces, stacks of weapons, pikes glinting. He could not issue a call in his own person. The Commune was urging him to action, but he could not do it.

Augustin and Philippe marched in. Max embraced them and started to question Augustin what had happened, where he had been taken. Augustin brushed that off. "We have only a few hours to act. We must call out the sections! The Guards assembled below are asking what to do."

"How can we call out the sections? In the name of the Convention? The Convention voted our arrest." Max shook his head.

"In the name of the Revolution. The Convention has sat too long. The war goes well. Enemy troops are off French soil. The Constitution is overwhelmingly popular, so we'll use it to found a new government. We'll call for elections." Augustin sat down to draft an appeal to the sections.

Elisabeth came in as they were working on the appeal, but Philippe sent her home, to safety. She left weeping. Philippe turned to Augustin and Max. "It's all well and good to call up the sections, but we essentially disbanded them, when the Hébertists were trying to rouse the people. We broke up the women's groups. The apparatus for fast response isn't there—but it's worth trying."

Messengers ran off through the rain to deliver their call. The Commune wanted to attack the Convention, but Max hesitated. How many times could Paris rise and destroy its government, before a people became essentially ungovernable? "What will the army do?" he asked.

Saint-Just had finally been located and released. It was almost midnight. At last two officers carried in Couthon in his wheelchair. Saint-Just answered for the army. "How they act depends on whose interpretation reaches them first. We must send word at once."

"In the name of whom? We cannot sign for the Convention," Philippe said patiently. "They just issued warrants for our arrest. We can't attack the Convention and pretend to be the Convention at once."

"We will sign in the name of the French people," Max said. He had no problem with that. He was the voice of the people.

"We need more troops," Saint-Just said. "It's pouring. What good are a handful of men? There are cannons with no one to man them."

"A handful of men?" Augustin looked out onto the dark square. Most of the troops had left. "I'd better talk to the ones who are left."

Max nodded. "Yes. Hurry. Make them understand what's happening!"

Couthon wrote the appeal to the armies and they dispatched it to the various fronts. Saint-Just peered out, his hands clasped behind him. Without turning, he said, "If the army doesn't stand with us, we have no chance. Those pitiful few cannon can't match one real company of artillery."

"We can't risk civil war again," Max said.

"If the sections don't rise quickly, we die." Saint-Just turned to face him, stoic as ever. "I'm prepared."

Philippe cursed. "You two are half in love with death. We should have acted at once and arrested Barère and Amar and Vadier and the two damned Committees. Then it would be their heads."

"Enough heads," Max said. "Enough of everything."

Augustin came slowly in, wet and disheveled. "I can't hold the troops. Without Hanriot, there's no one strong in charge. It's raining hard and I can't give them orders. They're leaving."

"What's happening with the sections?" Max rubbed his hands together. Exhaustion was a drug buzzing in his veins. "Why are they taking so long to respond?"

No one answered. Saint-Just was staring out. Augustin was trying to dry himself at the fireplace. Philippe was sitting at the table with his head in his hands muttering. Couthon was dozing in his wheelchair, exhausted. His mouth had fallen open. The day had been hard on his frail health.

"Wait, more Guards are coming," Saint-Just said from the window. "In strength."

"The sections at last!" Max sank into a chair in relief. They were rising. It was the people's choice, not his.

Saint-Just turned. "It's not the sections. It's the Convention forces, and our own troops have gone home. We've had it."

Philippe rushed out to the hall. Downstairs the first troops were bursting in. A bailiff from the Convention saw him. "Stop! You're under arrest." A shot was fired from below but missed. He ran back into the room and slammed the door. "They're in the building!"

Augustin stood at the window. "There's no way out."

They could hear fighting below, but only seventy-five defenders remained in City Hall. Philippe took two pistols from his coat. Calmly he loaded each of them. "I do not care to be displayed. It's more dignified this way." He handed one pistol to Max and put the other to his head. The shot rang out. Gore and matter stained the wall. Philippe fell dead beside the table.

"I'll talk to them," Couthon said. "They know us. It isn't as if we're aristocrats." He wheeled his chair to the hall. They heard him scream. There was fighting outside, men cursing, bodies falling, an occasional shot. Saint-Just stood at the table with his arms folded, looking slightly bored. Augustin wrestled the window open. "Maybe I can make it. If I fall well." He climbed onto the sill and stepped out. Max rushed to the window. Augustin lay below writhing on the pavement. A man turned him over and then let him drop. Max called to him but he did not answer.

Soldiers forced their way in. Max had no time to consider his action. He lifted the pistol that Philippe had given him, loaded and cocked. He fired at the same time that a soldier fired at him. He fell, a terrible pain in his face. He did not know if he had shot himself or if the soldier had shot him. His jaw was broken and he could not speak. Blood ran down over his waistcoat and shirt. Blood ran down into his ear and caked in his hair.

They carried him out. The guards marched rapidly to the Tuileries. Max was thrown on a rough wagon along with Couthon, whose crippled legs had been smashed, and Augustin, who had passed out. Max was groaning but could not speak as he was jolted over the pavement. Finally he recognized the courtyard of the Tuileries. He was roughly handled up the Queen's Stairway, dropped on the green baize table where the Committee had worked so many days and nights. Couthon was brought in half-dead. Saint-Just said, "The kind gentlemen pulled him out of his wheelchair and threw him down the stairs."

Max tried to ask how Augustin was, but he could not form words. His jaw was smashed. He tried to assess the damage, but when he touched his face, he almost fainted with pain. With his hand he kept tracing an A in the air until Saint-Just understood. "Augustin's still alive. His hip is broken. He's partly paralyzed." Saint-Just was the only one unwounded. He seemed detached, icy. They lay on tables or desks in the Committee room while messengers passed by and people made jokes and insulted them. Someone spat at him, the gob landing on his hand. He could not turn his head to see who the coward was. Someone else came, quietly cleaned him up and put a pile of papers under his head so that he would be in less pain. It was one of their secretaries, a very young man from Marseille. "They have conspired against you," he whispered. "But the people will never forget you."

He could hear the surviving members of the Great Committee drawing up lists of Robespierrists and Jacobins to execute. Sanson would be busy. Security was issuing hundreds of arrest warrants. The Jacobin government was over.

Toward dawn a physician came and treated their wounds as best he could. He argued that they should be taken to a hospital, but he was ignored. At dawn they were hauled to the Conciergerie. Thanks to the law of twenty-two Prairial, they need only be identified and a trial could be dispensed with. They were prepared immediately for execution. Sanson complained bitterly of the extra work, since only Saint-Just was able to sit on the stool. The others had to have their shirts torn, their hair cut and their hands bound behind them where they lay on the muddy stone floor, where boots had tramped in the night's heavy rain. Augustin groaned and Couthon lay in silent agony. Max spent his remaining strength trying not to moan or cry out.

In the tumbrel, Saint-Just stood erect, immaculate. He exuded a stoic calm. He was quite beautiful standing straight in the cart, not even swaying with the rough jouncing. Couthon lay in a heap of mangled limbs. Max sat up but could not stand. The pain roared in his mind. The route lay down the Rue Saint Honoré past the Committee, past the Jacobins, past the Duplays. The house was shuttered. Someone had thrown red paint or blood on the closed gates to the courtyard. Upstairs, he saw the shutters open a chink. Eléanore looked at him. He could hear Blount barking furiously. He could not turn his head to keep her in sight. The tumbrel moved on through a crowd shouting for his death as they had cheered him so often.

"It is important to die well," Saint-Just said quietly. "We are exiting and entering history at once. This is the last act over which we have any control."

At least the pain would stop. He had often thought of what he might say as he faced death. Now he could say nothing.

He was the last. Couthon took the longest. Max wished he could have pleaded with them to handle him less roughly. It took them a full quarter hour to force him onto the plank. Again and again Max tried to make himself heard, to beg them to be gentler. The drums rolled. People shrieked. There were twenty-one of them, a common number in a batch: Hanriot, the officers of the Paris Commune. Now the others went faster. Saint-Just was called just before him, walking with dignity onto the scaffold and bowing his head briefly to the crowd as if in recognition of applause. Then they led Max up. It was exactly a year ago he had agreed to serve on the Committee of Public Safety.

Sanson yanked the rag bandage violently from him so he could not help crying out, a short scream. He could not close his jaw now and it hung open, blood streaming down. He was impatient for it to end. He lay down on his stomach and waited. They had bungled. They had failed. He knew the Revolution would not survive them. But there would be other revolutionaries and other revolutions. There would be others. He only wished he had time to figure out exactly what he had done wrong. He felt as calm as Saint-Just had seemed. There was nothing he could do now; he was free of the doing. He heard the blade released and the people cheer. In a moment Sanson would grin, holding up his head with the shattered jaw. He was thirty-six years and two and a half months of age.

EIGHTY-THREE
Pauline

❧

(August 1794)

PAULINE wrote to the Tribunal reviewing their case, "It is my sole desire to devote myself to domestic duties, to the happiness of my husband and the education of the children we wish to have, in the service of our great country." She had heard that garbage from the delegates who had banned the RRW and from the Jacobin Club, when the men turned against them. She could write it by the yard. Working against Théo and her was that they had been far left, and these days the open road was to the right. Working for them was that Robespierre had put them inside, and any enemy of Robespierre's might have friends in power.

Claire said, "I just can't say those lies. Besides, we may be safer inside. The people are being disarmed."

"Claire, the Terror is over. They repealed the law of twenty-two Prairial. No more assumption of guilt. Every day more people are freed."

"I've noticed more keep arriving."

"You're afraid to hope. That's defeating yourself. I'm full of hope." Pauline also suspected she was filling up with something else, but she would not say a word to anyone, least of all Théo, till she knew for sure.

Claire had been transferred to the Luxembourg. She had already set up a business, along with Momoro's widow. Almost every day Victoire came to Claire, but Babette had not been to see them in weeks. Claire could get things for people. Prisoners put in requests for food—a chicken, salad greens, good red wine—and gave them a deposit. Victoire could get deals in used clothing. They had contacts among former RRW members, Enragés and Hébertists. Some Hébertists were still in power, although the Commune had been purged and more than a hundred Robespierrists had gone to the guillotine. She and Théo had friends in the government, agitating to get them out. Théo's army officers and buddies were demanding his release, saying that his regiment needed him.

That day, the midwife came in to examine Pauline. Then Pauline added a note to her appeal. "I am with child, and I think I would be a better mother if I could raise this child among good citizens. I intend to breastfeed my son and raise him to be a soldier."

"But you're not pregnant. You don't think you've laid it on a little thick?" Théo asked. His own plea was full of martial ardor and fervent promises to be a good officer and stay out of politics.

"I don't think it's possible to lay it on too thick for them. Whoever *them* is this week." Everything was unstable since the fall of Robespierre. Different factions were vying, but basically a coalition of Dantonists and those further right were in power. Former terrorists—agents on mission whom Robespierre had recalled and condemned for excesses of brutality or corruption—had moved to the right and were busy persecuting their old allies.

"If you claim to be pregnant, they can bring in a doctor," Théo warned.

Pauline stood very straight beside their little table. "They are free to examine me. They'll find I'm with child."

Théo's face cracked open in an enormous grin. Gently he laid his hand on her belly, as if he could feel anything yet. "Now we really have to get out of here. Do you think I groveled enough? I'll swear to anything." He hugged her, carefully. "How do you feel?"

It was a hot summer, little rain. The last hard rain had been the day Robespierre had fallen. They were sitting in the garden under a tree when the warden sent for them. "Good news. You're out today. Get packed."

Pauline kissed Claire goodbye. "You'll be free soon," she prophesied.

"I'm not so sure. They seem to find me dangerous still."

Claire was no longer dressing in the RRW mode, pantaloons and jackets, but more like a bourgeois lady. It suited her in prison. Théo wanted Pauline to wear better clothes. While they were still in prison, he had a seamstress make her up a blue-and-white dress. The seamstress called it à la anglaise. It was less comfortable than her normal clothes; when she tried it on at a mirror, she looked like an elegant stranger. Théo said to save it until they got to his regiment and she met the other officers and their wives. "Remember, you'll be an officer's wife." He ordered another like it in white and red.

An officer's wife. She was alarmed. If she had married Henri and followed him to the wars, he was the lowest sort of soldier. She could not quite imagine what her life was to be like, or whether she could manage to get along with the other officers' wives. It sounded daunting.

"I have no idea what we're going to find outside," Théo said. "But if the Terror is really over, everything should be easier."

Hand in hand Théo and Pauline walked out of the Luxembourg. They had to get a cab to move their bed, their table, their linens and clothes and utensils and books. The streets looked different. Nobody was wearing the red cap of liberty. Many men and women dressed like ladies and gentlemen—not as fancy as the old nobility had dressed, but fine enough. Private carriages rushed through the streets. She saw a few men she recognized. Lawyers who had dressed like sans-culottes when she had gone into prison, now wore waistcoats, culottes, silk stockings, standard bourgeois finery. Shops catering to people with money seemed to have plenty to display, whether silks or lamb chops or gloves. Ladies were wearing enormous hats covered with flowers and birds. The carriage driver had not addressed them as "tu," but rather used the polite "vous."

On the walls instead of the revolutionary posters denouncing or exhorting, there were notices of dances, of balls, of fairs, of plays and galas. When they came into her old neighborhood, everything looked different too, but not gayer. The people scurried along as they used to before the Revolution, nervous, wary. Lines stood before bakeries and butcher shops. Little was displayed. The contrasts between neighborhoods were far more marked than in the spring. All the barriers of class seemed back in place. She was reminded as the cab pulled into her little street that she had married a man from a higher social class than her own. Would he regret this? She had never thought of him as having a class, because they were political together. Only the line you followed mattered.

The chocolate shop looked strange. She heard sawing as they approached. The doors and shutters were flung wide and a man came out carrying a pile of planks. "There's someone in the shop!"

Théo leapt out before the cab had come to a halt and ran up to the open door. "What are you doing in here?"

A swarthy man with his sleeves rolled up paused in his sawing. "What does it look like I'm doing?"

Her shop had been rented out from under her. Now she understood why Babette had sent her a message that she had her things. Théo and Pauline entered the tavern warily, not sure what it all meant. Men were slumped at the tables drinking sullenly in the middle of the day, a sure sign of unemployment. Newspapers lay around but no one was reading them aloud. Instead of the animated political argument she had grown used to, the men were mumbling in low voices. Babette's mother motioned them toward the back. Babette was sitting at a table with her leg on a chair.

"Forgive me for not getting up, but I can't. The fucking bastards broke my leg."

"Who broke your leg?" Théo leaned on the table.

"Those bastards, Gilded Youth. They're gangs of fancy thugs. You'll see them. They dress like fops, with skin-tight pants and high cravats, sort of like Saint-Just used to wear. They keep their hair long and braided in back. They carry sticks with lead weights and they beat you up. They're terrorizing all the sans-culottes and the Jacobins and everybody they hate. The streets belong to them. If you see a bunch of them coming, run for cover. . . . Anyhow, that's why I haven't been to see you. I can't get around. They raped me. Then they beat me up and broke my leg."

Babette began to weep and Pauline held her. She wiped Babette's face gently and patted her shoulder.

Théo was still trying to find out about Gilded Youth. "So who are they? Pimps? Mercenaries?"

Babette's mother answered, from behind the counter. "They're accountants, lawyers' clerks, all the kids who got out of going to the army. We should have finished them off when we had the chance."

Babette's brother shushed her. "Police spies," he said. "They're everywhere."

Babette did have Pauline's things.

"We'll sell them at the market. We'll keep the bed and some linens, your clothes, anything worth hauling. The rest we'll sell off," Théo said. "We're leaving Paris as fast as we can. I just want to collect my papers. Then we'll join my regiment. Your chocolate business is gone. Time to clear out with what we can carry."

They stayed in a cheap inn for the next week, while they wound up their affairs. Pauline sold off the furniture. She bought a horse and a simple wagon. At Théo's insistence, she got some clothes, skirts, chemises, aprons, a new shawl. Victoire found exactly what she needed.

She was having morning sickness but otherwise felt fine. Théo reported that the army was a sanctuary for radicals. She would be an army wife, traveling behind the regiment. There would be other women like herself, sans-culotte women, women of Paris, he explained, because many of the new officers were men who had been raised up by the Revolution. Some might even know who she had been. Her mother had never taken her father's name—lots of sans-culotte women didn't—but Théo had expected her to take his. Perhaps it would be safer for her and the child, if people didn't know that she had been a revolutionary leader. She began signing herself Femme Leclerc. Leclerc was a common name. They would disappear into the army. Gilded Youth could rage in the streets and the prisons could fill up, but they would be out of it, on the frontier or in another country. If the army won, victory could be sweet. They would always have enough to eat, no longer the case in her old neighborhood. She stopped dreading army life and began to look forward to it.

The day they left Paris, she sang to Théo, old ballads her parents had taught her. She sang to her husband, her husband—think of it. In his uniform, he looked slim and handsome and perfect. She sang to her unborn child. It felt almost like going on an extended day off, into the country. Théo was armed. He took his musket, pistol and sword back from a friend who had been keeping them. She felt safe and excited. People had been telling her that nowadays, in the days of victory and the army reorganized, the officers did pretty well. She had landed on her feet. She might call herself Femme Leclerc now, but she was the true daughter of her hardworking mother and father, who if they were given half a chance, would manage, would come through.

EIGHTY-FOUR
Claire

❀

(August 1794–August 1795)

CLAIRE could read the political complexion of the government by who entered the prisons and who left. Victoire never tired of petitioning the various bureaucracies for her release, but months passed, summer into winter, and she was still a prisoner. Elisabeth Lebas and her baby boy were locked up in the Luxembourg, along with her sister, Eléanore Duplay, who had been Robespierre's fiancée. Eléanore was intense and very quiet. She observed Claire carefully for two weeks before beginning to speak to her.

"My mother hanged herself. My father's in La Force prison. When the news came that Philippe was dead, my sister fell into a dead faint. Her baby had to be put to a wet nurse. She was unconscious for two days. We thought she'd die. She had just come to and got her baby back when we were arrested."

"Your crime was giving a home to Robespierre?"

"We all loved him," Eléanore said. "I most of all. His idiot sister Charlotte renounced him. I will never cease to be faithful."

"Being faithful to a dead man is useless to both of you," Claire said. She did not bother telling Eléanore how much she had grown to mistrust Robespierre and his virtue.

"If you loved a great man, would you ever be satisfied with a little man?" Eléanore asked, her dark eyes glittering in her thin pale face. "He is my fate." She seemed pleased to have settled that for herself.

Claire was not only making more than she was spending in prison, she was laying by money that she gave regularly to Victoire. They were going to live together if she ever got out. Every day Victoire came, bringing her news, hope, affection, supplies to sell. Victoire was her life line. Never before had she depended on another as she depended on Victoire. For a time it frightened her, and then she grew used to that dependency, that connection. Without it, she would not survive. Winter was hard in prison because they must keep warm. Every fireplace had six beds huddled around it. Claire had no connections for firewood. Outside, people were starving. Babette told her, "Since they took off price controls, the price of bread has skyrocketed. Besides people dying of the terrible cold and hunger, there's something new. Three women in the neighborhood killed themselves. Mimi walked into the Seine with her little daughter by the hand." Babette came regularly to see her, hobbling on her crooked leg. She remembered Babette dancing.

"Why? What's wrong?" Claire could not imagine the women who had fought so hard, those bawdy strong women killing themselves.

"Despair," Babette said. "Despair is what's happening."

She did not like to tell Babette that there was no starvation in the Luxembourg. The official rations had been cut, but almost everybody here had resources. Many of the better off had been released. Still the prison was always full. Elisabeth was getting help from the family of her dead husband. His brother came up to Paris to see her every month. He was working hard to secure her release.

"He looks so like Philippe," Elisabeth said to her. They were sitting together picking over dry beans for maggots before they made a stew. "Do you remember how handsome my husband was?"

Elisabeth had regained her color. She was far prettier than her sister, although less bright. She was a good mother, and Claire expected she would go on being Elisabeth Lebas, but with a different brother, after she got out.

Sometimes one of the new society ladies would visit friends in the Luxembourg, wearing the latest fashions. They were simple in line, but made of almost transparent fabrics. Sometimes the outlines of the breasts could be clearly seen through the white gauze. Fashions seemed to have gone from everyone dressing in working-class styles as if they were about to saw wood or do the laundry, to dresses that suggested every woman was a courtesan. Tallien, one of the conspirators who had overthrown Robespierre, had married his mistress who was setting the fashion. Her salon was the most renowned of the new ones.

In late spring, Victoire came to see her, as she did daily, but with new excitement, catching Claire's face between her hands. Victoire was lit up, shining. "Claire, your case has been reopened. Things are moving."

"But in what direction?"

"Somebody bribed them. Suddenly they can find all your paperwork. Suddenly there's a hearing next week. I'm told it's a formality."

Claire could remember when a hearing was tantamount to a short ride to the guillotine. People were still being executed in droves. Only the personnel in the tumbrels had changed. Now they were almost always sans-culottes or Jacobins or former radicals from the sections. This was called the White

Terror. It was even more widespread in the provinces. The prisons there were packed, but the new trick was for a prisoner never to reach jail. Instead he was ambushed on route after arrest; or he just disappeared as if yanked upward by a deus ex machina: except that a week later, his body would be found riddled with shot beside some deserted country road. In other places, whole towns were under reign of those who wanted revenge for the death of relatives, their own imprisonment, or just the lack of respect they had received from their inferiors. The low had been high; now the high were high again and the low were low, and they were going to see it stayed that way.

A carpenter went to the guillotine because he was heard saying, "I miss old Robespierre. Under Robespierre, we had blood, but we also had bread."

Claire was half-reluctant to leave prison, where she had managed to set up a comfortable life. People depended on her to supply them. She felt safe and needed. She had no idea what it would be like outside. She had been in Luxembourg for ten months, and she knew the guards and the ways to finagle what she needed. Little bribes had slowly become a way of life. After Thermidor—the fall of Robespierre—bribes had gradually turned into the usual grease for the wheels of the whole society. It was going to take some getting used to. If Robespierre had put his puritanical stamp on the time of the Terror, Tallien and Fréron, both corrupt, both venal, had spread their attitudes abroad through the new society. If you asked a favor, you passed money. You tipped afterward.

The day before Claire was to be released, she had a surprise visitor: the still very handsome Mendès Herrera. He embraced her formally. "You're looking fresh," he said.

"Are you the one who bribed the court?"

"A few tokens of my esteem. Wine from Bordeaux is always appreciated."

"I appreciate too—that you'd help me. What's happened with you?"

"Things were dangerous for a while, but we kept our rights. We're citizens. The import-export business had gone to hell with the British blockade, but I'm in wine now. I was able to pick up a good vineyard in the sales. . . . I'm helping you for old times' sake." He was keeping his distance and she behaved demurely also, waiting to see what the price was.

"There isn't anything I want from you," he said, as if reading her mind. "I'm married. She comes from an old Sephardic family, she's nineteen and beautiful, and she brings me a dowry of gold and olive oil. I learned of your problems. No one else need know. You've become a little notorious, Claire. I don't know if you can turn it to your advantage on the stage. I wish you luck. You're as beautiful as ever, but I'm a family man again."

Then he was gone. She was entirely brushed off, but she did not mind, for if he had his wife, she had hers: faithful Victoire, with whom she walked out of the Luxembourg into a cool overcast May day. She brought her things back to Victoire's room, and there they pondered what they should do. That night in the sagging double bed, she made love to Victoire as if she were a man. She knew such love existed, but she knew nothing more about it than that it was a scandal and everybody said it was a sin. Everybody said a great many things were sins, but they did them anyhow. This, she thought, should be a sacrament. "I marry you, I marry you, I marry you," she said to Victoire in the dark room where the candle had long ago guttered out leaving an acrid smell of smoke. The scent of their love-making hung in the air along with the stew they had made in the fireplace.

"I marry you," Victoire said back. "I've loved you forever."

"We must be very careful," Claire said. "Or we'll end up back in prison, this time both of us. Don't tell anyone, not Babette, not anyone, what we are to each other. Outside this room, we're friends. Inside here, we're married. We know that, but nobody else must."

Claire set out to see if she had any contacts left for a job. She wondered if Collot d'Herbois had gone back to the theater, for he hadn't been in the Committee of Public Safety since September. She assumed he'd managed to protect himself, after bringing Robespierre down. But she learned he was being tried for crimes under the Terror, along with the melodious-voiced Barère, who had sung paeans to the army, and Billaud-Varenne, whom she remembered from the Cordeliers Club before he had served his time on the dreaded Committee. Swiftly they were condemned to life imprisonment in Guiana. Convicts died there like poisoned sheep. So much for Collot.

The mighty had fallen all over the place, but then, they had only been mighty a matter of months. The guys with carriages and silk stockings were back on top. After three weeks of making the rounds, she got a job. Political plays were out. The Gilded Youth served as informal censors. If they didn't like the politics of a play or of an actor or actress, they would make so much noise they disrupted the performance. If that didn't work, they attacked the patrons. They liked to beat people up. They were protected by Fréron. They were an unofficial police corps of the reaction.

She was worried about how they would respond to her. It was a melodrama of bourgeois virtue vindicated, one of the sort Collot had used to put on in the provinces. She was the villainess. She was set for a month. One of the patrons of the theater asked her out to supper at the Palais Royal after the Saturday performance. She went warily. Perhaps she wouldn't have a month's work. It would not be worth it if she had to fuck the patron.

The Palais Royal was changed. Nobody was making speeches. She saw not one person who would classify as a sans-culotte or an artisan. It was the province of Gilded Youth, who celebrated the downfall of Robespierre with Lobster Thermidor, a new dish that was all the rage and cost a small fortune. In luxury restaurants and refurbished cafes, the clientele was composed of financiers, middlemen, deputies, purveyors to the army, big landlords, the courtesans who pleased them, their mistresses. The patron was not interested in bedding her; rather she had caught the eye of a certain manufacturer of boots, who he said was well connected and a personal friend of Tallien.

"Alas," she said theatrically. "The gentlemen who procured my liberty has also procured my favors. I could not be unfaithful to him."

"I heard that was a Jew from Bordeaux."

"He was merely the middleman. I'm sure you understand the need for discretion."

"Of course." The patron looked properly impressed. He did not push her further; neither did he invite her to have dessert. That was too bad; she had wanted to try the Tortoni everyone was talking about.

This was a Paris of new fashions in food and drink, of elaborate parties, of finery and jewels, of dubious taste and ostentatious consumption. But this was not the ancien régime. Birth meant little. People with money had power, generals had power. There was a class of politicians whom everybody wooed. Actors and Jews and Protestants kept their rights. But women were losing theirs. They had gone three steps forward and two steps back. The only women who mattered were mistresses or wives of men with power. Life on the bottom seemed little changed, except that the people had learned what they wanted and might not forget it. They were crushed, disarmed, policed and kept down, but they met in quiet conspiratorial groups and talked of freedom, of equality, of a just society. They told their children stories. In low voices in the Dancing Badger, the men mumbled of politics, the women muttered to each other. By now, they knew their local police spies.

When the melodrama closed, Claire had trouble finding another job. Managers seemed to have remembered who she was. The only thing she could locate required her to pose nude in a pantomime, and she thought she was getting a little too old to stand that long in a draft. However, she had a job offer from a company based in Nantes. Victoire and Claire decided they had little to keep them in Paris, so they would follow the job. Victoire had skills as a seamstress.

"I was born in Beaujolais, in Morgon," Victoire said. "Maybe someday we can buy a little piece of land near there. It's good country."

"I figure I have two, three years left for the stage. I'm no great actress."

Claire was packing her wardrobe into a battered trunk that had traveled all over France.

"But you're a great woman," Victoire said. "If you hadn't given those years to the Revolution, you'd be famous today as an actress."

"Maybe, maybe not. That was my life. Now we have our life. A quiet one, I hope." She took Victoire's round face between her hands. She could see the stress of the last year etched around her lover's eyes. For Victoire, waiting and worrying, perhaps it had been harder than for her. "We have to save our money. Plan for the long haul. At least people like us can buy land now. The Revolution took the lid off."

Victoire took a brush and let down Claire's long dark hair. "After you leave the stage, we'll set up in business together. Between us, we can manage."

Claire let her eyes close, enjoying the brushing that made her feel like a purring cat. "We'll be safer out of Paris. And we have one great gift: we can trust each other."

EIGHTY-FIVE
Claire

❦

(Fall 1812)

CLAIRE was sitting with Victoire and their visitor, Pauline Leclerc, in the courtyard of the yellow stone farmhouse she and Victoire owned, in southern Beaujolais near Lyon. They had run a cafe in the city for twelve years, but three years ago, they had sold the business and retired to their land, a piece Victoire had inherited. Another chunk they had bought. They had a vineyard, chickens, ducks on a small pond, ill-tempered geese, three goats, peach and plum trees, raspberries, vegetables.

"Isn't it hard work for a couple of women in their forties? I don't think I could go up on a ladder in the trees the way you do," Pauline said. If Claire had turned wiry and Victoire had wrinkled like a white-haired raisin, Pauline had gone round as a pumpkin. She was a plump prosperous-looking lady dressed in blue silks and perspiring, mopping her face with a dainty lace-edged handkerchief in the modest heat. At her throat she wore a sapphire. They were sitting in the shade of an arbor of table grapes.

"We have help," Victoire said, "and we like to stay spry."

"Why did you give up the cafe?"

Claire said, "We feel safer here. Some people in Lyon know who I was." Moreover, something in both of them had said, This is the good life: a plot of land, some animals, to sit under their vine and drink their own Beaujolais and be at peace. They wanted to take the two girls and the boy they had adopted, street orphans all, out of the city.

"Sometimes Théo thinks of going back into politics, but I always put my foot down. We had enough of that."

"Isn't his job political?" Claire knew Théo was an official in the Napoleonic government set up in northern Italy.

"Just administrative. We keep our noses clean."

"What brings you to Lyon this time?" Victoire asked. She was a little wary of Pauline, because of Théo's old affair with Claire, because Pauline had been close to Claire before Victoire. They had wondered together if Pauline recognized the nature of their relationship. Claire thought that Pauline must know, but Victoire insisted Pauline would not consider the possibility.

"We're on our way to see Théo's folks. And he had an uncle in Lyon who died recently. We're paying our respects."

"Do you get on any better with his family?"

Pauline snorted. "After seventeen years? After three sons and two daughters? They've had to accept me. I'm a fact."

Pauline was stout and she waded through the humid air instead of marching, but she was still a force, energetic, loud, cheerful, radiating a kind of centered strength. Claire smiled at her. "We didn't get what we wanted, did we? What we imagined for women. Freedom, equality."

"We survived. I have Théo and my kids. But yes, women got shunted aside. That's Napoléon."

Claire noted that Pauline gave herself leave to criticize the Emperor. It was a pleasure to hear her. "There's so few of us left."

"More than you think," Pauline said. "Théo and I have raised our children to be good revolutionaries. Napoléon won't last forever." Pauline helped herself to more of the plum cake that had been one of Victoire's specialties in the cafe. "Both my girls are getting an education. Aimée has a gift for languages. Who'd think a daughter of mine would speak English and Italian at age eleven? She's a little genius. They're all smart, and I don't just say this as a mother. . . . Don't you ever wish you had children?"

Victoire's eyebrows rose. "What do you call André, Colette and Marie?"

"I mean, of your own." Pauline was looking at Claire.

"They are my own," Claire said quietly.

Pauline sighed. "I hope you forgive me for Théo. If only you'd married, I'd feel less guilty. . . . But you never did. . . ." She shrugged. "I never imagined you'd end up a spinster, but if you like it . . . ?"

Claire looked at her lover, who looked back at her. Well, that answered that question. "Don't bother feeling guilty, please. We like our life. By the way, we're supposed to be war widows, sisters-in-law. There are so many widows nobody thinks anything of women alone."

"I'm glad Théo went into administration. The mortality rate in the army is incredible. We're killing off a whole generation. Don't believe what you hear about the glorious victories. Ever see a battlefield?" Pauline waited for Claire and Victoire to shake their heads no. "It's just a big butcher shop, like that area near Les Halles where they used to cut up steers and calves, where the gutters ran thick and red. It's a bunch of guys who died in horrible pain, body parts everyplace. You can take the glory of war and stuff it. . . . But Théo has done all right."

"So have we," Victoire said. "When I think of the women from our group who are dead already. . . ." She sighed, and their eyes met.

"Sometimes I remember, Pauline, all the people we knew. I think of Jacques. Olympe de Gouges. Danton. And that boy who never grew up— Desmoulins with his pretty, silly wife. None of them ever got to be middle-aged. They were all so young. We were all so young. Even Robespierre. Do you remember when you had a crush on him, Pauline? I met his girlfriend in prison. She got out not long after I did."

"The best thing he ever did was land reform," Victoire said. "That's changed the face of this country forever. All the peasants who could manage it got a piece of land. No one's starving. They don't expose babies any more or have to send all the girls off to the cities to work as scullery maids, the way my parents sent me."

"We thought we would make a new just world where we would all be free," Pauline said. "We were naive."

"We did make a new world," Claire said. "Just not exactly the one we intended. It's a bigger job than we realized, to make things good and fair. It won't be us who finish it. But we gave it a pretty good start before we lost our way. Now, as Voltaire said, we cultivate our garden. A small place where we can be ourselves in peace."

"Still," Pauline said, "I remember and I make sure my daughters know, it was old biddies like we are now and young women who brought the King down. We were the Revolution, ladies, and we carry it in our blood to the future."

They all sighed, smiling ironically at each other, and had another piece of plum cake under the arbor.

CAST OF CHARACTERS

MAX

MAXIMILIEN ROBESPIERRE	Oldest child of Francois de Robespierre; lawyer; orator, leading revolutionary; Jacobin
CHARLOTTE	Max's sister, second-born
HENRIETTE	Max's sister, third-born
AUGUSTIN	Max's younger brother, fourth-born; also called Bonbon
THE CARRAUTS	Max's mother's family; local brewers
BISHOP OF ARRAS	Powerful bishop, controlled scholarships at Louis-le-Grand school; involved in a scandal with the Queen; also known as Cardinal Rohan
CAMILLE DESMOULINS	Student at Louis-le-Grand school; friend of Max and later of Georges Danton
JÉRÔME PÉTION	Student at Louis-le-Grand school; later Mayor of Paris
CLEMENTINE	Client of Max
MLLE DESHORTIES	Distant cousin of Max, whom he courted
LAZARE CARNOT	Acquaintance of Max; Jacobin; later member of the Committee of Public Safety
DR. GUILLOTIN	Delegate to National Assembly; inventor of the guillotine
JEAN MOUNIER	Delegate to the National Assembly
DUC DE NOAILLES	Delegate to the National Assembly
COMTE DE MIRABEAU	Deputy of the Third Estate in the Assembly; important leader in early Revolution
M. DUPLAY	Carpenter in whose house Max lived; Jacobin
MME DUPLAY	His wife
VIVIENNE DUPLAY	Their youngest daughter
ELISABETH DUPLAY	Their middle daughter; later to be Elisabeth Lebas
ELÉANORE DUPLAY	Their oldest daughter

COUTHON	Delegate in the Legislative Assembly and the Convention; Jacobin; ally of Max; later member of the Committee of Public Safety
DUKE OF BRUNSWICK	Led Austrian and Prussian troops against the French Army of the Rhine; fought to restore power of the King and the Church
ANTOINE SAINT-JUST	Colleague of Max; youngest deputy in the Convention; later member of the Committee of Public Safety
PHILIPPE FRANÇOIS LEBAS	Jacobin; colleague and friend of Max; married Elisabeth Duplay
VARLET	One of the Enragés, also called Mad Dogs
HANRIOT	Supporter of Max; head of the National Guard '93–'94
AMAR	Member of the Committee of Security; anti-feminist
VADIER	Member of the Committee of Security; also called "The Old Inquisitor"
DAVID	Artist; Jacobin; friend of Max
CATHERINE THÉOT	Arrested for prophesying that Max was the messiah
TALLIEN	Important delegate in the Convention
FRÉRON	Ally of Tallien

CLAIRE

CLAIRE LACOMBE	Youngest of five surviving children
ANNE-MARIE	Claire's mother; laundrywoman
YVETTE	Claire's older sister
PAPA	Claire's father; bricklayer
PIERRE	Claire's brother, the only one who lived at home
GRANDMÈRE	Claire's grandmother; Protestant
JEAN-PAUL	Actor in a troupe that visited Pamiers
JEAN COLLOT D'HERBOIS	Actor; playwright; Jacobin and Cordelier; later member of the Committee of Public Safety
YVONNE	Actress in Collot's theater company
JULIETTE	Actress in Colot's theater company
MADAME	Collot's wife
LUCIE DE FONTANELLE	Actress in Collot's company

MME ABIEL	Actress in Collot's company
FRANÇOIS	Actor in Collot's company
MENDÈS HERRERA	Jewish merchant in Bordeaux
HÉLÈNE	Friend of Claire from the Paris theater
SANTERRE	Brewer; leader of guards; revolutionary
JACQUES ROUX	Friend of Claire; radical priest; one of the Enragés
THÉOPHILE LECLERC	Young army officer; one of the Enragés
MOMORO	Cordelier; one of Hébert's group
MONTGOLFIER BROTHERS	Built and flew hot air balloons

NICOLAS

MARIE JEAN NICOLAS CARITAT, MARQUIS DE CONDORCET (NICOLAS)	Mathemetician, philosopher, social scientist, feminist
JEAN LE ROND D'ALEMBERT	Friend and mentor of Nicolas
JULIE DE LESPINASSE	Jean's best friend; led an important liberal salon
VOLTAIRE	Philosopher and author; friend of Nicolas
DIDEROT	Encyclopedist; author
AMÉLIE SUARD	Married woman in whose house Nicolas lived
ANTOINE SUARD	Her husband; editor; friend of Nicolas
BARON TURGOT	One of Louis XVI's chief ministers; friend of Nicolas; reformer
MALESHERBES	Minister under Louis XVI; chief censor
NECKER	Minister under Louis XVI; Protestant; Swiss-born
BENJAMIN FRANKLIN	Envoy from America
BUFFON	Naturalist; rival of Jean d'Alembert
JEAN-PAUL MARAT	Doctor; radical journalist; revolutionary
MESMER	Doctor who used electricity and hypnotism to cure
DU PATY	Older friend of Nicolas; liberal who sought justice
SOPHIE DE GROUCHY	Daughter of du Paty's in-laws; later wife to Nicolas; also called Grouchette
CHARLES	Sophie's little cousin
MME HELVÉTIUS	Widow of philosopher; adopted Dr. Cabanis who was courting Sophie's sister; led famous liberal salon
ADRIEN DUPORT	Wealthy magistrate and member of the Parlement of Paris; Committee of Thirty met at his house

GILBERT LAFAYETTE	Marquis de Lafayette; soldier and politician; friend of Nicolas; helped fight for independence in America; commander of the National Guard
ABBÉ SIEYÈS	Member of the Committee of Thirty and the Estates General
JEAN-SYLVAIN BAILLY	Astronomer; Nicolas' rival for admission to the Academy; leader in the Third Estate; later Mayor of Paris
NICHOLAS BONNEVILLE	Revolutionary; editor of *Iron Mouth*; associated with the Social Circle and the Girondins
ABBÉ FAUCHET	Revolutionary priest, associated with the Social Circle
DR. PIERRE CABANIS	Sophie's doctor; adopted son of Mme Helvétius; courted Sophie's younger sister
CHODERLOS DE LACLOS	Chevalier; ex–army officer; novelist; Jacobin; wrote *Les Liaisons Dangereuses*; secretary to duc d'Orléans
TOM PAINE	Englishman; pamphleteer; involved in the American revolution; friend of Nicolas; associated with the Girondins
ETTA PALM D'AELDERS	Dutch feminist; associated with the Social Circle
ELIZA	Daughter of Sophie and Nicolas
ROEDERER	In charge of defending the Tuilleries, August 10, 1792
ROBERT LINDET	Radical; in the Convention; member of the Committee of Public Safety
CHAMBON	Jacobin Mayor of Paris
BARÈRE	Jacobin; Cordelier; in the Convention; member of the Committee of Public Safety; orator
CHABOT	Demanded that Nicolas be arrested for sedition
MME VERNET	Had an apartment where Nicolas lived in hiding

MANON

MANON PHILIPON	Maiden name of Mme Roland
SOPHIE CARNET	Lifelong friend of Manon
GRANDMÈRE	Manon's grandmother; lived on Île Notre Dame
M. PHILIPON	Manon's father; master craftsman
MME PETRIE	Manon's wet nurse and friend

MME DU BOISMOREL	Aristocratic lady for whom Grandmère worked as a governess
MIGNONNE	Elderly maid of the Philipon family
JEAN ROLAND DE LA PLATIÈRE	Older government bureaucrat whom Manon married; later associated with the Girondins; minister of the Interior
MARGUERITE FLEURY	Maid to Manon
EUDORA	Daughter of Manon and Jean
DR. LANTHÉNAS	Friend of Manon and Jean; associated with the Social Circle and the Girondins
BOSC	Young botanist; friend of Manon and Jean
DOMINIQUE	Canon; Jean's brother
LAURENT	Another clerical brother of Jean
JEANNOT	Poor peasant in Thiezé
JACQUES-PIERRE BRISSOT	Young journalist who corresponded with Manon and Jean; member of the Assembly and the Convention; associated with the Social Circle; more or less head of the Girondins (also called Brissotins)
HENRI BANCAL	Friend of Manon; political man and lawyer; associated with the Girondins
FRANÇOIS-LÉONARD BUZOT	Young revolutionary; Jacobin; associated with the Girondins; member of the Legislative Assembly and the Convention
PIERRE VERGNIAUD	Orator; Girondin; Member of the National Convention
GENERAL DUMOURIEZ	Talented general; minister; Girondin
RENÉ HÉBERT	Put out the popular far left journal *Pere Duchesne*; associated with the Paris Commune
CHARLOTTE CORDAY	Girondin woman who assassinated Marat

PAULINE

PAULINE LÉON	Older of two living children
THE LÉONS	Ran a chocolate shop near the Cafe Procope
MARIE-THÉRÈSE	Pauline's younger sister
MAMAN	Pauline's mother; also called Marthurine Telohau
THE FOSSE FAMILY	Friends of the Léons; lived upstairs
ANATOLE FOSSE	Father; water carrier

SANSON AND HIS SON	King's executioners; masters of torture
HENRI	Pauline's boyfriend; apprentice to a hatmaker
BABETTE	Pauline's friend; worked at the Dancing Badger tavern
AIMÉE	Pauline's friend; married; coffee vendor
OLYMPE DE GOUGES	Butcher's daughter; dramatist and pamphleteer; wrote *Declaration of the Rights of Women and Citizens*
VICTOIRE	Old-clothes woman; revolutionary; first divorcée
MARTIN	Victoire's husband
DE BRETEUIL	King's replacement for Necker as chief minister
MAILLARD	One of the heroes of the Bastille
THÉROIGNE DE MÉRICOURT	Peasant girl who became a well-to-do courtesan; strong supporter of the Revolution; warrior feminist; associated with the Girondins
OTILE	Babette's mother; ran the Dancing Badger tavern with her husband
JEAN-BAPTISTE LOUVET	Girondin; in the Convention; wrote novel *The Adventures of the Chevalier de Faublas*
HÈRAULT DE SÉCHELLES	Ex-aristocrat; revolutionary; Jacobin; later member of the Committee of Public Safety

GEORGES

GEORGES-JACQUES DANTON	Orator; politician; lawyer; president of the Cordeliers; member of the Legislative Assembly and the Convention
VINOT	Solicitor for whom Georges worked as clerk
FRANÇOISE	Widow from Champagne; friend of Georges
M. HUET DE PAISY	Kept Françoise; sold office to Danton
FRANÇOIS-JÉRÔME CHARPENTIER	Proprietor of the Cafe d'Ecole; Georges' father-in-law
MARIA	Wife of Jérôme; Georges' mother-in-law
GABRIELLE	Daughter of Jérôme and Maria; Wife of Georges
MME DUPLESSIS	Wife of a bureaucrat; courted by Camille Desmoulins

FABRE D'ÉGLANTINE	Friend of Georges; law clerk; poet; pamphleteer; dramatist; later member of the Convention; Cordelier
JULES PARÉ	Friend of Georges from school; revolutionary
LUCILE DUPLESSIS	Daughter of Mme Duplessis; wife of Camille Desmoulins
DE LAUNAY	Governor of the prison at the Bastille
PANIS	Lawyer; friend of Georges; in the Jacobin government
SIMONNE ÉVRARD	Common-law wife of Marat
FRANÇOIS AND LOUISE ROBERT	Husband and wife who ran a revolutionary paper; Cordeliers
LEGENDRE	Butcher; Cordelier; friend and supporter of Georges
LAMETH BROTHERS	Close to Lafayette; Feuillants
MANUEL	Prosecutor at the Paris Commune
MANDAT	Head of the National Guard in August 1792
ANTOINE FOUQUIER-TINVILLE	Camille Desmoulins' cousin; the public prosecutor under the Commune during the Terror
BILLAUD-VARENNE	Cordelier; radical; later member of the Committee of Public Safety
SERVAN	Minister of war in Girondin government
CLAVIÈRE	Finance chief in Girondin government
FRANÇOIS-GEORGES, ANTOINE	Children of Gabrielle and Georges
THE GÉLYS	Lived upstairs; friends of Gabrielle
LOUISE GÉLY	Girl from upstairs who took care of Georges' children; his second wife
LE PELETIER	Education reformer; Jacobin
FREI BROTHERS	Austrian-born financiers

NOBILITY

KING LOUIS XV	1710–1774, King of France
KING LOUIS XVI	1754–1793, King of France
MARIE-ANTOINETTE	Queen of Louis XVI, daughter of the Austrian Hapsburg dynasty
THE DAUPHIN	Eldest survivng son of Louis XVI
COMTE D'ARTOIS	Youngest brother of Louis XVI; later Charles X

COMTE DE PROVENCE	Brother of Louis XVI; later Louis XVIII
PRINCE DE CONDÉ	King's cousin
MME DU POMPADOUR	Mistress of Louis XV
MME DU BARRY	Mistress of Louis XV
DUC D'ORLEANS	King's cousin; developed the Palais Royal, Jacobin, in the Convention; later known as Phillipe Égalité
AXEL FERSEN	Swedish nobleman; reputed to be the Queen's lover
COMTESSE DE POLIGNAC	One of the Queen's favorites
PRINCESSE DE LAMBALLE	One of the Queen's favorites

ORGANIZATIONS

CORDELIERS	Radical club for the common people
JACOBINS	Radical club with many delegates and lawyers
SOCIAL CIRCLE	Drew men and women of the educated classes
FEUILLANTS	Lafayette, Lambeths. Broke away from Jacobins when that club became more radical
REVOLUTIONARY REPUBLICAN WOMEN	Organization started by Claire Lacombe and Pauline Léon; first entirely women's political organization, started by women, with women officers, a radical feminist agenda and membership consisting only of women
ENRAGÉS OR MAD DOGS	Informal faction of the left who agitated for price controls, higher taxes for the wealthy, economic reform, more democracy and more power to the sections; Théophile Leclerc, Jacques Roux were among the characters associated with the group, as were Claire Lacombe and Pauline Léon; Hébert was sympathetic to its political goals

The Cordeliers, Jacobins, and Feuillants were named for the former monasteries in which they met.

ESTATES GENERAL	Body of the Three Estates called by Louis XVI
NATIONAL ASSEMBLY	What the Estates General turned itself into

LEGISLATIVE ASSEMBLY	Subsequent elected legislative body
NATIONAL CONVENTION	Successor of the Legislative Assembly; the body that ruled France under the First Republic
GIRONDINS	Delegates in the Legislative Assembly and then in the Convention who were first part of the left and then the moderate faction; constituted the government from the June uprising in 1792 until brought down by another demonstration a year later; also called the Brissotins after Jacques-Pierre Brissot, considered by outsiders to be their leader
THE MOUNTAIN	Delegates of the left in the Convention (Jacobins and Cordeliers), so called because they occupied the upper seats
THE PLAIN	Delegates in the Convention who did not belong to either the Mountain or the Girondins; the swing votes
COMMUNE	Elected body that governed Paris
COMMITTEE OF PUBLIC SAFETY	Group of twelve deputies from National Convention; wielded executive power
COMMITTEE OF SECURITY	Police committee, set up before the Committee of Public Safety; less powerful sometime rival to that Committee